# ABOUT



James was born in Suffolk in the UK. He travelled the world extensively, worked as a journalist in the 1990's and then turned to his passion for the great outdoors, designing and building gardens for several years before returning to writing.

James moved to North Yorkshire where he lived between the Yorkshire Dales and the Yorkshire Moors. It inspired him to use these beautiful areas as the location for the EDEN CHRONICLES series.

In 2013 James rowed across the English Channel and the length of the Thames to raise money for MND and Breakthrough Breast Cancer.

www.jameserith.com
james@jericopress.com

facebook.com/JamesErithAuthor
twitter.com/jameserith
instagram.com/edenchronicles
goodreads.com/jameserith
pinterest.com/jameserith
amazon.com/author/jameserith

# COPYRIGHT

**Eden Chronicles Series, Books 1-3**
**The Power and the Fury, Spider Web Powder, The Chamber of Truth**

First Edition published 2017


Cover: Tom Moore (tom@beatmedia.co.uk)


ISBN: 978-1-910134-15-3 paperback

# ALSO BY JAMES ERITH

The Dragon's Game - Eden Chronicles, Book Four

Lightning Source UK Ltd.
Milton Keynes UK
UKHW011316041120
372791UK00001B/2

9 781910 134160

# EDEN CHRONICLES: BOOKS ONE TO THREE

---

THE POWER AND THE FURY, SPIDER WEB POWDER, THE CHAMBER OF TRUTH

JAMES ERITH

*For Charlotte*

*It started out as a story for my Godchildren:*

***Isabella, Daisy, Archie, Iso and Ernest.***

# EDEN CHRONICLES BOOKS SET, BOOKS 1-3

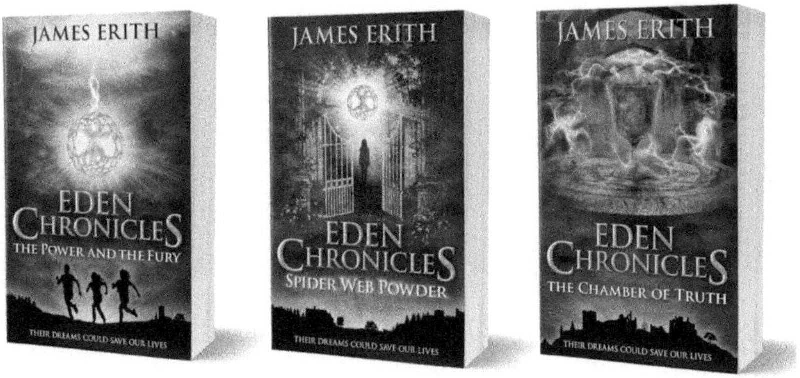


**THE POWER AND THE FURY**
**SPIDER WEB POWDER**
**THE CHAMBER OF TRUTH**

by JAMES ERITH

# CONTENTS

# THE POWER AND THE FURY

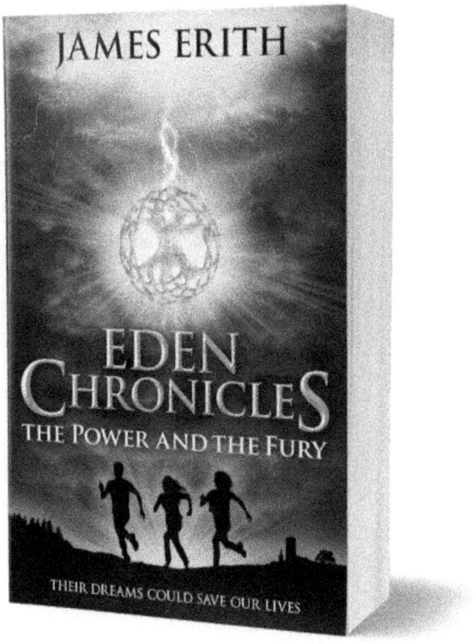

# 1 A DREAM IS GIVEN

Archie tensed.

*No, it was nothing*, he thought, *just a gust of wind rattling a loose tile on the roof, or the strange 'yessss!' sounds that his twin, Daisy, shouted in her sleep. Then again, it could be Isabella sleep-talking about her science experiments.*

He took a deep breath. Her last sleep-talking dream was something to do with atmospheric pressure and barometers or some other weird weather-related thing.

Archie smiled and rolled over; who else but his sisters could dream of such odd and opposite things – football and science. Crazy.

He rubbed his eyes and yawned. His heavy eyelids began to close but, just before they locked tight, he noticed something unusual above Daisy's head that forced them open.

A shudder ran down his body.

He closed his eyes and counted, very slowly, to three.

ONE.

TWO.

*THREE.*

Then he opened them just a bit.

It was still there!

*But it couldn't be! An angel ... when had anyone seen an angel, really seen one?*

His brain whirred.

*Maybe it was a ghost. But ghosts didn't exist. Or did they?*

A cold sweat broke out over his forehead.

And now he looked harder, it was more like a huge, strange species of spider covered by a thin, opaque jellyfish spraying blue forks of electricity from its midriff.

Archie didn't want to stare but he couldn't help it. He exhaled as quietly as he could, desperate not to draw attention to himself. And now that his eyes were adjusting to the light, Archie could see delicate claw-like contraptions at the end of the *thing's* long slender legs, and they were moving in perfect time with Daisy's every breath.

As if the claws were somehow *feeding* her.

Archie's heart pounded as a flurry of questions crowded his brain:

*Does it hurt?*

*What if it's poison?*

*What if it comes towards him – what then?*

*Will it do the same to me, the same to Isabella, Old Man Wood, Mrs Pye – everyone in the house?*

A nauseous feeling churned in his stomach.

*What if it's an alien and hundreds more are about to drop out of the sky?*

Shouldn't he *do* something?

And then another thought struck him and, absurd as it sounded, it felt ... possible. Really possible.

*What if this creature had a connection with the strange dreams he'd been having? What if it was giving Daisy a dream?*

As if hearing his thoughts, the spidery-angel turned its head and stared at him with deep black eyes like cavernous empty holes. Archie froze as a chill rushed into his brain and in the very next moment the creature had vanished.

Gone. Just like that.

Archie stared out into the dark night air as his heart thumped like a drum in his chest.

Gradually, the iciness began to thaw but Archie remained stone-still, terrified that the *thing* might reappear directly on top of him. After what felt like a month, he sat up, shook out the arm he'd been lying on, and wiped the sweat from his brow.

All he could see was the fabric of the large drape, perched like a tent above him, and the outline of the thick old wooden rafters beyond. And opposite lay Daisy, fast asleep, snoring, as though nothing had happened.

Had the spidery creature been in his head, a figment of his imagination – another dream?

He pinched himself and felt a twinge of pain.

So what was it doing to Daisy with those tiny claws on the end of its long legs? Sucking her brains out? Archie chuckled; no one in their right mind would steal those. Daisy's feet were wonderfully gifted for football and running, but her brains? Nope.

Archie replayed the scene in his mind again and again, as though scrolling through a film. He remembered the way the creature waited for her inhalations and then, as she drew air into her lungs, its tiny claws spun like crazy.

Each time, he returned to the same conclusion; it wasn't *taking* anything from Daisy, more *giving* her something. And whatever it was, she had drawn it deep inside.

Archie flicked on the bedside lamp and a gentle yellow glow filled the attic room. From the far wall, Isabella yawned and rolled over. Archie waited until she had settled, then slipped out from under his duvet.

He tiptoed silently towards Daisy's bed, a couple of wooden planks moaning in protest as he went.

He knelt down and surveyed her.

She was silent and at peace. She looked as pretty as anything with her golden hair tumbling wildly over the pillow, her mouth parted.

He smelt her sleepiness.

Leaning in, his face was just a few inches from hers as he inspected her nose, her chin, her lips, her cheeks and ears.

But there were no odd marks or stains, no bruises, no bleeding, nothing amiss.

Archie put his head in his hands.

*Perhaps he had imagined it – perhaps it was just another nightmare.*

He rubbed his face and readied himself to go back to bed when suddenly Daisy gasped as though she'd been stuck underwater and burst through to find air.

She groaned and tossed her head from side to side. Then, without warning, she sat bolt upright as though a massive electric current had smashed into her, her face missing his by a whisker.

Her wavy hair brushed his nose.

Archie's eyes nearly popped out of their sockets. He could feel her breath marking his cheek. He swayed to the side and noted that her eyes were shut tight.

She was asleep!

Now she was mumbling, but he couldn't make out the words. He listened harder.

What was it ... "odd", followed by "wo-man?"

She repeated it, this time louder. This time the word "odd" sounded more like "blood" or "flood". And there was something else. Yes, a word like, "a-shunt" before "woman" and then a word like ... "bread". That was it.

But what did it mean?

"Blood – a-shunt – woman – bread?"

A car accident?

Again Daisy said these words, again and again, growing louder and louder. And now it sounded like, "flood an shunt woman Fred"."

'Flood an shunt woman Fred?' Archie repeated.

What was she talking about?

In a flash, it came to him.

Archie reeled; he knew he wasn't mistaken. Now he said it with her. The first word was definitely "flood", followed by, "Ancient Woman ... dead".

Archie felt the blood drain from his face.

He stood up and stared at his twin, his mouth open.

It wasn't possible – it couldn't be. How could she have access to his very own nightmare, the exact same dream he'd had over the past few nights; the flooding and the haggard old woman?

*Was it a twin thing?*

No. Twin things never happened to them.

He noticed tears falling from Daisy's eyes, eyes which were wide open and staring at a fixed point across the room.

Without warning, Daisy screamed.

Archie automatically ducked and covered his ears.

She began to shake.

Then, her hands reached out as though clawing at an invisible figure.

Words spilled out incoherently.

A moment later she stopped, and, with a look of absolute dread and fear mixed upon her face, she spoke, her words faint, like whispers.

Archie leaned in but wished he hadn't, for her next words stabbed him, as though a knife had been plunged deep into his heart and twisted round and round.

'No, no, please don't do it, Archie,' she implored, repeating these words over and over and louder and louder until she was yelling.

'DON'T DO IT, ARCHIE ... NOT HER,' she cried. **'PLEASE.'**

And then one final plea.

**'PLEASE, ARCHIE ... NOOOO!'**

# 2 THE ROUTE TO SCHOOL

Archie swung the bag over his shoulder. 'I'm going the forest route,' he announced. 'Anyone want to come?'

'Not today,' Daisy replied while staring at her nails. 'Saving my energy for the big match – if I'm allowed to play. It's the announcement in assembly.'

'Oh yeah, of course. *The announcement*,' Archie said, dragging his fingers through his black hair. 'I'm sure you'll be fine.'

'Promise me you won't get covered in mud or torn to bits with brambles,' Isabella yelled from behind her curtain. 'It'll be detention if you do. And I *will* make sure you do it.'

Archie pulled a face.

'I can tell exactly what you're doing, Archie de Lowe,' Isabella said. 'Ten pounds says you're making a face.'

Archie stuck his tongue out and waggled it towards her curtain.

Daisy laughed.

'Hilarious,' Isabella said, as she popped her head out. 'I'm on a mission to tidy you up. Up until now you've ignored everyone. But it has to change.'

Archie rolled his eyes and, with a smile where the corners of his mouth curled up mischievously, he winked at his twin, turned, sneaked out of the door and down the stairs to the landing below.

This morning, the stairs creaked more than usual and every single floorboard Archie stepped on whined back at him. Why was he surrounded by old things that groaned and moaned all the time, like Isabella?

As Archie walked, he noted a single shaded light bulb dangling rather sadly from the ceiling which reminded him of his experience in the night.

Daisy had screamed loud enough to wake people in Northallerton ten miles away. And she'd slept through it all.

But what nagged him most was what Daisy knew.

Why had she screamed his name?

Why was it so familiar?

He'd ask her later – if he remembered – but not now. He didn't have the will and, deep down, he was pretty sure she'd give him one of her dismissive looks with her big blue eyes and say, 'Sorry, no reveally', and he'd feel like a bit of an idiot. And he hated feeling an idiot, especially when it came from Daisy.

He toyed with the idea that instead of asking Daisy about her dream, he'd tell her that he'd had a dream that sounded, well, similar.

He stopped as he reached the bottom step.

Then again, why should he? Daisy wouldn't be interested and anyway, he was over-reacting, right?

He scrunched his eyes shut in frustration. I mean, the spidery-angel thing he'd seen was scary – and real, very real – but it was, he reminded himself, only a dream.

If only it had felt like a dream.

---

ON HIS WAY OUT, Archie poked his head around the door of the kitchen where Old Man Wood and Mrs Pye were washing up breakfast.

'Just off,' he said, 'see you later.'

'You're going early,' Mrs Pye said. 'Anything the matter?'

'Nah, just fancy a walk, that's all.' He spotted Mrs Pye placing some apples in the fruit bowl. 'Ooh. Can I have one?' he asked.

Mrs Pye gave him a look.

Archie sighed. '*Please.*'

Mrs Pye selected one and lobbed it over. 'Now don't you go getting them clothes ripped again or go tripping down any holes or burrows or bigger holes like those badger ones on them slopes. I'm fed up with constantly mending your things and darning your clothes and washing, young Archie, I am.'

Then she smiled, although to most people it would have looked like a grimace.

'But what am I telling you that for, eh? You're quite old enough to know better.' She grimaced, or smiled again.

'Whatever you do,' she continued, 'don't go breaking any of them bones of yours. Understand? It's your football tomorrow and you know how Daisy would be disappointed.'

Archie smiled.

He loved it when she rambled on. He grabbed his bags, opened the thick oak door and slipped outside.

He drew in a large breath of air as he watched the first rays of light slowly creeping up over the vale, smearing the base of the thick cloud in a fiery orange glow.

At first he followed the stony path towards the ruin but, before long, he cut along a makeshift animal track that weaved through the long grass before it met the forest and the steep slopes that ran down to the river.

For several minutes he hurdled fallen branches and jumped rabbit warrens and fox holes, untangling brambles from his clothes as he ducked through thickets and bushes. Every so often he would stop and pluck a few blackberries or scavenge for hazelnuts on the ground.

He chewed them as he went, savouring the tastes – be it tangy and sour or over-ripe and juicy – smearing his hands and lips with red berry juice.

In the semi-darkness beneath the forest canopy, he found long creepers dangling down and swung on them, pretending to be a pirate boarding a ship. One gave way in mid-flight and he tumbled to the ground but he picked himself up and brushed his clothes down.

He fingered a tear in his blazer and another in his trousers and shrugged.

Nothing he could do about it now.

He wished Daisy was with him. She loved this kind of thing, even if she didn't like to admit it. She only came out in the holidays – when her friends weren't around worrying about their looks and their make-up and nails and hair, and boys.

When Daisy was out here, she went wild; her blonde hair tangled up in brambles and grass, her face smeared by mud and berries and blood.

She wasn't that into all the girlie stuff. In fact she wasn't into anything particularly, except football.

His thoughts were interrupted by a fly buzzing round his head. Daisy and her passion for football. Strange that, really. A girl up here on the moors playing football with farmers' sons and country boys; she had to be good – and tough.

Yep, he thought. Daisy was equal and better on both counts.

He loosened his clothes as his body warmed up and before long he came to a huge grey boulder three times his height. In his mind's eye, he measured the distance and set off at a sprint towards it. At the last moment, he sprang up and grasped a stony outcrop just high enough to haul himself up onto the top of the boulder where he sat down and gulped in mouthfuls of morning air. Removing his rucksack, he reached into his bag and flipped open the lid of his bottle, grateful for the cooling effect of the water.

The day wasn't hot, just sticky, like a Turkish bath without the heat.

He rubbed an apple on his jumper and took a bite, wiping his lips on his sleeve.

Nonchalantly, he stared out over the valley. His eyes focusing on the buildings of Upsall – particularly the school – perched above the flood plain at the foot of the moors.

Above the school he noted the rugged, menacing, dark forest and jagged rocks that jutted out of the steep slopes like angry faces. In stark contrast were the manicured green stripes of the school playing fields, laid out symmetrically below.

He smiled. *Man's doing down below,* he thought, *God's above.*

He cast his eye along the valley, where large weeping willows marked the course of the meandering river at perfect intervals, as though guarding the valley floor like sentries.

From here, Upsall appeared so much grander and more important than it was, close up.

At school, there were constant reminders of the school's monastic heritage. The quadrangle with its grey stone and red-brick colonnade were relics of an age when it was a vital refuge for those heading north or east over the harsh Yorkshire moors.

The buildings had medieval emblems of security and style. Solid chunks of masonry, a huge circular rose window inlaid with delicate stained glass, a huge oak door and, most obviously, a tall, square tower that soared into the sky.

This must have been a welcome sight for weary travellers as they came off the hills.

Raised on a platform above the river sat a jumble of buildings in varying shapes, sizes and colours. The occasional facade was rendered in plaster but most were finished in grey stone or red bricks typical of the area. And surrounding the village the high slopes of the moors protected these dwellings like a shield.

The effect was of chocolate-box charm but with no real order or sophistication.

Old Man Wood often told them that the ruin next to Eden Cottage was far older than the rest. Archie spun to his right, towards the sheer rock face that rose high above him.

A great position for a fortress up there, he thought, hidden away in the forest, but at the same time imposing and bold – as a castle should be – with a view that stretched way into the Vale of York.

Today, something was missing.

He searched his mind. Nothing came.

No one really knew about their ruin, not from the school at any rate. Perhaps it was a bit too rustic, or too hard to get to, Archie thought.

Mr Solomon, the headmaster, called it, 'the hinterland', but for the de Lowe children the battlements and ancient earthworks gave endless possibilities for games – and battles.

And then it shot into his brain. He stared at the rock face again. Where were the eagles and buzzards that soared high above? He listened. Not a birdcall in earshot. Not a wingspan in sight.

He checked his watch and groaned.

Archie slid off the boulder and followed an animal track through the brambles. A little while later the shimmering silver of the river cut through the red, yellow, amber and brown colours of the leaves and before long he was in the green meadows adjacent to the river.

---

ARCHIE RAN ALONG THE TOWPATH, over the bridge, across the playing fields and towards the chapel. As he neared the stone steps, he dusted himself off and, noting the time, slipped in through the oak door.

Head down, he sped over the large flagstones until he found his row. Then, he squeezed his way to the middle, where he sat down and caught his breath.

He turned to see Daisy chatting to several of her friends. He caught her eye but she frowned and turned away. What did that mean? Was it about the team?

For a brief moment he experienced a feeling that he was being watched, just as he had with the spidery-angel the previous night.

His instinct was right. On the platform at the far end of the hall stood Mr Solomon, the headmaster, whose eyes bore into him.

Archie's heart sank. Another inspection.

Those who had even the tiniest scuffs or tears, or buttons missing, were being entered into his dreaded red book..

Archie gave himself a once-over.

A shambles, possibly the worst ever.

He felt for his tie halfway down his shirt and pulled it up. He drew up his socks and dragged a hand roughly through his hair, pulling out tendrils of a creeper and a few small strands of grass.

Archie knew he had a couple of seconds to run out. But as he thought about it, a familiar voice boomed through the hall.

'Good morning, school,' it said. 'Please rise.'

And automatically, everyone stood up.

# 3 GOOD & BAD NEWS

'Quiet ... please,' Mr Solomon roared, patting the breast pockets of his coarse tweed suit.

Wasn't it strange how the noise level always seemed to rise as conversations were rushed to a conclusion? He removed his glasses from his round, ruddy nose and glared around the hall.

'Thank you, children. Please, sit down.'

Two hundred and seventy-two pupils sat down on the hard wooden benches, lined out row upon row, the noise drifting high into the rafters of the vaulted ceiling.

On either side the walls were lined with large portraits of headmasters, interspersed with dark wooden panels where the names of past scholars, captains, and musicians were remembered.

Above, tall cross-beams supported large chandelier lights that hung from thick metal chains.

Mr Solomon stared out over the throng, cleared his throat before peering like an owl through his glasses to inspect his leather-bound clipboard.

'School dress!'

There was a groan.

Archie felt a strong urge to disappear.

'I see some of you shaking in fear,' Solomon said, his eyebrows raised as if he were all-seeing and all-knowing. 'And rightly, too,' he continued.

'There has been a marked deterioration in dress standards since the beginning of term. After half term, those who fail to comply with school regulation uniform will be given detention. Now, to show you what I'm talking about, no one is shaking more this morning than Upsall School goalkeeping hero, Archie de Lowe.'

A cheer went up.

'Archie, please stand.'

Archie sat stone-still in disbelief. *Not again.*

He felt a jab in his back and then another from the side.

'Come on, Archie. Up you get,' the headmaster prompted.

Archie stared down at his worn shoes and, taking a deep breath, rose from behind the large frame of his old friend Gus Williams.

Every pair of eyes stared at him. Archie could hear girls giggling nearby. His face reddened, the heat of his blush growing by the second.

He didn't dare look up.

Mr Solomon continued: 'Archie, I hate to make an example of you, but this morning you have beaten your spectacular record of being a complete and utter shambles.'

A ripple of laughter filled the hall.

'In all of my time at this school, your attire is by far the most dreadful I have ever come across. In fact it is almost the perfect example of how not to dress. Your shoes are filthy; you have no belt, which shows off your very splendid and colourful underwear, and your socks are around your ankles because there are no elastic garters to hold them up.'

Mr Solomon paused as laughter pealed into the high ceiling. 'Your shirt has lost buttons; your tie is halfway across your chest, and I'm not sure how this could have happened, but you seem to be wearing the wrong coloured jersey. Please turn around, de Lowe.'

Archie shifted, pretending to slouch like a tramp and in the process getting a laugh. It somehow made the humiliation feel a fraction more bearable.

'Yes, just as I suspected,' Solomon continued. 'Blazer ripped and, of course, your hair is the usual bird's nest.'

Everyone was laughing.

Archie feigned a smile while trying to pull his attire together. On Solomon's instruction, he sat down.

Isabella would be livid with him; only this morning she'd told him to sort out his appearance and he'd completely ignored her again. It meant he'd not only be faced with more detention, which was bearable, but he'd finally have to go shopping. And Archie detested shopping. He bowed his head and didn't dare look up in case he caught her eye.

Then he turned to see Daisy staring at the floor.

Solomon's tone softened as he smiled, showing his small, tea-stained teeth. 'Let this be a lesson to you, Archie. Today, and only today, you are excused because you're an important member of our glorious unbeaten football team. And this, of course, leads me on to the main item on this morning's agenda.'

With these words the mood in the hall changed and the noise level increased.

The headmaster raised an arm for quiet before starting again.

'Most of you are aware of our situation. As a small school our selection for teams is limited, and I regrettably endorsed that a girl could play in the boys' team. This team has subsequently gone on to great things, to the very great credit of our school. However, I ... we ... were found out.'

The headmaster pulled out a letter from the breast pocket of his jacket and waved it in the air.

'Let me read you the important parts of this letter I received yesterday from the president of our Football Association.'

He unfolded the letter and nudged his glasses into the correct position on the bridge of his nose and thumbed his way down the page.

'Ah-ha. Here we are: *Now, what this all means*,' he read, '*is that we would expect boys and boys only, to play*.'

A slightly confused murmur spread around the room.

'*However*,' he continued to read, '*under rule 12.7.1 there is a clause which reads: Any team member who has played ten matches consecutively has the right to appeal for an impartial ruling if a matter of disrepute has been reported.*'

Mr Solomon put the letter down on the lectern and removed his half-moon glasses. He peered around the room.

'What they are saying, therefore, is this: has Daisy played ten matches in a row this season?'

He spied a raised hand from one of the girls at the back.

'Sue Lowden, do you have the answer?'

'I believe she's played in twelve, sir. Thirteen if you take into consideration the friendly against the Dutch school.'

'Thank you very much, Miss Lowden.'

An audible buzz passed around the room.

The headmaster donned his glasses once more and turned back to the letter.

'*It is our opinion*,' he read, '*that Upsall School has seriously abused the goodwill of this league. However not one opposition team member reported or noticed Miss de Lowe's disguise until the information was passed to us by way of an anonymous letter*.'

Several heads turned towards a group of boys sitting on the left side of the room. A hissing noise started.

Mr Solomon continued to read, this time in a slightly louder voice:

'*As this happened prior to the National Northern Under 14 Cup Final, and Miss de Lowe has played in every round, we have decided to impart the following. Should Upsall School win, then we will recommend, with the full backing of the Football Association, that Miss de Lowe be allowed to continue playing for Upsall School and the rules be changed with immediate effect*—'

A roar of cheers and whooping noises filled the air.

'*However*,' Mr Solomon read, raising his hand for quiet, '*should Upsall lose*,' and here, his voice went so quiet that you could almost hear a pin drop, '*then it will be Miss de Lowe's last game for the school*.'

Silence spread over the assembly.

Mr Solomon picked Daisy out of the assembly, peeled off his glasses and spoke directly to her.

'So there we have it, Daisy. I have spoken to the authorities to make sure we are absolutely clear about the situation. You will play in tomorrow's final against Chitbury Town, but with no disguise. Do you understand? It's bitter-sweet, but it's not all over by any means!'

Mr Solomon addressed the children crashing his fist down on the lectern. 'Now, let's make sure as a team and a school that we jolly well win!'

Solomon waited for the noise to settle.

'Kick-off tomorrow is at 11am. There will be no assembly, but there will be a chapel service for those of you who wish to get rid of your sins, so I'm expecting a great deal of you. One final thing. I'd like to see all three de

Lowes afterwards for a moment, and prefects, can you ensure that everyone leaves in the usual orderly manner.'

---

KEMP MOVED QUICKLY to cut her off.

'I can look after myself, Kemp,' Daisy said coolly. 'There's no point trying to intimidate me. That's what you boys always try and do, and as you know, I don't feel pain—'

'I'm sorry,' Kemp butted in. 'What did you say, de Lowe, intimidation, pain?' He laughed. 'We wouldn't do a thing like that, would we boys?' he said, addressing his mates, Mason and Wilcox. 'Not really my style, de Lowe.'

Daisy leaned in towards him, taking him off guard, and whispered in his ear, her breath soft on his cheek. 'Only your foul breath could truly frighten me.'

In a flash she tried to push through a gap but Kemp recovered his wits and, with a big hand, grabbed her arm and twisted it behind her back.

A stabbing pain crashed into her shoulder.

'I haven't finished,' Kemp said. 'Now listen up, Daisy de Lowe. My mates at Chitbury are SO looking forward to it, especially the second half.'

'Tell your mates I'm looking forward to it,' she spat, staring him coldly in the eyes.

Taking him off guard, she fluttered her eyelashes, pouted her lips and spoke to him in a high-pitched girlie voice.

'You know what, Kempy-wempy,' she started, 'you really are super macho with your big muscles and your fat lips.'

Wilcox and Mason looked at each other and sniggered.

Kemp glared at them.

Daisy whispered very faintly in his ear. 'Deep down, I think you fancy me, don't you, big boy.'

Kemp looked ready to explode. He twisted Daisy's arm higher up her back.

Daisy squirmed. 'Let me go, loser.'

Kemp put his mouth to her ear. 'Don't even think about it, de Lowe.'

'What? Me and you?' she replied.

Kemp loosened his hold. 'No, stupid. The football. They're in a different league – at least soon they will be, so wave bye-bye to your football career, and hello to mine—'

'Back off, Kemp!' It was the large figure of Gus Williams closing in. 'The de Lowes are wanted by Solomon. Didn't you hear? Or are you deaf as well as dumb?'

Kemp released her. 'You're asking for it, Williams—'

'Fine,' Gus replied, his eyes bulging with excitement. 'Any time, just you and me, this afternoon—'

Daisy had had enough. Without hesitating, she aimed a vicious kick at Kemp's shin.

Kemp howled and hopped up and down rubbing his leg.

Gus flashed his big friendly toothy smile at Daisy and turned to Kemp.

'Kicked by a girl. That shouldn't be painful for a big, tough lad like you.'

# 4 KEMP'S STORY

'What was that about?' Archie said, as Daisy joined him at the other side of the hall.

Daisy ran her hands through her hair. 'Oh, nothing, usual stuff,' she said flatly. 'Kemp being a creep, telling me how much of a kicking I'm going to get and Gus, heroic, as usual.'

She sighed. 'Why does Kemp hate me so much?'

Archie rubbed his freckled nose and laughed. 'Because he's a thug and he's jealous of you. Because everyone likes you and hates him.' He frowned. 'And possibly because you – a mere slip of a girl – booted macho-man off the team.'

Daisy shook her head. 'But he was useless – always giving away fouls and kicking people off the ball. And anyway that was last year—'

'But he's like an elephant who never forgets—'

'Well, it's ridiculous,' Daisy complained, 'elephant or not.'

Archie grabbed his sister playfully by the waist. 'Strange thing, the way he looks at you.'

Daisy gasped and a smile lit up her face. 'Yeah, right!'

'He likes you. It's kind of obvious.'

She pushed Archie away. 'Eeeuk! No way! I promise you, Archie. Not in a million years!'

Archie grinned and stole a glance over to the far end of the hall, where

Kemp was talking to his friends. They locked eyes for a moment, then Kemp reached into his pocket for his mobile phone.

Archie turned back to Daisy, his face concerned. 'Probably a huge mistake to kick him though; other people feel pain in their legs, even if you don't—'

'I wonder,' Daisy said, staring into the distance, 'would Kemp even know me if I didn't play football? I mean, is there another side to him that's not horrible or gross or stinks like a skunk. How did he end up being such a dickhead?'

Archie shrugged. 'Kemp's alright, he's got problems—'

Daisy's eyes nearly popped out. 'Yeah! You're telling me—'

'No, seriously,' Archie said. 'He told me about it in a boring session of detention last term and made me swear not to tell anyone.'

'Well, go on, then,' Daisy urged. 'You can tell me.'

'Of course I can't, it's a secret.'

'Don't be silly,' Daisy implored. 'He's just tried to break my arm and his friends are going to kick the life out of me.'

'No.'

'Yes,' Daisy insisted. 'For curiosity's sake and because it's often best to know your enemy.'

Archie wavered for a second and then shook his head, even if Daisy did have a point. 'Sorry.'

'*Pleeease*,' Daisy begged.

Archie sighed. 'No.'

'*Pleeease*, winkle.'

'God. OK – as long as you swear you absolutely won't tell anyone. And you stop calling me winkle.'

Daisy wobbled her head inconclusively.

'I mean it,' Archie said, 'don't tell anyone.'

'Alright – I swear.'

Archie eyed her carefully. 'You do realise, Daisy, that if he finds out he'll rip my arms off or suck out my eyes. Or both.'

Daisy flashed him a look. 'Yeah, yeah, I know. Not a soul.'

'OK, so the thing is, Kemp's parents died when he was little – very suddenly – and he keeps very quiet about it. He never talks about it. Now he lives with his aunt, who he can't stand.'

'That's awful,' Daisy said, her eyes wide. 'How?'

'What do you mean, how?'

'How did they die?'

'Oh, I see,' he said. 'A car crash. Something happened up on the hills in the forest towards Dalton.' Archie's voice turned to a whisper. 'The rest is really grim.'

'Go on,' Daisy urged, leaning in. 'You've started so you've got to finish.'

Archie sighed, looked over his shoulder, and saw Kemp heading towards the door at the far end of the hall. 'Apparently, both lost their heads. Their car plummeted into a ravine and blew up. Some charred and disjointed remains were found scattered in the woods weeks later.'

Daisy whistled. 'My God. I can see why he doesn't want anyone to know.'

Archie nodded. 'Shocking, isn't it. And the worst bit is that they only found parts of one body.'

Daisy stared at the floor. 'So you like him, don't you?' she said.

'Yeah, I suppose, apart from when he's a jerk to you two.'

Daisy was intrigued. 'Come on, tell me more, I mean he's probably organising my death right now.'

Archie glanced down the hall and hesitated. 'God. OK. Beneath all that macho stuff he's actually quite soft – it's a barrier he puts up to protect himself, well that's what his shrink says—'

'*Shrink?*' Daisy blurted. 'He has a shrink?'

A few heads turned their way. 'Yes, shrink, psychiatrist, whatever – keep your voice down.'

'He gets counselling?' she whispered. 'They're not doing a very good job.'

Archie shot his twin a look. 'Tell me about it. He seems to snap in and out. I mean, when he told me all this in detention he cried buckets and went on and on about wanting a normal life with a normal family. And then he thumped me really hard on the shoulder and told me not to tell anyone. Remember that massive bruise I had when I said I'd fallen out of a tree.'

'Oh yeah, I thought that was a bit odd.'

'I couldn't move my arm for a week. Anyway he's basically sad, bored, and to be honest, lonely. Everyone hates him and he knows it.'

'Even Mason and Wilcox?'

'Those freaks don't really like him. They pretend they're best mates but it's fear that glues them together. Ever seen how they jump to attention when he's around or their heads get cracked together? One moment he's charming and funny, the next he's pure evil. It's as if there's a switch that flicks in his head. And he's really strong for his age, the only person who can match him is Williams—'

'And there were sparks flying between them earlier,' she said. 'So why does he like you?'

Archie smiled. 'Because I don't annoy him, and I'm probably not worth beating up,' Archie raised his eyebrows. 'And because I don't deliberately *piss him off.*'

Daisy thumped him playfully on the arm. 'He's a loser, Archie. Why doesn't he try being nice for a change?'

'Apparently it's something to do with offloading emotional pain. That's why Solomon and the teachers leave him alone so he can do what he likes. They're terrified he'll go even further off the rails. Apparently it's pretty common. I mean, think about it. If our parents got killed we'd probably go a bit nuts, although to be fair,' and he pinched Daisy on the cheek, 'you're at least halfway there.'

Daisy smiled, sarcasm screwed on her face. Then she sighed.

'Our parents are never, ever around, so it's almost the same thing,' she said.

Archie was glad that he wasn't the only one who missed them. 'Are you sure you're alright, you know, about the match?'

'Yeah,' she said. 'Thanks, Arch. I'll miss wearing that stupid wig. It felt kind of lucky – something I could hide behind.'

'Tell you what,' he said, changing the subject, 'why don't I cut your hair, make you look a bit more like a bloke?'

Daisy laughed as an image of a moustachioed Archie, wearing a white apron, with a pair of scissors in his hand, popped into her head.

'No bleeding way, winkle. You'd probably cut my ears off—'

'Well they're big enough, and anyway, STOP calling me winkle.'

They both smiled.

'Look, do you remember,' he began cautiously, 'anything about last night?'

'Last night? What do you mean?'

Archie felt himself reddening. 'You were having a bad dream.'

Daisy looked confused. 'Did I wake you?'

'Yeah! You were screaming, for starters.'

Daisy shook her head. 'Screaming? Loudly?'

Archie nodded. 'You probably woke the whole of Northallerton.'

Daisy grinned. 'Now you mention it,' Daisy began, 'I had this nightmare about being covered in water, as if I was in a huge storm.'

'That's it? Nothing else?' Archie teased. 'Nothing about me?'

'Nah.'

'You sure?'

'Sure. Why?'

'Well...' Archie hesitated.

'Well, what?'

'Oh, it's nothing really – just that ... you mentioned me, and told me not to do something.'

Daisy turned thoughtfully to the ceiling. 'Sorry. Can't really remember. You know, dreams—'

Archie could barely hide his disappointment and Daisy saw straight through him. The reality was that she'd had a terrible, terrible night – one she'd rather forget entirely.

'Actually,' Daisy began, scrunching up her cheeks, 'maybe there was—'

'Daisy, Archie, there you are,' said the headmaster. 'Now, where is that sister of yours?'

'Over here,' said the figure of Isabella heading towards them.

'Just been finishing off some science work with Mrs Douglas. You can't believe how ...' and she turned her eyes up as if searching for the correct term... '*loose*, some of these theories are.'

# 5 A WORD FROM THE HEADMASTER

The headmaster ushered the three of them into the adjoining corridor.

'Look, just a quick word, if I may,' Mr Solomon said as he leaned against the painted stone wall, his voice kind and his manner fatherly, but firm. He looked over them sympathetically.

'It pains me a very great deal to say this, but this morning I received an email from your parents who are somewhere in the Middle East. They will not be back for the football match or indeed for the whole of half term.' He scanned their disappointed faces. 'It appears they have discovered something rather important.'

Archie and Daisy exchanged glances.

'What does it say, what are they doing?' Isabella asked as she attempted to read the headmaster's notepad upside down.

The headmaster folded the pad into his large midriff.

'Well, it's light on detail – in fact there's hardly any information, which, given the circumstances is the very least you deserve. To be honest I'm not at all happy about this situation—'

'But we've got—' Isabella started.

'Yes, I know you're fortunate enough to have your caretakers at Eden Cottage – but looking at your appearance, Archie, I have to ask myself, are they up to the job?' The headmaster paused for effect.

'This is the third time I've had to reprimand you in the last two terms. Your parents have an obligation to you and this school beyond the callings of their work and the responsibility of others.'

Solomon sighed. He hated telling children off for something that wasn't their fault; they'd been deserted by their eccentric parents, and not for the first time.

But at least he knew that their caretakers – an old man and a lady – did their best for the children.

The old man, whom he knew as Mr Wood, had looked old when they first met years ago, and he never seemed to get any older.

The housekeeper, Mrs Pye, was another strange looking creature; large and pale, with a mop of ginger hair that hid a scar on her forehead, though she appeared entirely capable of looking after them.

He made a mental note to schedule a visit to see them in the next few days to make sure everything was as it should be.

Mr Solomon was fully aware of the long and established ties the de Lowe family had with the school and village. Their lineage could be traced back for centuries; at least, that was the claim.

The de Lowes from Eden Cottage even had a large stained glass window in the church in memory of a distant ancestor who was rumoured to have slain a local dragon. Solomon scoured their young faces. That particular gene had clearly died out a long time ago.

His gaze settled on Isabella. 'How old is your Great Uncle, Mr Wood? He must be well into his eighties, if not nineties—'

'He's getting on a bit,' she replied, 'but he's fit and well and Mum and Dad have every confidence—'

'And,' Archie butted in, 'Old Man ... er ... Uncle Wood's an awesome first aider. He's always patching me up brilliantly.'

'And,' Daisy said, 'Mrs Pye's amazing at cooking things and washing and cleaning and stuff. She's, you know, super-capable.'

'I am quite sure she is,' Solomon replied, not rising to Daisy's burst of enthusiasm. 'But who is going to get Archie to the shops for school uniform? And what if there's another emergency, like there has been in every holiday period over the last two years? Neither drive and you're two miles up a deep, steep, narrow track that's camouflaged by bushes and brambles. Your house is surrounded by thick forest – it's in the middle of nowhere! Frankly, it'd be a miracle if anyone could find you.'

Mr Solomon raised his eyebrows and peered over his half-moon glasses at each of them in turn. He wondered what condition the inside of the house was in, dotted up there on the hillside by the ruin.

'And what if your helpers were to have an incident, like a heart attack or a seizure or a fall?' he continued. 'What would you do? The place would be swarming with police and social workers and, trust me, they would be considerably less forgiving.'

The children didn't really know what to say so they remained silent and stared at the floor. To them, Old Man Wood and Mrs Pye were nothing but the best, so what was the big deal?

Isabella finally broke the silence. 'Sue's mum is taking us over to Northallerton on Tuesday. We'll get Archie smartened up then. Mrs Lowden's brilliant at helping out; I'll ask her tonight.'

Mr Solomon nodded. 'Very well, but before you go, Isabella, I'm going to entrust you – as the eldest – to take a letter back for your parents. Come and collect it before you go from my office. You are to give it to them so that this unacceptable situation is on record and does not happen again.'

Mr Solomon cleared his throat, which signified that the matter had been dealt with. He turned to the twins. 'I have some simple Religious Education homework for you two over the break. It's Genesis; the book right at the very beginning of the Bible. Have you heard of it?'

The twins nodded.

Mr Solomon smiled. 'Jolly good. The bit I want you to pay particular attention to is where God creates the universe in seven days – with Adam and Eve – remember?'

The twins nodded again.

'After creation, one of Adam and Eve's children, Cain, kills his twin, Abel, and is sent away. So God decides they're a pretty rum lot and sends a flood that wipes out everything on the earth apart from their descendant, Noah—'

'Who built the ark and put the animals in it two by two,' Archie finished off.

'Precisely,' Mr Solomon said. 'Now, Daisy, as your academic record is simply appalling, I'd like you to actually read it and then think hard about it – preferably before you dream up some kind of hare-brained scheme that gets Archie battered into pieces. Understand? You may find the chapter a valuable resource for your essay after half term entitled, *Did God create the universe, or did the universe create God?*'

Then, in one movement, as though suddenly aware of the time, Mr Solomon straightened, raised his bushy eyebrows and looked over the top of his half-moon spectacles. 'Now, for goodness' sake, over this half term period, behave yourselves, children; I cannot and will not have the Social Services chasing us around with your parents nowhere in sight. Please do not get yourselves into trouble. Understood?'

'Yes, sir,' the children said in unison.

'Excellent. Very best of luck with the football tomorrow morning. There will be a big crowd cheering you on and some members of the press will be present. The circumstance surrounding this game, and the fact that the final involves our larger rivals, seems to have caught the imagination of the entire region.'

He darted a look at Isabella. 'So, best behaviour please.' He hoped his message was clear. 'Now run along.'

Archie and Daisy scampered off down the corridor, the noise of their footsteps echoing off the old sandstone walls. Mr Solomon looked at his watch, mumbled something about the time and, as he turned, he noticed Isabella lingering.

---

'EXCUSE ME, SIR,' she said.

'Yes, Isabella,' the headmaster said impatiently, 'what is it now?'

'Well, it's the weather, sir.'

Solomon sighed. 'Yes, what about it?'

Isabella hesitated. For the first time in her life she didn't know what to say; it was as if her brain had jammed. 'I've made a barometer, to study the weather,' she spat out.

'Yes, congratulations on your skilful endeavour,' he replied. 'Mrs Douglas notified me. I'm told atmospheric pressure isn't even on your syllabus—'

Isabella ignored him. 'From my readings,' she began, 'there's going to be a simply massive—'

'Storm?' Mr Solomon interrupted with a sly smile. He bent down a little. 'Well I'm pleased that your readings match up with the area forecast, but I don't believe there will be anything to worry about. A bit of rain and some thunder perhaps. But just as a precaution, please remind your class to take their umbrellas and waterproofs as I mentioned in assembly.'

The headmaster scratched his chin and smiled at her. 'While you're here, let me remind you that it would be a very bad idea to go racing on to the pitch as you have done in the previous two football matches. You must leave events on the pitch to the referee and other officials – whatever the circumstances and however difficult.' Solomon smiled in a fake, head-masterly way and straightened.

'I expect nothing less than immaculate conduct, Isabella. There will be serious repercussions if you do it again.' He paused for effect. 'Do I make myself perfectly clear?'

Isabella nodded.

'Good. Now, thank you for your concern but I really must fly,' he rubbed his hands together. 'Geogo test with year eight.'

The headmaster marched off down the corridor, his steel capped shoes tip-tapping on the old stone floor. That girl was one of the finest pupils they'd ever had – bright as a button and eager to learn. He liked that a lot. And she was loyal, with a temper that could flare up like a storm, especially with incidents surrounding her twin brother and sister. And there were a surprising number of incidents.

He chuckled as he thought about his analogy of her and a storm. Well, it was perfectly sweet of her to warn him but he had a leaving party and other pressing things to organise.

Nothing would stop his celebrations; certainly not a little storm and a warning from a pupil with a homemade barometer.

---

ISABELLA CUT inside one of the main doors and burst into the changing rooms, which she knew would be empty at this time in the morning. She went directly to her locker and sat down on the wooden bench in front of it, pulled her knees up to her face and closed her eyes.

Why hadn't she been able to spit it out?

She looked at her watch. Science started ten minutes ago; Mrs Douglas knew she was seeing Solomon and, anyway, they'd argued about her homework already and Mrs Douglas got so cross Isabella thought steam would come out of her ears. She won't mind, Isabella thought; in fact she'll probably be rather relieved I'm not there.

Her thoughts turned to Archie. Why hadn't she given him a once-over and tidied him up before he'd gone in to assembly? She hated that their behaviour seemed to rebound on her all the time. How come the twins were polar opposites of her? Daisy, popular and sporty, and Archie, well, he was nothing short of a total shambles.

Isabella shook her head. What was the point of being popular if it made you late or scruffy or dumb? Why did she feel so responsible for them just because their parents were always away? They were only two academic years beneath her, it wasn't that much. Why should her desire for excellence be pulled apart by the twins at every step?

Maybe she shouldn't watch the game tomorrow morning; why should she damn well bother? She'd leave them to their football match and have a lie-in. She'd slept so badly recently, with a strange repetitive dream – a nightmare so clear and real that it felt as if she'd been transported away to a different place.

She hardly dared tell Sue that it sounded almost identical to hers. Could best friends share dreams? Sue had been really affected – shocked even. Should she say something? No. Sue would only think she was making it up to make her feel better.

Isabella closed her eyes, trying to forget the nonsense of it all, but no matter how hard she tried the strange images just wouldn't go away.

---

SUE LOOKED up as Isabella opened the door. She noted how, when her straight brown hair hung like a curtain over her forehead, it made her look slightly older. She was frequently told how similar they were and the joke went round that they were more twins than Archie and Daisy, who looked nothing like one another.

They were alike in so many ways: top of the academic pile, both enjoyed intellectual challenges rather than sporting endeavour and their features were remarkably similar: Isabella with straight mousy hair, Sue wavy mousy hair. Both had narrow faces, straight noses and brown eyes, although Sue's lips were fuller and her eyebrows finer.

But Sue's appearance turned heads – she exuded sex appeal – and she looked after herself, her clothes and hair had a sense of style, whereas Isabella had a nerdy more academic air and her clothes often sat on her like cloth sacks. Isabella regarded boys' general infatuation with Sue as a complete waste of time.

What's up now? Sue thought. Isabella's scowl had pulled her brow over her nose as though it were held by an invisible clip. 'Is everything alright?' she said.

Isabella slumped into a chair. 'You won't believe what I did,' she began. 'I told Solomon there was going to be a massive storm.'

Sue gasped. 'You did what?'

'I told him about the barometer.'

'Are you insane?' Sue said, turning a little red. 'I hope you didn't tell him it stemmed from my dream?'

'Of course I didn't!' Isabella said, holding her head in her hands. 'It was so embarrassing – he said he'd seen news of the storm on the forecast. I mean, what was I thinking?'

'I can't believe you did that,' Sue said, draping an arm around her and trying hard not to smile. 'But at least you tried.' Sue ran her hand over the scientific instrument her friend had made. 'Maybe your barometer's faulty – perhaps the calibration's wrong.'

'It's not possible,' Isabella said, frowning. 'Every time I reset it, exactly the same thing happens.'

'Well, please don't spend too long fiddling with it,' Sue said. 'You've got to watch the football tomorrow. It might be Daisy's final game. In any case, I'm required to keep you under control after last week.'

Isabella felt a burning sensation filling her cheeks. 'I know, I know. Solomon reminded me. But I just don't seem able to help myself—'

'Well you must. You can't verbally abuse the referee and then get yourself manhandled off the pitch, screaming like a loon. And you've done it twice.' Her eyes flashed at Isabella. 'You'll be expelled if you're stupid enough to do it again.'

'But Daisy gets kicked and flattened more than anyone—'

'I know,' Sue said, 'But she doesn't make a squeak. It's a mystery she makes it through week after week and continues to smile as if nothing happened. It's half the attraction – what makes her unique. And the fact that she's a footballing genius.

'You need to do the same and control that temper of yours.'

# 6 STORM WARNING

'The thing is,' Isabella said, 'I've done some calculations and I'm beginning to think that you might be right!'

'You really think so?' Sue said.

'From what you've told me, I think it's going to be absolutely massive. Look, here's some data showing severe weather depression models exactly like—'

'Where did you get this?'

'I pulled it off the web,' Isabella replied. 'Hacked into the Met Office data bank and downloaded flood sequences and weather system models from around the world.' She ran her finger down the page.

'Look, here's the data from Pakistan a couple of years ago, and this one's from Queensland, Australia; and here, this one's from that super-storm in Eastern USA; and this one's from Eastern Europe. Can you see the similarities in humidity and cloud density; it's unbelievable – inches of rain – a proper deluge; potential for devastation on a huge scale.'

Sue sat down and whistled. 'You're predicting rainwater at a couple of inches every twenty minutes covering a surface area of say ten square miles – based on what I saw in my sleep! We'll be white water rafting in less than two hours—'

Isabella nodded. 'Scary, huh. You told me that the rain was so hard and heavy you felt you could hardly breathe – that it was weighing you down, right? So, I've tried to figure out how much rain that would be and then multiplied it by the area involved, the potential volume the land can absorb and the capacity of the river to drain it away. Then I've added in the tidal flow of the river at York, and the increased effects of a full moon—'

Sue was astonished. 'Look, Isabella,' she began hesitantly. 'Let's get this straight. I had a really bad nightmare about you and the twins and a flood here at school. It was very real, sure, but it was only a dream.' She looked straight into her eyes. 'All of this,' she waved a hand at the barometer, 'it's great – really amazing, but it's pretty mad too.'

Isabella stared back. 'I'm doing this because I believe you, Sue.'

'You do?'

Isabella drummed her fingers on the desk. 'Yes, of course.' She paused as if wondering what to say. 'If you must know, I've had a similar nightmare.'

Sue nearly fell off her chair. 'What! Why didn't you say something? How similar?'

'Well, most of it was to do with water, but the rest is sort of different,' she said. 'And it's been peeing me off. Anyway, who says you're wrong? The evidence stacks up in your favour, even if the weather forecasters are saying it'll just be a localised storm. I mean, what if we're right and they're wrong? They've got it wrong before. Don't you think we should say something?'

'Forecasters screwed up years ago, before they knew what they were doing – before they had satellites and computer models,' Sue said. 'And anyway, the problem is, you can't go round with a megaphone and announce that there's a storm coming that's going to rip through the village because of the readings on a homemade, slightly random, barometer and a couple of freaky dreams. No one will believe us. Just look how Solomon reacted. We'll be laughed out of school and just imagine what morons like Kemp would say? The humiliation would be—'

'OK, OK, I understand,' Isabella said, rubbing her brow. 'I'll keep my mouth zipped, for now at least, I promise. You sure you're alright?'

'Yeah, but I can't seem to get rid of those images in my head – however hard I try.' Sue lowered her voice. 'Bells, there's one really important thing I need to talk to you about—'

But before she had a chance to expand, the door was kicked open and smacked into the wall. Sue jumped and then groaned when she saw who it was.

'Aha!' said the voice she least wanted to hear. 'I've found the nerds.'

It was Kemp and his friends, Mason and Wilcox.

---

'OH, MARVELLOUS!' Sue said sarcastically under her breath.

Isabella straightened. 'What can I do for you, Kemp?' she said curtly. 'Come to break my arm like you did my sister's?'

Kemp went to a desk in the middle of the room, turned a chair around and sat down heavily. 'And what would you do if I did? Run outside and scream and scream and scream and tell me off, like you usually do?' Kemp and the boys chuckled.

'I've got a message from chief nerd, Mrs Douglas. She wants to see you,' he said. 'Seriously, it's a real request and I'm just being friendly.'

Isabella smiled but her eyes were narrow and icy. 'Kemp, thank you. You've delivered your message; now you can leave ... we're busy.'

Kemp opened a book. 'I'm fine staying here for a while,' he replied putting his feet up on the desk. 'I believe I'm allowed to—'

'Allowed to what?' Sue cut in.

Kemp ran his eyes up and down Sue's body. 'Fancy a date, sexy Sue? Take you to the cinema. There's a new action film just out.'

Sue stood up smartly. 'Listen. I will never be interested, Kemp. Besides, you're far too young. Now go away.'

'Woah, no need to be like that,' Kemp said, standing up and grasping his heart as though mortally wounded. He turned to his mates and winked. 'Oh well, worth a try. One day eh, you and me.'

Kemp extended his arm and patted Sue's bottom.

Sue rounded on him, slapping his face, the sound like the crack of a whip. 'Don't you ever, ever touch me you filthy animal, or I'll report you for assault.'

Kemp's happy face vanished and a look of anger flashed in his dark eyes. 'You'll do what? Tell on me? Tell on me ... again,' Kemp fumed. 'Yeah, well big deal! Do you have any idea the number of hours I've spent in detention because of you two—?'

'You deserve everything you get,' Isabella said calmly.

'Forty-two,' he said, ignoring her. 'That's how many. Forty-two wasted hours.' He thumped the table. 'The teachers must think you're making it up, the way you pick on me—'

'Pick on *you*. Get lost, loser,' Isabella said, 'you make me want to vomit.'

Kemp smiled and sat down. 'Well now, speaking of vomit, a little bird tells me you've made a ba-rom-eter?' He said the word very slowly and as he did he felt under the desk and pulled away some sticky tape. He held up a small recording device. 'Hello little birdie.'

Isabella shrieked.

'Brilliant isn't it?' Kemp said, turning the black box around in his hands. 'Superb reception for such a tiny thing. I'll tell you what I'll do,' he continued, rubbing home his advantage, 'just before the football starts I'll announce – perhaps with Coach's megaphone – that there's a big storm on its way which will devastate the whole area. What was it, boys?' he said to the sniggering pair. 'Ah, yes ... we're going to be enjoying a bit of white water rafting, won't we?' He looked triumphant. 'And all because you dreamt about it. Isn't that lovely.'

The boys laughed, thickly.

Isabella's face was like thunder. 'That's immoral and illegal, Kemp!'

He waved her protest away. 'Now, pray tell where this clever barometer thing is.' He took a couple of paces to their desk.

'Christ, is this it?' he said picking it up.

'Don't you dare—'

'A glass jar filled with liquid and a straw.' Kemp seemed genuinely disappointed. 'What a pathetic, terrible, useless piece of sh—'

'Put it down!' Isabella demanded.

'Why? If anyone saw this you'd be laughed out of school,' he said, winking.

'Put it down—'

'Give me one reason?'

'Because I asked you to, that's why.'

'Not good enough—'

'Because it's an important part of my module—'

Kemp sneered. 'No it isn't. It's not even on your syllabus.'

'Please—'

'What will you do if I don't?'

'Put it down!' Isabella roared.

The door swung open.

'Archie,' Isabella gasped, relieved, 'what are you doing here?'

'Oh!' he looked at their faces. 'I'm dropping off a book ... what's going on?'

Kemp held the barometer in the air. 'Archie, my friend. Your sister thinks she should tell the world about a huge storm that's coming based on this hilarious scientific instrument. What do you think?' Kemp placed the barometer on the edge of the desk where it swayed for a moment and then righted itself.

Archie frowned. 'Er, I don't know.'

'Well if you don't know, Archie, then I really should dispose of it – to save these girls showing it to anyone and making complete idiots of themselves—'

'No!' Isabella cried.

Kemp ignored her and raised an eyebrow, 'and of course, to protect the great academic reputation of Upsall School.' Kemp laughed and slapped the desk with his free hand.

'I don't think that's a good idea,' Archie said, trying to read his sister's face. 'Why don't you give it back?'

'What!' exclaimed Kemp, turning on him. 'Don't get me wrong, but I'm the one who's going to decide whether they can or can't have it back. Tell you what,' said Kemp, addressing the girls again, 'if Sue goes out with me, I'll give it back.'

'Never!' Both girls instinctively replied. Sue slid her chair back so fast it fell backwards and clattered on the floor.

'There are rules for a reason, Kemp,' Isabella said, regaining her composure, 'so listen up. Here's what happens. You put the barometer down and leave it exactly as it is, while we go and get Mr Bellwood. Do you understand?'

Kemp scratched his fat nose. 'Bellwood will never believe you – and I've done nothing wrong. Nothing. Your little brother can prove that, can't you Archie?'

Archie shrugged.

The girls gathered up their things and headed towards the door.

Kemp wasn't finished. He winked at Sue and blew a kiss to Isabella. 'Remember, Mrs Douglas wants to see you both in the science labs. I'm just the messenger.'

'You'll pay for this,' Isabella yelled, as she closed the door, 'if it's the last thing I do.'

# 7 SWEAR ON YOUR LIFE

'Christ alive, Kemp,' Mason said, 'you're asking for it, didn't you hear her? She's gone off to get Bellwood. He'll go mental.'

Kemp smiled. 'You really think so? Well I don't know how it got there – do you?'

Mason suddenly realised what he meant. 'Me neither,' he said, his voice as thick as dough.

'Nor me,' said Wilcox scratching his long chin.

'That leaves only one other person who could have witnessed it.' Kemp turned to Archie. 'So Archie, tell me. Did you by any chance see who dropped the barometer out of the window?'

'Well, I'm not blind,' Archie replied.

Kemp rolled his eyes. 'I don't think he gets it, lads. I don't think he quite grasps the seriousness of the situation. Look, Archie, all you have to say is that you didn't see anything. Get it?'

'Right,' Archie said, wondering why it was that Kemp was such a massive jerk when Mason and Wilcox were around.

'I won't say a word,' he said mechanically.

Kemp hesitated. 'I'm not sure that's really acceptable. Swear on your life that you won't tell anyone.'

'Oh come on,' Archie replied, 'I'm not a kid and I'm not a sneak. You know that.'

'Archie, I need you to promise – on your life – that you're not going to tell anyone, that's all,' Kemp insisted. 'I mean, unlike your sister, you can keep your mouth shut, right?'

'If you didn't want anyone to know,' Archie argued, 'why did you throw it out of the window in the first place?'

Kemp smiled. Wasn't it funny how threatening words seemed to cause Archie no pain and physical beating seemed to cause Daisy, his twin, no pain either?

He stepped in front of Archie and drew himself up.

'Your big sister hates me. She's responsible for putting me in detention pretty much every week for the last two years. She cannot be trusted. Prove that you're different.'

'Oh belt up, Kemp, you're just showing off to moron and muggings. My sister doesn't like you because you do idiotic things like throw barometers out of windows and put dead rats in sports bags.'

Kemp chuckled as he recalled the rat incident. When he'd found a dead rat by the river, it gave him one of his best ideas ever – pop it in Isabella de Lowe's games bag, and wait.

And every day he waited, getting more and more excited about the slowly decomposing rat. It remained there for the best part of a week, with everyone wondering what the terrible smell was in the changing rooms. Then, on the afternoon of the school cross country run, as Isabella put on her tracksuit bottoms, out dropped the carcass, dripping in maggots.

Dynamite. He didn't realise Isabella had a vermin phobia and she'd screamed so much and puked everywhere and caused such a scene that eventually one of the teachers had to call an ambulance. They had to sedate her and take her away. She'd spent three hours a week for the next six months in counselling, according to Archie.

But the best bit was that no one suspected him in the slightest, apart from Isabella. The enquiry determined that the rat had taken a nibble of poison and wandered into her bag. But Isabella, he felt, had never forgiven him.

Archie sighed. 'Look, if it means that much to you, I'll do it, but only if *you* swear on your life not to do any more harmful, stupid, bullying things to Isabella, Sue or Daisy. It's got to stop.'

Kemp stuck out his jaw and moved it from side to side while he thought about what Archie had said. At last he nodded his head and said, 'OK, I agree. On the condition that it lasts until she puts me into detention again. Well, come on then, you say it first.'

Archie sighed; it was like being a seven-year-old. 'Do I really have to do this?'

'Yeah. Of course – if you want me to.'

Archie shook his head. 'I swear on my life that I won't tell anyone that you dropped the barometer out of the window,' he said. 'Now you say it!'

Kemp grinned. 'I swear on my life not to harm your sister and not to play any more tricks on her. There, good enough?'

Archie nodded. In his book you didn't swear your life away just for nothing.

'Oi, Mason, Wilcox,' Kemp said in his thuggish voice. 'Go and see if a teacher's coming. I want to speak to Archie 'bout something private.'

Mason and Wilcox sloped out of the room.

Kemp's face seemed to lighten up and his tone was altogether different. 'Yeah, sorry Arch. I know. I've been a bit of a tosser.'

'You're telling me!' Archie replied. 'Why do you do it?'

Kemp shrugged. 'Dunno. Boredom. Can't seem to help myself when I see your sister. Look, do you fancy bringing your rod over at half term,' he said, changing the subject. 'I caught a six-pound fish last weekend. Took me ages to land.'

Archie smiled. 'Only if you stop being a total moron, everyone's sick of it.'

Kemp rolled his eyes.

Archie ignored him. 'Well, I suppose I've got nothing better to do. Mum and Dad aren't coming home – more work digging up bones in the middle of nowhere.'

'They're never at home, are they,' Kemp said. 'But at least you've got parents.'

'I know,' Archie said, drawing a hand through his hair. 'It's so rubbish, though. Solomon's getting really worried. He thinks we can't cope.'

'Well, can you?'

'Of course we can. Old Man Wood's brilliant at stuff even if he is the oldest man in the world.'

They both laughed.

'But admit it, Archie, you are the scruffiest person I've ever met. I'm hardly surprised he's worried. I would be.'

Archie grinned. 'And unluckiest,' he countered. 'I'd been running through the forest.'

'Yeah, but being Bear Grylls doesn't work well with headmasters.'

Archie's eyes lit up. 'Lucky he didn't ask me to take off my jacket. I'd ripped the jumper almost the whole way down the back.'

'Look, come for the day,' Kemp said. 'I'll get my aunt to knock up some sandwiches and you can bring some of that unbelievable apple juice your old man whatsit brews.'

Archie smiled. 'His name is Old Man Wood.'

Kemp repeated it.

'OK. Deal,' Archie said, 'BUT it's on condition that you keep to your word about my sisters AND you get your aunt to do those beef sarnies; the last lot were awesome.'

Kemp nodded. 'For you, Archie, consider it done. It's the only thing she's good at. Get round to mine on Monday morning – about 10 am?'

Archie had reluctantly begun his fishing trips with Kemp last year and much to his surprise, away from school, he found Kemp to be a totally different person. Quiet and a patient and knowledgeable teacher. Kemp showed none of his aggression and he had genuine skill with the rod and tying flies and reading the flow of the river and where the best pools were.

Archie wondered whether he wasn't in some way jealous of people who were better than him at things, which was why he loathed Isabella and Daisy so much. Or maybe it was the gentle, calming effect of the river.

'But you're not to mention your sisters,' Kemp said.

'OK. Deal,' Archie said. 'But seriously, are Chitbury really going to kick lumps out of Daisy?'

'I said don't talk about her,' Kemp fired back.

Archie sighed. What was it about Kemp and his sisters? Were they always going to hate each other?

---

'QUICK, BELLWOOD'S COMING,' said Mason, as he ran back into the classroom.

'Out of the window!' Kemp suggested.

They ran to the window and pulled up the blind, only to find they were looking directly at Isabella, Sue and Mrs Pike.

'Drat,' said Kemp under his breath, and he smiled pleasantly back at them.

'Kemp,' the old teacher hollered, 'and Archie de Lowe. Well, who would have guessed? What can you tell me about the glass fragments on the concrete floor?'

Kemp opened the window and looked out. 'Glass?' he said innocently.

'The mess, down here,' Mrs Pike replied.

'No idea what you're talking about,' Kemp said. 'Window's been closed all along. Someone must have left it lying there.' He shrugged again. 'What is it anyway?'

Isabella shrieked. 'Kemp, you know perfectly well what it is.'

'A milk bottle?' he offered.

Mrs Pike stared at him with her cold eyes. 'No Kemp. It's Isabella's barometer.'

'A bar-hom-tier,' Kemp said thickly. 'What on earth is that?'

'Archie, did you see Kemp with the barometer earlier?'

Archie stared at the floor.

Mrs Pike tried again. 'Archie, why don't you tell us what happened?'

'Dunno,' Archie said, running a hand through his hair.

'What do you mean, you dunno?'

'Dunno,' Archie repeated, this time turning a little red.

Kemp looked straight into Mrs Pike's eyes. 'Honestly, there's been no one around.'

'Great!' Isabella stormed. 'Kemp's made you swear not to tell or something equally childish?'

The classroom door swung open. 'What have you done now, Kemp?' boomed Mr Bellwood, striding in.

'Nothing!' Kemp said. 'I was trying to explain to Mrs Pike here that I haven't done anything.'

'Yes you have, Kemp,' Isabella shouted through the window. 'You were the last person to have it and now it's in bits. It must have been you.'

'Prove it,' said Kemp, thrusting his jaw out.

'I shouldn't have to,' Isabella yelled back. 'Archie,' she pleaded, 'all you have to do is tell us what happened—'

Archie shook his head.

'Kemp, you've got history with this kind of mindless vandalism,' Mr Bellwood added, his moustache twitching.

'He should be expelled,' Isabella shouted.

'I haven't done anything—'

'Of course you have—'

'But you can't prove it – can you?'

'I DID IT!' Archie yelled. 'It was me.'

There was a long silence.

'You did it?' Kemp said.

'*You?*' Isabella quizzed.

'Archie?' Mr Bellwood said.

'Yes,' Archie sighed. 'I was fed up with you two always getting at each other, so I thought I'd save everyone the trouble.'

He bowed his head. 'I'm sorry.'

Isabella looked confused. This wasn't the sort of thing Archie would do, so why was he taking sides with Kemp?

'What did you say to Archie, Kemp? It's like you've done a pathetic deal or something—'

Kemp bit his lip and stared hard at her, his eyes cold and narrow. Then he spun and marched out of the room.

# 8 STORM GLASS

'I don't know what to say,' Isabella said. 'Why would you do such a thing?'

Archie shrugged.

'Right. Gosh!' Mr Bellwood said. 'I think you two need to sort this out for yourselves. There's no point in my hanging around. You're with me in ten minutes, Isabella.'

Isabella smiled in about as fake a way as she could, while Mr Bellwood made his way out of the classroom. The two siblings were alone.

'Why, Archie?' Isabella pressed.

'I'm sorry, but this warfare between you is ridiculous,' Archie said. 'If you stop putting Kemp in detention, he might stop bullying. He's only doing it as a reaction. Don't you see that?'

Isabella sighed. 'But the fact is, Archie, he IS a bully and I don't see why any of us, especially me and Sue, should put up with it. We have to protect ourselves and others. It's pretty simple, Archie. If he stopped being so childish, there wouldn't be a problem.'

She clamped an arm around his shoulders. 'Don't take me for a fool. It's perfectly clear that Kemp did this and you've been put up to it, haven't you?' Her eyes widened. 'Haven't you?'

Archie kept his head down and refused to say anything.

Isabella sighed. 'Have it your way, Archie. I'm not going to believe you and I haven't got the strength to argue about it. I just don't understand how you can be friends with him when he clearly causes me and Daisy so much distress. Do you have any idea how painful it is?'

Archie took a deep breath. 'But both of you give as good as you get. Daisy kicked Kemp on the shin earlier. If it had been the other way round, Kemp would be in massive trouble. Give him a break and I'm sure he'll chill. He's not that bad underneath.'

'You know that's not going to happen, Archie.'

He shrugged. 'Well, I'm sorry about your barometer,' he said, raising his eyes to meet hers.

Isabella pressed her lips together. 'Don't be; I just wish you'd be honest with me. To be frank, the barometer wasn't reliable. Actually, I've stumbled on a better idea; I'm going to make a storm glass.'

'Storm glass?'

'Yes. It's an old-fashioned weather gauge – and as a punishment for your behaviour you can help me make it.'

Archie smiled. 'Cool. But why the craze about weather stations?'

'Well, if you must know,' Isabella said, 'there's a curious weather system brewing bang overhead – have you noticed how sweaty and smelly everyone is – and,' she hesitated a little, 'this may sound completely nuts but Sue and I have had a premonition, a dream about torrential rain and flooding.'

Archie was astonished. 'Do you always do this after a dream?'

'No. To be honest, I never really dream. But I've got a strong gut feeling and I reckon it's worth finding out more, that's all.'

Archie scratched his head and wondered if he should mention his dream – and Daisy's mutterings in the middle of the night.

'So how does this storm glass work?' he said.

'It's pretty cool, I think. It shows what's going to happen to the weather – in the liquid in the glass. So if the liquid in the glass is clear, the weather will be clear. If small crystal stars form, snow is on its way, and when a thunderstorm is coming the liquid will be cloudy with small star crystals in it and so on. I'll show you later, if it works. But first, I'll need a few ingredients – and this, bro, is where you come in.'

Archie nodded. 'OK.'

'First, go and bat your eyelids at Mrs Culver and ask for 10 grams of camphor, she should have some for flavouring food. Tell her you need some in chemistry to show how a compound can burn without leaving an ash residue. If she starts asking questions, start talking about oxygen. For some reason Mrs Culver can't bear the actual word oxygen. Then go and find Mr Pike in the Maintenance Department and ask for some distilled water – fill a large, old, Coke bottle if you can. I know he keeps some to top up his forklift batteries.'

Isabella scratched her forehead thoughtfully, making sure she hadn't forgotten anything. 'So have you got that? Camphor and distilled water. I'll find some ethanol and the other compounds from Chemistry later on – shouldn't be too difficult,' Isabella added – almost as a reminder to herself.

As she rushed off she turned and said, 'The science labs are free straight after lunch, we'll do it then. Meet me there.'

———

ISABELLA LET herself into the chemistry lab using the spare set of keys that Mrs Douglas kept in a jar outside the biology room. When Archie arrived, Isabella was talking animatedly to Sue. Both wore white lab coats, safety glasses, face masks and Lycra gloves. They reminded Archie of surgeons in an operating theatre.

Sue noted his curious look and threw over a lab coat. 'Got to look the part in case someone comes along,' she said, her voice muffled by the mask.

Archie pulled his ingredients from a carrier bag. He'd had no problem getting the camphor, but when Mr Pike asked him in a most suspicious manner what the distilled water was for, Archie stuttered a little and told him that Isabella wanted it. Without hesitating, old Mr Pike poured out the water from a huge plastic container and handed it over, with no further questions.

In no time at all, Isabella and Sue had measured out the required parts of each of the elements which now sat in glass beakers, neatly labelled, on the desk. Sue lit a Bunsen burner and began to gently warm the water. Isabella waited for a couple of minutes before adding the ingredients, with the ethanol and camphor going in last. When these had dissolved to her satisfaction, Isabella asked Archie to find a large test tube sealed with a cork. Archie looked underneath the desk and put the test tube upright in a holding device on the desk.

In silence, and as Archie and Sue looked on, Isabella added each component until the beaker was three quarters full.

Isabella asked Archie to clean the apparatus in the sink in the far corner. He did as he was asked, filled it with water and just as he was about to clean it, the door swung open. For some reason he couldn't explain, Archie ducked under the table.

It was Kemp.

'There you are,' Kemp said with big smile. 'Been looking all over for you two.'

'GO AWAY!' the girls yelled at him.

'Whoa! Calm down, I've only come to apologise.' He looked down at the desk. 'What's all this then. Doing some illegal experiments are we? That's exciting. Creating a bomb or some poison for me or a tiny bit of chemical warfare—'

'It's none of your business, Kemp. Leave us alone.'

'Come on, I'm offering an olive branch. Anyway, have either of you seen Archie?'

Isabella caught Archie staring at her from behind one of the desks, out of Kemp's eyeline. He was shaking his head vigorously.

'Er, no. Sorry. No idea where Archie is,' she said as she brushed an imaginary speck off her lab coat, her face reddening.

Kemp eyed her suspiciously and then his eyes moved to the test tube on the desk. He picked it up before either girl had a chance to react. 'So this is your experiment, is it? A test tube full of cloudy potions. Brilliant.'

'Thank you for your interest, Kemp,' Sue commented, 'but to be honest this is a very boring experiment dealing with the creation of crystals using camphor, ethanol, distilled water and a couple of other things you probably wouldn't understand,' she said in her most condescending manner.

But Kemp was interested like a dog after a scent and his tone changed. 'So, if it's so boring, why are you doing it in break time?'

'As I said, Kemp, it's a simple experiment—'

'I don't believe you.' He stepped closer. 'It doesn't add up.'

'Please go away and leave us alone,' Isabella said sweetly, remembering what Archie had said.

But her words fell on deaf ears. 'Why won't you tell me what you're doing?' Kemp quizzed.

Isabella snapped. 'Why should we?'

Kemp smiled back. 'Cos otherwise, I'll smash it—'

'You wouldn't dare. Give it back immediately.'

Isabella lunged for the test tube, but Kemp was too fast.

'So come on, what have you got here?' he said. 'A lethal poison, a nerve gas—'

'Don't be ridiculous.'

'I'm not the one being ridiculous.'

Isabella huffed. 'Well, if you must know, it's a storm glass—'

'Oh my God,' Kemp said slowly. 'You're not still going on about this storm, are you? When will you grow up and do what everyone else does. Go and watch the weather forecast. Oh, but hang on, don't tell me – you're so far up in the hills that you haven't even got a telly!'

'Of course we do,' Isabella raged, taking the bait.

Kemp thrust out his jaw. 'You lot are so backward – I wouldn't be surprised if your mum has to shave Neolithic hair off her body. But then we'd never know because she seems to have disowned you.' He cocked an eye at Isabella.

'And that old woman who looks after you has whiskers coming out of her face like a cat,' he laughed. 'I know! Why don't you make a potion for hair removal. Customers in your own home!'

Kemp was enjoying himself and brushed aside Isabella's howl of complaint. 'Now, let me fill you in. Last night the man on the TELLY,' which he said in a deliberately loud and annoying voice, 'said that there was going to be a storm at some point over the next couple of days – but not a very big one – and certainly NOT one with WHITE WATER RAFTING.'

He marched over to the end of the room where Archie was hiding under the table.

Isabella gasped.

'I tell you what I'm going to do,' Kemp continued, 'I'm going to do you a favour and put you out of your ridiculous weather misery. I'm going to spin this tube thing like a spinning top. You do know what that is, don't you? By the time you get over here, either it'll be smashed to bits on the floor ... or, by some miracle, you may have grabbed it. But if and when this happens, I'll be long gone out of the door. Then, you can go and do what everyone else does and watch the weather forecast on the telly. You'll find it comes directly after the news.'

Kemp put the test tube between the palms of his hands and drew them quickly apart. The tube span so fast and so true that for a moment everyone in the room was fixated by it.

Satisfied with his handiwork, Kemp walked quickly towards the door, switched off the lights and shut the door behind him.

The sound of the latch clicking seemed to accentuate the wobbling noise of the glass. Instantly the girls rushed over in near darkness, but in their haste they careered into the side of the desk and caught their feet on the chair legs, sending both of them sprawling onto the lab floor. A huge noise of scraping chairs and upturned tables filled the lab.

As the noise receded they heard the test tube slow to a stop, followed moments later by a crash and tinkle of glass.

From outside the door came a roar of triumph.

# 9 BROKEN PROMISE

'Ow! My head,' Sue groaned. 'Isabella, get out of the way.'

'I can't. I've got a chair leg in my face. I can't move; I'm wedged in.'

'Will one of you please turn on the light,' Archie hissed. 'I'm surrounded by glass.'

After a minute or two, and as the children's eyes began adjusting to the light, Archie could just about make out the shards of glass that surrounded him. Water was everywhere, as well as a warm, sticky substance.

Kemp opened the door and flicked on the light. His face was beaming. 'What's going on here, then?' he said in a mock policeman-like voice.

He looked around to see an empty room and then, slowly, Sue got up. Her hair seemed to have come apart all over her face.

Then Isabella rose, rubbing a bump on her head.

Kemp was in hysterics. 'Bloody brilliant,' he laughed as he pulled his phone out of his pocket. 'Smile at the budgie.'

He pressed the button and the camera clicked and flashed. Kemp inspected the image. 'Lovely, you two look gorgeous. Social media here I come.'

Archie stood up, brushing fragments of glass from his jacket.

'Archie!' Kemp exclaimed, his expression changing. 'Where the hell did you come from?'

'I've been here all the time, you idiot.'

Kemp's manner changed immediately. 'You alright?' He pointed at Archie's sleeve. 'Is that blood?'

Archie looked down at his hand – blood was pumping out from a gash at the base of his thumb and covered his hand and his arm.

'Satisfied?' Isabella said, as she tiptoed around the larger glass fragments towards him. 'Happy now?'

She held Archie's arm and inspected it. 'Sue, get the first aid box, we need to stop the bleeding. And Kemp, now that you've stopped having your fun can you for once be useful? Go and find a brush and a mop.'

Isabella led Archie to the tap. 'This might hurt,' she said soothingly as she ran the water and placed Archie's hand underneath.

He winced.

There's still a bit of glass in there,' she said. 'I need a towel and tweezers and then we'll need to compress the wound.'

Sue barged past Kemp who stood frozen to the spot.

Archie gritted his teeth as the water ran into his cut, his blood colouring the water from pink to burgundy. Sue was over in no time and Archie shut his eyes tight as she plucked out the fragment before applying pressure on the wound.

When Archie opened them, Kemp was still standing in the same position.

Archie looked him in the eye. 'You SWORE on your life, you wouldn't do this kind of thing,' he said. '*You swore – on – your – life*,' he repeated, his voice hard and accusing.

'I held my side of the deal, but at the very first opportunity you couldn't resist it, could you? It's now totally clear to me that you value your life as pretty much worthless. What would your parents think? Do you think they'd be proud of you?'

Kemp's face fell and the colour drained from his cheeks. 'Sorry, Archie,' he said. 'I ... didn't realise ...'

And with that, he turned and fled for the door.

---

THE GIRLS BEGAN to clear up the mess. But Sue noticed something a little strange as she swept the glass into the dustpan. The glass they were clearing up wasn't the test tube with the storm glass experiment in it, but a much thinner glass typical of a large beaker.

In which case, she thought, where was the test tube?

As he watched her expression, Archie's smile had grown until he was beaming at her. 'I know what you're thinking,' he said at last. 'So, come on – spit it out.'

Sue burst out laughing. 'Archie, you're impossible. One minute you're best friends with that oaf and the next you're ...' she sat down heavily on the table top.

'Right, come on, where is it?'

'What?' Archie cried with feigned shock.

'Where is ... what?' Isabella said. She hadn't clicked.

Sue tutted. 'Oh come along, come along, Sherlock Isabella. Time to use those famous powers of deduction.'

'Sorry, I have absolutely no idea what you're talking about—'

'The storm glass, silly.'

'In fragments in the bin.'

Sue bit her lip. 'That's beaker glass, isn't it, Archie?'

'Beaker glass?' Archie said, thickly.

'Well it's definitely not the test tube, is it? *You've* got it, haven't you?'

Archie grinned.

Very slowly he moved his gaze towards his trousers and pointed at his crotch. 'It's right here,' he said.

Then, very deliberately and very slowly he began to unzip his fly.

'Don't you dare!' Sue exclaimed. 'If you pull anything out that isn't a test tube...'

Archie reached in and very gently teased it out. 'DA-NAH,' he said, his eyes sparkling.

Sue had gone bright red.

Archie held the test tube up in the air. 'Sorry, couldn't think of anywhere else quick enough,' he said. 'Thing is, I had no idea quite how uncomfortable it would be so when I crouched down I lost my balance and wiped out the beaker.'

Isabella looked delighted but horrified at the same time. 'A storm in your pants, Archie. Now that must be a first. Be thankful the storm glass didn't break down there – or just think where we'd be plucking glass fragments from!'

Archie placed the tube on the holder.

Isabella wagged a finger at him. 'One more thing, Archie,' she said. 'Please give it a clean before either of us has to handle it.'

# 10 A POINTLESS EXPERIMENT

After school, the children walked up the long, steep lane home, stopping, as Isabella had promised, for a swing on the rope that hung off the great branch of the oak tree.

By the time they arrived home it was almost dark, the air heavy and surprisingly warm for the time of year.

They entered the stone courtyard which was flanked on three sides by stone outbuildings and waved at Mrs Pye whose head had appeared at one of the two windows in her flat opposite the cottage. Using the dim glow of the outside light, Archie and Daisy immediately set about kicking their football, the scuffing noises of their kicks and the thumping of the ball echoing back off the grey stone walls.

Isabella watched them play and her mind turned back to the conversations with Solomon and Kemp, who had both been so rude about their cottage. It wasn't that bad, she thought, as she studied the exterior.

OK, so it was a bit of a mishmash of a moors farm but it wasn't too unusual, was it? Constructed from local Yorkshire grey stone and old, thick timbers, the roof was covered in moss and lichen, which seemed to hang over too far as though it was in need of a haircut. And just by looking at the blackened and slightly crooked chimneys it was easy to see that it was old. Very old.

Her keen eye noted how the stones were generally larger than most other farmhouses in the area and she wondered if they had been taken from the ruin. In any case, Isabella liked the way the occasional stone-free area was in-filled with red brick or exposed timbers.

She reckoned it had a cosy feel, especially with the large wisteria that covered the end of the courtyard wall and with the windows which were squished here and squashed there out of proportion to one another.

It was as if the builder simply slapped it up stone by stone without any plans in the hope that it would turn out reasonably well.

Architecturally, she supposed it was a bit of a deformity, but perhaps these quirky anomalies helped it blend in to the rocks and the forest beyond. Somehow, she concluded, it worked beautifully.

Mrs Pye waddled out into the courtyard. 'You're finally back, come on in.'

They followed her inside, the cooking aromas filling their nostrils.

Soon, Mrs Pye was cutting and throwing a mixture of vegetables into a large pan.

Archie smiled. 'Wow that smells good – what's for tea?'

Mrs Pye tapped her nose. 'Wait and see,' she said, 'be ready in fifteen.'

The kitchen was the centre of the house and drew them in with its feeling of warmth – of being used and loved. On the floor were big worn Yorkstone slabs, which bore a glossy sheen from continual use, and above were huge, old, oak timbers – as hard as iron – that ran in neat lines above their heads like ribs protecting the room. A keen eye might notice that one beam, right in the middle, appeared to be missing.

Fixed into these large timbers were hooks of different sizes which held a range of kitchen assortments and herbal delights, like bunches of rosemary, lavender, thyme, dried meats and fruit.

Although the kitchen was a curiosity in itself, the children would point out to their friends that it wasn't entirely a throwback to medieval times. Yes it was large and tall and made predominantly from stone and wood, but it was always bright and snug.

This was helped in part by two old wagon wheels that were suspended from the ceiling by three strong metal chains. On each wheel rim were eight electric candle bulbs – and being on a dimmer, the light exuded real character, especially when turned down.

It was then that Old Man Wood's brilliant stories were truly brought to life, the wrinkles in his old face bursting with a wide range of expression and meaning.

Opposite the fireplace was a large white porcelain sink and above this was a Gothic-style window through which they could see for miles across the Vale of York towards the low peaks of the Yorkshire Dales.

On either side of the window were oak cupboards and drawers capped with thick worktops, like coffin lids, the grain of which Archie liked to trace with his finger. Above these, at intervals, were wall units where discreet lighting shone down from each recess, gently illuminating the work surfaces.

At the far end, on the wall, was the latest addition to the family; a large flat screen telly, which Mrs Pye polished more than any other item in the house.

Running down the middle of the room was a large, rectangular, dark-brown oak table with an immense richness of depth and shine, and surrounding it were eight matching high-backed chairs that were usually tucked in under the table's edge.

Next to this was a brick inglenook fireplace where the old cooker lived. It was an old-fashioned metal range fired by wood, which Old Man Wood lovingly filled up every day from the wood store next to the larder.

Knowing Mrs Pye didn't like to be disturbed while she prepared supper, the children slipped out, made their way through the hallway and up the large staircase, along the corridor past the bathroom and then up the top stairs to their bedroom, the floorboards creaking at every step.

---

'WELL, COME ON THEN,' Daisy said, slinging her bag on her bed. 'Show me this amazing thing that's been in Archie's pants.'

Isabella pulled her books out of her briefcase and stacked them neatly on her desk. Then she changed her top, slipped into a pair of cotton trousers and brushed her hair. Daisy and Archie watched her patiently from the green sofa, knowing full well it wasn't worth rushing her.

'Right,' Isabella said as she unwrapped the test tube from her scarf, 'let's have a look.' She leant the glass between two books on the table. Three pairs of eyes stared at it.

'Bit foggy, isn't it,' Daisy said. 'So, does that mean it'll be foggy?'

Archie raised his eyebrows. 'Don't be silly, Daisy, this is serious science.'

Daisy giggled and elbowed Archie as they continued to stare at the test tube.

'Ooh,' Daisy cooed. 'Look at those little stars. What do they mean?'

Isabella pulled out her crib sheet. 'I think tiny stars means that it might be stormy.' She read it out loud. '*A cloudy glass with small stars indicates thunderstorms.*'

Daisy coughed. 'Is ... is that it?'

'What do you mean, is that it?'

'Well, it's very pretty,' Daisy said, glancing to Archie for support, 'but if you wanted to know thunderstorms were coming all you had to do was look at the forecast on the TV. Are you telling me you've gone to all this trouble to find out something we already knew?'

Isabella stood up. 'That's exactly what that fool Kemp said. If you must know, I think there's going to be a terrible deluge. Sue and I dreamt about it, so I'm trying to prove it scientifically.'

'Don't get me wrong,' Daisy said, picking it up and turning it round in her hands, 'but how will this help.'

Isabella sat down heavily. 'Well, to be honest, I was hoping for something a little more dramatic, like the crystals speeding up or something.'

'But how would that change anything?' Daisy quizzed.

Isabella sighed. 'I don't know. I really don't know. Maybe I'm hoping it will give us a warning or...' she shrugged.

'Actually, Daisy, I haven't a clue. I've got such a strong feeling about this, that I had to do something.'

Archie took hold of the glass from Daisy. 'This must be the worst scientific experiment ever,' he said. 'If Kemp knew he'd tear you to bits.'

'Please don't tell him.'

'I'll never tell him anything again after what he did today. I don't know if I'll ever forgive him.'

'Children!' Mrs Pye's strange voice was calling them. 'Tea's on the table.'

Four bowls brimming with dumplings in a thick vegetable broth sat steaming on the table. The children slipped into their chairs and began sniffing it as though they had never smelt anything quite so amazing before in their lives.

Mrs Pye pulled up a chair and sat at the end of the table watching them, like a sentry.

'Have you heard?' Isabella said between mouthfuls, 'Mum and Dad aren't coming home.'

Mrs Pye's piggy eyes seemed to pop out of their sockets. 'What, my darling!' she said. 'No. Well I'm blowed – and I'm sorry for you.'

'Can't you say something to them when they get back?' Archie asked. 'It's like they're never here.'

'Don't you eat with your mouth full, little Arch,' Mrs Pye scolded. Then she sighed, 'You know it isn't proper for me to tell your folks what they can or cannot do. If they choose to be away, then it's for a good reason. They miss you just as much as you miss them.'

Mrs Pye said this with as much conviction as she could, but she could see the disappointment in their eyes and wondered what on earth it was that so completely occupied their parents' time. Something to do with old relics, something terribly important they'd told her.

She sighed. In any case she loved looking after them and she counted her blessings. Being here at Eden Cottage was the only thing she could remember. There was nothing else. Nothing apart from the memory of a sudden flash and a terrible pain that coursed through her body.

She only had to raise her left arm above her head or try and touch her toes to get a reminder. By all accounts it was a miracle that Old Man Wood had found her in the woods, miles up in the forest, in a heap, on the verge of death, her face and shoulder smashed, her clothes ripped to bits – hardly breathing – and he carried her all the way home, singing to her, trying to keep her alive.

Old Man Wood still sang it, though she had no idea what it meant. And over the years she'd picked it up:

*O great Tripodean, a dream to awaken*
*The forces of nature, the birth of creation.*
*Three Heirs of Eden with all of their powers*
*Must combat the rain, the lightning and showers.*
*In open land, on plain or on sea,*
*Survive 'till sunset – when their lives will be free.*
*But the Prophecy has started – it's just the beginning.*
*And it never seems to end, it never seems to end.*

For several months, Old Man Wood and the children's parents nursed her, slowly building up her strength, giving her every support, trying to help her remember her past. But there was emptiness in her memory as if a blanket covered her previous life.

She'd had to learn everything again, although it was true that some things came to her with little difficulty. She had no name, no address, no family, no lovers, no pets, nothing she could ever recall laughing with or crying at.

The first time she laughed was when the babies crawled to her bed and gurgled in her ear, especially little Archie, who was like melted butter. These were her first memories, and happy ones too.

The authorities had been contacted, but no one had come forward. And after a while she didn't want to go anywhere else and why should she?

She loved the children, she loved the quiet remoteness of Eden Cottage with its big views over the Vale of York towards the peaks of the Dales in the distance, and she felt safe being close to Old Man Wood who, although he came and went, seemed not to have a harmful bone in his body.

And it felt right that she should look after the children. A nurturing feeling ran through her core that was both instinctive and natural.

Besides, after she had been found, her face was not one to parade around the streets of Northallerton. Her nose seemed a little squashed to one side and she had a thick scar on her hairline that made her look a bit like Frankenstein's monster – or so she'd been told by Daisy. She couldn't care less, but she was mindful that her appearance might reflect on the children with name-calling and jibes.

As far as her name went, the children called her after the one thing she was a natural at; baking pies. So she was known affectionately as "the famous Mrs Pie", and somehow it stuck.

The children's parents tweaked the spelling to make it feel right and Mrs Pye she'd been ever since, living in the apartment on the top half of the old converted barn across the grey, stone-slabbed courtyard.

# 11 HEADMASTER VISITS

For such a big man, Old Man Wood moved graciously and unhurriedly like a very large gazelle. He was light-footed, although when he pulled himself out of an armchair he groaned in exactly the same way as any old man. But he rarely complained about his age. He popped his head around the door.

'Evening all,' he said. 'Smells marvel-wonderful.'

Isabella got up and gave him a big hug.

Old Man Wood hugged her back, closing his eyes. 'Now then, little one. I sense all is not as it should be.'

'Correct,' Isabella replied, wanting to burst into tears. 'Everything today has been awful. It's like the worst day in every respect.'

'No one died, though, did they?'

Isabella was a little thrown. 'Well no, of course not. But Archie cut his hand and Kemp's been a total jerk again and smashed my barometer and even Solomon gave us a talking to.'

'Oh dear,' he said kindly. 'Tell me again, what is a *jerk*? I find it hard to keep up with your words sometimes—'

'A moron, idiot, fool – someone who doesn't fit in,' Isabella rattled back.

Old Man Wood rubbed his chin as though absorbing this information. 'Any good news?'

'Suppose so,' she said softly, 'Daisy's playing tomorrow.'

Old Man Wood smiled. 'There. Good for you, Daisy, now finish your tea and then we'll talk about it. Must say, I can't remember such strange weather. Feels as though a storm is brewing right bang on top of us. An appley-big one at that. I can feel it in my old bones.'

Isabella slammed her fists on the table, making everyone jump. 'That's exactly what I've been trying to tell everyone. No one believes me; Solomon, Kemp, you two—'

'Woah! Chill, Bells,' Archie chipped in. 'It's just that your experimentation is a bit ... bonkers.'

Mrs Pye piped up, 'That nice man the weather forecaster on my big television said there might be a bit of a storm. Localised—'

'Arrggh!' Isabella cried. 'NO! NO! **NO**! Not you as well!'

Mrs Pye turned bright pink and looked as though she might burst into tears.

'That's enough of that, Isabella,' Old Man Wood said. For a moment there was quiet. Old Man Wood furrowed his brow as though deep in thought. 'What's funny,' he began, 'is that I've been having very strange dreams. Real clear ones about a great deal of rain, flooding, storms. Thing is, I'm so old it could mean anything'

'Really?' Isabella gasped. 'You've had dreams too?'

The children stopped eating and stared up at him.

'Oh yes. More than ever. Shocking stuff too. I should check those apples I gave Mrs Pye—'

'There's nothing wrong with those apples, I'm telling you,' Mrs Pye replied from the end of the table.

'If that's the case,' Old Man Wood said, 'maybe there's going to be a storm and three quarters.'

He reached across, grabbed an apple, rubbed it on his jumper and took a large chomp. 'Now, you're old enough to know,' he continued between mouthfuls, 'that once upon a time there was a great storm and then a flood. I'm sure you will have learnt about it.'

Isabella groaned. 'You wouldn't mean the Bible?' her voice was laced with sarcasm.

Old Man Wood seemed surprised. 'Ooh. Yup. That's the one. At least I think it is. You know about it, do you? With a man they called, now what was his name— ?'

'Noah?' Isabella added as though bored rigid.

'Ha!' Old Man Wood clapped his big hands. 'Just as I thought. Been muddling that one for a while. So you know about it. How marvel-wondrous.'

Isabella shook her head. 'Blimey O'Reilly – at least we know where Daisy gets it from.'

The conversation was interrupted by a banging at the door. The family stared at each other.

'Who on earth could that be?' Old Man Wood said.

Before anyone else could move, Daisy tore off to see who it was.

'You'll never believe who it is,' she said, as she rushed back in, excitement in her voice. 'It's Solomon!'

For a minute they looked at each other not sure what to do.

'Well, don't you think you should let him in,' Old Man Wood said.

The children headed towards the door.

'Mr Solomon, sir.'

'Hello, Archie, Daisy, Isabella. Just a brief visit – to see how you're getting along. May I come in?'

They led him to the sitting room where Old Man Wood was adding a couple of logs to the fire.

'Mr Wood, how nice to see you,' the headmaster said as he eyed up the old man. He was just as tall, big and wrinkly as he remembered and had the strangest little tufts of hair protruding from an otherwise bald but patchy scalp. In fact, if he wasn't mistaken, the old man looked identical to the first time he'd ever met him twenty-five years ago.

He remembered then thinking what peculiar clothes he wore. His trousers and shirt were made entirely of patches, as though he had never once been clothes-shopping. It made him look like a moving patchwork quilt and he immediately thought of Archie and his curious attempt at school uniform.

Solomon wondered whether these had been stitched together by Mrs Pye, who was loitering in the doorway.

He strode over and shook her hand. 'Isn't that road awfully narrow and steep?' he said as a way of breaking the ice. 'It must be devilishly tricky to navigate when the weather turns. Do those parcel couriers ever manage to find you?'

Mrs Pye froze and turned as pink as a lobster.

Old Man Wood rescued her by moving in and extending his hand. 'Now then, is everything in order? Perhaps I could offer you a glass of something, apple juice, tea, my special rum?'

'How kind,' Mr Solomon said, 'a glass of apple juice will be fine. I can't stay long.' The headmaster rubbed his hands against the fire – for a man his age, his handshake was like iron. 'Could I talk to you, er, in private.'

Old Man Wood turned to the children. 'Children, would you excuse us.'

The children headed out of the room while the men sat down.

'You are aware that the children's parents won't be returning until after half term?'

Old Man Wood nodded.

'As I explained to the children, this is highly unsatisfactory.'

'Rest assured,' Old Man Wood began in his deep, soothing voice, 'the children are in perfectly good health and are super safe here.'

'Good health, yes, safe, yes – there's no doubt about that – but can you give them the kind of assistance that should be expected if, and I hate to say this, if anything goes wrong.'

'What kind of wrong, Headmaster?'

'Well, if Archie was to break his arm again. How would you get him to hospital? And what if there's a fire? Are you capable of protecting yourselves? A fire engine would never get up your lane.'

Old Man Wood burst out laughing, his rich, deep, joyful voice bouncing back off the walls. 'They are strong children,' he said, 'and are quite capable of looking after themselves, with or without me.'

It had the effect of making Mr Solomon feel rather idiotic. 'With respect, Mr Wood,' he fired back. 'Archie's appearance is repeatedly way below standard. Can you explain this? And can you give me your word that Isabella won't disgrace the school by violently interfering with the officials during our remaining football matches as she has done in the previous two?

'I am in agreement with you that they are strong and capable, Mr Wood. Daisy shows this with her keen soccer skills, but she hasn't done a stroke of work the entire time she's been with us. She is on course to fail her exams – and then what?'

Old Man Wood didn't know what to say so he simply smiled back.

Solomon wondered if the old man had listened to a word. 'Mr Wood, I'll be frank with you. I have no argument with your family, in fact I am very fond of the children, and Isabella shows exceptional academic promise.'

He removed his glasses and rubbed them on a cloth before setting them back on his nose.

'The school exists on the legacy provided hundreds of years ago by the de Lowe family. Each successive headmaster has granted a generous bursary in favour of the family as set out in the original deeds. But I must tell you this: I am to retire at the end of the term, and I doubt my successor and his governors will be so generous.' Solomon paused and took a sip of his apple juice.

'In each of the examples, the children would have been severely reprimanded and perhaps even expelled.' Now Solomon spoke a little slower. 'And in each case, the bursaries would certainly cease. While they may look at the de Lowes as a special case, these are difficult times and there is every chance they won't.'

Old Man Wood nodded his head and scratched an imaginary beard. 'I'll make sure the children's parents understand the situation entirely,' he said.

'Good, thank you,' Mr Solomon replied. He cleared his throat. 'Please don't be offended, but are you fit and well enough to continue in the role as the children's caretaker? I worked out you might be nearing the heady heights of 90 years—'

'I may be old, Headmaster,' Old Man Wood said, 'but body and mind are ticking along just nicely, thank you.'

'I ask these questions for the sake of the children.'

'Mr Solomon,' Old Man Wood chuckled. 'When you are as old as I am, love, health and well-being are the things of importance. It is harder to remember things from one's youth but we are lucky to be in possession of excellent health and are blessed that Mrs Pye feeds us and nurses us. You're right to be checking up, though. We don't have so many visitors up here in the hills.'

Old Man Wood decided to change the subject. 'Have you plans for your retirement?'

Solomon seemed to relax. Perhaps it was the apple juice. 'Yes,' he sighed. 'As a matter of fact, I'm hoping to go to the Middle East to see some of the ancient tombs and archaeology – that kind of thing.'

A little while later, as they got up and made their way to the door they heard scuffling sounds heading off towards the kitchen.

Old Man Wood and Solomon exchanged a smile.

'Children,' Solomon said loud enough so they could easily hear. 'I have something to say to you, so you may as well come back here.'

They appeared from around the corner, looking sheepish.

'I am leaving Upsall School at the end of the term,' Solomon began. 'I have decided the time has come to retire. Please keep this to yourselves until I have made the official announcement after half term.'

He looked each of the children in the eye. 'I would be disappointed if any of you were to leave the school before me, so I suggest you work together to improve those areas that need addressing. For example, Archie and Daisy, as I mentioned before, learning the opening stages of the Bible story, the bits where Adam and Eve are ejected from the Garden of Eden.'

He gave them a knowing look over his half-moon glasses. 'I have a suspicion that this may well be the main topic in one of your exams.' He winked, knowingly.

'And the other thing is that I would like very much to win the football trophy tomorrow. I don't mean to put any additional pressure on you two, but it would be wonderful to leave the school knowing that we had reached the pinnacle in both sports and academics. So, the very best of luck.'

'We'll do our best,' Daisy said enthusiastically.

Isabella seized her opportunity. 'What about the storm, sir,' she cut in. 'If it breaks there's going to be a disaster. I just know it.'

Solomon's friendly manner evaporated. 'Isabella, I cannot possibly see how a small, localised storm will make the slightest bit of difference. The river has flooded once in the twenty-five years I have been with the school. They may just have to play in the rain and get a little wet. It's as simple as that.'

He smiled and headed out of the oak door.

Isabella wasn't finished. 'But, sir,' she exclaimed as the door closed in her face.

Old Man Wood drew the bolt. 'What a nice man,' he said. 'I wouldn't worry too much about what he said. You're doing well at school and you're fit and healthy and you're polite and you've got friends. What more could you want, eh? Talented littluns, aren't you. Now, off to bed, the lot of you.'

A rumble of thunder boomed high up in the night sky.

Old Man Wood sniffed the air. 'Something tells me tomorrow is going to be a big, big day.'

# 12 THE DREAMSPINNERS

If the three children had awoken and brushed the sleep out of their eyes and read the clock on the wall it would have told them that it was shortly after two in the morning. But they wouldn't wake, not now, for their sleep was long and deep.

It was the night-hour of dreaming.

Four dreamspinners, like the one Archie had seen over Daisy, arrived in a pinprick of a flash. The flash they made wasn't a flash any human could see, but to the dreamspinners it was a tiny, intense, burst of energy. They had come to see Genesis, the eldest dreamspinner, give the last part of the Prophecy of Eden – the Tripodean Dream – the final part of the most important dream ever created.

Using their eight delicate legs banded with grey, each spider-like dreamspinner picked its way over an invisible grid on the air until they were suspended above the children.

From where their abdomen should have been was a maghole, a round hole in which tiny streaks of lightning radiated in wave after wave of blue and white forks. It was through this that a dreamspinner could invert to any place it wished, almost instantly.

Above this maghole, a wiry tubular neck connected the body to a small head the size of a clear, white orange. On each face were three jet black eyes the size of quails eggs and in the recess beneath the middle eye – in place of a nose – was a dent, as if a tiny scoop of ice cream had been cut out. There was no mouth, well certainly nothing the children or anyone else would call a mouth, just a tiny slit the size of the edge of a small coin.

If the children had woken, opened their eyes and looked up, they would have seen the old oak beams holding up the roof above and the dangling lamp with its musty-coloured lampshade and the curtains and drapes that hung across their sections: the dreamspinners would not exist. To human eyes – they are invisible.

And neither can they be heard. The children would have caught only the gentle noises of the night outside; the rustle of leaves, or the scurrying of a mouse but never, ever, a dreamspinner.

---

GENESIS WAS the largest and oldest dreamspinner. She had spun more dreams than she could remember, right back to the beginnings of modern humans, but she knew her time was up – death creeps up on a dreamspinner just as it does on every organism. When the moment arrived, it had taken her by surprise; she had flashed into human view in the midst of offering a dream. It was unthinkable. Her end was close at hand.

How could this have happened? And why when she was delivering the most crucial dream in memory? Genesis could hardly bear to think about it. How had she grown so old and not noticed? Was this the cruel way in which old age announced itself; by failures in routines, failures of body parts – failures that could ruin everything?

Genesis counted her blessings that it hadn't happened a moment earlier, for she was the only one who knew how to spin the Tripodean Dream – the dream that showed the Prophecy of Eden.

She touched the burn marks where the boy's eyes had looked upon her. The pain was bearable. Now all that remained was the final part of the Tripodean Dream and then the Prophecy would be told. It was the last dream she would ever give.

Genesis studied each of her eight delicate claws one by one, as if paying homage to them for their service. For the first time she noted the wear; the way so many had turned grey where once they were bright white, how her slender knuckles and joints were worn down to delicate slivers of hardened bone.

As she seamlessly morphed each claw from needle to duster to holder and back to a claw, she was filled with a deep sense of foreboding. What if the Heirs don't understand the dreams of the Prophecy, then what? She shivered at the thought. Nature would never allow them to survive, she knew that much. And what if Cain reappeared?

Putting her thoughts aside, she sent out a communication via the tiny vibrations of her legs to the waiting dreamspinners, Gaia, Janana and Asgard.

'You are here to witness the last part of the Tripodean Dream, for there must be no doubting it. Their sleep pattern is deep and flowing. I am ready.'

Genesis moved her spidery frame deftly through the air as though walking on top of invisible threads. Dropping her head and two slender legs into her electrical middle – her maghole – she pulled out microscopic-sized granules of powder.

Momentarily, she was mesmerised by them. Fragments that hold so much power, she thought, realising that power was the wrong word. They were far more than that; they were the opportunity of life itself.

Taking one last deep breath, Genesis positioned herself so that four of her long, opaque legs dangled down either side of Isabella's sleeping head like anchors, holding her steady for the dream she was about to deliver. Her other four legs sat by Isabella's lips, ready in anticipation.

With her ovate jet-black eyes, Genesis stared at the girl. Instinctively she began to feel the rhythm of her breathing.

'Child,' she thought, 'interpret this dream as best you can for all our sakes. Try to understand. Try to make the right choices.'

Then, just as Isabella inhaled, two claws spun at amazing speeds, releasing a fine powder directly into her mouth, the dust being drawn deep into her lungs.

Genesis plucked more blue, red and yellow powders from within her maghole and then, at exactly the right moment and in precisely the correct amounts, the dreamspinner lowered her silky legs towards the child's mouth and once again filtered the dream powders to the sleeping girl.

Years of experience had taught her to understand every slight frown and flicker, every twitch and groan. After every breath, Genesis stopped and gauged her reaction, making tiny adjustments to the rate of powder in proportion to the volume of air drawn in.

So far, so good, thought Genesis. Already she tosses and turns. The dream powders have entered her mind. Now she begins her lucid and vivid journey. Nothing will wake her.

With the dream complete, Genesis walked through the air across the dark room and settled above Daisy, where she repeated the procedure, scrutinising every movement, looking for signals, making sure that everything was perfect.

Finally, it was Archie's turn.

Genesis had noted the strong, intense reactions of the boy, similar perhaps to those of the Ancient Woman. But his haunting, wailing cries were like those of someone else. Someone she'd hardly dared make the comparison with. Was it really so like Cain?

Genesis studied the reaction of the children, noticing that the noises they made were not just the anguished, crazed cries of their previous dreams, although these might come later. These were sounds that exuded certainty and confidence; Daisy laughing, Archie smiling, Isabella's face beaming with happiness.

Maybe the final part of the Tripodean Dream was a reassurance that it would be worth the trouble ahead. She dipped a slender leg into her maghole.

After all, she thought, there must be hope as well as fear.

Genesis, tired and aching, climbed into the middle of the room and addressed the dreamspinners, her legs flicking with subtle, silent vibrations.

'As you also know,' she said as she floated towards Isabella, 'the Tripodean Dream comes with a gift – a special gift – for each Heir of Eden.'

She dipped two sylph-like legs into her maghole and withdrew them, studying the ends. 'These crystals were passed to me before my mother died, as once they were handed to her. Their purpose? To help those who seek the rebirth of the Garden of Eden.'

She noted a strong vibration from Asgard but ignored him. 'If the Heirs of Eden succeed in the tasks set before them and open the Garden of Eden,' she said, 'the stock of spider web dream powders will be replenished and wondrous dreams may begin afresh for all life on Earth.

However, if Eden is not reborn, the dreams of hope, wonder and creativity, the dreams that offer a spark of life, will vanish. Everything in the living worlds will alter—'

'Why do we meddle?' Asgard snapped, his legs moving quickly, the vibrations aggressive and powerful. 'If the Tripodean Dream had not been spun, who is to say that life would not continue? Besides, the Tripodean Dream has been given to mere *children* of man. These riddles were made by Adam when he was strong and powerful, a wizard at the height of his powers. Children are not equipped to tackle what lies ahead; the storm will tear them to pieces, they will not survive. Furthermore they do not seek, or even know of, the Garden of Eden—'

'This is not the time to argue the rights or wrongs of it,' Genesis interrupted, her vibrations overriding his. 'The time has come for change. These children are the Heirs of Eden whether they like it or not, marked by their blood and their birth.'

She stretched out two legs and slowly drew them in. 'It is up to the Heirs of Eden alone to interpret the dreams that I have given them. And when the sky bursts and the thunderbolts rain down upon them, our lives and the lives of every living thing are in their hands, whether they like it or not.'

Genesis let her words sink in. 'The Prophecy tells that if they fail, rain will fall for forty of their days and forty of their nights. It will rain with such purpose that few will survive.'

Genesis shifted uneasily. 'To succeed, the Heirs of Eden must outwit the storm and seek out the tablets of Eden. Using their minds, their strength and their skills they will prove that mankind is ready for a new time. It is our role to herald in this new cycle of life, whichever way it falls. It begins now with these gifts.'

Genesis' silvery-grey, ghost-like body now sat directly above Isabella's sleeping face, her maghole emitting blue shards of light over Isabella's pale face.

There was a deep silence, broken only by the child's gentle breathing.

Quietly, Genesis began:

*'For the eldest, yellow spider web powder – for hands and feet.*
*Hands that guide, heal and protect.*
*Swift feet for running.'*

She transformed the claw-end of one of her legs into a needle so long it was like a slither of pure ice melting into nothing. With it she injected a tiny yellow speck into the soft flesh between thumb and finger on each of Isabella's hands.

Moving down Isabella's body, she repeated the action on her ankles, the needle entering the tender skin by her Achilles' heels.

As she withdrew the needle, Genesis noted a buzz of electric-blue energy that flowed through and over the girl's sleeping body. The gifts are undamaged by time, she thought.

Without hesitating, Genesis walked across the night air and was above Daisy, moving directly over her face. As she extended her legs she signed again, the vibrations clear to the onlookers:

*'Blue spider web powder, for eyes to see when darkness falls and ears to hear the tiniest of sounds.*
*With eyes so sharp and ears so keen, she will understand what others do not hear or see.'*

A minuscule blue crystal fragment sat at the very tip of the needle. With astonishing precision she injected the tiny fragments through the delicate tissues of Daisy's closed eyelids into the retinas of her eyeballs. Then, with two of her other legs anchoring her abdomen, she carefully slid two needles down Daisy's ear canals and injected the crystals directly into her eardrums.

On the withdrawal of the needle, Genesis noted again that Daisy fizzed momentarily with the strange electrical current.

So skilful was her technique that other than the gentle rise and fall of their chests, Isabella and Daisy did not flicker a muscle.

Now it was the boy's turn; the one she dreaded most. She sensed other spider legs vibrating nervously nearby. She stretched out a limb and drew it slowly back in.

'Dreamspinners,' she announced. 'The first of his gifts is to his heart. When the needle leaves it will trigger a reaction that will herald the start of the quest to open the Garden of Eden. From this moment forth, the clouds will deepen and build with rain. We do not know what will happen.'

Her vibrations were like a whisper. 'There must be absolute quiet.'

Genesis stood above Archie's chest, which heaved in front of her with his every deep breath.

A roll of thunder drummed high above them as she steadied herself and recalled the previous gifts.

*'Yellow for hands and feet,'* she said.
*'Blue to hear and see.*
*But red is the one – for heart and mind – for strength – and understanding what may be.'*

With her limbs aching, Genesis galvanised herself for one final effort.

*'Red spider web powder, a gift of power, when strength is needed.'*

And, on the word "strength", Genesis thrust her claw with the needle high into the air.

She paused and steadied herself, marking the exact spot on his chest where she would thrust it in.

She shut her eyes.

The needle swept down and pierced the boy's heart. His body fizzed. Genesis held it as long as she dared, making sure every last little speck of spider web powder was injected.

As she withdrew the needle, a terrific thunderbolt rattled the cottage.

Genesis trembled. Nature had awoken.

A sign from one of the other dreamspinners confirmed her suspicions that his sleep waves were changing. But a strange feeling filled her. A feeling of exposure, a feeling she had felt only once before. 'No!' she cried out, 'not my invisibility!'

She concentrated hard on the boy. *I must finish this*, she thought. She dipped her leg into her maghole and withdrew her final gift.

*'Red spider web powder.*
*The first for strength – another for courage.'*

A minuscule red fragment flashed into the tender flesh beneath Archie's chin. But before she could complete the task, she heard a gasp and felt a movement.

A burning pain seared into her.

Instantly her legs retracted as she looked up.

In front of her, on a face contorted by fear, were Archie's large brown eyes – staring directly back at her.

---

A SHORT WHILE AFTER THIS, candlelight filtered in to the corridor and a soft light spread through the door into the attic room. In rushed Mrs Pye, out of breath, her flame-red hair hanging down to her waist, her small sharp eyes accentuated by the glow of the candle.

'Goodness me! Oh my little Arch,' she said rushing over to him, 'I never heard such a terrible scream in all my life. I thought you might have died.' She looked over him lovingly, wiping away the sweat on his brow.

'I ... I had the strangest dream, Mrs P. I swear I was about to be stabbed by ... by a terrible eyeless, ghostly monster—'

'Is that right?' Mrs Pye said softly, 'and eyeless as well?'

'It had a blue hole in its middle—'

'Well, well, I never. Now, I think you're old enough to know better than to be troubling yourself with all that bunkum,' she continued as she helped him back to bed. 'Come now. Get yourself back to sleep.'

Mrs Pye sat on the edge of his bed and cradled him. She stroked his cheek tenderly as Archie closed his eyes. Then she lowered his head onto his pillow.

A gentle, faraway tune that blended with the rhythmical sounds of sleep came to her – the song that had once been sung to her by Old Man Wood – and she hummed it quietly, the music soft and soothing.

Before long, Archie's breathing slowed and he returned to a deep slumber.

Mrs Pye kissed the young boy on the forehead.

What was it, she thought, about this funny young boy; so scruffy, so underrated, so sensitive. And yet with a strange toughness.

---

WATCHING FROM THE CEILING, her invisible status functioning once more, Genesis the dreamspinner was relieved that the final dream had run smoothly, even if the boy might have missed out on the final part of his Gift of Eden.

If the children failed, would the blame be levelled at her?

Only time would tell.

Genesis drew her legs together and took comfort in the warm glow of electrical current that sprayed over her abdomen and nursed her burns where the boy's eyes had seared into her.

She wondered about the Tripodean Dream. Maybe Asgard was right; maybe the whole thing was foolish. And although she dared not admit it openly, she knew perfectly well this undertaking had never been designed for the children of man.

She closed her eyes and recalled what she knew – what she remembered. Nature's course must run as it always did.

Nothing could stop the Prophecy now. The Gifts of the Tripodean Dream had triggered the building of rainclouds. The great flood was almost upon them.

Nature had called for a new time. A time to wash away the old and bring in the new.

Would the children survive? Who could tell. It was impossible for them to have any idea of nature's fury. She shivered and her old legs rattled against one another.

Failure meant forty days and forty nights of devastation – for everyone – the planet wiped out. Even if the children survived the flood it would take nothing less than a miracle to find the stone tablets, let alone secure the key to the Garden of Eden.

Asgard wasn't stupid. Yes, perhaps *she* was the fool. At least she was wise enough to know that nature's wishes cannot be resisted.

And what of the old man – there to guide and help? He had forgotten everything. Time had taken its toll – he was old, but was he now – in a curious twist of fate – *a liability*?

She dipped her claws into her maghole. She would make sure he was given a dream every night that would somehow, *somehow* – however hard, however shocking, however desperate – stir him into action. Something had to click, it just had to.

With these thoughts, she inverted into her maghole and vanished into thin air.

# 13 CAIN'S LUCK

How could Genesis let it happen? Asgard fumed.

Could she not see that the whole Tripodean Dream was doomed? These were children. Simple, pathetic children. They had no chance of success, none whatsoever. The world of man had slipped into the sort of decline that had been talked about from the outset. The species deserved to fail.

Children to save the planet? Absurd. And what of Adam, Asgard thought. A bumbling old fool who had forgotten his mantra. It was laughable. Time really had got the better of him.

There was only going to be one winner in this shambles, and that was Cain, the Master of Havilah. Cain would finish them off even if their trials didn't. A ghost like Cain had enough tricks to see off these children one hundred times over.

Asgard knew what he had to do. He had to find Cain and somehow transport him from Havilah to Earth. Then Cain would mop up this sorry affair once and for all. He had a talent for this type of occasion. And anyway, what were the alternatives?

The dreamspinner toyed with the thought and dipped a couple of legs in his maghole, feeling the warmth. Why did it sound so right, yet feel so horribly wrong?

The world had changed so much; was there a need for inspirational, magical dreams from Eden? Was there a requirement for dreams that gave insight, or dreams that inspired change, or for dreams that solved puzzles or elicited love and joy? Did dreams have a place in the world?

Maybe – maybe not, Asgard thought as he cleaned a couple of legs by flicking and rubbing them rapidly. Did it matter? Not really. So long as dreamspinners kept spinning dreams, so long as they did not become extinct.

After all, this was the one great rule of a species: if you can't change, you die. It had applied to everything apart from dreamspinners.

Right here was their opportunity. Now, they had a choice. A choice almost every other species had had to make at some point. Asgard remembered spinning dreams to creatures trying to show a route out of their crisis – and then watched as they failed – and died.

Would dreamspinners fail and die out too? Did other dreamspinners see this? If they didn't, he'd have to educate them, that was clear.

Asgard worked out the chain of events: if the children were killed by the storm and Earth fell to the rains, he would be vindicated. Dreamspinners would harvest dreams from the spider webs across Havilah under Cain's watchful eye until the Garden of Eden opened again. So what if the dreams they gave were nightmares. At least they would be alive.

And then another thought came to him. What if one of the heirs was there – alongside Cain? Perhaps Archie. The boy heir might dilute Cain's power.

He toyed with the thought. Would it be possible to separate the boy from the other Heirs of Eden, especially when all three heirs needed to survive the storm?

Asgard could see a plan forming. Yes, tricky – but the more he thought it through, the more excited and fearful he became.

Asgard could feel his maghole expanding as the enormity of his plan hit him. But he'd made his mind up. He would take sides and align with Cain. After thousands of years, the dreamspinners – the most ancient and lasting species of them all – would no longer be neutral. But it must be done – for the benefit of all dreamspinners.

Asgard felt for Cain's vibrational energy field. A short while later he was locked on, ready to invert directly to that old devil, Cain, across the universes in Havilah.

IN NO TIME Asgard was in Havilah walking through the massive library in Cain's palace. Asgard remembered how grand it once was; the golden ceiling, the diamond chandeliers that sparkled so brightly they could almost blind, the windows made from cut jewels and shining floors made from complex patterns of coloured stones. Now it was covered in thousands of years of dust, a veil of grey smothering it like a blanket.

The dreamspinner walked through the air, wondering where the ghost might be. Cain's vibration was strong but ghosts could be hard to find. He found himself facing a huge piece of furniture with hundreds upon hundreds of drawers lined out row after row in neat columns.

Suddenly a drawer opened and its contents tumbled to the ground. It was Cain, searching as he always did for his branchwand.

Asgard readied himself to inject the ghost of Cain with a substance that would enable them to communicate by translating his signing into words.

Asgard jabbed at him, his leg shooting in and out so fast that Cain barely felt it.

'Who's there?' Cain called out. 'Which rapscallion of a rascal is it? Because I'll have you. I'll have you good and proper when I find my branchwand.'

Another drawer crashed over the floor.

Asgard materialised into the air above Cain's head.

Cain sensed it. 'Who are you and what do you want? I may be blind but I see things perfectly. Do not underestimate me.'

'I am Asgard the dreamspinner.'

Cain seemed to think about this. 'A dreamspinner, is that right?' he said at length. 'Well, well, well. Then it is lucky I am blind so I cannot look upon your ugly body.' Cain sniffed the air. 'You want to tell me something, don't you?'

'I come with news and a proposition,' Asgard began. 'The Tripodean Dream has been given, Master—'

Cain seemed to slip. 'The Prophecy of Eden!' he yelled. 'The dreams! You lie!'

'No. Clouds are building, the sky is preparing for rain—'

'And the Gifts of Eden? Have they been given too?'

'Indeed.'

Cain roared. 'While I am stuck here in this empty hole, Eden will be reborn and will inflict more useless creations on the worlds. It is infernal.'

Several drawers flew out and smashed onto the floor. 'Who are the heirs, are they strong, are they blessed with power and magic? Huh, tell me, dreamspinner.'

'They are children, weak sons and daughters of Adam. They have no magic and little sense of nature.'

'*Children?* You jest. It cannot be. Are you sure?'

'Indeed.'

Cain seemed to mull this over. 'Then they will not succeed. The tasks require immense strength and cunning. They may not make it past the storm.' Cain's voice petered off into the room. 'And what of the old man?'

'He wallows in self-pity. He remembers nothing. His time on earth has mellowed him. He may prove more of a hindrance to the Heirs of Eden than a help.'

Cain groaned, a noise of deep frustration. 'So, ugly dreamspinner, why are you here?'

'I may be able to help,' Asgard answered.

'You have my ear, dreamspinner, but there is the small problem of getting away from this damnable place.'

'I believe I have found a way of transporting you to these Heirs of Eden,' Asgard began.

'Yes, yes, yes, dreamspinner,' he said, his voice rising until it was booming. 'Don't you think I haven't tried *everything in my power* for the last however many thousands of years to get out of here? Now go away.'

Asgard let the echo die down. He had some explaining to do. 'Dreamspinners move freely throughout the universes – we go wherever we choose – on the feelings of vibrational energy. If a solid being goes through our maghole, our middle, perhaps we will die.'

'What's your point?' Cain shot back.

'You are not a solid being,' Asgard responded calmly. 'You are a spirit, a ghost. Therefore it should be possible for you to travel anywhere I designate.'

Cain instantly realised what it was saying. 'Are you saying that I could go through you, to other places?'

'Indeed.'

'My word. It is brilliant! Brilliant!' Cain roared. But after a few moments his tone changed. 'Why?' he asked. 'Why would you do this for me? What is the benefit to you, dreamspinner?'

Asgard paused and then signed rapidly, his claws flashing in the air. 'Like all dreamspinners, I am concerned with giving dreams. I do not worry where they come from, only that there are dreams to spin and that dreamspinners survive.'

'Clever, very clever,' Cain said. 'And this is on the understanding that the Heirs of Eden will fail?'

'Yes.'

Cain's enthusiasm dampened. 'But I am a ghost – I cannot do much with what is left of me. I have no eyes for magic or power, nor do I have a great physical presence.'

Asgard had been waiting for this. 'Yes. But what if you were to absorb the body of a man.'

'And tell me, how would this be possible?'

'If a being were to freely and willingly offer its body to you, you may join with it – in partnership. It would give you substance. You would be able to move with more purpose and have strength.'

Cain suddenly saw what he meant. 'Get a human to blend into me? Is this possible?'

'Of course. Though it cannot be forced. Perhaps, as the storm approaches, you might form an alliance with one of the Heirs of Eden.'

'Even cleverer, you clever, vile, little dreamspinner,' Cain replied, astonished by this huge stroke of luck. 'But surely it would harm you in your movements across the worlds, dreamspinner?'

'I cannot say,' Asgard said. 'If it was a child of man, it might not dominate your spirit, so movement may be possible.'

Cain chuckled. 'An Heir of Eden with me in harmony. My, you have a seasoned plan, dreamspinner. It is an opportunity I cannot afford to miss. Hear me out though: if it fails, will I remain a spirit in another place?'

'At least you would be on Earth.'

'Yes. It will be more interesting.' Cain dropped his voice, 'Do other dreamspinners know?'

'I am alone, for now,' Asgard said. 'I believe others may join me when they learn what I have done.'

'Indeed. You are bold coming here,' Cain clapped his hands together, although being a ghost it made no noise. 'Strange creature, I am willing to try your plan. You will be properly rewarded if this turns out as you suggest.'

Asgard shifted uneasily. Rewards were not what he wanted. 'Time is moving, Master,' he replied. 'On Earth the storm breaks in the morning when the sun is high in the sky and the heirs are in open ground. One of them is a boy named Archie. One of his Gifts of Eden ... failed.'

Asgard hesitated knowing he couldn't be absolutely certain. 'His "courage" will not be with him. Now, the boy sleeps, but he will wake shortly. He has seen the Prophecy of Eden in his dreams and he has seen the murder of your mother. You remember?'

'It has preoccupied my time for too long,' Cain replied. 'What do you suggest, Asgard?'

'Use her murder to manipulate the boy. He does not understand it. It confuses him – he is only a child.'

Cain guffawed. 'Excellent thinking. Hardly a stone unturned. But how will the boy believe a spirit? What if he does not comprehend the afterlife?'

Asgard hadn't foreseen this. 'It may not be enough if you are invisible. Can you wear a cloak?'

'I can – but not for long – an hour at a time.' The ghost scratched his non-existent chin. 'There is a long, but light, overcoat which I use to spook my subjects with. I'll see if I can find it.'

Asgard called after him. 'Hurry, Master. Make sure it is bland so it will fit in with human tastes on Earth. Bring anything else that you may require.'

Cain drifted away, his invisible presence marked only by the swaying movement of dust and papers lying on the floor. Shortly he returned wearing a trilby hat, a scarf and a long overcoat.

Asgard realised Cain had acquired a sixth sense of knowing where and what everyday objects were.

Cain sensed his thoughts. 'I have learnt to find things by understanding the energy within objects,' he said. 'It is amazing what you can see if you can't actually see, and what you can hear when you can't actually hear.'

Asgard stretched out a leg so it was touching Cain. 'Hold on to my leg – you will feel its energy.'

Cain held out an arm. 'I will pull you towards me. On my word, crouch down and dive horizontally, as though into a pool of water. Do this as fast as you can – understand?'

Cain felt a tingle fizzing through his ghostly frame. 'I feel you, it is powerful.'

'Good,' Asgard said. 'Now lower yourself and I will open myself up.'

Cain did as he was asked.

Asgard began the countdown. 'One, two, THREE!'

Cain thrust himself forward, like a diver off a high board. A mild burning sensation coursed through him and, following that, he found himself on a soft floor.

Cain picked himself up and began to dust off his coat. His face beamed with excitement.

'You do not have much time,' Asgard said as he turned invisible. 'You must do the rest alone.'

'Where will I find the boy?'

'Make your way up the stairs. The heirs sleep at the top of the house in a room in the shape of a cross. The boy is on the left side. I must go – other dreamspinners may be around. Return to the fireplace at the bottom of the house when you are done. Hide in the chimney. I will be back before dawn breaks, before the old man stirs.'

Cain stood up and prepared to go.

'Remember,' Asgard called after him. 'Make an ally of the boy. Use his fear of the murder of the Ancient Woman. Arrange a place and time to meet him before the storm breaks. Go in haste, Master.'

# 14 ARCHIE MEETS CAIN

Archie woke, his sleep disturbed. He lay in bed, wide awake, as segments of his dreams flashed back to him like flickers in an old movie. His heart raced as though he'd been running hard. He took a few deep breaths and stared at the ceiling, trying to piece the events together in his mind. Then he closed his eyes.

The images of the murder of an incredibly old and haggard woman came to him vividly in a sudden burst. Why was it always so graphic, so shocking? And then he'd experienced a feeling of drowning, of gasping for air, of swimming for his life. His heart pumped furiously, sending blood that seemed to flow like hot lava, coursing through his veins.

He exhaled loudly, opened his eyes and looked out into the blackness of their room. Was there someone at the foot of his bed?

'Daisy? What d' you want?' he slurred.

A windy chuckle came back at him. It was loud enough so that he knew instantly that it wasn't either of his sisters. Archie shuffled into a sitting position, yawned, stretched his arms out and searched the room. Before long, he could make out a figure, a human figure, masked by a long coat and a trilby hat.

Archie started to slip under his duvet, but then, for some strange reason he stopped, and called out, 'Who is it?' in a weak voice.

'Ah! Hello. I didn't see you there!' the voice said huskily.

Shivers raced up Archie's back.

'Now, are you the boy or one of the girls?'

Archie was baffled by this strange question. He couldn't think what to say so remained silent as his eyes gradually adjusted to the light.

'What can I ... er ... help you with, mister?' Archie stammered at length. He could make out a long coat and a hat. Was it an intruder? Were they being robbed?

'Ah! Forgive me for waking you,' said the croaky voice. 'I have something very important to share with you.'

With his head bowed, the man approached. As he neared, he raised his head.

Archie gasped. Underneath his hat, there was nothing there. Nothing. It was a ghost; he was having a seriously bad night.

Archie wondered if it was dangerous. His stomach knotted.

'Now, boy, I need to speak with you about a rather urgent matter. I need a favour.'

Archie reeled. 'Is this another weird dream?' he blurted, his brain trying to get a grip on what he was experiencing.

'I tell you what,' the ghost said, moving closer, 'is this one of your dreams?' And in a flash, the ghost whipped out a tiny dagger the size of a penknife encrusted with red jewels.

Archie froze as the knife floated through the air towards him. Moments later he felt a nick just under the left side of his chin and yelped. He put his hand up and worked the smooth velvety texture between his forefinger and thumb before it turned sticky.

He had been cut – violated – by a ghost! Archie's head thumped. He sidled back down his bed.

The ghost moved closer, as though inspecting the damage. 'Goodness me, a little human blood – I haven't seen any of that for years,' he said coldly. 'You do believe I exist, don't you?'

Archie's whole body was rattling. He could see straight through him. He nodded, his eyes bulging.

'Good. Let's be quite clear about that straight away,' the ghost said moving a little further from the bed. 'You might be aware that you are on the threshold of something rather extraordinary. There are mortal challenges you must face. I am sure you know of them through the images that have been given to you.'

Archie nodded. 'The nutty dreams?' he stuttered.

'Precisely,' said the ghost, chuckling. 'Nutty dreams.'

Archie shivered. 'But I don't understand them.'

The ghost sucked in a mouthful of air. 'You've heard about the Garden of Eden?'

Archie's brain fizzed. If it wasn't Solomon banging on about the Garden of Eden, it was a deranged ghost. I mean, the place didn't even exist, did it? OK, so it might have done six thousand years ago! Why was this ghost so interested in the Garden of Eden?

Archie kept as still and as quiet as he could, hoping like mad that the ghost would say his piece, not mutilate him further, and go away.

The ghost stared at Archie for a few moments as if trying to gauge his knowledge of the subject. 'Well, Eden's where life began, you must know this. But more recently it's been, how should I put it, on ... standby. The thing is,' the ghost explained, 'there's a slim chance it may operate again, which would mean terrible things must happen to my mother.'

The ghost paused as though taking stock. 'Everything clear so far?'

Archie couldn't think, let alone figure out what the ghost was talking about, but he nodded.

'Good. Now this forthcoming event is known as the Prophecy of Eden and it involves you, my boy. And I would like to help.'

The ghost leant in – almost earnestly – Archie thought, as if trying to gauge his reaction.

'In return, you can help me. You know, a tit-for-tat arrangement.'

Archie tried to remember to breathe. His eyes were straining to remain in their sockets. He blinked several times over and over, trying very hard to understand what was going on. It was madness; how on earth could this ghost know about his dreams which were still rattling around in his mind?

Archie sensed that the ghost was smiling thinly at him. Then it chuckled like an old motor. 'If the time comes, I will need you to take good care of the Ancient Woman – see that no harm comes to her.' His voice trailed off as he searched Archie's face. 'You do know about the Ancient Woman?'

Archie looked a little confused.

'Well, you see,' the ghost continued, 'she's my mother and she's a sad old woman hanging on to life. But she'll never see it again because she's blind, like me.' The ghost paused solemnly as if remembering her. 'To cut a long story short, Archie, she took the noble but worthless step of sacrificing herself in order to keep a spark alive.'

'A spark?' Archie quizzed, barely able to squeeze the words out. 'A spark of what?'

'A spark of life, I suppose.'

Archie thought he'd better play along and said weakly, 'And if you save your mother, will it mean you stop being a ghost?'

The ghost was thankful Archie couldn't see his face as he was barely able to control himself. What a naive thing to say, the boy didn't have a clue. 'Of course not,' he sobbed trying to hide the laughter in his voice. 'My body is gone, but my spirit is forever.'

'But it will mean I'll stop having dreams about ... about killing her.'

'If you help me, then I promise that is exactly what will happen.'

Archie was confused. 'What do I have to do?'

'In due course, you must protect her, no matter what,' the ghost said quietly. 'There are some that would want her dead. These people may think they are right to wish so, but rest assured they are mistaken. You must protect her from harm – do you understand? I'm asking so very little.'

Archie breathed out a sigh of relief. In the event that this entire conversation hadn't taken place in an unknown part of his brain and in lieu of his appalling dreams, looking after this Ancient Woman had to be the right thing to do. So, maybe the ghost was on their side, even if it was a bit knife-happy. Perhaps ghosts were like that.

Archie nodded, hesitatingly, but it was a nod.

'Very good,' said the ghost, whose gaze seemed to stare at Archie for rather too long.

Cain hovered into the middle of the room. The boy – this Heir of Eden – has no idea what is going to happen, he thought. His dreams are just images and he has found no meaning in them. Did people of Earth not understand dreams anymore? Asgard was right – these children would never survive the storm, let alone complete the other tasks of the Prophecy.

Now to put into place Asgard's plan.

If he could lure this boy into him – as part of him – he might be partially restored and utilise the boy's power. And, let's face it, he thought, it was a great deal for the boy, it would save his life.

Cain floated back to Archie's bedside. 'There is another way,' he began.

Archie didn't move a muscle.

'I want you to consider joining me – physically – as my flesh and blood.'

Tiredness swept over Archie. He yawned. 'Join you?'

'Not right now, of course, I'd like you to think about it. But joining me will save your life.'

Archie had no idea what the ghost was gabbling on about. Was it a deal of some sort?

'Sure,' he said, wearily. 'Whatever.'

'Good-good, I'm thrilled ... delighted,' Cain said, as he felt the weight of his coat. 'I am sorry about the knife,' he continued. 'I don't have time to explain things in great depth, so occasionally it pays to use ... other means.'

'But, Mr ... sir,' Archie said summoning his nerve, 'if I did this thing, er, what's in it for me?'

'What else, for you, Archie? Ah yes!' the ghost was thinking on his feet. 'What's in it for you apart from saving your life? Of course, how silly of me!'

The ghost drew himself up as best he could and faced Archie. 'I hold the secrets of ages past, Archie. I will offer you strength and courage, young man, so you are feared and respected. You will have the strength of a horse and the courage of a lion. I will give you my word that these rewards are genuine. All you have to do is meet me tomorrow morning – somewhere safe, where I can be with you alone. Then I will show you more and when you know the facts you will choose to join me.'

The ghost made this sound so easy – so obvious. But his voice turned darker. 'There is a terrible time coming, Archie, but I alone offer you salvation.'

Archie nodded again muffling a yawn. 'Yeah, sure, OK.'

'Excellent! Then you will meet with me in no more than nine hours and no less than eight,' the ghost demanded. 'Think of a place where no one will see us.'

'There's a back alleyway above the bank of the football field near the school,' he yawned. 'You'll know you've found it when you see two houses leaning in on each other. If you go up there it's normally pretty quiet.'

'Very good,' the ghost gushed. 'Make sure you wear a long overcoat like mine and a scarf. Do you have one?'

Archie didn't, but he said he did.

'And do you like sweets, Archie?'

'Yeah, a bit,' Archie replied. What a curious question from a ghost. 'Old Man Wood's the sucker for sugary things. He's always dipping his fingers in the sugar bowl and getting told off by Mrs Pye.'

The ghost, invisible though it was, seemed to flinch. 'Is that so? Yes, I had forgotten.'

Archie felt a little stupid.

A groan from the bed nearby signalled that Daisy was stirring.

'We meet in a few hours in the alleyway,' the ghost whispered as it drifted slowly to the door, struggling to keep the coat on top of him. 'Now remember, tonight's chat, young man, is our very own secret. Any tongue-wagging and the deal is off.'

Archie caught a glimpse of the knife.

As the ghost reached the door he was almost bent double. 'See you tomorrow, Archie. Be in no doubt that your life will change forever a few hours from now – the strength of a horse and the courage of a lion – you will never regret it. Now not a word to anyone, including the old man.'

Archie nodded. 'What ... what's your name?' he asked.

'Ah yes. I forget – the finer, little details.' His invisible eye sockets bore into Archie who felt as though his heart was briefly being sucked out.

'I am the ghost of Cain, son of Adam and Eve, brother of Abel. Maybe you've heard of me, maybe you haven't. Who knows what is taught these days.'

Cain stopped as if an idea had popped into his head. 'You have a cup of water?'

Archie pointed to the table just behind him.

Cain dropped something in which fizzed a little. 'You will need this. Drink and it will give you great strength. Until tomorrow, Archie.'

And with those words, Cain slipped quietly out of the door.

ARCHIE FELL BACK on his pillows, rubbed his eyes and wiped the beads of sweat off his face. What was that all about? What a dreadful, dreadful night; nightmare after nightmare.

In the back of his mind he wondered if this ghost was *the* Cain as in 'Cain and Abel' in the Bible story. Wasn't he the son of Adam and Eve? Crikey. Properly bonkers. Didn't Cain kill Abel or something and get turned away? He'd have to look it up.

Archie was so tired he felt it was almost impossible to know what was real and what wasn't. Anyway, the one thing he was sure of was that he wasn't going to meet the ghost. No way.

He studied the clock. Three thirty-five. He did a quick calculation. Eight hours from now and it'd be bang in the middle of the football match. Nine hours and the game would just be finishing.

He chuckled – a classic timetable clash. Well, at least the problem was sorted; there was no way he was missing the game and certainly not for a deranged ghost.

He smiled, relieved by his fortunate scheduling, closed his eyes and drifted back to sleep.

---

GAIA THE DREAMSPINNER HAD A FEELING – a vibration – that Archie was awake. She arrived in the room to find the ghost talking with Archie. From the corner, she listened in.

She was astonished to learn a couple of things. Firstly, that it was Cain, the Master of Havilah himself, forever banned from leaving Havilah, who had somehow found his way to the Heirs of Eden's bedroom only hours after the last part of the Tripodean Dream had been given. This was beyond comprehension.

Secondly, Cain knew about the children's dreams and was aware of the Gifts of Eden. Thirdly, Archie had no idea about his own gifts – but Cain knew enough to exploit him.

It was astonishing. Cain was clever and manipulative, but how was it possible?

Gaia thought it through, reaching the same conclusion again and again. One of the dreamspinners must have communicated with Cain. It was the only way. But dreamspinners were honour-bound to be neutral in all things. They did not meddle; this was engrained into their very fabric.

There were only four of them who had seen the dream and gifts given: Genesis, Asgard, Janana and herself. The most senior dreamspinners.

Genesis? Was she bitter about coming to light in front of the boy? No, it didn't add up. What about Asgard? He was the one who objected to giving the Gifts of Eden to children, but he was also the most passionate dreamspinner about dreams. Or Janana, the quiet one. Yes, Gaia thought, maybe it was her.

And then another thought whistled into her mind. Cain was a spirit so perhaps he had travelled ... through a dreamspinner?

Gaia reeled. In which case, a dreamspinner must have forged a pact with Cain.

But why?

Perhaps another dreamspinner was close at hand? She searched her vibrations. Nothing. Dreamspinners moved through the universes so fast it was as if they were fluid. This dreamspinner would have to be caught in the act.

Gaia looked down on the boy who turned his head on the pillow. The children had no idea what was about to happen. She moved in close and administered a deep space dream in the hope that the meeting with Cain might feel like it never happened. Whether it worked was up to Archie's subconscious to decide.

# 15 HAVILARIAN TOADSTOOL POWDER

Cain could feel his overcoat bearing down on his body, but he had an idea, an idea so brilliant he was determined to carry it out even if it meant he had to let the coat slip to the floor.

While searching through his cupboards, he'd stumbled upon a jar of grey powder. Cain pulled the jar out of his pocket and inspected it – wondering if the contents were still alive. He smiled. This was pure, evil genius. Havilarian toadstool powder. A lethal poison, designed to kill or reduce to nothing those who originated from the Garden of Eden. There was enough powder here to reduce the old man to a ghost just like himself – several times over. Old Man Wood's value would be nullified – not that he had much worth. The old man would very soon become a spirit just like him.

Cain reached the hallway. No Asgard. Good, he thought, better the dreamspinner doesn't know.

Cain cursed as his ghostly frame struggled under the weight of the coat. He let it fall. Now unburdened by the coat, he searched the vibrations of the objects in the room. Soon, a map started to appear in his mind's eye.

He sensed a room with a table in the middle. He could feel the resonance of plants and foodstuffs that hung from the ceiling. A little to the left were strong vibrations of a smouldering fire – a cooker perhaps. Good; he was in the right place.

As he moved about, he could feel the energy of the cupboards. He thought hard about sugar. Cain felt a surge of energy. There it was. Near to the cooker. He opened the door. The sugar grains were there, exactly as he suspected, nestled in a bowl exactly as Archie had mentioned.

Cain grinned. Easy to see, he thought, when one has had eons of time to master the energy that surrounds us. With considerable effort, and taking far longer than he anticipated, he opened the jar and poured the contents into the sugar bowl, which as far as he could tell, was half full. Perfect. As he did, he could hear tiny squeals coming from the powder.

Cain chuckled. Double luck. The Havilarian toadstool powders were most definitely alive.

Cain replaced the items and drifted out of the room back to the fireplace. He felt for the vibrations of the spider. Nothing. Damn.

Upstairs he could hear the yawns of the old man stirring in his bed and his feet padding on the ceiling above.

Come on, Asgard, where are you?

A moment later, the stairs began to creak very loudly under the old man's weight.

Cain didn't want to hang about. He knew he couldn't be seen but he absolutely didn't want to be sensed. He didn't want anyone to know that he had left Havilah, and was in the house of his father – the house of his greatest enemy.

As the footsteps got louder he heard a tiny noise. 'Master, it is Asgard. Dive now. Do nothing else.'

'About time,' Cain snapped just as he heard a small cough and the shuffle of feet of Old Man Wood entering the room. Without waiting to be prompted, Cain knelt down and dived.

'You cut it fine, dreamspinner,' he snapped.

'I cannot pretend it was easy, Master. One of the dreamspinners is suspicious. I must go. There are dreams to give and other dreamspinners to talk to. I cannot be found in Havilah.'

'Find me in eight hours as the storm breaks,' Cain said. 'With luck, I will get the boy. You know there will be no hiding place for you, dreamspinner, if this is the case?'

Asgard signed. 'That is why I must go. There are others I must talk to.' He inverted, leaving Cain in his great ballroom.

Cain gasped. A terrible realisation struck him; he had left the coat behind with the dagger in the pocket! But his shock soon turned to glee and then laughter.

Ha! The cut on young Archie's chin might be explained by a bump in the night but the coat will prove I was there, he thought. The boy *cannot* ignore it. Archie will see it and take it. Cain thumped the air. Oh, to see the look on his face! And now he will come to me, like flies to sugar.

Enjoying an image of a bowl filled with Havilarian toadstool powder, sugar and flies, Cain threw his invisible head back and roared with laughter, the noise echoing eerily down the passages and through the rooms of his huge palace.

# 16 SIMILAR DREAMS

Daisy woke twiddling her hair.

She pulled the duvet over her head, lay back and shut her eyes. She could feel the intensity building in her head once again and a sharp noise rang in her ears. Then the flashing started: images, like snapshots, of water, endless water, the feeling of drowning, flooding, trees and strange things that talked to her: a great chamber, skeletons, serpents, stone things like books flying through the air.

And then darkness. Following this was a feeling of evil that turned her body cold like ice. She shivered as her nausea grew, and her eardrums thumped and her eyes ached as if the lids had been smeared in hot wax that, having cooled, were heavy and uncomfortable.

And again there was the murder in cold blood – or so it seemed. Why was it always Archie?

She gasped and then her sobs filled the room. 'Ancient Woman!' she cried out. Why was it always the same haggard old woman?

---

ISABELLA CLIMBED OUT OF BED, ran across the room and closed her arms around her. 'It's me. Are you alright? You look terrible.'

Daisy burst out crying 'Why?' she sobbed, hiding her head under the duvet.

Archie joined his sisters. 'Daisy, it's me,' Archie said, trying to sound as supportive as he could. 'What's up?' But his question was met by an even louder outpouring of tears.

'Now look what you've done!' Isabella said, turning on him. 'This is so your fault.'

'But I haven't done anything. I didn't touch her – and anyway, it was you that set her off in the first place.'

'Nice try, Archie. The last time Daisy was this traumatised was when you put dog poo in her slippers three years, two months and sixteen days ago. So what is it now? Another one – or is it something else equally as vile?'

'Don't be ridiculous, you're completely over-reacting—'

Isabella faced Archie. 'Listen, Arch. This is a girl problem – so please, please can you give us a couple of minutes?' she smiled thinly at him. 'Be useful – go and see if you can get us a cup of tea or something?'

Archie rolled his eyes and walked off.

With Archie out of the way, she turned to Daisy and looked lovingly into her eyes. 'Right now,' she said, taking a couple of deep breaths, 'you look like you need a huge dollop of sisterly love.'

---

ARCHIE TRUNDLED down the creaking corridor, his face burning like molten lava. No one gives a damn how I feel. No one ever asks me what's been going on in my head. And why is it is always my fault? It's not fair. He stretched out his arms and thrust out his chin. As he did so, he felt the sting of a cut. He froze. Cloudy images of the previous night rushed back at him. Before he knew what he was doing he had dashed into the bathroom and was looking in the mirror. It was a small incision, just as he suspected.

Archie couldn't believe it. Ever since he'd woken the words of horse and lion had reverberated in his head. What was it again: 'The strength of a horse and the courage of a lion?' He shook his head. Nah – ghosts didn't really exist, did they? But why was his memory so foggy and why did the meeting he'd had in the middle of the night feel so wrong, but yet so right?

Archie put his head down, deep in thought, and headed towards the kitchen.

Mrs Pye, who was ploughing through a huge pile of washing, looked up as Archie came sloping in. 'You taking an elephant for a walk?' she said.

'Uh? An elephant?' he repeated. Archie realised what she meant and tried desperately hard not to break into a smile.

Mrs Pye leant against the sink. 'What's the matter with you lot?'

Archie coughed. 'Bells and Daisy had a bad night. They're talking about some, er, girlie things, you know ...' Archie mumbled. It was the first thing that had popped into his head.

'Periods?' Mrs Pye said very loudly. 'Daisy becoming a woman now, is she? About time, I suppose.'

Archie went bright red. Oh no. Was this what was meant by "girlie things"? He had no idea why he'd told Mrs Pye they were discussing "girlie things". Menstruation was just about the last thing on his mind. He thought he'd better change the subject. 'Er, my throat's really sore, Mrs P, and my head hurts; feels like someone's tightened a clip around my neck.'

'Come here and I'll have a look.'

Archie sidled over to the sink and Mrs Pye took his head very gently in her hands. 'What's this cut on your chin? You been playing with your knives again?'

'No. Of course I haven't,' he said, weakly. 'I fell out of bed and bashed it on something.'

Mrs Pye looked at Archie suspiciously. 'I won't tell – you know that. I know you like to disappear off to the potting shed and practice your throwing, though Lord only knows why.' She took his hand, and then felt his forehead and then the back of his neck. 'It's your sister who doesn't approve.' Mrs Pye had finished her medical. 'You is a bit sweaty, young man. Could be a fever coming on. And what with all that noise in the middle of the night – well, I don't know what to make of it.'

She rubbed her chin, thinking what might be the best cure. 'I reckon you need a couple of ...'

'Apples?' Archie said.

Mrs Pye raised her eyebrows. 'Yep, how do you guess?'

Archie forced a smile. 'Just a lucky guess, that's all.'

---

ARCHIE HEADED upstairs to break the news. 'Can I come in now?' he yelled from the top of the stairs.

Isabella opened the door. 'Sorry Arch, been a bit of a funny morning. Any luck with the tea?'

'Even better,' he beamed as he stepped inside. 'Huge breakfast en-route – thank you very much.' He looked rather pleased with himself and then he started to go red.

Isabella noticed. 'What have you done? You look ridiculously guilty!'

Archie pulled a face. 'I told Mrs P that you were having, er, girlie problems – you know, like, er, periods. It just popped out.'

Daisy exploded into laughter. 'Periods? You? OMG, hilarious,' she said, slapping him on the back. 'Winkle, that's a classic.' Her mood instantly lifted. 'Archie, I'm already a wo-man.' Daisy stood up, posed and strutted around the room. 'The person you see here is ALL woman.'

Archie laughed. 'You could have fooled me—'

Daisy ignored him and grabbed his hands, 'Wo-man, wo-man,' she said in a low growl which she hoped was cool and sexy. 'I am ALL WO-MAN.'

In no time the twins were dancing a kind of strange waltz in the middle of the room, occasionally tripping over each other's feet and crashing to the floor and laughing and singing, "WO-MAN!" over and over again.

Typical Daisy, Archie thought: one minute scared to death, the next it was quite forgotten about.

Mrs Pye rapped on the door. 'Give us a hand will you!'

Isabella rushed over, opened it, and her eyes nearly popped out of her head at the massive tray. It must have weighed a ton. On it were an array of plates and cups and dishes with poached eggs, bacon, mushrooms and tomatoes. A full rack of toast stood neatly in smart rows and pots of marmalade and Marmite were squeezed on top. Finally, there was a large pot of tea with a jug of milk.

Mrs Pye set it down on the table, drew in some large gulps of air and straightened up. 'Now then, which one of you has the girl problems?' she announced.

At which, Daisy fell about laughing as if it really was the funniest thing in the world.

AFTER THEIR UNEXPECTEDLY ENORMOUS BREAKFAST, and now that Daisy had calmed down, Isabella felt it was time to question her. 'Daisy,' she began quietly, 'earlier you called out, "Ancient Woman". Can you tell me why?'

Daisy took a couple of deep breaths to compose herself and as she did a shadow seemed to fall over her face. 'It was another nightmare,' she began, hoping she wasn't sounding completely idiotic. 'I've had three now,' she said, scratching her chin nervously. 'All totally disturbing, but last night's was the best ... and the worst ... and the weirdest.' She looked at her sister for support. 'They've been so real – I could smell things, understand everything; birds, trees, plants. They talked to me – properly talked! It's just so complicated, I don't really know where to begin.'

Daisy scrunched her face up and ran a hand through her hair, getting her fingers temporarily caught in a knot. 'And then – then there was this old woman telling me about a wonderful, beautiful place and ... also, yes, also there was a terrifying storm – a sort of endless hurricane that felt like it was after me. It had the lot: lightning, mudslides, tons of water beating me to death. I was drowning ...' she tailed off leaving a silence in the room.

'What is it, Daisy?' Isabella prompted.

'I dreamt I reached a sanctuary – and only then was I safe from the storm. It was like ... Heaven.'

Isabella couldn't believe it. Daisy's dream sounded so similar to hers. She had to find out more. 'Daisy, what happened to this Ancient Woman.'

'Well, I'm pretty certain this haggard old woman was trying to tell us something,' Daisy said. 'You see, in each dream she died—'

'Are you sure?'

'Oh yes,' Daisy said, her eyes wide. 'Really violently and every time in a different way. It was like being there – I could feel myself actually screaming – but I couldn't tell who'd done it,' Daisy said, burying her face in her hands.

She took the silence from the others as a green light to continue. 'Look, I know it sounds nuts, but this "Ancient Woman" knew about us ... she knew *everything* ... even though we were in a completely different world.' Her eyes searched her elder sister's, begging her to believe her. 'It's terrified the living daylights out of me.' Her bottom lip began to tremble and tears welled in her eyes. 'Every time I think about it, I think I'm going mad.'

---

ARCHIE STARED LOVINGLY at his twin sister. He loathed her for ignoring him when it suited her and for being better at sports and for her ridiculously carefree nature. But he loved her quirky manner and her honesty. If only he could muster the courage, like her, and say what he felt. If he did, perhaps everything would be clearer.

Then, without warning, tears began to well up in Isabella's eyes.

'Oh no. Not you as well!' Archie said.

'Me too!' Isabella cried, tears streaming down her face. 'Same – exactly.'

Archie's eyes nearly popped out of his head. 'But that's crazy—'

'I know – it's totally bonkers.'

Archie was confused. 'Just like Daisy's? Are you sure?'

'It's the truth,' Isabella insisted. 'I swear it. Three intense dreams like Daisy's: clear as glass – but making no sense whatsoever. I've never been so amazed or happy or terrified, and what's more, just as Daisy said, it always ends in death.' She burst into tears. Daisy handed her a tissue and she dabbed at her eyes before continuing. 'It's like flying into a cloud and every now and then, as you get used to it, you find yourself back in the cloud, trying to figure out what's going on.' She grabbed another tissue. 'And I keep seeing rain, torrential, terrible rain and lightning – you know how I've been going on about this deluge, well it's terrifying me ... it's as if this stupid storm targeted us alone.'

Daisy nodded in agreement.

Isabella touched Archie's shoulder tenderly. 'And I'm sorry I was grumpy with you, Arch,' she said, as she raised her eyes and offered him a quick smile. 'It's just a bit overwhelming and confusing.'

It was now Daisy's turn to ask the questions. 'What did you make of this "Ancient Woman"?'

Isabella thought for a moment. 'Well, she'd been stuck somewhere, as if abandoned, I think. She's a really sad, horrible looking thing, waiting for—'

'For what?'

Isabella shrugged. 'I don't know. Something. And her eyes had been gouged out so she could never be sure where she was—'

'That's it!' Daisy agreed. 'Exactly how I saw her. No eyes, but really nice and kind and full of love.' She pulled a bit of a face. 'She was disgusting to look at though, all shrivelled up, like one of Old Man Wood's prunes. I've never seen anything like it.'

'Probably more crinkly and withered,' Isabella added with a thin smile. 'It was very hard to believe how she was still alive. It was as if she held the key to something, something amazing, but I can't remember what it was.' Isabella frowned. 'Why are dreams so weird? Why can't I remember?'

Archie had become noticeably quiet over the past few minutes. As if by instinct, the girls turned on him.

'What about you, Archie?' they said at the same time.

Archie sat with his head against the window. He didn't dare tell them about the odd spidery kind of thing he'd seen hovering over Daisy, or the ghost of Cain. He turned and faced the girls, his face ashen.

'Yeah,' he said shakily. 'I've dreamt of this flood and this Ancient Woman on three occasions – just like you.'

The girls gasped.

Archie stared at them, his eyes red and brimming with tears. Then he dropped his head.

'Thing is, in each of my dreams, it's me who kills her.'

# 17 OVERCOAT

'Look. I know it's odd, really odd, but they are only dreams,' Isabella said. 'They're just part of our minds worrying about stuff in the night. They're not real – however extraordinary.'

'But if you don't think there's any truth in it,' Archie said, 'why did you go to such lengths to make the barometer and the storm glass? I mean, you must have believed there was something to it.'

Isabella thought for a moment. 'Sue had had a similar dream and it sounded like mine and I wanted to try something – anything, I suppose.'

'So, if this is a coincidence,' Archie said, 'do you think there's a storm demon out there putting dreams in our heads?'

'Don't be silly. Of course I don't, Archie. I never said that.' She drew her fists up to her temples. 'I don't know what to think. It's just a stupid dream.'

Daisy, who had been pretty quiet, suddenly piped up. 'Why don't we look at the storm glass? Maybe it will tell us something about this rain we've dreamt about. Where did you put it?'

Isabella stood up and plucked it out of the grate of the old Victorian fireplace. She placed it against the wall on top of the mantelpiece.

The children stared at it, as though it held the answers to their problems. 'It's still cloudy with loads of little stars,' Archie said, his voice a little glum.

'But is there any change from before?' Daisy continued, now focusing more intently on the glass tube. 'Blimey those little stars are moving quickly, aren't they? What does it mean?'

'Daisy,' Isabella sighed, 'the thing is, I don't really know what it means or what it's supposed to show. I don't know enough about it.' Isabella went back to her area and began to gather her things.

Daisy concentrated hard on the storm glass and as she stared, she could see hundreds of tiny stars darting around at high speed. 'Just out of interest,' she said, 'for simple-minded people like me who never saw it before, what was it like when you began this mad project?'

'Cloudy,' Archie said.

'Thanks Archie, very helpful,' Daisy said. 'Well, as far as I can tell, it's pretty zooming,' she said. 'It's way more than cloudy.'

Isabella strode over and stared at the storm glass. 'Nothing there,' she announced. 'Come on you two; time to get your things. You've got this big match to play, or had you forgotten?'

The twins returned to their areas and grabbed their sports bags.

'And we need to get a move on,' Isabella said, looking at her watch. She picked up the storm glass and slipped it into her pocket. 'My guess is that we're being freaked out by this strange weather and our brains are picking up some sort of random signal that's making us react oddly.'

Daisy frowned at Isabella. 'I realise I don't know about these things, but if I were you, I'd keep a close eye on that stormy glass thing-a-me.'

They filed down the stairs and found Mrs Pye at the bottom. 'Good luck you lot,' she said, giving each of them a hug. 'Goals galore for you, pretty Daisy, saves for you, brave Archie. And as for you, Isabella, just make sure you don't go running onto the pitch beating up the umpire – you heard what that headmaster said.' She gave her a nudge. 'Now, away with you – and I expect to hear heroic tales when you get back.'

---

THE CHILDREN HAD BARELY STEPPED out of the door when the familiar voice of Old Man Wood stopped them short.

'Best of luck today, little ones,' he called out. 'There's one heck of a big dark cloud over our heads. If lightning starts, remember to run for cover. You understand?' He was quite sure they weren't paying him the slightest bit of attention. 'Do you recall that ditty we used to sing about different types of cloud? Now, how did it go? Ah yes:'

*High and light, no need for flight.*
*Low and grey – stay away.*
*Grey and round – rain around ...*
*But black with a crack ... is the devil's smack.*

'So I'll see you early afternoon. Best of luck, Daisy. Your school is relying on you, you heard what Solomon said.'

The children waved.

'His stupid poems,' Daisy said quietly.

'Oh, *wait*!' Old Man Wood exclaimed, almost forgetting himself. 'Did any of you leave a coat? Found it on the floor of the corridor.' A large overcoat dangled over his arm. 'Nice coat too, with an interesting pattern on the lining. Sure I've seen it somewhere before – reminds me of something.' Old Man Wood scratched his head and then pinched his nose while he tried to remember.

Archie missed a step and stumbled, just righting himself before his head hit the floor.

Old Man Wood saw. 'Is it yours, Archie? Looks a touch big for you, mind. But you might have mistakenly brought it home last evening.'

Archie doubled back, his body trembling. Without looking at Old Man Wood he inspected the coat and ran his hand inside one of the pockets. His hair almost stood on end.

'Back in a second,' he yelled behind him as he flew up the stairs.

Archie ran into the attic room and spied the glass of water on the side. It was tinged slightly blue – exactly as he'd left it. In one movement he grabbed it, and in the next and in one gulp, he drained it. He wiped his mouth with his sleeve, and ran down the staircase.

'Everything alright, Archie?' Old Man Wood asked.

'Fine,' Archie answered gulping as though a burp was about to burst out. 'Forgot something, that's all.'

'Jolly good,' Old Man Wood said. 'Your coat?'

'Oh, yeah, it belongs to a friend. Must have taken it by mistake.'

'Big fella, is he?'

'I suppose,' Archie said as casually as he could.

Old Man Wood handed him the coat. But as he did so the ruby-encrusted knife slipped out of the pocket and fell with a clatter onto the paving slabs.

'A knife, Archie? You know you shouldn't carry one of those around with you at school.'

Archie's heart skipped a beat. 'Don't worry. It's only plastic – a stage knife, you know ... for acting,' he smiled badly. 'The bloke who owns the coat is the lead part, I think – in the school play; Macbeth or something.' He bent down, narrowly beating Old Man Wood to it.

'He certainly has an interesting taste in knives,' Old Man Wood commented, raising his eyebrows at Archie. 'Well on you go, young Arch, and remember to save those footballs.'

Archie smiled and ran on, not a full sprint, but not a jog either, to catch up with the girls. As he ran, his heart was thumping like a huge bass drum and his head buzzed with a mixture of dread and excitement.

---

OLD MAN WOOD waved at the children until they had slipped away down the track out of eyesight. Now wasn't that funny, Archie behaving like that. That wasn't a plastic knife, not a bit of it, not in a million years. He knew how to tell a cheap knife from a proper knife, because he knew all about knives. How, he didn't remember, but he felt it in his bones.

He'd certainly taught Archie about them, how to make one, the different shapes and handles and what they were used for and what certain carvings and notches meant. Not only that, but he'd shown him how to throw them as well, how to understand the balance and how the weight would determine the revolutions and power in the throw.

He mulled this over, wondering what light might develop in his brain on the subject. No, nothing there again – just a deep penetrating feeling, like toothache. But the instant he saw the knife drop from the coat, he knew it was a beauty; a knife worthy of a powerful man with a large hand. And from the clinking noise it made on the floor, he would have bet a trinket or two it was made from silver and hard steel and, from the way the light reflected through the stone and diffused onto the Yorkstone slabs, he'd have taken another wager the knife's stones were special – most likely rubies and pink diamonds. Plastic, never. He shook his head. There was no way in the world it was plastic.

So what was Archie doing with it – and what was it about that funny old coat with the curious markings?

Old Man Wood turned his head up to the sky and breathed in deeply. How dark was that cloud. Too dark by his reckoning, and growing. It now filled the sky from the moors to the dales like a great swollen bladder. It reminded him of Archie's horrid, swollen, purple and black eye from the beginning of the year when a fishing hook caught him on the flesh just beneath his eyeball.

He had a bad feeling about the cloud from deep in his gut, and this feeling hadn't been helped by the images from the infernal nightmares he'd been having – every night – for the past week.

He rubbed his chin. If he wasn't mistaken, they were about his past, fragments from years ago. Stuff he could never remember, not at his age. Things like flooding and a desperate old woman, ghosts and odd spidery creatures that looked like jellyfish with blue flames in their bellies. And a cave? Now that one had seemed more familiar but ... the problem was, there were just so many "buts".

Old Man Wood brushed a speck of dust off his coat. Nothing I can do about it now, he told himself, whatever it means.

He shut the door and his mind wandered back to the knife and the coat, as if the subject wanted to spend a little more time in his head.

What had surprised him was his reaction to the pattern on the lining of the coat. It had taken his breath away. Why? Was it the pattern? No, it couldn't be. He'd seen thousands and thousands of patterns of snakes and trees or snakes slithering up poles and the like all the way through his long life.

But why did this particular one send such a shiver up his spine? Why did it make him feel a little weak and thrilled at the same time? Was it was something to do with the fabric? Maybe that was it.

He replayed his memory to the moment he saw the lining for the first time. There it was – that curious feeling again. It was as if the snake had actually moved, had slithered up into the tree right there on the fabric itself. He shook his head, stood up and paced uneasily around the room.

And he'd noted the buttons too, with a matching crest of a snake winding through the branches of a tree. That exact pattern – where was it from? Maybe there was a copy of it somewhere in the house – perhaps on one of the many woodcarvings – in his room even?

Suddenly an idea shot into his head and it filled his entire body with a bolt of electricity as though in some way it was inspired by a greater power. My goodness me, he thought, it can't be.

He made his way into the sitting room and sat down in his large, rather worn, armchair which faced the fire. He cupped his face in his large, leathery, old hands and stared at the embers.

What if the fabric from that jacket wasn't actually from Earth? He felt dizzy. Now this was bringing back the past. He'd never seen a fabric that had the ability to change shape before here on Earth, but if he remembered correctly this could be something from one of those other places. And if it bore the marks of the snake and the tree, then could it possibly be from the Garden of Eden?

A surge of energy coursed through his body, making him feel strong for a second or two. He hadn't felt this for years. Another thought hit him. Perhaps it wasn't the Garden of Eden. What if it was the other place – the place he'd deliberately cast out of his mind?

Old Man Wood stood up, narrowly avoiding cracking his head on one of the lower supporting beams of the house.

Time to research those old carvings, he thought. He'd start on the stairs and then try his bedroom. He didn't know what he might find; he just had a sense about him that they might shed a clue on that strange garment's true home.

# 18 KEMP TRIES TO MAKE UP

Today was the last day before the long half term break. Not only was there the excitement of the big football match but the school had laid on exhibitions, a concert and a play so that almost half the children in the school were, in one way or another, involved in the celebrations. Aside from their earlier worries, the girls had a spring in their step as they headed down the steep track.

At the top of the hill, the banks at either side of the track gradually increased in height. As the children descended, it was like a steep gully, as if the lane had been cut out of the hillside by a giant digger. Overhead, the tree branches provided a thick canopy of leaves, like a covered tunnel, all the way from the top to the bottom.

On a clear day, sunlight flickered through, and when that happened, it was as if glitter was sprinkling down upon them. Today it was almost pitch black and the tree roots that supported the bank twisted through the rock and soil, reaching out at them like the arms and legs of decaying corpses.

The children were used to it; after all, it was their everyday walk to school. So the idea of it being in any way scary was beyond them. But Sue called it "the big graveyard ditch" and she was petrified of it. She was right in one respect; it took the water off the hill and even in the driest summer a constant trickle dribbled down from the moors at the top to the river below.

As the children walked down the hill, the girls asked Archie about the coat.

He shrugged and told them that it was Kemp's dad's old coat – he must have got it muddled up in the cloakroom. But his heart was thudding in his chest and his brain worked overtime as he tried to remember what had happened during the night.

The girls didn't bother to question him further. For someone as disorganised as Archie it was quite believable that he might have picked up the wrong coat. He was often turning up in strange woolly hats or with pens and pencils that he'd mistakenly pocketed.

A third of the way down the tree-covered lane they stopped by a vast old oak with a huge bough that leaned over the road. Daisy climbed nimbly up the steep, high bank using the large roots as hand grips. At the top she uncoiled the rope that was tied around the middle of the huge branch and tossed down the slack.

Although he didn't feel quite in the mood, Archie went first. He ran up the hill and, as he took off, he climbed up the rope until his feet settled on the large knot at the bottom. Then he swung rapidly backwards and forwards, the wind rushing through his hair. It was exhilarating. As the rope slowed, he climbed down, running to a stop.

Isabella went next. Her way was to sit on the knot and swing gently through the air. Finally it was Daisy's turn. She climbed up the rope and asked Archie to pull her up the hill as far as he could. She soared through the air, her hair flying behind her, until she was almost horizontal with the bank and crashing into the canopy.

She flew backwards, screaming in delight, and then she soared forward before bashing into the bank on the left and twisting to the one on the right. They laughed at her recklessness.

Daisy desperately wanted another go, but Isabella put her foot down. 'We'll be late. But I promise we'll have a go on the way back.'

'Oh sure,' Daisy said, sulking, as she tucked the rope through and around a protruding root. 'I bet we'll forget, or you'll be too tired, or it'll be too dark or some other rubbish excuse.'

'Daisy,' Isabella replied, 'it isn't possible for *you* to forget the rope swing.'

When they came to the rickety wooden bridge, they peered over the railings at the water beneath that had journeyed from the heart of the moors.

Archie was determined to see a fish but was dragged away by Isabella who pointed out how, in the strange light, the school tower to the left looked quite enormous compared to the tiny wooden boathouse at the foot of the hills by the river. She wondered if the boat in there was still sound and made a mental note to enquire about it with Mr Pike. It would make a great trip out before the weather turned.

The children skipped across the lush velvety green football pitch with big, bold, alternating stripes and tattoo-like fresh white markings burnt into the turf. Down each side were posts with safety ropes attached to keep the spectators at bay. On each corner, slightly recessed, was the headmaster's pride and joy, the moveable floodlight towers in a crisscross of metal thirty feet high. They were the first school in the North (as Mr Solomon often repeated) who played football when they liked and cricket when they liked.

Daisy ran ahead, pretending to do skills and dummies, commentating about the goals she was going to score all the way to the steep set of steps up to the school buildings.

---

AS ARCHIE FOLLOWED Daisy into their brightly lit form room, the rows of incandescent lights glaring down upon them, Daisy immediately rushed over to join a group of girls at the front. Archie noticed Kemp sitting quietly at his desk, reading a book. Let sleeping dogs lie, he thought, especially unpredictable dogs. So, without any fuss, he made his way to his desk at the other side of the room.

Archie draped the coat over the back of his chair, sat down and put his head in his hands. He desperately tried to remember what the ghost had said: a meeting, something about the strength of a lion and the courage of a horse and, after writing it down, he realised that it had to be the other way round. This and that he'd be saved. But saved from what?

Hadn't he agreed to do something as well; join him or enter into a partnership or something nuts like that? It didn't make any sense but, and it was a huge BUT, he was in possession of the ghost's coat and dagger here in this very room. So it couldn't be *that* nuts. Archie rubbed the cut under his chin – another reminder.

He pulled out a piece of paper and nibbled on the end of a pencil. "Possible options for the meeting place", he wrote.

Was it down by the boatyard or up by one of the big willow trees? He wrote both down but shook his head. No. Neither of those options rang true. He wondered if it was the alley above the football pitch and he wrote that down as well.

He underlined it a couple of times and leaned back in his chair. Yes, that one rang a bell. But what on earth was he going to do about it. He sighed. Nothing, he supposed.

His thoughts were interrupted by a friendly, but slightly painful, wallop on his shoulders. It was Gus Williams who had bounced into the room. 'Morning Archie. You're not by any chance writing a "to-do" list, are you?' he said, with a laugh that showed off his extensively large teeth.

Archie smiled. 'No, don't be ridiculous.'

Gus read the list. 'Lost something?'

'Nah. Just trying to remember a dream.'

'Oh, well that's OK,' Williams said cheerily. 'So long as it wasn't a very big and complex dream?'

'Well, as a matter of fact, yes it was.' Archie looked up, smiling. 'Now go away and leave me to think.'

'News alert!' Williams announced to the room, his grin almost completely covering his face. 'Archie de Lowe is thinking! Give him plenty of room, oxygen at the ready.' Gus leant down again. 'Next you'll be telling me Daisy's caught the same bug,' he whispered. 'Good luck!'

He smiled and sprang off like a big, energetic, happy puppy to his desk at the back of the room.

Kemp had been listening to Archie's conversation with Gus with great interest. He smiled. Archie was completely hopeless at organising himself; he would bet money Archie had forgotten something again. And by the looks of it, it was more important than usual.

He stood up quietly and headed over to him. 'Morning Archie, everything cool?'

Archie groaned. First Gus, now Kemp. What did *he* want? 'Not really, Kemp,' he said coldly. 'I had a very, very bad night.'

'Oh yeah?' Kemp replied as he perched on his desk.

'Yes. If you must know, I had a couple of very odd experiences. But I can't remember either of them.'

Kemp burst out laughing. 'Want to talk about it?'

Archie stared at Kemp's face and noted what a big nose he had and his ridiculously square jaw. 'I told you; I'm not talking to you after what you did yesterday.'

Kemp sighed. 'OK. You win. Look I had a think and last night I decided that I'm going to change. No more jokes on people. I promise—'

'You said that before – and immediately let me down. In fact you lied to me. Christ, Kemp, I had to own up for your stupidity and you made me feel like an idiot. Luckily Isabella didn't believe me.'

Kemp sucked in his cheeks. 'Look Archie, I've told Mason and Wilcox I don't want to be part of the gang. When I'm with them, I act like a ... like a moron. I don't know what comes over me and, bottom line is that I don't want to hang with them anymore.'

Kemp noted Archie's look of disgust. 'If you don't believe me, go and ask them,' he continued. 'Go on, they're over there in the corner, playing on their phones like two happy little bunnies. Seriously, I don't want to hurt anyone anymore. I really don't.' He dropped his voice and briefly stole a look over his shoulder. 'I want to be your friend.'

'Blimey, Kemp, this isn't the time. Right now, I've literally got a nightmare on my hands. And anyway, you're going to have to prove it. I'm not going to trust you until I know you mean what you say.'

'What do you want me to do? I promise I won't be nasty to either of your sisters. I'm going to put that behind me. I won't even speak to them if you don't want me to.'

'But I bet you've already arranged with your Chitbury mates that Daisy's going to get a kicking – haven't you?'

Kemp winced. 'Well there's not much I can do about that now, is there?'

'And the only reason you're being Mr Nice about it is because if they kick her out of the game we'll lose and she won't play in the team after half term, leaving room for someone else. And that person will probably be you.'

Kemp's expression had changed. 'You know what, Archie,' he spat. 'I meant what I said. Just throw it back in my face, why don't you.'

On hearing raised voices, Mason and Wilcox instantly towered over

Archie. Wilcox, with one huge hand, picked him up by his collar. 'Back off boys, let him be,' Kemp ordered. The muscle sloped reluctantly back to their desks.

The classroom had fallen silent but Archie wasn't finished. 'See what I mean, Kemp,' Archie fumed. 'If you want to be my friend you've got a long way to go. I swore on my life that I wouldn't tell anyone about the barometer and I kept my word. You ... well, frankly, you disgust me.'

Archie was pretty astonished the words had spilled out of his mouth and for a moment the classroom stopped and stared at him.

# 19 ARCHIE SPILLS IT OUT

The spell was broken by the bell and, moments later, the upright figure of Mr Bellwood came striding in, twiddling the ends of his moustache.

'As you know,' he boomed, 'there is no class-work today.' He stared around the room. 'Gosh,' he continued in a softer voice. 'Silence! Oh, hallelujah!'

The classroom remained silent.

'Have I missed something?' Bellwood continued, as his eyes flashed from pupil to pupil trying to make out what had caused this unusual lack of noise. 'No? Very well.' He peered at his notes. 'Our school day looks like this; footie for those playing footie. Can I have hands up for those who are likely to be watching.' The whole class except for Kemp, Mason and Wilcox thrust their hands into the air.

'Excellent. I take it you have other things to be getting on with, Mason?'

Mason shrugged.

'You know, you three aren't the best advert for this school and today is what we like to call an "open day".' Bellwood said.

Kemp stole a glance at Archie, who was still looking troubled. Just beyond him was Williams who was smiling his big toothy smile straight back at him and raising his eyebrows. Was Williams trying to provoke him with his eyebrows? He put his hand up.

'Yes, Kemp.'

'Actually, I'm watching the football as well,' he said.

'A change of heart, huh, Kemp.'

'You could say that.'

'Well, I'm glad to hear it.'

Kemp caught Williams' bulging eyes again. He knew exactly what he was implying.

'So Wilcox and Mason, just you two. Correct?' They nodded dumbly. 'In that case, you will report to Mr Pike in the Maintenance Department. There are leaves to sweep up and fences to paint.' On cue, the class burst out laughing. Mr Bellwood waited until the noise was bearable. 'Come on. Simmer down. Mr Pike is expecting you to be ready for work at kick off time, which will be eleven o'clock precisely.'

Mr Bellwood stuck his nose in the air and twitched his moustache. It was a signal that he was going to say something profound. 'Now, about the weather. There is a rather large cloud brrrewing right above us,' and as he said this he rolled the 'r' rather dramatically and then repeated the word, 'brrrewing.'

It was Bellwood's habit of dramatising a word for effect. 'To put your minds at rest, our headmaster has been in touch with the Met Office to find out if this might be a cause for concern. I am happy to report that, as far as they know, there are no serious worries. This morning and this afternoon, there is a high chance that we may get a little wet, indeed there may even be a possibility of a heavy downpour. Nevertheless, all school activities are to go on as scheduled.

'Daisy de Lowe, please remove that lipstick from your desk. Now remember, class, just in case lightning strikes, what would be the best course of action to take? Anyone. Ah, yes, Alexander?'

'Put up your umbrella, Sir.'

'No, you do not, Alexander. And stop laughing. And Allen will you desist from flicking paper balls at Daisy please.' He glared at the boys, 'Umbrellas, as you know perfectly well, are for repelling water. I'm talking about lightning strikes.'

Bellwood raised his eyebrows in anticipation. 'Kemp, what would you do?'

'I'd get the hell out of there before I was shrivelled to a burnt crisp.'

The class laughed.

'Well, it's better than holding up an umbrella, but where would you go?'

Little Jimmy Nugent put up his hand.

'Yes, Nugent.'

'I've been told that if you get in a car the rubber tyres would earth the strike, wouldn't it, sir?'

Mr Bellwood clasped his hands together. 'Very good, Nugent, and you're absolutely correct. Either get indoors or hop in a car—'

'My granddad,' Nugent continued, 'got killed by a bolt of lightning in 1983, while walking his bull terrier called Plank—'

'Did he, Nugent?' Mr Bellwood sensed one of Nugent's stories coming on. 'How very fascinating. Perhaps you wouldn't mind telling me about it after half term.'

He turned back to the pupils. 'Now, class, do the best you can today and make us all proud, and have a safe half term. You are dismissed.'

---

THE PUPILS instantly divided into several small groups, except Archie who remained in his chair twiddling his pencil.

Kemp came over to him again. 'Come on, Archie, it can't be that bad.'

'You have no idea,' Archie replied. 'Really, you would never, ever believe me.'

'Try me.'

Archie sighed. What did he have to lose? But then again, where should he start? Who on earth would believe a story about a ghost. 'OK,' he began. 'If you really want to know, I was visited in the night by something that, as far as I could tell, was a ghost.'

'A ghost?' Kemp chuckled. 'Really?'

'Yes,' Archie fired back. 'I told you you wouldn't believe me.'

Kemp eyed him suspiciously and raised his hands. 'Sorry. Don't worry about me ... carry on.'

Archie rubbed his forehead. 'Well, this ghost promised me stuff if I met up with him.'

'Yeah? What did you say?'

'I kind of agreed. I mean, what would you do?

'I'd probably agree too,' Kemp said. 'Was it a nice ghost or a nasty ghost?'

'Bit of both, I think, although it was wielding a knife, but at the same time I'm pretty sure it wanted to help.'

'Well that's alright,' Kemp said, sounding like an authority on the subject. 'So it had a knife and it didn't kill you. That's a start – where were you going to meet up?'

'That's the problem, I can't remember. I thought it was a dream, so I agreed to everything and said the first thing that came into my head.'

'So what makes you think it wasn't a dream?'

Archie pointed at the coat. 'This.'

Kemp looked at it. 'An old overcoat! Bleeding heck, Archie.' Kemp wondered if Archie hadn't entirely lost his marbles.

'I know,' Archie said, quickly realising it must sound idiotic, 'but I swear it's the same coat the ghost was wearing. Look at those buttons with the snake slipping up a tree.'

Kemp thrust out his jaw and furrowed his brow. 'How do you know it isn't Old Man Whatshisface's?'

'Old Man Wood,' Archie said. 'His name is "Old Man Wood".'

'Yeah right, chill your boots.' Kemp held the coat up in the air. 'I mean it's pretty big – about his size – are you sure he wasn't ... giving it to you? You know, offloading it before he took it to the charity shop.'

Archie shook his head. 'No, definitely not. Old Man Wood doesn't have that many clothes, certainly not an overcoat like this one. Anyway, there's more.'

'More? Great.'

Archie turned his head and indicated the cut on his chin. 'Look at this.' Kemp leant in. 'It's from the blade of the knife I was telling you about—'

'From the ghost?'

Archie nodded.

Kemp inspected it. 'Nah, I don't believe you, you could have got that from a bramble or a branch when you ran to school yesterday.'

Archie shook his head. 'No, honest to God, it definitely arrived in the middle of the night.'

'You one hundred percent sure?'

Archie nodded.

Kemp guffawed. 'Ghosts don't carry things like knives or hit people. Everyone knows that.'

'This one did,' Archie said.

Kemp was trying not to laugh and only just managed to restrain himself. 'Don't get me wrong, Archie, but it doesn't stack up. Why would a ghost want to harm you?'

Archie thought for a minute. 'To prove it was real, I suppose.' Archie felt in the coat pocket and slowly withdrew the knife, shielding it from prying eyes with his hands.

'Look.'

Kemp's eyes fell to the gap under the desk where Archie held the knife and he swore under his breath. 'Blimey Archie, that's a beauty.' Kemp could hardly prise his eyes away. 'So what did this ghost say?' he asked.

'That's where it gets a bit blurry,' Archie began. 'He said he was on a mission to save his mother, that she was going to die and that I had to help protect her at all cost.'

'Epic. Sounds good to me,' Kemp said. 'I'd do anything to protect my mother.'

Archie realised he'd hit a raw nerve. 'Sorry, Kemp. I didn't mean—'

'Chill, Archie, I know you didn't.' Kemp was intrigued. 'So what's in it for you?'

'Well, as I said, a partnership of some sort. I told you, I can't really remember. I'd find out at this meeting but,' Archie laughed and turned a little red. 'Thing is I think I said I'd meet him bang in the middle of the football match – not that I'd go anyway.'

Kemp chuckled. 'Your planning skills are very poor, Archie.'

Archie ignored him. 'Somewhere along the line, he was banging on about power and strength or something equally crazy.' He shook his head. 'Oh, I can't remember.' He thumped the desk. 'Maybe it's my lack of sleep?'

Kemp was intrigued but also a little worried about his friend. It might be madness and completely made up, but you had to hand it to them, these de Lowes were nothing less than interesting.

Archie studied Kemp's face, and quickly reached a conclusion. 'You think it's bollocks, don't you?' He put his head in his hands. 'I've been sucked in, haven't I?'

Kemp shrugged. 'Probably your Old Man thingy playing a joke or something—'

'Or perhaps a hallucination from one of his strange apples – or another nightmare?' Archie added.

'Yeah,' Kemp said as though it was perfectly normal. He'd heard about the old man's curious apple collection. 'Probably one of those – can't believe you didn't see it all along.' He slapped Archie on the back. 'You ought to be getting along, don't want to miss your warm-up.'

Archie cocked his head and looked at his watch. 'RATS! Is that the time?' He started gathering his bits together. 'Hey, Kemp, thanks for the chat – please don't think I've turned into a nutter – and promise me, you won't tell anyone about this?'

'You de Lowes are all nutters,' Kemp said. 'But you, Archie, are the only one worth their salt.'

Archie noted the look in his eyes had gone cold. Maybe he was bored or had turned his thoughts to Daisy.

Archie ran to the door. 'See you later.'

Kemp winked. 'Sure.'

---

KEMP SHOOK HIS HEAD. Those de Lowes are properly nuts. There's something distinctly odd, unsettling and eccentric about them. If it wasn't strange scientific experiments or an infatuation with ghosts or girls being brilliant at games designed for men, it was some other random thing, like extraordinary disorganisation, or manic recklessness.

Mr Bellwood re-appeared. 'Time to lock up the classroom,' he said. 'Please gather your things as it won't re-open until after half term. Make sure you take everything you need.'

Chairs scraped against the floor as the remaining students stood up. Kemp slipped into his overcoat and gathered the contents of his desk, dropping them haphazardly in his bag. He tucked in his chair and headed towards the door with the others.

'Kemp,' Mr Bellwood called out, 'haven't you forgotten something?'

Kemp looked puzzled.

'Your coat?'

Kemp hesitated. 'Oh, yeah. Sorry, wasn't thinking.' It was a little odd that Bellwood hadn't spotted he was wearing his own coat in the first place. Oh well, he'd take it for Archie, and give it back later. He returned to the chair, picked up the coat and put it on over the one he already had on. Then he saw the slip of paper on the desk in Archie's scrawny handwriting. Kemp scanned it for a second and noticed the underlined location. It must be where he was meeting this so-called ghost. Kemp read it again, folded it up and put it in his pocket.

'Jolly good,' said Mr Bellwood running his hand over his chin. 'Now, let's go and watch that football match, shall we.'

# 20 A STORM IS COMING

Archie tore around the corridor when he almost collided with Daisy. She was talking with her girlfriends.

Archie reddened. 'Daisy, er sorry, but shouldn't we be getting ready?'

'Oh, I thought we had plenty of time.' She studied her watch. 'It's only just gone ten – we've got at least half an hour, haven't we?'

Archie reddened even more and shook his wrist. Stupid watch. 'Yes. Sure. Right, yeah – of course, er ... whatever.' It wasn't going well. Why did he feel so intimidated around groups of girls? Individually they were fine but a pack of them scared him to death. 'Look, I'm going to see if I can find Isabella. Want to join me?'

'No. Not really.'

Archie's face went purple. 'Please,' he squeaked.

Daisy caught his eye, turned and addressed the girls. 'OK ladies,' she said, 'I'm off to do battle with those big, bad, beastly boys and kick the house down.' They shrieked their approval. 'Wish me luck.'

Each of the girls made a big play of kissing her on her cheek and then broke into a chant;

*'GO, GO Daisy de Lowe! GO, GO Daisy de Lowe! GO, GO Daisy de Lowe! Go Daisy! Go Daisy! GO Daisy ...'*

Daisy put one hand in the air as she waltzed away, her other fluffed up her wavy blonde hair and she wiggled her hips.

Archie put his head down, trying to ignore his sister, although it was virtually impossible. How would anyone believe Daisy was such a talented footballer when she hung out with the "chicks" and did idiotic dances like this?

As the twins turned the corner the chanting changed to the old *Queen* anthem: *'D-D-L, D-D-L, D-D-L – SHE WILL, SHE WILL ROCK YOU!'*

'You coping, Arch?' she said. 'You're very glum-faced.'

'Moron-faced, more like.'

'Oh no, what have you done now?'

Archie groaned. 'Oh, Daisy. I think I've done something insanely foolish. I told Kemp about my nightmare. He must think I've totally lost the plot. I don't know why I did it. He'll probably tell everyone, like he usually does.' Archie caressed his temples with his fingers. 'It's social suicide.'

'Yup.' Daisy pinched him playfully on the cheek. 'When will you ever learn? He's a jerk and you're best off keeping well away.'

They found Isabella in the physics lab with Sue, running over an experiment, their heads buried in some calculations.

Daisy was full of bounce. 'Ready to go, girls?' she said.

Her jollity didn't really have the same effect on the science students.

'Daisy,' Isabella said, in her most serious tone. 'I want you to wear these, on your boots.'

Daisy looked at her in amazement. 'On my bits?'

'Don't be so stupid. Your football boots.'

She fingered the rubbery, gooey material. 'What is it?'

Isabella peeled off her lab glasses. 'In short, it's a de-energising unit we've created.'

'A what-erising-humit?' Daisy said. 'Why?'

'Just in case, that's why.'

'I don't understand?'

'Just do it, will you,' Isabella demanded. 'One for each boot.' She handed her a second one. 'You too, Archie.'

Archie studied it. 'What's it for?'

Isabella squealed. 'In case either of you gets hit by lightning. It might help, that's all.'

Archie stuck the strips to the soles of his boots. 'Aren't you're taking this a bit far—'

A huge roll of thunder shook the building. The windows rattled and the children's hair stood on end. They looked at each other.

Isabella raised her eyebrows. 'We're not, Archie. These could save your life—'

'Where's that storm glass thing?' Daisy cut in, her tone serious. 'I want to see what it's doing.'

'Next to Isabella's desk,' Sue replied.

Daisy picked it up, studied it and quickly put it down again. 'I don't mean to be rude, sciencey nerd folk, but have you analysed this lately?'

Isabella marched over as though it was a complete waste of time. 'What?' she snapped.

Daisy put it down. 'This test tube. Have any of you noticed a) how hot it is, and b) that it's literally crammed full of crystals moving very, very fast.'

Isabella grabbed it, stared at it for a moment or two before laying it down on the bench. 'I have no idea what you're talking about, Daisy. Yes, it's a little warm – but so what? As I said, I'm not sure how it works.'

Daisy shrugged. 'Well, you two know what you're doing. But I'd keep an eye on that if I were you.' She stretched out the gooey strip. 'Can I put this in my hair?'

'Please, Daisy,' Isabella said. 'It must be on the bottom of your shoe. Attach it on the underside of your boot using the Velcro.' Isabella sounded a little irritated by the intrusion. 'Now go away – run and get changed or you'll be late.'

Daisy skipped off, singing to herself and punching the air.

As her footsteps receded down the corridor, Archie picked up the storm glass. Immediately he put it down again. 'Woah! It really is hot, seriously. Touch it.'

'I've just done that,' Isabella said.

Sue put her finger to the glass. 'OW! Scorching!' she sucked her fingers. 'Bells, it's steaming.'

'A mild expulsion of water vapour, that's all,' Isabella said nervously.

'You think so?' They started backing away.

'No, not necessarily.'

The test tube was beginning to glow, steam pouring out of the top.

'Has anyone added anything to it?' Isabella asked.

Archie and Sue shook their heads.

The activity in the test tube increased. They could hear the crystals popping against the glass.

'Get out!' Isabella yelled. 'Crickey. It's going to blow!'

They ran for the door and shut it firmly behind themselves and threw themselves to the floor. Seconds later, the storm glass exploded, sending fragments to every corner of the room.

Sue shivered. 'What does it mean?' she asked.

'I think it means we were right all along.' Isabella's voice quaking. 'For here above us, beginneth the storm from hell.'

'It couldn't be a mistake, could it?' Sue said – a tinge of desperation in her voice.

'Possibly,' Isabella replied, as another roll of thunder boomed and shook the walls. 'But I very seriously doubt it.'

---

'RIGHT, THAT'S IT!' Isabella said as she barged past Sue. 'Out of my way!'

'Where are you off to now?'

'To see Solomon and have it out with him. This time properly.'

'Oh no,' Sue said remembering the last time she'd seen Isabella like this. She'd torn into Mrs Douglas, the science teacher, and ended up being severely reprimanded – and very nearly expelled. 'I'm coming with you.'

As Isabella marched off, her eyes hard and her chin up, Sue had to run alongside to keep up. They wove through the maze of old school buildings, up worn stone stairs and down dark corridors, until they reached a large, dark brown, studded wooden door that sat below a striking Gothic arch. Opposite this was a small, elegant courtyard with a fountain, like a bird bath, in the middle.

Isabella thumped on the door, the noise echoing back at them. 'He must be in,' Isabella said. She turned the handle of the door. It creaked.

'You can't just let yourself in,' Sue whispered.

'Watch me – I'll wait for him inside. Then he can't get away from me.'

'You're being ridiculous—'

'Now then,' said the familiar voice of Mr Solomon as his head appeared around the door. He pulled it open and peered over the top of his glasses. 'Isabella, Sue, how nice to see you.' He smiled a thin and rather fake smile as he studied their faces. 'Is everything alright – what can I do for you?'

Inside, Isabella saw books piled up on tables and crammed into shelves from the floor to the ceiling and stuffed into every nook and cranny of the room; old reading lamps offered light to large leather armchairs and exercise books with piles of marking were stretched out across the floor. Odd curiosities and portraits of headmasters dotted the walls.

This room of learning had the immediate effect of dampening her temper.

Solomon caught her staring and invited them in. 'Can I get you both anything – a cup of tea, perhaps?'

Isabella hesitated. 'No, thanks.' She turned to Sue as if for encouragement. 'I'll, er, get straight to the point if I may. You have to call off the football match.'

'Whatever for?' the headmaster replied. 'You're not still worried about this storm?'

Isabella reddened a little. 'Yes, sir. I'm not only worried about it; I'm petrified about it. You see, I ran some programmes on global weather data with specifics exactly like those we have above us, and then I did another experiment which confirmed my suspicions—'

'How fascinating,' said Mr Solomon with a plastic smile. 'Tell me about it?'

'Well, I built a storm glass – and it has just blown up—'

'A storm glass?' Solomon interrupted. 'A 17th century version of the weather forecast?' Solomon laughed dryly. 'I haven't heard of one of those since I was a student. In fact, I'm sure we had one here once upon a time. It was in a cabinet – as a curiosity. I'll have to dig it out.'

Isabella frowned. Solomon knew about storm glasses. She felt a rush of uncertainty.

'You're concerned about this horrid cloud again, aren't you Isabella,' Solomon said gently, noting that he'd unsettled her.

She nodded.

'Well, rest assured. I am too.'

'You are?'

'Indeed. In fact I have just this very minute put the phone down from a conversation with a senior forecaster at the Met Office. According to them, there's little to worry about. It's a localised cloud – at worst we may hear several growls of thunder and see a few flashes of lightning and perhaps experience some heavy rain, but nothing unusual for the time of year. And they assured me that it was unlikely to break until this afternoon. Satisfied?'

'But—'

'There you have it, Isabella. I'm afraid there's nothing more to say about the matter. The match is on and the other performances will continue as planned.' His tone changed. 'I am particularly busy at the moment organising today's celebrations before the start of the match, so please don't pester me with this again. You should know by now that I have everyone's best interests at heart. Safety, as you are well aware, is my number one priority.'

Isabella stared at the headmaster. He wasn't telling the truth one bit – she could smell it. 'Can I ask who you spoke to at the Met Office, sir?'

Solomon paused and glared at her. 'If you must know, it was a man by the name of Mr Fish.'

With that he ushered them out of the door and shut it firmly behind him.

---

SOLOMON LEANT on the oak door and listened as their footsteps receded down the corridor. Then he let out a sigh. Had she believed him? He couldn't be sure. It was hard to read her expression, although he noted there was more of a frown on her face than before.

Why did she keep coming back to him about the storm? Did she really believe there was going to be a disaster? If she did, he thought, it was very over the top.

Solomon picked up his schedule folder and sat down in one of the leather armchairs. Her persistence was admirable, even if it was misplaced. No, no. Nothing was going to stop today going ahead, not a big storm or even a few drops of rain.

Goodness me, he thought, this is Yorkshire, the finest county in all of England – God's own county they called it – where thunder and lightning went hand in hand with the rough landscapes of the moors and dales.

These kids were getting too soft.

He chuckled to himself. Met Office? He couldn't think what had made him come up with that nonsense. He simply knew that the only way he'd be able to stop her in her tracks was to throw something scientific back at her.

But why Mr Fish? It was an implausibly good name for a weatherman. In any case, he had a busy morning ahead; press turning up, television and newspapers, new parents and old, and this was his big – and last – chance to showcase everything he had done over the past twenty-five years. The crowning day of his headship.

He smiled and busied himself sorting out the place names for the banquet later on in the old school chamber. It was an evening he'd anticipated for years – and wouldn't it be sweeter still if they won the football.

How he hoped like mad that sister of hers, Daisy, would play her heart out again. What a player! He'd never seen the like. She was George Best and Pele and Ronaldo blended into one slender pop-tart of a girl – brave as a soldier, tough as leather and as quick and slippery as a salmon.

He sighed and shook his head before returning to the matter of wondering who he should sit next to. Geraldine Forbes. Yes, perfect. The star of Summerdale, the TV soap star famed for her gritty Yorkshire one-liners, but in reality she was a delightful, attractive lady, who had simply the most beautiful green eyes he'd ever seen and lips as full as cushions.

He pictured it in his mind; the hall decorated to the nines in the school's light blue and scarlet colours, bright candles accentuating the Gothic arched windows and the trophies and cups in gold and silver from the vaults sparkling in the light. Magnificent!

And afterwards, he'd make his speech of retirement and receive warm, generous and heartfelt thanks from those whose lives he had touched. Yes, he mused. It was to be his swan song and nobody, certainly not Isabella de Lowe, was going to stop it.

And then he laughed even harder, his mood turning from happy to jovial. Mr Fish. Ah yes, he thought. There really had been a weather forecaster called Mr Fish, if he recalled correctly. Wasn't he the one who told the nation there was no storm coming shortly before the devastating storms way back in the nineteen eighties?

Solomon laughed out loud and wiped his brow. Now won't that be hilarious if Isabella rings up the Met Office and asks for Mr Fish.

Whatever will they think?

# 21 ON THE WAY TO THE GAME

'Sue, we need a plan,' Isabella said. 'Solomon clearly doesn't want to know, so we're going to have to either disrupt the match or figure out how to get away—'

Sue couldn't really face direct action. 'Away would be best—'

Isabella was on a roll. 'If I can get Arch and Daisy over the bridge, then I think we'll be fine. When we get to the lane, the canopy of the tunnel will protect us. It's you I'm worried about.'

'*Me?*'

'Yes, you.' Isabella confirmed. 'How are you going to get out of here? You'll need to get home fast. Have you ever driven a car?'

'No. Stop being ridiculous—'

'I'm not. You could steal one.'

Sue glared at Isabella who shrugged back. 'Look, Bells, I'll think of something, OK.'

'Well thinking isn't good enough,' Isabella snapped back. 'You need a plan. Why don't you come back with us!'

'I can't. My mum wants me home.'

'Well, in that case, start engaging that brain of yours.'

As the two girls trudged slowly back from the science laboratories in silence they could feel the buzz of the crowd making its way down towards the bridge.

'Why do I feel so edgy about this match?' Isabella said as a couple of boys ran past nearly knocking her over. 'What if Daisy gets a huge kicking and can't run and they lose and then the storm breaks and she can't get home? And what about Archie? His mind seems to be all over the place, have you seen him? He looks sick, poor boy. I'm worried he won't save a thing – he seems even more scatter-brained than usual.'

'Well it is the final—'

'I know that,' Isabella said. 'It's just that I've got an awful feeling deep inside me that everything's going to go wrong.' Isabella closed her eyes and shook her head. 'You know, I'm not sure I even like football—'

'Rubbish. You love it,' Sue replied, 'you're just a little jealous of Daisy like everyone else. Just look at Kemp. He's dying to play, but he sees Daisy as his barrier. He simply can't accept that girls can be superior in what is essentially a man's game. And Daisy's a babe too, so it's kind of doubly awful. And that, basically, is why he hates her so much.'

'But that still doesn't mean I like football—'

'Sure, but as you're her sister and sporty as a mole, it's natural for you to want her to do well.' Sue looked up at the sky and her heart seemed to skip a beat. She whistled. 'It really is the biggest, blackest, purplest, most evil-looking cloud I have ever seen, Bells. Even Solomon's hilarious floodlights are on. Every time I look up, my whole body starts shaking like a jelly.'

Isabella laughed nervously; she had the exact same feeling too.

Sue inspected her watch, 'We've got five minutes.' She slowed and grasped Isabella's arm as if setting herself up to say something important. She stared earnestly into her friend's eyes. 'Listen Bells,' she began, 'I've been meaning to tell you something important—'

'Really?' Isabella noticed that her friend had gone a little pale. 'Did you put the wrong mix in the storm glass—?'

'No. It's not about the storm glass ... it's about—'

'So you DID—'

'Bells, I haven't touched it. In fact I'm quite sure it did what it did perfectly naturally.' Sue added. '*It's about you*. It's personal.'

'Me?' Isabella's mind whirled. 'You've got a boyfriend and you haven't told me—'

'For goodness' sake, you know full well I haven't got a boyfr—'

'OK, someone out there fancies *me*—'

'NO. Listen, Isabella – it's got absolutely nothing to do with boys—'

'You sure?'

'YES.'

'Good,' Isabella said, 'they're a waste of—'

'It's *about* you,' Sue said.

'Me?' Isabella said. 'OMG. You ... fancy ... me?'

Sue shrieked. 'For crying out loud, Bells, NO! *Will you just let me speak.*' She took a deep breath trying to control herself. 'It concerns YOU, in fact it concerns all of you de Lowes. You, Archie and Daisy. All those things I told you about in my dream, well, there's more.'

'More?'

'Yes! The storm – the rain. You see, I'm pretty sure that in some way you're linked—'

Isabella was a bit confused. 'Us, linked?'

'Listen! SHUT UP, just for a minute.' Sue tried to compose herself. 'What I'm trying to say is that—'

Sue heard the long shrill of a whistle and the roar of the crowd. She followed Isabella's eyes towards the floodlit football pitch.

'OH NO! We're late!' Isabella cried and smacked her hand on her forehead. 'Your watch must be slow.'

Sue tapped the face of the dial and compared it to the clock on her mobile. 'Oh help! Sorry.' But already her friend had gone.

Isabella tore off down the track. What was I thinking? I bet someone's scored. 'Come on, keep up!' she yelled over her shoulder as she took off down the shingle path. She felt Sue draw close. 'Look, tell me later! I mean it's not like it's life or death, is it?' she yelled.

'But there are things you absolutely ... must ... know,' Sue said, her voice trailing off as she watched Isabella fly away from her at a simply extraordinary speed. In fact she couldn't remember seeing Isabella run faster in her whole life.

Sue felt sick, the moment lost. Everything in the last hour had started to confirm that what she had seen and heard and felt was going to come true. And if there was even the tiniest chance of this happening, then she absolutely had to tell Isabella everything.

She gritted her teeth. Why was it that every time she tried to say something to her, it never seemed quite the right time – as though there was some kind of force preventing it from happening?

Because the thing was, it really was about life or death.

---

KEMP REACHED into his pocket and pulled out the paper with the scribbles Archie had made. He wondered if what Archie had said had any truth in it. Nah, even though Archie banged on about it – as though it really mattered – he was probably nervous about the football or something.

Kemp dismissed it.

Then he wondered if it was an elaborate set-up for a fight with Gus Williams; the work of one of those girls – Daisy or Isabella de Lowe. He could smell them all over this.

Kemp leant against the stone wall outside the school hall and held the paper up. If that Old Man Wood, or whatever his name was, was old enough to play a prank on Archie and give him this old coat to wear, then what were the others capable of?

Maybe that's what they did up there in the hills; they dreamt up hilarious jokes because they had nothing else to do apart from tell stories and get freaked out by ghosts or the weather. He glanced up. It was ridiculously dark and it was a ridiculously huge cloud. He wondered if Isabella's experimental madness with barometers might have some foundation.

Kemp's eyes returned to the paper. He looked at the middle option, the one which was double-underlined. It read:

*'Alleyway behind kissing houses.'*

Kemp thought about it. It was a good choice. If he was to meet a knife-wielding ghost in a quiet spot which not too many people seemed to know about – but wasn't too quiet – AND with the advantage that you could get out of both ends – AND close enough to the playing fields for a quick getaway, it was a very good choice. He nodded. Clever old Archie, not just a scruffy little boy.

Then he clenched his fist. It was also the perfect place for a fight.

He remembered the look on Williams' face. He wanted a battle; he could see it in his eyes. Kemp twisted the fabric on Archie's coat; at least it was nice and strong – and light too. Another layer of protection – just what he'd need if Williams came at him.

Kemp sucked in his breath. That was it. They would fight – him and Gus Williams, the two of them – and he'd show him who was the strongest.

Yeah. Finally, Gus Williams was in for a beating like he'd never had before.

# 22 KEMP'S FIGHT

From the road above the football field, Kemp could see the crowd that lined the entire perimeter of the pitch. In places they stood four deep from the touchline. How could so many turn out for a silly game of football? But it was a hollow thought for, deep down, Kemp ached to be part of it – to have them cheer *him* on.

Anyway, he'd never play alongside that girl. It was a step too far; at least it was for him – there was absolutely no way he could play in the same team as her. That annoying, self-contented, plucky, idiotic Daisy de Lowe.

It made him feel like puking just thinking about her, even if she was Archie's sister. That was unfortunate. Archie was kind of cool – laidback and easy. She was a show-off and she got under his skin like a pus-filled boil.

Anyway, his friends at Chitbury would have the last laugh with Daisy de Lowe in the second half. That was the plan.

He kicked a loose stone on the ground which skipped across the raised pebbles and smacked a small boy in the knee with a sickening thud. The boy collapsed in agony on the path as Kemp clenched his fist. Nice shot, he thought, wishing it had been de Lowe's knee.

Kemp looked down on the illuminated pitch. That's what they need out there, strength, leadership and character: me.

He walked further up the slope towards the houses which sat above the playing fields, slowly passing the crowd by until he was on his own high above the pitch. As he walked, he thought about how he could occupy himself over the break with his dreary aunt. Last time, he'd nearly died of boredom, being dragged around endless museums, antiques shops and flea markets. All he ever seemed to do was look at dead things; stuffed animals, bones, and fossils.

Sure, his aunt was kind and nice and tried hard for him, but she was almost too nice; too wet, too soppy.

The very thought of her made him cringe. He wondered whether, if his real parents had still been alive, they would have done things which were more fun – things he'd actually like, stuff they could get stuck into together, like sailing or mountaineering or holidaying abroad.

He smiled as he imagined a camping trip by the side of the river next to a large, warm fire and looking at the stars, his mother singing – her notes filling the air in a sort of magical way in time to the crackle of the burning wood. His father smiling at him proudly.

It was a fantasy, of course – the idyllic family life he'd never have – and every time he thought of it, it brought a tear to his eye. He couldn't remember if his mother used to sing to him or not and he had no idea what his parents looked like, but it felt right.

But how the reality hurt.

A long booming rumble distracted him. He spied another round pebble and took a mighty swipe with his heavy, black boot, connected sweetly – delighted with the way it flew through the air – skipped a couple of times and then, on the last bounce, it lifted quickly and seemed to whistle past the head of someone lurking by the lamppost near to the alleyway.

Oh hell! What was an old bloke doing standing over there in the first place? And he didn't even flinch. Bloody weirdo, probably missed him – must have missed him or he'd have been knocked out cold.

Kemp put his head down and sauntered on as if nothing had happened. He leaned against a tree. Maybe it was the ghost Archie had told him about. He shook his head and smiled. Nah, more like a lucky escape.

A few paces on and Kemp noticed a figure just inside the entrance to the alleyway where moments earlier he was sure no one had been there.

His heartbeat quickened.

Kemp studied the person while pretending to read Archie's bit of paper. It was the same figure of a hunched old man, shrouded in a long, dark cloak, a thick scarf wrapped round his chin and nose and a kind of loose-fitting trilby hat pulled over his head in such a way that he couldn't make out a face. The figure was leaning on a stick just like a blind man.

Maybe *this* was Archie's ghost.

A roar rang out from the football pitch. Kemp turned his attention back to the game. He picked out the chant of 'Daisy de Lowe, GO, GO, GO'.

He smacked his fist into his hand. Typical. That idiotic girl must have scored.

---

KEMP WATCHED as Chitbury kicked off and mounted another attack but after a couple of passes a shot flew high over the crossbar of goalkeeper Archie.

He reached into his pocket for his phone but, as he did, his hand touched a waxy piece of paper, like a sweet wrapper. With a frown on his face he tried to work out how it had got there. He smiled. Of course – it was from one of the packs of Haribos he'd stolen from Poppy – one of de Lowe's girlie friends – at break. He'd stuffed it in his mouth and nonchalantly tossed one of the wrappers into the headmaster's rose garden, where it stuck rather comically on a thorn and flapped in the breeze. He smiled.

But how come this one was folded?

Out of curiosity, he pulled it out, opened it up and stared at it. Strangely, the sweet paper was covered in random scribbles like a pile of spaghetti plonked on a plate.

Just as he was about to trash it, a few of the lines looked familiar. They're kind of ... faces.

Kemp scanned it and turned it sideways and round again. And then three figures came out at him, like a "magic eye" puzzle revealing itself on the wrapper.

There were three clear faces staring back at him.

Then it struck him. It was the de Lowes! Absolutely, definitely, them; all smug and cheerful and ghastly. But, as he studied it, their faces seemed to melt away into the paper, like slush dripping through a gutter.

The next time he blinked, he was staring at nothing. Not a damn thing.

He turned the sweet paper over. It was blank.

Kemp felt a surge of excitement run through him. Was he seeing things? Was this some kind of joke?

He slapped his face and rubbed his eyes. Then he tried hard to remember what Archie had said, and scoured the area for a mysterious old man?

He looked at the wrapper again. It was changing gradually from white through grey to almost black, like the colour of the vast cloud above them. And then the words "HELP ME" started to appear in the form of tiny molten streaks of lightning on the paper, as if burning the words into it. He crumpled it up and thrust it in his overcoat pocket.

Kemp's heart beat so fast that for a moment he felt as if he would vomit.

Instinctively, he started walking, faster and faster; as if walking might make it go away.

A few minutes later, he skipped up the series of wide Yorkstone steps to street level and tentatively made his way towards the houses that leaned in as though they were kissing. He peered down the dark alleyway but as far as he could tell it was empty, save for the black wheelie bins guarding it like sentries.

As he took his first step under the buildings, he noted how the oak-beamed houses on either side all but touched each other as if challenging one another like fighters. It reminded him of his duel with Williams.

He spun towards the football pitch below him as he heard a groan from the crowd. He tried to figure out what was happening. Had Chitbury won a penalty? Certainly it looked as if there were bodies lying all over the pitch. He smiled.

Was that Archie staring up at him? He almost felt like waving.

Then Kemp turned and headed into the alleyway.

---

HALFWAY DOWN, he slowed. He sensed something creeping up behind him.

His heartbeat quickened. There was no doubting it, someone was definitely there, someone really quiet. But who? This was strictly out of bounds – how would he explain himself? Was it a teacher? Nah, unlikely. They'd be watching the football match or making last minute plans for the performances later on. In any case they'd have said something.

Kemp thought quickly and it came to him: Williams. He almost said his name out loud. It must be Williams. It had to be. He was free this afternoon and it was exactly his style to creep up on people.

Kemp curled his fist into a ball and very precisely said, 'Williams, if it's you, I'm warning you. Stop, and walk away, NOW.'

There was no reply.

He could feel him coming closer.

Kemp bent down, pretending to tie his boots. His pulse raced. He readied himself. He sensed the person behind him was now only a couple of paces away.

'I've been waiting for this,' Kemp said, and in one movement swung around and threw his biggest punch.

But it wasn't Williams, it was the old man. And it was too late to stop.

His momentum carried him forward, his fist unstoppable. But instead of connecting, the arm careered straight on and propelled him on to the hard grey stone.

Kemp's head cracked the paving as he went down. His left leg and arm throbbed.

'You don't have to do that, Archie,' said a gravelly voice from behind the scarf. 'We're on the same team now.'

Kemp was struggling to get to grips with what had happened. Was it Archie's ghost?

'Believe me, it is excellent news that you've arrived on time.' The old man moved almost directly above him, his face covered by the scarf and hat. 'And I sense that you have brought my coat. Very well done; did the Old Man find it?'

Kemp was horrified and for a moment simply didn't know what to say. 'Yes, he gave it to me,' he lied. His voice stammered as a terrible chill swept through him.

'Are you ready to join with me, Archie de Lowe?'

Kemp's skin crawled. Everything Archie had told him was completely true.

He needed more time. 'Join you?' Kemp said, scuffling backwards, trying hard to keep his face hidden. 'Er, can you remind me again? I was very tired last night.'

The ghost hesitated. 'Well, let me put it this way. I've got what you want.'

Kemp shivered. What I want? No wonder Archie was freaked out. 'What do you mean?' he stumbled.

The old man moved to one side and appeared to look up towards the sky. 'Why me, of course.'

'You?'

'Yes, me,' said the ghost. 'You see I'm the only one here who can help you escape from this place. And you have only about fifteen minutes in your time to decide.'

Kemp's brain went a little fuzzy. Fifteen minutes? In *your* time? Decide what? Kemp stole a look down the alley.

He needed to get away, fast.

The old man sensed his unease. 'You see, in a very short time the skies will open and it will rain for forty days and nights in a way you cannot even begin to imagine—'

Kemp looked confused. 'What ... forty days and nights?'

'Yes. That's what I said, forty days and nights—'

'Forty days and nights—?'

'Yes!'

'What ... like Noah's Ark—?'

'STOP repeating what I say and listen!' the old man spat. The words seemed to smack Kemp around the face. He lost his footing and slipped.

'If you think what I'm saying is any way over the top,' the old man said, bearing down on him, 'I can assure you that in a short while, all of this – everything here, everything – will be destroyed.'

The old man gestured, almost triumphantly, Kemp thought, towards the playing field.

'Archie,' the ghost continued, his voice mellow once more, 'there will be nothing but devastation. There is a shift happening, a shift in time, a shift in the way of the universe and it is happening right here, right now. You are part of this, Archie.

'The wheels are turning and they cannot be reversed.'

# 23 THE GAME

Shortly before the whistle blew for half time, Isabella dashed down the touchline and found Sue.

'Sue, thank God I've found you,' she said. 'What's up with you? We're on drinks duty in the catering cart, or had you forgotten?'

'Ah,' she said. 'You're right. My watch ...'

They rushed over to the old Volkswagen Combi ice cream van, known by the children as the "catering cart", which acted as the half time refreshment centre and mobile sweet shop.

Isabella and Sue and a couple of others pulled out a few tables and lined out paper cups for jugs of orange squash. As they did so, a steady stream began queuing to buy drinks or chocolate bars or crisps.

Sue took the money while Isabella handed out cups, but Sue could barely keep up.

Isabella was working at an astonishing speed, darting here and there, handing out confectionery and drinks and talking to everyone about the score or Daisy's brilliant goals or the curious weather or who was next. It was an orderly, efficient operation.

'How did you manage to serve all that in ten minutes?' Sue said, as she squeezed a few more cups into the overflowing bin bag. 'We must have made a killing.'

She wiped her brow and breathed a sigh of relief. It had been a welcome distraction and with no rain thus far perhaps Solomon was right. Maybe the cloud would break later on that afternoon. And anyway, with everyone chatting and milling around and surging towards the orange juice and chocolate bars, she hadn't had a moment to think about her predicament, and it was some time after the whistle had sounded for the start of the second half that she focused her attention back to the pitch.

From inside the van she looked out over the scene. The crowd was still three or four deep the entire way around the pitch and she could just make out the steep rise of the bank on the far side that led up to the village.

The floodlights shone down onto the pitch, giving the players a strange quadruple shadow. If it hadn't been nearly midday, there would be no reason to suspect that they weren't playing a night match.

'Isabella,' she called out. 'Get a place left of the halfway line. I'll join you in a minute. I'm going to cash up.'

---

THE VERY FIRST attack after the break, Chitbury scored. Isabella stamped her feet in frustration. 'Exactly what we didn't need,' she said. 'Come on, Upsall!'

Sue looked up at the vast black cloud that seemed to be growing thicker and sinking lower as if someone was filling it up with an enormous hose. The feeling of dread she'd experienced before was building inside her; she knew she should get out, run to higher ground, but in her heart, she was swallowed up by the football and the drama, and swept away by the team led by Daisy de Lowe, who blocked and tackled and encouraged her players to keep going with her relentless drive and skill and energy.

A heavy challenge sent Daisy flying. The crowd swayed and spilled onto the pitch.

The noise increased.

'That was late. Too damn late,' Isabella shouted, peeling off her scarf.

'Listen, Bells. Watch it,' Sue said firmly. 'You mustn't go nuts. You'll get expelled. I promised Solom—'

'It was deliberate and dirty—'

'**NO**, Isabella!' Sue snapped. 'Hold your tongue.' She grabbed her arm.

'But they're targeting Daisy exactly as Kemp said they would. They're going to kick her out of the game!'

Sue closed her eyes. Great, just what she needed; Isabella going out of control, again. She looked at her watch. Ten minutes to go. Isabella was already sizzling like a firework.

'What's that noise?' Isabella said.

'The gargantuan cloud should give you a clue.'

'Th ... thunder?' Isabella said, momentarily removing her eyes from the action.

Sue nodded.

Some of the crowd started to leave; others were gesturing towards the sky and gathering themselves to go. This is it, she thought. This is where it starts – exactly as I saw in my nightmare. *It feels the same too.* I've got to tell Isabella. I've got to tell her NOW.

A ghastly feeling of panic prickled her. They should stop the game.

Her thoughts were interrupted as Daisy stole the ball and sprinted down the field. She skipped inside one tackle and then slowed, looking for support. The crowd roared their approval but, from nowhere, a couple of Chitbury boys smashed into her from opposite angles. All three lay on the ground as the ball was kicked away by another Chitbury player.

Play continued, but it was a poor decision.

'That's another foul. Yellow card,' yelled a senior boy. 'C'mon ref!'

The atmosphere turned. Late tackles and players being kicked indiscriminately out of sight of the referee.

Then one of the Chitbury strikers stole into the penalty area as a massive crash of thunder reverberated around them. At that exact moment, little Jimmy Nugent, chasing back, tapped the forward's foot and the player fell head-first into the turf.

The whistle shrilled.

'Penalty!' Isabella spat. 'I don't bloody believe it!'

The ball was placed on the spot.

'This is it,' Sue said quietly, 'the end of Daisy's dream ... Bells, what on earth are you doing?'

Isabella was scribbling furiously in her notebook. 'Just watch for me a minute – you know, commentate like they do on telly.'

She didn't need to. The groan told her everything.

'What happened?'

'The ball trickled past Archie – he should have saved it. All he had to do was put his foot out. Two-all. Ninety-nine times out of a hundred he'd have had that.'

Isabella stood up and thrust the paper into Sue's overcoat pocket. 'Ye of little faith, Sue Lowden,' she said. 'You'll see. Daisy will score again. I'll bet you a real barometer she does!'

Another roll of thunder boomed and cracked. More spectators headed off.

Sue's stomach lurched. It was now or never. She grabbed her friend and faced her. 'Bells, we must get out of here. I mean it. But listen to me first. If it starts raining, this pitch will be a river in less than ten minutes. It's important—'

'Please, Sue. Just shut up!' Isabella snapped as she turned back to the game. 'Get the ball to de Lowe,' she screamed. 'Give it to Daisy!'

She turned to Sue. 'Listen, hun, tell me whatever is so damn important at the end, OK. There's less than five minutes to go and it's two-all in the most important match of my brother and sister's life. Just give it a break for five minutes. Five minutes.'

And with that, Isabella sidled out onto the pitch, ran down the touchline and dived in among some spectators further down.

---

ARCHIE STOMPED around the penalty area, his face burning with shame.

For some reason, just before the Chitbury player stepped up to hit the penalty, it came to him; the person he'd seen way up on the steps heading into the alley was Kemp. It could only have been Kemp. For a start, his hair was a complete giveaway and secondly he was wearing a long coat – Cain's coat – that dragged along the floor.

Instantly, he knew Kemp must have been checking out whether there was any truth to what he'd told him earlier about meeting Cain.

Intense confusion filled him. All he wanted was to run up there and find out what Kemp was up to.

In the very next instant, the ball trickled past him into the goal, even though the Chitbury striker had totally miss-hit the ball. The whistle shrilled as a collective groan eased around the ground. Daisy would be furious with him. Isabella's reaction didn't bear thinking about.

If Cain *was* there and Kemp had gone to find him, would Cain know? Would he care? But surely *he* was the one who was going to receive the power of a horse and strength of a lion, not Kemp.

He grabbed the upright and kicked the base of the post again. He felt he'd accomplished nothing – only given things away, like a vital goal and the opportunity for something extraordinary.

The more he thought it through, the more certain he was that Kemp was still there. And the angrier it made him feel. All I ever do is look on hopelessly, he thought. When will I stop being so average and pathetic?

A slow-burning fury started moving through his body. It was an anger borne of frustration and annoyance and it was beginning to consume him.

---

'NOW, LOOK,' Kemp said pulling himself together. 'If you ask me, you need help.' He drew himself up, his confidence returning. 'All that forty days and nights rain stuff happened a very long time ago in this book called '*The Bible*'. But I don't see any ark or animals.'

'Look above you, Archie,' the ghost said.

'Yeah, right,' Kemp said. 'A few dark clouds. Big deal. Hey! Is that a lion?' He pointed down the alleyway. 'And look – two kangaroos and a couple of woolly mammoths. Excuse me, freak, but I'm outta—'

'No – you – are – not,' said the old man, spitting each word out so severely that Kemp fell back on the ground. 'Out of all the people on this puny planet, I've selected you. So be grateful, Archie de Lowe, because I'm giving you the chance to save your life. There is no other way.'

Kemp squealed and looked down the passage. What was holding him back? Why didn't he run? Why didn't he say that he wasn't Archie? But he felt oddly dizzy – as if a force was holding him against his will – like an elastic band stretched out only to rebound.

'You need convincing,' the old man said, his voice as smooth as honey once more. 'This has come as a shock, so I'm going to show you something to ... reassure you. All I'm asking for is a little co-operation.' The old man took a step back. 'Please turn your attention towards the dark sky. Watch it closely.'

Kemp stood up, his knees barely able to hold him.

'You see, I'm going to tell you the story of what has happened so far and then I'm going to tell you what will happen next. Do you understand?'

Kemp nodded.

'Good. Firstly, let me tell you about that piece of paper in your pocket. Then I'll explain who you are and how you are going to help me.'

---

ARCHIE WAS ABOUT to kick short from the goal kick, but, from out of the corner of his eye, he saw Daisy in yards of space on the halfway line, catching her breath after the last attack. Could he reach her? It was worth a try. He pushed the ball ahead, ran up, and thumped it hard. The ball rose high into the air.

Daisy saw it and ran ahead, her eyes never leaving the ball. She took it down in her stride and, with a burst of speed, she tore past one player then another. Then she stopped so suddenly that another over-ran and she side-stepped one more who fell over. The crowd roared – this was Daisy at her best.

*'D-D-L, D-D-L, D-D-L – she will, she will – ROCK YOU!'* the crowd chanted.

Daisy side-stepped another and with a burst of speed headed towards the penalty area with real menace. Four Chitbury players lay sprawled on the floor, only one more to beat.

'Go on Daisy, you can do it,' Archie screamed.

Archie watched as the remaining defender was sold a beautiful dummy, which Daisy seemed to do with such ease it was laughable, and as she pushed the ball past and effortlessly made her way around him, the defender slid out a leg and tripped her – quite deliberately. Daisy stumbled and fell but she wasn't giving up. She crawled towards the ball and then, even as she lay on the ground, with the ball wedged between her knees, she somehow still managed to keep moving.

But a cry went up as three Chitbury players and the goalkeeper converged on Daisy. It felt as if Daisy had fallen into a trap as the Chitbury boys cocked their legs back and kicked out, striking more of Daisy than the ball. And then they kicked her again and again in a kind of frenzy, with Daisy refusing to give the ball up.

The crowd swayed and screamed and then fell silent. They could quite clearly see Daisy's face contorting as kick after kick rained in on her.

A boom of thunder echoed around the silent field as the crowd watched in startled amazement.

---

ARCHIE COULDN'T BELIEVE IT. Where was the referee? This wasn't football, it was violence.

He thumped the goalpost. How had he missed saving that penalty? He shook his head and looked up. The giant, angry bruise in the sky now stretched above him like a vast, black, monstrous airship. It sagged so low he felt he could jump up and burst it as easily as pricking a balloon. Perhaps Isabella's experiments weren't so crazy after all.

The heady smell of damp filled his nostrils as another crack of thunder escaped. Archie felt the blood boiling inside him. Now there were five of them surrounding Daisy. She managed to stand, but one of them pushed her over.

That was the final straw. Anger flooded through him. No one, Archie seethed, does that to my sister.

He gritted his teeth, but he couldn't control himself. He found himself running down the pitch, the crowd baying, the referee shouting, desperately trying to separate the players, but everyone, it seemed, was fighting.

'NO! Don't retaliate, Archie—' he could hear someone yelling. But it was too late, he was already there and it seemed as if hell had broken loose.

One of the Chitbury boys was holding Daisy's hair and leering at her, screaming at her. Archie grabbed him by the collar and threw him away, as if he were a doll. The boy sailed through the air and landed in a heap on the ground. Then Archie punched another hard on the nose and he thought he heard crunching sounds, then found himself receiving blows but he couldn't feel them.

Blood coursed through his body and he felt strong and powerful – invincible. A couple of Chitbury boys jumped on him but he easily beat them off. Then he found another hitting Alexander. He smashed the boy hard in the stomach and threw him away like a piece of litter.

The whistle shrilled.

Finally a sharp, stern voice rose up out of the melee. It was Isabella. Archie could see her marching towards them. Uh-oh, he thought. He was in for it now.

Archie looked around and found a couple of Chitbury boys and the referee staring at him with their eyes wide open. Were they looking at him in fear? It was a sensation he'd never really experienced before. He noticed the four boys he'd hit still lying in agony on the floor. Blimey, he'd done that.

Archie wiped his brow and allowed himself a smile. It felt strangely good.

---

FOR THE FIRST time in her life, Sue could feel the sensation of utter panic building up in her veins like a bubbling chemistry experiment. A series of flashes filled the sky, mirroring the extraordinary scenes of fighting on the pitch. Lightning fizzed and crackled in the dark cloud, forming – for a brief moment – a picture.

Sue gasped. A boy.

Then a thunderclap smashed overhead so loudly that the crowd cried out. Shrieks and screams filled the football field.

Sue fell to her knees, barely able to think, her body shaking. No! It can't be! It's not possible. It's ... it's ... Kemp's face – the lightning was Kemp's face super-imposed in the cloud. But how, how was it possible?

She looked around. Where was Isabella? Had she gone already; left her? Surely not. She followed the eyes of the crowd.

Oh NO! Isabella was striding towards the fighting on the pitch.

'STOP! ISABELLA, STOP!'

There was no reaction.

Without thinking, she took off after her. 'Isabella, LISTEN!' she screamed as she ran. '*It's you*!'

She ran on further.

'The dream is about your family, the de Lowes.' She sensed Isabella slowing down. 'You must ALL survive until sunset. Do you understand? SUNSET. YOU MUST STAY ALIVE.'

Her voice was petering out as she realised she was screaming herself hoarse. She sucked in a deep breath.

'Find clues in your house – Eden Cottage. *You must find the clues.*'

Sue coughed and then repeated the last part, adding, 'GO! GET HOME! NOW!'

She noted some of the crowd staring at her as if she was a madwoman. But she didn't care, not one little bit.

---

A LOUD ICE-CLEAR voice cut through the air: 'STOP IT – NOW!' It was Isabella's and she was striding towards the players with a sense of purpose.

The teams almost instantly ceased brawling. Isabella's direct approach had that effect on people.

'You're pathetic – all of you,' she shouted, pointing at various individuals. 'It's like a wrestling match for the Under 5s. Chitbury – especially you three – should be utterly ashamed of yourselves.'

Isabella scooped up the ball. 'And as for the refereeing – it's a disgraceful display. Twelve deliberate fouls by blue totally unaccounted for and you haven't even got the balls to book them, let alone send them off for repeated violent conduct.'

The football smacked into the referee's hands. 'What has the world come to when—?'

Before she had a chance to finish she was grabbed by Coach and Mr Bellwood who hauled her off her feet and away to the sidelines.

---

THE REFEREE RESPONDED by pointing rather belatedly at Isabella. 'GET HER OFF!' he yelled. 'You'll be dealt with later by the authorities.'

He blinked, trying hard to pull himself together. Why couldn't he remember the procedure for dealing with a brawl? It felt as if his brain had emptied.

'And along with that madwoman, Upsall numbers one and eight, and blue players five, seven and four,' he said pointing at the Chitbury players. 'GET OFF THIS PITCH.'

The referee waved his red card at the players and scribbled in his book.

Another huge slap of thunder exploded almost directly overhead. A terrible feeling crept right up his back sending his hairs erect.

The ground shook.

'Direct free kick to red,' he said, quickly pointing to a spot just outside the penalty area. 'And the quicker we're out of here, the better.'

He studied his watch. Less than a minute to go, thank the Lord. The girl was right. It had been a dreadful performance. He couldn't think why. Maybe it was this huge cloud that was sitting bang on top of his back.

Whatever it was, by God, he wanted this game finished with.

---

ARCHIE SHRUGGED AND STARTED WALKING. Moments later he was running. He couldn't complain – more than anything, he had to find out what Kemp was up to – and fast. If he was right, there wouldn't be much more time left. His stomach churned as a darkness seeped into his bones that something terrible was about to happen.

The clouds crashed and boomed. Spectators began to flee to the school buildings. Without looking back, Archie sprinted off the pitch towards the steep bank that led up towards the town.

# 24 THE PROPHECY

There was more, Sue thought, much more, but she'd said it; she finally said what needed to be said. Thank goodness she'd had the presence of mind to scribble down her dreams the moment she'd woken up. Now she had to get out of there – and fast.

'GO! Run! – run, all of you,' she yelled at the spectators. '*It's going to break. The storm's going to break.*' Thunder rolled out of the sky. She ran as fast as she could up the slope towards the buildings. She had to find a way out.

As she passed the top end of the ground she spied Gus leaning on the lamppost near to the kissing houses. She sprinted towards him. 'Gus. What are you doing?'

'Following Kemp – he's been acting weird all afternoon. Are we winning?'

'Listen Gus,' she said as she caught her breath. 'Rain ... like you've never seen ... you've got to get out of here and fast.' Her hand touched some paper in her pocket and she pulled out Isabella's note. 'You've got to believe me.'

Gus rolled his eyes. Had she gone completely doolally?

She started to read it out loud:

'*My best friend, Sue, there's a boat in the old shed. Key under a pot by door – oars on side. Canopy in cupboard ... just in case. Love you. Be safe – Bells.*'

Sue kissed it in relief; clever, brilliant Isabella.

Gus grabbed the note. 'What's up with you two?'

'Look at the sky, Gus. When that 'thing' bursts it will rain harder than you can possibly imagine. In minutes the water will flash. I had a premonition – I'll tell you about it—'

'A premonition? Blimey. Cool. You sure?'

'Absolutely. No one has a chance. Can you drive? Do you have access to a car?'

'Of course I don't!'

'Nor me,' she fired back. 'Some of the kids have gone but I'm being picked up later, after the music.'

'Same,' Gus said, trying to keep pace with her.

'Then we're stuck, Gus,' she said. 'Screwed. There's no way out.'

'Stuck? What are you talking about? Why should we be stuck?'

'Look, Gus,' she said. 'I promise you I'm not crazy, I'm deadly serious and I'm right. This cloud isn't holding an ordinary storm, when it lets go it will be utterly catastrophic. Come on, keep up.'

Gus frowned. 'You really are serious, aren't you?' he said, the smile slipping off his face.

'Never more so.' She stopped to catch her breath again. 'Please, Gus,' she began, 'I need your help. Will you help me? Please?'

Gus scratched his nose. He liked Sue even if she was a bit of a nerd, not that it really bothered him; at least she was a pretty nerd. The person who bothered him was Kemp and, more than anything, he'd like to knock him down a peg or two. Gus carried on thinking; he had certainly never seen her quite so animated. 'OK. I think I'm going to have to trust you on this one. Where do we start?'

'Oh great! Thanks, Gus,' Sue said, moving in and hugging him. If she was going to do this, better to do it with big, strong Gus Williams than by herself. 'First off, provisions. Food; high-energy snack bars, chocolates, lemons, dried fruit, tinned food like tuna and baked beans, sweetcorn, a couple of lighters, bottled water,' Sue rattled off, 'blankets – if you can find any. Anything you can get hold of. Come on,' she urged him to keep up. 'You're the Scout leader, aren't you? So you know – stuff we can survive on.'

'To the shop, then,' Gus said, smiling his rather big, toothy smile and suddenly feeling rather important.

'I've got about eighteen pounds from the footie snacks and drinks. I'll pay it back later.' Sue did some calculations in her head. 'Actually, that's probably not enough. Have you got anything?'

Gus shoved his hands in his pockets and pulled out some change, 'Just short of four pounds.'

Sue grimaced. 'In that case, Gus, I hope you don't mind but you're going to have to steal – come on, there's not a minute to lose. When we get in there, grab some bags and start filling them. Don't hesitate or stop but do not be stupid about what you take. When it's done I'll drop the money on the counter and we run. Alright.'

'Blimey, Sue. What if we get stopped?'

'We won't. Oh, and if necessary, use force. Do you understand?'

Gus nodded and handed over his money. His eyes were bulging with surprise. 'Where are we going afterwards?'

'The boatshed.'

'Boatshed? What boatshed?'

'The old shed by the river.' She waved her hand in its rough direction. 'We should have time to sort out some kind of cover and find some survival things ... then we're going to have to hope for the best. I don't know what we'll find when we get there but at the moment it's our only chance.'

Gus smiled. He loved a girl who meant business even if it was clear she had no idea about survival. And, he supposed, if there really was to be a disaster, this girl had the whole thing planned – that's if she wasn't completely crackers.

---

ARCHIE SCAMPERED up the steep bank, pulling himself up on the longer tufts with his hands and using his studs to give him grip. At the top of the bank he caught his breath and looked about. A huge roll of thunder shook the ground as he watched Isabella being marched off the football pitch by a couple of adults. People were streaming away, pointing skywards.

Wow. What a mental couple of minutes. He couldn't believe his strength and the fact that he had actually *hit* someone and then thrown two guys two or three metres as easily as if they were pillows. He shook his head; Archie de Lowe, most laidback human on the planet, had hit someone. Archie smiled. And the odd thing was, it hadn't felt so bad. Was it the strange glass of water left by the ghost?

He spied the alleyway and ran over, the studs of his boots clacking on the stone beneath him. He thought for a minute about taking them off but wondered whether there was any point.

This Cain, he thought, this ghost, couldn't really exist, could it? He peered down the alleyway and saw two shapes.

A sudden burst of lightning brought the pair to light and he could make out Kemp's red hair and another figure beside him bearing a long coat and a kind of trilby hat. Archie's heart pounded. They were making their way towards him.

OK. OMG. Wrongo. So what if Cain *did* exist and Kemp had got there first. Was this a good thing or a bad thing? Oh hell!

Archie shrank down, wondering what to do, and wiped the sweat off his forehead. He needed to think fast.

---

AS HE CROUCHED DOWN, urging his brain into action, Archie was struck by a thought. Cain was blind, wasn't he? He'd gone on about the fact that he didn't have any eyes – like the Ancient Woman, so if Cain was talking to Kemp, perhaps Cain couldn't see him. Using the same logic, another thought struck him: what if Cain thought Kemp was him! But the ghost couldn't get it that wrong, could he? I mean they were completely different.

Archie stood up from behind the wheelie bin so that only his head might be seen. Kemp was about ten paces away and Archie could definitely make out that the figure next to him was a ghost by the simple fact that he didn't have any shoes on and his face was covered – rather oddly, he thought – by a scarf. A crackle of lightning fizzed above them and, from the light it threw out, Archie was able to see – just for a flash – Kemp's face. It was a picture of utter terror.

Archie gasped and his heart thumped like a drum.

Kemp had seen him – his eyes widened, and for a brief moment their eyes met.

Kemp and Cain moved nearer and nearer. All the while Archie could discern the ghost's words like "power" and "magic" and "strength". Archie was stunned; did Cain think Kemp was him?

By the look of things, he did – although Kemp looked deathly pale.

A dark thought dashed into his mind: wouldn't Kemp be dying to get all of those things – power, strength and magic? Then Archie realised that the ghost was holding Kemp tightly around his left arm. Was Kemp moving them slowly out into the open or was it the other way round? Who was moving who?

Archie listened harder as they stopped just the other side of the wheelie bin.

He heard Kemp's quivering voice. 'Tell me again about the Prophecy. I need to be absolutely certain before I make my final decision.'

Cain seemed unimpressed. 'Did you not listen, Archie?' he complained.

Archie gasped. Cain *did* think Kemp was him! So what was Kemp playing at? And why was he asking Cain to tell him about this Prophecy one more time – it seemed a pretty odd thing to do. Was it for his benefit?

'I need to be perfectly sure,' Kemp replied.

'Very well.' Cain turned his head to the sky as though sniffing it. 'But a shorter version. We are running out of time.'

Archie stole another look at Kemp from around the corner of the wheelie bin. When he caught sight of Kemp's face, tears were streaming down his cheeks. Archie recoiled. Why? Why was Kemp crying? Was he trying to tell him something?

He crouched down and listened to Cain's deep, powerful voice. 'There is a great shift that occurs every now and then in the way of life, Archie,' the ghost began. 'Humans, who are at the top of this chain, evolve slowly but every now and then there is a big change. A change in physical attributes, a change in relation to surroundings, the infinite and beyond. The processes of these changes are shown in the form of dreams. The dreams that start this process have been given to you and your siblings. These dreams are the Prophecy of Eden, for you are the Heirs of Eden, the anointed ones.'

Archie's gut turned. JEEZ. Anointed ones! From their dreams. Why – why them? He remembered the strange creature above Daisy – he had been right all along – it *had* been giving her dreams. But it didn't make it any easier to understand.

The ghost coughed and carried on. 'It is complex – this is not the time to tell you the ways of the universe. All you need know is that the Heirs of Eden face fearsome challenges.' He turned his face to the sky. 'The first of which begins with a terrible storm aimed entirely at you. If any of you do not survive the storm, it will rage for forty days and forty nights and wash out the world, bit by bit.' Cain sucked in another lungful of air. 'When the waters recede there will be a different world with a new beginning.

'I tell you now. You children stand little chance – there is no ark to save you, nor any place you can go that you will not find yourselves shot at by lightning or washed out by torrents of rain. The earth will slip down hillsides, the rivers swell and trees crash down. There is nowhere you can hide. I do not tell you this with any joy, but the storm was designed when men were strong and lived long and knew how to fight with nature through other means, like magic. You are about to enter a time you are not equipped to cope with. Do you understand?'

Kemp nodded and his eyes bulged. 'Why?' he asked.

'Aha! Young man, the Prophecy is a measure – a test, if you like, to see if the people on this planet are ready to move into a new age, a new age of human enlightenment – the next step – if you like. The Prophecy was designed to test the strength, courage, intelligence and skill – to see if mankind is ready.' Cain stopped for a moment and chuckled. 'You and your sisters, the Heirs of Eden, must survive until sundown. On the absurdly small chance that you make it, the destructive force of the storm will cease...' Cain tilted his head skywards. 'There is no more time,' he barked. 'It will break in a few moments.'

Now Archie was trembling. Everything Cain said rang true; he'd seen it in his dreams, though of course it had meant nothing. And Isabella had been right all along!

Archie could hear Kemp's voice, strangely muffled saying, 'So ... there's little hope for me and my sisters.'

'There is always hope, young man,' the ghost replied. 'But in comparison with the thickness of a rainbow, the chances that the three of you will survive are but an atom wide. You are a child. You have neither the strength nor the skills to combat what lies ahead. You know no magic and you do not understand nature. What chance do you have?' He paused for effect. 'None. That is why you must join me now, Archie. The world will be washed away, but I offer you the chance to escape through me. You have the opportunity, through me, to start again. All I need is the use of your body.'

'And will this help save your mother?' Kemp stammered.

The ghost seemed a little surprised. 'Yes, as I told you. You have seen her and you know that she holds a great secret within her that others seek to destroy. By joining me, Archie, she will be saved. I guarantee it.'

Cain was laying on the charm. His persuasion intoxicating. 'Here, the suffering will be great but together, Archie, we can build a new future. I am nearly useless without you and you are helpless without me.'

Kemp looked over at Archie whose terrified face had risen from the other side of the wheelie bin. 'But I still don't understand,' Kemp whimpered.

Cain growled. 'These things are beyond your understanding. Open your mind; you have seen it in your dreams.'

Suddenly, Kemp tried to make a run for it. He attempted to loosen the grip on his arm by charging at the wheelie bin. 'GO!' he screamed at Archie. 'RUN!' But the ghost held him tight and forced him to the floor. Kemp whimpered in pain.

The ghost moved into Archie's path in front of the entrance to the alleyway and began to unfurl the scarf that covered his face. 'I see,' he began. 'There is another one.' He sniffed the air. 'And one of you is Archie. You have tried to deceive me,' the ghost said calmly.

'So there is a choice. Archie, if you choose to come with me, the world will be saved. My mother will be saved. You will be saved. If you run, you die.' He released Kemp who fell to the floor. 'Which will it be?'

Kemp looked utterly petrified – his face red, his cheeks streaked with tears. He caught Archie's eye, and stared at him – imploring him, begging him to understand. And then Kemp began to speak very slowly. 'Kemp, you are my only friend,' he said, 'and not long ago, I swore – on my life – that I would never hurt you or your family. I failed.' Kemp's eyes opened wide, desperate for him to understand.

Archie frowned. What *was* Kemp talking about? Had Kemp worked out that the ghost was blind?

Kemp began again, 'Run Kemp; save yourself. GO!'

'Uh?' Archie said, still confused.

'Yes, Kemp – you moron – get out of here! Get to safety.'

Archie stared at Kemp.

And then Kemp said it again. 'Look, Kemp, you great big oaf. Go now while there's still a chance. Leave this to me, but promise me one thing.'

'What?'

'Look after that fishing rod.'

'Fishing rod?'

Kemp couldn't believe Archie. 'Blimey Kemp, how stupid are you?' he said. 'Go! Now. Run you idiot – GO!'

Archie stared deep into Kemp's tear-stained eyes and could see a spark of light. Deep down, both suspected they were doomed, but Archie was sure that Kemp was trying to tell him that while there was even a tiny slither of a chance Archie had to try and make it through to dusk.

Archie curled his fist into a ball and punched his friend lightly on the shoulder. He winked and mouthed the words, "Thank you".

'So long, Archie,' Archie said, 'see you in the next world.'

And taking a deep breath, he turned and ran for his life.

# 25 CAIN'S BODY

Daisy dragged herself up and flicked a fleck of mud off her shorts.

What a crazy match; her being kicked to bits, Sue screaming at Isabella, Isabella going mad again and screaming at everyone else, Archie missing a total sitter and then beating up the opposition like a prize-fighter – and getting sent off – deafening thunder crashing overhead, lightning fizzing – everything so loud.

Her head was ringing.

She noted the ref looking at his watch. And now, with the last kick of the game, she had a chance to win the match. Boy, pressure kicks don't come much bigger than this, she thought. Better make it a good one. I'll curl it over the wall – the floodlights are so poor it's got every chance.

'Come on, Upsall. Come on, Daisy de Lowe, you can do it,' roared the small section of crowd still remaining before starting the repetitive chant of '*D-D-L, D-D-L, D-D-L*'.

Daisy bent down and rubbed her tired, bruised legs and drew her hands through her muddy blonde hair. She fixed her boots and as she did so she selected a slightly raised patch of turf on which she carefully placed the ball, which glowed like a full moon.

She stood back and studied her route to goal. Twenty, twenty-three yards? Perfect – just as she'd practised time and time again with Archie.

She rubbed her eyes and concentrated hard on the ball. It was now or never.

Everything she'd ever played for came down to this one shot.

She sucked in a large mouthful of air and blew it out, her eyes focusing on the ball so intently that she felt she could actually see the entire trajectory of the ball and the precise spot of where to kick it.

The whole atmosphere, the crowd and the rumbling sky for a moment seemed to disappear leaving a strange quiet.

The referee blew his whistle.

It was time to step up and smack it.

---

'IT HAS STARTED,' the ghost said, his hat angled upwards towards the sky. 'Something more powerful than you can possibly imagine has begun.' He raised an arm towards the lightning and thunder.

'If you want to see your friend for the last time, follow his path. I doubt he will last long. You too may run now, but you would be a fool, Archie.'

Kemp moved to the end of the alleyway, wondering if he should run for it. People were scattering everywhere even though the players were still on the pitch.

He watched as Archie hared towards the steep bank and went out of view as he vanished down it. He reappeared, running flat out, waving his hands in the air. By the way people were looking at him, it was as if he was screaming at the top of his voice. Now he was sprinting onto the football field.

Kemp shifted his gaze. Daisy was striking a free kick and...

**CRACK!**

With a deafening roar, a massive thunderbolt flashed out of the sky right on top of Archie. Kemp's heart missed a beat as he watched Archie fall to the floor like a ragdoll, his body spasming one moment, still the next.

Smoke drifted out of his friend.

Kemp recoiled and collapsed. Everything the ghost had said had happened; the sweet paper, the lightning in his own image in the cloud and now the thunderbolt aimed at Archie who lay dead on the ground.

Archie didn't deserve this; laidback Archie with his scruffy hair who was always late for everything. Archie who didn't really do anything; harmless, quiet Archie, his fishing pal, the only person he'd ever told about his parents. And he'd sent him to his death.

Kemp turned to find Cain directly behind him.

'I am nothing more than a sad ghost. I was stripped of my flesh and bones, but not my spirit. It means that I cannot move or touch with any great purpose, so I require flesh and blood to partially restore me. This is where you come in – where you can help me. I cannot do it alone.'

The ghost removed his clothing until all that was left was the overcoat that covered his body and the hat on his head. He sniffed the air around Kemp who felt a coldness on his face and stumbled; was he going to be ... eaten, or have the life sucked out of him? He felt dizzy and sick and paralysed with fear.

'Rest assured,' the old man said softly, 'I know you are not Archie. I have no intention of taking your life, only *borrowing* it for a little while. When my work is done and my mother is saved, I will put you back near this very spot. That is my solemn promise. But nature's curse is upon us.'

The ghost took a step towards the quivering body of Kemp. 'You must freely decide if you will help me. You must choose now. I doubt you will get such an offer from the storm.'

---

KEMP FACED him head-on for the first time. All he could see was a transparent gap beneath his hat. His teeth were chattering. 'If I don't—?'

'You'll almost certainly die or be drowned in the rains or in the landslides or the tsunamis which will sweep through the land destroying everything—'

'Will you kill me?'

'Kill you?' the old man chuckled. 'No. As I said, I'm just going to *borrow* you for a while. Why would I kill you when my purpose is to save so many? You must *trust* me.'

Kemp looked up at the sky. It was fizzing with electricity like an angry nest. A terrible boom rattled every bone in his body moments before a thunderbolt smashed into a nearby chimney pot. Terracotta splinters showered them.

His head shook.

He stared down the path, readying himself to run. But as his eyes focused on the dark shadows between the buildings, he found himself looking at a familiar face. It was Gus Williams laden with shopping bags! They locked eyes for several seconds before Williams simply ran off, as though someone had called him away in a hurry.

'Dreamspinner!' the ghost barked impatiently. 'Open up. It is time to go!'

'Wait,' Kemp croaked. 'What do I have to do?'

'Put on the coat and hat that covers me. Quickly.'

Kemp's mind was made up. In a flash, he threw both of his overcoats to the ground and moved in close. As he did, he felt a strange coolness wash over him.

'Ignore that I am here,' the ghost said as Kemp fumbled. 'Put it on, like you would any other.'

Kemp grabbed the collar of the coat and pushed in his arm, amazed by the sudden intense freeze that enveloped it. Then his other arm slid in. Kemp had a wonderful feeling of enormous strength building up in him as though he was being filled with electric charge.

It started in his fingers, moved up his wrist, through his elbows, to his shoulders. All too soon it was spreading down through his loins and into his legs and feet. It was as if a thick liquid, like freezing treacle – stuffed full of power – was coursing through every vein, into every muscle and sinew.

Kemp drew the coat across his chest and the curious feeling leeched towards his heart and lungs.

Now he cried out and stretched his arms wide as the ice-like treacle rushed into his vital organs and washed through his body. He shouted out a cry of pure ecstasy, his cries echoing back off the old houses.

Kemp only had one more thing to do. He lifted up the hat and pulled it down over his head. Very quickly he could feel the cold charge oozing up his neck and through his mouth. For a few seconds, he shut his eyes, enjoying the extraordinary tingling sensations of the liquid ice entering his brain and slowly dispersing through the back of his skull, tickling parts he never knew existed.

Then the surge of power rounded the skull and headed towards his eyes.

When it flowed into his eyes, everything changed.

With a rapidity that took him completely by surprise, Kemp felt a searing pain enter his head, and it grew like a balloon filling with air.

'What's happening?' he screamed. 'It's burning me ... MY GOD, *my eyes*!' He desperately tried to pull off the hat and wrestle out of the coat, but it was too late, they were stuck on. 'My head's being blown apart. What – have – you – done – to – me? Help me! *HELP!*'

The ghost chuckled as Kemp carried on screaming.

'Welcome to me,' Cain said, his voice laced with triumph. 'Welcome to the burnt-out body of Cain.'

# 26 THE STORM BEGINS

Confusion reigned as players and spectators ran hard towards the cars and houses above the football field. Screams filled the air.

Archie blinked, opened his eyes and tried to focus. His head was pounding from the noise of the blast and he smelt burning hair. When his eyes focused, all he could see was a burning net and smouldering goalpost.

Daisy sprinted over. 'Archie! Winkle!' She kissed his forehead. 'Thank God!' she said, cradling him. 'I thought you were toast. Say something – are you hurt – can you move?!'

Archie smiled dumbly and mumbled several inaudible words. Then very slowly he moved his arm and rubbed his eyes. His fingernails were black and smoking.

Daisy carefully pulled him into a sitting position. 'Your hair's gone all ... all spiky—'

'ARCHIE!' Isabella screamed as she tore across the pitch to him. 'Please, Archie.' She ran directly over and placed her hand on his forehead. She felt for his temperature, then checked his pulse and inspected his tongue.

He smiled weakly.

'PHEW! I can't believe you're OK – you are OK, aren't you?'

Archie nodded, but his eyes were not focusing right.

'My strips must have saved you!'

'UH?'

'The strips I made you put on your boots.' She handed him a bottle of water. 'Daisy, why don't you get the tracksuits, while I make sure his internal organs are functioning.'

Isabella gave Archie a short examination and declared that Archie was well enough to take a couple of little sips. Daisy returned with their tracksuits and she slipped into hers before helping Archie into his.

'Victory!' Isabella said, 'You did it!'

'Don't be ridiculous,' Daisy scoffed as she pulled Archie's top over his odd hair.

'I'm not,' Isabella replied. 'The ball's in the net. It was blown into the goal. You scored!'

Daisy didn't know whether to hit her sister or cry. 'No,' she said furiously. 'I missed and Archie got fried. Look at him – it's a miracle he survived.' Daisy felt a dullness consume her; her limbs were tired, sore and defeated. She could hardly bear to look at her sister.

'He's fine, aren't you, Archie?' Isabella cried. 'Anyway you're wrong. Admittedly your shot was heading towards the corner flag but the lightning bolt deflected the ball into the goal – I swear it. The charge of particles must have generated a force to hit it in precisely the right spot to divert it without blowing it up. It's a miracle. It's the goal of the millennium—'

'Shut up! Please,' Daisy said sharply. 'Stop it, Bells.'

Coach was running over towards them and he went straight to Archie where he spent some time checking him over.

'WOW-ee,' he whistled. 'That's one lucky escape, young man. I thought you were brown bread for a minute. It looks like the Gods spared you – you may feel a little groggy, but you're gonna be alright. Try standing if you can.'

Archie smiled and, with the aid of a person on each side, he stood up.

'How do you feel?'

Archie grinned. He couldn't quite hear or see them, but he was improving by the second.

'That's the match-ball in the net, isn't it, Coach?' Isabella asked. 'I've taken a picture of it on my phone – for safekeeping.'

Coach clapped his hands. 'You're right! Looks like we ruddy well won. We're only the bleedin' champions!' He slapped Daisy on the back, almost knocking her over. 'Quite amazing ...' But he stopped mid-sentence and turned to the sky, his tone serious once again. 'Listen, if you think you can make it, Arch – you'd better get off now up that funny track to your cottage. Otherwise I'll give you a lift back, via the school.'

'Don't worry, Coach. We'll get him back in one piece,' Isabella insisted. 'I promise – it's not so far. Anyway, you're not that bad are you, Archie?'

Coach eyed them. 'You sure? You'd better get going then. Best scarper before another of them thunderbolts gets us.' He patted them on their backs. 'And fast as you can! I reckon it's going to bloody piss down.'

Coach skipped off towards the car park singing loudly. Then he yelled back at them. 'Great goals, Daisy and bloody brilliant hairdo, Arch. You're legends!'

---

ARCHIE WAVERED a little and Daisy caught him. 'You really think we can get back home?'

Archie was trying to say something. But it came out slightly askew.

'What is it?' Isabella said softly.

'Storm! Go,' he replied.

Angry rolls of thunder boomed around them.

'Is anyone else finding this very loud?' Daisy asked. 'I've had to put tissue in my ears. Look!' And she pulled out the paper. Suddenly Daisy's face went pale.

Isabella spotted it. 'What is it?'

'I think there's another in-coming thunderbolt.'

'*What!*' Isabella said.

'RUN! NOW!'

They grabbed Archie round the shoulders and set off.

'I can hear the particles gathering in the cloud, I think. Sounds like a build-up of collisions.' Daisy stopped. 'DIVE!'

A moment later, a massive crack tore across the sky and unleashed a lightning bolt that smashed into the exact spot where, moments earlier, they had been huddled together. The ground smouldered.

'Bloody hell,' Isabella whispered, her knees buckling. 'That was close. It's like it's after us.'

'It is,' Archie mumbled. He closed his eyes and tried to work more saliva into his mouth. 'We have to survive ... until dusk.'

'That's exactly what Sue was yelling about,' Isabella said. 'Survive till sunset.'

'Where do you get that nonsense from?' Daisy said. And then she twitched.

Isabella noticed. 'What is it, Daisy?'

'Another one – I think I can hear it!'

They reached the tree and slipped under the branches.

'We should be safer here.'

Daisy held her hands over her ears as a couple of tears rolled down her cheeks. 'My God. Here it comes!'

A lightning bolt crackled and smashed into the branches. The children screamed as a huge branch sheared off and crashed a couple of metres away.

They ran out hugging each other.

**'OH, NO!'** Daisy cried, her ears screaming in pain.

'What now!?'

'It's like ... a power shower has just been switched on.'

A warm wind swirled and nearly blew them off their feet. Then the first few large rain drops like mini water balloons began to plummet out of the cloud.

'We need to move, NOW!' Isabella cried. 'This is the storm from hell we predicted—'

'*Predicted?*' Daisy yelled.

'Yeah, Sue and I ...' Isabella's voice trailed off. 'OMG,' she said, 'we've got about five minutes before this playing field becomes a river.'

'Oh, well that is simply marvellous,' Daisy yelled.

Isabella and Daisy put their hands under Archie's armpits and folded his arms across their shoulders so he was properly supported.

'You've got to move your legs, Arch,' Isabella implored. 'HURRY!' she screamed, forcing the pace. The rain intensified as the wind blew in several directions at once. In no time, in front of them, on top of them, and behind them, a wall of water sluiced out of the heavens, pounding them, beating them hard on their heads and shoulders and backs. Isabella removed her coat and draped it over their heads. For the moment at least, it acted like a shelter.

'Where's the bridge?' Daisy shouted above the din of the rain. 'I can't see ANYTHING!'

Isabella slowed and stared at the ground. Water heads downhill, so it's got to be this way. If we get to the path, we'll find it. Without knowing why, she pointed her free arm ahead of her, closed her eyes and allowed it to guide her.

Soon the feel underfoot of soft wet turf made way for hard gravel. They followed it, but every step was tricky and they couldn't be sure exactly where they were going. Isabella rubbed the ground every so often with her foot to feel the hard path underneath. By the time they reached the bridge, the children were cold, soaked through and exhausted. And, more worryingly, water was spilling out of the river at an alarming rate – up to their ankles and rising fast.

'Bind – tighter – scrum!' Isabella yelled, 'We've got to move together, rhythmically, in time. I'll count.' She realised they couldn't hear her so she signed with her fingers: ONE, TWO ... THREE and then she flicked out her thumb.

'Where's the bridge?!' Daisy screamed, before suddenly losing her footing. She screamed again as Archie hauled her to her feet.

Isabella shook her head, imploring her to keep going. 'DON'T FALL.' She turned to Archie to see if he understood. He nodded.

Isabella counted each agonising step, the force of the water gaining by the second, pushing hard at their legs. Every breath was a struggle and their heads were bowed from the pressure bearing down upon them.

Isabella had no idea where she was headed. She simply trusted her hands and, as if by a miracle, they guided her to the rail. She breathed a deep sigh of relief. They shuffled onto the bridge, still huddled together, their feet searching for the wooden boards.

Daisy suddenly went stiff, holding the others back. She turned to the others, her eyes bulging.

Collectively they realised what she meant.

'RUN!'

They scampered up to the brow of the bridge, Daisy leading the way holding Archie's hand on one side, when suddenly she dived, hauling Archie forward with all her might.

Bits of wood splintered around them, the noise deafening. Daisy picked herself out of the water, her feet grateful for the feeling of land, and discovered Archie next to her. He was fine; but where was Isabella?

Daisy called out but it was hopeless; she wouldn't be heard over the din. As she listened, the only thing she could hear was the roar of the rain and rushing water flushing everything downstream.

# 27 ISABELLA DISAPPEARS

Isabella found herself slipping and falling. The water took her as her world went blank. When she came to, her body was numb from the shock of the lightning bolt and, although she hadn't received a direct hit, every nerve and sinew tingled like a spectacular case of pins and needles.

She coughed and gasped for breath, spluttering and ejecting the water trapped in her lungs. Her hands and feet kicked, her arms and legs moving faster than she could have possibly imagined just to keep her head above the torrents. Already, her feet were unable to feel the bottom of the river – had the water climbed so high in such a short time?

The problem was finding enough oxygen to breathe. There wasn't a single bit of air anywhere. Her hand touched something and she grappled with it and tried to pull herself up. But it was a loose root and it fell away.

She plunged back under the surface and was pulled down river. When Isabella rose to the surface, she wondered how long she could keep floating helplessly like this and how far she had travelled.

She needed to touch down on the cottage side of the river. If she made land on the valley side, she was surely doomed – there would be little chance of crossing. Treading water as best as she could, she did a quick calculation: if the water was running from the moors down into the valley, she had to land on the right side as it flowed towards her. Isabella kicked hard until she could feel the water pushing her and then twisted to the right with all her strength, swimming at an angle into the current.

Moments later she touched on something that felt like a shrub. She put her feet down and was relieved to find herself waist high. She scrambled across the bush, her legs getting scratched to bits, and kept moving until her feet hit on solid ground.

Almost immediately, Isabella coughed and spluttered and then retched the water she'd swallowed. It felt as if her insides were coming out. She gasped for air and headed uphill for the cover of a nearby tree. She found one, leaned into it, put her head in her hands and breathed deeply.

She closed her eyes. And now it was exactly like her nightmare, except this time it was for real, the premonition she dreaded. Tears built up and for a moment they rolled freely down her cheeks. Daisy, Archie! They'll probably think I'm dead.

She imagined them waiting for her. Please, please, no; every minute spent waiting for her was a minute wasted.

And she wondered what had happened to Sue. Did she find the boat? In any case, would a little boat survive a storm like this? Never; it would fill with water and sink in minutes.

Isabella felt herself welling up, but a ripple of water washed against her shins. The water was rising fast. She had to keep going – finding the others was futile now – she was on her own. She'd head uphill, from tree to tree and use whatever cover she could find.

Only there would she find safety.

---

DAISY WAITED for what felt like hours, although she knew it was little more than a few minutes. She shivered – grateful that the rain was not particularly cold. It was tepid – probably from being stuck up in that big cloud for so long, she thought. But Daisy knew that even warm rain quickly chills, and there was just so much of it endlessly pummelling them.

She ventured from side to side of the path as far as she dared, yelling and screaming for Isabella, but she knew it was hopeless; visibility was zero and she could hardly hear her own voice.

With every movement, her bones ached and her joints screamed out. If only she hadn't just played a game of football. She just didn't have the energy reserves for this kind of physical trial. If a thunderbolt didn't get her or the rains sweep her away, she'd surely succumb – eventually – to the cold.

She stamped her feet and jogged up and down. She concentrated hard on the water further down and for a moment she was sure that she could see, much further down on the river bank, a body, someone climbing out of the water. She shook her head – it was impossible, she must be seeing things – like a mirage in the desert.

She put a hand round Archie and hugged him close. His body warmth was like a hot water bottle. He seemed better – his eyes were clearer – maybe he was back to full strength – although she smiled as she touched his odd spiky hair – especially when hers was smeared all over her face and head like the tentacles of a jellyfish.

He seemed in shock. Numb, as though his tongue had been cut out. Was it the lightning strike, or was it something else?

What he had said earlier was very odd – that the storm would come after them until sunset. How did he know that? But she didn't need him like this, she needed him on full alert, thinking – helping. Perhaps, she thought, he needs another shock. She slapped him on the cheek as hard as she could.

'Blimey, Daisy!' he yelled rubbing it. 'What did you do that for?'

'Got you back,' she mouthed, kissing his forehead. 'I'm sorry – necessary.'

'There's no need to hit me,' he yelled.

But Daisy hugged him tight and spoke into his ear. 'Aw, but it did the trick. Keep moving, Archie – can't wait here much longer – freezing.'

Archie nodded and pointed towards the track.

'But what about Bells?' Daisy cried.

'She's a strong swimmer,' he said and he drew Daisy's head in to his chest. 'She'll be fine.' But as he said it, he frowned. He looked at his watch. Only two-thirty. Jeez. What had Cain said: Nature will throw its full fury until sundown? Should he tell her that they had at least another two to three hours of this?

———

EVEN THOUGH THEY walked up and down the track almost every day – in winter, spring, summer and autumn, now, it was impossible to find.

At every turn, with the rain pounding on their heads, unable to see anything, they found themselves walking into the bank or into bushes or into trees. Eventually Archie discovered a section of fencing that had been washed up. He broke it up so they could use it on top of their heads but even then, keeping their arms in the air was exhausting and the rain stabbed at their fingers. At long last, Daisy recognised a big boulder that was just inside the bottom of the covered tree track.

A mini triumph, Daisy thought, as a long booming roll of thunder crackled gruesomely overhead. She covered her ears, wincing at the pain, but after only a few paces she realised there was a far bigger problem. She bound closely into Archie. 'Mud!' she yelled at Archie. 'Look – thick mud and stones – rushing down.'

Every step forward was like walking over barbed wire; the path was laced with branches, brambles and rock.

And ever present was the thick mud and water speeding down the narrow track. Worse still, the canopy that sheltered them was being smashed in by the rain, so that branches were falling down on them – not just twigs and dead branches – but branches as thick as a man's wrist. Even though they'd only stepped a few metres in, it was becoming obvious that the canopy was close to breaking point.

Archie tried to skip over a large branch that was heading directly towards him. He slipped as he landed and cried out, the muddy water dragging him down the hill. He dug his fingers into the bank alongside, grabbed on to a root and managed to pull himself upright.

Daisy climbed up onto a large root on the side of the bank and waited for him to catch up. For the first time in ages she wasn't being pounded by the rain. She looked down the track, and could see Archie struggling. For every two steps forward, he was pushed one step back.

'COME ON!' she screamed.

Archie hugged the side of the track but found that every time he did, it simply folded in on him. Not only that, but his ankles were being stripped bare by the mud, stones and wood being flushed down. At last he made it to Daisy's position and climbed up next to her.

He gasped for breath and rubbed his badly scratched ankles covered in blood. 'We're never going to make it. Not like this.'

'We have to!' Daisy replied. 'Do you think it'll be any easier out there, getting pummelled by the rain?'

'But it's acting like a ditch,' Archie complained. 'A gigantic storm drain; all the water is cascading down here. The branches are about to collapse, several are already breaking off. It's about as dangerous a place as you could wish.'

'Then what's your suggestion?' Daisy fired back at him.

Archie thought through his next move. 'Up the bank and crawl along the top,' he yelled.

'But it's over a mile of crawling—'

'I know. But that's one mile of not being swept away and dying, sis. And we can use the cover of the trees. There's no other choice.'

Using the roots of the big oak they were sitting on, they climbed up the bank. On hands and knees they made their way slowly uphill, brushing aside branches and thorns which tore into them. After several minutes, Daisy collapsed under the cover of the next large tree.

She rubbed her body, which was pierced by blackthorn and dog rose. 'Great idea, Archie!'

'Look at the track!' he replied.

She looked down and, through the veil of rain, she could just make out a moving torrent of mud and branches halfway up the bank. It was flushing downhill at great speed.

'OK, OK. *Good* decision.' Daisy drew in her breath. 'How far up the track are we?'

'Keep going and we'll come to the big oak with the swing rope. We can rest there.' Archie had no idea, but he knew he must give her a goal. He could see she was struggling by the way her eyes kept closing.

Another huge boom of thunder clapped overhead, followed by a lightning bolt that crashed down nearby.

They crawled on. The foliage was thinning and once again the rain smashed down, pummelling their backs. Archie led, with Daisy closely behind. But, after a short while, when he turned, there was no Daisy.

He backtracked and found her, hanging halfway down the bank, which had quite simply subsided into the water. Only the thick tendril of a rose and a large bush that was slipping into the mud was holding her. She was dangling above the muddy, rushing waters. He needed to act fast.

He grabbed the base of the rose and tried to swing it. But the huge old rose was near to breaking point and sinking under the pressure of the rain. The thorns were digging into the flesh on his hands. He screamed out.

There had to be a better way. He shuffled to a nearby hedge and saw a small tree. That was it! He bent down, put his hands around the trunk and pulled with all his might. The roots started coming away. One more heave and it broke free. Archie turned it round, ripped off some branches and lowered it to Daisy. She grabbed hold and Archie tugged her out.

They moved under a nearby tree and gasped for breath.

'OK, so we've learnt two things from that,' Daisy yelled between gasps. 'The first is that the bank is collapsing and the second is that you've been working out without anyone knowing.'

Archie shrugged and looked at the small tree. For a boy of his age it was a seriously impressive show of strength.

---

TAKING A WIDER berth away from the track, they continued crawling.

The rain did not cease for one moment and as they inched forward they were consumed with dread. Danger surrounded them: danger from branches snapping and falling, the dreaded thunderbolts, landslides, mudslides or simply being washed down onto the track and down the hill.

They came across a badger sett, which was now a huge hole and had to be circumnavigated. Eventually they struggled up to the large oak, the one they loved to play on, the one with the rope, which now dangled down.

Archie pushed Daisy on and up she went, her hands gripping one after the other as though her life depended on it. Archie was right beneath her, shouting encouragement.

The rope was tied around the thickest branch which hung over the lane. Where the branch met the trunk, a huge bough seemed to curve over, like a mini cave and, for the first time in ages, it offered them almost complete protection from the rain. Archie sat with his back against the trunk and Daisy sat in front of him, leaning into him. They both took deep breaths and shut their eyes.

In no time, Daisy, through sheer exhaustion, fell asleep.

Archie didn't mind. He looked at his watch. It felt as if they had been crawling and sliding and fighting for days, let alone hours. And yet there was still an hour or so to go. If only he could remember what time the sun went down.

The problem with being stationary was the cold. The sheer amount of water made it feel like they were in a fridge even if the water itself wasn't so cold. And it had soaked in to their bodies, like a sponge, right to their bones.

He wrapped his arms around his sister. She was freezing and her body rattled like a spluttering engine. A rest was a good idea, but at some point they were going to have to keep going, whether they liked it or not.

# 28 OLD MAN WOOD FINDS A CLUE

As the morning wore on, Old Man Wood was consumed by a feeling of utter dread, as if a toxic stew was brewing in his stomach and a splinter was stuck in his heart. Whatever he did, it would not go away. What was it? He marched around the house looking for something, anything, that would alleviate this terrible feeling. He studied the carvings on his wall and traced his fingers over the rich detail in the wood panelling in his room. He inspected the old pictures for a clue. Anything that might not only shed some light on the nightmares he'd had, but also cure the interminable worry that filled him from the top of his head to the tips of his toes.

The pictures and carvings had been there since he could remember. Didn't they mean something? If so, *what*? He knew there was a vital clue missing and it was probably staring him in the face. The more he played with this notion, the greater and deeper the feeling of despair grew, like a slow-growing cancer.

Old Man Wood headed outside to see if his brain might clear from a walk up to his cattle. He wondered for a moment if he shouldn't go down to the school and watch the football match, but it didn't seem right. The children would tell him what happened in detail later, not that he understood much of it. Besides, he didn't like to show himself in public, he'd been around too long for that. Instead, he headed up to the ruin to check on the sheep and cattle.

They seemed quiet and tetchy, jumpy – like him, he thought, and wondered if they, too, sensed something unusual. He made sure that the shelter built from old rocks was sound in case the storm broke, and he counted them: eleven sheep, three cows, six bullocks and Himsworth the bull. He'd tried to milk the cows at their usual time, the crack of dawn, but their milk had stopped. Were they sick?

Old Man Wood sat down on a grey boulder at the head of the ruin and looked out across the vale. In front of him was a sheer drop of solid rock that disappeared down to thick forest for seventy metres or so before reaching the valley floor. He could just make out the river curving around the rock face and, from there, it slipped around the corner and along and up into the moors.

Old Man Wood shuffled his boot in the dirt. He was too old for this; too old for riddles and memories. His brain couldn't cope. He shook his head as he wondered what it all meant. Why the dreams every night – what were they trying to tell him? And why did he have a strong feeling in his bones about something that he hadn't felt for ages? He stood up as a deep roll of thunder boomed and crackled through the valley. He kicked a stone which flew off the ledge and sailed through the air before crashing into the canopy of the trees way below.

He could make out the school buildings in the distance although the top of the tower was smothered by the deep black cloud that sat directly overhead. He was lost in his thoughts when a lightning bolt shot out of the sky right into the heart of the village, and then another and another. Each one with a blast of light so bright and crack so loud that he covered his ears.

Then a searing pain walloped into his chest. For a moment he thought it was a heart attack. He bent over and cried out. The sky fizzed with lightning as another huge bolt crashed out of the sky directly onto the playing field. This time the pain was unbearable and he crouched low, clutching his chest, struggling for breath.

There was no danger of dying, he was absolutely certain of that. In fact there was no danger of him ever dying. So was this pain linked to the storm? Perhaps it was telling him something important. Whatever it was, he needed to lie down.

Old Man Wood straightened up as best he could and tottered back down the pathway, stopping occasionally to view the storm playing out over the school. Wasn't it funny, he thought, how the storm seemed to focus only on the school? He had a stirring inside him that the children might be in terrible danger. And, as he concentrated on this, the feeling began to grow and grow. He hurried back, certain that rain would follow. By the time he opened the door he was drenched from head to toe. He couldn't remember anything like it; torrents of water literally pouring out of the sky.

He lay on his bed and massaged his heart, trying hard to understand this feeling, when another thought crossed his mind. How would they get back? The river would be swollen in no time and the track would act like a storm drain. What if they were trying to get back and got swept away? He dabbed his handkerchief on his forehead. He had to *do* something.

Just as he was preparing to get up, Old Man Wood felt a yawn wash over him and a powerful urge to close his eyes. His head fell back into his large pillows and a moment later he was snoring.

---

GAIA THE DREAMSPINNER appeared in Old Man Wood's room and found him lying on the bed.

Had he forgotten so much? Had he forgotten his entire reason for being there in the first place? How, when the children needed him so badly, could he be so utterly hopeless?

Old Man Wood hadn't reacted to any of the dreams given to him and Gaia worried that if Old Man Wood could not understand and believe his dreams, what chance would the children have with theirs? Were the dreams too complex, too terrifying? Was the approach wrong? Were the dreams too old, suitable for a different time? Perhaps their dreams needed to be more obvious, like action sequences linked together.

She dipped a leg in her maghole. Did the Heirs of Eden have any idea what they were up against? Did they stand a chance? No, probably not, she thought. They were mere children, unprepared for this onslaught that was designed for the best of men. And years ago those men would have used additional powers.

Gaia rubbed a couple of claws together. This wasn't the time for reflection – that would come later – and anyway, the children were alive, for the time being at least. The storm would not relent until sundown, so, if Old Man Wood could find them, then surely they would have a greater chance of survival.

She would give him a dream of action, and in it the old man would be struck by lightning. Yes, that was it. Perhaps it would re-energise him, get his brain working, jog his memory. She would not consider defeat, not yet; there was still too much to play for.

In no time, Gaia was over the old man, spinning a sleeping draft directly into his mouth. It worked fast. Moments later the dreamspinner was plucking tiny specks of dream powders out of her maghole and feeding them to the old man as he breathed in. Gaia added an ending – a reminder of a potion Old Man Wood had stored away a long, long time ago. Perhaps the old man would find it, perhaps not, but it was worth a try and it was the very best she could do.

As soon as it was done, Gaia stared down at the old man. She desperately hoped it would do the trick. Then she flashed inside her maghole and vanished.

---

OLD MAN WOOD tossed and turned as the dream filled his head.

He looked down and found himself wearing a pair of shorts and he was running. It was a lovely feeling, the air filling his lungs. And he had hair! How wonderful. He dragged his hands through it and it was silky. He felt young, like a child, the same age as the twins. His skin was smooth and his mind was ... alert.

On his feet he wore a pair of football boots, just like Archie's. He looked up. A football was flying towards him and his immediate reaction was to run out of the way. But out of the corner of his eye he spotted Daisy yelling at him. What was she saying? Pass it? He went towards the ball but it was too fast and bounced off his boot straight to an opponent. This wasn't as easy as it looked.

Daisy swore and chivvied him to chase the player.

He took off and was moving at speed. Much to his delight, Old Man Wood found himself gaining. He lunged for the ball but tripped the player.

The whistle blew. 'Do that once more and you'll be in the book,' the referee said.

Old Man Wood caught his breath and brushed the mud off his knees.

Daisy was there in an instant. 'What do you think you're playing at?' she said. 'There's hardly any time to go. Don't make stupid fouls like that. We've got to win or we're never playing again.'

The other team lined up a shot and the ball was cruising towards the goal. But Archie danced into the path of the ball and caught it smartly. In a flash he punted the ball wide.

One of his players passed it to him. This time he managed to control it and he slipped a neat pass through to Daisy. Daisy, now on the halfway line, jinked past one, and then sped past another, her blonde hair bobbing up and down as she went. Boy, she was quick. He found himself sprinting just to keep up with her.

A defender forced her wide and she played the ball inside to him. Looking up, he passed it to Isabella on the other flank. He couldn't remember Isabella ever liking football but she neatly passed it back to him just as she was clattered by an opposition player. He couldn't help laughing at the horrified expression on her face.

Now Daisy was screaming for the ball.

But Old Man Wood found himself running with it and it felt brilliant. He did a jink – just as Daisy had – beating the man in front of him. He knocked the ball forward, finding Daisy, who held off a challenge and stood with the ball under her feet.

In a flash she turned on a sixpence, the ball rolling under her other foot, totally foxing the defender, and headed towards the goal. Old Man Wood felt himself sprinting into the area as Daisy smashed a shot at the goal. Old Man Wood held his breath as the ball sped toward the goal. It whacked against the post and rebounded directly into his path. Out of the corner of his eye he could see a defender running towards the ball. He had to get there first, so he sprinted harder; he knew what he had to do. He cocked his leg back and kicked the ball as hard as he could a fraction before the other defender got there.

The ball screamed into the roof of the net, tearing a hole in the netting, and was still rising just as the defender crunched into his foot.

A heartbeat later and a lightning bolt smashed out of the sky directly into him. A surge of energy fizzed through his entire body, through every sinew and fibre of his being.

It took his breath away and when at last the sensation wore off, he peered down to find a bottle of gold liquid on his lap.

And then he woke up, with a start.

---

OLD MAN WOOD opened his eyes and thumped the air.

'What a goal!' he shouted, and then, 'Ouch!' He stared up at the ceiling, a big smile on his face, his head sizzling as though a rocket had gone off in it and his body was tingling like mad. 'What a marvel-tastic dream,' he said out loud to the empty room.

His foot throbbed. He looked down and found he'd walloped the end of his bed. Must have been when he scored that amazing goal. He looked a little more closely and found a hole in the wooden sheet that covered the bed-end. He studied it, pulling a few of the fragments away and chuckling at the absurdity of it all – he'd certainly struck the ball with awesome power.

Old Man Wood wiggled his toes, grateful that he'd lain on his bed with his shoes on. As far as he could tell, nothing was broken or too badly bruised. Then he heard the rain pounding outside and his heart sank. His earlier worries flew back at him. He kicked the broken piece of wood as though recreating the goal might lift his spirits. But it wasn't the same.

He climbed off his bed and peered out of the window, but the rain was so heavy he could barely see out. Were the children safely tucked away in the school? What if they were outside trying to get home? Would they survive?

His heart filled with heaviness. If something happened to them, he was responsible, but what could he do? There was no way of knowing where they might be. With no answers, Old Man Wood walked slowly back to his bed and lay down.

He looked at the hole in the wooden panel. A tiny flicker of light, like a dim torch whose batteries were running low, seemed to leech out from behind it. Now wasn't that strange, he thought. Maybe it was a trick of the light. But none of the house lights were working – he'd already tried them.

Maybe he should crank up the generator – at least it would give him something to do. He swung his feet off the bed and as he did the light from behind the wooden panel intensified.

He inspected the hole a little closer and found that there was indeed a faint glow emanating from behind it. He prised it open with his fingers and, feeling more than a little intrigued, began to wrestle with the wooden surround that covered the large bed-end. But it was stubbornly attached. He found a torch, switched it on and rushed out of his room past the wide staircase to the tool cupboard, where he selected a crowbar before returning to his room.

Moments later, Old Man Wood wedged the crowbar in behind the panel and was attempting to lever the wood away by leaning on it as gently – but firmly – as he thought necessary. But whatever angle he tried, the panel would not budge. Furthermore, he was conscious that if he was too heavy handed he might damage his beautiful bed carvings.

He scratched his head and slipped out of the room, returning moments later with a flat head screwdriver and a hammer. Old Man Wood thrust the flat head into the tiniest of gaps and gave the end a smart whack with the hammer. The nails securing the panel lifted, just a fraction.

Placing the crowbar in the new gap, he levered it once more and after a few more whacks, the panel popped off.

He rubbed his chin. 'Well, I'll be blowed,' he said as he ran his fingers over the three panels that now stared back at him. 'What in the apples do we have here?'

In front of him were three beautifully inlaid panels that seemed to glow like three small monitors – rather like the children's computers. The difference was that these ones were inlaid into the bed itself and surrounded by carvings that matched those on the bed.

He stared at them for a while, his face a picture of confusion, the wrinkles on his forehead deeply pronounced. Every now and then the images in the panels moved and, when they did, Old Man Wood could feel his heart racing. And it kept on happening with all three panels, randomly. Was he was seeing things, he wondered?

He noticed that the overlying image was hazy – like looking through heavy rain. Maybe it was mirroring the weather right now, he thought, as if it were in some way, however ludicrous, a weather forecasting unit. As he became more accustomed to the panels, the images on them became a little clearer. On each panel was a figure. Three panels, three figures, one on each "screen". And why did each one look so familiar?

He studied the carvings to the sides of the screens. The first was an ornate pointer in the shape of an arrow. He touched one that faced away from the first panel. To his astonishment, the panel seemed to move the image out, exactly like a zoom on a camera. He did the same with the next panel, this time pressing on the arrow that turned in. Once again the picture moved, but this time closer. He studied it with increased fascination.

The person he was looking at appeared to be drenched and walking up something – tripping every now and then – as though trying to negotiate a pathway, but the image was still so hazy. He rubbed his hand over another carved icon adjacent to the arrow, which he thought looked rather like a cloud. He pressed it and magically the picture transformed, removing the rain.

Old Man Wood gasped as he stared at the new image. That balance and gait could only belong to one person, and that person was Daisy. He pressed the inward arrow a couple of times and he could now see her in quite extraordinary detail.

A thrill passed through him. He was looking at the children, right now, in real-time, and he realised that, if he could determine which buttons to press, he'd be able to see exactly where they were. He did the same to the panel on the right, this time pressing the cloud and zooming out with the away arrow.

He clapped his hands. It was Archie, definitely Archie, with a kind of spiky hat on his head – and he was standing right next to Daisy. And, just like her, he was trying to walk through something and that something, he concluded, was not in the slightest bit helpful. It was like a river of goo sliding towards them. So where were they? He pulled out and saw an image of a gully with low branches bending down.

The track! It must be the track. He clenched his fists. My goodness me! But where were they on the track? He pulled out even further. Apples alive! At the bottom! His heart sank. At least the twins were together, but what about Isabella?

He scoured the left panel and sighed with relief as he saw her outline. He honed in and pressed the cloud icon. It cleared the screen. He pressed the outward arrow to try and work out her position.

She was heading towards a large object with a sheer face, pushing past bushes and through trees. He zoomed out. Behind her, he could see something creeping up on her. Was it water? It had to be. My goodness it was flooding fast. He thought quickly. The only sheer rock he could think of was ... was underneath the ruin. So how come she was separated from the others?

It didn't matter. She was where she was.

Old Man Wood breathed a sigh of relief. They were alive. He looked at his clock. How long was it since he'd been out for a walk? Two hours? He trembled.

Had the children been out in this for that long? Goodness gracious. Not much would survive in that.

His heart thumped. He needed to find them before they were battered and drowned in all that rain.

# 29 LIGHTNING BOLTS

Daisy dozed, her head resting on Archie's chest. Her mind swam. She dreamt fleetingly of the cottage, of Old Man Wood and their parents. She dreamt of scoring a goal with a sensational bicycle-kick and Archie making a flying, fingertip save. The storm seemed a million miles away.

Suddenly she woke. A noise had clicked in her brain. She studied it, her eyes shut tight. Then she realised what it was.

'MOVE!' she screamed at Archie.

Archie opened his eyes. 'Eh? What?'

'Incoming. I can hear it. MOVE!'

'Where?' Archie replied.

The noise was building somewhere miles above them.

'Down the branch. NOW!'

Archie did what he was told and shuffled his bottom as fast as he could down the branch, the rain smashing down on them once more.

'Further,' she screamed. 'As far as you can.' She was skimming along, almost bouncing when she stopped, wrapped her hands and legs around the thick branch, and hugged her body into the wood. She hoped for the best.

Archie continued on, oblivious to Daisy's action. From out of nowhere, a terrific surge of power smashed into the tree. The branch was severed like a head being cut off by an axe and it crashed down, bridging the track just above the flowing mud. Archie flew into the air and came down into the torrent. He sank underneath the waterline.

---

DAISY CONVULSED with electricity and was filled with pain, particularly her ears. She uncurled her body from around the branch as the rain crashed onto her back and head.

Regaining her composure, she turned round. Where was Archie?

She tried to call out his name but not a single sound came from her mouth. She knew it was hopeless. Even if she could scream for help, he'd never hear her. She scanned the area. Suddenly she saw a hand struggling to grip the end of the branch. And then it fell away, caught in the torrent.

She shrieked and desperately fished her hand down into the water but felt nothing but twigs and leaves and the occasional bush flashing beneath her.

Daisy thumped the branch, tears streaming from her eyes, blending with the rain. How much more she could take? Her eyes dipped.

And now she was all on her own.

---

ARCHIE WAS CATAPULTED into the air. He landed in the middle of the torrent and plunged into the water. He felt his body being whipped away. He battled with all his might and when he surfaced, directly in front of him was the huge branch which straddled the track.

His lungs burned.

He reached up, but however hard he tried, he couldn't get a hold on the bark and after several attempts he felt a pain as though the nails on his fingers were starting to detach. The force of the water was so great that he had simply no option but to give in. He let go.

He was swept away. He desperately needed to breathe. He struggled to keep his head up and every time he did, it was battered down again by the rain. And all the while he searched for buoyancy – a branch or a tree he could grab that might keep him afloat.

He thrashed out with his feet like a madman, kicking the water beneath him in a last massive effort to survive. Something caught around his left leg, possibly a root. He succumbed, shattered and beaten. He smiled ironically as he let himself go, Cain's words coming to him as he floated away: if it wasn't the thunderbolts and it wasn't the rain, it was the landslides.

But, much to his surprise, he remained bound by this thing that had snared around his leg. The current pushed him towards the bank and he made a grab for a protruding root, twisting his body round and keeping his head up. He sucked in air, coughing water out of his lungs. He gave his foot a yank and found it unyielding.

He tried again, this time holding the root on the bank with his other hand. It moved! He did it again and again. Now there was just enough slack to allow him to climb up. He bent forward to see what was around his ankle and felt into the water, pulling his left leg towards him.

He touched something coarse and thick. Archie's mind was working overtime. Then it struck him. It was the swinging rope attached to the big branch.

He pulled harder, knowing that if Daisy was still attached to the tree trunk she couldn't possibly know it was him. The rope came away a little more. Now there was enough slack for him to try and untie it. He reached down and figured that the end had knotted around his ankle. It wasn't the trickiest knot he'd ever seen, but the rope was thick and the current was pulling him and the rain beating down and every time he thought he had it, the slack was withdrawn and he was back to where he started. He gave the rope an even bigger tug. The whole branch moved. This time the rope gave and slipped off his foot. He grabbed it, and tied it around his waist.

And then he heard a scream. Even above the roar of the rain and the torrent, it couldn't be mistaken.

It was Daisy, screaming;

**'IN-COMING!'**

---

ARCHIE KNEW EXACTLY what he had to do.

Daisy was still on the branch – he was sure of it. He tugged with all his might and felt the branch yield. He pulled again and again. Slowly the branch twisted off the bank and slid towards the torrent below. There couldn't be much more time. One more pull was all it needed.

He harnessed the rope around his shoulders and yelled out, pulling like crazy. Suddenly the branch broke free and shot forward, just as a thunderbolt crashed into exactly the place it had been resting. Archie wondered if he'd done enough – if Daisy had managed to get out of the way. But he had no time to think, for the big branch began slipping down the slope, joining the torrent that was flushing down the lane.

Archie was whipped away behind it, trying desperately to keep himself above water, holding on for dear life as the branch joined the main body of the river. As it did, he pulled himself closer and put his left leg out, using it as a rudder. It seemed to work and the great branch pitched towards what he hoped was the bank on the left hand side.

---

ARCHIE PULLED himself up onto the log, shut his eyes and gritted his teeth. The rain slammed down on his back and head as if it was beating him to death, slowly and surely, with blunt nails, like Chinese torture.

Maybe he should slip back into the water to take the pressure off his body. But what if he did that and was swept away? It wasn't worth it. He didn't know if either Daisy or Isabella were still alive. If they were, it was a miracle. How much longer could he last? He felt his eyes closing and he thought he heard a voice. Was it Old Man Wood? No, similar but different. Cain? Archie lifted his head and swore he could see something sitting near him on the branch. 'Daisy – Daisy,' he groaned.

'Come with me,' a voice said. 'You can be saved, Archie.'

'Saved,' Archie repeated. It was the best offer he'd had for a while.

'I can lose this other boy. Say yes, and it will be done.'

Was it Cain? With Kemp? Everything Cain had said was true. What did he have to lose?

His brain swam. All he could think of was his sisters and nothing else. The branch jolted and snapped him out of his trance.

No. Archie knew he had to get Daisy off the log and find Isabella. There was no other way. They'd die together. But better to die together trying to save the world than not to try at all.

'I'd rather be with my sisters than join with you,' he spoke into the rain.

The voice laughed back at him, 'I will return, Archie. You may need me yet.'

# 30 ISABELLA GETS TRAPPED

For every step Isabella took forward, she seemed to slide back two more. And when she was out in the open she found herself pushing blindly through sheets of water with no idea where she was heading.

She needed guidance and wondered if she could find the strange sensation in her hands that she'd felt when guiding them to the bridge. She extended her hands in front of her and felt a gentle pull, one way and then the other. With each step, her feet touched on harder ground. Sometimes her hands swung her at right angles and every so often she had to backtrack. But she trusted in it, for it was the only thing she had.

The one thing that terrified her was the thunderbolts.

Daisy had been able to hear them forming – or so she said – and it was true. Every time Daisy screamed and they ran, a thunderbolt crashed onto the spot where they had just been. But now there was no Daisy, and Isabella sensed that it was only a matter of time before another would come. And she had a deathly feeling in her gut that it would come directly at her out of the blue.

She moved forward, all the while waiting for the crack or the blast. And, as fast as she went, the trickle of water around her ankles kept gaining on her, so that for every surge she made forward out of the water, in no time it had caught up with her, sometimes as high as her knees. She hurried on.

Isabella had a sense of a thunderbolt generating in the clouds above. She didn't know why, it was simply a terrible, stomach-wrenching fear that filled her.

She crawled fast, scampering over fallen branches and through brambles up to the base of a large tree that offered her decent protection from the rain. Almost immediately Isabella stretched her hands into the air above her head, her palms facing outwards, her fingers touching. She channelled every ounce of energy into protecting herself. She didn't know why, but it felt as if her hands were her only hope.

She closed her eyes and waited and waited. Sure enough, and only moments before Isabella was thinking of putting them down, a thunderbolt sliced out of the sky directly upon her. A fraction of a second after she heard it break, Isabella slammed back at it.

She could feel its power pushing her into the ground as the immense voltage made to slam into her head. She gritted her teeth and pushed out harder, her hands red hot as if burning rods of molten iron were being welded into them.

And then it was over.

Isabella's body slumped to the ground, her hands smoking, her eyes closed, a look of peace fixed on her face.

---

IT WAS the water licking at her lips that brought her back.

Isabella opened her eyes and shivered. The thunderbolt! She'd survived! How long had she been out, five minutes – half an hour? She pulled her hands up to her eyes. Even in the dim light she could make out large black circles, like burn marks, on her palms. Her body tingled, the electrical charge still running through her. How – how had she done it? It didn't make any sense. By rights, she should be frazzled.

She checked her limbs one by one. They worked, but her whole body ached like crazy and her head felt as if it was full of wire wool.

'Keep going,' she heard. 'Move, now.'

It was as if someone was with her, egging her on, trying to lift her. Was this her spirit, begging her not to give in?

She forced herself forward and fell flat on her face. Again she heard the voice. She picked herself up and wondered who or what it could be.

She crawled on, finding a steady rhythm that made her progress faster than before. Soon she was above the waterline and she kept on going until she cracked her head on a large black rock.

'OW!' she cried, as she rubbed her head. She noted that the rain had ceased pummelling her. It was a sheltered spot under a rock shelf and, for the first time in ages, she felt a little safer. She sat back, stretched out her legs and cradled her head in her hands. Where would the next meal come from, she wondered – that's if she remained alive long enough. She was lonely, terrified, lost and starving.

Isabella pulled herself together and tried to take some bearings. She was pretty sure she was on the cottage side of the river but she could be anywhere – who could tell how far she'd drifted – and the hills carried on for miles and miles. She picked up a rock. At the very least she could narrow it down by working out where rocks like these came from.

Moments later there was a terrible explosion of noise, like the sound of a train smashing and crunching into another right above her. The sound got closer and closer until it was right next to her and all around her. She shut her eyes and put her hands over her ears.

Out of the sky, a deadly surge washed over the rock. Isabella shook. She didn't have the strength to put her hands up to protect herself, but if she had, it would have been useless. Through the veil of water something else was pouring out of the sky – darker, and deadlier – directly onto the area from where she had crawled.

It took a while for Isabella to work it out. It was a landslide. Even above the noise of the water she could hear cracking and crushing and splintering sounds as everything in its path was obliterated.

For several seconds the cascade rattled on. Isabella's heart thumped; she wouldn't have stood a chance. Eventually, the cacophony ceased. She ventured out into the rain and, only a couple of metres from where she had been sheltering, she encountered a vast pile of boulders, rock, mud and splintered wood.

She slunk back to her sheltered position as a terrible thought began to wash over her.

If she was underneath a cliff face the chances were that it was either a landslip off the top of a hill or, and she thought this more likely, a section of the cliff face had simply fallen away. That would explain the boulders.

The only place she knew where that had happened before was below the ruin.

In her mind, she pictured the geography of the area and the position of the cliff face. She knew from several attempts to climb it that surrounding her probable position was a ledge and, above this, a sheer wall of pure rock.

And then, like a thought one doesn't want to think about but cannot avoid, she realised that she was completely and utterly trapped.

# 31 GUS' CANOPY

Gus was sure he'd seen Kemp, and that he looked nothing less than terrified. And who was that odd chap he was with? Oh well, what the hell. Whatever he was up to, Kemp was probably best left to his own devices. Right now he had more pressing things to be getting on with.

He hurried after Sue, his arms nearly dropping off with the weight of the shopping bags. It had been so embarrassing. In the shop he'd rushed round and shovelled everything he could find – pretty much the entire contents of two shelves – into three carrier bags, much to the shopkeeper's increasing curiosity. Sue was the other side doing the same, before running up to the counter and literally throwing money at the shopkeeper. The notes fluttered in the air and the coins sprayed like confetti all over the counter. She spun on her heel and fled out of the door with Gus right behind her.

'Stop! Thieves!' the shopkeeper yelled out, but even though Gus turned round and shrugged his shoulders as a sort of apology, he'd run away as fast as his legs could carry him, down the hill. And when he took a little breather, that's where he'd seen Kemp.

The boathouse was clad in old weatherboard wooden planks with big, square, open windows at either end. Gus thought it looked like a mini wooden barn. On the river side, the shed had a section removed with just enough room for a boat to be pulled in and out.

Sue was trembling so much she couldn't lift the plant pot under which the key sat and eventually Gus put his bags down and calmly did it for her. The key was old and rusty and got stuck in the lock, turning only fractionally. He forced it first one way and then the other, loosening it gradually until it clicked and fell around. If that was the condition of the lock, he thought, then what sort of condition will the boat be in?

The door whined as it opened, as another crash of thunder and lightning crackled in the sky overhead. Gus shivered and brushed a few old cobwebs out of the way.

'When was the last time this was used?' he asked.

'No idea,' Sue replied, searching for a light. She pushed the switch and a solitary dangling light bulb flickered into life.

In the middle, and covered by a large tarpaulin, was the boat, which sat on two large pieces of wood on the dry ground. It was a rowing boat with three bench seats and Gus reckoned it was probably twelve feet in length and four feet wide. He laughed. 'And this piece of junk is going to save us? It should be in a museum!'

He dragged off the tarp and shook it. Dust flew everywhere. 'Help me fold this up and stow it,' he said. They opened it to find that it appeared to be twice the size of the boat. They folded it quickly and nestled it inside the boat. Gus whistled as he inspected the vessel. Layers of varnish had peeled off and the wood was covered in a thick layer of dust. He wondered how much weight it would take.

'We need to build a canopy,' Sue said.

'Why?' Gus quizzed.

'So the boat doesn't fill with rainwater and we don't spend the entire time bailing it out, that's why.'

Gus pulled the oars off the wall and nestled them in the rowlocks before searching the boathouse for wood. He found a few decent lengths of 2 inch by 4 inch cut timber.

'How long did you say we would be stuck in this?'

Sue shrugged. 'How should I know? A day, a week—'

'A week?'

'Maybe a month?'

'Jeez. A month.' For the first time, Gus was taking their situation seriously and he sprang into overdrive. He ran round the room finding things that might be useful and tossed them into the boat; rope, bits of wood, a couple of buckets, a crabbing line and a fishing net. He found a handy looking wooden box and a plastic container with a sealed lid. He told Sue to give it a quick clean before putting in the matches and anything else that needed to be kept dry.

Then he had a thought. How would they anchor down the canopy? And what would they sleep on? And what would they drink? He yelled over to Sue who was still busy cramming the tarpaulin under a seat. 'Really, a month! You think so?'

A huge crack of thunder smashed overhead.

She put her hands out. 'How long is a piece of string?'

Gus spied four fifty-litre plastic containers. He ran over and smelled them. No foul odours. Good. He took two to the tap, rinsed each one out and filled them before heaving them up onto the boat, which creaked ominously under the weight. He hoped the wood was sound.

'Make room for these,' he instructed Sue, 'one at each end.'

Gus tied the two empty ones to either side to act as bumpers or emergency buoys.

With this task complete, Gus stood up. As he did, the rain suddenly started to cascade out of the sky, thumping like a carnival on the tin roof. Within moments water was spilling through the cracks. Gus wished he had a bit more time. He spotted a couple of loose planks on the far wall. He marched over and, without hesitating, began levering the first one off. As it fell to the floor Gus stared in disbelief at the rain. Holy moley, he thought, she really is right. Rain was falling out of the sky like a sheet.

He pulled two more weatherboards away and slipped them into the boat. 'Hammer and nails,' he yelled out. 'Have you seen any?' He mimed hammering a nail.

Sue pointed in the direction of an old workbench.

It was a long shot but if there were any it might make all the difference. He went through the drawers and cupboards, finding paint and rags and paintbrushes and sandpaper. He dragged out a thick canopy and laid it aside. But there was nothing suitable for attaching it. To the right was another pile of bits and bobs covered in two large, old dust sheets. He picked them up, shook them out and handed them to Sue.

Beneath this was a selection of woodworking tools. Gus thumped the air. What an astonishing stroke of luck. Clearly someone had set out to repair the building and left everything.

Right, Gus thought. I reckon I've got approximately fifteen minutes to build a world class, life-saving canopy.

---

GUS STRETCHED THE CANOPY, which in truth was a thick, heavy-duty plastic sheet, the length of the boat from bow to stern. It fitted perfectly. To make the main beam, he placed a long length of wood under one side and a matching length above it, so that it sandwiched the plastic sheet. He used two 2 inch by 4 inch sections, about four feet long, to connect to the main beam – one at each end. Then he nailed in two more sections at each end from the side rim of the boat to the main post, which levered the canopy up to form a tent shape.

It was a tad uneven, Gus thought, but it would do. He listened to the downpour. It needed to be super strong. He'd take more wood and prop up the mid section if he had time later, once they were underway.

Next, he nailed two rough planks on both the port and starboard sides, leaving a gap in the middle for the oars. As fast as he could, he nailed a baton to the side of the canopy on the outside of the boat. He repeated this on the other side so that, in no time, the boat was covered in a tight tent and better still – if it worked – water would run off the canopy and out of the boat, not into it.

Sue looked on in awe. Gus didn't come across as the brightest spark in school, but my goodness he was practical. He was a credit to the wood-work department. She ran round pulling bits of the canopy tight while Gus hammered and sawed and stretched the plastic sheeting. So immersed in their project were they, that they hardly noticed the water seeping in and over the floor.

'Almost time to batten down the hatches,' Gus cried, smiling.

Sue ran up and hugged him. 'I couldn't have done this without you,' she said, and she genuinely meant it. Sue climbed into the boat and sat under the canopy as a deep sense of foreboding filled her. She desperately hoped she was doing the right thing. And she hoped like anything that Isabella and the twins had got away safely.

Gus slipped a few remaining planks into the boat and a couple more of the 2 inch by 4 inch sections, grabbed the remaining nails, the hammer, a saw, a small axe and a chisel and threw them in the box. Just before the water covered the whole floor, he scanned the shed looking for anything else; Sue's umbrella for starters, a couple of old empty paint pots with lids. More rope, string, a whole reel of strimmer cord, another large dust sheet, this one neatly folded. He rummaged through the cupboards like a man possessed and found an untouched bag of barbecue briquettes. He threw them in. When they landed, they'd need fire.

Sue packed them away. Then with a few last minute alterations as the water reached the upper limits of his boots he clambered in, praying like mad there were no holes in the boat. And he prayed that with their weight and the fresh water and the timber, they wouldn't drop through the bottom.

Slowly the boat rose with the rising water level. It creaked, but so far so good. No holes nor rotten timbers – as far as he could tell. Sue shook as thunder and lightning blazed outside. It felt as if they were waiting in the depths of the Coliseum before being fed to the lions in front of an angry, screaming crowd. The boat rose further still before finding its buoyancy. Then it started to drift.

'Here we go,' Gus yelled. 'Hold on tight.'

But, a moment later, the boat clunked into something. Gus looked confused and squeezed past Sue to the bow. He looked out and muttered something under his breath.

'What is it?' Sue cried. 'Is there a problem?'

'Technical difficulty,' he said, scratching his chin. 'Pass me the axe.'

Sue scrabbled around in the box and handed it over.

Gus disappeared and set about trying to smash the weatherboards. A short while later and Gus' banging stopped. 'It appears,' said Gus, popping his head back under the canopy, 'that the water has risen higher than the gap the boat was meant to squeeze out of. In short, we're stuck!' and he smiled his toothy grin again.

'For crying out loud,' Sue howled. 'Can't you get the boards off?'

'What do you think I've been doing? Knitting?'

She rolled her eyes. 'So how are we going to get out?'

'There's a window directly above, so panic ye not. I've got an idea,' he said. 'Pass me the saw, and move to the other end – please.'

Gus took the saw and stood on the seat right at the prow of the boat. He began sawing as fast as he could through the timbers surrounding the window, the boat sloshing from side to side.

After several minutes of sawing and whacking, Gus put his drenched head back under the canopy. 'Don't think that's going to work, either.' He smiled again. 'Rain's quite warm, so that's cool.'

Sue looked appalled. 'What are we going to do?'

Gus stretched out his legs, closed his eyes and took a deep breath. 'We wait.'

'Wait!' Sue roared. 'You must be joking. We'll drown if we stay in here. Can't you see that?'

Gus ignored her and smiled toothily again. It seemed to act as an anger-deflecting shield. 'You know what we haven't done?' he said, his large eyes sparkling.

'What?' Sue snapped.

'Named our vessel.'

Sue eyed him warily. 'Seriously, Gus, before we start thinking up names, do you actually think we'll get out of here?'

Gus raised his eyebrows and nodded.

'How?' Sue said, raising her eyebrows back at him. Getting a straight answer out of Gus was proving to be a bit of a nightmare.

Gus pointed upwards.

'God?' she yelled, sarcastically.

Gus laughed and his whole body galloped up and down. He moved close to her so they could hear each other without yelling. 'No, you banana-cake; through the roof. So long as the water continues to rise,' he peered out of the end of the boat, 'and it is, just as you said it would, then we go up.'

Sue grimaced. 'Really? You sure it'll work?'

'Oh yeah. Far easier this way. There's corrugated iron sheeting up there, they'll lift off and then, whoosh – away we go.'

Sue couldn't help but admire his confidence, although she wasn't entirely convinced. Wasn't corrugated sheeting incredibly heavy? 'So what do we do now?'

'Well, let's see. We could start by naming our boat. It's definitely good luck before a maiden voyage. You got any ideas?'

'Not really. You?'

'Yeah,' and he smiled his big smile again.

'Oh no, what is it?'

Gus opened his eyes wide. 'I think we should call it the "The Joan Of".

'That's it?' Sue said. She looked mystified. 'The Joan of ... what? What does that mean? It doesn't make any sense. That's not a name for a boat.'

Gus feigned a look of shock. 'Now, come along, brainbox. This little teaser shouldn't be difficult for a super-smart girl like you.'

# 32 TO THE RESCUE

Old Man Wood hadn't taken his eyes off the panels. It was impossible. But increasingly he knew in his bones that he absolutely had to do something. More than anything, he was amazed and thrilled that the children were alive. He couldn't fathom how they'd managed it. How could children so young survive the tumult out there? They're only little, he kept thinking, as tears formed in his eyes.

He knew Daisy was tough and had a very high pain tolerance – the purple bruises she wore after football matches gave him the proof of that. But Isabella? Archie? No. No chance. They were soft – like all the children he'd ever known of that age.

What could he do? He felt helpless and, worse still, he wasn't even sure if he could help. He viewed the screen; Daisy and Archie were sitting in each other's arms up a tree. Now that was clever – keeping warm, out of the rain. He clapped his hands together. If they stay just as they are, they'll be fine – he'd go and find them.

In a second it changed. He saw them shuffling up the branch as though something was coming to get them. He zoomed out. Was it a predator, a big cat or ... ? He scratched his chin. Suddenly a huge flash burst onto the screen. Old Man Wood fell back. Lightning? Sweet apples! His skin prickled with a cold sweat. Daisy lay on the branch as it crashed into the bank – where was Archie?

He watched the scene unfurl: Daisy hanging on for dear life – Archie being swept away. Archie held up by something and, as though in a huge panic, straining on the rope with all his might while Daisy lay on the branch. What was she doing? Screaming? He couldn't take his eyes off the scene. Then another flash struck directly at Daisy. Old Man Wood shrieked and felt for his heart. He could hardly bear it. Then he watched as the entire branch of the tree hurtled down the makeshift drain towards the swollen river, Archie dragged behind, under the water.

Old Man Wood yelped and clasped his head in his hands. Much to his astonishment, Archie resurfaced and climbed onto the log. How did he have the strength? – he must be possessed.

Daisy lay still, just as she had before. She hadn't moved since she'd screamed. Her screen flickered, as though it was faulty. Old Man Wood gave it a pat, as if that might restore it. But it flickered again, little lines cutting through the clear picture. A terrible feeling rushed over him and the colour drained from his face.

'NO!' he yelled out. 'Don't give up, Daisy. Whatever you do, DO NOT EVER GIVE UP!'

---

OLD MAN WOOD was spurred into action. He had to get down there and fast. What should he take? He turned on the torch and shot off towards the shed. His heart and mind racing, he grabbed a rope, a small axe and his hard helmet with a built-in torch on the front. He dashed into his cold room where he stored his huge variety of apples. He selected eight rather small ones from the special box he kept far from the door. These would fill them up. In the cloakroom, he found his long, waterproof coat and his walking boots, which he slipped on to his large feet as fast as he could.

He returned to the bedroom and stared at the screens.

Archie was cradling Daisy, he could see that. Tears were running down his face. 'Oh you poor things,' Old Man Wood cried. 'Keep her warm and speak to her, little Arch – don't let her drift off.'

At least they had found somewhere to disembark. It was on what looked like a huge pile of rocks. And Daisy's monitor was back to normal, for the moment at least.

Now, where was Isabella? He furrowed his brow. Blimey, she's in a funny place. Bang next to a rock face and surrounded by boulders. She's shivering, crying. No wonder. How did she get there? He zoomed out and pressed the cloud button which cleared away the rain.

'Apples alive!' he said. 'They're on either side of the same great heap of rocks. With all that rain they'll never discover one another, unless by chance!'

He zoomed out further on Isabella's monitor. 'I know exactly where it is!' he exclaimed, his eyes almost bulging out of his head in excitement. He checked his watch. Ten minutes before four o'clock or thereabouts. Just over an hour before nightfall. He'd have to hurry.

He darted out of his room, bursting with an energy and purpose he hadn't felt in years, when an idea shot into his head. He turned on his helmet light, made a detour and skipped down the cellar stairs. Now, which one was it? He headed along a very musty brick corridor that smelled of old wet rags and stopped outside a low, thick wooden door laced with metal studs right at the end. Cut into it were the markings "II" – Roman Numerals for cellar No. 2.

Now, he thought, how did the door open? There wasn't a key, he was sure of that – it was something smarter; keys could be lost or discovered by nosey children or unwanted guests. He strained his brain trying to work out what it might be. 'Aaarghh,' he cried. 'Why does my head always go blank at times like this?' In his frustration he thumped his fist on the wall. One of the bricks shifted. His eyes darted up and he groped about, pushing the bricks to see if anything would happen.

Nothing.

He screwed his eyes up. He couldn't even remember the last time he'd been down here. From the corner of his eye he spotted a piece of stone protruding from the wall. Maybe that was it. He pushed it.

Again, nothing.

He left his hand there as he tapped his forehead on the wall in utter frustration. The stone moved! He pulled it further and heard a soft click. He twisted the metal ring on the door and the latch came free. He was in.

Inside, it looked exactly like a room which had been forgotten about for centuries. It smelled of dust and linseed oil. Old Man Wood brushed past the cobwebs that drooped from the ceiling and shone his helmet torch around. There, lying on shelves surrounding the walls, were hundreds upon hundreds of glass bottles and jars filled with liquids, each one covered in a thick layer of dust.

Starting at one end, he picked each one up and blew the dust off to reveal the writing which was neatly etched into the glass. Names like, Spindle Sap, Ogre Blood, Wood Ox, Willow Potion and Oak Spit. He hoped like mad that when he saw it, he'd know.

A flood of memories rushed in, almost overwhelming him. These were his bottles. HIS! From a time ... well, from a time he'd lost, a time he'd forgotten. He continued along the row, reading out the names as he went until he found what he was looking for. Three full bottles with the words "Resplendix Mix" pronounced in bold writing on each. He pulled one off the shelf and brushed it down. In the torchlight, the colour was like liquid gold, and as it moved, little sparkles of light, like diamonds, danced within it.

His heart was beating like mad. Maybe he really could save them. He shoved the bottle into his pocket and rushed out of the room.

---

OLD MAN WOOD closed the back door and was instantly set upon by the water. He breathed a sigh of relief that he'd found the hard hat with the light to protect his bald head.

Every step he took involved wading through shin-deep water. What was the best way to the bottom of the cliff, he wondered. He scratched his chin. The lane from the house was acting like a drain, so the road was impassable. Maybe he could lower a rope from the ruin and let himself down. He felt the coils bound around his torso. But he knew the rope wasn't long enough and what if he was swept off the top? No, it would have to be across country, though the woods and then somehow up and onto the ledge.

He'd need a lot of luck and he'd need to hurry.

# 33 CAIN RETURNS

After the euphoric sensation of the icy power sluicing through his every sinew, Kemp experienced a pain like he had never felt before. His whole body raged with fire, the burning excruciating but, as he dissolved into Cain, Kemp kept repeating his name and his birthday, and his mother's and father's names and his school and his favourite colours and everything happy that he could ever remember.

The last thing he remembered was diving head-first towards the electric body of a weird spidery creature and then being sucked into a void. He must have passed out.

When he opened his eyes it was as though he was seeing through a grey filter. He could see shapes and objects, but nothing clearly; no detail.

He sensed he was lying on a bed. He shut his eyes, and tried to see if he could lose the pain – a constant, driving, nagging ache. He could sense that he was in a body that was gently rising and falling – his body – but it was surrounded by something else. Ash? Soot?

Cain was sleeping. He was sure of it. Kemp felt woozy and weak, and utterly helpless. Nothing he did seemed to make any difference. He had no control, but maybe he could use this time to think – as himself – while Cain slept.

Now Cain was stirring. Suddenly Kemp felt his entire body taken over and his brain and eyes and everything seemed to be fading away, like a gas lamp being extinguished.

---

FOR THE FIRST time in ages, Cain woke feeling like a different person.

What a wonder, he thought, rubbing his non-existent eyes. Sleep. I had forgotten how invigorating it is. I feel marvellous and now I'm hungry. That boy inside me needs sustaining.

'Food!' he yelled out. 'Schmerger, I require food. WHERE IS MY FOOD?'

From the door, Cain could make out a shape which stopped at a respectable distance and bowed. 'Your Lordship,' the bent figure of Schmerger said, 'you haven't eaten for thousands of years. Are you yourself today?'

Cain picked himself off the bed and marched up to the servant. 'I require food, immediately; a huge feast.'

The servant had a look of shock and confusion on his usually featureless face. 'There is no kitchen,' he replied.

'NO KITCHEN?! What kind of palace is this?'

Schmerger was completely taken by surprise. 'May I be bold and say that ever since I was assigned to your highness, there has never been a kitchen. Your highness banned them.'

Cain thrust out his arm, picked the man up by the throat and threw him at a table which splintered over the floor. 'Is that so?'

The servant held his throat and, in shock, wondered how Cain had acquired his new-found strength.

Cain drew up to him. 'How and *where* do you eat, Schmerger? Show me.'

The servant bowed and led the ghost down the wide main staircase through a corridor and several doors before entering a small room.

Cain followed, delighted that for once he could see outlines of people and rooms and his bed and even his dim profile in the mirror. And though it was a shame he couldn't see with any detail, it was a great deal better than nothing at all.

Schmerger picked up a wicker basket. 'From Mrs Schmerger, Sire.'

'Tell me,' Cain quizzed, 'what is in it?'

Schmerger thought this was quite ridiculous. 'It was my lunch, Sire,' he lied. 'There is no more.'

'Do you take me for a fool?' Cain said as he thrust his hand into the basket. He pulled out something black and stodgy and, without hesitation, stuffed it in his mouth. For the first time in ages he chewed, although he had to admit it wasn't really for him. Aside from a tingle in his mouth, it tasted like soot. But he was sure the boy found it favourable.

Schmerger backed out of the room, trembling, leaving it to Cain.

Cain pulled another piece of food and popped it in his mouth. This time, it crunched and splintered. Cain spat it out. 'Schmerger,' he yelled, 'what is that?'

'It is the leg of a bird,' the servant said. 'One does not ordinarily eat the bones.'

Cain crashed his fist down on the table. 'What is there to drink?'

'There is nothing but water, Sire,' Schmerger said. 'Your Majesty has never had a requirement for any.'

'I do now. Bring me some this instant. I have a thirst.' Cain marched out of the room. 'Let me see this palace of mine. Bring the drink to me, and more food.'

Cain crashed through the doors and found himself at the foot of the grand staircase. Then he had an idea. 'Dreamspinner, dreamspinner, dreamspinner,' he called out. It was their agreed way of contact.

Moments later Asgard appeared, his maghole tingling as usual with electrical current.

For the first time, Cain could just about make out his outline. 'Let us see how the Heirs of Eden are surviving. And let me try and persuade Archie to come with me.'

Asgard opened the hole and Cain bent down and dived through.

---

ASGARD TOOK him to the big log that straddled the track and, as he emerged, he surveyed the scene. Cain was frankly amazed that the Heirs of Eden were still hanging on to life.

They looked desperate, pathetic. He could tell their struggle was nearly over. Their bodies could not take much more of a pounding. And where was the old man? Ha! He didn't even know what was going on. Sad. Truly.

Cain realised that this was possibly his last chance to tempt Archie to go with him. He could lose the one inside him and have Archie instead. In one easy step it would resolve this theatre, this charade, that these puny Heirs of Eden might survive.

He would put them out of their misery.

Everything would be resolved.

# 34 HOLDING ON

Archie stared at his watch: gone four. When was sunset, five, half five?

He crawled over to Daisy and cradled her in his arms. 'Come on, Daisy,' he whispered as he sheltered her face. 'Don't give up on me. There's only a little while to go, you know. And I'm going to keep you alive, if it's the last thing I do.' He put his cold hands on her face. He was cold but she was icy.

Gently, he massaged her heart, he didn't know why, but it just seemed the right thing to do. 'Please, Daisy, you've got to come back. Don't you dare back out now; I don't know what I'd do without you. And if you go, we've all had it; everyone, not just us.' Her eyes flickered and he saw the corners of her cut lips turn up.

Thank goodness, he thought, a spark of life.

He'd keep talking and somehow he had to keep her listening. 'Right, here's what we're going to do,' he said, quite aware that there was probably no way she could hear him. 'I'm going to pick you up and start carrying you over these rocks and stuff, OK?'

Very gently, he picked her up and tried to find a foothold in the debris. He took one step and then another, swaying each time to keep his balance. Every so often he studied her face to make sure she was still with him and carried on, leaping from one rock to the next, disregarding the rain, disregarding his own discomfort, worrying only about each step and the well-being of his sister.

As he climbed, he carried on talking. He talked about what was going to happen and how safe they were going to be in only a little while and anything else he could think of. When he ran out of things to say, he started singing. The first song that came into his head was a song their mother taught them when they were young. With chattering teeth, he sang it as best as he could. When he forgot the words, he hummed it, his voice shaking with cold.

After a few minutes of this, Daisy's eyes flashed open. He looked down at her and smiled, trying to hold back his tears and continued his humming. But he could feel her tensing. Now her eyes were wide open, as though telling him something. What was it? Her eyes rolled back.

Archie tensed. Oh no. It can't be.

NOT ANOTHER ONE!

Instantly, Archie threw Daisy over his shoulder in a fireman's lift, which helped to centre his balance. He reached the top of a boulder and tried to see beyond it, but there was nothing but the steady veil of rain. 'Daisy!' he cried out, 'I've got to jump and I don't know where we'll end up. If this goes badly, just remember that I love you.' He had no more time.

Archie sucked in as much air as he could and closed his eyes. He bent his knees and jumped as high and as far as he possibly could – into the dark unknown.

---

ISABELLA COULD REMEMBER IT WELL. It was her first skiing trip, high up in the Alps a couple of years ago, and the day had been beautifully hot with a bright blue sky. At lunch, she stripped off her jacket, threw off her hat and ditched her long johns giving them all to her mother who crammed them into her rucksack. Then they'd jumped on a chairlift that headed right to the top of the mountain. Halfway up, it stopped and swung in the air. They stayed like that for ages – an hour, maybe more. Then the weather changed.

First the clouds blew in, followed by an icy, biting wind and after that, snow. She sat there freezing, with nothing but her father's arm around her to protect her while, in the seat behind, her mother was holding the bag with her clothes in. An hour later as they skied off, every bone in her body, from the top of her head to the tip of her toes, ached with cold. She remembered how it took two hot chocolates before she could move her jaw enough to say anything. What she would give for a hot chocolate now.

What had her father said? *Keep moving, girl.* That was it. *And if you can't keep moving, hug someone. Hug them nice and tight.* A warm feeling filled her as she remembered how Archie thought this was the perfect excuse to go round hugging people and everyone had thought him rather cute, even Daisy.

Isabella tried to smile although her jaw was impossibly cold. Even though she was under the cover of the boulder and out of the rain, she had been still for some time and the cold had begun to creep into her, just as roots burrow into soil.

She needed to move. Using her hands as a guide along the face of the stone, she felt for jagged bits or protruding rock so that she might get a decent foothold. She found one, lifted herself up and then felt for another further up. She'd done enough climbing to know that planning a route up and making sure one's feet were stable was the key. The problem was that she couldn't see and there was so much water and she was so numb that she couldn't feel if her grip was true or not. She slipped back and landed with a wet thud on the ground. Isabella shook her hands vigorously in front of her and slowly the blood began to return. She jogged on the spot, her wet trousers sticking to her legs, and rolled her head on her shoulders. She needed to search further along.

Once again she followed the face of the rock, guided by her hands, her legs now knee-deep in the water. A little further on – to her right this time – she found the perfect spot: an outcrop of stone concealed by bushes.

Moving them aside, she found not one but two easy steps. She pulled herself up, placing her foot carefully on the first and making sure it was solid. Then, hugging the rock, she tested her weight slowly on the next. It felt solid, like a step, and she wondered if it had been purposely carved out of the rocks.

Her arms searched around in the rain trying to find another. She found it and levered herself up. She did the same again, noting that the steps curved around the rock face. She found another, and then another, and as she reached out for another, she realised she was on a flat ledge.

With the rain driving at her, she had lost her sense of direction. She sat on the ledge trying to fathom the angle of the steps in relation to the rock face. She crawled on her hands and knees in the direction of the cliff face, scanning for any sudden gaps or boulders. Aside from pebbles, it felt smooth. She crawled on further before she realised the rain was subsiding a little. Then it stopped altogether. She was under the cliff face itself! She wiped the water from her face, and leaned into a big, round rock behind her. Isabella felt strangely elated, as if she'd completed a task.

In the dim light she could make out that what she was leaning on was a huge round rock. She examined it and figured that it sat directly under the cliff face. The question was, how would she get out from here? The logical answer was to head out to the right – above which their cottage sat. But she wasn't sure if it was such a clever idea. The light was failing fast and the rain wasn't letting up. Maybe she'd have to stay put until the morning. At least she'd be dry and safe from the water. It couldn't rise this far, could it?

And anyway, what had Archie said right at the start? That the storm would go at them until sunset, or something like that. She dismissed it, stood up and stretched her back.

And then they came out of the sky.

She hardly had a chance to react – just to duck down.

Two lightning bolts smashed into the rocks near to where she'd just been.

Oh my God. What if there's one for each of us! Were those for Archie and Daisy? In a heartbeat she knew exactly what she had to do and she threw herself off the ledge. As she went, a huge bolt spat out of the sky and smashed into the exact spot she'd been standing on.

Isabella tumbled into the water, her heart beating like crazy. She sank down as low as she could go, amazed at how much the water had risen. But Isabella knew that this section of water was secured by the boulders of the landslide.

It was now a deep pool, where the current wouldn't whisk her away.

She stayed underneath as long as her lungs could hold her, hugging the cliff face as splinters of rock and stone punched the pool like deadly shrapnel.

# 35 THE BOAT HEADS OUT

'Oh, *ARK*!' Sue exclaimed. 'As in, *Joan of Arc*.'

Gus nodded. 'Blimey. At long last. Remind me never to partner you in a pub quiz. Ever.'

'You mean,' Sue said, 'you've actually been to a pub quiz?'

'Of course; every Friday night with my dad.'

'Really? My parents never do that kind of thing. What's it like?'

Gus wondered if he should make it sound really exciting. 'Well, it's OK. Actually it's quite nerdy – you'd probably do pretty well.'

Sue's eyes sparkled. Gus was full of surprises. Just goes to show, she thought, you really can't tell a book by its cover. 'So what subjects are you good at?'

Gus pulled his brainiest face, which made him look pretty stupid. 'Particle physics, geography, English history from 1066, current world affairs and, er, yeah, modern American history.'

'You're joking me!'

'Try me. Go on,' Gus said, looking like a dog after a bone.

Sue didn't know what to think. She screwed up her face as though deep in thought and asked: 'Which President of the United States of America wrote the American Declaration of Independence?'

Gus scratched his chin and made lots of quite odd-looking faces. 'Abraham Lincoln—'

'Ha, wrong—'

'Won the Civil War,' Gus continued, ignoring her. 'Thomas Jefferson was the main author of the Declaration of Independence.' He tried very hard not to smile. But he did raise his eyebrows. And they were very big eyebrows.

Sue couldn't believe it. 'Correct,' she said, trying to think of another question. 'Name the English monarch who came after William Rufus?'

'You can do better than that, sexy Sue.' He pulled a serious face. 'William Rufus, heir of William the Conqueror. Shot by an arrow by a noble who thought he was a total nob-end. Succeeded by Henry, as in Henry One, also a son of the Conqueror, who sat on the throne for a middle-age marathon of thirty-five years.'

Sue shrieked. She couldn't believe it. 'Gus, you're brilliant at this. Why are you such an idiot in class?'

Gus shrugged. 'Low tolerance to teachers—'

A loud clunk stopped them in their tracks. Gus raced up to the bow step. 'The Joan Of has hit the roof,' he yelled. 'Here we go.' Gus ducked his head inside the canopy. 'I hope you're ready for this. Pass me that long bit of wood and sit at the end. And Sue...'

'Yes.'

'Whatever you do, please don't scream – it really won't help.'

Gus had never really expected the water to rise quite so high, nor so fast. In fact he was pretty sure they'd stay in the boathouse quite safe from anything outside. Now, it was very different. He grappled with the piece of wood, eventually holding its base, and thrust it up towards the corrugated sheeting directly above. Come on, you little beauty, you've got to move. Nothing happened. He changed his tack, trying to lever the roofing off. Move, you little sod, he murmured, as he pushed the wood with all his might.

But, as he pushed, he noticed that the entire building had begun to move of its own accord. Gus stopped hammering on the roof and watched as the shed began to lift up and drift off into the flooding all on its own. He couldn't believe it. He wondered if, incredibly, the buoyancy of their boat had given buoyancy to the whole building – and now it had gone adrift with them inside it. That, or he was suddenly immensely strong.

The only thing he knew for sure was that the whole unit was moving very quickly into the swollen floodwaters. As far as he could tell, they were safe. In fact, he rather suspected they were safer than any place they could otherwise have expected to end up in – so long as The Joan Of wasn't rotten. He ducked down under the canopy. Sue was crying hysterically.

'Everything ship-shape and dandy, Capitan,' he said, saluting.

Sue looked confused. 'What's happening, Gus, I'm scared.'

Gus shrugged. 'I pushed the roof and the entire shed came away. Funny thing is, I always suspected I had superpowers.'

'Is it ... safe?'

Gus looked at her blankly. 'Truthfully? I've no idea, but so far, so good. Now, how about another brainteaser.' He sat down and put his legs up again. 'Can't wait all day.'

Sue peered up at him. She simply couldn't believe his brazen attitude to the disaster unfolding around them. The boat lurched and her eyes widened. But Gus rubbed his eyes and yawned.

'You are ridiculous, Gus Williams. I don't know how you do it.' She took a couple of very deep breaths as if to control herself. 'We're on the verge of plunging into Armageddon and you want another teaser, Gus?'

Gus nodded. 'Yeah. Absolutely.'

'Good Lord.' She took a deep breath. 'OK. Physics question – you said you were good at physics, right?' He nodded. A question popped into her head. 'Where does bad light end up?'

Gus put his feet up on the seat in front, confidently, grinning like mad, which Sue later discovered was a sign that his brain was working. 'OK,' he began cagily, 'either it's in an ohm?' Sue giggled but shook her head. 'OR,' and there was quite a long pause. He clicked his fingers, 'In a prism?'

Sue clapped her hands. 'Brilliant! You big strapping genius.'

Gus was bursting with pride. Big, strapping and genius – in the same sentence – from delicious, sexy Sue; he hardly dare tell her he'd read the answers in a magazine at the dentist. 'One for you,' he said. 'What did the male magnet say to the female magnet?'

Sue burst out laughing. 'I'm seriously attracted to you?' She turned purple on the spot.

Gus caught her eye. 'Not bad. Want another try?'

Sue shook her head. 'Tell me.'

Gus looked quite serious. 'From your backside,' he began. 'I thought you were repulsive. However, from the front I find you rather attractive.'

Sue clapped her hands and laughed as Gus punched the air.

Suddenly, a terrible noise, like the body of a car scraping along a road, stopped both of them in their tracks.

Gus slipped out at the front. Then he dived back in and dashed toward Sue at the rear. 'Move up front,' he ordered.

Sue shuffled up as Gus headed out of the canopy at the bow.

Seconds later, he reappeared and, without hesitating, sat in the middle of the boat and grabbed the oars. He started to row, pushing the oars in to go backwards, as fast as he could.

'What's going on?' Sue cried.

'Our time has come. The Joan Of has landed.'

With a terrible crunching noise, the back end of the shed began to lever high into the air as if the nose had plunged in to the water. Gus took a deep breath. 'We're on our own. Let's pray that The Joan Of holds together.'

With a massive effort, Gus continued to row the little boat backwards, creeping under the raised end and out into the river. For the first time, the rain whammed into the canopy and the boat rocked in the water. The sound was deafening. Sue screamed.

After a couple of minutes, Sue bravely put her head out as far as she dared and tried to survey the scene. But the only things she could see were faint outlines of cars, wood and sections of plastic, bobbing along beside them.

She ducked under the canopy, her face ashen.

'Everything alright?' Gus yelled, noting the distress in her face.

She shook her head. 'Isabella, Daisy and Archie are in this – with no protection,' she yelled back. 'They haven't got a hope.'

'They'll be fine,' he yelled back. He looked down. 'Sue,' he screamed, his voice only just heard above the sound of the rain smacking down on the canopy. 'Get a bucket and start bailing!'

# 36 A LEAP OF FAITH

When Isabella surfaced she noticed a big difference. The water level was near to the ledge and it was almost dark. She pulled herself out and sat down, her feet dangling in the pool. She shivered and stretched her hands out in front of her.

There was something else and she couldn't think what it was. Then it struck her. The rain had almost stopped! It was like a miracle and she smiled through chattering teeth.

The remains of her clothes stuck to her like cold, soggy slime and she still had to make it through the night. How was she going to do that? The temperature would drop – it always did at about this time of year – and there was no hope of a warming fire.

In the next breath, her thoughts turned to Daisy and Archie. There had been three huge thunderbolts, one designed for each of them. Why, she had no idea, but it seemed right, even if it was absurdly illogical and absolutely terrifying.

She shuffled along in the darkness and called out their names.

*'Archie. Daisy – are you there?'*

She listened, but heard only the swishing sounds of the running water beyond.

Again and again she called out and listened.

But no reply was forthcoming.

---

ARCHIE HAD no idea what he might land on: rock, mud, a piece of wood, an old section of metal? But a broken leg was preferable to being fried to death by a lightning bolt.

To his shock – and relief – Archie, with Daisy over his shoulder, had landed in a pool and sank down to the very bottom at the exact moment two lightning bolts smashed into their previous position. The brutal force of the energy splintered the rock, sending shards and pebbles and larger stones flying towards them, shaking everything to the core. Archie stayed down, holding Daisy, cradling her head for as long as he dared until her eyes opened wide as if she was on her last reserve of oxygen.

Archie winced as the first stone hit him on the shoulder. Then he felt himself being peppered as if from a machinegun at close range. He had to get to the surface to breathe, to get Daisy out. As he rose to the surface, a large rock whacked him on the head. He fell back into the pool and saw stars.

The pool and the torrential rain were blurring. Now he saw Daisy. He imagined the branch spinning in his head, like a ride at the fairground. The feeling accelerating.

With a last effort, he pulled himself over towards the rocks and, feeling his feet touch firm ground, he pushed Daisy up as far as he could. Her body slumped and fell on what he desperately hoped was a safe place.

Now his head spun so fast that in no time he felt himself go, his body slipping away to a place of softness and light. A feeling of great calm washed over him, a warmth – a comfort – like a cuddle brimming with love in the arms of someone who truly adores you.

With his last breath of consciousness, Archie had the wherewithal to reach up and grasp a rock. And then his mind slid into the darkness of a black and deep abyss.

---

ISABELLA WOULDN'T GIVE UP. Deep within her, she sensed they were near, but it was so hard. She was so tired, so cold, so hungry. She knew she had to pull herself together. Come on, she told herself, no time to be lazy; look for them. A thought kept returning: what if they were a few feet away and died in the night because she couldn't be bothered? She crawled along the ledge as far as she dared, all the while making sure she kept a firm grip of the surface, and calling out for them in turn, '*Daisy*' and '*Archie*'. Then she listened, but every time, there was nothing, just the lapping of water splashing up against the rocks.

Had Daisy and Archie been blasted to smithereens by the bolt? Had they been swept away? What if they had never been close but found their way home? She knew that was impossible. She ran her hand through the water and then through her hair, removing the strands that were stuck to her face. With defeat threatening to overwhelm her, she dragged her aching body to the rock face, out of the drizzling rain.

The problem now was survival. She had all night to wait out until the dawn of a new day.

She shivered, her lips quivering involuntarily as she stared out into the darkness. Occasionally she heard a sound like a groan but it was hard to tell if it was the crunching of metal on metal, like cars or sheds being washed down the river and colliding with each other, or whether it was from people or animals. Tears built up and an overwhelming sense of sadness began to leach into her, her feeling of helplessness almost complete.

As if in response to her cries, a tiny sliver of light appeared on the lip of the horizon and threw a grey light over the water. Isabella peered at it and, for a short while, thought that she must be dreaming. It looked so beautiful, like the gentle sparkle of light catching the rim of a silver bracelet. She blinked and shook her head. The moon? It was moonlight!

Now, instead of the pitch darkness, she could distinguish the outlines of the boulders and the ledge and. looking up, she could make out the sheer sides of the rock face curving above her. She scoured the valley and was struck by a curious sight; a dull, watery reflection, gently flickering, which extended on and on in front of her.

As the moon rose, its brightness lifted her spirits further; now she could walk where before only crawling was possible. A renewed sense of hope swept through her – maybe she'd be able to find a way out. She scoured the ledge. The round boulder she had leant on before the lightning struck was reduced to rubble, save for several large chunks that had been hewn into rough, awkward shapes. But the area behind it seemed unnaturally dark.

She approached, wondering if it was a result of the strike – perhaps it was the exact spot where the lightning had smashed into it? With every footstep, she grew more curious, her feet crunching through the debris. Was there something behind it, something hollow and open, or was her mind playing tricks on her again?

She sidled closer, gently pushing on the split sections that might be unstable, until she found herself peering up at a perfectly symmetrical entrance. It was a cave.

Without hesitating, she placed one foot ahead of the other and, holding on to the side, she made her way in.

---

ISABELLA TRIED to see what was inside. A breeze was blowing out of it, and for a moment she caught it on her face – warmth? Hot air?

Cautiously, she took another step, hoping that her eyes would adjust to the moonlight. Oh, how lovely and warm it was, like being in front of a hairdryer. But how come? This bit of rock wasn't thermal, like a volcano – or was it?

Isabella was about to take a further step in when she heard a strange cry from near the ledge. Her heart skipped a beat. Daisy? Archie?

She scanned the area but found that the ledge was only just higher than the river and it was hard to tell where one stopped and the other started. She heard it again, a groan followed by a cry and a tiny cough.

Her heart beat faster as she scoured the ledge again. She concentrated, feeling that if she could find one of them, she might very well find the other.

She ran to the right, urging her eyes to peer deeper into the night sky.

Nothing.

She walked cautiously to the left.

Nothing.

In front of her, all she could make out was a blob. A blob, almost black in colour, like so many of the other rocks and bits of debris. As she approached it, the blob stirred. Isabella's heart leapt. She was there in a second.

The body was barely covered by clothes. It was smeared in dirt intermingled with bloody cuts and angry bruises. The legs and arms were as white as a sheet. Isabella's heart sank. As she turned the body over, the arms folded round limply and splashed helplessly in a puddle.

The eyes were closed.

Isabella screamed. It was as if someone had ripped her heart out. She had never seen anyone look deader.

It was Daisy.

# 37 STUCK ON THE CLIFF

At every step, Old Man Wood was forced to hold on for fear of being pulled down and swept away. Twice he lost his footing only to slide fortuitously into a nearby tree. And on another occasion he thrust his axe out and wedged it into a tree trunk. He pulled himself up and hugged the tree like a long lost brother who had saved his life.

Every so often, Old Man Wood stumbled into a rock he was familiar with or a tree he knew, even when the tree had been uprooted. And from these small signs, he was able to gauge his direction towards the cliff face beneath the ruin.

The problem building in his mind was getting up on to the ledge. Usually it was done by means of some steps at the base of the cliff. Why they were there, he had no idea, but he knew that by now they had to be submerged. He'd make his way along a rocky seam further up and see if he could climb across and downwards.

Before long, Old Man Wood was at the point where he needed to start down the steeper, sharper cliff face.

Old Man Wood faced the rock and shuffled along, happier in his step where the mud gave way to stone. As he angled across the cliff face there were sections that sheltered him from the downpour, while other parts showered him with mud and loose rock. He dug his fingers into every tight crevice and small hole – moving along as carefully, yet as fast, as he dared – unclear of his position, but hoping like mad he hadn't started too high.

Shortly, he was able to take stock of his position under a deep overhang where he found a decent foothold. He gulped in huge mouthfuls of air as he leant into the stone. Should he drive a bolt into a suitable crevice so he could attach the rope – just in case?

He found a hole, delved into his pocket, found a quick release bolt and thrust it in. It expanded instantly and fastened into the rock. He put his weight on it and it held. Good. He tied the rope to the end, and attached the rest around his body.

As he turned to inspect his next footholds, a huge electrical pulse flashed out of the sky below and to the left of him. He looked on in shock. Then a second bright charge, the noise piercing his eardrums.

The valley lit up and he saw everything move like a huge grey beast filled with water. Apples-alive, he muttered under his breath as his heart raced. He was too high above the ledge.

He felt for a footing, making sure his hold was solid. He tested his grip and bent down but, in the very next moment, a huge thunderbolt smashed out of the sky directly into the cliff face beneath him.

For a second Old Man Wood held on for dear life.

*There they were!*

He could see the children.

Isabella diving into a pool, Daisy further round, and Archie. But Archie was struggling.

He had to get down there fast.

---

IF HE TRIED to scramble down, the overhanging rock extended too far over on one side and there was every chance he'd suffer a serious injury on the sharp edges.

No, it would have to be a far more radical route. He climbed along as fast as he could, letting the rope out behind him. After several metres he tensioned the rope and started to descend, being careful not to slip and fall. The old man sucked in his cheeks.

Right, he thought, here we go; nothing like a bit of adventure. He wondered how high he was above the ledge. Six feet? Ten feet?

He braced himself and pushed out with his feet. The rope swung out.

Moments later, Old Man Wood was flying through the air, rain smashing into his face.

He began preparing himself for the landing. It was going to hurt, he thought. Rather a lot.

The rope swung out again, this time gaining speed. Moments later, he was back to his starting position, like a pendulum. This time, as he reached the limit of his arc, he noted that the rain had suddenly stopped.

The shock of the lack of rain, and the fact that the moon now offered just enough light to see below, forced him to hold on and he let his momentum take him out one more time. He was ready to jump. But as he looked down, he could see Isabella directly below him, walking towards a broken rock.

He swung back, holding on for dear life – but it was one swing too many. The bolt disengaged from the rock, and the rope and Old Man Wood hurtled downwards.

Old Man Wood flew through the air and crashed to the rock ledge where he cried out in agony. As he landed, a pain shot into his ankle and his back. He attempted a parachute roll, but skidded and smacked into a large rock.

He lay in a heap, his breath knocked clean out of him. The old man tried to pick himself up using the rock as a prop. But the burning sensation in his ankle meant that the joint was refusing to take any weight.

He watched Isabella walking out and bending down. He heard her scream. Then muffled cries. Was he too late? Had she found one of the children? Daisy?

Old Man Wood couldn't believe it. Had he come this far only to fail? Oh apples alive, he cursed, how could he be so hopeless. He summoned his strength, trying to ignore the searing pain that coursed through his legs.

He urged himself on, but his body would not co-operate. He slumped back down and pulled up his trouser legs. Already his ankle was swollen – full of blood, huge and tender, like a juicy summer pudding.

His eyes watered as his fingers probed the swollen flesh. Was it a tear or a break? Had it twisted on landing? He wondered if his back was equally shot. He turned his head and his back screamed out as if a knife was stabbing at his vertebrae.

Even his hands were hurting. He studied them and found that blood was pouring from a cut in the middle of his left palm.

What a pathetic, hopeless disaster. What had he been thinking? Swinging on ropes at his age, he wasn't a child who was able to play football. He couldn't even bring himself to laugh at the madness of it.

And now his body was beginning to shut down. It was in shock – Old Man Wood knew it well. Then it struck him – how come he hadn't thought of it earlier? Resplendix Mix! Of course! He'd self-medicate.

At least he'd know if it worked. With his swollen hand he reached into his pocket. There it was. He transferred it to his bleeding left hand and attempted to remove the lid. Did it twist off?

Old Man Wood set the bottle down and attempted to hold and turn, but when nothing happened apart from his hand slipping round the rim, he inspected it.

No lid.

Harrumph. Maybe it needed a sharp pull, so he tried, but there was nothing to pull on.

Old Man Wood shook his head in frustration. No shaking or twisting or pulling or yelling would make it open.

He felt his eyelids becoming heavy and struggled to keep them open. He wondered if he shouldn't try and break the top off by smashing it on a rock. But his thoughts vanished like vapour on a window as a deeper yearning for sleep filled his mind.

He tried to fight back, but it was hopeless.

And then his mind slipped away.

# 38 BETRAYAL

Gaia, the dreamspinner, flashed back to see Old Man Wood as regularly as she thought appropriate, returning as near to the old man as she dared. Once she understood what the old man was doing, or not doing, she inverted into her maghole so that her movements would not be seen, nor her presence missed.

Gaia knew it was nearly impossible for one dreamspinner to follow another, simply because each one went wherever they chose by simply thinking about their destination and flipping through their magholes to get there. So unless another dreamspinner had access to her thoughts she was safe enough, but in these strange times, who knew who was checking up on who?

Every dreamspinner, Gaia sensed, fully understood the events playing out with Isabella, Archie and Daisy. And they knew that what happened now would affect them. It wasn't a game, it wasn't coincidence, and it wasn't something they could ignore.

She sensed a strange atmosphere of nervousness around the Great Atrium – the vast chamber where the last specks of dream powders were stored. On top of this was another sensation that she was not familiar with at all. She wondered if this was the feeling humans called fear?

Dreamspinners knew their purpose was now threatened. If they had no more dreams to give, what would become of them? Would they spin only bland dreams and nightmares? But why? Why fill the world with dreams of anguish and sorrow and mediocrity?

Wasn't the point of dreaming to let the dreamer reach out to something magic or beautiful or bewitching; feel a sensation that was out of the ordinary? Wasn't it another way of understanding the universe and the complexities of life?

Gaia flicked a couple of her legs. The story of the Prophecy was commonplace. News was spread by the gossip in the great chambers where the dream powders were made and stored. The dreamspinners knew of the loss of Archie's gift of courage, and whispers abounded that the Heirs of Eden were not really the Heirs of Eden at all, but just three children who happened to be in Eden Cottage with the old man. Gaia had put them right. They were the Heirs of Eden alright – it was their birthright.

As for the old man, well, Old Man Wood had never expected to live so long. He might be doddery but he was the only one who could help them. And, with any luck, he still would.

The trouble was, Gaia thought, that dreamspinners had never meddled in the lives of others, however terrible the mess, however easy it would be to make a situation better – or worse. That was how it had been since the dawn of time itself. Nature and the forces of the universe might interfere as they wished, but not dreamspinners. They span webs to make dreams but they never toyed with the consequences.

How dreams were interpreted was up to each individual. As Gaia thought about this, she crossed and re-crossed her long, slender legs, occasionally dipping one in her maghole. She knew that dreamspinners could make a difference, if they wanted, but now that the dreamspinners understood how serious the situation was, would their approach change? Was this, she wondered, a sign that the dreamspinners were finally evolving too?

Gaia dipped two legs in her maghole. What was Asgard up to? Where was he? She sniffed the air and reached out into the cosmos to see if she could pick up a vibration. It was a long-shot. She'd have to feel the vibrations of a physical place where a dreamspinner might be.

A strong vibration from Cain's palace in Havilah came to her, particularly from the roof of the ballroom perhaps the fireplace. Dreamspinners loved fireplaces. It was exactly the sort of place Asgard liked to be. Why such a strong feeling?

Gaia didn't want any other dreamspinner to know of her actions, so she had two choices. The first was to turn up invisible and expect the other invisible dreamspinner to see her. If so, she'd turn the deeper rings of grey into white, like a young dreamspinner, and hope her identity would remain a secret – at least from a distance.

The second option was to arrive in a solid, physical form, in which case only those who were in the same state would be able to see her. But few dreamspinners would dare. If they were looked upon by a human it could leave a burn and her dream spinning abilities might be tarnished for good. She recalled how unlucky Genesis had been with Archie – on two occasions – and wondered if she should seek her advice. But Genesis was old and in pain and her help would be japes and jibes which would not help.

Gaia needed to act fast. She thought of a place where she could be painted white with ease, but which would not hinder her movements. A white powder, perhaps, that was so fine with a colour so pure.

She knew exactly where to go, thought about the place and inverted into her maghole, vanishing out of sight.

---

GAIA FLASHED out of the sky and onto the ceiling of Cain's ballroom. Had she done enough to camouflage her body? She wondered whether the tiny specks of white powder rubbed over her dark parts masked her deep-grey age-lines. She'd have to see.

Young dreamspinners acknowledged the senior ones by means of a simple, subtle and quick movement, a nod of the head, the flick of a leg or a flaring of the mouth. In return, the senior dreamspinner would return the gesture.

Gaia reminded herself that, now she looked a thousand years younger, she would have to remember to do this first rather than in return. If only she still felt as slight and as fast.

There — a tiny flicker of light. And now she looked closely, masses of dots of light, like faint pinpricks, flashed by the huge, open hearth of the great fireplace.

Was this an organised gathering?

She plotted a course for the vast chimney and inverted. Inside, it was crammed full of dreamspinners.

'Friends,' said a familiar low vibration. It was Asgard, just as she suspected. 'I trust you have not given yourselves away?' A shared vibration went round and Gaia had no option but to hold it and pass it on. Each dreamspinner sent a vibration back. Gaia tried to guess how many there were, three hundred, a thousand – more? She wondered if her vibration would be picked up. Her physical disguise was not so bad, but she hadn't thought to conceal her vibrations. She tried to muffle them, hoping they would slip through unnoticed.

Asgard's vibrations continued. 'There are many here, so shrink your bodies. Now, I will tell you the bitter truth.'

More arrived. Gaia retracted her maghole.

'The Heirs of Eden,' Asgard vibrated solemnly, 'are on a course to fail.' A gasp vibrated around the chimney.

A vibration shot back from nearby. 'You know this, Asgard? You have proof?'

'Are they are dead?' another quizzed. The air was humming.

Asgard let the questions shoot around. 'There is not long to go,' the dreamspinner began. 'Reports come to me regularly.'

'How can you be certain?' said another.

'It takes just one of them to die,' Asgard continued. 'I am informed that two of them are on the brink of expiring.'

In vibration terms, the chimney exploded into an uproar. Gaia stuck a leg out and heard a few, feeling the expressions of shock and anguish and worry, but she kept her head down, and hidden. She needed to find out what Asgard had planned.

'I know how you feel,' Asgard said, his vibrations rising up above the clamour. 'The chance to open up the Garden of Eden once more – after so long – is slipping away like the lives of those children. The new time we hoped for will not be. The heirs have failed, and failed at the very first test.

'A child of man is never going to be strong enough to survive the ravages of nature, let alone the three great tasks. I told this to the great Genesis who ignored my pleas. But I have been proved right, as I knew I would. Perhaps in her great age she is no longer in touch.'

Uneasy vibrations flew around.

'Be sure of this, dreamspinners,' Asgard continued. 'There is nothing I would desire more than for their success, but by this time tomorrow there will be no dream powders to inspire man, no dreams of wonder or evolution—'

'Then what do you suggest?' came a vibration.

'What I suggest is that it is time to regard our options,' Asgard said. 'Do we wait until the time of the next Tripodean Dream? And who knows how long that might be – a hundred days, a thousand years, or a million years? It may never happen, and if this is the case we dreamspinners probably won't even exist. Perhaps, then, we should join with Cain here in Havilah and spin the dreams from the spider webs of Havilah in the hope that he might find a route into the Garden of Eden in the meantime.'

The chimney exploded with furious vibrations.

'An alliance? With Cain, never!' cried one.

'We are independent,' shouted another.

A strong vibration shot down from near the top. 'We will never do the bidding of others. Never!'

'Do we wish,' said a loud vibration from the side, 'to spin nightmares and painful dreams for the rest of our days?'

'What has it come to if we do this?' said a deeper vibration.

Asgard waited until the furore had calmed down. 'If this is what you believe, then you had better consider my words.' The chimney fell silent. 'You are here because each one of you is fearful for the future. Has it not once entered your mind that perhaps now is OUR time?'

'Time for what, exactly, Asgard?'

Asgard pounced. 'Time to evolve, dreamspinners.'

Vibrations of both agreement and disagreement shot back and forth.

'We dreamspinners are the only species ever created who have neither reached forward nor plunged back. We have never needed to embrace change, either by desire or necessity. The failure of the Heirs of Eden is, perhaps, a sign that we *must* alter our ways.' A series of strong vibrations shot out in agreement. 'If not, we will end up with no purpose. And we all know what happens to creatures that have no worth.' Silence filled the room. 'Don't we?'

Asgard could feel opinion shifting towards his position. 'And that is why I am helping Cain, because at the end of this, he is the one who will surely come out on top. The dreams of Havilah will be the only ones left for us to spin.'

Angry vibrations shot out once more.

Gaia was bursting with rage. 'But they are not dead yet,' she seethed, 'and dusk is falling. If they are alive – if there is but a *murmur* of a heart-beat in them, the heirs will have prevented the destruction of the land. You are fools to write them off.'

'Who speaks so?'

Before Asgard could find out, there was a tiny flash and one of the dreamspinners had vanished.

'That dreamspinner has made the wrong choice,' Asgard vibrated. 'Be sure you do not make the same mistake.'

---

INSTANTLY, Gaia was above the battered body of Old Man Wood, who was desperately trying to prise open the lid of a bottle. In no time, she was spinning the old man a dream. Seconds later Old Man Wood was fast asleep.

Good, she thought, the powders are working fast.

So, it was Asgard who had betrayed them, just as she suspected – and he had brazenly admitted it! "Helping Cain!" he'd said it, just like that – as though it was the most natural thing in the world. Traitor! Gaia poked a leg in her maghole. In which case, she was going to add balance to the drama.

She needed Old Man Wood to wake up. The dreamspinner hovered around the body of Old Man Wood, waiting – for there was nothing physical she could do to aid his recovery. Shortly, the old man stretched his arms out wide and yawned. Then he screamed in pain. Gaia watched as the old man shuffled, his face contorting in surprise as he found the Resplendix Mix. Then he studied it as he realised exactly what it was.

Now let us see how he does it this time, the dreamspinner thought. Gaia watched as the old man placed the bottle top to his lips, closed his eyes and kissed it. Instantly the top of the bottle opened.

Excellent, Gaia thought. It worked.

# 39 A CRY FOR HELP

Old Man Wood smiled, put the bottle to his mouth and took a couple of drops, barely wetting his lips. Immediately, a heat like the glow of a hot fire and the burning sensation of eating a hot chilli, coursed through him. Those parts that were damaged or hurt burned with more savagery, the heat intense like a soldering iron welding him back together. He gritted his teeth as the Resplendix Mix set to work.

Shortly, now the heat was bearable, he had the urge to stand. He rolled his head and breathed deeply, the air filling his lungs like bellows. Aside from the glow of the Resplendix Mix, he felt wonderfully well and invigorated. He coiled up the rope and scoured the moonlit ledge. The bottle of Resplendix Mix had re-sealed itself and he slipped it in his pocket.

Right, where were they? Isabella – he'd seen her below him on the rope, but the other two? Old Man Wood headed out onto the ledge. There was Isabella, bent down and holding something. What was it, a body?

Old Man Wood scampered over. As he neared, a terrible wailing noise, the worst suffering imaginable, was coming from her. He prepared himself and coughed as he approached.

'Looks like you could do with a hand,' he said solemnly.

ISABELLA TURNED. 'OLD MAN WOOD!' she flung her arms around him. 'Am I glad to see you? Look! It's Daisy – I think she's, she's ...'

'Oh, little 'Bella, let's see what we have.' Old Man Wood bent down and ran a hand over Daisy's brow. He felt only coldness. He searched for signs of breathing, nothing. 'My goodness, she's had a terrible beating,' he said, trying to locate the Resplendix Mix in his pocket. He noted how her lips were a pale crimson – bloody pink – against her white skin. He felt for a pulse and his heart nearly stopped: he couldn't feel one. If it was there, it had all but gone. He could sense Isabella staring at him, searching his face for answers.

'Now, Isabella, there is only one thing I can do.' He showed her the bottle. 'She needs just a couple of drops from this bottle of Resplendix Mix. I'll tell you about it another time, but all you need know is that it's a very old remedy of mine for healing. Thing is,' he continued, a deep frown filling his forehead, 'the bottle will only open if the potion within can heal the person whose lips it touches.'

Isabella frowned. It didn't make sense. 'Anything, Old Man Wood – hurry!'

Old Man Wood lowered the bottle to Daisy's mouth and pressed the top against her lips.

'Why don't you just open it?' Isabella growled, mostly in frustration.

'As I said, I can't. The bottle will open if it can heal – otherwise I am afraid we have lost her.'

He shook his head.

'What is it?' Isabella cried.

Old Man Wood's lips trembled. 'I'm so sorry, but I fear it isn't going to work.' A tear rolled out of his eye and landed on Daisy's cheek. He wiped it off, and inspected the top of the bottle, which remained closed. 'I am too late.'

He picked himself up onto his knees, his eyes watery. 'I'm so sorry, little Daisy. So terribly sorry.' Another tear dropped out. Old Man Wood was bent over, dumb with shock.

Isabella stared numbly at her lifeless sister. A feeling of intense anger rushed into her until she felt she simply had to do something.

She directed her hands towards Daisy, closed her eyes and screamed, 'STOP BEING SO STUPID, DAISY DE LOWE, YOU WILL NOT

DIE ON ME. IS THAT PERFECTLY CLEAR? I WILL NOT ALLOW IT!'

A strange, pink glow emanated from her hands, cocooning Daisy's body.

'YOU WILL NOT GIVE IN,' she continued.

Daisy's eye's flickered.

Isabella reeled. Blimey, she thought, it worked. What had she done? Had her words really had that effect?

Whatever she'd done, she suddenly felt desperately tired. She stumbled and collapsed to the ground.

Old Man Wood put the bottle to Daisy's lips and found that it opened. He gasped. 'Come on now, just a drop is all you need.' Moments later, they could see the colour in Daisy's cheeks returning.

Isabella smiled weakly and tried to hide a huge yawn.

'I think you could do with a drop of this too,' he said, and he applied the Resplendix Mix to Isabella's lips. 'Is there any shelter?' Old Man Wood asked. Isabella pointed towards the rock.

Old Man Wood scooped Daisy off the rocks and carried her in to the cave. Isabella followed. As soon as she stepped inside, the warmth made her feel drowsy and tired and hungry. She sat down and closed her eyes.

Old Man Wood shone his torch around the chamber and gasped. The whole place was covered in paintings that seemed familiar – as if he'd seen them somewhere before, a long time ago.

In the middle he found a small, circular recess – like a large fire pit, but empty. It seemed a good place to rest and, more importantly, as he stepped inside to inspect it, it was deliciously cosy and warm, a covering of a soft, sandy, dust-like substance on the bottom that was as fine as talcum and soft as a mattress.

He lowered Daisy in, making sure her head was propped up, and started back out of the cave. From the corner of his eye he spotted Isabella, slumped and fast asleep on the floor. He moved her into the same pit. It seemed the right thing to do – a place where they were warm and away from danger, where they might sleep – while he searched for a way out.

Two were alive by the skin of their teeth. Now, he had to find Archie.

ARCHIE WAS SPINNING SO FAST that he felt he might start doing some serious damage, not only to himself, but to anything unlucky enough to cross his path. Now his body twisted, then steadied, and as he levelled out he realised he was flying. He soared like a bird, swooping first one way then another. He shot high into the air, twisting as he went, enjoying the marvellous sensation of weightlessness. Each gust of wind caressed his body and he cried out at the freedom and the speed. Now he was diving, and flying fast, as fast as an arrow. He screwed left and found himself heading, at breakneck speed, towards a rock face, a large boulder, as if he *was* a bolt of lightning. Maybe he was a bolt of lightning. He couldn't stop, he couldn't turn fast enough and there wasn't enough room for him to manoeuvre. But he wasn't afraid. He would wallop into it with his head. That's right – it wouldn't hurt at all.

BANG! The rock shattered into several pieces.

In place of the boulder was the entrance to a cave. He looked inside. Isabella and Daisy were there, with Old Man Wood. They were so excited and wanted to tell him something. They beckoned him, teasing him to step in and join them. They were laughing and smiling and looked so happy and content.

He raised his foot and carried on through the entrance. But as he did he felt the anger of Cain smash into him and he fell to the ground. Cain started kicking him – smashing him in the ribs, in the chest, and then to his face.

He gasped, struggling for air.

Why would Cain want to hurt him? They were on the same side, right? He felt air leaking out of him like a balloon with a small hole that was getting bigger all the time. He gulped. He needed to breathe so badly, so badly it hurt, like his body was crying out ...

Archie surfaced and thrashed the water, desperate to find a hold. His fingers touched on a rock. He pulled himself up. He felt sick. He vomited, expelling the water from his gut – but it felt as though he'd swallowed a full bathtub and he retched and hacked until it felt as though his internal organs might come out as well.

He lay panting on a stone. His head throbbed like crazy. He could feel drops of rain on his face, though not as hard as before. His stomach churned and he shivered. Daisy? Isabella? He couldn't see anyone close by, in fact, he couldn't see anything at all.

He shuffled out of the water, and slowly up onto a boulder where he pulled his legs into his body. Cold, so cold.

In his mind he wondered if he could hear things. 'Help,' he called out. But he had no way of telling if the word was coming out as a sound.

He wanted to yell out for one of his sisters, for Old Man Wood, but instead, he knew there was only one person who could help him.

Cain.

'*Cain!*' he yelled. 'CAIN, HELP ME!'

And through the cracks in his eyes, he swore he could see someone appearing. Was it Cain? It had to be. Perhaps he would survive after all.

And then it went black.

---

ARCHIE'S HEAD SWAM. How long had he been out cold, minutes, hours? In fact, was he actually alive? A vicious pain rocked through his skull, like an out of control pinball. He felt his head and found a bump the size of a golf ball at the base of several of his hair spikes.

Something must have hit him hard ... he couldn't remember. Did you get headaches when you were dead? He tried to think, but he couldn't. In any case, surrounding him was a warmth and dryness and softness that was comforting and soothing – like his bed at home.

He slipped away but was jostled back. He stirred. Maybe the warmth meant he was in Hell.

Then again, perhaps Cain had rescued him after all.

He tried to open his eyes but they were stuck down, as if with a powerful glue.

What time was it and ... Daisy? What about Daisy? He swore he could smell her sleepy smell, the one he'd noticed when the strange creature was over her.

# 40 WHY CAIN?

Old Man Wood sat on the edge of the pit and studied the children who lay sleeping in the strange soft substance in the base of it. The sound of their gentle breathing was the sweetest music he had ever heard. He reflected on his extraordinary fortune. It was a miracle that he'd found them, he had the curious bed panel to thank for that, and then there was the amazing re-discovery of the Resplendix Mix.

He whistled. The torrential rain, the lightning, the mud slides and the cold. Old Man Wood shook his head. How, in all the apples in the world, were they alive? And how had Daisy come back when he'd felt no pulse. Had Isabella clawed her back from death's door, or had Daisy done it through sheer bloody determination?

And what about Archie? He'd seen a body at the other end of the ledge on top of a rock. As he approached, his heart had fallen; the boy was delirious, curled up and shivering, his mouth foaming and his eyes staring wildly in different directions. His body was battered to bits.

But what was so strange was that, with his first glance, he could have sworn it wasn't Archie at all, it was his friend – the one with the ginger hair who was always so unpleasant to the girls. That's right, the boy Archie liked to go fishing with. The boy called Kemp. He wondered if he'd been washed up on the shoreline – the first of many, he presumed.

He'd rubbed his eyes and looked out over the water. In the next blink of his eye it was Archie. And Archie was calling out '*Cain, Cain*,' over and over again. But who on earth was this Cain, and why did that name strike a chord deep within him that was not at all pleasant?

Old Man Wood searched his memory. Why did Cain seem so important to Archie and, oddly, to him as well? That one name, *Cain*, dredged up a confusing sense of love and anger and it didn't feel comfortable at all.

Now the children were asleep, he lowered himself into the pit and studied them in more detail. The bruises and cuts on their bodies were quite simply astonishing. On each he found signs of terrible burns; no doubt from the lightning bolts. How in the blazes had they survived them? Daisy's legs were entirely black and blue, criss-crossed with cuts – some deep and some sharp, like punctures, and others raked by thorns. Her fingernails were black, and on her ring finger and index finger the entire nail had detached leaving only bare, raw skin. Her shoes had long gone and her feet looked as though they had been forced through a blender. Her tracksuit bottoms were non-existent apart from the elastic, and one of her football stockings was attached by a few threads and it flapped off her bright red and raw shin.

Old Man Wood wondered if he should give her some more Resplendix Mix. But, then again, he knew deep down that any more so soon wouldn't be a wise idea. Resplendix Mix was powerful stuff, and powerful potions, he suspected, needed careful portioning.

But as he thought about it, his attention drifted back to Archie. Like Daisy, the boy had been battered, beaten and pulped to within a millimetre of death. But there was one significant alteration to his appearance; Archie's hair stood on end in spikes exactly as he'd seen in the panels, when he'd thought it was a hat. The effect looked similar to a medieval mace club the children had pictures of in their history books.

He ran his hand across Archie's head and was amazed to feel that the spiky parts were fused together. It was as if it had been done with superglue or a whole pot of Daisy's hair gel. Old Man Wood couldn't understand it. He tried to bend a section of hair but it was set tight.

He inspected Archie's hands. They, too, were terribly cut and bruised. He suspected a broken finger or two by the way his digits were angled. And on his palms there was a raw streak, like burning – probably from pulling the rope, he thought. His head bore the blows of rocks as did his body – as if he'd been sprayed by a rock gun. Some of his cuts seeped, others had congealed already. Old Man Wood sucked in a deep breath. How on earth had he survived?

Most extraordinary of all, perhaps even odder than Archie's hair, were Isabella's hands. The palm of each one bore a hole that looked as if they had quite simply been burnt through. The marks looked so symmetrical that it was as though they had been painted on with black marker pens. And the flesh around each one had been burnt through as though punctured by a red hot poker, so that he could see light coming through on the other side. Old Man Wood stared at them for some time.

He shook his head. How would they get home? They'd be safe enough here for a while – he certainly wouldn't attempt it now – not while they needed to sleep and recover as best as they could. He'd address their wounds in the light of morning and they'd need another drop of Resplendix Mix. Then he would have to find a way out. He climbed out of the pit and headed towards the cave entrance, grateful for the moonlight flooding in. The water reached near to the top of the stone ledge in front of him, gently lapping at the edges. If the water continued to rise, would it reach into the cave and fill it? No, it was impossible.

He returned inside and searched for higher berths, just in case. Good, there were plenty. They would do in an emergency. He slipped back out to the cave entrance and pulled himself up onto a higher rock to the side and sat back.

Using the grey moonlight, he tried to envisage how far the water must extend; two hundred, three hundred metres, perhaps more – a mile or two? And everything in its path destroyed in the space of a few hours – just like that. The power and the fury of nature, he thought.

Why did he feel so especially linked to it?

---

BEFORE LONG, Old Man Wood found himself dozing off, his mind racing from Archie's shouts about someone called Cain and the boy with the red hair, to the terrible injuries of the children. And then his dream flashed to the strange bed panels and his old cellar and the pictures on the cave walls.

He was awoken by a fizzing, gurgling noise. He opened his eyes and his first thought was to wonder how long he'd been asleep. He checked the sky, and the moon had disappeared behind a cloud higher up. Rain was falling again, slightly harder than the drizzle earlier and, as he jumped down, his feet splashed in the water. His heart missed a beat. Apples alive, he thought, how had the water level risen so high so fast? Had he been asleep for hours?

The children! He'd left them in the pit! He sped round to the entrance from where the peculiar sound was coming. A strange mist floated out, like a huge, billowing steam cloud. Cautiously, he peered in, his face a picture of confusion. Where was it coming from?

He entered the cave to find that it was dry inside. Water was flowing rapidly along a neat, straight channel that led, he presumed, directly into the pit. Old Man Wood's heartbeat raced. He followed the channel on his hands and knees through the thick mist. As he crept closer the colour of the water changed from blue to pink and it was gently bubbling. He put his damaged hand in and touched it. The water tingled on his cut and sent a warm buzz through him.

He leant over the edge of the pit, his heart thumping. He couldn't bear to think what had happened to the children. Were they still alive?

He pulled his hand out and gasped. The wound was healing in front of his very eyes.

Then he heard a voice. Or was it laughter?

'What on earth are you doing?' Daisy said.

Old Man Wood reeled.

Daisy giggled. 'Hey, why don't you get in?'

Old Man Wood felt himself choking up. 'Goodness me. Daisy!' he cried. 'Is that you? Is that really you? I can't see you.'

'Yeah, it's me alright. Come on in. It's gorgeous and warm and fantastic,' she replied. 'And it smells delicious, like lavender and pine needles.'

'Are you alright in there?'

'We're absolutely fine,' Isabella said. 'Come on in – see for yourself.'

Old Man Wood was confused. 'Are ALL of you fine, I mean, well, in there? Isabella, Archie?'

Old Man Wood heard a splashing noise and Archie's strange head popped out. 'Yeah. You ... alright?'

'Apples alive! It IS you.'

Archie smiled. 'Well, it's good to see you too. How long have you been here?'

'Your head?'

'Yeah, I know. Something's happened to my hair. I think it was a lightning bolt.' And he patted his spikes before drifting back into the steam.

Old Man Wood didn't know what to think. Perhaps he was dreaming. 'Isabella?'

'Uh-huh,' she responded lazily.

Old Man Wood's heart leapt for joy. It was impossible; a miracle. He had to see it to believe it. 'Right then, you lot, I'm coming in.'

He could hear them laughing. 'About time too, there's masses of room!' Daisy said. 'And watch yourself as you get in or Archie will puncture you with his idiotic hairdo.'

# 41 BAILING FOR THEIR LIVES

How many more bucket loads could she do, Sue wondered? It felt like she'd scooped out enough water to fill an Olympic-sized swimming pool three times over. Her arms ached so much she thought they might simply drop off.

Gus had started out holding onto the oars just to keep the boat steady in the water. Then, he tried to row with the flow but the current was too strong and, besides, he had no idea where he was going.

When he stole a look from under the canopy he was met by a wall of water sluicing from the sky. He pulled in the oars, inspected the canopy and drove a couple of nails into the areas where he sniffed a weakness. Then he returned to the bench and helped Sue bail water out. And, for the amount coming in, it needed both of them working flat out.

Sue couldn't believe how vital Gus's canopy was. If it hadn't been there, the boat would have filled with water and plummeted to the river floor. What a stroke of luck she'd bumped into him.

As The Joan Of pitched through the waters, the storm smashed down upon their tiny vessel so hard that Sue couldn't help thinking about Isabella, Archie and Daisy. They wouldn't stand a chance out there in this, and every time she imagined them trying to soldier on or getting swept away in the flooding, her heart sank. She hoped like crazy that they'd managed to get home in time, but it didn't seem possible.

She bottled up her grief and concentrated on keeping herself and Gus alive.

Every so often, the boat would bash into something hard and solid, like a wall or a car, and they would be thrown forward. It was at these moments that both of them knew the strength of the boat would be tested. All it would take was a crack or a small hole and that would be the end of it. At other times, The Joan Of seemed to grind against something, or spin as it diverted off an object, the water tossing the boat one way and then the other.

Several times, Gus managed to lever the boat away with an oar, pitching it back into the swell. Gus would grab Sue and hold her, staring into her eyes reassuringly – his eyes wide but not so much in fear, she thought, but more in excitement. To her, Gus seemed to be having the time of his life. He seemed to be almost ... enjoying himself. When he started singing a hearty sea shanty as he tossed the water out with his bucket, his singing got louder and louder until it was in direct competition with the rain. Sue didn't know whether to laugh, cry, join in, or hit him. But, for a while, at least it stopped her thinking about the disaster and her friends.

After three hours, Gus pointed upwards. The rain seemed to be a little less brutal. He sidled up. 'I think we've moved away from the main rain belt.' She nodded in agreement. 'Problem is – how far do you reckon we've gone?'

She shrugged. 'No idea,' she said. And it was impossible to tell.

Gus put his head out of the canopy and took a look around. 'Still can't see a thing,' he reported back, 'apart from muddy water. Fancy some grub?'

Sue was starving. Gus opened a tin of tuna and a bag of salt and vinegar crisps and took a swig of water. When they'd finished, he had an idea.

'Look, Sue,' he began, 'one of us had better have a kip – we're going to need to sleep at some point and there's not much room. If we do it this way, the other can keep look-out.'

Sue hadn't thought of this. 'Good idea, brain-box. On sailing boats, I think they do four hours on and four hours off. Want to give it a try?'

'Sure,' Gus said. 'It's five-fifty now. Have a sleep till half nine – if you can. Then I'll look out till one and do the early morning shift at four or five. Sound OK?'

With a bit of a shuffle, Gus pulled the planks he'd stowed from the bottom of the boat and made up a bed – of sorts – where at least one of them could lie down. Gus unfolded a plastic sheet and laid it on top of the wet boards so they wouldn't lie in the wet. Sue lay down and he spread the dust sheets over her. It wasn't great, but it would have to do.

Sue closed her eyes. She didn't really feel like sleeping, but having a rest now after all that bailing out was welcome. And Gus was right, one of them needed to be on look-out – especially if there was a place they could land – and it would be a disaster if they were to miss out while they slept.

---

GUS MOVED out to the bow of the boat and breathed a big sigh of relief. Quite amazingly, it seemed, they had got over the worst and the makeshift canopy he'd erected had saved their lives. He laughed. He'd have won the DT prize for that; just goes to show what you can do when the pressure's on. He wondered if Sue had any idea how close it had been, and then he thought of his mum and dad. Mum would be worried sick, but his dad would be chuffed to bits with him, he reckoned. He hoped they hadn't gone looking for him – there was nothing he could do about it if they had. Anyway, what a surprise it would be when he got home.

He caressed his temples. At least they had food and water and could keep dry. And so long as the boat held together they had every chance. Plus they made a good team. He took a deep breath as the last gasps of daylight started to eke away. Yeah, they made a very good team.

If only they had some way of telling where they were. He thought for a minute if it wouldn't be worth dropping the oars and trying to make it to land by rowing hard to one side. Or maybe he could drop an oar at the back and use it as a rudder. But, then again, what if he didn't have the strength to handle it and dropped the oar into the water. No, it wasn't worth the risk. He wiped the rain, which was now bearable for more than a minute, off his face. Best keep on and hope the boat might bank somewhere where they could make off to safety.

He ducked inside and, as Sue dozed, he slipped past her, grabbed a bucket and started the process of bailing the water out all over again. How long would the rain continue? Perhaps they were over the worst, but what if the deluge came back? He shivered. They had been lucky – astonishingly lucky, he'd never seen anything like it – but he didn't fancy their chances if it happened again.

---

AT THE CHANGE-OVER, the boat continued to float freely, bumping into driftwood and other debris being washed out. Occasionally, The Joan Of spun and pitched, but not with the same force as earlier. Gus wondered what they were going to eat for supper, before resisting the temptation to devour a Mars Bar. He headed to the front of the boat where, every so often through the drizzle, he imagined he could see a spark of a light in the distance.

When Sue woke, they tucked into a cold pork pie and shared a few pieces of chocolate. Gus was very strict on the rations, stating that until they had some idea where they were, they needed to conserve every morsel. Sue complained bitterly, but Gus made it quite clear that this was non-negotiable. By the time they had given each other a few more teasers, and told each other stories about their childhoods, it was ten o'clock. Gus reluctantly lay down on the planks while Sue kept look-out.

At midnight, Sue was frozen. And she was bored of looking out onto the dark sky and being spat on by the rain while the boat bobbed along. She climbed under the canopy and shivered. A big yawn engulfed her and, instinctively, she lay down next to Gus, who was fast asleep. She nestled up to his warm body, rearranging the dust covers over herself and inhaling the boyish smell of his clothes. Before long, the gentle rocking of the boat sent her fast asleep.

---

THE JOAN OF rocked gently one minute and then seemed to climb up a bank and then skid down. For a minute, Gus thought he might be at a funfair. But what was that terrible screeching noise? He yawned, opened his eyes and found himself looking into Sue's sleeping face. He smiled; what a very pleasant way to wake up. She must have got bored in the middle of the night and slipped under the dust covers. Oh well. And then he wondered what his breath must be like. Probably gross. Heck.

Trying not to disturb her, he shuffled down to the end of the boat, popped his head out, closed his eyes, stretched his arms and took a huge lungful of fresh air.

Then he opened one eye and peered about. Then the other.

His head felt dizzy. OK, so this was interesting.

He pulled himself right out of the boat, and stood on the step while leaning on the canopy. Then he whistled.

Sue was stirring inside the boat and Gus could hear her yawns.

'Good morning, Captain Sue.'

'Oh, morning, Gus,' she said rubbing the sleep out of her eyes. 'Everything alright?'

He popped his head down. 'Fine and dandy-ish.'

'Any idea where we are yet?'

'Ab-so-lute-ly none. Have a peek for yourself.'

Sue crept down to the other end and leant out.

'Oh!' she said calmly. A moment later she ducked her head inside, her eyes wide open and her face as pale as milk.

'Oh? Is that it?' Gus said.

'Yes, Oh!'

'We're miles out to sea with no way of knowing where on earth we might be and all you can say is "Oh".'

'Yes, oh,' Sue began. She took a deep breath. 'Right, Gus. I've never sworn at anything or anyone before in my life – but I've heard my mum do it and I think this is the perfect time to finally give it a proper go.'

Gus looked a little confused. 'Oh?' he said.

'You see,' Sue continued, 'every time she swears, it always begins with, "Oh".'

Gus raised his bushy eyebrows. 'Oh,' he said again.

And with that, Sue returned out of the canopy and screamed at the very top of her voice. **'OH $*%@!'**

# 42 THE BUBBLING POOL

Old Man Wood dipped his foot in the water, which felt like a winning combination of champagne and cream.

Ever so slowly, he lowered his body into the pool and the water bubbled up around him. He closed his eyes and let himself drift under. Almost immediately, he felt the bubbles caress his aches and pains, as though targeting each one individually. When he resurfaced and opened his eyes, the children were beaming at him.

Old Man Wood laughed. 'You did it, you survived! HOW in apples' name ... how? And are you better – Daisy, Archie – truly?'

The children floated over and hugged him.

Old Man Wood inspected Archie, looking for the cuts and bruises on his head and on his hands and body. He did the same with Daisy, but their skin was clear and smooth. It was as if the battle through the storm had never happened.

'I can't believe it. I simply can't believe it,' he repeated. 'In all the world I thought you were as good as dead, you twins. Battered to bits you were and now look at you. It's a miracle.'

The children looked at each other blankly. It was indeed strange that their cuts and bruises had all but gone, but maybe they hadn't been hurt that badly. Anyway, wasn't that what thermal springs did, heal? This one, they decided, must be a pretty good one.

Isabella asked. 'So how did you find us?'

Old Man Wood hesitated as he tried to work out how much he should tell them. 'I was up at the cottage watching the storm blasting out of the sky and thinking to myself that if you were trying to get home you'd be in a spot of trouble. There wasn't a word from the school so I thought I'd better try and, er, find you. It took a while, mind, slipping and sliding. By the looks of you lot when I found you – you know exactly what I mean.'

'I can't remember much,' Daisy said, playing with her hair, 'apart from being very cold and very tired. That's it really. Oh and holding on to a branch for dear life and some big, nasty flashes.' Her eyes sparkled. 'Did we win the football?'

Isabella laughed. 'Really, Daisy, of all the questions. You don't remember?'

Daisy shook her head.

'Well, I'll tell you. With the last kick of the game, you hit possibly the worst free kick the world has ever known,' she raised her eyebrows. 'Still not ringing any bells? Fortunately for you, the ball was deflected by a thunderbolt into the goal and, in the process, fractionally away from Archie's brain, short-circuiting his hair.'

The four of them roared with laughter, while Archie tried to bend his new strange mace-like hair.

'Daisy,' Archie said, a tone of uneasiness in his voice, 'could you really hear the thunderbolts coming?'

'Yeah,' Daisy said. 'Couldn't you?'

The others shook their heads.

'Oh.' She seemed genuinely surprised. 'It was a funny crackling noise miles up in the sky, the sort of noise you get when you put wet leaves on a roaring bonfire. It was quite easy to recognise after a while. Are you *sure* you couldn't hear it?'

There was a small silence.

'Anyway,' Isabella continued, trying to sound a little more cheerful. 'I can remember is seeing you, Old Man Wood. After that I must have fallen asleep. And when I woke up I was sitting in a wonderful thermal bath with you guys. I thought we'd arrived, you know, in Heaven.' The children laughed. 'All my aches and cuts and bruises had vanished.' She opened the palms of her hands, 'Apart from these.' She showed them her hands.

The black burn marks had gone, but the indents were still there with the hole through the middle.

'Ow!' Daisy said. 'How did you get that?'

Isabella winced. 'I think I managed to deflect a lightning bolt.'

'*You did what*? But that would have killed you.'

'I know, I put my hands up to protect me and ...' Isabella was confused. It didn't make sense to her, and furthermore, she didn't want to elaborate. 'Anyway, we haven't heard from you, Archie, what happened to you?'

'I honestly don't remember a great deal,' he said as a cheeky smile grew on his face. 'Did I really punch one of the Chitbury players?'

'Punch?' Daisy said her eyes wide, 'yeah, big time, you went bonkers, like you were possessed.'

'Blimey.' He fell quiet. 'I've never hit anyone before.'

As he tried to recall the moment, the image of Kemp and Cain came flashing back and a dark scowl crept over his face. 'Can't remember much more – apart from pulling that massive branch off the lane and getting tangled up in the rope, and then I think I got whacked in the head.' He inspected his head. 'Feels fine now.'

Archie ducked under the bubbles and when he re-emerged he blew the water out of his mouth at Daisy. She retaliated by flicking water at him and a water fight developed, which was a welcome break from telling their awkward survival stories.

But there was one thing Daisy wanted to know. 'Archie, do you remember you said just before the storm broke – that it was going to come at us and wouldn't stop until the sun went down? How did you know? I mean, that's exactly what happened. All those thunderbolts came at us, didn't they? And Isabella told us the heavy rain stopped just as the sun disappeared.'

Isabella leant in. It had been playing on her mind too.

Archie felt pretty uncomfortable. Thinking about it made him go cold. How could he explain it without sounding like an idiot? Maybe he'd tell them later. He just wanted to eat something and go to sleep. He yawned. 'I dunno,' he said and shrugged his shoulders. 'Just a hunch, I suppose. I'm starving.'

'You're hiding something, aren't you, winkle?'

'I hate it when you call me that,' he said and splashed his twin with water.

But the girls knew there was something he wasn't telling them.

---

OLD MAN WOOD LISTENED ATTENTIVELY, noting that they had survived direct strikes from lightning bolts. It was impossible – so how had they done it? He rubbed his chin; there must be something special about them – was this what his dreams were trying to tell him? And what was it about the awkwardness in Archie's face – it was the same expression he'd seen when he handed him the coat. And what was it about the "Cain" person he'd called out for? He wondered if Archie would ever elaborate.

He remembered the apples. 'I've got just the thing,' he announced, rummaging in his coat pocket. 'You must be starving, so I took the liberty of bringing you something. Afterwards, it'd be a good idea to grab some rest. After all, we've still got to figure out how we're going to get out of here.'

Archie cupped some of the water. 'The delicious water in here's filled me up a bit,' he said, 'but a nice chocolate brownie – preferably with chocolate custard – would hit the spot.'

'Or a huge plate of Peking duck pancakes with plum sauce, cucumber and spring onions,' Daisy said.

'Or a huge slice of banoffee pie, with thick cream,' Isabella added, licking her lips.

Old Man Wood pulled out the apples.

He could see the disappointed looks on their faces. 'Now, before you start complaining, these are my special apples, so make sure you eat the whole thing, understand. Pips and all. They'll fill you up. Trust me. Don't know why or how, but they will.'

He threw an apple at each one of them. They all bit in hard and were rewarded with the taste of golden syrup, honey, apple pie and raspberries flooding their mouths. Delicious.

The children pulled themselves out of the pit and wrung-out their tattered clothes. The cave was beautifully warm and their bodies – now devoid of cuts and bruises – quickly began to dry. From the multicoloured glow of the water, which seemed to generate its own light, the children searched the room for somewhere to lay their tired heads and bodies. It soon became evident that there were four ledges, like stone benches, off the floor, as though individually made for them.

Daisy sat down heavily on the one in front of her and, in the next movement, she pulled her legs up so she was lying down. 'This is lovely,' she announced, scrunching her hand in the soft velvety texture. Daisy sank into it and, before long, she was snoring loudly.

The others did the same, and they too experienced the extraordinary sensation of the warm silky powder, softer than feathers, that moulded perfectly around their bodies.

Within moments, the Heirs of Eden and Old Man Wood were sound asleep.

# BOOK 2 - SPIDER WEB POWDER

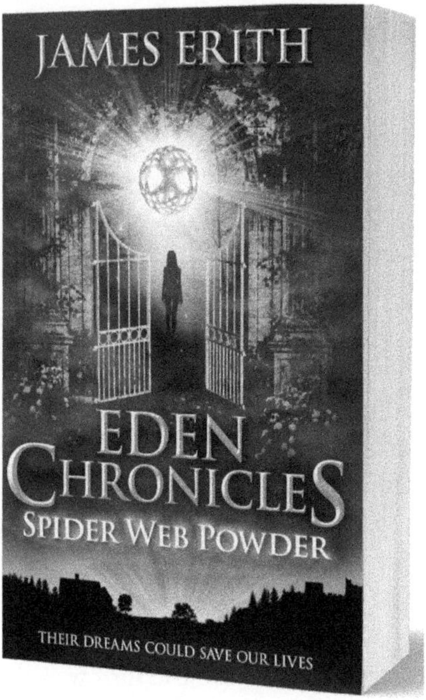

# 43 AFTER THE STORM, INSIDE THE CAVE

Daisy popped her head around the entrance of the hidden doorway. 'Oh for goodness' sake,' she eventually yelled out. 'I've been up and down about a thousand stairs. It really isn't hard to find—'

'I don't have weird eyes like you, remember,' Archie shot back. 'Only stupid hair.'

Daisy ignored him. 'Look, it's over here!' She beckoned them to a tiny, almost invisible, gap that looked identical to the cave wall from all angles.

'Clever, isn't it?' she said. 'It's recessed so that when you squeeze through, you have to turn sharply, like this.'

Archie's fingers found the entrance and he eased himself in. 'It's a bit tight.'

'Just mind your head,' Daisy quipped, 'or you'll damage the walls. Anyway, there's a far bigger problem at the top.'

Archie shot her a look.

'You'll have to wait and see – if you're fit enough,' she said. 'It's miles up and up and up. Prepare to be disappointed.'

---

OLD MAN WOOD'S frown grew until the furrows appeared almost black and white. 'How am I supposed to get in there?' he complained. 'And what about my things?'

The children could see his point. The opening was wide enough for them, but tight for a large man like Old Man Wood.

'Crawl – on your side – you should be able to make it,' Daisy said, trying to be helpful.

Old Man Wood continued to stare at the gap. He was an old man, not a bendy child.

Isabella reappeared through the small slit in the wall and held out a hand. 'Your hard hat,' she said to the old man. 'Archie, as you're the smallest, grab his rucksack. Come on, let's go, I can't wait to get out of this ridiculous place.'

---

ISABELLA HADN'T TOLD the whole truth. The moment she woke, an unnerving sensation, as though she were being watched, made the hairs on her neck stand erect and her brow damp with fear. She connected the sensation to her nightmares in which large, green, alien eyes penetrated her mind and this queer feeling grew stronger and stronger until she'd woken up terrified and shaking and soaked in sweat.

Isabella tried to calm down by taking deep breaths, but her body sagged like a sack of potatoes and her brain felt like squishy dough. Perhaps this was the aftershock of surviving the great storm?

Her thoughts turned to the twins. She'd found them on the stone ledge at death's door; unconscious, frozen and lacerated with cuts that sliced into their bodies like whip lashes. So, their recovery in the pool was nothing short of a miracle.

In the cool light of morning, Isabella wondered if the whole thing had been part of another nightmare.

Or, could it be the downside of the powerful medicine Old Man Wood had given her? What did he call it, Resplendix Mix? A gold, sparkly liquid in a curious old bottle that didn't have a lid – or a *use-by* date. She'd taken just two drops on her tongue. And boy did it hurt – like rolling around in stinging nettles on the outside with burning hot coals inside.

Medicines that instantly healed didn't exist in the real world – or did they? But she did know that the trade-off with a powerful medicine was often a vile side-effect.

The children wound their way up and up the dark stairs, each foot feeling for the narrow risers, their feet scuffing like sandpaper. After several minutes, Isabella stopped and held her sides. 'Phew!' she said. 'This is exhausting.'

'You're seriously unfit, Bells,' Daisy said.

'Actually, I'm seriously hungry and freaked, OK? And I just want to get out of here.' Her heart thumped. 'It's like the whole of yesterday was some kind of weird, crappy dream – as if we were stuck in a game where we had to stay alive—'

'Yeah,' Daisy said. 'But at least we survived.'

Isabella rested a hand on her sister's shoulder. 'I know. That's what's so crazy. You actually sort of died, Daisy. Did you know that?'

Daisy leant her head casually on the tight riser above her. 'Can't remember much.'

'Lucky you,' Isabella said as she recalled how Daisy had lain on the rocks, her body limp, her face pale, her eyes shut. When Old Man Wood couldn't feel a pulse, a kind of anger had filled her and she'd screamed at Daisy with all her might not to die. And then a strange thing had happened ...

'I thought it was Old Man Wood's medicine,' Daisy said. 'You know, Repulsive Mix, or whatever—'

'He calls it Resplendix Mix,' Isabella said. 'For some reason it wouldn't work on you.' She turned to Archie. 'What about you, Arch? Do you remember anything?'

Archie thought for a minute. 'Think I got fried—'

Daisy burst out laughing, the sound bouncing off the walls of the stairwell and echoing eerily back at them. 'Yup, you sure did, bro. And landed unbelievably weird hair—'

'Archie's hair isn't remotely funny,' Isabella snapped. 'Nor are your red eyes or my hands.'

Daisy scowled back. 'Who said it was funny? I just said it was odd.'

'Well yes, very odd,' Isabella agreed. 'You know, Daisy, when you told us the lightning bolts were coming, did you really hear them or were you making it up?'

'Of course I heard them,' Daisy said crossly.

Isabella twisted round a sharp edge and perched on a step. 'Well, it's illogical,' she said. 'This whole thing. Water poured from the sky at a velocity far greater than Sue and I calculated – I'm convinced of it.'

Isabella sucked in a breath. 'And we couldn't see, or hear, anything, could we?' They climbed on, their footsteps almost in time. 'I still don't know how I guided us across the playing field to the bridge.' she said. 'Just imagine the devastating scene out there.' No one answered.

'Well, let's say the river is fifteen metres above sea level,' she continued, 'and we had five hours of water at a couple of inches of rain per minute. That's nearly ten metres of water! Then, augment that with water pouring off the hills and the spring tide and lunar situation...' Isabella frowned and her voice dropped. 'It'll be underwater,' she continued, 'totally submerged. Only the top of York Minister—'

'Can we please get on?' Daisy interrupted. 'I just want to go home, Bells.'

The children shuffled on, picking their steps carefully as Isabella continued. 'You know, I shouldn't have been able to swim against the water that swept me off the bridge, and I escaped a mudslide,' she said. 'Something egged me on. Perhaps that's what having "spirit" means.' She looked up at the climb ahead. 'Blimey. These stairs go on forever.'

'Tell me about it,' Daisy said. 'I've already done it once.'

'But you're fit—'

'Bells, stop gabbling on with theories about our great escape, and keep climbing,' Daisy said, as she pushed her sister ahead. 'Seriously, this is just the start.'

---

AT LONG LAST, they emerged out of the top of the narrow stone stairwell and into a dimly lit cavern. Beams of light filtered through tiny, random holes in a large, circular pattern at the far end of the cave, around twenty paces away.

As the children caught their breath, their eyes searched the chamber. Beneath them lay a smooth, gently undulating rock floor that gave way every now and then to a patch of mud or a pool, formed from water dripping from the ceiling, which echoed in the quiet.

From the cavern roof, which was as high as a small house, jagged rocks forced their way out of the stone like misshapen teeth. Along the sides, water had shaped the rock into small alcoves creating, Archie thought, mini sleeping areas. Perhaps early humans, like Neanderthals, had lived and slept here thousands of years ago.

'See the problem?' Daisy said.

Now, as their eyes had adjusted, they stared at a vast boulder whose rotund expanse sat in the ground like a massive egg in a massive eggcup. The problem was obvious; they were stuck, with no way out.

A deep boom echoed up the stairwell.

'What on earth was that?' Isabella said.

Archie turned to his twin, Daisy, and raised his brows. 'Fifty pounds he's stuck.'

'You don't even have fifty quid,' Daisy said.

They hurried back to the hole.

'Are you alright?' Archie called down.

A few moments later an echo returned, the sounds crashing into one another.

'I'll go,' Archie said, heading down. After a couple of minutes, encased in the musty darkness of the stairwell, he slowed. 'Where – are – you?'

'Still – at – the – bottom,' the old man replied, taking in to account the reverberating noise. 'Jammed – in, good – and – proper.'

---

OLD MAN WOOD lay half up the stairs and half wedged in at the foot of the stairs. *Sweet apples alive*, he thought as he ran his leathery hands over the walls, trying to find a nodule to grip so that he could push himself back down and out. He groaned. The problem was that the more he struggled the more stuck he became.

If he could get back down – and it was a big "if" – he had no choice but to head out into the swirling waters thick with flotsam and jetsam, and swim for his life. And Old Man Wood hated swimming.

He wriggled his torso, twisting one way then another and managed to slip down a step. His outstretched foot touched a protruding stone knob and, using it to lever himself round, he pressed down hard – only to feel the stone retract into the step.

Before he had time to gather himself, a clunking noise filled the stairwell, followed by grinding, crunching and crushing sounds. Old Man Wood covered his head with his free arm, waiting for the inevitable rocks to come crashing down.

None came and, much to his astonishment, the stairwell walls began to pull back until a crashing boom sounded and the noise echoed eerily until eventually it ceased. The stairwell was now at least a foot wider.

*Well, well, well,* he thought as he sat down on a step and mopped his brow. That stone must have been a gear cog slipping into place. Now there's a nifty bit of engineering – and just in the nick of time. What sort of person would design something like that? And why?

Old Man Wood dusted himself down, pulled himself together and stood up.

'What's – going – on – down – there?' he heard.

'Don't – you – worry,' Old Man Wood said. 'I'm coming up, littluns! Nothing doing!'

He trundled up the stairwell, finding a rhythm, stopping on three occasions to catch his breath. At the summit he sat down, taking large gulps of air as the children gathered around. 'Two hundred and twenty-two steps. Phew-ee! Apples alive! And they're high steps and all.'

'What happened?' Archie asked him. 'How did you get the stairs to widen?'

Old Man Wood wiped his brow. 'Touched a lucky stone, that's all.'

'A lucky stone?' Isabella repeated.

'Ooh yes,' Old Man Wood replied. 'Very lucky, I reckon.'

---

ISABELLA LEANT on the boulder at the entrance of the cave and groaned. It was huge – six feet high and eight feet wide with a significant amount stuck in the ground – and it stood between them and freedom.

Stains marked the boulder's surface with streaky patterns where the rainwater had leached down – the light grey stone now lined with blue and black hues.

*How on earth were they going to move it?* she wondered. Maybe it was one of those things that only needed a tiny push. Isabella stepped back a couple of paces and charged.

A moment later she shrieked and rubbed her shoulder.

Daisy laughed. 'I told you—'

'Shut up, Daisy,' Isabella barked. She swivelled towards Old Man Wood. 'You're good at getting out of things, aren't you, Old Man Wood?' she said, as if he might solve the conundrum for them. And then she turned, gritted her teeth and tried to push the boulder again.

Archie could hardly believe it. 'What *are* you doing? That's up there with the stupidest thing I've ever seen. Not even Daisy would try something as moronic as that.'

Daisy nodded.

'I know,' Isabella sobbed. 'It's just that ... just that I'm hungry and I want to go home and I want to know if Sue and Gus survived and ... this is so ridiculous and unfair and infuriating after everything we've been through.'

'But running at it isn't going to help,' Archie said quietly. 'Think about it. That boulder must weigh more than ten tonnes. You are a fraction in comparison. You're the scientist – do the maths.'

Isabella frowned, sat down and let her straight brown hair fall over her face, hiding her tears.

Archie began pacing the floor as an idea formed in his mind. He turned to Old Man Wood. 'You said you touched a lucky stone. Was it a lever or a knob – did you push it in, pull it, or did it fall to the side?'

Old Man Wood thought for a second. 'Pushed it with my foot. A chunk of rock, like a lever, I suppose—'

'Well then, if one opened the stairs up, why not another to loosen the boulder?'

Isabella looked at him curiously. 'You really think so?'

Archie shrugged. 'We haven't got much else to work with, have we, unless you've got a better idea? Whatever this place is, it's been designed by someone pretty clever – so chances are that he built more than one. What do you think?'

The others shrugged.

'I suggest we start hunting for odd pieces of rock that stick out—'

'Stick out?' Isabella said.

'Yeah, you know – like you see in the movies.'

'Cool,' Daisy added, as she un-twiddled a blond curl from her finger.

They selected different parts of the cave and applied weight to rocks that stuck out and pushed every little cavity. But nothing worked. Not a wobble, a flicker, or a nudge. The big boulder remained exactly where it was.

---

DAISY SLUMPED TO THE FLOOR, defeated. How long had they been searching in the gloom? An hour? Two? Her tummy rumbled. 'This is nuts,' she said. 'Whatever we're looking for isn't here, I'm sure of it.'

'Well, what do you suggest?' Archie said.

'What if Isabella has a point,' she replied. 'Maybe we should *all* try and push it out of the way. Who knows, it may be hinged—'

'Hinged?' Archie said. *'Hinged!* Doors are hinged, Daisy, not blooming great boulders.'

Daisy shot him a piercing look. 'But we haven't tried it and anyway you pulled a tree out of the ground so who says you can't move a boulder?'

'Well I can't, and anyway that was ridiculous.'

'No it wasn't.'

'Yes it was! It's like saying that Isabella could move it with her hands.'

'Well maybe she can—'

'I didn't mean that—'

'Stop it you two,' Isabella ordered. 'We need to think, work it out logically.'

Aside from the trickle of water, silence filled the large cavern as the four of them sat down on the stone floor and racked their brains.

'OK,' Archie said eventually. 'Let's try. All of us—'

Isabella wasn't convinced and rubbed her shoulder. 'It's huge, Archie, you said it yourself.'

Archie shrugged. 'I've got nothing better to do, don't know about you.'

Archie walked over to the mouth of the cave and stood in front of the round, grey bulk. 'Well, come on – or do I have to do it on my own?'

Reluctantly, the others joined him.

Old Man Wood and Archie took up central positions with Isabella and Daisy on either flank.

Archie counted them in. 'On the count of three. One, two ... three!'

They heaved until their faces were puce, but the boulder didn't budge.

They fell to the floor.

'Anyone want to try again?' Archie said. They shook their heads. Just as Isabella said, the attempt was hopeless.

Moments later, Daisy spoke up. 'Oooh. I've got an idea,' she said, and she ran the length of the cavern. 'Back in a mo,' she yelled behind her as she disappeared down the dark stairwell, her footsteps echoing behind her.

Archie stood up as though he understood what Daisy had been thinking. 'Old Man Wood – where were you when you touched this "lucky stone"?'

'Now then,' the old man began. 'I hadn't got very far. First steps I reckon—'

'That's it!' Archie cried. 'We're looking in the wrong place! The clue must be on the walls in the chamber, *down there* – not up here.'

And without hesitating he shot off down the stairwell after his twin sister.

# 44 THE PICTURES IN THE CAVE

When Archie appeared, Daisy was studying the paintings on the walls. Her lips moved as if she could read the story like a book, her eyes fixed in concentration as she scoured the simple artwork. Occasionally, she moved in to dust off the image or icon, then she'd step back and take in the whole scene. Archie was fascinated by her intensity, and followed her eyes which shone as though a bright red light had been switched on inside her head.

The first section of the mural began with a circular tree and ended with figures carrying gifts. Then, the mural divided into two and kept dividing as the story progressed around the walls.

Above, and running the length of the mural, was a storm, depicted by jagged lightning bolts and strong lines for heavy rain. This concluded with mountain peaks poking through water. Archie gulped.

Below this "storm mural" stood three figures in front of a setting sun and directly above them the rain lines were less dynamic. Archie instantly recognised this, for when the sun went down the night before, or so he'd been told by Isabella, the torrential rain that had sluiced from the sky abated to no more than a drizzle.

He moved on to the next mural which showed the same three characters holding a rectangular stone tablet encrusted with ornate carvings. It was not much bigger, he guessed, than a paperback book.

Here, the mural divided, as it did with each new tablet that had to be found. *Three stone tablets in all*, Archie thought, *one for each of the three figures*. And as far as he could make out, if any one of them died – and at any point – then they would end up in a place of skulls and withered trees: death would come to all.

Now that Archie studied it, it reminded him of levels on a computer game: win a level – move up a level. The difference in this game was that if one person lost a level, everyone died.

So, if these pictures were somehow connected to them and if one of them had died in the storm, then the rains would have continued on to destroy the planet until only the mountain tops were spared. A shiver ran up his spine.

He followed the mural to its conclusion where three figures basked in glorious sunlight, as if they had succeeded. Beyond the basking figures, and extending over much of the rocky vaulted ceiling, in the shape of a circle, was the outline of a vast tree showing both roots and branches. On its upper half, animals and birds and plants and fruit hung in and around the foliage. Below, beside the roots, swam creatures of the sea.

Archie recognised some – like the seahorse, whale, elephant and crocodile – but he had no idea what the double-headed snakes were or what the birds with forked tongues and huge sharp claws were called. In fact, most of the creatures seemed to belong to an alien or medieval make-believe fantasy world.

He turned his attention to Daisy who was captivated by this strange tree. She stared at it for some time, her mouth open, a frown creasing her forehead. Archie tried to work out what she was so struck by and looked harder until he noticed, just behind the tree, the faint outline of a cross-legged woman with a crown of leaves resting upon her head. In place of eyes were dark patches, as though they had been coloured in, and a cushion sat in her lap. Resting on the surface, in the shape of a heart, was a locket.

Archie's mind raced and his heartbeat quickened. Was this the Ancient Woman? Was this the haggard old woman they'd dreamt of, the same person he had repeatedly killed in his dreams? Was this the same woman he'd promised Cain he would look after?!

Archie rubbed his front hair spike. He noted how his follicles had hardened together like steel. So, if this was them, were these cave-images ... their destiny?

Archie suddenly felt rather weak and insignificant. It made him think of his friend Kemp. Kemp, who had lost his mother when he was so very young, and he tried desperately to remember what Cain had said to them in the alleyway, but the whole thing had happened so fast. If only he could find Kemp, Kemp would remember and tell him – that's if his friend was still alive.

Archie shut his eyes. Cain told them that they were the anointed ones, the Heirs of something-or-other and that everything hung on their staying alive till sunset. Wasn't that the heart of it? So if the murals were correct, he, Archie de Lowe, a rather shambolic and disorganised twelve year old and his two nutty sisters had just saved the world. Wow.

But he didn't feel like a superhero.

And then it dawned on him that perhaps the whole thing was in his head – his imagination – part of a very long, extended dream. A fantasy. Yeah, that was it. Not a bit of anything that had happened was REAL. It couldn't be. Not even the paintings in front of him truly existed ...

'You done?' Daisy said, waving her hands in front of his face. 'Woo-hoo! Anyone there?'

'Sorry, miles away,' Archie replied, returning to earth.

'Have you taken all of this in, absorbed as much as you can?'

Archie was a little confused. He looked around. 'God. Er ... yeah. Suppose so.'

'Good,' she said, rubbing her eyes. 'As you are fully aware, my brain is completely rubbish, so from now on, I'm relying on you.' Daisy ran her hands through her curls and noted Archie's blank expression. 'Want me to explain?'

'Explain what?' Archie looked confused.

'What's going to happen, numpty.'

Archie nodded.

'Cool. Right, you see that little picture at the base of the stairwell.' Daisy pointed at it.

'Uh, right,' Archie replied, squinting. 'Yeah, didn't see that.'

'Well that shows us how we get out of here – stroke of luck Old Man Wood pushed the other one, hey?'

Archie stared at the wall. He couldn't see anything. 'Sure,' he said dumbly.

Daisy eyed him. 'You have no idea, do you?'

'Nah. All looks like white-wash to me.'

Daisy sighed. 'Please tell me you've noticed the cave entrance recently?'

Archie reddened. He turned and his eyes led him from the steaming, bubbling pool along the stream to the entrance.

Daisy couldn't believe Archie was being such a moron. 'Jeez, Archie. This cave – *where we are right now* – is underwater. There's some kind of plastic film or glass barrier or weirdo trick holding the water back.' She marched over to the entrance, put her hands on the strange glass film and smacked it with her fist. A hollow, thick ring like a church bell replied.

'Yup, resin or glass or something,' she said nonchalantly, as though this kind of thing happened every day.

Now that his eyes had adjusted, Archie could see right through the transparent barrier to the murky, swirling mass of water behind it. He felt sick. 'How did it get there?'

Daisy shot him a look. 'How the hell do I know?'

Archie's voice creaked. 'What's it doing?'

'Dur! Holding back the water! Come on, Archie! What do you think it's doing?' She hit it again, this time harder. A louder "dong" rang out.

'Blimey, Daisy. Don't do that.'

'Why not? It won't break.'

'How do you know that? It might.'

Daisy ignored him. 'Look, Winkle,' she said, 'when it breaks, we're dead. Very, very, very dead.'

'Just what I was thinking,' Archie said.

'But it's not going to, quite yet.' She paced back to the wall. 'So these marks,' she continued pointing to a very faint blur on the wall, 'tell us there are two levers. One to widen the stairwell and the other to release the boulder—'

'Of course,' he said rubbing his chin, 'just as I suspected.'

She moved in closer and pointed at them. 'These marks ... here.'

'Yeah,' said Archie moving in too high.

'No,' she said, 'these two.'

Archie shook his head. Was she playing with him?

'Now the problem is,' Daisy said, 'there's a bit of a problem.'

Archie nodded dumbly.

'Well, you see these funny looking icons next to them?'

Archie bent down. 'Actually, no, not really.'

Daisy tutted. 'Well they seem to indicate that the moment the boulder lever is pushed the staircase begins to retract.'

'Wow, cool.'

'No, Archie. Not cool.'

Archie frowned. 'Why not?'

'Because when that happens, Winkle, the barrier breaks and water pours in.'

Archie grimaced. 'OK. Yup, not so cool.' He turned to the entrance. 'So that glass thing—'

'Collapses. The brain is stirring,' Daisy said, rather triumphantly. 'It's all here on the walls – I can't believe you're so blind.'

Archie didn't even attempt to counter her. Silence filled the cavern as they thought through their situation.

'So, if you're right,' Archie said at length, 'we're dead, whatever we do.'

'Yeah. Probably.'

'Have you got a plan?'Archie stuttered.

'What? Other than seeing what odds Isabella would give for survival? Nope. Look, that barrier is protecting a pretty big hole and as brain box kept on telling us, there's one hell of a lot of water out there. The cave entrance is a few metres above the river and the water level is higher than the top of the cave, which means water must stretch for miles above the Vale of York. And water, as you know, always finds the easiest route—'

'Hold on a minute,' Archie said trying to catch up. 'You really think water stretches across the valley?'

Daisy shot him a look as if his brain had a leak. 'Well, yes, of course it does,' she said. 'So,' and she pointed at the covered entrance, 'when it goes—'

'The pressure of water flooding in would be like firing a tsunami hosepipe up the stairs,' Archie concluded.

'Correct-a-mundo,' Daisy said punching him lightly on the shoulder. 'Now you're getting the picture.'

They stared at each other.

'And the longer we wait here,' Archie whispered, 'the higher the water rises and the greater the pressure.' The magnitude of what they'd worked out was beginning to sink in.

'Yeah, Winkle. Something like that.'

'God almighty. Even deader,' Archie said. 'We need Isabella's brains on this one. And, Daisy.'

'Uh-huh.'

'Please stop calling me Winkle.'

# 45 ISABELLA'S CHALLENGE

Daisy headed up the two hundred and twenty-two steps of the stairwell with Archie in pursuit.

Isabella and Old Man Wood stood waiting for them and, the moment they heard them coming, leant over the stairwell firing questions.

The twins held their sides, doubled over, as they caught their breath.

'So, there's good news and bad news,' Archie gasped. 'Which do you want first?'

'The good news.'

'OK,' Daisy said. 'Give me a sec.' She flexed and stretched out her legs. 'Right, the good news is, I've found the lever to activate the boulder.'

Isabella clapped her hands. 'Brilliant. And the bad news?'

'We die if we activate it.'

'Die? Really? That's pretty drastic. Are you quite sure?'

Daisy raised an eyebrow.

Isabella examined her siblings. 'You're ... you're kidding, aren't you? It's another of your silly little jokes?'

Their serious expressions said otherwise.

'But I never saw any of this,' Isabella countered. 'Why didn't I see it?'

'I did though, Bells,' Daisy said. 'Look, sis, I'm not really sure how these eyes work, but it's scribbled on those walls, I promise. On my life.'

Isabella listened as Archie and Daisy explained. Then she repeated it, just to be sure. 'So what you're saying is that one of us has to press this lever and run like mad up two hundred and twenty two stairs while the whole thing starts closing in and falling apart and water starts crashing through the cave opening. And then, and only then, will the boulder open.'

'Yup,' Daisy said blankly. 'And if we fail, it screws the world. Apparently.'

Isabella wrinkled her nose and played with her straight brown hair and then stamped her foot hard down on the ground. 'This is ridiculous.'

'Well, yes it is,' Daisy agreed, 'but the longer we wait, the greater the water pressure, the harder it gets. Anyone going to volunteer?'

Old Man Wood put his hand up. 'I'll do it.'

Daisy smiled sweetly at the old man. 'No, you're far too old, big, and much too slow. Sorry. Anyone else?' she looked at the receding faces of the others.

Isabella cut in. 'Daisy you're nimble, quick ... fit. It's got to be you—'

'Why don't I do everything?' Daisy replied, crossly. 'Look, my legs are pretty stiff after yesterday's match and I've just climbed up here for the third time. That's six hundred and ... er—'

'Sixty-six.'

'Yes, I knew that,' Daisy fumed. 'Why don't you do it? You're two years older for goodness' sakes and you've only done it once.'

Isabella was running out of excuses. 'Archie. Come on – this is just up your street.'

Archie shook his head. 'I'm slower than Daisy and I've done it twice.'

Isabella smiled – her lips wavering. 'Oh ... oh, God! All right. As usual it's going to have to be me.' Her lips quivered and then she burst into tears. 'I hate this,' she sobbed. 'I hate this kind of stupid thing. None of this makes any sense, it's ... it's—'

Old Man Wood moved in and enveloped her with a big hug like a comfort blanket. 'Now then, young Bells. I'm not sure we have a choice, do we? You've always been a strong runner so you'll be just fine. I can feel it in my bones.'

This only made Isabella cry louder.

Archie couldn't bear it. 'Look, if you're going to be such a wetty about it, I'll do it!'

Isabella wiped her eyes. 'No, I'm the eldest,' she sobbed, trying to compose herself. 'And you're right, you've done it twice. It's only proper that it's me.'

Daisy smiled. 'I don't mean to be a spoil-sport,' she said, 'but the longer we wait—'

'Yes, yes I know. You've already told me,' Isabella said. 'Oh, Daisy, you're finally finding some brains!' She gave her sister a big hug, took a deep breath and steadied herself.

'Old Man Wood – you stay here with Archie. Daisy – you'd better come with me and show me how these lever things work. When I've got it, get back up the stairs. When you're at the top, yell down. Everyone got that? I'll depress the lever, yell, and run for it. OK?'

Daisy spoke gently. 'No waiting, Bells, understand? When it goes, scream a warning then go as fast as you can, sis. And good luck, I know you can do it.'

Isabella smiled and turned to Archie. 'Archie, if I don't make it, please do something with that hair.'

Archie's face was as white as snow and his hair rigid. 'You'd better make it, sis,' he said softly. 'Go like the wind.'

Old Man Wood furrowed his brow. His eyes watered. 'Good luck, young 'un,' he said, folding her into him again. 'Believe in yourself, little Bells, and you'll be fine.'

Quietly, Isabella turned and began the long walk down the steep, winding stairs with Daisy following on behind.

---

AT THE BOTTOM of the stairs, Isabella and Daisy came out into the bubbling cave entrance. All they could hear was the water of the pool frothing, while steam floated to the ceiling. Otherwise, a nervous quiet hung about them. Isabella's heart thumped.

She searched around and found that the twins were right, the cave mouth was being covered by a most peculiar screen and beyond it, murky water swirled about. Isabella would have loved to study this extraordinary material and scrape off a few cells so she could analyse how it worked, but she was interrupted by Daisy.

'Right, Bells,' Daisy said, taking a deep breath. 'Here are the levers. That one,' and she pointed to the top protrusion, 'is the one Old Man

Wood pressed with his foot. The bottom one – here – is the dude you need to push.'

Isabella nodded. She shook like a rattle.

Daisy noticed and reached out for her hand. 'Then run, Bells. Run like you've got a seriously massive great monster after you. Got it?' Isabella's eyes were wide with fear. 'Fast as you can,' Daisy continued, 'and don't stop. Understand?' She noted how pale her sister had turned. 'Look, are you sure you can do this? I mean, I'll do it ... if you can't.'

For a brief moment Isabella very nearly gave in. 'No, no, Daisy,' she said as she pulled herself together. 'You must be shattered. Get back to the cave. Call down when you're there. It'll give me time to compose myself.'

Daisy smiled, trying hard not to betray her nerves, and moved in close to give her sister a hug. 'Look, you can do it. Easily,' she said, her voice croaking. 'Piece of Mrs Pye's cake, sis. Easy-peasy.'

---

ISABELLA SMILED as Daisy's footsteps receded up the stairwell like distant whispers.

She stared at the drawings on the wall for some time, just as Archie and Daisy had, thinking hard about what they'd been through and if these cave pictures had any bearing on their current circumstances. *Wasn't it a coincidence*, she thought, *that everything on the walls seemed to bear out what they'd been through?* But why them? In particular, why her?

She wondered about her best friend, Sue. Had she sent her to her death by telling her about the old rowing boat? What had she done? Suddenly she missed Sue like mad and her tears stained the dry stone floor. She would give anything for her to be here now; they always had a way of working things out.

She returned to the bottom of the stairwell, wiped her eyes and listened. *Daisy must be nearing the top by now*, she thought, and almost immediately she heard a croaky, eerie voice echoing down, which sounded nothing like her sister's voice.

*Time to push the stone.*

She ran her fingers through her hair, conscious that she was shaking almost uncontrollably. She inhaled deeply and tried to remember her relaxation classes. *Centre yourself, be calm,* she thought.

*Breathe.*

She moved out into the cave once more for a last look at the quiet, gentle pool and the curious murals and the extraordinary seal covering the entrance.

She stretched her legs and moved in front of the protruding knob of stone. A terrible nausea swept through her.

*OK. Here goes, time to do it.*

She put her hand on the stone and leant on it with all her weight, waiting for something to give, something to click – anything.

But however hard she pushed, nothing happened.

# 46 KEMP, IN CAIN

Trapped inside Cain's ashen body, the boy, Kemp, twisted in pain.

Why hadn't he died? He should have run off like his friend, Archie, rather than bend to the crackpot desires and charms of a deranged ghost. He would have been better off dead – rather than endure this ... this relentless torture.

Cain had wanted a body in which he might move and be free and Kemp had willingly given his.

*So,* Kemp thought bitterly, ***why didn't Cain damn well look after him?*** The ghost had no understanding of rest, or the needs of human beings, and now every action forced upon him was as if rods of red hot iron had permeated every nerve, muscle and sinew in his body.

Kemp remembered the moment in the alleyway when he knew that the words spoken by the ghost were neither in jest, nor madness.

The de Lowe children, Isabella, Daisy and Archie, the ghost said, were the Heirs of Eden and had to negotiate a prophecy that originated in the mists of time. He'd laughed at first, but then the storm began to crash about and bolts of lightning smashed onto the rooftops and splinters of tile and brick flew through the air like shrapnel and the deafening noise made every hair on his body stand to attention and he had never been so frightened.

Kemp felt a burst of heat on his leg. He moved and the pain faded.

How could those ridiculous de Lowe siblings save the world? I mean, they were crazy, nutty kids. Super-heroes ... them? Even now, the thought would have made him chuckle ... if only he wasn't so filled with pain.

A test of Mother Nature, the ghost had said. Madness the lot of it, but here he was, trapped inside the spirit of a ghost, his body reduced to ash. He'd witnessed the storm, seen the raging fury of the lightning and rain and, by all accounts, the de Lowes had made it alive to sundown, but only just – at least that's what he'd thought he heard Cain say. The muffled sounds of being stuck inside another body made it so difficult to hear.

If they survived, the ghost told them, the storm would cease. And when that actually happened, a flash of heat shot through him so powerfully that he swore he smelt his hair burning. They must have survived.

Kemp felt his fingers burning as though currents of molten wires extended to his fingertips. Why wouldn't the ghost leave him alone for just one minute? He tried to scream but Cain didn't hear him. He needed sleep, desperately, and food and water too. How long had it been? A day or two, three? It felt like a week – a month even. He yawned and felt his body moving off, his legs clumpy as if filled with wet sand. Every time he stopped a surge of intense heat smashed into him and he had no choice but to keep moving.

Kemp could see, though not well, and the sickly vapours of singed hair and fried flesh caught at the back of his throat. Every sound was muted, like being underwater. Soon his thoughts turned to death. If he refused to go on and died within Cain, then what? He'd be burned alive, probably. But would Cain remain trapped inside him until he decayed into dust or would Cain simply slip away like the spirit he was? Kemp groaned. Cain wouldn't die – he couldn't die – he was nothing more than a spirit who might leave him at any time.

But why had Cain tried to swap him for Archie towards the end of the storm? For a moment he'd been released – tossed out naked onto the rocks and deluged by the rain. He'd seen Archie, battered and smashed, his body covered in cuts and bruises, his head bloodied from a gaping wound, his body motionless, pale, deathly.

Tears came to him then, but they would not flow.

He thought instead of Archie's strange hair. Kemp managed a wry smile. He knew then that his friend was too far gone to make the choice of joining Cain willingly.

So did Cain.

He remembered how the storm had lashed him with such violence that he knew he didn't stand a chance, certainly not while naked, burnt and hungry. He had no choice but to give himself, freely, back to Cain. He regretted it. He should have refused then and there, died in the storm and let Cain drift off to be a ghost again.

Now, here he was, living in the darkness of the body where burns streaked him like a spray gun of hot oil. It was like being trapped in space, he thought, with no one there to hear him scream.

---

'LOOK AT US, BOY,' Cain whispered. 'Here ... look at me. Isn't it magnificent!'

Cain studied his body in a tall mirror ringed with dull gemstones. Morning light shone through a vast window. He stood alone. 'You're here, boy,' he said, as his voice echoed off the walls. 'Right here inside me – that's right; half ash, half man ... or boy ... only a fraction ghost.'

Cain examined his reflection. His borrowed eyes weren't anything like the proper article – his vision filtered by a grainy film – but what a sensation to see anything when, for thousands of years, he had tuned into the vibrations and presence of things using his highly developed other sense – his sixth sense.

He studied his hands and turned them over. Then back. He clapped, the noise a muted thud. Ash puffed up and floated quietly through the air.

*Oh, the joys of having a body*, he thought, *whatever form it took.*

Cain removed his overcoat, took off his hat and returned, naked, in front of the mirror. His figure was the same size of the boy and his torso was covered in layers of flaky ash in every conceivable hue of grey. *How utterly remarkable*, he thought, as he rotated from side to side.

His chest was a boyish replica of the one he remembered, though his pectorals and abdomen were not so hard and toned as perhaps they once were, and the sinews and muscles on his thighs, calves and buttocks were pleasingly accentuated by the light.

His feet, he noted, were unusually large. He sprang up on his toes only to find that a couple of digits simply dropped off. Cain stared, fascinated, as they instantly re-grew.

In the reflection of the mirror, Cain moved close. His face appeared sallow and partially skeletal, with a flaky grey chin that jutted out more than he cared. He nudged his thick plump lips, prodded his flat nose and admired his eyebrows. He touched his hair that sat in a matted mass of ash swept back off his forehead and he admired his eyes that sparkled like polished coals.

Then he noticed a strange cluster at the top of his legs. Wasn't this awfully important? As he reached for it, to his horror – and just as he remembered its original purpose – the appendage severed and slipped through his fingers to the ground. Cain squealed.

His concerns were short lived. Quickly it re-grew and he and his organ were re-acquainted. Cain's mood brightened. 'Thousands of years without one,' he roared, 'and the first one falls into a million pieces!'

Cain was a living body of ash – a by-product, he realised, of being burnt to death all those years ago. His eyes narrowed. How could he forget the burning, when his powers were taken away from him. The deal, he remembered. Oh yes, The Deal. Part of *his* Punishment.

Cain flexed up and down on his knees. He had movement – real gravity-based movement and physical presence. Utterly marvellous. None of this floating around nonsense any more, none of this walking through walls and doors and people – although it did, from time to time, have its advantages.

He wondered if the boy would interact with him and how their relationship would work in their combined state. Would the boy do as he commanded? Who controlled who? Who was master? Cain threw his arms up in the air and clapped his hands as a shower of ash fell over his head. So far, he had been in control, no doubt about it.

All of a sudden, a feeling of heaviness overcame him. Was the boy asleep again? Cain clenched his fist and found that when his concentration focused on that movement alone, the fingers pulled themselves together, like it or not.

Cain pressed one foot down, followed by the other. He felt a modicum of resistance, like a badly-fitting drawer that needed forcing. He willed his leg to move. 'Come on, boy – we need to be able to use these, and to good effect.' But the movement felt sluggish, sleepy. He pulled his leg back and thrust it forward in a loose kicking motion, ash spraying. 'Good lad!' he said. Now he flailed his arms, moving them faster and faster until the boy trapped inside him did exactly as he wished.

'We've places to go, my little friend, and there's not a moment to lose.' Cain said out loud. He couldn't tell if the boy inside him could hear, but a feeling told him that the boy wasn't entirely deaf. 'Do my bidding, little friend of Archie de Lowe,' he said, 'and everything will work out fine. Just fine. You never know, we may even get to like one another.'

Hard as he pushed and cajoled, the boy inside him soon slowed to a standstill. Maybe sleep was required. A couple of hours should do the trick and then he'd be off again; Cain has returned from the ashes, the rumours said. Cain the Cruel, Master of Havilah is back, the cry went round. He could almost taste their fear, smell it. The inhabitants of Havilah were terrified of his apparent re-existence, he'd been told.

Cain knew instinctively that he needed to make the most of his presence, his new form – and fast.

---

CAIN RAN through the sequence of events of the past few days. Archie de Lowe, that scrawny young boy, deceiving him before the storm broke. Running off, cheating death. How, in the name of Eden, had the boy and his sisters survived? Battered and broken, they made it to sundown by the very skin of their teeth and with no magic except for the special gifts they had been given by the dreamspinners. But they were children. *Children*, for goodness' sakes! How many human years? Fourteen for the eldest, twelve or thirteen, perhaps, for the other two, the twins?

*When men lived to be a thousand years*, he thought, *children of this age would be considered little more than babes*. Cain smirked. Maybe these days they simply grew up faster. But even so, it was hard to fathom. The whole area ravaged; destruction and death on a horrific scale, but these de Lowe children, the pathetic Heirs of Eden, survived. Were they possessed with luck, he wondered, or had he underestimated them? Maybe they had escaped because they were too small, too weak.

Cain enjoyed the thought but his mood turned darker, a rage building in him.

The boy shifted.

And how, he wondered, had the old man arrived? What did they call him now, Old Man Wood, or something preposterous like that? That bumptious, bungling old fool had dragged them into the safety of the cave where the water would mend them; of that he was certain. Cain gritted his ashen teeth, noting how they disintegrated and fell away, re-growing instantaneously. But did the children, these supposed Heirs of Eden, have the faintest idea what they were doing or what awaited them? Did they really understand?

Cain sighed. No, how could they? The riddles for the finding of Eden were designed for grown men, versed in magic, educated in battle, long in wisdom and the ways of nature.

He listened for the boy inside him and heard, faintly, snores coming from within. It had a strangely calming effect. Luck – that's what it was. Maybe they had been blessed with the vagaries of fortune. But fortune, he reminded himself, never hung around for too long.

And thinking of luck, what a huge slice that Asgard, the Dreamspinner, had found him. Dreamspinners, the most ancient and mysterious of creatures, who spun dreams to living things, but were hidden from all ... apart from him. Who would have thought he might travel through the blue electric middle of a dreamspinner – through its electric maghole – across the worlds?

Astonishing, really.

Cain watched as a section of his ashen finger fell and collapsed in a puff of ash on the floor. Big, ugly, spidery things, dreamspinners, like peculiar angels, or silky, spidery clouds with long, thin, opaque legs and cavernous, oval-shaped black eyes.

Cain allowed himself a wry smile. Asgard also knew the prophecy of Eden was not meant for children and, now that the dream powders in the Garden of Eden were finished, Asgard had the wisdom to understand that the only way to keep dream powders coming was to seek the help of Cain the Cruel, Master of Havilah.

Cain noticed, for the very first time, a gentle, rhythmical beat within his chest cavity.

*A heart.*

My goodness, he had a heart. He placed an ashen hand over it and pressed gently, feeling the steady rhythm of its beat. It reminded him of his mother, the Ancient Woman, stuck forever in the Atrium of the Garden of Eden. She would need protecting, but the Heirs would fail before it got to that point. In any case, Archie had sworn to protect the Ancient Woman.

He'd hold that boy to his promise over his dead body.

*So what next?* Cain thought. He removed his hand from his chest, shut his eyes and took a deep breath. What followed flooding? Cain smiled. Disease. Yes, of course. Disease came next. Now the memories flowed: the Heirs of Eden had seven earth days to find three tablets and understand the riddles they posed. Seven days to save the planet and the human race as they knew it. Actually, Cain calculated, if they escaped from the cave, it would be more like five and a half. Probably less.

Cain wondered what the ridiculous Heirs of Eden were doing. Still stuck, no doubt. Ha! The clues were painted on the walls of the cave, or so he'd been told. And it required great skills of observation, strength and speed to get out. Oh, happy, happy days, he mused. With any luck the little children would end up buried there with dear, forgetful Old Man Wood. Maybe he should pay them a visit and see how they were getting along.

Cain felt an arm stretch out wide. It was the boy in him, moving his limb without him. It felt quite marvellous, thrilling. He felt a long breath of air fill his new lungs as the spark of an idea gathered in his dark mind.

*If the disease starts where the storm began*, he thought, *then maybe he ought to make things a little more lively, speed things up, put the humans out of their misery a tad earlier.*

So ... what if he were to add some of the disease particles to human dreams?

He listened to the silence of the night air, thrilled with his idea. He'd work on it. If he was right, the children would be too busy trying to figure out what was going on to be in the least bit concerned.

And besides, by the time most of the world had received dreams from his dream powders made from the spider webs of Havilah, there wouldn't be a world worth saving.

Cain opened his eyes and stared through the large window, his mind buzzing with a sense of excitement he'd long forgotten.

And then the road would finally be clear, he mused. Yes, after the longest time imaginable, he would lay claim to the greatest prize of all: the Garden of Eden.

# 47 THE PROTRUDING STONE

At the top, Archie and Daisy listened, their ears straining, the silence unbearable. Archie nibbled his fingernails until he'd run through both hands. Occasionally he wondered if he'd heard a sound, like a click or thud, and he'd peer nervously down the stairwell.

Daisy shook her legs out, shut her eyes and imagined Isabella readying herself to push the stone lever, urging her to do it. She found that when she focused, she heard, quite clearly, Isabella's gasps and groans and mutterings, but the words bounced off the walls, reaching her ears as garbled sequences of noise.

The minutes passed. Daisy slumped down the wall. 'What if she can't do it?' she whispered.

Archie shrugged. 'What if she's not doing it right?'

'There's nothing to do wrong.'

'Maybe it's stuck – you know, jammed,' Archie said. 'It must be pretty old—'

'Nah. I reckon her brain's stopped ... or she's had a breakdown ...'

They leaned their heads back on the hard stone and closed their eyes.

'What do you think, Old Man Wood?' Archie asked.

The old man stared at the wall as though completely lost, miles away, and shook his head. 'Don't know, littlun,' he said, a worried look on his face. 'Think I might have to go and help her.' He picked himself up and stretched out his arms.

The twins shook their heads.

'Sorry, Old Man Wood,' Daisy said sweetly, 'but it's up to Isabella. There's no way you're going down there.'

And so they waited as a dreadful eerie stillness washed over the twins who sat, heads in hands, alert for any strange noise. But all they could hear was the quiet hush of the cave and the occasional drip-dripping where water had seeped in through the ages, making small pools and streams which disappeared through cracks in the rock.

Shortly, the twins heard a strange noise, a throaty, purring, rhythmic sound that reverberated around the cave.

Archie stood up smartly and swivelled his head, trying to pinpoint where it was coming from, but Daisy pulled at the threads of his loose, tattered shirt and pointed towards the old man who sat sleeping. The twins caught each other's eye and smiled. Snores. Great big ones like a throbbing motorbike engine.

Archie sat down and closed his eyes.

'It must be fifteen minutes,' Daisy said, nudging him. 'Do you think she's alright?'

'Yeah. I'm sure she's fine,' he lied.

Daisy stood up and walked over to the stairwell. 'She's down there all right – I can hear grunts and scrapes – as if she's moving a stone or a rock, or something.'

Archie joined her. 'I can't hear anything at all,' he said. 'Are you sure?'

'Yep. Quite sure,' Daisy replied. 'It's not right, Archie. Something's terribly wrong.'

---

ISABELLA STEPPED BACK into the cavern, took a lungful of air and tried to compose herself.

Why wouldn't the damn lever move? Perhaps she simply wasn't strong enough.

She'd spent every last morsel of energy pushing down until her arm and leg muscles cried out, but it hadn't worked. Why not?

Now she shuffled about, head down. 'Calm down, Isabella,' she said out loud, her voice mingling with the soft bubbling tones of the chamber. Isabella's hands were shaking badly, very badly.

She stretched her arms out, took a couple of long breaths and returned through the hidden door to the step. She stared at the two protruding rocks – the *supposed* levers.

What if it was stuck? Jammed in some way? She slammed her right foot down on it for the twentieth time, gritted her teeth and pushed as hard as she could. But still it would not yield.

She sat down on the stairs, exhausted. Should she ask the others? Daisy might be able to figure it out with her silly eyes or Archie with his supposed super-strength, but it would make her look such a total failure. She groaned. And then she'd get only endless taunts from the twins about how weedy and hopeless she'd been.

*There's no option*, she thought. *I've got to do it myself, use my brain and work it out logically*. She gathered her strength and approached the protruding stone from a fresh angle, positioning herself so that her foot lay directly in line with the angle of the stairs. It didn't work. In frustration she pulled and pushed and heaved again, each time getting more and more irate until a rage bubbled up inside her.

'Right, you evil, stubborn, stupid rock,' she said to the protruding knob. 'I know what you need: a bloody great whack.' She marched into the cave and looked around. On the floor lay a variety of good sized stones.

'If I use a heavy one,' she said, as she found a nearly square grey lump of rock, 'and drop it from height, the downward force will be tenfold what I can do with my body mass alone.' She smiled. *Triple that*, she thought, as she factored in the speed and mass.

And if that fails, then – and only then – will I let Archie or Daisy have a go.

With considerable effort she rolled the rock across the floor and squeezed it through the narrow entrance. So far, so good. On her knees, she manoeuvred it onto the first step and, wary that it might topple off, quickly heaved it up to the second step, followed by the third. On the fourth it wobbled and she caught it, pushing it back on the ledge. She took a couple of deep breaths.

Four more steps to go and, with the correct aim and allowance for the circular stairs, she'd roll it off and nail the knobby stone.

Her mood lifted.

At the sixth step, she wondered whether it would be enough. Quickly she did another mass and velocity sum in her head and tried to work out if there might be enough momentum and downward force to utterly pulverise it.

Probably not. She cursed.

Up to the seventh step. Now the eighth. She was hot and angry and so utterly fixated on completing her task that she had almost forgotten about her worries. She stretched out her back and flexed her fingers.

'Right. Here you go – you horrible little, annoying, stubborn, nasty knob of rock.' Her fingers slid underneath the overhanging stone.

'You're going to be smashed into tiny little bits!'

---

EVER SINCE SHE'D returned to the top, Daisy had been nagged by the thought that she may have misinterpreted the icon – the tiny, delicate picture on the wall. Perhaps the faint round markings above the image represented a touch by something like a pebble or a stone, and now that she thought hard about it, it made complete sense.

She swayed at the top of the stairs, wondering whether to run down and tell Isabella. She tapped Archie on the shoulder. 'Winkle, I think I know why Isabella's struggling.'

Archie groaned and opened his eyes.

'She needs to hit it with a pebble – a stone – something hard. I've figured it out. I've got to tell her – all it needs is a tap.'

Archie woke up. 'Whoa, Daisy! Hang on! What if she sets it off while you're halfway down and the walls start folding in?'

'Well so what? She's still got to run up.'

'But you've been up and down like a yo-yo and stretching your legs and stuff – they must be like jelly,' Archie said.

Daisy ruffled her hair. 'Tough. Sorry, Winkle, but she needs to know. Otherwise we're going to turn to dust.'

Archie had a bad feeling about it. 'OK, but promise you'll only go down far enough so that she can hear you. The last thing we need is for you two to get in each other's way.'

Daisy nodded, and for the fourth time headed down the two hundred and twenty-two steps, the noise of her feet scuffing the stones as she descended.

---

ISABELLA STARTED to lift the mini boulder, her back straining, her fingers raw, when a voice echoed off the walls.

Daisy. It had to be. Isabella stopped as she tried to comprehend the message. 'I'm – doing – it,' she yelled back.

Isabella suddenly found the rock unbelievably heavy and, much to her horror, the square lump slipped through her fingers and crashed first onto the step below and then the next, gaining momentum.

Isabella stared in disbelief, helpless to do anything. The stone spun, touched the corner of the next step and launched into the air. Isabella gasped. She hadn't figured that it would bounce! What if it missed?

It clipped the stair below and, as it passed by the protruding knob, a tiny stone fragment sliced off it before smacking into the wall and shattering over the floor.

Isabella groaned and put her head in her hands. 'After all that,' she cried, 'the rock missed.' She sank to the floor, defeated.

Idiot – what a fool. What would the others say ...

And then it happened.

Suddenly, everything shook.

Chunks of stone sprayed from the ceiling. Isabella wrapped her arms above her head, protecting herself, the shaking throwing her into the wall where she struggled to keep her footing.

Then a grinding noise: the gear mechanisms whirling, groaning and crunching all around her.

For a moment Isabella didn't understand. The next rumble threw her off her step and she crashed down to the foot of the stairwell. Had she engaged the lever or was it an earthquake? She poked her head into the chamber and gasped.

Water seeped through cracks in the film protecting the cave entrance. Her heart thumped wildly.

My God, she'd done it.

She needed to move, but another rumble sent her sprawling against the wall. More debris flew. She felt a crack on her head. Dazed, she stood up, disorientated, giddy. Isabella closed her eyes. Her head swam. She leant into the wall.

The water touching her ankle snapped her round. She opened her eyes and retched. It made her feel better instantly.

'RUN, RUN! WHAT'S WRONG WITH YOU?' she heard.

The water was up to her knees. Isabella swore and started up the stairs, one at a time, then two – onward, upwards.

Then a boom, like a giant wave crashing into the chamber, filled her with a dread she had never believed possible.

The panel.

Isabella ran, faster and faster.

The water gaining. The passage narrowing.

She focused hard and before she knew it her hands and feet sprang off each step like a great cat until she was bounding, round and round the stairwell, faster and faster, up and up, like a blur.

Nearly there, but now the walls on either side were so tight her sides were being scraped like cheese in a grater. A blast of wind caught her now, water rushing beside, overtaking her, carrying her to the peak.

She took a last gasp of air, stretched her arms in front of her and pointed her toes like a ballerina.

When she smashed into the ceiling, her hands padded her impact but she felt herself crumple in a heap.

Her arms ached. Water sprayed everywhere.

She landed on something soft.

Then a big black veil swept over her and she felt no more.

---

DAISY WAS a quarter of the way down when she heard the gears shift. Isabella had done it! But instead of rushing off she waited until she heard her sister's scream, for while the passageway was rumbling and shaking it was otherwise silent.

And it remained silent.

Something must have happened. She ran down as far as she dared and screamed.

Daisy knew what was coming, she could hear it.

She waited as long as possible then fled up the stairs, taking them two or three at a time, urging her exhausted body on, praying that Isabella was not far behind. She feared the worst.

Near the top she could hear a noise like a dam bursting, water flashing out, gaining, chasing her. She missed a narrowing step and fell, the hard stair-lip cracking her shin. She howled but limped upwards, the rock ripping, tearing her sides.

If this was what it was like at the top, Isabella had no chance.

A massive gust of air blasted up through the stairwell blowing her on. She knew it heralded the arrival of the water. When the water hit her she had only a few steps to go and, using its momentum, she flung her body out of its path and into the cave.

She stood up and gasped. Water poured from the ceiling, spraying the cavern like a fire-fighter's hose. Seconds later, she was flattened by an object that rebounded off the ceiling like a rubber ball.

Isabella's blood-soaked body.

# 48 SUE AND GUS AT SEA

Sue scanned the endless horizon and whistled. 'Sublime and ridiculous.'

'What do you mean?' Gus said as he wrestled with a penknife and the lid of a can of tuna.

'We survive a monsoon in a geriatric rowing boat – with a ridiculous name—'

'There's nothing wrong with calling a boat *The Joan Of,*' Gus said, smiling.

Sue raised her eyebrows. 'Anyway, thanks to your sublime woodworking skills we're still alive, but like fools we wake up in an ocean possibly miles from anywhere in another perilous situation. Therefore, ridiculous.'

Gus flashed a toothy smile and poured the brine off the tuna and into a cup. 'Well, if you hadn't fallen asleep at your post, none of this would have happened.'

'Gus, are you blaming me?'

'Of course,' he mocked. 'I entirely blame you. You should have woken me up rather than snuggle up.'

'But you looked so sweet.' Sue couldn't believe she'd said that and her face instantly turned bright red.

Gus didn't know if he should read anything into her comment. He'd never had a girlfriend – he'd never given girls any serious thought before, but here he was, nearly thirteen and mature for his age, and most of his friends had dallied in some form of relationship. He thought about his interaction with girls and found that although he was friendly with many, like Daisy 'delicious' de Lowe and Poppy in his class, Sue was the first girl he'd ever really properly talked to about stuff. Stuff like life and parents and feelings. Up till now, girls could have been aliens; they did different things – odd things – and even talked in a strange way.

Gus offered Sue first go at the brine liquid that lay on top of the chopped fish.

'Oh really, do we have to?'

'Yes. Everything that can be eaten must be eaten and that's an order. No wastage allowed.'

Sue rolled her eyes and pinched her nose, sipping the tangy bitter juice. It stuck to her gums.

She handed the rest over to Gus.

'You know, I've never had a proper boyfriend,' she said, moving next to him and leaning on his shoulder.

'And I've never had a girlfriend,' Gus said, cringing. He felt himself tense. God she smelt wonderful, like fresh fruit. And seated so close to one another there was no way of denying it; she was fabulous, even if her breath smelled a bit ... fishy.

He sipped on the brine and spluttered.

She stared into his eyes. Gus was the most amazing person she'd ever come across. He'd saved her life. Not only that but he'd kept her smiling and it had given her a whole new perspective on life. If they didn't make it, he'd smile right to the bitter end, she thought. Wasn't that amazing? For some reason, she'd felt safer just being with him than anyone else she could think of.

---

GUS STARED BACK into her eyes which shone like jewels. He took a sharp intake of breath. Oh my goodness. His heart raced, blood pumping fiercely through his veins. A strange kind of electrical current passed through him. What was going on?

She leaned in and kissed him – just a peck on his cheek and she held her mouth close. He felt her breath on his cheek. It felt so perfect, so timely. Gus felt his head swim, stood up and cracked his head on the wooden frame of the canopy above them.

'Blimey,' Sue said, chuckling. 'You've never kissed anyone before, have you?'

Gus rubbed his head. Now it was his turn to turn beetroot. 'Yeah, of course I have,' he lied, badly.

The corners of Sue's mouth turned up mischievously. 'Who?'

Gus couldn't think fast enough. His head was in a muddle. 'Oh God. Do you really have to know?'

'Yeah! Absolutely! Come on!'

Gus played for time and rubbed his head. 'Er, no ... I can't—'

'Go on!' Sue demanded. 'I insist!'

'OK. It was, er, Daisy,' he said, not knowing why he'd said it.

Sue reeled. 'Daisy de Lowe, Daisy Chubb or Daisy Martin,' she fired back.

'Oh, ah, um, the first one,' he mumbled.

'Well now, you're a sneaky devil, aren't you?' she said. He was lying through his teeth like most boys his age. 'Daisy de Lowe, huh?'

Gus reddened. 'Er, yeah. Didn't last for long,' Gus said, trying to sound casual while busying himself in the food box.

Sue frowned. Boys loved Daisy because she was beautiful and cool and sensational at football. But she was aloof, off in her own little world half the time. And anyway, she knew Isabella and the de Lowes better than she knew her own family and the whole thing seemed ... unlikely. She reckoned Gus might have had a crush on her.

'Now, Gus,' she said. 'Let's be honest, that wasn't a great start. We could give it another go if you'd like?'

Gus drooled. His speech deserted him. He nodded like a puppy dog.

Very gently they leaned in.

The moment their lips came together, Gus smiled and tried very hard not to snicker. He lurched forward and bashed his teeth on hers. There was a clank which sounded a great deal louder to both of them than it really was.

He pulled away. 'God, sorry. That was rubbish, wasn't it?'

Sue smiled. Before he could move again, she looked deeply into his eyes, put a finger over his lips and slowly replaced her fingers with her lips.

---

GUS WAS SO SHOCKED that it took him a while before he joined in. Was it revolting or nice? *It was most definitely slippery*, he thought, *and a bit fishy*. His tongue appeared to be battling a mini eel.

Either way, he couldn't decide, but all of a sudden a strange shot of energy passed straight through him, like a stab of electricity. An *electric eel*, he thought.

He broke it off – a smile on his face. 'Tuna?'

Sue looked confused. 'Tuna?'

'Er. Yup.' Gus couldn't think why he'd suddenly blurted it out. Maybe it was because he felt a bit out of control, getting aroused on a boat – or more likely because he'd just opened a tin of their prized food and he was famished. Kissing could wait.

He noted her disappointed face. 'Oh no. I ruined it, didn't I?'

'No,' she said, looking a little embarrassed. 'Well, yes, you did a bit.'

'Sorry. It's just ... you, er, surprised me and ... I'd just opened—'

'Don't say a word,' she said. 'I'm utterly starving. Let's eat.' She prodded him gently on the arm. 'Plenty of time later!'

Gus divided the tuna onto the two paint pot lids they used for plates and handed out two biscuits and half an apple. It wasn't really enough, but it was better than nothing. Gus realised that running out of food was a real possibility so he divided their foodstuff into meals that might stretch to two weeks. Realistically, he doubted they could hold out that long. If he could work out how to catch fish, it would, as their sports coach said, be a "game changer".

And so long as it continued raining and the three big water containers were topped up using his upside down umbrella water-catching device, they would survive. If it stopped raining for more than three days, then they were in trouble.

After chewing the food as best they could and swilling it down with a cup of water, Gus tried to not think about kissing and the quite extraordinary buzz that tingled all the way through him and set about thinking about how they could get *The Joan Of* back to land.

They talked as he went about his tasks, the first of which was trying to make a sail. Occasionally he would ask Sue to hold things or to pass him a nail or a piece of wood. Then he gave her a length of string and Sue threaded it down a section of the tarpaulin which he'd cut with his penknife and as she did this he wrapped it around a long length of wood which was to be the mast. When this was done, he wedged the upright tight between the seat and the prow of the rowing boat so that it stuck up in front of *The Joan Of*. For good measure, he nailed the timber into the prow and bound it with rope.

The course they sailed would be the direction the wind blew and he hoped like crazy they'd catch an easterly wind which would blow them back to the English coast.

Wherever they were going, perhaps now they would get there faster.

---

WHILE GUS MOVED up and down the tiny boat, making adjustments and checking his ropes and trying to get wind in his sail, Sue reached into the wooden box stowed under the main seat and fetched out a fishing line. She remembered a conversation between Archie and Kemp when they'd been discussing their fishing tackle. Something to do with sweet corn as bait and shiny objects that she thought looked like large earrings. Lures. She looked in their supplies. Three tins.

She checked the nylon line. It seemed fine, as far as she could tell. She found a rounded, double hook that looked like a tiny anchor which curved back on itself. Surrounding it were some faded feathers with a hint of sparkle. She opened the tin and popped two corns onto the spikes and a couple in her mouth with her fingers and savoured the sweet juice.

Carefully she removed one of her own earrings and, using the fishing line, tied it close to the hook below the feathers. Very slowly she let the line out, further and further until the lure disappeared behind a gentle roll of water.

Gus popped his head down. 'Everything OK? Mind if I squeeze past? I've just got to tension the mast and then we're done.'

Sue shuffled along as Gus stood up, threw the rope above the canopy to the other end and scuttled after it.

The moment he pulled the rope, the wind caught in the tarpaulin and the boat lurched forward.

'Wa-hey! It works,' he exclaimed. He reached down and squeezed her shoulder. 'We'll get somewhere in no time,' he joked.

'Or is that nowhere in some time?' she threw back at him.

Gus beamed. The sea was calm and the lapping of water as the waves bent around the bow of the boat was a truly positive sound.

He sat down next to her. 'Now, would it be alright if we go back to just before "tuna"?'

She giggled, turned to him and they kissed, briefly.

But now Sue broke away. A look of panic filled her face.

'What is it now?' Gus said.

'Fish!'

'What?' This time it was Gus' turn to be confused. 'Where?'

'FISH!' She pushed him away. Her arm was outstretched at a ninety degree angle.

Gus stared at her with a puzzled look on his face.

She stared back. 'Help me!'

'Uh?'

'Look.' She pointed to where her other arm pointed out to sea. 'I think I've got a fish!'

Gus suddenly understood. Gently he helped her wind in the nylon line around the plastic unit. His hands on hers, keeping a steady rhythm.

'Not too fast, but you've got to keep it moving.'

'I think it's a big one,' she said, turning pink.

Gus didn't notice. 'Let the line slack a bit and then pull it in again. Don't lose the tension!'

She did as he said and slowly started to bring it home.

'You can do it!' he said. 'Go on, land it yourself!'

Sue's arm was about to fall off and she shot him a look of panic. 'It's too heavy!'

Gus' hand came back on hers. 'OK. When you think you can, we'll pull it firmly in one fluid movement into the boat.'

The fish was close and angry. Sue could see it thrashing in the water. She wound the line twice round the plastic coil, stopped and turned to Gus.

His face was beaming. 'Keep going, it won't bite!'

Sue could see its dark silvery coils, its black eyes staring back at her. Two more twists. Her fingers hurt. She pulled gently, wondering if her muscles could take it. Gus, with his big hands on top of hers, steadied himself.

'One more and then up and into the boat,' he said. 'Ready?'

Together they heaved and the fish slipped out of the water and thudded into the boat.

The fish thrashed, its tail flapping and sliding and thudding against the wooden planks, until Gus grabbed a hammer and bashed it on the head. The fish stopped, its battle lost.

He beamed at Sue. 'You did it, Sue!' he cried. 'First go.'

He had no idea what kind of fish it was but it meant that, if they drifted out to sea, at least it would give them more time. They wouldn't starve. Brilliant, brilliant Sue.

'Sushi for tea?' he said.

'Yeah! I love sushi,' Sue replied, grinning from ear to ear.

# 49 THE BOULDER

Archie fell to the ground. Rock and stone dislodged from the ceiling and thudded down over the cavern floor. He rolled under an overhanging lip as the tremors shook. His heart pounded.

'Old Man Wood!' he screamed. The old man stood in the middle, covering his head. 'Move! Here!'

When the tremor ceased and the noise of the gears kicked in, he wondered what sort of hell the girls must be going through deep down in the depths of the cliff.

Another tremendous rumble forced his hands over his ears. The boulder at the front of the cave began to move. Slowly, incredibly, it rose up from out of the ground. Archie jumped out from under the ledge and thumped the air.

'Come on! Keep going, keep going!' he yelled.

But as quickly as his euphoria started, it ceased, for the boulder simply stopped. And there it sat, the same size, the same width, but with no part nestled under the ground. It was perched in the entrance.

Why didn't it roll away?

His attention was grabbed by a ghostly noise whistling up the stairs.

Hell, the girls.

He ran over. He could feel the wind, stronger now, as an awful, swirling noise grew louder and louder. Without warning, and just as Daisy threw herself out of the small hole, a huge jet of water smashed into the ceiling. Archie ducked as spray douched the cave.

In the following moments, all hell broke loose. Going at the speed of a cannonball, Isabella smashed into the ceiling and crash-landed directly on top of Daisy.

Both lay on the ground. Motionless.

Archie's heart nearly stopped. He ran to Isabella and found her smothered in gashes – some deep, dark red, others pink where skin had been peeled away by the rock. Blood ran through her hair and streamed across her face, her arms and her legs. Her body was limp, her arms shattered and bent over like towels over a washing line.

'QUICK!' he screamed at Old Man Wood. 'Quick! The girls – your potion.'

Together, they carried the girls to the far end of the cave, away from the spray, and laid them down on a stone slab.

Archie turned and swore. The cavern floor was already filling with water, the boulder acting like a seal, holding the water in.

---

OLD MAN WOOD'S face was as pale as milk as he nursed Isabella. Her clothes were shredded to bits, her arms dangling.

He moved both girls as high as he could and pulled out his little bottle of healing liquid which he placed to their lips. The Resplendix Mix would mend and make them stable. He didn't know how – but it would – so long as it opened.

Almost immediately, Daisy opened her eyes.

Now Isabella's turn. He pushed the bottle to her lips and she gasped as the first drop hit her tongue, coughed on the second and screamed as the third drop set to work.

Old Man Wood kissed her forehead. 'Be brave, young Bells,' he said soothingly. 'Healing, littlun, is a painful business.'

*And this*, he thought, as he studied her, *was going to hurt*.

---

ARCHIE WADED THROUGH THE WATER.

He had to move the boulder and fast. But how? He weighed it up and heard Isabella moan, then scream in agony. It spurred him on. He had to try – even if it was impossibly large. There was no other alternative.

If he could turn it a fraction, jog it a couple of millimetres, then at least some water would rush out.

He waded around to the side of the huge boulder, put his hands and chest in the water and tried to find a hand-hold. Too smooth. By the time he'd worked his way round to the other side, water lapped at his chest. He dived down and this time his fingers touched on a little ridge. Perfect. He stood up and took as big a breath as he could, sank down under the surface, bent his knees and, with every ounce of strength, he heaved. And he didn't stop lifting until every particle of oxygen in his frame departed.

Archie resurfaced, with only his head and shoulders above water. He gasped, drew in a huge lungful and went again. He found his hold and heaved once more.

He felt something shift. It definitely moved.

He kept it up until, once again, he had to surface for air. Archie stood on his tiptoes, gulping.

One more go. It had to be this time.

He ducked under. His fingers grasped the stone hold and he crouched low, bending back on his haunches. Gritting his teeth, he heaved.

Soon, Archie resurfaced, treading water. So, so close. Maybe he had time for one more try if he had enough strength left in his body. Treading water wasn't helping. Could he do one more? He swam up to the boulder and, as he looked up at the sphere, an idea struck him.

Why not shove it from the top? He'd have more of a hold. Perhaps he could rock it – create a gap for the water to wash out and away.

He swam to the side and climbed on top of the stone, so that while he pawed the ceiling with his hands, his feet gripped the crown of the boulder.

Archie sucked in a couple of huge mouthfuls of air, bent his knees and pressed.

Nothing. He felt hopeless.

At least Old Man Wood had clambered up onto the stone ledge with the girls. He had a couple more minutes.

Archie shut his eyes as an image of him trying to push a boulder came into his head. How could he possibly be expected to move a boulder?

He grinned and then chuckled as again he saw himself, in his mind's eye, doing something so dumb, so stupid, so ridiculously impossible, that it was hard to believe.

He chuckled louder, seeing himself – a boy on a boulder, trying to move it. Then he started roaring with laughter. He smacked and kicked the boulder in total hysterics.

'What a stupid, stupid fool you are, Archie de Lowe,' he sang, between howls of laughter.

As he did this, he reached the top of the boulder and, using the ceiling as a prop, he pushed and pulled in a rocking motion, singing and laughing like a maniac.

He was still laughing when he felt the extraordinary sensation of movement. Then a wobble, then a feeling of water flashing by.

Archie held on to the top of the cave like mad and only when he realised what was happening did he allow his grip to lessen.

'OH MY GOD! It's moving!' he screamed. 'HEEELP—!'

And in the nick of time, as the boulder started to rotate, he hurled himself off and landed in a pool of muddy water.

As the roar of water rushed by, he watched the huge boulder smash everything in its path as it thundered down the hillside, the cave water following closely behind.

# 50 MRS PYE'S STORM

A heavy drizzle from low grey, clouds in the failing light matched the de Lowe's sombre mood. Looking around, it was hard to imagine the place they knew so well could look so smashed, pulped to bits, beaten up. And it had all happened in a few wretched, brutal hours, almost exactly one day ago.

Boulders, rocks, sand, mud, trees, bushes and branches lay scattered and splintered randomly, with no care or enterprise. When they stumbled on a few paces and rounded a large, protruding section of rock, the valley opened up beneath them and, even in the dank gloom, they gasped. From their vantage point on top of the hill, the surroundings were significantly less mangled than in the valley where the water had obliterated everything in its path. Beneath them, a moving body of water stretched as far as the eye could see like a big, flat, silvery-grey monster. In the distance, where the tops of the gentle valleys of the Vale of York rolled, small hillocks had emerged like little islands, stretching out like the backs of crocodiles lying in a river.

When they turned towards the school, only the reflective grey of the water and the distinctive school tower and chapel roof reached up into the sky.

For several minutes the four of them stared, agog, at the extraordinary sight. This was destruction on a terrifying scale and, from where they stood, it seemed quite possible that only they had survived.

Archie looked on while holding Daisy's hand, who in turn held Old Man Wood's hand who carried Isabella over his shoulder.

A sudden emptiness and helplessness threatened to overcome them.

'It's so quiet,' Daisy whispered, 'so, sort of ... dead.' Her strange red eyes bulged, full of tears. 'Like we've discovered a different planet.'

'No birds, not a twitter,' Archie said. 'Everything churned up as though it's been in a gigantic mixer.' He felt sick.

Isabella woke, and moaned. The accelerated healing effect of the Resplendix Mix potion had knocked her out, and the pain had dropped off to mildly less excruciating. Already, astonishingly, the multiple scuffs and lacerations over her body were beginning to close. She too wanted a look.

Old Man Wood set her down, and for a while the four of them sat quietly on the fallen bough of an old oak and viewed the landscape, a gentle wind brushing their faces.

'I hope the house is still in one piece,' Daisy said at length. 'And Mrs Pye's not been flushed out.'

Old Man Wood groaned. 'Only one way to find out. Ready to go?'

Collectively, they turned away and limped slowly on, their feet squelching in the mud. Old Man Wood hoisted Isabella back over his shoulder and picked out a path, mindful of larger puddles and steep banks of slippery mud.

Before long they came over the brow of the hill and looked out over where the cottage should have been.

'It's gone,' Old Man Wood said, wiping away a tear.

'No it hasn't,' Daisy said. 'Don't be daft.'

'Daisy, it isn't there anymore,' Archie said.

'Trust me, please,' Daisy said. 'It is. You're all being very dramatic.'

And there, as they approached, perfectly camouflaged amongst the debris at the top of the hillside, sat their stone cottage, its roof covered by moss and lichen, blending in seamlessly with the greens and browns of the forest. An impressive oak tree now leaned into the courtyard in such a way that the crown of the tree enveloped the house, making the buildings all but indistinguishable from the carnage around.

Only Daisy, with her extraordinary eyesight, could see it.

For a while their thoughts were of the worst, but when Daisy spotted a thin plume of smoke curling out of the chimney they exchanged glances and smiles, their eyes sparking into life. They knew that Mrs Pye was safe and that comfort and food and warmth and sleep were not far away.

Never had the rough, misshapen, stone house in the middle of the forest on the edge of the Yorkshire moors been a more welcome sight.

---

MRS PYE WAS SITTING in the kitchen, fretting when she heard scuffling noises in the courtyard. *Must be my imagination playing tricks again*, she thought. The sound of a soccer ball being kicked over the paving slabs, a sound like sandpaper on wood, was a noise she associated with Daisy and Archie. That and shouts and laughter: happy sounds of the children.

She tried to put it out of her mind and concentrated on lighting the fire again.

Then her ears instinctively pricked up again, just as they had at every sound since she'd caught a glimpse of the old man leaving the house the day before wearing a builder's hard hat. What an astonishing rainstorm – blasting out of the sky hour after hour. She'd never seen or heard anything like it. And as the hours slipped by she didn't dare go to bed, just in case they returned. In any case, the lightning was simply terrifying. So she went round the house, cleaning and mopping up water and singing loudly. For in her heart she knew something terrible was happening.

An ache, like a stubborn splinter, pierced her and, for the first time in years, the long scar beneath the mop of bright orange hair on her forehead throbbed, giving her a pressing headache. She pined for the children. It was as though a cord had been severed between them, as though part of her soul had become detached. She tried to put these feelings behind her and soldier on. She had to. They would return, she was sure of it. What would she do if they didn't?

A staggering amount of water had poured down the various chimneys dotted around the house. Mrs Pye had waddled round as fast as her legs would carry her, placing buckets in every grate and under every chimney flue. She'd been entirely preoccupied with mopping water out of each fireplace, rolling up the hearth rugs and adjacent carpets and then emptying the buckets outside or down the sink. Round and round the house she went, from the children's bedroom in the attic to Old Man Wood's room to the parents' room, then downstairs to the kitchen and sitting room and the study, across the courtyard through sheets of rain to her apartment and then back again, and again. Each time drenched to the bone. She was thankful that the house sat at the top of a hill and had a big, oversized roof which made the water run away. Or else, she thought ... or else.

In Old Man Wood's room, near to where the water had spilled over from the fireplace, she noticed five rectangular rugs that sat on the floor, each the size of a hearth rug. She folded them up and took them to the back door to give them a bit of shake under the wide roof trusses. As she did, plumes of dust flew in every direction.

*How revolting*, she thought. *How vile*. She'd give the old man a good talking to when he returned – if he returned. They were caked, like knotted dreadlocks, their colour a blend of silvery-brown and dark green, and the patterns submerged beneath years of dirt. As the rain belted down upon them, a black sludge dribbled out, like slurry. Mrs Pye left the rugs in the deluge for a few moments and then decided to bring them in, draping them over a wooden clothes horse under the rickety old porch. *If she left them outside*, she thought, *Lord only knew where they might end up*.

Night fell and, to her great relief, the deluge subsided. She mopped the remaining water from the fireplaces and laid a fire in both the kitchen and the sitting room, which she lit. Covering herself in a blanket, and quite overwhelmed with tiredness and worry, she nodded off in the rocking chair in the kitchen, next to the warm metal range beneath the thick oak beams.

Hours later, she woke suddenly and for a moment wondered where she was. She yawned and for a second thought she could hear tiny, shrill voices. She looked around. No, there was nothing there. Just imaginary things, like the noise of a football being kicked in the courtyard.

The house was as black as night, so she opened a box of matches and struck one. The flame briefly shone, the bright light extending its reach into the large room before dying back. Mrs Pye felt a chill. The fire was on its last embers. She added a handful of kindling and placed two dry logs on top, stood up and stretched out, feeling the stabbing pain in her shoulder that had been with her all her life.

She took the candle and trundled to the door, made her way to the sitting room, added several logs into the large, ashen grate and sank down onto the sofa. She sighed. Where were they? What had become of them?

She played with various scenarios. Maybe they were at school and playing with their friends, Archie with his black hair and cheeky look, the freckles around his nose that made him look naughtier than he really was and his dark lively eyes. She'd get him a whole new uniform when their parents returned. She'd insist on it. No more patched-up clothes – he was too old for that.

Then she thought of Isabella. Isabella so upright and straightforward, so bright and busy. Her straight brown hair that fell over her face when she was embarrassed, just like her mother. Her straight pointy nose and thin lips. Her alertness and confidence. Oh, and her temper!

And then there was Daisy. Funny, pretty Daisy with her blonde wavy hair and red cheeks, her keen eyes and her warm smile. *Why, they all had warm smiles*, she thought. Nice teeth and warm smiles. Decent, well mannered kids, too. She let a tear roll down her cheek.

*Where were they?*

Had they been caught in the storm trying to head home? She shivered and pulled her woollen blanket tight. Wasn't there anything she could do?

Mrs Pye had no idea how long she'd been asleep, but she woke suddenly to find a dim light filtering in through the windows and the fire smouldering in front of her. She checked her watch and, with a groan, pulled herself up. The house was as quiet as she could remember and she wore her sense of loss like a ball and chain.

In the kitchen, she put the kettle on the stove and stared out of the windows as morning light rose over the Vale below her. She gasped. My goodness me, she thought. A lake – or was it sea that filled the valley below?

Nearer, trees lay prostrate in a wretched jumble. Her heart sank.

She hobbled about, wondering if she should go outside and call out for them. But what if they returned only to find an empty home? That wouldn't be right and, in any case, the old man would bring them back, wouldn't he? He had a knack of doing that. After all, he'd found her all those years ago, barely alive, so they said, deep in the forest at the bottom of a gorge. He'd carried her home, apparently – for many miles. He'd do the same with the children. She felt it in the marrow of her bones. There was something right about this feeling, something special about the old man that she couldn't quite lay a finger on.

If he couldn't do it, who else could?

She continued with her chores; she made bread and finished off the washing. She added more logs to the old iron stove to bring it up to heat, and then shuffled out of the back door where she moved the wooden clothes horse and gathered up the five rugs which, to her great surprise were, mildly damp and not at all saturated with water.

Strange little things, she thought. Like hearth rugs but lighter and, as she realised when she gripped the fabric, far stronger. She knew Old Man Wood didn't like her in his room, and duly stayed away, but why hadn't these been washed before? She had a good mind to either throw them in the rubbish bin or pop them in the washing machine. She tutted. Without any power they would have to wait. No, she'd let them finish drying and pop them back in Old Man Wood's room, dirty though they were, and give them a proper clean when the power came back on.

---

WITH HER JOBS done and the house as spick and span as she could remember, the sweet aroma of fresh bread filling the kitchen and the dry, though filthy, rugs replaced on the floor of Old Man Wood's room, Mrs Pye sat down in her rocking chair with a mug of hot water containing a sprig of mint. She swayed, backwards and forwards, for a minute or two, lost in her own world as she hummed Old Man Wood's peculiar song. Then her eyes began to close and she slept.

For some strange reason, she thought she heard Old Man Wood's deep tone.

Her eyes opened. She'd imagined it – must have – or she'd been dreaming. She closed her eyes, and as she did, she heard it again. But this time there was another voice, higher in pitch. She stood up straight away, conscious of the blood rushing into her heart. Could it be possible? Had he returned with the children?

By the time she reached the huge, studded door her pulse was racing. She withdrew the large, black iron bolt and yanked on the brass knob. The door yawned open. There, in front of her, stood the old man with the three children. One was draped over his shoulder, covered in blood and littered with an assortment of cuts and bruises. The others were hanging on to his coat, shivering, almost naked, their remaining clothes hanging off them, torn to shreds. One had strange spikes on his head and the other had hair matted to her face.

'It's a miracle, it's a damned, ruddy miracle,' she cried as she opened her arms, her voice cracking with emotion. Daisy and Archie folded into her large midriff, tears falling freely down their cheeks. 'Oh my poor, dear children,' she cried. 'You're safe. Safe now.'

Mrs Pye ushered them in and, while making a terrible fuss, sat them down in front of the fire and produced a basket crammed with soft, downy blankets and pillows. Shortly after that a saucepan full of thick, milky chocolate appeared. She returned with homemade flapjacks and sandwiches bulging with butter and raspberry jam. Archie and Daisy tucked in, but Isabella was too sick, too broken by the looks of things, to eat. Old Man Wood was seeing to her next door.

Mrs Pye talked and cried in equal measure as she went. 'Do you have any ideas what a terrible, terrible time I've had?' she said repeatedly. 'Do you have any ideas how it's been for me, huh? Watching the storm out there and worrying meself sick,' she complained. 'And do you have any ideas how difficult it is being alone in the house with no one here?' At this point, she turned on Old Man Wood. 'What were you playing at – leaving without telling?!' she shouted through to the next room. 'Left me on my own to worry – and worry I did, every minute of every night and every second of the day.'

And then she exploded into tears and told them all how much she loved them and how she would never let it happen again – over her dead body – and that she knew they'd be alright and she knew they'd come back.

Mrs Pye was normally a woman of few words so this tirade was borne out of complete and utter love, and the children knew it.

Archie and Daisy exchanged smiles as if to say, "If she really knew what had happened ... what then?"

# 51 SUE REMEMBERS HER PHONE

It was all very well catching the fish, but another matter altogether gutting it and cutting it up.

The meat came away from the bones with a lot of fiddling and a great deal of mess. Sue thought it might be a sea bass whereas Gus was convinced it was cod. It wasn't that delicious – too salty and slimy – and they joked that it would have been miles better deep fried in batter with chips, but it filled the cavernous hole in their hungry tummies. They washed it down with an additional ration of water using one of the empty baked bean tins as a cup.

As night began to fall, the rain beat a little heavier and it reminded Gus to set up his upside down umbrella rain catcher. He'd discovered Sue's umbrella on the bottom of the boat, opened it out and punctured two holes right in the centre where it met the stick. Then, he'd twisted the lid off the water container and aimed the upside down umbrella's spike at it and pushed it fully inside. Then he tied the handle to each side support. When this was secure, he laid the wooden planks down the middle of the boat and they clambered on top, the rain tapping gently on the canopy above.

Doing nothing on the boat was exhausting.

'Pity we haven't got a camera,' Sue said. 'This should be recorded for historical purposes.'

'The intrepid adventures of Gus and Sue,' he replied. 'Survivors of the Great Yorkshire Storm.'

Sue laughed, before sitting bolt upright, her head missing the cross-beam by millimetres. Then she slapped her hands together. 'Of course! I've been incredibly dumb – I do have a camera. On my phone.'

'You forgot you had a phone,' Gus said. 'How?'

'Well, I only use it in emergencies.' She shrugged and began rummaging in her coat pockets. She pulled it out, kissed it and held it in the air as if she'd won the World Cup.

'I'll call someone – let them know we're here, wherever here is,' she said.

She pressed the power button. The lights flashed and the start up mechanism buzzed into action. They stared at it for a while. 'Oh. No reception,' she said quietly, her mood deflating.

She groaned and lay back, the presence of the phone giving her a reality check. 'I wonder if Isabella made it back – they were still playing the football match when we went past with the shopping. They had a fight on the pitch, Archie slugging away – can you believe it?'

'Archie?'

'Yeah. And Isabella doing her mad referee-bashing thing.'

Gus laughed.

'Do you think they had time to get over the bridge and up the lane to their cottage?' For the first time, Sue's heart filled with a sense of loss. Before she knew it, tears were rolling down her cheeks. 'I'm sorry,' she cried, wiping them away. 'It's just bloody awful, isn't it?'

Gus put a reassuring arm around her. 'I don't know,' he said. He knew it would have been a tall order to survive. 'I'm sure loads of people are perfectly fine,' he lied. 'And more than likely Isabella's tucked up in bed with a hot chocolate having stories told to her by that nice old man who lives with them.'

Sue smiled. She knew he was being kind. As she searched the depths of her soul, it didn't feel as if she had lost her friend. 'Do you think anyone survived?'

'We'll only know if we get home, I suppose.' Then he had an idea. 'Sue can I have a look at your phone.' She handed it to him. He stared at the screen for a while. 'Actually,' he said, 'better if you do it.'

'Do what?'

'Find an app with a compass. So we can start figuring out which way we're going.'

Sue started going through the various menus. 'Here, is *this* what you're after?' She handed it back to him.

Gus stared at it as if it were gold. 'Brilliant!' His big smile radiated back at her. He twisted the phone in his hands and the compass point moved.

'What does it say?'

Gus beamed back. 'We're heading south.'

'Is that good or bad?'

He shrugged. 'I don't know. Good, I suppose – better than heading north. Ideally, we want to go west.'

'How do we do that?' Sue said.

Gus grinned. 'A rudder for steering would help and we need to change the position of the sail.' He shifted his position and untied the sail rope before moving it into a new position on the other side of the boat. *The Joan Of* altered course slightly.

'Turn your phone off for now. We may need it later.' He clapped his hands together. 'I'm going to make a rudder with one of the planks. Can you dig out the tools?'

While Sue rummaged around at the bottom of the boat placing the tools on the seat, Gus began mapping it out. 'I'll attach a small section of plank to a longer section of 2 by 4. Then at the bow I need to hook it over the end so it stays in place and then lever this side so that moves it one way or the other.'

Sue looked confused.

Gus smiled back. 'Just pass me things and tell me about that dream you had while I figure this out.'

As Gus set to work, Sue told him about her premonition. How she'd woken up and written down as much of her dream as possible and then studied it, altering it where she might have got it wrong. And although it made little sense, the nightmare scared her so much that she confided to Isabella. And then Isabella went berserk trying to prove it was actually going to happen. Which it did.

'And the thing is,' she said, 'Isabella had a dream about it too.' She strummed her fingers on the seat. 'Isn't that freaky?'

She paused as Gus bashed in a couple of nails and then continued.

'Most of this nightmare centred on the de Lowes and what really got me most was just how incredibly real the images appeared. It was like watching TV.'

'Give me an example,' Gus said.

'Where do I begin?' she said. 'OK, the coming of the storm, the lightning, oh, and here's one which I didn't think much of, but it felt important at the time, that they had to stay alive till sunset.'

Gus looked up. 'Well, the storm certainly happened,' he said. 'Did you tell them about the other bit?'

'About the sunset?'

'Yes. Pass me the saw.'

Sue reached into the box and handed it over. 'Yeah, but only right at the end before I ran off the pitch. I don't know why I put it off for so long. I wasn't sure I believed the nightmare would come true. It seemed too mad. And there was also another part ...'

'Go on,' Gus encouraged. 'I'm all ears.'

'They had to find some clues to find three tablets or something in that old house of theirs. It was about as much as I could remember at the time.'

Gus began sawing the plank, the noise drowning out the conversation. It gave Sue time to think. 'Thing is, by the time I told them, the de Lowes were either fighting, being kicked or being hauled off the pitch.'

She ducked as Gus turned the rudder around. 'What do you make of it – do you think I'm crazy?'

Gus picked up the rudder and studied his handiwork. 'Who knows, there might be something in it. I mean you were spectacularly right about the storm, and if you remember, when nightfall came, the deluge gave way to spitting. So if they did survive, then maybe what you saw really was a premonition of some kind. Spooky, huh?'

Sue looked at Gus quizzically. For a boy he was an amazingly good listener. But she needed to get one more thing off her chest. 'Thing is, Gus, why did I have a dream about another family? And why did it feel so heart wrenchingly real?'

Gus relaxed, put his tools down, and faced her. 'Maybe you're related to them,' he said.

Sue guffawed.

'No, listen,' Gus continued. 'Don't get me wrong, but you're incredibly similar to Isabella. You're the same height, you have the same hair. You both like the same stuff. You're as clever as each other and both of you are terrible at sport. You're just prettier.' The moment he said it, he blushed.

'Oh, that's so sweet, but I don't know about that,' she said, noting Gus' discomfort. 'She's way smarter than me with a vicious temper.'

Gus smiled broadly. Isabella's sharp tongue was legendary at Upsall school and he'd been on the receiving end a couple of times. 'So what?' he said. 'Twins aren't always exactly the same—'

'Twins?'

'Yes. Maybe you're Isabella's twin. You know, separated at birth. Stranger things have happened.'

Sue had heard this theory before. 'No, I don't believe that. Loads of people look the same and act the same.'

'No one looks like me,' Gus said.

'Well, you're one of a kind,' she said, punching him playfully.

He raised his bushy eyebrows. 'Why don't you text Bells and remind her of all those things you said? If we get in range and they're alive, you never know, it might help. There's nothing to lose apart from a bit of battery power. More than anything, she'll be overjoyed to hear from you.'

'For a boy,' Sue began, 'you're quite clever.' Sue ran her fingers over the keypad while she punched in the texts. 'Tell you what, I'll send three. The first to say that we're OK, the second with all the things I've told you, and a third to my dear old mum.'

# 52 ISABELLA HIDES AWAY

Where the previous day had stretched their bravery, strength and courage to the absolute limit, the following day, mental torture grabbed at each of them like a bloodsucking leech.

The world as they knew it had caved in. It was now a world where nothing made sense. The magnitude of their survival felt like a punch that simultaneously winded and broke their noses.

More so for Archie and Isabella.

Archie couldn't stop thinking of his visit from the ghost called Cain.

Every time he thought of the ghost, his heart raced because everything Cain had said had come true: the fact they were the "anointed ones" with special powers – as he'd seen in the cave paintings – the fact that the storm would break and target them – as it did – and the fact that he'd seen a picture on the cave wall of a woman. Was this woman Cain's mother whom he'd asked him to protect at all costs, or the hag from his dreams?

Anyway, who was Cain and how did he fit in? Archie couldn't figure if the ghost meant well or if his words fitted another agenda. He sensed that several parts of the puzzle were missing. Why did Cain really need him to protect the old woman? And how? I mean, she was a product of his imagination – his dreams – wasn't she?

And when he thought of the ghost, he worried about what had happened to his friend Kemp in the alleyway. Had Kemp joined with Cain and merged with him as Cain had demanded? Had Kemp been dazzled by Cain's promise of power and strength? *That was the problem with Kemp*, he thought, *he simply couldn't be trusted.*

Archie's hair was as tight as steel and he stroked his foremost spike, odd memories returning. What about the creature that hovered over Daisy? It had to be connected to her yelling, her crazed sleep-talking. He replayed the images of the white, spidery creature with the blue electric middle again and again until he felt a headache coming on. It must have been giving her a dream – or a nightmare.

He shut his eyes tight, trying to erase the memory, but it persisted like a stubborn head cold. Were dreams given? Was that possible?

Archie was so confused and exhausted that for a day he simply shut down and slept and mooched about the house, avoiding everyone. Although he was dying to tell Daisy about Cain, ever-present in the back of his mind was his promise to Cain that he wouldn't tell a soul.

Deep down, a persistent nag told him that Cain might resurface at any time and the idea of Cain visiting him made his stomach churn. And if he did say anything, Daisy would only tease him for "being silly" and Isabella would think he'd gone mad. So for the time being, at least, it wasn't worth mentioning.

Archie ran a hand over his head and shuddered. He didn't like his ridiculous new mace-like hairstyle – or wire-style – but it filled him with curiosity. When he relaxed, the fibres softened, but when threatened or angry, the follicles tightened hard like steel. They seemed to act like antennae for his mood, for his defence.

When this happened, he noted how a curious physical strength built up in him, combined with an awesome sense of power, of being indestructible.

And though he dared not admit it, this strange new feeling felt wonderfully good.

---

ISABELLA'S HANDS touched on the soft cotton bed sheet and she allowed herself a smile.

She couldn't remember much, just the terrible panic in the stairwell and then a pain in her arms. She clenched her fist, amazed to find there was feeling in her fingers, although a strange, painful, electrical current tingled through the palms of each hand and through each digit. Hadn't she smashed her wrists? Then it started coming back to her: the storm, the ordeal in the cave, waking up and looking over the broken Vale of York. The excruciating pain.

It made little sense.

Her mind clouded and a frown built on her forehead like ripples in sand. Hadn't they been stuck in the water? She opened her eyes and saw the familiar sight of her section of the attic room. Home! And what of their friends, what of Sue? With a cry, she sat up. Her body ached like mad and she examined her hands. A chill ran through her. *The holes*. The holes where the lightning bolt had smashed into her. She sank back into the soft pillows. She needed to sleep and think it through, work it out logically. Work it out like a scientist.

Perhaps then, it would go away.

She made her way over to the desk, and wrote in big, bold letters on a piece of A4 paper:

*'DO NOT DISTURB.*

*DO NOT TALK TO ME*

*DO NOT FEED ME.'*

She pinned the note to the outside of the closed, thick velvet curtain that set her area apart from the rest of the attic room and shuffled back into bed where she slept, sometimes deeply, mostly fitfully, until midday.

---

'COME ON, BELLS,' Daisy said, from the other side of the curtain, as she read Isabella's notice. 'You need food. Lunch is on the table.'

Isabella groaned. She didn't want to see anyone, and she certainly didn't want to talk to anyone. Couldn't Daisy read?

'You missed breakfast and you didn't eat anything last night. You've got to eat.'

Still no response.

Daisy persevered. 'You can't hide away in your bed all day.'

*I can*, Isabella thought. *And I will.*

Daisy opened the curtain and strode in.

'GO AWAY! Can't you read?'

Daisy ignored her and sat down on the side of her bed. 'How are your arms?'

Isabella rolled over so she faced away.

Daisy sighed. 'Look, Einstein, you can't stay here all day – you'll get bed bugs and—'

'Please, Daisy. Go away. Just leave me, please.'

But Daisy was in a stubborn mood and she was bored. 'Make me.'

Isabella pulled the duvet over her head.

Daisy smiled, stood up, fluffed up her blonde hair, puckered her lips and made her way to the mirror. She stared at her red eyes. 'Freaky, but kind of cool, huh? What do you think?'

Isabella groaned.

Daisy turned her attention to Isabella's neat bookshelves. 'Where's your Bible?'

'Please, Daisy—'

'Think I might do that homework – you know, the Creation story, the bit Solomon's been going on about.' Still no response. 'God, you and Archie are so boring, feeling all sorry for yourselves.' She flicked through a copy of Shakespeare's plays, read aloud two passages, folded it and tucked it under her jumper. 'Old Man Wood's disappeared again. Gone to check on his cattle – how about a game of something?' She sat down heavily on the bed and traced a finger up Isabella's body.

Isabella popped her head out. 'If I give you the Bible will you GO AWAY?'

Daisy cocked her head to one side. 'Might,' she said, pouting her lips. 'On one condition – that you come down later for tea. Mrs P's knocking up a stonking curry. Helped her put the ingredients in – eleven in all – and I slipped in an extra chilli. Gonna be a corker. *And*, Banoffee pie for pudding, which is your favourite.'

Isabella stirred.

'Anyway, Mrs P's been droning on and on about my eyes, it's sending me nuts. She's talked more in the last few hours than the last year put together. Hey, look at these.' Daisy popped on a pair of thin, metal-rimmed pink-tinted glasses. 'Lush, eh? Found them in Mum's drawer.'

Isabella's head popped out. She pointed at the bookcase. 'Second row. Says *Bible* on it,' she said, as her head flew back under the duvet.

Daisy stood up and traced her fingers along the spines of the books.

She pulled one out and sat down on the bed. 'So which bit is it? Genesis, creation or something—'

'For goodness' sakes,' Isabella cried. 'It's at the beginning of the whole thing,' she said. Did her sister have no concept of how insane the last forty-eight hours had been? Was she unaware of the scale of the disaster? 'GO AWAY!' she hissed.

Daisy stood up. 'Sure, you boring boffin. If you want to talk, chat about anything – I'm, you know, around. Not too busy today. Diary pretty much empty.'

Isabella cringed and realised Daisy was only trying to help. She popped her head out again. 'Look, I'm sorry, Daisy. I know you're trying to help ... it's just that I'm not ready.'

Daisy smiled. 'Yeah, cool,' she said as she turned to leave. 'You know, Bells, whatever happened, happened. We can't change it and we don't know what's coming. That's it really. Sometimes you just have to go with the flow.' Daisy opened the curtain. 'Laters, right?' she said as she drew it behind her.

Isabella gripped her duvet in her fist. Why couldn't she go with the flow like Daisy rather than be tormented by questions and riddles and trying to make sense of things that didn't make any sense? Go with the flow – if only it was that simple.

Isabella closed her eyes and thought of Sue, her best friend in the whole world.

Tears streamed down her cheeks. She had sent Sue to her death by slipping her a bit of paper with details of a rickety old boat in a rundown boathouse. A stupid little old boat no one had even looked at for years – what was she thinking? She pictured it in her mind. Sue alone, cold, wet, begging for help, drowning. She wouldn't have stood a chance, not three minutes against that storm – not a chance in hell.

Oh Lord, she'd only tried to help – if only she'd known, if only she could have done something else.

Isabella cried until her tears ran dry as she mourned for her friend.

---

THANKS to the strange sparkly potion called Resplendix Mix, which Old Man Wood had found in the cellars beneath Eden Cottage, Isabella's injuries had very nearly healed up. She hadn't known it but, when she exploded out of the stairwell and smashed into the ceiling of the cave, both her arms fractured under the pressure, though incredibly, her hands had perfectly cushioned her head and didn't bear a single scrape or a blemish aside from the existing holes in her palms. Her skull, shoulders, hips and arms bore scuffs and lacerations and a patch of hair had been removed by the rocks and her face looked as if someone had taken a cheese grater to it. But, overnight, her bones were as good as new and her scabs had all but disappeared.

Isabella, though thrilled to have mended in astonishingly quick time, was a little confused and concerned as to how Resplendix Mix worked, and what the likely long-term side-effects might be. In all the science and medical journals she'd ever read she had never heard of anything like it. Had the potion manipulated the cells in her body to recreate the bones and tissues? Was it a form of genetic science working at a hitherto unknown level, or was this a reversing potion of sorts?

But more importantly, what was Old Man Wood doing with it in the first place? Was Old Man Wood a scientist like her, or some sort of amazing chemist?

When they quizzed Old Man Wood about how it worked or what its properties were, he replied that he had no idea whatsoever, and this was the truth. And when asked where he had got it from, he took a deep breath and told them that it had been given to him a long, long time ago, most probably by an apothecary. And this was also true. But although Daisy accepted this as perfectly normal, Isabella's suspicions grew, namely because apothecaries didn't exist anymore. They were now called pharmacists or chemists.

Whatever their suspicions, the potion was like magic and, Old Man Wood told them, the faster an injury was acted upon, the quicker it healed. Hence, Isabella's arms had healed almost instantly in contrast to Archie's cuts on his legs when he crawled up the lane during the storm. The one negative effect was that, as it mended, the pain was excruciatingly hot.

Archie thought it was like pouring antiseptic on an open flesh wound and eating a hot chilli at the same time, multiplied by at least ten. So when Old Man Wood had held the bottle to Isabella's lips in the cave, she had blacked out as the Resplendix Mix went to work.

As they sat down at the kitchen table for Mrs Pye's curry, Isabella moved her arm back and forth, testing her limbs, and said, 'I have a question for you, Old Man Wood. Why isn't Resplendix Mix prescribed in hospitals or doctors' surgeries?'

Old Man Wood raised his head for a minute, shook it before gathering a forkful and cramming it in his mouth.

'I mean, look at me,' she continued, 'almost fully healed apart from these stupid holes. If it was readily available to everyone, what a huge burden it would take off the National Health Service. Think of the enormous benefits – benefits that could be used right now – out there,' she said, waving towards the window, 'and its properties could probably be transferred to other schools of medicine—'

Daisy groaned. 'I preferred you when you were asleep.'

Isabella shot her a look. 'No, seriously. No hospital waiting lists, no injuries that couldn't be dealt with. No nasty scars.' She nudged Old Man Wood. 'Do you know what's in it?'

Old Man Wood shook his head.

'I'll analyse it,' Isabella said. 'Then we can manufacture it here and sell it worldwide. We'll make a fortune.'

'I don't think Mum and Dad would be too happy with that,' Daisy said.

'But they're never around, so they wouldn't know.'

'They'll be back,' Mrs Pye said. 'And at least we know they must be safe and sound.'

'Yeah, but they don't know *we're* safe, do they?' Archie added.

Isabella ignored them. 'Well, I'll do it when I'm a little older, in America or somewhere like that,' she scoffed. 'There are tons of excellent commercial scientists over there who would bend over backwards for this kind of thing.'

'Bells, I'm not sure you've thought this through,' Archie said. 'If you did make this stuff, then in one go you're wiping out all the hospitals and doctors and nurses and physios and first aiders. I mean what would all those people do?'

'And they'd brand you as a witch,' Daisy said, mischievously. 'They'd burn you alive.'

Old Man Wood hummed. 'Thing is,' he said, 'I'm not sure it works with everyone. And I've a feeling that, in the wrong hands, it's downright lethal.'

'Ha! So you do know what it is,' Isabella said.

Old Man Wood furrowed his brow. 'Nope. Not really littlun. It's just a feeling.'

Mrs Pye beamed at him. 'Your Old Man Wood has a ton of remarkable strings to his arrows.'

Daisy coughed. 'Isn't it, strings to his bows?'

'Or arrows to a quiver?' Archie added.

Mrs Pye shot the twins a beady look. 'Bloomers. You two getting all clever on me? You know what I means. Now eat up.'

The children didn't know what to say to this, but the medicine was part of a broader subject that needed examining and it was proving extremely difficult to expand Old Man Wood's general lack of knowledge on these things.

# 53 ISABELLA DOES NOT BELIEVE

The children's sense of confusion centred around the dreams they'd been given, and now that silence filled the kitchen, aside from the clanging of cutlery and the odd loud slurp, Archie thought it might be a good time to revisit the topic.

'You know when we talked before about our dreams,' he began, 'when we figured out they'd been the same?' he searched around the table to see if anyone was listening. 'Well, do you think they might be coming true?' he paused. 'I mean, the flooding happened, and we all saw it coming, especially you, Bells, and don't get me wrong but there's no way we should have survived. It was only through our, you know, efforts and the other strange stuff that—'

Mrs Pye broke in. 'Well, now that you're on talking about dreams, that means bed, and I is pooped. So I leaves you and loves you to get some dreams in meself.'

Old Man Wood stretched his arms wide. 'And I'm going to sit next door – softer, there.'

The children thanked Mrs Pye for the delicious curry, hugged her goodnight and shut the door.

They sat down again.

'Good point, Arch,' Daisy said, leaning across the table. 'But I don't get what the old woman we dreamt about – the one you killed in my dream,

Archie – has got to do with it. Maybe we've got to protect her or something so that she won't be killed.' She flashed Archie a look. 'What do you think?'

He shrugged. 'Maybe you're right,' he said as his thoughts turned to his conversation with the ghost, Cain. Archie rubbed a hard spike on his head. He didn't know what to make of the woman either, but Cain wanted him to protect the Ancient Woman so perhaps that was what they had to do. The last thing he wanted was her death on his hands. 'What if there's a deeper meaning?' he added. 'Something else.'

'Cool, have you thought of anything?' Daisy said, wiping the side of her mouth.

Archie shook his head. 'Not really, Daise,' he said. 'But I was hoping we could talk about it—'

Isabella leaned back in her chair and flexed her hands. 'Come on, kids, this is ridiculous—'

Daisy put her hands up. 'Only thoughts, your brainy-ness—'

'I'm sorry, you guys,' Isabella sighed. 'Frankly, it's too much for me to get to grips with right now, so I'd rather we didn't talk about the old woman.'

Daisy shot her sister a look. 'Well actually, boffin-brains, I think we should. We're in this together and dreaming of the Ancient Woman is our only common denominator.'

'No. I'm sorry,' Isabella said, amazed that Daisy knew what a "denominator" was. 'It's not going to happen.' With a loud scraping sound, Isabella slid her chair back and stood up. 'You two – by all means discuss it to your heart's content and do whatever you feel you've got to do. Me? I can find better things to get on with, like study.' She grabbed her plate and made her way to the sink.

'Hang on!' Archie said. 'What about Sue—?'

'And the fact that I sent her to her death!' Isabella snapped.

'You don't know that—'

'There's no way she survived—'

'*We did—*'

'That was luck, Archie,' Isabella shot back. 'Pure luck. I can spell it for you if you want.'

'No, it wasn't—'

Isabella shook her head. 'I'm sorry, but I don't understand which bit of the last day you think wasn't.'

'That's ridiculous, you know what happened – you were there!' Archie said.

'Yes, of course I was. But there's no reasonable, logical explanation for it, is there? *No truth.*' She washed her dish, placed it in the rack to the side and dried her hands on a tea towel. 'To be honest, I'm not even sure it happened.'

'*What?*'

'It's an illusion, Archie,' she said staring at their shocked faces. 'Hasn't it crossed either of your tiny minds that what happened might not have *actually* happened? That it's entirely a figment of our imagination.'

'Rubbish—'

'Guys, seriously.' Isabella smiled. 'It might have been a drug – or the vapours from the storm glass I made that led us, unwittingly, to imagine it.'

Archie shook his head. He could feel his hair turning steely. 'OK. Let's talk about the storm glass, Bells. When it blew up, you thought it was important enough to go off to see the headmaster, didn't you? And blocking a lightning bolt and getting holes in your hands isn't simply a matter of luck. Look at my head and Daisy's eyes. I don't remember the cave being imaginary – do you, Daisy?'

Daisy shook her head. 'Nope. Nor the fact that the flooding stopped when Archie said it would.'

'Or a Jacuzzi that miraculously healed us—'

'And that I can hear lightning forming,' Daisy added, 'and see stuff you can't, and you can run up two hundred and twenty-two steps in the time it took me to go an eighth of the way. And, let's not forget, that you also repelled lightning.'

Isabella had been dreading this conversation. Her features darkened. 'These freaky things,' she said as she whirled her arms in their direction, 'can be explained by science. I'll grant you, there may be some scientific wonders we experienced that aren't known as yet, but it's only a matter of time. Very soon, everything that happened to us will be seen as perfectly normal.'

'Bullshit,' Daisy said. 'That's utter rubbish.'

'No, it isn't, Daisy. Your hearing of strange, acute things must be something to do with heightened vibrations in your ear drum. Your hair, Archie, or wire or whatever you want to call it, must be an amalgamation of the electrical particles and the chemical atoms of the leather or rubber of the football combined with the huge voltage of electricity that narrowly missed you, and my hands – well, that's simple. It must be related to the anti-lightning conductor I made with Sue in the lab shortly before the football game.' She smiled triumphantly at them. 'So no, it isn't some kind of hocus-pocus weird dream magic as you're suggesting.'

'But Bells,' Archie fumed, 'look outside at the wreckage. The whole country has been utterly mangled. You – YOU dreamt about it—'

'Listen, Archie. It was a once-in-a-lifetime storm. They happen. Globally, big floods really do occur. America, Pakistan, Australia, China; they have massive meteorological activity just like this. It's quite possible that we somehow sensed it in our dreams – and remember, twins, these are *only dreams*. DREAMS for goodness' sakes. And dreams tell you what you fear, so it was perfectly natural for me, as a scientist, to make the connection.' She smiled at their furious faces, but her eyes were hard. 'It's your subconscious playing games with you, mucking about inside your head, telling you things—'

'So how come,' Daisy butted in, 'we saw the same things—?'

Isabella sat down. Her eyes sparkled. 'Because people dream about the same things all the time. Dreams repeat themselves time and time again like ... like songs on the radio. Why do you think there are hundreds of books on dream interpretation?' she offered the question to the table. No one replied. 'It's because people have the same kind of dreams every single day, that's why.'

A silence descended. Isabella looked from one twin to the other.

'The trouble is, Bells,' Daisy said quietly, 'that no one knows what dreams are actually for – it's unclear what the purpose of dreaming really is.'

Isabella scoffed.

Daisy ignored her. 'Dream scientists who map our subconscious and study sleeping patterns and REM come to only broad conclusions because, hard as they try, they don't know why we dream.' She looked from one to the other. 'So it may be possible that ***our*** dreams have a purpose.' She slipped her pink glasses on and raised an eyebrow.

'Oh, how awfully clever, Daisy,' Isabella spat. 'Suddenly you're an authority, are you?'

Daisy stood up and fixed her with an icy stare. 'Yes. I looked it up on the INTERNET. Do your own research.'

The girls eyeballed each other across the table.

'In any case,' Daisy said running her hands through her hair and puffing her cheeks out, 'I simply can't understand that you have the inability to link the dreams we've had about a storm, finding stuff and the murder of an old woman, with the pictures in the cave which quite clearly showed the first part of that exact same sequence.'

Isabella chortled. 'You're talking about those cave paintings?'

'Yeah, Einstein. Of course I am,' Daisy said.

'OMG. How typical, how cute that you managed to find a story in them. I hardly looked at those stupid pictures—'

'They were NOT stupid—'

'Oh, how sweet of you to think they had *meaning*,' Isabella responded. 'Of course they were cave-man scribbles! How dumb can you get? You honestly think you can derive a story, a narrative, from them? They could be interpreted in any number of ways—'

'Really?' Daisy snapped. 'If you'd actually bothered to study them, you would have seen our dreams drawn out perfectly—'

'And,' Archie added, 'it showed us with our odd features—'

'And the Ancient Woman,' Daisy said.

'And the flood—'

'STOP IT!' Isabella screamed. 'STOP IT!' She hid her face behind her hands, her hair hanging like a veil over them. 'Stop going on at me,' she sobbed. 'Why are you two always having a go at me—'

'We're not—'

'Yes you are! Ganging up like ... like Ant and Dec.'

Archie and Daisy exchanged glances. 'Ant and Dec don't gang up on anyone.'

Isabella flapped her arms about. '... Thinking how funny you are all the time.' She wiped her nose with the back of her hand. 'Do you have any idea what it's like picking up the pieces after you two,' she raged, 'covering your backs?'

Isabella stood up, picked up her chair and threw it in the corner. 'None of this makes any bloody sense,' she yelled. She turned on Archie. 'God, look at you,' she seethed. 'You're a mess, and you,' she said, directing her ire at Daisy, 'are a stupid, idiotic tart. And you're thick. You're no better than that oaf, Kemp.'

She picked up a glass and, for a moment, Archie thought she was going to throw it at one of them. Instead, she slammed it down, turned, and stormed out of the room.

# 54 A PROBLEM OF DIET

Kemp detected another surge of Cain's energy tugging on his tendons and yanking at his muscles, threading into the fibres of his body. The heat radiated from the nerve endings of his fingers down to the tips of his toenails.

Kemp shrieked as it hit him harder, forcing him out of his slumber, heat blasting over him as if he'd been tossed into a bath full of scalding water, burning him.

Why wouldn't Cain let him be? Did he have any idea of the damage he was doing?

Today, after another short sleep, he woke up so weak that putting one leg ahead of the other was like wading through treacle. Tiny morsels of food and little or no water had passed into his stomach the entire time he'd been within Cain – nearly two days. It felt like a month. Kemp seriously doubted that the excuse for water really was water. It had the texture of slime and the smell of sulphur, like chemically manufactured eggy farts.

Every time he ate, and he tried everything, he spewed it back out.

Kemp stared at the breakfast – foodstuffs like nothing he'd ever seen before; slug-like creatures that wriggled, foul stinking jelly and cakes consisting of insects and flies; foods he did not recognise. Desperate for something, Kemp picked up a slippery purple ball. He could hardly bear to think about it. He shut his eyes and put it in his mouth. It tasted like tapioca with an outer shell as gritty as bark. His stomach heaved. He tried another – a thin hard-backed slice of cake with a soft gooey centre that smelt of oil. He put it towards his mouth. The odour was too awful. He shoved it in and chewed with his half teeth.

'... why ... eat ... slowly?' Kemp heard every second or third word, muffled, but he had no way of responding.

'Come ... much ... ... little time ... world ... ... genetically useless ... to sort ... hurry ...'

Was Cain talking to him again, urging him on?

Kemp chewed as best as he could. As he ground the cake between his teeth, a liquid suddenly burst out of the bark and flooded his mouth. He involuntarily vomited.

Kemp's swollen stomach gave a sharp pain, like the tip of a wooden stake jabbing his gut. His legs felt like lead weights. His head throbbed.

Kemp knew that his body was failing, as if his body wasn't even there. The pain of the burning seared him as if being sizzled in a frying pan and now his strength had gone, every last bit of it.

He stumbled and fell.

Then only blackness.

---

CAIN'S ashen exterior struck the floor and a large plume of ash soared into the air.

'What now?!' Cain screamed. 'There's something wrong, I cannot feel the boy,' he yelled. 'Schmerger, Schmerger – where are you?'

Cain's chief of staff arrived. 'You called, Master?'

'This damnable boy is not working,' Cain said from his position within the ashen body prostrate on the floor. 'Do you think he does it purposefully? Does he do it to spite me?'

Schmerger made his way over, grabbed what he hoped was an arm and manoeuvred the ashen bundle into a chair. Stepping back, the servant coughed and dusted himself down. 'I am unsure as to how you mean to continue your relations with the being.'

'What are you talking about, Schmerger?'

'It appears the boy may have requirements of which, Sire, we are unaware. Can you feel if the boy is alive within you or dead?'

'I am unsure,' Cain replied, checking his limbs.

Schmerger rubbed his long black beard. 'How does your relationship with the boy work?'

'Work?' Cain said.

'Sire, I need to understand how the boy operates. It has come to my attention that he has barely ingested any of the food I have laid out for him. Maybe these humans do not eat what we eat. Or it might be that he requires another source of energy? All living things must feed to create energy, Sire. Or they fail.'

In his excitement Cain hadn't stopped to think this through. 'Then we must find out – and soon – for having this being within me is an absolute wonder, Schmerger. You have no idea – I *must* make it work. I have no magic, not yet at least, for I do not have eyeballs, but at long last I can see and my presence is as real as any other being. Do you have any idea how invigorating it is after so long?'

Schmerger was astonished by recent events. Never in his wildest dreams had he imagined that Cain would in some way come alive. Now he sensed the power, the presence and the aura that once surrounded him. He understood the stories of Cain's imperious majesty and power.

Cain hadn't seen his palaces, his lands or the seas or the mountains for thousands of years. Even when he left the great palace for months at a time, roaming the lands of Havilah in his invisible form, he would return and continue searching for his branchwand. The branchwand which Cain believed might return a fragment of that old power.

Now that Cain had stumbled upon the boy, an energy and purpose had returned to his master that was both thrilling and awesome. And his futile, eternal search for his branchwand had been put on hold.

When Schmerger told his family of Cain's newfound body, they had told their friends who had told their friends and so on. Before long, the news spread across the planet of Havilah that Cain was back.

A sense grew that this strange ruler of theirs, dormant for so many thousands of years, might finally help them. Schmerger wondered if it was fate. The people on Havilah had been weakening for some time, rife with disease and illness, and it wasn't because of anything particularly different, more that their bodies hadn't been able to modify, to change or evolve, since Cain's disappearance.

Havilah, once the melting pot of all the worlds, a hubbub of liveliness, a place where vices were ignored and ruthlessness admired and riches abounded, now groaned in collective decay, a land slipping into waste.

'I've had the boy two days and now he is collapsing. What is wrong?' Cain asked. 'Why is Havilah failing? Why do the people here wallow in pity, why is there no life, no zest?'

Schmerger wondered if, like all the inhabitants of Havilah, this boy from Earth bore their sickness. He moved closer, inspecting the pile of ash. 'My Lord, this is a most unusual situation—'

'Of course it is, you fool,' Cain snapped. 'And I employ you to look after my unusual situations. How can I restore Havilah if the boy is faulty?'

Schmerger knew to tread carefully. 'The boy is made of flesh and blood? A human—'

'Of course.'

*'Then perhaps he requires a diet to fit mankind?'*

Cain was amazed he hadn't thought of this before. 'Of course! You're right. Just because I have no need of sustenance ... what is the diet of man, Schmerger?'

'Our insect and fungus diet is not suitable, that is plain to see.'

'Obviously, you idiot. The boy needs earthly foods – where are they? He needs them NOW.'

Cain detected a faint glow of the body he had taken over. 'It is weak,' Cain said quietly as a terrible feeling washed over him. 'If the boy fails ...'

'Surely you can remove yourself?' Schmerger asked.

'Indeed I can – and go back to how I was. But it is not good enough. No! I need a body that will *willingly* be a part of me. Understand this, Schmerger. It may not happen again. If I were to release the boy and he recovers, would he give himself to me again freely?'

Cain realised he had been reckless. He needed to act quickly.

Schmerger looked on anxiously. 'Is there anyone we can contact as to the boy's health?'

Cain thought for a minute. 'Are any types of humans actually living here in Havilah?'

'There are some in the caves, but they are the old type,' Schmerger replied. 'Ancestors of the early people. They are troublesome and barbaric – they would not help.'

Cain groaned. 'Who else?'

'Perhaps you could return him to Earth, Sire, in the manner by which you arrived, through ... a creature?'

'Alas, servant,' Cain said, 'Asgard the dreamspinner is reluctant for me to use his maghole as transportation until our plan is complete.'

Schmerger stroked his long black beard, contemplating the situation. Suddenly a light sparkled in his eyes. 'As a spirit, Sire, a ghost, you are part of another world. You might summon a human spirit to advise you—'

'Yes,' Cain said, as the idea sunk in. 'Brilliant, Schmerger. Of course. But who?'

'A spirit connected with him, one of his ancestors. Humans die so young there must be many.'

Cain sat and thought. 'You're right, humans have a bond like no other. I will call for them, Schmerger. You may live another day but be warned, you should not be here when they arrive.'

Every day since he'd returned, Cain had threatened to kill him, part of the job, he suspected, but Schmerger partially heeded his master's advice, turned and walked to the door where he waited. If it got bad, he would leave.

The room fell into silence. Cain began chanting, his voice calling out into the universe.

> 'Spirits awaken, spirits come near.
> Spirits come close you have nothing to fear.
> I call to those who connect with this boy.'

He stopped and waited.

> 'O spirits from the reaches of time and of space,
> Come hither to connect with me here in this place.'

Schmerger trembled as he felt a wind envelop him. He hated it when Cain joined his ghostly companions. He looked about, but there was nothing to see. But Cain looked upon a host of Kemp's family whooshing in and around the building.

'Spirits of this boy,' Cain called out, 'I call upon you as a spirit myself. I cannot ascend into the sky or feel the land but I will always live. This child of man, your relative on Earth, willingly joined with me and in return I have saved him from the great tempest on that planet.'

Cain looked up at the spirits who floated round him. *What an ugly bunch*, Cain thought, *with matted hair, thrusting chins and thick red lips sweeping around the room.*

'The boy is failing fast. I have fed and watered him, but I did not understand his needs,' he called out. 'The child requires your help. I call on the newest of you to reveal yourselves now.'

In an instant, a silvery, opaque-looking man appeared, kneeling in front of them.

Cain noted the spirit's sadness – his youthful, bent head, his mournful face. 'Thank you. And you are ...'

'I am the spirit of the boy's father,' he said, his voice deep and blowy like the wind.

*The boy must have lost his father young,* Cain thought. 'There is no more ideal person, other than a mother.'

'Indeed,' said the ghost. 'His mother lives, though she knows not of her child. I was taken when our son was an infant. We were together in an accident ...' the voice tapered off.

Cain suddenly realised that this information answered the question the boy had posed when he'd told him he had to save his mother – *because he'd never known his own mother*.

In the next second, Kemp's father reached into the ashen body, his body following.

Shortly, he flew out and settled over it. 'What have you done to him?' he roared. 'He is a child. His body is poisoned and burned almost to death. It is fortunate he is strong.'

Cain kept calm. 'Be assured, I did not mean to harm him. The boy means more to me than you know.'

The ghost snivelled. 'If this is true, you have only one option. Return him to Earth where they can nurse and nourish him. Can you do this?'

'I will try,' Cain said.

'There is little time,' the ghost said. 'The alternative is that he comes with us.'

'Should he go to his mother's side?'

The ghost shot into the air and swirled around before floating down.

'No. She may reject him. She does not recall ever having a son. Her mind was damaged in the car crash. And he is too sick.'

'Then where shall I leave him?'

'Somewhere he will be found and helped.'

'And there is no one else?' Cain asked.

Kemp's father swayed one way and then the other, like a flag being waved, testing the vibrations. 'His friends will have the answers,' Kemp's father said as he drifted away as though on a breeze. 'His friends,' he repeated as he spiralled higher and higher and eventually away through the ceiling.

Cain watched him go. Spirits were a curious lot, but they did generally have their bloodline's best interests at the top of their limited agenda.

Cain mulled over the ghost's words. Was he referring to that confounded Archie de Lowe as the boy's best friend? Cain could hardly bear to think about the de Lowes. He'd come so close to having Archie, with his power, within his grasp. The Heirs of Eden, children, surviving the great storm by the skin of their teeth. It was preposterous. But Cain knew that the prophecy demanded a great deal more; finding the three Tablets of Eden was an altogether different matter.

---

'DREAMSPINNER, DREAMSPINNER, DREAMSPINNER.' Cain shouted.

A second later and Asgard the dreamspinner appeared, long, slender slivers of legs dancing by his silvery, opaque body and the blue maghole of lightning burning in his middle in place of an abdomen.

'Ah-ha, my ugly friend,' Cain began. 'It appears I am within the dying body of a boy.'

Asgard walked on his eight legs across the air as if treading on an invisible grid. 'Then you must return him.'

'Yes,' Cain said, 'but how can our plan work if there is no flesh on me?'

Asgard dipped a couple of claws into his electric-blue, burning maghole as if thinking. 'The boy may recover and come back to you if he has access to the one thing he desires most in the world.'

'And, pray tell,' Cain replied, intrigued, 'what is that?'

'It is for you to puzzle,' Asgard said. 'There is no time to lose. When the boy lands on Earth, you must return immediately. I am unable to transport at will any more. There are problems—'

'What kind of problems?'

'The boy burns me. I cannot be sure of survival.'

Cain's good mood evaporated. 'Then find me spiders who will sacrifice themselves for the cause,' he demanded.

Asgard stared at Cain. He did not like taking orders, especially from a spirit. Maybe he had to get used to it. 'The consequences are difficult for dreamspinners. We are not familiar with other species, other worlds—'

'If you are unable to transport me, Asgard,' Cain snapped, 'find others who will. If you want the Garden of Eden to open, if you want to keep making your dreams, I suggest you give me your wholehearted support. Use another.'

The ultimate sacrifice – death? This shocking idea had not even entered the mind of the dreamspinner. Asgard knew dreamspinners would have to change, but he didn't realise how drastically. He recognised that the dreamspinners, the oldest curators of life, the givers of dreams, faced a stark choice: back the three children or line up behind Cain.

Asgard had been there when the children were given the Tripodean dream – the prophecy of Eden. But he knew the prophecy had been designed for the best of mankind, men who were strong, clever, and wise in magic and nature. This prophecy heralded a new era for mankind and, as Asgard realised, for dreamspinners too.

Without dream powders of inspiration from the Garden of Eden, was there any point in being a dreamspinner? Asgard had seen it many times; species who failed to contribute to the fabric of life very quickly ended up extinct.

Havilah was now the only place that offered spider web powders of any note. Even if these spider web powders could only be spun into dark dreams, or nightmares, they were just as powerful as dreams from the Garden of Eden – depending on how they were interpreted. And although these dreams were not as fun to deliver, at least dreamspinners would continue to exist.

'Perhaps,' Asgard signed with his long, slender, opaque claws. 'Perhaps it can be done, for the greater cause.'

'Indeed,' Cain crowed. 'If you are to change, dreamspinner, then you must accept choices you do not like.'

Asgard knew it was so, but right now he needed to get them back to Earth. 'Master. Awaken the boy. There is one last thing to do. Dive through me once again. This time, save your strength, for you shall bear the boy's weight and steer him through my maghole.'

Cain softly reached inside and, for the very first time, did not force the boy awake. He talked to him gently, as if to a child, and a glow – which wasn't particularly nice, nor unpleasant, just unusual – ran through him. He had to work with the boy, not force him, he reminded himself. Cain's thoughts turned to the puzzle Asgard had given him: what would make this human come back to him? What was the one thing the boy desired most?

Cain thought of the conversation with the spirit. His mother is alive, and the boy doesn't know it. The father who died in a car crash when he was an infant with his wife by his side. All this time, and the mother survived!

Yes, it made perfect sense, and Cain chuckled. It is the answer. I will search her out and when the boy is fit and strong he will come back to me, because I will give him his mother. And he will come willingly and I will look after him.

Cain's plan was building in his mind and already it pleased him greatly.

The boy woke and started to move as Cain gently coaxed him on. 'Together, little Earth being, we will start afresh. Together we will rule the universe.'

'Where shall I take him?' Asgard asked.

'Back to where he came from, dreamspinner. To a place they cannot fail to find him.'

'Then let us go with haste. I am ready.'

With the boy stirring, Cain summoned every ounce of his ghostly strength and threw himself and Kemp through the dreamspinner's middle.

# 55 DAISY TRIES TO WORK IT OUT

Daisy picked up the chair and pushed it under the thick, wooden table top. 'That is one seriously confused chick,' she said, 'with a terrible, terrible temper.'

Archie looked pained. 'You think Isabella's wrong?'

'Doh, yeah. Of course she is, Arch!' Daisy replied. 'Come on, no one in the world has hair like yours or eyes like mine, or holes through their hands, for that matter.'

'True. Cool glasses by the way – they suit you.'

Daisy grinned. 'Bells has only to look at her hands to realise something odd is happening. It's just too freaky for her.'

Archie grinned. 'So what next?'

'Well, for starters,' she said smiling at him, 'you need to start wearing a hat.'

'Ha, ha!' He replied. 'No way!'

Daisy pulled a black hat out of her pocket and threw it at him. 'Try this – one of Dad's. Found it while rummaging around upstairs.'

'Have you been through their entire wardrobe?'

'Yeah, pretty much. Go on, try it.'

'No way!'

'Way! Pleeease!'

Archie put it on and Daisy clapped her hands. 'Fan-tastic!'

'I can't go round with a black beanie on my head.'

'But it's cool.'

Archie took it off and examined it. 'You sure this is OK?'

'Winkle, it's got *you* written all over it.'

'Don't call me Winkle.'

Daisy laughed. 'Look, seriously,' she said, 'if we really think that our dreams actually mean something, we're just going to have to figure out the next part.'

Archie sighed. 'Great. Now *I* feel confused.'

'Well, let's start with those "cave-man" paintings on the wall,' she said. 'Did you study them?'

'They were just odd,' Archie said.

'No, they weren't. They were all about finding some tablets or books or pieces of rock. I've been searching already.'

'Found anything?'

'Nope. Just these glasses, your hat, and these cool, fingerless, studded leather gloves for Bells. What do you think?'

Archie couldn't believe it. 'They're so not her.'

She laughed. 'You think? Me too, but they might toughen her up a bit, make her look a little less like a nerd.'

Archie couldn't help himself and laughed. 'But I still don't get it,' he said.

Daisy put an arm round him. 'Don't worry, Winkle. Trust me, it's a piece of cake. All we've got to do is get to the next stage.'

'Next stage?' Archie queried. Daisy's confidence was staggering.

'Yeah,' Daisy said slapping him on his back. 'Not sure how we do it, but don't worry, we'll figure it out. Somehow.'

---

'WHAT DO YOU THINK, Old Man Wood?' Daisy said as they entered the living room.

The old man was looking particularly pale and the lines on his face were deeper and more ingrained than usual. He simply continued to stare straight ahead at the wall. No words came out of his mouth.

'Woo-hoo. Anyone there?' she said, waving a hand in front of his face. 'Anyone home?' Old Man Wood blinked and rubbed his face.

Daisy shook her head, her hair bouncing in the firelight. 'A right load of zombies in tonight,' she said as she threw herself on the sofa. She opened the Bible, flicked through to the first pages and started to read.

Archie looked at her with his mouth open. 'You alright, Daise?'

'What do you mean?'

'Archie raised his dark eyebrows. 'Reading ... *the Bible?*'

Daisy shrugged. 'Why not?'

'For starters, I didn't know you could read.'

'Ha-ha, hilarious aren't you? It's the Genesis story Headmaster Solomon's been banging on about – might as well get it over and done with,' she said. 'And anyway, in the cave you said we may have saved the world from forty days and forty nights of rain, right? Well then, in that case, the Bible's probably a pretty good place to start.' She turned the page, 'I've got a hunch, Winkle. There's something in here. Something we're missing.'

Archie looked baffled. 'Missing?'

'Yup,' Daisy replied. 'And when things are missing, you need to look for them. Got to start somewhere.'

Archie slouched down by the fire. 'But what makes you think it's got anything to do with the Creation story?'

'As I said, it's a hunch, but there is an awfully well-known flood-event in the Bible and the Koran and other religious tomes,' Daisy said, mimicking Isabella's intellectual voice. 'You know, Noah, animals in two by two, and all that jazz. When I think of those cave paintings I reckon we've hooked into a very old and very bonkers adventure that goes way back.'

Archie pulled a face. 'You really think so?'

'Yup,' Daisy said. 'Dunno why it's us, though. Beats me.' Her eyes sparkled. She rather enjoyed Archie looking confused. 'There's definitely a link between our dreams, the storm and the pictures in the cave; the images on the walls clearly showed we had to find stone tablets or books, or something.'

'And what if we don't find these tablets?' Archie said as he threw another log on the fire and dropped into an armchair.

Daisy scratched her nose, rubbed her eyes and ran a hand through her wavy blonde locks. 'Well that was the weird bit. It showed that if we didn't find the tablets we'd die—'

'As in the pictures below the images of the rain—'

'Precisely.'

A shadow crossed his face. 'So how do you think we're going to die? From plague, or with giant hail stones beating us to death?'

Daisy stretched her arms out. 'No idea,' she said. 'I couldn't make out what it was. But we definitely die—'

'Great—'

'...Unless, of course, we find these tablety things,' Daisy added. 'Don't worry, Winkle, it'll be just fine.'

'Oh, why should we worry, Daisy,' Archie said crossly. 'when we're only going to die?! I mean is there anything else you'd like to share?'

'Come on. It's not that bad.'

'Yes it is! It's called *death*. The end of this thing we do called *living*. And stop calling me Winkle. You're just as bad as Kemp!'

Daisy pouted and returned to her reading.

Archie studied her. 'You actually think we're going to survive, don't you?'

'Yep.'

'How come?'

'Because, Winkle,' she said, completely ignoring his name request, 'we beat the storm and it can't get any harder than that, can it? I also know that I very nearly died – and that you two got a zapping from lightning bolts, hence your hair and Bells' hands. But I didn't die, thanks to you two. And I'm convinced that if we do this together, we're much stronger because, if any of us fail, we're screwed. After all, that's what the pictures showed.'

'But Bells doesn't want to know. She's given up.'

Daisy closed the book and shrugged. 'Then we're dead already.'

Archie leaned forward in his chair, his chin resting in his hands. 'You think she'll come round?'

'Sure. She's having a wobble, that's all.'

Archie shook his head. Daisy didn't sound in the least bit worried. 'Aren't you terrified?'

'Nah,' she replied, momentarily opening the book. 'What's the point? Go with the flow, Winkle. Go with the flow.' Daisy nodded at her words of deep wisdom and returned to her reading.

Archie looked dumbfounded. 'Any idea how long we've got?'

Daisy lifted her head out of the page. 'What, before we die? Nah. No idea.'

'In that case,' Archie said, 'I'm going to write a last letter to Mum and Dad.'

'You do that,' mumbled Daisy, who was now concentrating hard.

When Archie returned several minutes later with a pen and a pad of paper, Daisy was busy writing.

'What are you doing now?'

'Just had an outstandingly groovy thought,' she replied.

'Well, what is it?'

'I can't tell you till I'm certain ...'

Archie scowled and began his letter, glancing up to study his pretty sister who was immersed in the Creation story and intermittently scribbling. He'd never seen her like this and wondered for a minute if this was the same Daisy he'd grown up with.

He couldn't bear it. 'Come on, Daise. Tell me, please?'

Daisy held the palm of her hand up in the air towards him and continued writing. Every so often she turned the pages forward and then flicked a few back before returning to her notes.

'Well,' she said at long last. 'You asked me how long we had, so I had an idea. In here there are loads of references to the creation of the world so I thought I'd count the numbers.'

'All I meant,' Archie said, 'was that supposing this is real—'

Daisy shot him a look. 'Winkle, it is real. You're going to have to wise up about this. Furthermore, I'm sure the cave pictures are related to something in the Bible, and my hunch is that the creation story is somehow linked to all of it. It's like the whole story is a massive clue. But in a weird way.'

'How?'

'How should I know?! It's a hunch, right.'

'Oh,' said Archie. He was beginning to wonder which of his sisters was more insane.

'So let's say,' Daisy began, 'that the storm represents a new beginning aimed at wipe out the world for some reason. In here, it says that the Creation took six days plus a day of rest. That's seven days, OK. And there are more references to seven. Seven this, seven that—'

'Seven deadly sins,' Archie offered.

Daisy looked muddled. 'I'm not sure that's got anything to do with it, Arch.' She'd lost her train of thought. 'The thing is Archie, bottom line, I'm pretty sure we have seven days to sort this out.'

---

ISABELLA LAY on her bed and stared at her cream-coloured book shelves crammed with books, all stacked alphabetically. She liked the regimented order of it, the neatness, the simplicity of her cataloguing. She noted that one of the books was upside down. How odd. The only person who'd been in was Daisy. She couldn't have rummaged through her bookcase again, could she? Isabella stood up, picked out the book and studied it. '*Evolution of Man.*' Goodness. What was happening to her sister? Isabella put it back the correct way up and sat back down on her duvet.

It was time to think; everything that happened could be linked scientifically and logically, surely? But her arguments had logic holes the size of France. She sighed and rolled over. She wished Sue was here to talk it through, then it would be clearer, she was sure of it.

Sue had this skill of making complex problems easy to understand, like her explanation of particle physics, which she'd struggled to get her head around. Sue asked her to imagine how it was possible to look inside two cars that have no windows or doors. She replied that it was impossible, but Sue told her that the answer was to smash them together. And that, in a nutshell, Sue explained, was what physicists were doing with particles in an attempt to find out what lay beyond.

Isabella swung her legs off the bed, stood up and sought her reflection in the mirror. Didn't her face look a fraction thinner, her rather pointy nose a bit sharper than usual? Maybe it was worry. She looked tired and her eyes had a watery sheen on them, from crying. As she brushed her hair, she mulled over the argument with her brother and sister.

To the twins, the events of the past twenty-four hours weren't a dream or a nightmare of any kind. They were real and deserved to be treated as such. These impossible things had happened. She held up her right hand and looked through the neat hole in the middle of her palm.

Perhaps she shouldn't have been quite so hard on them. After all, the twins were only trying to work it out and they were a lot younger and not nearly so clever. She'd apologise, especially for the chair-throwing bit, and make sure they didn't tell mum and dad about it whenever they returned. She picked up a picture of the family that sat in a simple, silver frame by her bed. *So odd our parents not being here,* she thought. Not a word, either. She wondered if they had even the smallest inkling of what they'd been through and if they missed her even a fraction of how much she missed them.

The evening light outside had a creamy texture now that the sun's dappled rays had sneaked under the sheet of grey-stained white cloud that covered the valley. She opened her drawer in search of a hair clip and noticed her mobile phone. She'd put it there before she left for school on the day of the storm.

Now, as she stared at it, she knew it might give them contact with the outside world but as nothing had worked – no power, aside from the petrol generator, no communications and no TV – her hopes weren't high. And anyway, what would she say? After all, they were alive and probably in a better condition than most of their friends. Her heartbeat quickened at the possibility of receiving news. Terrible news, she suspected. More importantly, she wondered if there might be a message from Sue or their parents. Could she take it?

She placed the phone back in the drawer, pushed it closed and walked away.

Then she hesitated, ran back and opened it again.

She pressed the power button and the phone loaded. First one, then three signal bars came up and the battery indicator showed that half the charge was available.

Messages bleeped in.

Isabella read the first and bit her lip. It was catastrophic. She trembled and levered herself off her bed; she'd need to walk around for whatever they'd been through. Others, it appeared, had experienced the same or worse and many were still going through a terrible time.

The difference was that while they were alive, most of the messages were about whether anyone had found Jimmy or Gus or Charlie or Poppy or Lara. These were heart-breaking messages from desperately worried people. The families of their friends who were in a frantic search for their loved ones. And she knew most would never get replies.

She'd recharge the phone with Old Man Wood's generator in the morning, but how long would the mobile signal hold? In no time at all,

Isabella was downstairs and heading towards the living room. She poked her head around the door.

'Daisy, Arch,' she said, her voice quivering with excitement.

Daisy was still reading on the sofa and Archie was sitting in the smaller armchair, opposite Old Man Wood looking bored.

'Firstly, I'm sorry I had a go at you,' Isabella said. 'I ... was wrong to yell.'

Daisy turned her eyes up from her book and smiled. 'It doesn't matter. We'll work it out – you'll see.'

'You're reading?' Isabella said. She couldn't remember ever seeing Daisy read. 'Is that a book in your lap?'

Daisy rolled her eyes. 'Yeah, yeah. I thought I'd give it a try. Nearly at the end of the flood bit.'

Isabella shook her head and moved in to the middle of the room. She sat down on the floor next to Archie's chair by the fire. 'The other thing,' she said, her voice quaking, is that my phone's working – I've got some reception and there's a little bit of battery.'

Daisy and Archie's ears pricked up.

'Any messages?' Archie asked.

'Yes, tons.'

In a flash they were around their elder sister peering over her shoulder.

'Hey! Wait a mo,' she said, 'probably best if I read them out. I warn you, there's no good news. Seriously, we might need tissues.'

Daisy got the message, dashed off and returned with a roll of kitchen paper.

'Right,' Isabella said quietly. 'Our weird, bad week has just got officially worse.' She looked them both in the eye. 'Are you sure you want to hear this?'

Daisy and Archie nodded.

'OK, put your arms around my shoulders, we need to be strong.'

Isabella took a deep breath and let the air out slowly. 'Here goes: first up, a message from Alice: Mr Beattie's body floated past yesterday – face down, so couldn't be sure – but identical blue and red tracksuit, same build.'

Daisy gasped. 'Coach ... dead,' she said under her breath, her eyes welling. 'He can't be.'

'I'm so sorry, Daisy,' Isabella said. 'I know how much he meant to you. And just to think, Archie so nearly went with him after the game.'

For several minutes she read on. Without exception, these were heart-breaking messages of lost children and desperate parents. And between them they knew every missing child or adult.

As she read, the others stared into the fire, lost in their thoughts, tears rolling down their cheeks.

'Are you sure you want to hear more?' Isabella asked, worried that this might not be helping them.

Archie and Daisy nodded, desperate to hear news of their friends.

'Another from Alice. She doesn't think they'll make it through another night. She reckons they've had it,' her voice began cracking. 'It's the rain that's getting them. There's nothing but wet and cold and they're starving – there's nothing to eat and only poisonous sewage in the water. Disease is beginning to spread.' Isabella dabbed her eyes with a paper towel. 'Here are the people missing or drowned.' She read out Alice's list, choking and holding back her tears until she couldn't go on.

Now there was a long silence, the only noise the gentle crackling of the fire, the slow, deep snores from Old Man Wood and the tip-tapping of rain on the windows, which fell heavier tonight. The light from the flames licked the inside of the old room.

Finally Daisy spoke. 'Any news from Sue?'

'No, nothing, no,' Isabella said.

'What about the teams?' Archie said. 'They must have been the last ones out of there.'

Isabella scrolled down. 'Chitbury bus discovered five miles downstream.'

Then she read out another school message. 'Missing: Anderson, Petre, Hill, Allen and Alexander. Gus Williams missing too. Kemp's coat found, but no body.'

'This is terrible,' Daisy cried. 'What about little Jimmy Nugent, Jo and Cassie?'

'Sorry, Daisy. No word on them, I'm afraid,' Isabella said as she scrolled on. 'Here's one from the headmaster.'

'SCHOOL ABANDONED DUE TO FLOOD DISASTER. WILL NOTIFY IN DUE COURSE. GOD BE WITH YOU ALL IN OUR HOUR OF NEED – SOLOMON.'

'I'll reply that we're safe. At least they'll know.' Isabella began tapping away at the tiny keyboard.

'I wonder if the school even exists anymore,' Archie said as he recalled the storm. 'It happened so fast – the football match was mental—'

Isabella suddenly stood up and began pacing the room. 'That's it!' she exclaimed. 'THAT'S IT!' The others watched her, intrigued. 'OK, it might look like I'm backtracking,' she said, 'but you know Sue and I had been working on a worst case storm situation in the event of this phenomenon—'

'Uh-huh,' Daisy replied. 'The whole storm glass thing.'

'Well, yes. You see, Sue dreamt about the flooding as well, and she ... she...'

'What is it?' Archie cried.

'Oh my God,' Isabella whispered, going pale and stumbling. 'It's ... it's so obvious—'

'What is—?'

Isabella sat down. 'Sue—' she began before stopping.

'Bells, are you all right?'

Isabella scrunched her eyes tight. 'Sue told me about her nightmare about a flood at the school. She said it was the most real and terrifying dream EVER. I told her I'd had one too, so we looked into it to see what might happen on a physical level. But she kept on wanting to tell me something else and I kept avoiding it – I thought it was something to do with a boy's crush—'

'Why was it so important?' Daisy asked.

Isabella stood up and resumed her pacing, talking as she went. 'OK. The thing is, Sue is meticulous about note-taking. And believe you me, she records loads of strange things. So the moment she woke from her nightmare she wrote it down, step by step, until the images in her mind blurred. It meant that she had a pretty clear idea of what she'd seen, whereas ours were basically a frightening assortment of images which were confusing and scary. And this stems partially from the fact that none of us wrote them down. Agreed?'

'Absolutely,' Daisy said.

Archie smiled. 'So are you saying now that there might be some purpose to our dreams?'

Isabella flashed him a wry smile. 'No, I'm not there yet, Archie.'

'So this would explain,' Daisy said, 'why she yelled at you on the football pitch?'

'How do you know that—?'

'I can hear everything, remember,' Daisy reminded her with a knowing smile, 'just before you did your "beat up the referee" act, she ran on after you.'

Isabella stopped still. 'You're right!' she said. 'I heard her too. What did she say? You've got to remember!'

Daisy rolled her eyes.

'Look, please try and remember, Daisy,' Isabella said. 'It's important.'

They sat down in front of the fire, the firelight flickering at their features as Daisy ran through what had happened. 'OK, I'd been hacked to the ground and lay still, trying to keep out of the way when little Jimmy Nugent ran in and everyone started fighting. Archie joined in and threw one of their guys about four feet in the air – unbelievably cool – and I was probably the only person who wasn't getting stuck in. Then I heard a voice. Sue's voice – yeah, definitely, now I think of it, screaming something like: *the rain – it's all your fault*.'

The three of them looked at each other.

'Our fault. OUR fault,' Archie said. 'That's pretty full-on. You sure?'

'No,' Daisy shrugged. 'Something similar, though.'

Isabella slumped to the floor. 'The thing is, she desperately wanted to tell me something, and I kept putting her off—'

'No, wait!' Daisy exclaimed. Her eyes were literally glowing. 'I've got it wrong.' She slapped her forehead. 'It was about *you*. That's it. It's "*ALL ABOUT YOU*". That's what she yelled.'

'Anything else?'

'Yes,' Daisy said, turning to Isabella as it flooded back to her, '*you're the only ones who can stop it*.'

'*Me? Stop it?*' Isabella said incredulously.

'That's close, but it's not quite right,' Archie said, standing up and clasping Daisy's shoulders. 'What she said was: *only you and your family – the de Lowes – can stop it*.'

'Stop the rain?'

Archie shrugged. 'Yeah, I suppose. The storm, the rain, everything. That must be what she meant.'

Daisy clapped her hands. 'And,' she said, as more flooded in, 'that we, *must find clues in Eden Cottage*.'

'Clues? To what?' Isabella quizzed.

Daisy shrugged. 'I don't know. I thought she'd lost her marbles.'

'Maybe she had,' Isabella said. 'Maybe you two are making it up. It's not that convincing—'

'Perhaps,' Archie said, 'she was referring to the clues to finding the stone tablets that were in the pictures in the cave?'

'*You really think so?*' Daisy said, winking at Archie.

Isabella sighed. 'Look, I really don't think it's fair to jump to conclusions about Sue's mental health state at that point by instantly linking Sue's words with your cave-man pictures. Do you mind if we don't go there right now?'

'But you just said how important it was—'

'Yes, I know I did. But before you two think I'm going to believe you, I need further proof, and proper science-based proof at that, not some crazed shouting in the middle of a football match or dubious links to Neolithic art. Sue could have been trying to say any number of things. It needs to be much more convincing if it's going to have any sway with me.'

'Yeah, right,' Daisy said, her voice cold. 'We've got seven days to find whatever we've got to find and you being like this really isn't helping.'

# 56 GENESIS QUIZ

Sometime later, after they'd read every message about the tragedy unfolding in the valley beneath them, Isabella read a message that had just arrived:

'THANK YOU FOR UPDATE. CAN ONLY APOLOGISE 4 NOT LISTENING TO U ISA. WISH I HAD. GR8 U SAFE. TERRIBLE LOSSES. ARMY ON SCENE. HELP TAKEN AGES 2 ARRIVE. SEEMS WE R LUCKY ONES. DISEASE RIFE. STRANGE POISON IN WATER. D & A WHY NOT LEARN GENESIS FLOOD – S.'

'I don't believe it!' Archie cried, 'half the school are dead or missing and he reminds us to do homework. The man's extraordinary.'

'No,' Isabella answered, 'he's a teacher. At least he apologised for getting the weather so spectacularly wrong. And the creation story is topical,' she said, 'and not exactly difficult. Everyone in the universe – even mice – know about Adam and Eve, the serpent and the flood.' She looked down at her sister. 'Please tell me you have an outline understanding about the Flood, with Noah?'

'Of course I do,' Daisy said, staring at the floor. 'I've just been reading it.' Her eyes had narrowed and her red irises were like pinpricks. She hated it when Isabella tried to make her look brainless and foolish.

Isabella clapped her hands as an idea popped into her head and almost immediately a bleep from the phone meant a new text had arrived. Isabella studied it, her hair falling over her face like a curtain. She squealed in delight and thumped the air.

'What is it?' Archie demanded, leaning in on her.

Isabella removed the phone from his line of sight. 'Right you two,' she said, her face beaming, 'if you want to know about the contents of the text, and I absolutely promise that you do, you'll have to battle it out in a Creation quiz.'

'You've got to be joking,' Archie scoffed. 'I'm not doing that.'

Isabella grinned back. 'Why not? This text is fantastic news.'

Archie's face sank. 'Because it's boring, and I'm not in the mood, that's why.'

Isabella looked at him earnestly. 'Arch, you're going to have to do it at some point. Why not do it now while we're actually thinking about it so I don't have to pester you with it ever again? And Daisy's just read it so it'll be fresh to our new scholar and if you don't know the answers I'll explain,' she said. 'That way you too might actually learn it and then pass the exam. Because if you remember, school disaster or not, you are both hanging on by a thread to your school places.'

Archie looked appalled. 'I'm not doing some stupid RS quiz.'

But Isabella wasn't going to let it go. 'Look, it's a bit of fun to kill the time.'

'I'd rather play ... cards!'

Daisy joined in. 'Come on, Arch, let's do it – you can play cards anytime.'

Archie shot a disbelieving look at his twin sister. 'Daisy?'

Isabella knew Archie wouldn't argue with both of them.

'God. OK,' Archie said, knocking his head against the floor and denting a floor board. 'On condition that you never, ever mention it again.'

'Fine!' Isabella replied. 'It's a deal.'

A deep groan came from the armchair as Old Man Wood stirred. He yawned, stretched out his arms, blinked and rubbed his eyes. He smiled as he saw the children around him and stretched out first one leg and then the other.

'Ah, good,' Isabella continued, 'now you're awake, Old Man Wood, you can judge.'

'Hmmm. What was that? A judge?' Old Man Wood said through half a yawn. 'Why, yes, of course – what sort of judge?'

'It's a homework quiz – and you can help me decide who wins. You know, you can be a quiz master—'

'Quiz master? What the apples are you going on about now, young 'un?'

'Keep the score, see who comes first,' Isabella said. 'Like they have on buzzer rounds.'

'Buzzer rounds?' The old man had no idea what she was talking about.

'Yes,' Isabella said. 'Archie and Daisy will pretend to press a buzzer by making their own buzzing noise. It's pretty simple. All you have to do is tell me who gets there first – OK?'

Daisy and Archie proceeded to make strange buzzery noises.

Old Man Wood rubbed his hands and then his eyes. 'You and your games, hmmm. Apples alive. Whatever next? Well, before I do any judging of buzzery things, let me attend to the fire.' With a couple of groans, Old Man Wood pulled himself up, made his way over to the fireplace and thrust a long, steel poker into the embers a few times. He added a couple of lumps of coal from the brass scuttle and retreated into his armchair, the springs groaning under his weight.

Shortly, golden flames danced out of the fireplace. Daisy and Archie snuggled up to the old man, sitting either side of him on the arms of the armchair, listening to the gentle crackle of the flames as Isabella rapidly scribbled out a selection of questions.

A flash from outside made their heads turn towards the window. For a moment, lightning illuminated the shiny wet flagstones in the courtyard, and they could see the outbuildings beyond, glistening from the water. Inside, shards of blue light bounced off an assortment of metal curiosities on the dark wood-panelled walls.

Now that Isabella was ready, she stood up, drew the curtains and returned to her position on the hearth rug.

'Archie, for goodness' sake stop reading and pass it to me,' Isabella said. 'Right, Bible quiz on Genesis, are you ready?'

'Oh. So it's the Bible you're practising?' Old Man Wood said, his deep, grainy voice blending with the storm outside. 'Interesting choice. I can't remember the last time—'

'OK, quiet,' Isabella said. 'Question one on chapter two. Are you ready?' Isabella gave Daisy a look as if to say, *come on, concentrate!*

'When God made the universe, there were no plants on the earth and no seeds. Now, Daisy, is this true or false?'

'True.'

'Correct. One nil to Daisy. Second question to Archie. What substance came from beneath the surface of the earth?'

'Um, it's er ... water, isn't it?'

'Nice one,' Isabella said, raising her eyebrows and ticking her score sheet smartly. 'You see it's easy-peasy. So far, so good – one all. Right. Fingers on your buzzers,' she said, glancing to Old Man Wood who leant forward in anticipation. 'Who came first, Man or the Garden of Eden?'

'The Garden,' Old Man Wood said, rather surprised by his instant response.

'You're the judge, not the contestant,' Isabella said scolding him. 'And anyway, you're wrong; it says here it was "Man".'

'Are you sure?' he replied.

'Yes,' she said.

'That can't be right,' he added.

Isabella sighed. 'Well, that's what it says here.'

Daisy tilted her head. 'So – is the Garden of Eden a real place? Can you actually visit it?'

'No,' Isabella sighed, 'you can't.'

'Then, what is it?'

Isabella leaned back knowingly. 'This is the big question. No one really knows,' she answered. 'The Garden of Eden is a curiosity, a mythical place that if it did exist today archaeologists reckon it would be in Iraq.'

'Where Mum and Dad are?' Daisy said.

'Yes, I suppose,' Isabella said. Their parents never seemed to give them any precise locations, simply because they were constantly on the move from one archaeological dig to another. But in the last postcard their parents said they were in Mesopotamia and the children had figured out that it was almost certainly in Iraq, even if the postcard wore a Jordanian stamp.

Isabella spotted Daisy's confused look. 'Look, if there once was a place of lush green vegetation there's nothing there now but desert and a river that swells during the rainy season. That's why it's a myth. OK?'

It was Archie's turn to look baffled, but Isabella continued. 'The other way of looking at it is that the Garden of Eden is an allegory – a story – of how early man settled in the pasture-rich valleys of the area; also known as the paradise of the Garden of Eden. Carbon dating on bones and fossils tells us that man inhabited the Earth for literally tens of thousands of years before. So you might think of Biblical creation as a method by which the writers and storytellers start our understanding of God.'

'Then it's all made up?' Archie said, wrinkling his nose.

'I suppose,' Isabella said. 'It's more than likely, but it depends on what you want to believe. Some people actually think that the world started at this point, some don't. Science has shown us that life has been evolving constantly for millions of years. So it depends on your religious belief and how you interpret the story.'

'What about the flood?' Archie asked. He'd never realised how complex it was. 'I'm sure I've read that a real flood happened.'

'Good point, Arch,' Isabella said, as she thought out her reply. 'Flood stories have been recorded across different cultures – from Ancient Chinese to Aboriginal Australian, from India to the Middle East, so who knows, there might be something in it. Some experts reckon there was a meteor strike that created a series of tsunamis. Mum and Dad are basically experts about this – you should ask them.'

'I thought they were archaeologists, looking for relics and stuff,' Archie said.

'They are, but in a way it all amounts to the same thing,' she replied. 'They're trying to piece our history together. It's the sort of stuff they're mad about.' Her eyes turned to the book. She wondered if she should ever have started this. And all she really wanted to do was tell them her stunning news. 'Back to the quiz,' she said, scouring the page, her finger tracing down the text. 'Where in the Garden of Eden do the trees of life and knowledge live?'

'In the middle,' they said at once.

'Correct.'

Old Man Wood furrowed his brow and shrugged his shoulders, suggesting a dead heat. Isabella fired the next question.

'What does the tree of knowledge represent?'

'Er ... knowledge,' Archie said with a silly smile on his face.

Isabella glared at him.

'Alright – *understanding* – the clue's in the name.'

'Nope,' Isabella said, 'it says here in the text: "knowledge of what is good and what is bad".'

'Hang on,' he said. 'That's the same thing.'

'No it isn't—'

'Yes it is. Of course it is. You must have knowledge to understand what is good and bad?'

Isabella thought for a while. 'A bit dodgy, but I see what you mean. Half a mark.'

Isabella fired in the next question before either could protest. 'OK. A hard one. How many rivers did Eden divide into?'

Archie and Daisy stared at each other blankly.

'Two?' Archie tried.

No response.

'Four or five,' Daisy said, trying hard to remember.

'Four,' Old Man Wood said softly, as if not thinking. He scratched his bald head. None of this seemed right at all. But why did it feel wrong? Why did it throw doubt in his mind? 'There are four rivers,' he repeated, his brain in a spin.

'Correct,' Isabella said with a tone of surprise, 'but please don't answer – how are they supposed to learn anything?'

'Sorry, just slipped out—'

'And can you name any of them?' Isabella asked.

Archie stared at the ceiling rolling his eyes, while Daisy made an ooohing sound, as though it was on the tip of her tongue.

Isabella took this as a "no". 'Neither of you has a clue,' she said. 'The first river is called Pishon, which flows around the country of Havilah. And if you're lucky enough to be passing Havilah, you'll find gold, rare perfumes and precious stones. I am so going there when I'm grown up.' Isabella smiled. 'The second river is Gihon, which flows round the country of Cush, the third river is the Tigris which flows east of a place called Assyria. The fourth is the Euphrates.'

Just then, Old Man Wood exploded into laughter and long, deep guffaws echoed from his large, barrelled chest. As the quiz had gone on, fragments of memories had returned and his extraordinary dreams were at last beginning to make some kind of sense, as though he'd found a vital piece to the jigsaw puzzle.

A thunderbolt crashed over the cottage. Isabella ducked and Archie and Daisy instinctively threw themselves behind the armchair, but Old Man wood stood up and roared with laughter as if he hadn't a care in the world.

Isabella, Archie and Daisy stared at the large man with their mouths wide open, their hearts fluttering. Had the man they loved so deeply finally lost his marbles? Was it his eccentricity or simply the effects of his great age?

Suddenly a gust of wind shot down the chimney and blew out all the candles. The children froze as though darkness, like a thick cloak, had dropped out of the sky. As their eyes adjusted, the flames in the fire flickered with rich and vivid colours, the noise of the storm sounded louder.

'Are you alright, Old Man Wood?' Archie whispered.

'Fine, my boy. Fine,' Old Man Wood replied, returning to his chair and then leaning forward towards the flames. 'Something smouldering in the back of my mind suddenly burst into flame when you were talking about those rivers,' he said. His weathered, bony features were greatly enhanced by the firelight, and his eyes seemed to shine like the stars and his wrinkles were deep and filled with experiences. 'It reminded me of ... well, something from a long time ago, that's all.'

'Right,' Isabella said, gathering herself, trying not to explode with joy. 'Since there's no light and you both did reasonably well, would you like to hear who the text was from?' Daisy and Archie moved in next to her, trying to catch a peek at the screen.

'It's from Sue!' she exclaimed.

'Sue? You're kidding?'

'NO! She's alive!' Isabella started dancing in front of the fire, punching the air. 'In fact,' Isabella continued, 'it's better than that. She's with Gus!'

'No way!'

'Yes way! Together they made it through the storm.'

Archie was astonished. 'But how? Are they in hospital—'

'No, no, it sounds incredible,' Isabella said, her voice singing. 'I scribbled on a piece of paper about the boat and shoved it in Sue's pocket. When Sue ran off, she bumped into Gus and persuaded him to join her and she found the note. They looted the shop, Gus built a shelter over the boat and, because of that, they survived! Apparently Gus has been nothing less than heroic. They're out at sea and she just caught a fish!'

'Blimey,' Archie said. 'That really is incredible.'

'It's brilliant news, sis,' Daisy cried, and she hugged Isabella who was already hugging Archie.

'And there's more.'

'What do you mean, *more*?'

'Oh, so much more.' Isabella could hardly stop giggling. She found herself blushing and pushed her siblings away.

'What?'

Isabella found tears welling in her eyes. 'They've fallen in love.'

Archie reeled. 'No Way! Gus – are you sure?'

'Gus, with Sue?' Daisy added. 'Never.'

Isabella shook her head. 'They've kissed!'

Archie reddened just thinking about it.

'They've been snogging?' Daisy laughed. 'Epic!'

'Yup!' squealed Isabella. 'Snogging!' she repeated.

'Ooh-eeee!' and the girls squealed in delight.

---

WHILE THE JOYS of Sue and Gus' love affair dominated the conversation, Old Man Wood quietly picked his way around the room and re-lit several of the candles. Then he slipped out of the room to do the same in the hallway and kitchen.

For the first time in ages, his whole body fizzed with energy. It was as if a touch paper had exploded a great big memory-rocket right inside his mind and information had flashed in. It was almost too much to bear. He had forgotten so much – and yet so much still remained locked inside. How and when would he tell the children, and would they believe him? If they didn't, then what? Would it ruin everything? The old man was swamped by questions.

One thing had come to him with clarity. The answers to some of his questions lay with some special old friends who he needed to find – and fast. From what he had remembered, they might be able to fill in the blanks.

Maybe, he thought, his time had finally come.

---

ISABELLA WAS PUTTING the finishing touches to her text reply and the twins were discussing the revelation of Gus and Sue's kissing, which Archie thought sounded quite disgusting.

'Tell me,' he said, 'how do you actually snog?'

'OK, so what you do,' Daisy replied in a very educational manner, 'is put your lips together with your friend, shut your eyes, open your mouth a bit, poke out your tongue and swirl it around against the other one.'

'Oh my God!' Archie said. His look of revulsion said it all. 'And that's supposed to be nice.'

'Yeah. I suppose,' Daisy replied.

'What if you start dribbling?' he asked. 'And what if you bash your teeth?'

'You won't—'

'How do you know?'

Daisy pouted her lips. 'Cos I do.'

'And anyway,' Archie asked, 'if you're swirling away, how are you supposed to breathe? Isn't it all just a bit uncomfortable and awkward and what if the person you're kissing has bad breath, like Kemp?'

'God, Archie, *you're so ten*, aren't you?'

Archie frowned. How come Daisy knew all this stuff? 'Have you actually done it?'

'Might have,' Daisy replied coyly.

Archie eyed her suspiciously. 'I don't think you have, you're telling me a big fat porky pie, lie.'

Daisy winked at him with a smile on her face. 'That's for me to know, and you to find out.'

Old Man Wood returned and coughed. The children fell quiet. 'Time for bed. I'll put the generator on in the morning,' he said. 'But would any of you like to hear one of my special stories?'

'Oh yeah! But only if it's got absolutely nothing to do with snogging,' Archie said.

Old Man Wood's stories were fantastic tales full of heroes, magicians and witches, evil overlords and brutal wars. They nearly always contained adventures about Tree-men, who were always the bravest and noblest of creatures. The way he delivered them was like fire and ice blended perfectly together; his ancient face alone, full of wrinkles, seemed to express the meaning in the story. And when the stories were happy his eyes sparkled like the bright Northern Star. When they were sad, dark clouds cloaked his eyes and his wrinkles grew deep and long and the shadows from the wavering firelight dramatised the effect so much that the children would ask questions for days after, such as, 'What happened to the Warlbist, when her husband gave in to the Floak?' or 'How did the Spurtle get its fur?'

Daisy smiled. 'How about the Iso story?'

'We always have the Iso story,' Archie whinged.

'Because it's beautiful and she is so incredibly cool.'

'But it's sooo girly—'

'It's an excellent choice,' Isabella added. 'Just what we need – as long as it's only the beginning.'

'Ah, yes, the Iso story,' Old Man Wood said, winking at the girls. 'A story of love and friendship and derring-do! But afterwards, no questions, it's straight to bed.'

# 57 OLD MAN WOOD AND THE FIRE

Old Man Wood had always been old. His face was deeply lined by the journey of time; his teeth worn to dull stumps, his remaining hair random and straggly, his skin blotched and wrinkled. For this reason he was affectionately called Old Man Wood; because he looked as weathered as a rough piece of bark from a tree like an old birch.

Old Man Wood studied his rectangular four poster bed which jutted out into the room like a big wooden box. He noted with interest the strange patterns and shapes of the carvings on every upright and beam and wondered if they offered any clues. He examined the three rectangular panels at its foot, showing live pictures of the children. Old Man Wood scratched his chin. If it hadn't been for the panels he might never have found them ... hadn't that been a stroke of luck?

On the floor lay five brown, dirt-ingrained rugs. Standing behind them stood a large wardrobe where he stored his few clothes and in front of the window sat a brown leather sofa. Opposite the door, an old metal fireplace with intricate scrolls saw regular activity during the colder months.

Classical wooden panelling, made from many different tree species, covered the walls and it glowed with an unlikely variety of colour. How unfussy it was, how strangely beautiful; how well it suited him.

Every night since the rain had begun he'd fallen into a deep sleep and later woken, sweating and yelling, gripping his sheets until his hands hurt –

his fingernails digging into his palms. And last night it was the same: blinding flashes, searing heat followed by intense cold. Goosebumps appeared as he thought about the spider; that horrible, ugly, white, ghost-like thing with a blue ring of fire in its belly. He closed his eyes but the snapshots refused to go away.

Old Man Wood moaned. He stared out of the window at the dark early morning, with its dirty charcoal colours filtering through the grey clouds, and tried to make sense of it all. With nothing forthcoming, he frowned and stretched his arms out wide. Maybe he'd be better off in front of the fire in the living room with an early morning cup of tea. *Might just fix my head and settle my nerves,* he thought. He shuffled into the kitchen and boiled the kettle. With his brew in hand, he ambled into the sitting room, grabbed some kindling and a couple of logs and placed them on top of the embers. The fire smoked before a small golden flame danced nervously around the wood as it tentatively took hold. Old Man Wood sank into his armchair and stared at the fire, trying as best he might to understand the images in his head.

He spied the local newspaper on the side table next to him. He read about a burglary in last week's Northallerton News where a thief, on making his getaway, had slipped on a banana skin and fallen down an open manhole into the sewer. Old Man Wood chuckled.

Then, out of the corner of his eye he noted that the fire needed a bit of a poke. A tune had jumped into his head and, feeling in a better mood, he reached out and grabbed the steel fire prong.

'Whoooosh, hummmy, sshhhhh,' he began humming. He didn't know why, but the song felt etched into him like a tattoo and came with ease. As he sang, he reached out and prodded the burning logs, enjoying the way the flames danced and licked yellow and tangerine with greater intensity. He hummed the tune a little louder, with more vigour, liking how it blended seamlessly with the rhythms of the crackles of the fire. He turned it up a notch until his singing was coming from a place deep within him, the tune filling him with a kind of inner strength that began in his loins and spread to his heart and then out to his fingertips and toes.

As he stared deeply into the fire, a curious rectangular object grew and appeared to be coming directly at him. *In all the apples*, he thought, *what is it?* A box, a lump of stone? Mesmerised, he found himself drawn towards it and, moments later, the sound of humming still coming as if like a chant, he found himself stretching out a hand. And now his fingers touched it and much to his surprise he found that it was cool, not hot at all, and solid – as if it were made of a kind of stone. He stopped singing and pulled, but the object would not yield.

'Now then,' Mrs Pye's voice called out, shattering his concentration and the song. 'What do you think you're doing?' She stared at him from the doorway.

Old Man Wood suddenly felt the heat. 'OUCH! Blasted thing!' he cursed, rubbing his hands.

'You alright?' she said. 'Messing with fire, and at your age too – you should be more careful.'

Confused, Old Man Wood stood up and marched around the room rubbing his chin, humming to himself, trying to think. Then he made his way into the boot room where he donned his cap, threw on his green waterproof coat and, after a great deal of groaning, wrestled his boots onto his large feet.

After he'd seen to the cattle, it was well past time, he thought, to seek out his old friends.

# 58 SEARCHING FOR THE BUBBLING BROOK

Archie woke with a start. Darkness filled the room. He yawned, removed the sleep from his eyes and looked at his watch. Five o'clock. A bit early – but for the first time in ages he felt refreshed after a long and nourishing sleep with no dreams. In any case, he had knives to throw. He dressed quickly and, trying not to disturb the house, he trod exceedingly carefully on the ridiculously creaky floorboards and crept out of their attic room, down the stairs, along the corridor, down the main stairs and into the kitchen.

He wasn't the first up. 'Morning, Old Man Wood,' he said as he poked his head round the kitchen door. 'You're up early. Everything alright?'

Old Man Wood waved a hand in Archie's direction. 'Morning, littlun. Peculiar stuff going on in 'ere.' He pointed to his head and then stretched his arms out to pull down the cuffs on his coat. 'Very, very strange things,' he tapped his head again. 'I've been to see the cattle,' he said, changing the subject, 'give them more feed. My, oh my, they looked utterly terrified – which is hardly surprising, I suppose. None of them have eaten a great deal and I squeezed only a few drops out of Bernice and Burger, dear things.' He stopped and stroked his chin. 'It's as if they're trying to tell me something.'

He turned his attention back to Archie. 'What are you doing up so early?'

'Might go and throw my knives, take my mind off stuff,' Archie replied, rubbing the front spike on his head. 'Are you off out again?'

'Yes, littlun, I need to clear my head,' the old man said as he studied the boy. 'Is there anything I can help you with?'

Archie looked up at Old Man Wood. 'Actually, do you mind if I join you?' he said weakly. 'It's just I could do with some grown up company. I'm really missing Mum and Dad.'

'Of course you are,' the old man replied. He pulled him in for a hug. 'I've noticed that none of you lot are playing. Lots of arguing and funny conversations. What's up?'

'It's the rain, I think,' Archie said, wishing he could say more, 'and being stuck here and feeling utterly helpless and worrying about our friends and ... and things like the cave and the pictures and my stupid hair that don't make any sense.'

'Hmmm,' Old Man Wood said. 'Think I know what you mean.'

'Where are you off to?' Archie asked.

Old Man Wood scratched his chin. 'I'm off to find some old friends – they might be able to help at a time like this.'

'Friends? Where?'

'Well, I don't know, down there, somewhere.'

'You're, er, quite sure about this?'

'Oh yes, Archie. I'm not fooling you.'

Archie thought for a while. 'Please can I come too?' he said.

Old Man Wood rubbed his mottled head. Taking Archie to find the Bubbling Brook could be a big mistake, foremost because he had no idea where it was. 'I'm not sure you're ready to come along, little Archie.'

'Yes, I am,' he said instinctively.

'If you come along, you're going to have to swear to me, Archie, that you won't mention it to your sisters. Especially Isabella. I heard her earlier.'

'Why?'

'Because I'm asking you, that's why,' he replied. 'Just for the moment.'

'I don't understand,' Archie said.

Old Man Wood felt himself getting tangled up with the words. 'Well, it might upset you, that's all,' Old Man Wood said gently. 'It would most definitely upset young Isabella.'

Old Man Wood draped an arm round Archie's shoulders. 'Many, many moons ago when the flood waters rose above the old steps by the base of the cliff, I discovered something and it struck me that I might find it again.'

'By the cave?' Archie looked puzzled.

'There or thereabouts.' Old Man Wood said. 'Somewhere in the valley.' The back door creaked open. 'If you come along, Archie, you're going to have to open up your mind.'

---

DAWN THREATENED as a soft murky light filtered out across the vale. In front of them the floodwaters stretched like a vast flowing silver lake starting behind the hedgerow in front of the currant bushes in the vegetable garden below. After slipping and sliding down the steep track, and squelching through the saturated fields, they were soon at the water's edge. Old Man Wood took a couple of deep breaths, shook some mud from his boots, furrowed his brow and peered into the rain.

'Now, where are those funny old trees?' he said out loud.

'Trees?'

Old Man Wood nodded.

Archie shivered. 'Blimey, we're looking for trees and you don't know where they are. There are thousands. Do you know what type they are?'

'Ooh yes. Willows, a great big clump.'

'Willows?' Archie said, avoiding a large puddle. 'The valley's littered with willow clumps.'

Archie scoured the vast expanse of grey water intermittently punctuated with bushes nearer the water's edge. 'Most are underwater. What if it's one of those?'

'Must be easy enough to find, I reckon,' Old Man Wood said as he strode off, his boots squelching in the mud. 'Something tells me the clump's just around the headland towards Upsall. Come on, Archie, this way.'

Archie studied the expanse of water with tree clumps – mainly willows – popping out, like miniature crowns. *This is utterly ridiculous,* he thought. Talk about a wild goose chase.

---

AFTER A COUPLE of unsuccessful attempts at entering the thick brambles surrounding one clump, and then doing exactly the same thing with another, Old Man Wood began to wonder if he had gone the right way. He stamped his boot down in the sludge and a shower of sloppy, brown water sprayed over a clump of sodden ferns.

He stopped to think. It wasn't brawn that would lead them to the Bubbling Brook, it was brains, just as he often told the children. But Old Man Wood was well aware that his brain took a while to get going. In fact, he was amazed that his head worked at all considering his vast age.

He found an old tree stump, sat down, closed his eyes and concentrated.

---

ARCHIE WATCHED Old Man Wood with a mixture of curiosity and growing anxiety. His excitement bordered on madness, real madness. It was like watching a child at a fairground who couldn't work out where his favourite ride had gone.

Old Man Wood stood up and sat down again, all the while mumbling to himself. Then up. Now down. Without warning he shot off, following the waterline towards Upsall. Archie hurried to keep up. Most of the clumps that followed the line of the water were identical, their leaves stripped from the branches by the rain. Defeated by the first two clumps, they waded through the water, where at length they met a huge clump of brambles and fallen trees with twisted, smashed branches.

Close by, a mudslide with deep water pockets blocked their path. The pair slipped and climbed and squelched back up the hill towards the ruins, reverting down to the water's edge as soon as they could. Old Man Wood stopped every now and then and sniffed the air – or so Archie thought – as though searching out the best route before shooting onward at such a speed that Archie struggled to keep pace.

They walked along in silence for many minutes. Soon, they came across a willow clump consisting of new shoots and whips and three huge, old trees. It was impassable. On one side, several large and small trees stood half-submerged in the floodwater, on the other a mess of trees and rocks and brambles had collected where the ground had slipped away.

Archie caught his breath. 'Look, there's no way we'll get through there,' he complained. 'Why don't we head back—?'

Old Man Wood groaned. 'Maybe I'll use a bit of beef and bludgeon me way through the middle,' he said, ignoring Archie.

In no time, the old man had shinned up one of the large outer trees and was balancing on a thick branch that leaned directly into the middle of the clump. Archie climbed up after him and watched as the old man – his arms outstretched as if on a tightrope – moved one foot in front of the other along the branch.

Archie noticed that, within the clump, directly below the trunk they stood on, was a crater filled with water. A creepy mist swirled around as if it was somehow protecting it. Archie took a deep breath and pulled himself along.

---

'BLAST!' the old man cried, staring at his feet. He sat down on the branch. 'I thought there was something wrong. Look! A hole!' He bent his leg round, removed his boot and a stream of water splashed into the pool a metre or so below.

As Old Man Wood wrestled his boot on, he eyed a route across. It would take a couple of acrobatic leaps. Was he nimble enough? Apples alive, why not? Of course he could do it.

The old man took a deep breath and puffed out his chest. He leapt onto a low branch, which swayed ominously, before jumping on to the next one. He was halfway across.

'Hey, be careful!' Archie shouted. 'You sure you're alright?'

'Never been better,' Old Man Wood replied. 'Come on! It's a piece of Mrs Pye's cake.' But at that moment, for no real reason, he lost his balance and throwing his arms wildly in the air like a windmill, he swayed first one way and then the other and then back again, like a pendulum. Each time, Archie's heart leapt. Then, with a look of total surprise on his face, the old man disappeared into the pool beneath him and under the surface.

Archie, in spite of his gloominess, exploded with laughter and held back his sides for fear of falling in himself. But, seeing Old Man Wood struggle in the water, he realised the pool was deeper than they'd thought.

'Over here,' Archie said, offering his hand, tears blurring his vision.

When his feet touched the bottom, Old Man Wood recovered his wits and waded carefully towards him until he was within reach of the branch. Suddenly, he disappeared under the waterline again, as though he had walked off a ledge. Shortly, he re-emerged looking, Archie thought, like a drowned rat and, after plenty of splashing and coughing, he held onto the branch, spitting water out of his mouth.

Archie heaved him up. 'I think you swallowed some water,' Archie said, as he thumped the old man's back a couple of times.

'Thank you, Arch,' Old Man Wood replied. 'I most certainly did. That's better. Now out of the way while I shake myself dry.' The old man stood up and, like a dog, sprayed water in all directions.

---

ARCHIE SIMPLY DIDN'T KNOW what to say. The surprised look on Old Man Wood's face made Archie's shoulders gallop up and down with laughter.

The old man wiped his face with his sodden clothes and sat down beside Archie on the branch. He shook his head. 'Getting a bit old for this kind of thing, I reckon,' he began.

Archie's frame hurt.

Suddenly, Old Man Wood's head twitched from one side to the other. Then he stood up and sidled further along. 'Is someone there?' he turned to Archie. 'Did you hear that, Archie?'

Archie scanned the pond.

Just the drizzle and the mist and drops of water splashing down from the branches overhead. He shook his head.

'Apples alive, there are more,' the old man whispered. 'Laughing like crazy. All round.' Old Man Wood's head shifted from side to side. 'Laughing like I've never heard.'

'I can't hear anything. You're sure you're all—?'

Old Man Wood had had enough. He climbed up onto the branch and folded his arms. 'You think that an old man falling down is amusing, do you?' he said furiously to the empty pool. 'Well, when I find you lot, I'll show you another type of entertainment!'

# 59 KEMP'S RESCUE

Daisy woke, sensing a movement in the bedroom. It didn't take long to figure out that it was Archie. She felt a strange hollowness in her stomach. She laid her head back on the pillow, her curious thoughts staying with her. Sometime later, she sat up with a start. 'I've got to find Archie,' she said out loud. 'Something's happened.'

'He's fine,' Isabella yawned from behind her curtain. 'Don't worry—'

'No, Bells. It's not right. Not right at all.' She climbed out of bed. 'I can ... kind of ... sense it.' She flipped on the light which, much to her surprise, flickered into action. The generator was working.

As she slipped into her jeans and shirt she tapped on Isabella's duvet. 'Bells, put your phone on charge. There's power but it won't last for long.'

'You do it. It's downstairs,' Isabella groaned before disappearing back under her duvet.

In the living room, Daisy plugged in the phone and headed into the kitchen where she found Mrs Pye doing the ironing in front of the telly. The hum of the generator and the drone of the morning news filled the room.

'The telly!' Daisy exclaimed. 'When did it come back on?'

Mrs Pye looked up. 'Good morning, Daisy.'

'Oh! Morning, Mrs P.'

Mrs Pye scrunched up her face. 'Now then, about ten.'

Daisy smiled. Mrs Pye never referred to time in its entirety, so it could have been seconds, minutes, hours, or days. Sometimes even months or years.

Daisy grabbed a bowl, ladled in a couple of spoons of porridge from the saucepan on the range cooker and sprinkled it with salt, stirring it in. Then she pulled up a chair and watched the screen as a banner ran below it with the words; *Yorkshire Disaster.* And next to it was: *helpline number.* Daisy wondered whether it was worth a call. Then again, they were fine, so why bother? By the look of things, others were in a far worse state than they were.

*'... experts are saying that the unprecedented flood in the north of the country is partly due to the effects of global warming. But what is baffling forecasters is that this freak storm did not blow in, it simply mushroomed out, growing at alarming speed from a position just to the west of the North Yorkshire Moors.'*

The camera panned to show a village almost totally submerged. Daisy gasped. It looked like Kettleby, just down the road. Only the spire of the church and a few rooftops were visible. *'This is the picture throughout the whole of Yorkshire, Cleveland and Lincolnshire. There is no power, no fresh water and sewage fills the streets. Disease is now a real threat.'*

The picture returned to the studio and a man stood next to a graphic of a map of the North of England. The presenter looked glum. *'It appears that a freak depression has settled directly over this area.'* The TV graphics changed. *'The problem, as you can see from our satellite image, is that this extraordinary weather doesn't appear to be letting up. Although there has been no torrential rain like we saw on Friday afternoon which, by the way, was the hardest rainfall recorded anywhere in the world – and for the longest sustained period of time – there is more rain forecast, which will cause further havoc as water levels continue to rise. And exceptionally high spring tides at York, with an already saturated water table, means the rising water doesn't have anywhere to go.'*

The screen snapped to helicopter imagery of the flooding. *'Early casualty estimates range from 3,000 to 30,000 victims. According to the emergency services, it's impossible to tell. Ten counties are in an unprecedented state of emergency. Survivors within this huge area have been evacuated to the higher ground of the moors and the Yorkshire Dales. The death toll looks certain to rise as news filters in from stricken towns and villages across the country.'*

The picture reverted to the news anchor. *'We'll have regular updates throughout the day, but right now we can go to our reporter in the submerged North Yorkshire town of Northallerton. Some of these pictures are of a distressing nature.'*

Mrs Pye watched the screen, transfixed, her face even paler than normal.

*'This pregnant woman was saved when a neighbour managed to break through an upstairs window and get her onto the roof. She was one of the lucky ones—'* The woman, looking frightened and pale, told her terrifying story. Daisy recognised her as Sue's babysitter.

The reporter continued: *'Now that a partial service has resumed for many mobile phone networks, the emergency services are urging people to call the national emergency number to let them know of their whereabouts. Please be aware that the network operators have told us that only a limited service will be available.'*

Daisy was about to go when a news story flickered on the screen. *Breaking News.* The broadcaster cocked his head, listening to the mike in his ear. *'We're getting news of an extraordinary story of a boy who has been found at the top of a large tree.'* He smiled at the camera as he focused on his news feed. *'The boy, winched to safety by the North Yorkshire air ambulance, was found naked, hanging onto a top branch of a tree in the middle of the vast area of flooding. I'm told that it was close to the epicentre of the storm, near to the ravaged village of Upsall. This remarkable footage has just come in from members of the helicopter crew.'*

The screen showed a helicopter cockpit and a man with a jumpsuit and mask. Through the windows, the chopper blades blurred. Below lay a huge expanse of water and, as the pilot took the helicopter down, right in the very middle of the picture sat the crown of a huge bare tree. Suddenly, muffled noises from the crew cut across the whorl of the rotors. The camera lens cut back to the crew within the helicopter who were gesticulating wildly with their arms.

The camera panned back to the tree as the helicopter banked and then the lens zoomed in. For a moment there was a strange silence as the crew and viewers tried to see into the bare branches of the tree. As the helicopter swung to the left, there, draped over a bough, was a human figure hugging a thick branch.

Mrs Pye grabbed Daisy's arm and gripped tight.

Now the sound cut out altogether. The camera zoomed in even closer to show the boy, unmoving, his naked white flesh clearly visible against the dark water beneath him.

Daisy gasped. Who could have survived the storm and the flooding and then climbed up a huge tree? It didn't seem possible. Daisy could hardly breathe as the camera lens reached in until the only thing on the screen was the head and shoulders of the boy, gaunt and white, so utterly beaten. The boy had not a hair on his head; bald, like a big baby.

A shiver raced up her. The jawline, so familiar. And those fat lips. Like ... who? In a flash it hit her. Kemp. It was identical to Kemp. She could tell his face from a mile away. But if it was Kemp then where was the thick ginger hair? So it couldn't be, could it? Her dislike for Kemp lightened. She wished the boy, whoever he was, hope.

She snapped out of it. If it was Kemp, Archie needed to know. Archie would confirm her suspicions.

Seconds later, the images on the TV disappeared altogether. The satellite connection failed. Mrs. Pye waddled over and gave it a smack. She moaned at it and then returned to the ironing. Daisy swore she could see tears falling down Mrs Pye's ruddy cheeks.

Daisy slipped out of the kitchen to the boot room and noted that both Old Man Wood's and Archie's boots were missing. Maybe Old Man Wood had gone to look for him as well. She donned her oilskin and lifted the hood over her tangled blonde mop and headed out into the rain.

---

OK, Daisy thought, *if I was Winkle, where would I go? Dad's shed in the haunted garden? Not a bad place to start. Quiet. Dark. Horrible.*

The shed by the haunted garden was part of a derelict area near the vegetable patch at the bottom of the garden. The children's father and Old Man Wood grew potatoes here but never stayed late. 'It's as if I'm being watched,' their father often said. 'Whoever it is, it doesn't like the fact that I'm there, and as a result I'm not too keen on staying either.'

Daisy knew exactly what he meant. She looked at the cold, damp, miserable place, intermittently wiping rainwater out of her eyes. 'Archie,' she called out. 'Archie. I think they've found Kemp!'

In the distance, the drone of the whirring blades of a helicopter forced her to look up into the thick clouds. *Must be the rescue mission,* she thought, *swinging into action, moving people to high ground.* But they'd never come up here, where the forest was impenetrably thick and littered with broken trees and mudslides.

Behind the plum trees lay an expanse of thick bushes in the shape of a horseshoe. Daisy made her way gingerly towards the drooping, skeletal branches, her boots squelching noisily. Here, a small opening led to an old rusted gate.

She stopped and studied it for a moment. I don't remember that gate. Where can it have come from? *More importantly,* she thought, *where does it lead?* She looked up at the dark morning sky and wiped rainwater from her cheeks and eyes, removing a couple of sopping hair strands at the same time. Then she entered the pathway towards the gate.

Suddenly, she glimpsed a light glimmering on something in the bushes beyond the gate. Daisy peered at it, intrigued. A tiny jewel – a diamond? She walked closer until she was in front of the gate whose scroll-like pattern appeared strangely familiar, like a circular tree with its roots showing.

She noted that the jewel looked more like a pearl in the shape of a tear drop. It sparkled. She liked the thought of it around her neck, against her pale skin.

Daisy gave the gate a push. It was stuck, jammed by foliage and creepers. She tried again with the same result. It hardened her resolve.

*Come on, Daisy,* she whispered. *On the count of three: One, two ... THREE!*

She slammed into the gate, but instead of meeting resistance, the gate flew open and Daisy hurtled straight into the bush. As she tumbled, she reached out for the jewel and before she knew what was happening, she crashed into a ditch full of water.

Daisy sank under, entirely submerged. Moments later, she surfaced, waving her arms and spluttering violently.

Phleaux, tchuch, she spat, coughing out the metallic, coppery-tasting water that had a hint of strong cheese. Her head swam and a dizziness overcame her, as though a bee had shot into her brain and was struggling to find a way out.

She fell to the ground as a terrible thought washed over her. What if she'd swallowed the deadly, poisonous sewage-water like the man said on TV?

She dragged herself up the bank on her elbows and knees, moving to a patch of dry grass. She lay still with her eyes shut and wondered if this was how the poison worked. A gentle, warm wind blew over her as the buzzing sensation between her ears grew more comfortable and then ebbed away entirely.

*Perhaps*, she thought, *she'd died and gone to Heaven.*

---

AFTER SEVERAL MINUTES, her eyes still shut tight, Daisy placed her hand over her chest. Her heart thumped. She sat up and slowly opened each eye.

Stretching out in front of her was an area about twenty large paces across by twenty wide tapering in the further away it went. On each side sat three wide-trunked and curiously gnarled old trees covered in pink, white and yellow petals. Behind these showy trees, sat a line of thick, impenetrable-looking thorn bushes. Daisy realised that no one could see in and she couldn't see out.

At the far end, adjoining the space, stood a kind of old dilapidated greenhouse bereft of glass. In it sat a peculiar object, like a big Victorian garden roller with a curiously large handle.

She turned over and stared up at a rich blue sky. Bright rays of sunshine warmed her.

Daisy shot to her feet and dashed around frantically. 'WHERE ... am I?' she shouted out. But her cries were lost in the foliage and the blossom and the gentle wind.

She sat down and threw a handful of petals into the air which caught on the breeze and fluttered to the ground nearby. Maybe she was hallucinating – 'Am I dead?' she yelled out.

She tried again. 'Is this Heaven?'

Still no answer. She kicked a pile of pink blossom, then ran over and did the same to the white and yellow piles, repeating it again and again in a frenzy until petals filled the air and snowed down over her.

'WHAT IS GOING ON?'

Daisy lay down on her back and turned her face up to the sun as the last few petals fluttered to the ground. She wiped them off and sank back, enjoying the warmth on her skin as if it were a hot spring day by a swimming pool. She listened to the rustle of wind blowing through the petals and leaves and removed her wet coat, trousers and shirt, which she hung over one of the gnarly old trees. She took off her boots.

*Since no one can see me,* she thought, *and I can't see anyone else, I can't offend anyone.* So she lay back on the bed of petals in her underwear, took a couple of deep breaths and stretched out her arms. With the sweet fragrance of the blossom overwhelming her senses, she basked contentedly and considered her fate.

*If this is Heaven, I'm sure it'll be fine to lie here a little longer. I wonder if Archie and the others will miss me,* she thought, a lump growing in her throat. *And I never said goodbye ... to anyone. Will Mum and Dad even notice ...*

Old Man Wood might. Just.

I hope they play football in Heaven.

Daisy wiped a tear from her eye and looked around.

*But I don't feel very dead.*

She re-arranged herself in the blossom and inspected her body. *This bump*, she thought, feeling her shin, *feels like me*. She stretched her neck up. *The wind blows in my hair and I can feel it.* She sniffed the air and grabbed a handful of petals; *my nose senses the perfume and my skin feels the warming rays of sun in each pore. So perhaps being dead is like being alive. Maybe that's what Heaven really is.* Daisy smiled. Got to be better than hell.

But it's a bit boring.

After a short while, she pulled herself up and scanned the area. She studied the bushes that fenced her in; thick hawthorn and blackthorn, bearing inch-long needles, interwoven with brambles and nettles. She groaned. They would tear her apart with or without clothes. The only other way out – and even then she wasn't certain of it – was to follow the line of the ditch under some bushes that looked like evil barbed wire. Definitely a last resort.

'So,' she asked out loud, having completely forgotten that she was searching for Archie, 'what happens next?'

'You're after the Atrium, right?' a voice from the side answered back.

Daisy shrieked and covered her body with her arms and hands. She looked around. There wasn't anyone there. 'Er ... who's that? Who's there?'

The same voice spoke out again. It wasn't a nasty voice. This was a kindly old voice, rich in resonance. 'You're here for the Atrium?'

'What? I mean, pardon. I mean, I'm terribly sorry,' Daisy started burying herself under the petals, 'I don't understand, your Godliness.' If this was Heaven, she reckoned she should be as polite as possible.

This time, another higher pitched voice joined in from the other side. 'You're here for the Atrium, are you dear? That's all we need to know.'

Daisy tiptoed towards the tree where she'd left her clothes. 'What ... what Aytreehum?' she said. Daisy was beginning to think her mind was playing tricks on her. 'Are whoever you are, angelic?' she asked. 'Perhaps you're the angelic invisible host?'

Daisy thought she could hear laughter, certainly sniggering. Her face reddened. Wrong question. She grabbed her jeans.

'The creature hasn't a clue,' said the higher pitched voice.

'Typical,' said the first, low, kindly voice. 'The first person who comes along for an age, and it's by mistake.'

'What do you mean?' Daisy said, a little exasperated. '*Mistake? What creature?*'

Then a voice from right beside her said, 'Don't be alarmed, dear.'

Daisy nearly jumped out of her skin. 'Alarmed!' Daisy shot back. 'Of course I'm alarmed. Who are you?'

'Poor thing,' the kindly first voice said. 'I believe she's lost.'

Daisy, now with her top on, marched about peering around the trees. 'Where are you?'

There was a pause. Daisy listened. She could hear a kind of whispering.

'Now, a quick introduction,' said the voice that had come from next to her. 'We are the Cherubim of the Rivers of the Worlds. We guard the entrance.'

'Oh no. I'm dead, aren't I?' Daisy said.

'My dear,' said the higher pitched voice. 'I don't think you look dead. Do you think you're dead?'

'No, not really—'

'Well there you have it—'

The strange voices laughed again.

Daisy was confused. 'Hang on. Where ... what entrance?' she said.

'Why, just look in front of you!'

'But all I can see is three gnarled, old, fat trees and a kind of greenhouse—'

'We're time-worn, NOT fat!' the second, higher voice shrilled.

Daisy felt as if her head might explode. *Either it's one hell of a dream,* she thought, *or a wicked hallucination.* Dead or alive, what did it matter? She lay down in the scented petals, put her fingers in her ears to block out the noises that continued to babble on, and basked in the sunshine.

Shortly, thinking that the sun had disappeared behind a cloud, Daisy opened her eyes to find the tree with pink blossom leaning directly above her.

'Joe-crockers! You moved!' she said out loud to the tree.

The tree straightened, a flurry of petals swamping Daisy. 'Oh yes indeedy! I haven't done that for a few thousand years. Apples it feels gooood.'

Certain that the tree had been talking to her, Daisy sat up and brushed off the petals. She shut her eyes and thrust out her hand. 'Hello, my name is Daisy de Lowe, from Eden Cottage, which I think is somewhere over there.' She found herself pointing randomly.

'I have absolutely no idea what's going on, or how I got here, but I'm looking for my brother Archie. He's about my height with strange spiky hair. And he's a little bit shy. You haven't seen him, have you?'

Then, as an afterthought, she added, 'And, your Godlinesses, please can you clear one thing up for me? I'd be most grateful if you'd tell me if I really am actually dead or alive?'

# 60 OLD MAN WOOD FINDS HIS FRIENDS

The laughter, for Old Man Wood, grew and grew. 'Haaahaaahaaaahaaa! Haaaaaaa! Ha! Woah-ha ha!'

His eyes darted from one direction to another. Old Man Wood crouched down and coughed the remaining water from his windpipe. 'They're laughing at me, Archie. Masses of them – in hysterics.'

'Cor, this is the most hilarious thing I've seen for years,' said a voice.

Old Man Wood's ears pricked up. 'Someone spoke. There! There it is again!' he boomed. 'Can you hear them?'

'Hear who?' Archie quizzed, trying to find the source of Old Man Wood's outburst. 'You sure you're alright?'

'Uh—? You can't hear it?' Old Man Wood whispered. 'You must be able to!'

'No, there's nothing—'

'There! There they go, loads of them. Laughing, talking, hum-humming.'

Archie strained his ears, 'Hum-humming? I can't hear anything – only rain.'

Old Man Wood scrambled across a branch, his head turning to and fro trying to locate the source of this invisible sound.

'You know,' Archie said, 'maybe you're hearing things. Is there water in your ears?'

Old Man Wood stared at him, his eyes bulging quite madly. He shook his head. 'Definitely not.'

'Look,' Archie insisted, 'there isn't anything here. I think we should go home for breakfast.' He scoured the clump. 'Really, there's nothing.' He watched Old Man Wood shuffle up another trunk.

'Oh yes there is, Archie.'

Archie sighed. 'Let's get back, please? You'll catch pneumonia if you hang around too long.'

But Old Man Wood had abandoned his boots and was now scurrying around the trees and bushes like a man possessed; dashing around the thicket, wading through the pools and peering through, under and around the trees.

'Reveal yourselves!' he cried. 'Where the devil are you?!'

---

ARCHIE WAVED and shouted at Old Man Wood. On his third attempt to grab his attention, Archie decided that the old man had totally and utterly lost the plot.

*Brilliant!* He thought. *One half of our grown-up team has gone nuts.* What would headmaster Solomon say if he saw this? They'd be whisked from the cottage and taken into care, exactly as Solomon said. He snapped off a wet, dangling branch and tossed it in the water and stared at Old Man Wood who was still bouncing around the pool, ducking here and peering there behind the trees.

Archie felt empty inside. *He's going to have to go mad all on his own,* he thought. Making as little fuss as possible, Archie scrambled over the fallen tree trunks and returned out of the clump the way they'd entered, back towards Eden cottage.

---

TO OLD MAN WOOD, the giggling continued. Then, slowly, it came to him as his old brain cells started functioning.

'Is that you?' He turned his head to the sky. 'Is it the sound of the old trees?'

This time, the trees collectively seemed to agree. And their laughter was now more of joy at seeing Old Man Wood than roaring at his antics.

'Archie! Here! I think I've found them. I told you so,' Old Man Wood yelled out before turning back to the brook. 'How come I can hear you old sticks?'

'Well, hello to you, too, Old Man Wood,' was the reply from the willows. 'The water is sooo high, way up, up over those steps, hum-hum. With any luck, we have ourselves several days of the loveliest special water, hum-hum,' said a voice from the largest of the weeping willow trees. There was a general murmur of approval. 'Can you see us yet?'

Old Man Wood strained his eyes.

'Have yourself another good sip, dear old friend; you must have had a lil' taster in the pool to hear us laughing at you, hum-hum. By Heavens above, that was one funny sight, you still can make a tree laugh, old man.'

Old Man Wood cupped his large, old, leathery hands and brought the water to his mouth. It tasted metallic and bitter, as though laced with iron and sulphur, and the liquid fizzed and made his eyes wobble for a few seconds. He shut them as a buzzing sensation rolled in and tumbled about his mind. When he opened them again, he looked out over the brook.

Where before he noted an array of stems and boughs, now, and perched on each tree, were tiny elf-like figures no bigger than shoe boxes, with small, pointed ears and sharp noses.

Each of the tree elves had rough, coarse skin like bark and their tiny bodies were shrouded in mini clothes the colour of willow leaves. Tiny arms, like twigs, protruded from either side of their bodies and each had sharp eyes, like polished wood, that darted from place to place.

'Aha! Apples alive!' Old Man Wood exclaimed. 'The spirits of the trees. I see you!'

The old man noted that the larger trees had bigger elf-like creatures attached to them, and the young ones on the smaller stems ran up and down the trunks, their little legs disappearing into the wood and sometimes disappearing into the trunk of the tree altogether and then reappearing at the end of a branch dangling from their heads, or sitting at the foot of the tree trunk by the roots.

'Crimpers!' Old Man Wood said, as he hugged the biggest tree enthusiastically, the strange elfin creature standing with one foot attached to the tree and the other on Old Man Wood's head. 'How many are you?'

'We're now a family of sixty-seven,' said a deep voice from behind him. 'Loads of new little whips and a couple of small trees and, hum-hum, us big 'uns just keep on growing.'

Old Man Wood closed his eyes. 'Let me see if I can remember. Bethedi ...'

'Well, well, well, hum-hom. Isn't that something?' said a wiry, elderly tree-elf dangling off a big tree to the side of the brook. 'He remembers my name! So your memory is still intact, huh?'

'There's the thing,' Old Man Wood replied. 'It isn't. It's been an awful long time—'

'You mean,' the tree-elf said, ducking into the tree and reappearing at eye level with Old Man Wood, 'even with this great rain, you don't know what's happening?'

Old Man Wood groaned. 'I feel a yearning – an ache in my bones, but my brain gets all clogged up. And strange nightmares that I don't understand, with bits here and there that seem familiar and others that are a mystery. I've forgotten everything.'

'But you *do* know who you are?'

Old Man Wood frowned. 'I'm not really sure anymore.'

The noise of *hum-homs* and *him-hims* erupted around the brook as the elves absorbed this information. 'You quite sure about this?'

'Yes!' Old Man Wood replied.

'Then, hem-hem, you've come to the right place,' said a soft, higher voice from the third large tree on the far side of the brook. 'And in the nick of time, it would appear. Do you remember me? I'm Crespidistra, hem-hem?'

'Crespidistra,' Old Man Wood repeated, nodding. He propped himself up on the tree and looked over the water as the slender, feminine willow-spirit continued. 'We lost Jonix a few seasons back,' she said. 'He died from a painful canker, but he had time to pass on his knowledge. We miss him dearly ... but lately, a whole raft of new willows sprouted. Let me introduce you to our saplings.' The elegant willow spirit turned to the nursery. 'Say hello to our oldest and dearest friend, Mr Old Man Wood, hem-hem; the greatest and, indeed the only, being of his kind on this planet!'

With that, a huge 'Hello Mr Old Man Wood,' in an assortment of high and low voices called out over the gentle spring waters, followed by a range of ***um-ums*** and ***im-ims***.

Old Man Wood beamed back at them, when he suddenly remembered Archie. He searched around. 'I've found them,' he yelled out, 'Archie, here, they're here,' he repeated. 'Come, look—'

'Your friend left a little while ago, while you were, hem-hem ... figuring things out,' Crespidistra said gently, before disappearing into the tree and re-emerging higher up. She looked out towards the hill.

Old Man Wood followed her gaze and glimpsed Archie looking down at him from a distance up the bank. He waved enthusiastically but Archie waved back rather half-heartedly, shaking his head. *Oh well,* the old man thought. *Probably just as well.*

'Can I say on behalf of all the willow-spirits, what a magnificent entrance that was, my old friend – you certainly haven't lost your style. Welcome to the Bubbling Brook, where all things speak as one.'

The smaller tree-spirits erupted into laughter, pulling their stems one way and then the other, so that, very shortly, the noise of twigs snapping and cracking on one another filled the Bubbling Brook, like applause.

'Took you a while to find us, though – the water's been high for a couple of days now,' the elf said as she sat at the end of a branch that hung over the water. 'It's been a long time since we last spoke, hem-hem?'

'I hope you've got some juicy things to tell—?' said another, named Willip. 'It's so boring here. Did you ever manage to find your way into that storeroom?'

'How is that vegetable patch of yours?' said another. 'Some of the birds told us you'd grown star-shaped carrots.'

'And what of that young lady?' asked an elf called Shodwonk who, as his name suggested, was a little lopsided.

'And did you ever hear back from that friend of yours with all those ideas?'

Old Man Wood looked startled and scratched his head.

'You know, him-hom, about five hundred and thirty-two seasons ago. Mr Len Vinchi?'

'Oooh yes,' Crespidistra added, 'such a nice young man, hem-hem. And how are your apple trees? The apple spirits don't like to get out, always claim they're too busy—'

'Now, hum-hum,' said the deeper voice of Bethedi, 'fill us in, won't you. How have you been getting along, dear friend?'

Old Man Wood clapped his hands together as a smile spread from one side of his gnarled old face to the other. He beamed at the curious clump with their little tree elves homming and humming. Then, after a bit of a fuss, he sat down respectfully on one half of Jonix's stump, took a deep breath and began by telling the trees about the children, and how he'd found Mrs Pye in the woods at the bottom of a gorge, mangled and covered in blood and that they still didn't know who she was, or where she'd come from.

He followed this by telling them about his beloved vegetable patch and his trusty cattle. He went into limited detail about his struggle with bolting purple spinach and how the answer to his carrot fly problem was to grow the vegetables in containers on the roof. All the while the willow spirits listened, asking questions when appropriate, and laughing at exactly the right moments.

Old Man Wood felt as if he was talking to his oldest friends. And, in a way, this observation wasn't so far off the truth. For no matter how ancient Old Man Wood grew, the willow trees had the ability to remember in astonishing detail each and every word he'd ever told them, from the day they had first met. And this knowledge had been passed on from generation to generation.

These willow tree-spirits were information sponges – a perfect living memory bank. And if Old Man Wood asked a question about his past they would tell him because they held the answers within their sap ... but this information would never be given freely.

If Old Man Wood wanted to know something, he had to ask the right question.

---

JUST THEN, two ducks flew through the branches and, with a minimum of effort, dropped into the middle of the pool of water. Automatically, the ducks dunked their heads and, moments later, surfaced shaking their heads from side to side.

'Hey! You gnarled-old-pieces-of-timber,' the first duck said. 'What do you give a sick bird?'

'Tweetment!' the other said, before any of the tree spirits had the chance to respond. 'Hey, and did you see that duck who came in here? He really ... quacked me up! Whoaaa! I'm on form today,' the duck continued. 'And what about the owl, huh?' said the second duck. 'He couldn't give a hoot!' They both quacked with laughter. 'Ha-aha, oh boy, oh boy, oh boy we're good,' the first duck said, 'anything to liven up you boards. Whoa, geddit – *boards* – that's terrific, ha ha!' the birds sang as they lifted themselves out of the glade.

'Cres,' Bethedi said, 'can't we stop those blasted ducks flying in here, telling their appalling jokes?'

'You know there's nothing we can do and they're a great deal better than the blackbirds who simply repeat things over and over again if they like the sound of it.'

Old Man Wood shook his head and laughed – the sound of his rich voice echoing around the brook. He'd forgotten how wonderful the world was when everything could talk – and spell – given the right circumstances.

He was overjoyed to be with old friends.

Right now, however, he needed to put the trees' memory to the test and think of some good questions.

But where would he begin? And what sort of questions would be most helpful to all of them?

Just thinking of this quandary made his head pound and his eyes heavy with worry.

# 61 ARCHIE'S KNIVES

Archie squeezed between the old oak upright and the wooden door that had jammed tight against the cold concrete floor of the garden shed. Inside, he felt for the familiar course fibres of a pile of old empty sacks and fell heavily into them. His cheeks, red from running in the cold wet air, stung with the salt of his tears and the walk up the slippery hill had made his legs burn. He found the light on his watch. Not yet ten. It felt like lunchtime, especially as he'd forgone breakfast. Archie tried to get himself comfortable, to settle his mind, but he couldn't think clearly for the noise of the rain, which now drummed hard on the tiles above his head.

He reached behind one of the sacks, feeling for a bundle tied in a package of cloth.

Archie untied the layer of cloth, pulling out five stunning silver-coloured knives. He ran his hand over the sharp tips and shivered as he thought about the strange ghost, Cain, and the ruby-encrusted knife. He touched the scar on his chin. *The power of a horse and the courage of a lion*, he thought – ridiculous – even if he couldn't get it out of his head. And he smiled as the image of himself, deeply muscled, entered his mind and he wondered if somehow, impossibly, he really had acquired strength of some sort. How had he managed to pull that tree out and carry Daisy and push the boulder out of the way? And yet, here he was, still his reasonably puny self. He tensed his arms and the muscle bulge wasn't impressive. He patted his head and felt his spikes, which were hard. Maybe it had something to do with his spikes – something to do with being partially hit by lightning?

Archie's knives were like secret friends. He knew how to hold them, care for them, balance them and hide them away. It was his one secret, albeit a badly kept secret, for Isabella knew and she hated them with a passion that Archie thought was way over the top.

He remembered the day he found them. It was two days after his seventh birthday and they were playing a game of hide and seek in the ruin. He spied a dark space beneath an outcrop of stone and, without thinking, crammed himself under it, working his body under until he had all but disappeared. As he scraped the earth furiously to give himself more space, his hand touched upon a cloth.

Instantly his curiosity was aroused. As he feverishly reached in and dug further, he realised that inside this cloth lay hard objects. Treasure? He remembered his excitement but, just then and much to his annoyance Isabella rounded the corner, saw one of his feet and dragged him out. He had left the bundle there, but even now he wondered why he hadn't brought them out and shared his excitement with the others. Somehow, this was his own little secret. His, and no one else's.

A few days later, he returned. His fingers touched the bundle again, and the same thrill passed through him. Using a trowel from Old Man Wood's potting shed, he teased the package from the hard earth. Bit by bit, more and more came. And as he scraped, he found that the cloth was bound deep in the chasm holding the treasure within it. Archie pulled until eventually the bundle popped out like a cork from a bottle. With the evening drawing in he ran home and hid his treasure under the bed. Archie's excitement meant he could barely talk through supper and the following day, with the girls in town, he opened the package.

The cloth itself felt unusual, certainly like nothing he'd seen before. Wound neatly round and round, the fabric was light and strong even though he'd tried to rip and pierce it. Inside were three knives, each one about ten inches in length, made from slender sticks of metal. The knives shimmered as he touched them.

The tips were slender, with sharpened edges leading to a point, like leaves off a plum tree. The handles, were flat, like a wider version of an ordinary kitchen knife. And he noted that as no water had penetrated the metal, no rust or discolouration showed, so he figured that no air had entered either – or the metal wasn't steel. As he inspected them, right in the middle of each one, he found a pattern, a circle of lines swirling – mirrored – top and bottom.

It took him several days to work out how they should be used. As hunting knives they were all wrong; the blades weren't long enough and the handles ungainly. In the woods, as he ambled along figuring it out, he held one in his hand, balancing it. As he rounded a corner, there, beside the carcass of a rabbit, was a rat. Without thinking, Archie cocked his arm back and let the knife go. It flew through the air and landed with a thud, killing the rat instantly. Archie stared in shock as a thrill passed through him. How had he managed to do that?

From that moment on, he knew knife-throwing would be his thing. He wanted to be the best in the world. At first, when the house was empty, he threw the knives from the end of his bed onto an old cork notice board that he kept hidden under his bed.

What he discovered, by a process of elimination and frustration, and with the help of Old Man Wood, who he'd secretly confided in, was that each knife had a different weight, and he figured that each one had to rotate through the air at either a different speed or at the same speed but from a different distance.

Archie spent hours trying to work it out. And slowly it came to him. Soon he could automatically judge the weight and the throwing speed of each knife. Then one day, much to his surprise, he rubbed the emblem in the middle and, as if by magic, a smaller knife unfurled itself from the body of the big knife. The same thing happened on each, but as with the larger knives, the smaller ones bore different weights. Now he had six knives to play with; three heavy and three light.

Archie played with the smaller ones indoors, against his cork board, and the larger ones on an old wooden log in the forest. He didn't want anyone to know because he sensed that all hell would break loose, and he was right. In the end, it did.

One day, in the woods, while Archie thought the others were fooling around in the house, he set up a target which consisted of a woolly mop head and one of Daisy's old shirts which he'd pinned against a tree. Archie had mastered his throw from ten feet and now he was attempting a new distance – thirteen feet, which meant holding the knife the other way round. The first two had clattered into the bark and fallen to the ground. Archie weighed up the final one. The heaviest of all. He pulled his arm back and, throwing a little harder, let go. But at that exact moment, Isabella's head suddenly appeared by the tree.

Archie gasped.

The knife whistled through the air and, to his enormous relief, with a gentle thud, the blade nestled into the wood. For a fraction of a second, Archie wondered whether Isabella knew what he was doing. She looked at him curiously. Then her eyes followed his – to where he was looking. She moved around the tree and saw the end of the knife – straight through the breast pocket of Daisy's old shirt.

Isabella went berserk, screaming at him for being reckless and stupid and for plotting to kill them. Archie protested but Isabella gathered the knives and ran inside.

From that moment on, his knives were forbidden and it was made clear that they would not be tolerated in, or around, the house. Finally, on his eighth birthday he was allowed to have them back on condition that he always told a grown up when and where he was throwing, and never, ever, anywhere near Isabella.

---

IN THE DIMNESS of the musty, rickety shed, Archie focused on the large log. He balanced the first knife in the palm of his hand, a sparkle of gleaming metal catching a ray of light that had crept nervously under the gap in the door.

Thud.

The knife flashed into the thick wood. Archie wanted to throw it quicker – venting this curious anger that kept welling up in him.

He rubbed his front hair spike that stood as hard as iron. He knew he would have to throw it twice as fast. The next kicked out a splinter of wood. *Nice one,* he thought, *much better. Exactly in the right spot.*

And while he did this, it gave him time to think, time to reflect, time to work out what his dreams were all about.

---

ON THE ONE HAND, his dreams had made him feel like a bloodthirsty thug intent on the destruction of everything. Then, a moment later, he remembered how the sensation departed and he'd be laughing and joking with his sisters and friends and he couldn't remember being happier. And then his dreams would swing back to violence and this curious desire for power, which made his bones shiver because Archie's violent feelings were contrary to his laidback approach to life.

He was an average kid; scruffy and carefree; "horizontal" and "chilled" were words often associated with him. He was friendly too, to ... well, everyone; he got on with people – he always had – preferring to walk away, or talk, rather than head into a fight. Perhaps that was why Kemp liked him?

What shocked him most was how utterly real his dreams were, particularly the nightmare of the murder in which he had killed the Ancient Woman with a strength and anger he could not resist. He couldn't tell how he'd done it, but she had died by his hand. And yet, in a strange contradiction, he wondered if this Ancient Woman wanted to die, enticing him to kill her, even if she meant no wrong.

And did Daisy's dream – where she had screamed at him as though possessed by demons – mean that he was different? And what about the ghost of Cain, the weird spirit who had visited him, the ghost he'd run away from? How did Cain fit the puzzle? Cain knew all about them – and about the Ancient Woman and this crazy Prophecy of Eden – but if Cain truly existed, where the hell was he from? Could Cain really be the same spirit left over from the Bible story, the son of Adam and Eve?

*If so,* Archie thought, *what did Cain want? And how did Cain know about the "strength of a horse and the courage of a lion".* Archie toyed with this thought. He had strength, yes – possibly. But courage? No, not really.

It didn't add up.

Archie twisted the knife in his hand, flicking the dull blade around his fingers. He didn't have Isabella's cleverness to try and work it out nor Daisy's easy going nature to forget. To Archie, these confusing thoughts filled his soul with darkness.

And now, to top it off, Old Man Wood had gone totally stark-raving bonkers. Sure, you could talk to trees in dreams, but at 8:30 in the morning – to a clump of willows?

They'd have to get the old man seen to – proper medical help. Northallerton had a decent geriatric ward, at least that's what Gus Williams said. He used to visit his great-grandfather who got everything muddled up before he passed away.

The unfamiliar anger brewed in his veins again; his neck throbbed as a pain shot into his head. 'Why?' he said out loud to the dank air in the shed. 'I'm a twelve, nearly thirteen-year-old boy, and I'm sitting in a cold potting-shed in North Yorkshire, scared out of my mind. Why me?

'WHY ME?' he yelled. 'WHAT IS HAPPENING TO US?'

Annoyed that there were simply no answers, he weighed up his heaviest knife. He summoned every ounce of strength in his body and, with a cry, threw it as hard as he could at the old stump.

Archie walked across the floor and ran his hands over the two foot-thick log which now lay on the ground, split clean in half.

He smiled, picked the knife off the floor and, for a reason he couldn't explain, rubbed the centre over his jeans. He looked at it again and, just as he was returning it to the cloth, he realised he'd seen it before.

In the centre of the knife lay the circular emblem of a tree, with branches arching out above and roots mirrored identically below. The emblem of the Tree of Life.

He'd seen it in the cave, the exact same emblem. His heart beat quickened. The emblem at the beginning of the mural bearing fruit, and in the middle depicting death and finally by the images that reminded him of rebirth – of a new beginning.

Archie gasped and for the first time he wondered if the words of Cain should be taken with deadly seriousness. In his mind, he ran through the meeting in the alleyway again and again trying to remember every word until he realised his bones were aching.

Cain told of a prophecy – that the storm was only the beginning. It blended in perfectly with what he'd seen in the cave.

Niggling at the back of his mind was another thing; what had become of Kemp? Did he die, or run to high ground, or, and his pulse raced at the thought, did he actually join with Cain? Poor Kemp. Whatever happened, it must have been a nightmare. He was probably better off dead.

He rolled his neck and took a deep breath.

Whatever was going on, Daisy was right. All these things were somehow linked and they were right bang in the middle of it. And if only he could remember the general gist of Cain's speech to Kemp because, he realised, it was absolutely pivotal to the outcome.

Like it or not.

# 62 THE MIRACLE BOY

With his mouth and nose enclosed by a clear plastic breathing device, Kemp sucked in a large mouthful of oxygen and opened his eyes. Slowly, Kemp's brain began to wonder where he was.

He listened. A gentle churning noise, like the dull throb of an engine, of machinery gently running through its processes, followed by a regular bleep.

His body felt lighter and, as he ran a check over his anatomy, he noticed the burning didn't hurt compared to the agony he'd experienced before. Perhaps he'd died after all.

Kemp searched his body for signs of Cain.

None.

For a moment his mind and body leapt for joy. Then he remembered that Cain might be asleep. And Cain never slept for long. His eyes felt heavy again.

His ears picked out noises nearby.

He listened. Voices, deep voices, whispering, occasionally louder. Concerned, anxious tones. One higher pitched than the others. He tried to move his hands but they felt leaden, as though fixed down by weights. He yearned for someone to hold him and love him, for the comfort of a warm hug, of gentle words and soothing kisses. He pined for the mother he never knew.

A terrible sadness sank into him and a tear rolled down his cheek. He needed to sleep.

Kemp felt his mind drift off once more.

---

PRIME MINISTER KINGSFORD was basking on his sun lounger in Italy when the news broke. Three days into his break and the phones went crazy. *Typical*, he thought. Of all the weeks! Here he was with his family, gradually unwinding from the rigours of government, when there's an emergency of simply epic proportions to deal with.

*It was true; you never got time out in this job,* he mused, and with an election looming, he had needed a week to recharge his batteries. And now this. Oh well, what did he expect? *Running the country,* he thought, *was like looking after thousands of plates spinning on sticks and making sure that each person twiddling a stick kept it moving.* If one plate fell, it became an event or an outcry or a scandal. When a whole pile of them crashed, the pointing finger of the media spotlight inevitably turned on him.

He caught a helicopter the following day to find out what was happening. By the time he arrived, the damage had been done and England's heart lay in ruins. As the chopper flew north from London, he saw at first hand extraordinary scenes beneath him. From as far south as Lincolnshire, through the Midlands, into South Yorkshire then on and up through the Vale of York between the Moors and Dales, he looked out of the window to find a country underwater. Entire towns were submerged, fields transformed into huge, muddy lakes, only occasionally interspersed by protruding islands of high ground.

His leadership hung by a thread. It was typical, he thought. Those damn media people. What on earth could he do about a biblical-style freak flood? Furthermore, the damage had been so sudden, so brutal. Coordinating a rescue effort in these conditions and setting up COBRA, the emergency government council, took time. Time which they didn't have. To the rest of the country, their efforts appeared disorganised and uncoordinated ... *'Too little action, too late'* the papers screamed. *It must look,* he thought, *like a shambles.* But they were doing everything they could.

Victims of the storm were being found every hour, bloated and floating in the waters, thousands of people displaced, homes ruined, infrastructure wrecked, businesses destroyed and lives shattered. The difficulty was that the rains hadn't let up enough to enable the waters to recede, while high tides meant the water had nowhere to go. From his vantage point in the chopper, the Prime Minister fully understood how desperate the situation truly was. The military faced an uphill battle to coordinate a salvage operation in such adverse conditions. But, as the hours went by, fingers pointed accusingly at the Prime Minister.

Worse still was the latest development. A deadly virus was spreading. World governments and the media were clamouring for updates and yet there was very little he could tell them. The only option was to meet the experts in North Yorkshire, find out what they knew first hand, so he might understand what they were up against.

Soon enough, he found himself wearing an anti-contamination suit and staring through thick glass at a sick bald boy in an isolation unit; the miracle boy, found naked in the top of a tree right in the middle of a huge expanse of water. The images, already a sensation around the world, represented a glimmer of hope; a good news story, amongst the carnage, as the disaster spiralled out of control.

The Prime Minister recognised this and wondered how long he could put off facing the press and their questions. The media were baying like hounds for a story, and he needed it to be a positive one. The boy's survival remained top priority.

---

DR ADRIAN MULLER instantly struck everyone who met him as a kindly man. His sharp nose, thick mop of dark hair that flopped across his forehead and his jutting jaw line that moved from side to side when he talked, gave him a curiously academic air. He took hold of the clipboard and ran his finger down the boy's chart. Without meaning to, he raised his thick, dark, eyebrows which dislodged his half-moon wire-framed glasses. He nudged them back into place without even noticing.

He studied the data again. The boy's survival simply didn't make sense. 'Are you sure these are correct?'

The nurse, her mousy hair tied behind her head in a bun, confirmed the data. It had been triple checked she told him. And, keeping her voice low, she said, 'His condition is unlike any of the other flood victims. Typically, what we're noticing is a combination of hypothermia and a form of viral infection. This is nothing like that. Now that he's come out of his coma – we're hoping to talk to the boy later today.'

Dr Muller shook his head as he looked beyond the sheet of glass in front of him.

The boy lay on the bed, his mouth and nose covered by a plastic mask, his arms pricked with drips that dangled from him like flexible plastic straws. Littering his body were bandages, liberally administered, as if he were part human, part Egyptian mummy.

Two other men stood next to the medics in the gallery room with the window that looked in on the boy. One was Charlie Stone, the tall, thin, silver-haired Police Commissioner and chief coordinator of the flood relief, and the other was Prime Minister, Ed Kingsford.

And the PM was more than a little irritated by the whole thing.

---

'HE'S BEEN LOOKED over by the pathologists,' the doctor said.

'Good,' Commissioner Stone nodded. 'When will their findings be available?'

Dr Muller cocked his head. 'In roughly two to four hours,' he replied. 'They're working on it now.'

'And is this the same illness as the others?' said the Prime Minister.

'We don't know, sir,' the doctor replied, his jaw jutting one way and then the other. 'At the moment, it appears not. The symptoms common to the majority of victims are not evident – at least not yet. That's what makes him intriguing. We have the world's leading scientists evaluating this type of influenza, yet the boy here has none of the rashes, skin discolouration, acute vomiting or bowel dysfunction seen in the others. This little fella's main problem is malnutrition, poisoning and burns.'

'Burns?' Commissioner Stone quizzed.

'Indeed,' Dr Muller replied. The news of this had surprised him too. 'Small burns covering all four limbs, front and back and around the neck up to the ears. We think his hair has been singed off – not a single follicle can be found on his body. In his mouth, we discovered traces of soot and burn-blisters. It's as if this boy has been in a fire or been sprayed with a flammable substance.' The doctor raised his eyebrows. 'Were any fires reported?'

Commissioner Stone thought for a minute. 'Further south from where the boy was found there were two big blazes. But the boy would've had to swim or row a raft several miles against the current to get to where he was found. And remember, he was found naked. Are there signs of hypothermia?'

Dr Muller shook his head.

'And no major flesh injuries,' the nurse added. 'Not even minor scratches or bruises, just burns.'

The doctor strummed the glass with his fingernails. 'When his samples come back, we'll know if he's a carrier. If he is, then we might be able to monitor the effect of the virus through his body. We'll try and trace the viral elements and isolate it. At the moment, he's our mystery boy and the only hope for a cure.'

'What if he came from somewhere else?' the nurse asked.

'Are you suggesting he fell out of the sky, like an alien?' the Prime Minister said with sarcastic bite.

The nurse blushed.

The Prime Minister noticed and immediately regretted his sharp tongue. 'Oh, forgive me, I'm sorry,' he said. He smiled badly. 'Doctor,' he said, 'how many patients have symptoms of this ... disease, and how quickly does it affect them?'

The doctor stared at the floor. 'It acts fast; ten to thirty hours at most from incubation to death, depending on the severity of the strain and the constitution of the patient. There are sixty-two dead at the moment, each victim pulled from the water, all with the tell-tale skin rash and signs of acute vomiting and diarrhoea. In truth, Prime Minister, we have no idea how many are infected.'

'Is there any way of knowing?'

'None, I'm afraid. We don't know if it's waterborne or airborne, or both. And we don't know where it originates, but our guess is somewhere near to the epicentre of the storm, possibly the village of Upsall.' He raised his eyebrows and looked over the top of his spectacles. 'At the moment we can't tell whether it's an animal-based virus or a toxic chemical released into the floodwater.'

The Prime Minister sucked in a breath. 'What about some form of chemical or biological agent?'

'Unlikely,' the doctor replied. 'Though there are similarities to the untrained eye.'

'Have the initial life-savers, doctors and nurses shown any of the symptoms?'

'No, not yet, but many are in the containment zone, just in case,' Dr Muller continued. 'The common factor is that it appears to tie-in with those in contact with the floodwater—'

'Which is being analysed as we speak,' the Commissioner added. 'And the boy has obviously spent time in the floodwater, which makes him unique.'

A nervous quiet fell over the gathering. Then the PM asked, 'Do you know where he comes from?'

'No, I'm afraid not, Prime Minister,' Dr Muller said. 'No distinguishing marks, no clothes, nothing. We can't even tell what colour his hair is, though, from the paleness of his skin, we suspect he's a redhead.'

'And strangely,' the Commissioner said, 'no one has come forward to claim him, even though footage of the boy has been shown repeatedly on every single TV channel in the world.'

The team continued to stare at the boy, working out the next move.

'Alright, hear me out,' the Prime Minister began. 'The boy's story has captured the imagination of audiences around the globe ... and you think he might come around in the next few hours. Is there any way we can use this as a media event so we can buy some time until we have a clearer idea what this disease is? I mean, if it's contagious, we'll need to work around the clock to start the process of containment, correct?'

'Indeed, Prime Minister,' the doctor said. 'Can I suggest that before the scientists divulge their reports tonight, we start the process of sealing-off the infected area. If we take into account the movement of people during this time, the cordon needs to cover a significantly larger mileage than just the flood zone.'

Commissioner Stone nodded. 'With the known geographical spread of the flooding stretching for such a vast distance, this operation will be bigger than the evacuation of Dunkirk during the war.'

The Prime Minister coughed. 'Hang on a minute!' he said, a frown covering his face. 'Let's not run before we can walk, eh? Shouldn't we wait until the scientists report back? What if this *thing* is imminently curable?'

The doctor twiddled his thumbs. 'Prime Minister, I urge you to start the process as soon as possible. This outbreak is from an unknown pathogen and more cases are being reported on an hourly basis. We are fighting a battle with an unfamiliar enemy and time is against us. The flooding is spreading, therefore the disease is spreading. It is not going to get any easier.'

Prime Minister Kingsford had gone pale. The potential calamity of the situation was sinking in fast.

Commissioner Stone noticed. 'We have already begun it ... quietly,' he added. 'The last thing we need is a media-led panic. I have taken the liberty of putting in place a "containment zone" around North Yorkshire – travel bans to the area for everyone and I've cancelled leave for all civil servants, doctors, nurses and emergency crews. I realise this goes above my jurisdiction, but as the flood disaster tsar I had to trust my judgement.'

A murmur of agreement.

The Prime Minister's mood lifted a little now that a plan appeared to be coming together. 'Good thinking. Well done, Stone. Use whatever powers you feel necessary to get to the bottom of this bloody mess. I will make sure all the relevant authorities are aware.' One of the Prime Minister's personal private secretaries scribbled on his pad and slipped out of the room.

'So, first things first,' the Prime Minister continued. 'We invite selected media in and show them the child,' he turned to the doctor. 'You happy with that, Dr Muller?'

The doctor moved his jaw and nodded slowly. 'Sure. We can try to get the boy talking, it's a long shot but worth a go—'

'Don't you think it might appear a little bit see-through, a touch desperate?' the Commissioner asked.

The Prime Minister turned on him. 'Look, Stone, we've got the world's press outside clamouring to know what the hell's going on,' he snapped. 'Many are already sniffing about and jumping to conclusions. If the word gets out before we have any evidence, think of the consequences. Think of the panic. Imagine the morning's headlines. "*Britain – Quarantined*".' The Prime Minister paused for effect. 'In the rush to leave the disaster zone, the disease may go with it and that, my friends, will be a total catastrophe.

We need to buy time.' The Prime Minister kneaded his temples. 'The fact is this: it's our very own biblical mess and we're going to have to deal with it. It's as simple as that.'

'You're correct,' the doctor said. At last the officials were now taking the situation with the deadly seriousness it deserved. 'Good to hear you're right behind us.'

'Call a press conference for midday,' the Prime Minister ordered. 'You'll have the boy's blood results by then, so see if you can add a positive spin. Expand on the fact that this boy was found against all odds, burnt and naked up a tree, a miracle among the carnage, to give you added time. Speak to the press team. Commissioner Stone – you've got a day – more if we're lucky – to find out as much as you can and continue the "quiet" work you've started. After that – and when there's a fuller picture – the COBRA team will put a wider containment plan into action.'

Dr Muller nodded and nudged the Prime Minister gently to the side. 'If it is the start of an epidemic, Prime Minister, you are aware that you have been in an infected area and you must go through a de-contamination programme? For safety's sake, I urge you to do this at once and leave immediately after the press conference.'

The Prime Minister cocked his head. Years of being in the firing line of politics had given him a nose for judging people. 'Is there something you haven't told me, doctor?'

Dr Muller shifted and drew the PM and the Commissioner out of earshot. 'So far, we've only been able to reach a small number of people – namely those from Northallerton. We have no knowledge of the situation in the smaller villages which have been all but eradicated.' He frowned as his voice fell to a whisper. 'Early reports indicate that animals too have been found with plague-like symptoms almost identical to the human condition.'

'What is the relevance of this in relation to the outbreak?'

'Well—'

The Prime Minister stared at him open-mouthed as the truth hit him. 'You're saying that the disease – or whatever it is – is wiping out everything in its path.'

'Perhaps ... we can't rule it out,' the doctor replied. 'As I mentioned, these are only rumours and, of course, we don't know how the virus spreads – who is likely to catch it – or the conditions of infection. It could be—'

'Why was I not briefed about this?' the Prime Minister snapped. 'Have COBRA been notified?'

'There's a unit heading towards the village of Upsall – they left this morning. They are due to report back this afternoon.'

'God have mercy upon us,' the Prime Minister said under his breath. 'Isn't this the place where the storm started?'

'Indeed. Satellite recordings show that the weather system came from directly above the village—'

'Yes, I heard it was unlike any other storm formation ever recorded. What do we know?'

'As far as we're aware, it's the location of a well-known local school that inhabits an old monastery and the village is a popular tourist attraction for walkers in the summer. My cousin happens to be headmaster there. Man called Solomon.'

The PM pursed his lips. 'We need a thorough investigation of this place, and I mean *thorough*. Anything suspicious, anything ever recorded – police records, hospital records – must be analysed and re-analysed. We'll need details of farms, cattle stocks, any previous outbreaks of disease, bird populations ... anything and everything.'

'I have a team working on it already,' Stone said.

'Good. All survivors must be brought into the containment area and questioned. We need answers and quickly – like yesterday.'

The commissioner nodded.

'And pardon the pun, Stone, but leave no stone unturned. If this Godforsaken crisis cannot be explained by usual methodology, we need to work on something outside the box. Understand? And if the storm and the disease both spilled out of Upsall, then I want to know why. Is this perfectly clear?'

Stone smiled. 'Yes, sir. I understand completely.'

The Prime Minister nodded. 'Call on anyone – and I mean *anyone* you need in order to assist you. Let nothing get in your way. As far as I'm concerned, Stone, you have whatever power you need to get the bottom of this.'

# 63 ISABELLA MAKES A DISCOVERY

For a considerable time, Isabella remained under her bed covers, waking up. She'd slept like a log. She sat up and rubbed her eyes before stretching her arms out and yawning. *There must be a reason for all these odd things,* Isabella thought. *I'll work it out logically, starting with Sue's dream and then go through everything I can remember. Then, when I'm done, I'll present a logical, scientific report to the others.*

As she headed downstairs for some porridge, she grabbed her notebook and a pen and began to think hard about the chain of events that led up to where they were now.

She decided to concentrate on what she had discovered from the others, write it down and then work out which bits were linked and why they were connected. She opened her notebook, took the lid off her pen and began to write.

A LIST, **OF WHO IS / ISN'T IN MY DREAM(S).**

***Parents:***

*Not involved. Definitely remember seeing them, but can't place them anywhere.*

*Daisy hasn't mentioned them and Archie nothing. So they are fairly hopeless in not being here to help!!!*

***Sue:***

*Hasn't appeared in my dreams – WHY NOT?? So why did she have a dream ... friend??*
*Is she relevant? Probably. Don't know why.*
*She predicted the rain and knows about something we have to do ... according to her, it's our fault! Why are we to blame for the rain? Don't think so – IF SO, HOW?*
*Something else about clues ... ? in Eden Cottage. Have to find something. What? Tablets? Paintings?*
*Is Gus involved – NO. (Don't think so.)*

***Old Man Wood:***

*VERY VERY important.*
*Crops up all the time. Seems to be more than one of him, but why oh why would Old Man Wood want to be in my dreams??*
*Resplendix Mix is weird (but amazing). From an apothecary, apparently (they don't exist). Need to get a sample. His funny apples are a bit weird, too.*
*Somehow found us in the rain. HOW WAS THAT POSSIBLE???*
*Looks freaked out by what's going on. But not bothered by the ridiculous pool and Resplendix Mix.*
*Why did he laugh when doing the Bible quiz?*
*How old IS he?*

***Mrs Pye:***

*Comes into it at some point (I think) though is it actually her? Something not quite right about her. Don't know what it is.*

***Ancient Woman:***

*Vital to the whole thing. Daisy's common dominator (!!) but keeps on*

*being killed. Mainly by Archie. URGH? No idea why. She seems lost, desperately ill and frail.*
*Where is she from??*

***The Cave: (According to the twins)***

*Paintings on the wall similar to Sue's comments about finding ... what - tablets? (according to D). V Odd healing water.*
*Gears on stairs and boulder at top. Must have been designed. But WHO designed them and WHY?*

***Daisy:***

*Can hear acute things like lightning bolts forming and see astonishing detail, (though is she making it up?) Scientific explanation: Electrical charge from lightning bolt altered nerve motors in these areas. Eyes and ears suffered semi-permanent damage?*
*Also, utterly convinced that cave paintings are relevant ... D was dead? All V. odd.*

***Archie:***

Moved the boulder – though would it have gone anyway?
Hair stiff and wiry like a mace club. Scientific explanation: A mix that happened when the lighting struck between the particles of the football and lightning strips we gave him.
Very freaked out by murder of Ancient Woman.
Knew about sunset and rain ceasing. HOW? Did he dream this or ... ? Seems to know something else.
Is a bit lost and has doubt

ISABELLA READ her list and realised that she still had no idea. It struck her that she needed to interrogate Old Man Wood and quiz him relentlessly until he gave her proper, reasonable answers.

She'd start by grilling him about Resplendix Mix, which was both real and yet totally extraordinary. Then she'd ask him what he knew about the Creation story and also try to figure out how old he was.

Why not run a couple of tests on the Resplendix Mix to see if she could identify some of its properties? But then she realised she'd need a lab and light and heat and test tubes and all manner of things.

Realising her frustration, she thumped the table and threw her notepad across the room.

She'd just have to find out what she could, and prove – beyond doubt – that these were freak events that they were caught up in and nothing else.

And then she remembered that the old man said he'd been dreaming too. Perhaps she'd ask him about that as well.

---

ISABELLA TOOK off up the main wooden stairs towards his room and knocked on the solid oak door. 'Old Man Wood, are you there?' she began. 'I really need to talk.'

There was no reply. Isabella knew he wasn't in. When he was at home, either huge snores would reverberate through the door, or he'd be padding about, or rustling a newspaper on his great big bed; or the curious odour of pine-scented smoke from his homemade pipe with its strangely reassuring woody aroma would drift into the corridor from under the door.

Isabella waited a moment longer and turned the door handle. She peeked behind her, entered the room and closed the door. In the middle sat Old Man Wood's great bed. She tiptoed over the musty little carpets and jumped high in the air, landing in the soft pile of the feather-down duvet and cushions.

With her head propped up by large, soft pillows she lost herself in thought, and stared at the rain tracing its way down the windowpanes. Her attention turned to the beautiful wooden carvings that depicted strange scenes and images of animals and creatures which adorned every upright and joint on the old four-poster bed. She smiled as she remembered how, as younger children, they had spent hours creating outrageous stories with the wooden characters and, now that she thought about it, the carvings were never quite the same from one day to the next. *Probably*, she thought, *just their childish imaginations running wild.*

Isabella studied the three wooden panels at the foot of the bed. She couldn't remember seeing these before. Three panels, each the size of a large, rectangular place mat. The harder she looked, the deeper the array of colours; dark and light reds, pale and ocean-deep blues, soft and rich browns and a mixture of subtle creams and yellows. But overall, if you looked quickly, the wood was light brown.

Isabella pulled herself up and helped herself to a sip of water from Old Man Wood's glass. Then she lay back again.

Hang on! The figure in the first panel moved!

Oh. No, it didn't.

She smiled. But as she journeyed down memory lane, she stared at it again and noticed a girl sitting in a bed. She laughed. It looked quite like her, but probably prettier and thinner. Weird or what?

She turned her attention to the second panel, the wood lighter in colour than the others. The harder she looked the clearer she could see another girl lying down, somewhere where the sun was shining. The girl sunbathing but lying in snow in between three fat, rather deformed, trees.

Isabella felt a little jealous. *How nice to feel the sun,* she thought, but odd that the girl was semi-naked in snow. Just as Isabella lifted her head to see what else was on the bed-head, she detected a movement in the panel.

It changed! It definitely changed. She laughed nervously. Come on, Isabella, don't be an idiot. Bed panels don't move. She shut her eyes and lay back. But a part of her brain wouldn't let the imagery go.

She looked again and it was still. She breathed a sigh of relief.

Then the image moved again.

In shock, Isabella felt her head going numb. She stared, her bottom lip hanging, forgetting to breathe.

At length she exhaled. 'It's moving. It's really moving ... like a...' she muttered. Isabella sat bolt upright, shut her eyes and swung her legs off the bed. 'Like a ... telly.'

She walked past the wooden panels and over to the window where she sat down in Old Man Wood's armchair and shook her head. She must be seeing things.

After a few minutes, she reaffirmed that she was normal. There was nothing wrong with her eyes or her brain, and although her stomach felt hollow she took herself back to the bed.

She lay back, closed her eyes and then slowly opened them, hoping like mad that she'd been seeing things. But, to Isabella's horror, the girl in the wooden relief stood up, walked first one way and then the other before heading towards the frame of something that resembled a large greenhouse.

Isabella felt sick. However much she didn't want to believe it, she couldn't tear her eyes away.

The girl, now clothed, walked into this strange looking area where, across the floor, lay another object, rather like Old Man Wood's old-fashioned garden roller but with a flat ledge, like a table. If it wasn't a roller, what was it?

Isabella rubbed her eyes, swung her legs off the bed again and this time faced the mirror above the fireplace. She looked deeply at her reflection, particularly at her eyes. Then she pulled her hands up to her face and slapped each cheek as hard as she dared.

'OW!' she cried, surprised by the force. 'Wow, that hurt,' she said, rubbing her cheek, feeling a little foolish.

'OK. I'm real and this is real and that slap was definitely real,' she said to her reflection. 'So how has Old Man Wood managed to do this?' she continued. 'Is he a secret agent, a spy? Does he work for a space agency or something?' Isabella laughed. Old Man Wood as a spy, hilarious. Spaceman – even more hilarious. She walked across the room and lowered herself into his armchair.

A frown filled her face and her eyes narrowed. What if he's a wizard, or a witch doctor, or an ALIEN?

A thrill swept through her. It would explain the Resplendix Mix.

Isabella returned to the bed, full of trepidation, and settled back in the cushions. She closed her eyes and then half opened them, hoping the images had gone. They hadn't.

So, this time, she sat up and examined the subtle movement of the panels and the more she studied it, the more enchanted she became.

*If it's a kind of wooden telly,* she thought, *then it must have power going to it.* She began searching for wires, or a transmitter, or anything that might make a bit of sense. But again, she drew a blank.

Isabella sighed, clambered back onto the bed and returned to her viewing. For some time, the girl in the middle panel sat on the roller-object and nothing happened. Every now and then, her arms were thrown in the air in a familiar gesture that Isabella recognised from somewhere. Then the girl stood up and, with considerable effort, began to pull the roller-object's handle and, as she did so, a hole opened up where the table had been.

*This is more like it,* Isabella thought, pleased to see some action. The girl in the panel returned to the space where the table had been and appeared to look at it. Then she knelt down and swivelled as if she was talking to someone.

I'm sure I know that bum, Isabella thought, and the way that body bends forward so easily, like a doll, but who is it?

Isabella moved her attention to the third panel at the end of the bed which, up until then, had remained lifeless. But now that her eyes were accustomed to the colours, she could make out the outline of a body curled up in the corner of a darkened room.

Suddenly she saw a movement – an arm cocked back and then slammed quickly forward.

'Whoa!' she cried. 'What's that all about?' She watched again and shuffled closer to the screen. Moments later, the exact same motion happened. She suddenly realised what she was looking at.

'It's Archie!' she whispered, her heart racing, 'with his stupid throwing knives. I knew he hadn't got rid of them.' She watched closer. The figure stood up and there, on the top of his head, were his extraordinary hair spikes.

Isabella put her head in her hands. If that's Archie, then the middle one ... she looked at the picture of the girl in the sunshine again. That bum! Of course! It was ... *Daisy's bum!*

Isabella clapped her hands together. The third panel is Archie. The middle panel with the roller-object and that lovely bottom is Daisy's, so the last panel is ... she threw her hand in the air and the image on the relief copied her.

*It was her!*

A strange dizziness started to rush in.

It's me! Here, in Old Man Wood's bed!

Isabella stared back at herself, hardly daring to move. A dull ache jammed her brain.

Keep calm, need to think. Come on, brain; what ... OK ... who was Old Man Wood, really? And why this bed? For spying on them? Why though, for Heaven's sake? For perving on them? No. It couldn't be. Old Man Wood wasn't a pervert, not one little bit.

Perhaps it was a kind of child-monitor while the parents were away? No – way too expensive and ridiculous and impossible.

But why did he have it and what did it mean? Why did it exist?

Her heart thumping, she turned back to the wooden screens. Archie's arm flashed forward, throwing another stupid knife. By the dinginess of it he's probably in that horrible old woodshed.

But where was Daisy? On the panel it appeared as sunny, whereas outside, and she looked out of the window, it was dank, rainy and horrible. In her mind's eye she ran through every place on the farm and by the ruins but no place came close.

She took a deep breath and, totally absorbed by the spectacle, viewed her sister. But a moment later, Daisy disappeared.

One minute she was there and the next ... *where is she?*

A lump grew in Isabella's throat and her heartbeat quickened. Was the panel faulty?

Suddenly the wooden screen came back to life.

Phew. Panic over!

Isabella breathed a sigh of relief as she watched Daisy scuttle about on her hands and knees trying to move the roller thing.

She's talking again.

Then Isabella watched as Daisy stood up like a sentry and pointed towards the ground, her mouth open wide as if ... screaming.

Slowly, her body lowered into the ground; first her legs, then her chest, until all that remained was her head. Moments later she vanished entirely.

The screen went blank.

Isabella stared at the panel for several minutes, transfixed, until her large eyes filled with tears. But there was no mistaking it; while she and Archie remained on their panels, Daisy's wooden panel lay empty and lifeless and dull, like an ordinary section of their dining room table.

Daisy, she realised, had quite literally vanished.

# 64 A BEE AND A LEAF

Daisy squeezed her eyes shut and sucked in a lungful of air as if it were her last.

Suddenly her legs were pulled from under her as she tore off, a combination of whizzzooming at breakneck speed down the fastest water chute in the world, being thrown around in a tumble dryer and blown about by an enormous hairdryer all at the same time.

Two seconds later, she found herself lying on a cold, dusty floor, her heart racing.

*Those ridiculous trees encouraged her,* she thought as she gathered her wits; *and she'd taken their advice! Idiot!* She should have tackled the undergrowth by the ditch like any normal person.

With her eyes clamped tight and her head spinning, she spread her fingers and collected a thin, velvety substance on her hands. Dust. Fine dust. She pushed her hand in. A lot of dust. She sniffed the air. It smelt like a combination of decayed cheese and old newspapers.

Slowly, she opened her eyes. 'Where am I?' she whispered.

Her voice echoed back to her several times, eerie and ghost-like. She shivered as a deathly silence surrounded her.

Daisy picked herself off the dusty floor and began to survey the area. The first thing she could tell was that there was no one around, simply a flat surface that went on and on and on. Apart from the indentations of her marks in the thick layer of dust, there were no other footprints or signs of life.

She turned and gasped. About fourteen football pitches away, a huge wall shot up from the floor, reaching high into the air. Under closer inspection, at the foot of the wall, a series of huge arches concealed dark mouths.

Daisy looked up and squinted, her eyes adjusting to the change in light. She was in a vast cathedral-like room, bigger than anything she'd ever seen – so big that she couldn't make out where the sides ended and the roof began.

*If I'm really dead, and this time I absolutely must be,* she thought, *I don't think this is Heaven, or Hell for that matter. Maybe God couldn't decide so he left me in between. In purgatory*.

Some way off, near to what she suspected was the middle of this vast, dull construction, stood a strange-looking dust-laden object. Daisy imagined it looked like an old grey tree with, as far as she could tell, spindly branches that poked out rather sadly, as if they were dead. Like a skeleton tree.

She stood up and headed towards the gaping holes along the walls. Some were big enough for a ship to pass through and took minutes to walk past, their cavernous openings cold and black, while others were as small as fox holes. She walked gingerly down a tunnel that could have easily accommodated a pair of elephants but, after a short distance, found it blocked by rocks.

She tried another, and another, but they too were sealed. After five tunnels Daisy felt lonely, frightened and lost.

'What ... what is this place?' she said, her teeth chattering as her words echoed back. 'How do I get out?'

She took off towards the strange grey tree but after a few steps she jumped in the air and squealed as something underfoot snapped. Her heart raced. Underneath the dust, lay a skeleton. She worked the dust away from the bones and found it to be human. Daisy winced; someone died here a long, long time ago.

'Sorry,' she said out loud. 'Didn't see you there.'

As she studied the bones, her senses on high alert, she heard a rasp – a strange wheezing noise.

Was it the ghost of the skeleton? She listened again, putting all her concentration into it. The more intently she listened, the clearer the sound. Now there was a grating – a kind of breathing – getting closer.

Fear grabbed her.

She had to get out. *But how?*

The beginnings of a panic attack grew; the combination of hopelessness and fear, like a feeling she'd had in her nightmares. She ran towards the wall.

In the next moment, a terrible CRACK cut through the air like a huge branch snapping in two. The crack was followed by a scream and its shrill echoed around the huge room like deathly, wailing spirits.

Every hair on Daisy's body stood to attention. Her eyes bulged.

'I'm not alone!' she whispered to the room. 'The devil's coming to get me!'

She went faster. First towards the large holes to the side and then blindly, searching for a glimmer of light, a way out – a place to hide. After a few minutes, she drew up in front of a slightly different tunnel with worn markings surrounding it and caught her breath.

She wiped her forehead and listened. The sound of wailing, or screaming, filled her eardrums. How the heck would she get out?

She took a deep breath and readied herself to go when she noticed the stonework. It was a real arch, not the crude arch of a cave hole, but more a built arch – made from stone – with carvings. Under the brow of the arch was the outline of a gate and, below this, a familiar looking motif, like a crest you might see on a shield, with the curious, circular tree emblem exactly like the ones in the cave.

Below the circular tree were two distinct icons. She studied them. One bore a leaf, like an oak's, and the other, the picture of a bee.

As she looked around she heard a new noise, a terrific shrill that seemed to be growing.

*The oak leaf and the bee,* she thought. She realised she'd seen it before, but where?

She stared hard, her heart thumping. Where and what did the bee and a leaf mean?

She concentrated on the images as the piercing, high-pitched noise filled her ears. She had to work fast. Then it struck her like a bolt of lightning – it was a clue from her dream. She remembered it now. She had to join the images! That was it!

"BEE-LEAF."

'Bee leaf,' she said out loud. It struck her. 'It's about BE-LIEF! That's it!'

*All I have to do is believe!*

Without looking back, she took a deep breath, shut her eyes and walked straight towards the doorway without hesitating, thinking only of Eden Cottage.

---

THE NEXT THING SHE KNEW, the wind was blowing and the rain pouring down. She was back in a ditch, but this time the other side of the gate, way below the house. She shrieked with relief and punched the air as if she'd scored the best goal of her life.

She didn't care that she was drenched through. She laughed aloud and splashed the water, crying with joy. Daisy de Lowe had just escaped from Hell itself.

She had to tell the others. But, as she went, doubt filled her. What if they don't believe me? I mean, it's a bit ... nuts. *Actually,* she thought, *it's totally bonkers.* But they must believe me. *They have to.*

And if they didn't, she'd make them, whatever it took, and then they'd start making sense of things and then they could begin the search for the tablets.

Daisy ran, slipping and sliding as fast as she could up the hill towards Eden Cottage.

# 65 THE YORKSHIRE STRAIN

Commissioner Stone was proud of his accomplishments on the Force, proud that he had the respect of his team and proud that, at the age of fifty-two he could still fit into the suit he had bought with his first pay cheque aged nineteen: a sharp black pinstripe. He prided himself on his fitness, his well-being, and his full head of hair. He liked the fact that others complimented him on his sense of fair play and his ability to understand and uphold the rule of law in an uncomplicated manner. He liked the way ladies half his age stole admiring glances at him. But this, this silent and deadly enemy, which was growing at an alarming rate, terrified him. Nothing, no charm offensive nor training manual could combat it, even if operations for this kind of "natural event" had been planned years in advance.

Biblical happenings here in God's own county of Yorkshire. Storms! Plague! It was unbelievable.

Ironically, he'd been looking forward to the day for some time. His older cousin, known only by his surname, Solomon, was headmaster at Upsall school and had sent him an invitation to a banquet in celebration of his twentieth anniversary in charge. Rumour had it that it was to be quite an occasion.

In any event, he didn't get as far as his local town of Masham, on the edge of the Yorkshire Dales.

Only an hour after the rains began, he found himself stranded. Fortunately, it was as he drove past the front drive of the Swinton Park Hotel that he decided enough was enough and took refuge.

It was a huge stroke of luck.

Geographically, the hotel was perfect. Directly across the Vale of York from the village of Upsall, the hotel was isolated enough to prevent unwarranted intrusion and perched high enough in the dales to be out of danger from flooding. Furthermore, the hotel was big and comfortable; able to house the army of experts summoned at short notice from around the UK.

Over the following day, as the hotel guests were airlifted out, his team and their equipment moved in. The luxurious facilities were turning into the headquarters of the largest police and medical operation ever seen in the country.

He stroked his moustache as he drew himself up, patted his pressed uniform and addressed the team in front of him.

'Right. I need speech analysts to try and fathom what the boy was trying to say. If it was the word "Algae", maybe the boy is referring to the water, so I want results from those water samples today, please. I need to know what the "Dunno" is – if it's a thing, a person, a piece of rock or if the boy simply cannot speak clearly. I want teams to work on his family, figure out where he's from: blood samples, DNA screening – whatever it takes. Understand so far?

'I need an up-to-date on the boy's burns – who or what could have given them and how. And we need to understand if this is a terrorist attack on the country – a form of international sabotage or simply a freak, biblical phenomenon. Find out what you can – even if there's a possibility it's an alien attack – is this all perfectly clear?'

The officers nodded. Two ran out of the room.

'OK. Has everyone arrived for the briefing?'

'Yes, sir. They've been flying in all morning. The last guest put down ten minutes ago.'

'Good.' He made his way out of the reception area and into the grand hallway where a large, white sheet hung neatly over the paintings of the past owners of the once-grand ancestral home. Crammed in the hallway were a mix of scientists, the military and civil servants. Top brass. Commissioner Stone made his way up the wide staircase.

'Ladies and Gentlemen – Doctors, Generals, I appreciate your coming here at such short notice. I trust you saw the scale of devastation from your helicopters. You'll appreciate we don't have much time.

'The situation, in regards to the viral infection, is far worse than anticipated.' Stone paused as he caught the eyes of the people spread out below him. 'In fact, it's worse than our biggest nightmare. Not only is the contagion rate astonishing, but worse still, we have no idea how it is spreading. I'm handing you over to Chief Medical Officer Harries. He'll give you the latest update.'

Harries was one of the thinnest, leanest men you could imagine, with a pointed nose and a large, ill-fitting pair of spectacles on his nose. His thinning, scraggly hair made him appear far older than his forty-five years and the way he wore an almost permanent frown didn't help matters. But he was the leading authority on viral strains in the country, if not the world. He made his way to the front, a bundle of files tucked under his arm and nodded to the projectionist. The lights dimmed and the white screen above them burst into life.

'This plague, the Yorkshire strain or Ebora, from the Latin *Ebor* meaning *York* – and I do believe that this will become the common noun – is a most curious one,' he said as the first slide came up. 'Here are the strains of the virus that we've been able to map so far. You will notice how many there are.' A new image slid into place. 'Now, here is the Yorkshire strain in comparison with the Plague of Athens, Spanish flu and Ebola?'

'These pandemics are spread through touch or via carriers – the virus moving from one organism to the next. The difference of the Yorkshire strain is multi-fold. Our Ebora strain is smaller and considerably more aggressive. Moreover, it appears to mutate both randomly and rapidly. As I've shown you, we have already identified several varieties of the strain. And we believe there are many others out there.' The slides moved on.

'See here the effect of the Ebola virus on a victim in twenty-four hours. Now compare it with ours.' A loud gasp came from the onlookers. 'Yes, indeed, the Yorkshire strain is a great deal deadlier. Worse still, we've found animals – cattle, foxes and birds – bearing similar symptoms. So it appears that this outbreak doesn't stop with humans. It has the ability to attack every living thing.'

Another slide came up. Harries straightened. He looked pale and drawn. 'This slide will try and explain our current understanding of how the virus spreads.' He pointed his cane at the newest image. 'The known area of infection is coloured in blue.'

The map showed the entire area between the dales and the moors, reaching from Teesside at the top to Nottingham at the bottom. 'Two hundred miles and counting. This inner red ring is a five-mile radius around the likely source at Upsall, the exact same place as the epicentre of the storm. We don't know why, or even if there's a connection, but we're working on it.'

On the slide, a geographical map showed the flooded region of Yorkshire. 'Now here's the truly worrying part.' On his signal, a translucent sheet was placed over the map. 'This,' he continued, 'shows us the known victims as of early this morning. The lighter green circles around the dots indicates the victims' approximate movements.'

On the map were a number of random marks stretching north, south, east and west.

A voice rang out. 'sir, what does it all mean?'

'I was getting to that,' Harries barked. He straightened and smiled thinly. 'In simple terms, we think it means that the virus is spreading arbitrarily.'

A murmur spread around the room. Harries raised a hand in the air. 'The virus is spreading in a way we haven't seen before. By contact, by wind and by water. Perhaps, it is a combination of these. The incubation period is like nothing we have ever come across. There will be thousands of people with the symptoms already and I am afraid that, until we know more about it, we are at its mercy.'

An explosion of questions shot out. Harries absorbed them and then raised his arms for silence. 'We can only work with what we know,' he said. 'Scientists from all around the world are battling night and day to try and understand how this virus works so that a vaccination can be hurried through. But, as I mentioned, the Yorkshire strain is mutating fast and the sequences are enormously complex.'

'How long have we got?' yelled a female voice.

'In two days,' Harries said, 'the virus has spread uncontrollably. I'm afraid I don't have an answer.'

'Do you have any leads, any positive news?'

Harries looked glum. 'Even with the best scientific minds working flat out, we are unable to pinpoint the cause and effect of this strain. The common denominator is the fact that the outbreak appears to have started at the storm's epicentre. And that, my friends, is the small village of Upsall.'

# 66 ISABELLA RUSHES OUT

Isabella hoped like mad that, when she looked again, the panels wouldn't be there. She opened her eyes.

They were.

She groaned. She could see her outline in the first panel and Archie's in the last, but the middle panel showed only a blank, empty space. She waved her feet in the air and the panel reflected her movements. *If the panels were a true reflection of them at this exact point in time,* she thought, *then where was Daisy?*

She leapt off Old Man Wood's bed and raced down the wooden stairs three at a time and into the hallway. Then she dashed along the corridor, through the door to the kitchen, where she all but crashed into the table. 'Have you seen Archie or Daisy?' she demanded, as her eyes searched the room.

Mrs Pye was not impressed. 'Good day to you, too, Isabella,' she said.

'Well? Have you?'

Mrs Pye puffed out her chest and faced her. 'Good afternoon, Isabella.'

'Oh. Good afternoon. Well—?'

'Why, not for a little while. Archie went out early and ...'

Isabella didn't need to hear the rest. In a flash, she was pulling on her boots and donning her coat. She found her leather, wide-brimmed hat and as she drew the toggle under her chin she flew towards the door, inadvertently slamming it behind her. As she turned the corner she narrowly avoided smashing into Archie.

'Oi! Watch out!' he said.

'There you are!' she said clasping his shoulders. 'Great! Good! Fantastic!'

Archie reeled. 'What's going on?'

'Quick question – honest answer,' she panted. 'I'm not going to be cross.'

Archie didn't know what to say.

'You've been throwing your knives, haven't you?'

Archie bowed his head. 'Er, well—'

'You have – great!' she said. 'That's fine, excellent, good. Next question. Have you seen Daisy? She went off looking for you ages ago.'

Archie shook his head.

'OK. Didn't think so,' she said. Isabella knew that, if what she'd seen was correct, Daisy wouldn't be found anywhere. But she had to be sure.

'Where are you going?' Archie asked.

'Up to the ruin and then round the farm. I'll meet you in the cupboard, in twenty minutes ... I've got to find Daise. It's important.'

Archie was confused. 'Right round the farm? It'll take you an hour at least. If you want Old Man Wood, he's in a bunch of willow trees by the water's edge. He's gone totally dotty.'

But Isabella wasn't listening and, in a flash, she'd shot off towards the ruin.

---

ISABELLA THOUGHT hard about which direction to take. She'd head up to the ruin first, check around the rocks and then make her way back down the hill, circumnavigating the garden.

She charged off, gritting her teeth and running as fast as she could through the mud and spitting rain, jumping and hurdling branches and boulders with ease. She was amazed at how little time it took her to get there, how her feet seemed to take on a life of their own. She knew the distance was about five hundred metres. And she reckoned it took less than a minute. Was that right? She did a quick calculation. That's around thirty miles an hour. That's faster that Usain Bolt!

She stood by the remains of the old stone wall, which jagged here and there, its grey stones covered in ferns and creepers and small trees that had tucked their roots deep into the crevices. The battlements jutted out before disappearing into the grass below, then rose up like dark shadows until they ran along at twice her height for several metres.

Isabella followed the stones, looking for footprints. Had only two days passed since they had limped home from the cave? It felt like a lifetime; so many confusing, bewildering events crowding her brain. She stopped by a section of masonry, half-submerged in the ground, layered with moss and lichen. Was this the entrance into the old body of the castle? A gateway? She checked for footprints. There weren't any, just large, tyre-track markings, that weaved in and out of the scattered boulders. *Maybe,* she thought, *these were the residual patterns made by the movement of water finding its route.*

Isabella called out, but the sound of her voice bounced back off the walls. She hurried on. It was hauntingly silent, too silent, even with the rain pit-patting onto the leather rim of her hat.

She walked through the centre of the ruin towards the gnarled battlements on the far side. As she went she wondered where the cave entrance might be.

She followed the thicker walls, turned the corner past the low-lying walls, until eventually she was back in the same place. Had she missed it?

Isabella circumnavigated the ruin again, this time paying even closer attention. No gaping holes nor tell-tale tracks where a boulder had once been were in evidence at all. But the cave had to be there – the old ruin wasn't that big – and there were only three places where the walls were thick enough or tall enough.

Isabella sat on a rock and stared out into the valley at the hulking grey body of water. Had they imagined the cave or emerged from an alternative pile of rocks? She turned her hands over and for a brief moment her heart leapt as she thought she saw skin covering her palms. Her heart sank. The neat, symmetrical holes were still there, reminding her.

What if some parts were real and other bits ... made up, invented? What if the terrible experiences they'd had, had made them imagine things? What if they had some kind of post traumatic stress disorder? She'd read about this kind of thing in her textbooks. The brain was a powerful tool, a living computer with an unlimited ability for imagination.

Perhaps that would explain the dreams and things like the bed and Daisy disappearing.

She took a deep breath, put her hands out on the rock and leaned on them. As she did, a strange noise interrupted her thoughts. She gasped as a terrible chill ran through the very marrow of her spine and the image of a vast serpent with glazed green eyes flashed into her head. Her skin prickled and instantly she vomited, a nauseous feeling washing right through her.

She started walking.

*It's only in your head,* she told herself – *in your imagination.* She stood tall and stretched her arms out wide, then swung them around in a windmill motion as if to swish away the awful feelings.

It didn't work. She still felt nauseous and the chill remained deep in her bones. She hardly dared admit it, but the flash was identical to the image she'd dreamt about before the storm. Every bit the same, if not worse. The beast with the same green eyes that had latched on to her mind, and made her head swim. But why here, of all places?

And worse, what did it mean?

She looked around. Had the light dimmed? She noted another cloud brewing overhead. Wasn't it strange how this once happy place now had such a deep aura of evil, of darkness?

A rustling noise further along reminded her to check on Old Man Wood's cattle. She followed the strange tyre-track markings a short distance until they ran under a large rock. She thought briefly about her theory of how channels of water made the marks. But if this was the case, then wouldn't the tyre-track marks be in a different place?

She hurried on and, before long, came to the other section of the ruin, a large, rectangular courtyard dotted with crude rocks and the occasional scraggly bush and tree. Almost certainly this would have been the outer courtyard to the main castle keep. At the far end in the corner was a shelter for the herd, crudely constructed by Old Man Wood from large rocks and tree trunks and covered by a moss-covered roof of jumbled slates and tiles.

As Isabella approached, a terrible noise erupted – a frantic mooing and bleating building up and up. She crept forward, wondering what had unsettled them, only to hear a stampede of hooves as the cattle bolted, scattering in different directions, mud flying.

Isabella knew the animals well; they were never afraid of her. But now they looked terrified, their eyes wide and shining more than she could ever remember. She talked to them in a soothing voice, and slowly they calmed down. As the noise abated, and they moved back under the shelter, she counted them.

Two missing. How come? She counted them again. Perhaps the noise of the storm had incited two of them to bolt. They might escape from the rough enclosure of the courtyard, but the ground slipped away sharply on each side. In poor weather they always came up here.

Isabella tried to work out which ones were missing and, holding her nose, she took a step inside to see if they were hiding at the back. No luck. She made a mental note to tell Old Man Wood and offered some comforting words to the herd. Then she headed back towards the house.

And still, no sign of Daisy.

# 67 DAISY'S DISAPPEARANCE

Isabella quickly removed her waterproofs. Noting that the kitchen was empty, she reckoned Archie had sought the warmth of the cupboard.

"The cupboard" drew its warmth from the flue-pipe of the range cooker directly below in the kitchen. It was a small room, used by Mrs Pye as a walk-in airing cupboard, for drying and storing towels, sheets and linen, and the children used it as their own personal snug – for chatting, hiding and warming themselves up on a cold winter's day.

Isabella approached, knocked on the door three times and rattled off last week's password, 'Carrots, cauliflower and courgettes.'

Archie clicked open the latch, which was screwed on from the inside so that, when they occupied it, no one could barge in.

'Any luck finding Daisy?' Archie said.

Isabella settled in her corner on a soft bean bag and stretched her legs out. She shook her head. 'But I know where you've been.'

Archie reddened. He knew this was coming. 'Me?'

'Yup. I saw you curled up in the shed, Arch, throwing your knives.'

Archie frowned and felt his hair starting to wire up. 'Bells, there's no way you could have seen me in the potting shed. You saw me coming in and before that you were in bed.'

'You were in there, though, weren't you?'

'So what?'

Isabella didn't want to upset him. 'Look I'm not going to go mental on you, OK.' Her eyes widened. 'But aren't you curious to know how I know?'

Archie was confused. 'A wild guess?'

'Nope. You could have been with Old Man Wood for all I knew.'

'Well, I was, until he went crazy. He went to find some weirdo trees ... have you seen him—'

'No. And it's him we need to have a talk about. I'm afraid there's properly bad news.'

'I know. He needs putting in a geriatric home.'

Isabella smiled. 'Spot on.'

Archie cringed. 'Bells, you're not making sense,' he said. 'First you say that you've seen me throwing knives and then we need to talk about Old Man Wood. What's up?'

'Well, I don't know how to explain it,' she started, her voice barely controllable, 'but Old Man Wood has been tracking us ... spying on us, and ... and I've found out how he does it—'

'What are you talking about?' Archie said. 'That's ridiculous. He'd never do such a thing. I'll admit that he has gone insane, but he's our best friend and he wouldn't harm a bug.'

Isabella leaned in. 'You may think so, Archie, but I have evidence.'

'Get real!' he replied. 'Why would he do anything like that?'

'Listen to what I've found – and trust me, every single word of what I'm about to tell you is true.'

Archie's hair had now achieved full wire status. He was agitated. It didn't feel right.

Isabella went on. 'I was bored and wanted to ask him a few questions, so I went down to his room. He wasn't there, so I let myself in and jumped onto his bed. At the end of his bed are three screens that show every move *we* make. EVERY SINGLE MOVE, for each one of us, Archie.'

Archie sat listening, stroking his hair-spikes.

'And that's how I know you were in the potting shed, bundled up in the corner feeling sorry for yourself, throwing your stupid knives. On the final panel was Daisy. I could tell by the way she moves, by her bottom. And me, I was there on one of the panels, sitting on the bed.'

Quiet filled the small cupboard, only broken by the faint sounds of the range cooker drifting up to them and the hum of the generator.

'You've gone mad,' Archie whispered after a while. 'Just like Old Man Wood.'

'No I haven't, Archie. I couldn't make this up. I don't have an imagination, you know that.'

Archie groaned. 'Well, if you must know, I think we're missing a link to Old Man Wood.'

'What do you mean?'

'Well, our freaky dreams showed that Old Man Wood is connected to us, so there has to be a reason for his odd behaviour.'

'Archie, if Old Man Wood is spying on us then something is definitely not right. He might not be who we think he is—'

'But really—'

'Look, I'm serious – deadly serious,' she said, her voice quivering.

'Old Man Wood?' Archie chuckled, his memory fresh from Old Man Wood's fiasco with the trees.

'Yes! Maybe he's part of some sort of conspiracy—'

'So why not ask him?' Archie said. 'I mean, he's hardly likely to deny it.'

'That's exactly what I was going to do,' Isabella fired back. 'I mean, think about it. That medicine of his, the way he blunders about looking like he's lost at sea, staring aimlessly at the walls—'

'But he used the medicine to help us, didn't he? Look, I just can't believe he would do anything that would in any way be harmful—'

'There's more,' Isabella interrupted. 'You know I told you about these panels with each of us on.'

'Yeah. So?'

'Well here's the shocking bit—'

'Shocking—?'

'Yes. Just listen,' Isabella demanded. 'One minute Daisy looked as if she was sunbathing—'

'Sunbathing? She couldn't have been.'

'No, really, she was. One hundred percent the truth. And can you please stop interrupting me. Then she talked to someone or something and then she totally ... disappeared.'

Archie stared at Isabella. 'You have completely lost the plot—'

'No I have not, Archie. Her screen went blank – I'll show you. And anyway, why do you think I tore off round the farm, huh? To find her, of course, and she wasn't anywhere. I checked the place over.'

'But why would she disappear—'

'Ssshh!' Isabella said. 'What's that noise?'

Below them they could hear the sound of the door shutting followed by voices, as though the telly had been turned on. They listened.

'It's only Mrs P,' Archie said.

'It isn't. Mrs P headed off ages ago. Old Man Wood doesn't watch telly and Daisy's missing.'

Archie frowned. 'Then I think we'd better investigate,' he said.

They flicked the latch and slipped quietly down the stairs.

---

THE KITCHEN WAS in its usual immaculate condition but with no sign of Mrs Pye.

Splashes of neon from the TV lit the otherwise dark room as the latest news bulletin showed pictures of the disaster.

Archie and Isabella sneaked in.

Archie crept past the oak table and chairs, past the island and looked beyond it. Nothing. He moved farther forward, turned to Isabella and shrugged.

Then they heard a sniff. Archie took a pace forward as Isabella went for the light.

In a wet heap on the floor beneath the island sat Daisy, watching the news. Archie gasped. She looked terrible.

She turned her head as she heard him but quickly refocused on the news, ignoring him.

Archie didn't know what to think. She was drenched from head to toe, and shivering, but she wouldn't take her gaze off the pictures.

'You alright?' he said softly.

'Sssshhh,' she replied and with a shaking hand she pointed towards the screen.

Archie turned his gaze up.

On the screen, the image of a room inside a hospital showed a patient lying in a bed. The patient's eyes were open but dulled. A caption ran along the bottom of the screen in big letters.

LIVE: FLOOD CHILD OUT OF COMA

Archie sat down next to Daisy – offering her a couple of drying up cloths. Daisy grabbed them without taking her eyes from the screen. *Why,* Archie thought, *was Daisy so preoccupied with this bald, sick-looking boy covered in drips and bandages?*

The news continued.

*'Earlier on today,'* the commentator said, *'the miracle boy who has been nicknamed Jonah by the medical team, came out of his coma. The boy, his real identity still unknown, his body hairless and covered in mysterious burn marks, was found hanging on to a branch at the top of a tall tree surrounded by the floodwaters. Jonah, thought to be a local boy, was discovered by the air ambulance team earlier this morning suffering from serious malnutrition. Police and medical staff are urging anyone who might know him to ring this hotline number.'*

The camera panned in on the boy who happened, at that moment, to blink, quite slowly.

Archie reached in a little. That movement.

Then the boy smiled faintly, his lips parting a fraction. Archie gasped and peered in even more, and turned to see the reaction of his sister. She was doing the exact same thing.

The camera zoomed in even closer. The screen filled with the lips and eyes of the child, who had no hair, no eyebrows, nor eyelashes and who bore a curious red rim mark on his head as if he had squeezed into a hat that was too tight.

The boy closed his eyes. It appeared that he was trying to speak. He swallowed, struggling to form a word. After a great effort, a sound emerged.

It was barely audible, but sounded something like *Arjjie.*

Archie and Daisy knelt forward, watching keenly.

A voice from one of the medical team, her face covered by a white medical mask, gently said, 'Hello. Can you hear me?'

'*Algae,*' the boy repeated. His eyes opened wider, the struggle to talk seemingly beyond him. '*Dunno,*' he said before closing his eyes.

The boy swallowed again, the camera highlighting his considerable effort. '*DUNNO,*' the boy said again, with as much urgency as he could muster. Then the boy collapsed back on his bed as a machine above him started to bleep and a team of medics rushed in, surrounding him.

Immediately, the TV pictures cut out and shot back to the studio, where, emblazoned in big writing along the bottom of the screen were the words:

*THE PRIME MINISTER WILL ADDRESS THE NATION AT 18:00hrs GMT.*

# 68 HEADMASTER SOLOMON

Commissioner Stone stood up. 'Thank you, Chief Medical Officer.' He faced the throng of anxious faces. 'You now have an understanding of the situation. Coming round the room is more information – essential documents – in regards to what are the likely outcomes. Also, there is an outline of the strategic operation that is about to come into place. None of it makes for easy reading. All of you have been assigned roles in relation to your skill set. When this meeting is over, please collect your briefing papers from the drawing room which is along the corridor.

'These papers contain sensitive information, links and passwords to several Government archives and the main COBRA operations portal on the web. In order for this to remain out of the public domain, you will sign official secrecy documents before you depart, or you will not leave Swinton Park. Is this quite clear?

'Ministers and civil servants are being briefed as we speak. Regional and emergency councils are gathering. The main headquarters for the operation will be here and at Downing Street, London. As the virus spreads, operational headquarters will be situated in locations like this outside Cardiff, Exeter, Manchester, Cambridge and Edinburgh. The heads of all the emergency services are meeting in strategic locations shortly. Across the country, emergency stores are being placed in aircraft hangers and distribution systems are being organised. In our hospitals, isolation units are being prepared. Non-life-threatening operations have been cancelled. Every town and village will run their own health centres manned by local doctors, nurses and volunteers. Only dire emergencies will be accepted into hospitals.

'Later this afternoon, the media will be thoroughly briefed by the Prime Minister, who will then address the nation. You will not talk to the media from this moment on. All press and interviews in regards to the virus and operations will be made through official channels.

'Most of you will be flown out of here to help. You will be given smartphones that run on a special service connection so you can be kept up to date. Parliament went into an emergency session early this morning and the Prime Minister is chairing a cross party emergency cabinet. At the moment, other heads of state are being briefed, particularly our neighbours in Europe and in the United States.

'At eleven o'clock this evening, all airports, ferry crossings, railway stations, waterways and motorways will be closed. Travel in or out of Great Britain will be prohibited unless authorised by one of you. As of midnight tonight, there will be a total media blackout. The Internet will be temporarily suspended, with access at specific times to be announced. Television and radio stations will play films and repeats and be the source of all news updates. Supermarkets will come under state supervision and armed military units are already moving in to areas where civil unrest is likely. Yes, we do envisage serious panic in towns and cities as people rush for supplies.

'To that end, a curfew will come into play in every town and city across the country and a zero tolerance approach will be forced upon the citizens of the country.' The commissioner could feel the sweat on him. 'You will need to work fast. The security of the country is at stake.'

Stone remained standing, looking into the eyes of the people below him. 'We believe that so long as the disease is confined to the north of the country, these measures might contain the spread, both south and farther north. Every available expert is working on a solution right now.'

He pushed his glasses along his nose. 'As Britain goes into lockdown, be assured the world is watching with bated breath, and even then, it may be too late.'

THE COMMISSIONER DREW in a deep breath and mopped his brow. The stunned crowd in front of him began to disperse, heads buried in folders.

'Is a chopper available?' he said to the smart young officer next to him.

The officer, Dickinson, made a quick call. 'Ten minutes and it's yours,' he said as he hung up. 'Can I brief the pilot where it's headed?'

'Short trip – Upsall. Want to take a look for myself and there's someone I need to get out – the headmaster at the school, name of Solomon. Can you run a check and see if he's made contact with anyone?'

'It's bang in the middle of the zone, sir,' Dickinson said. 'The area suffered badly.'

'I don't care,' the commissioner snapped back. 'I need that man out of there, dead or alive!'

Dickinson raced off. Stone glanced at his watch and dusted down his jacket. He studied his mobile. *Still no word from the scientists. When would they come back with something – anything?* They were so lost in their own world, scientists, what they needed was a bang on the head to sort them out. He spotted Dickinson returning.

'This Headmaster, Solomon,' the officer said, 'actively used his mobile when the signal became operational. Nothing since 21:00 hours yesterday. Maybe he ran out of battery.'

'Good. At least we know he survived. Are we ready?'

Dickinson nodded and, knowing that the Commissioner liked to stride more than walk, marched quickly ahead.

---

'GOOD HEAVENS,' Stone muttered as he viewed the distant, brown smear of water and debris that was once the fertile green fields of the Vale of York. 'Now, pay attention. I want details of everyone in this area, starting with Upsall. I want names and addresses. I want to know who is in the school, pupils, teachers, caterers, who runs the newsagents, who blows the candles out in the church. I want medical records, death records, birth records and a history of the place from as far back as you can get. I want to know the occupations of all the families that have been around the area, I want contractor information.' He paused as he waited for the team to catch up with their note taking. 'I want a pattern. Have you got that?'

'sir,' one of the officers nearby said, 'this kind of investigation takes weeks.'

Stone fixed him an icy stare. 'Understand this, money is no object. Hire everyone you can. Use the universities of Leeds, Durham, Newcastle – Timbuktu for all I care. We need results and we need to find something that connects Upsall to this plague, do you understand? We need this last week, Goddammit.'

The chopper wheeled to the right. 'And I want everyone, and I mean everyone, who was found in Upsall village put in quarantine. Are the military in there yet? Good. Make arrangements for a mass evacuation of all the people up into the moors.' He rubbed his chin. 'Try using the outcrop at Crayke – use the castle there.' He fixed each of the people with eyes that told them to trust him implicitly. 'Your status as part of this team means you can access anyone. *Anyone*,' he emphasised. 'So get on your phones and get about your business. NOW.'

In no time the crew were relaying messages from their communications devices.

A message came through from the pilot. 'We're approaching Upsall, sir.'

'Good. Can you get near the tower?'

The helicopter whirred and levelled out. Beneath them was a slurry of debris where the pretty village once stood. Grey water swirled below. Sticking out was the old tower of the school and the top half of the tall chapel.

Before long, one of the marines was being lowered down, onto the parapet. A couple of people were there welcoming him in.

One was the familiar figure of the headmaster, Solomon.

---

TO THE COMMISSIONER, his cousin looked pale and drawn. Weight had already dropped off him, and his face, rotund at their last meeting, was now angular and coated with a grey, stubbly beard.

'You have to get the others out,' the headmaster said. 'You can't leave them there. You don't know what it's like.'

Stone nodded and patted his shoulder reassuringly. 'We'll get everyone out, believe me,' he said and then added, 'I'm sorry about your party. I know how much it meant.' The chopper soared into the rain. 'Was rather looking forward to it myself.'

The headmaster shrugged. Tears welled in his eyes as he stared out of the window.

'I'm going to come straight to the point, Solomon,' Stone said. 'We've got a pandemic on our hands and it stems from here.' He stared out of the window as if sharing the older man's grief. 'You need to tell me everything you know about Upsall.'

The headmaster gathered himself together. 'Of course. I'll tell you what I know, but I'm not sure if it'll help.'

The chopper climbed high and from here the devastation was truly remarkable. Water stretched from Teesside in the north as far as the eye could see to the south. Dotted at various points were outcrops, islands, full of tents and makeshift dwellings, like mini shanty towns.

'Were there any unusual circumstances prior to the storm?' Stone asked.

Solomon thought for a while. 'None. We thought the storm was, for all intents and purposes, just localised. That's what the Met Office said.'

'So you called the Met Office?'

Solomon remembered the incident with Isabella. 'No. Not exactly. I watched the forecast on the television, but there was a girl – one of my brightest students—'

'She thought otherwise?'

Solomon admired the way his young cousin had the knack of picking up little leads like this. 'Yes, probably nothing,' he said. 'A smart kid. You know, just interested—'

Stone lent in. 'And she said what, exactly?'

'Well, she'd made a barometer and insisted there was going to be a terrible storm. Why, I don't know. But she did it on three occasions.'

'Her name?'

'Isabella de Lowe,' he replied without flinching.

Stone scratched her name in his pad and handed it to the officer next to him. 'Get this checked out,' he said. 'Find out if she's alive, what family she has.'

'Oh, I wouldn't worry about her,' Solomon said. 'Her parents are stuck in the Middle East – archaeologists—'

'Look, I need answers and, at the moment, there are none,' Stone said. 'Everyone, and I mean everyone, is being checked out.'

An alarm bell rang in Solomon's mind. 'But she's only a child—'

'I don't care if she's a bloody donkey. I need to know about *everyone*.' His tone was tough and unapologetic. 'Where is she from? Upsall or—'

'All I'm saying,' Solomon said in his most head-masterly way, 'is that this girl came to me wanting to talk about a storm, which she said was going to be bigger than everyone thought.'

'Why?' Stone pressed. 'Do all your students do this?'

'I have no idea,' Solomon replied racking his brain. 'Perhaps she was being intuitive. Some children are remarkable in that respect. She's a bright child, one of our best.'

'Do you know where she lives?'

Solomon didn't like the way this was going. 'In the hills,' he said, waving a hand roughly in the air. 'Extraordinary family, very eccentric.'

'In what way?'

Solomon had forgotten what a persevering human being Stone could be. It was, he realised, one of the reasons he'd climbed to the top. 'Look,' he said. 'I'm tired, exhausted and hungry and I don't think this is helping.' He turned his head away. The headmaster needed to think, to run the conversations through his mind before he'd give his cousin anything else to work on. He certainly wasn't going to allow Stone to hound his students. 'I simply think you're barking up the wrong tree,' he added.

Stone surveyed his haggard cousin. 'de Lowe. Is that the name?'

Solomon grunted disapprovingly.

Stone turned to the officer. 'Find out everything about the de Lowe family. History, academic records, family records – the whole damn lot. Understand?'

Solomon was too tired to respond. In his heart there was something about Isabella and her ranting that struck a chord with everything that had happened – as if she knew. But what and why her? How could that family, living in a curious old cottage perched high up on the moors, with the strange old man looking after them and a heritage as old as the hills, have anything to do with this disaster?

But, deep down, Solomon supposed that if anyone had a clue about strange goings on in Upsall – it might be them. He slumped back into his seat and shut his eyes. He'd find out when they landed and he'd slept, washed and eaten. Until then, the last person he would tell would be Stone and his cronies.

Stone had a fearsome reputation for extracting information and he wasn't ready to hand over his students, or his friends.

Not yet at any rate.

# 69 CAIN'S PLAN

Cain amazed himself with his supreme intelligence. And his latest ruse smacked of pure genius.

OK, so he lost the boy. But did he really need him? No, not right now. In a way, the timing couldn't have been better. You see, he'd discovered a way of speeding up delivery of the plague, so that the world was plunged into misery even before the water had receded. Four days early! That was the strange thing about those dream-giving spider things, the dreamspinners. They knew everything but, at the same time, they knew nothing.

And yes, he did miss having the boy around. What a wonderful feeling! Walking, dancing, beating people up, just like the good old days. When the boy was better, he'd return and tell him all about his mother – for a price, of course. He looked forward to it. But this time, he'd look after him and get the boy to utterly trust him.

Cain couldn't believe that he had ignored the boy's most basic needs. For a brief moment he felt a twinge of regret but his current excitement made him overlook that emotion. Next time, he'd find a way of talking, perhaps by opening up a path in his brain, and they'd communicate and wouldn't that be fun? And he'd feed him – like a king. Already, huge lists of foods were being sought out. Things he'd never heard of. Things with extraordinary names like *fish fingers* and *roast chicken* and *Coco Pops* and *prawn crackers.* A kitchen to prepare this food was under construction, along with a well of water sunk deep into the palace earth and filtered in exactly the way necessary for humans.

Next time, he wouldn't force the boy to do anything by burning him. He'd only burn him if he didn't do things *his* way. Sure, it might be tricky, but he'd communicate and then win him over.

Anyway, the boy would understand that he had an opportunity to wield real power. And, if he was honest, Cain wondered about letting himself be dominated, controlled like a sleeping partner – taking a back seat and seeing what happened. He could switch off for a year or two, have a break from being a spirit; take a sabbatical, become a non-executive.

Cain danced around and swished through the air even if it wasn't half as enjoyable as having an actual, real body to do it in. He thought about the Heirs of Eden and laughed. So they survived the flood. Big deal. They have seven days to find the three tablets and, as of day three, those wretched children are still moping around their strange little home while a very horrid plague is rearing its ugly head to the unsuspecting world.

And it's all their fault!

He laughed. Well, they were just kids. The only person who could guide them was the old man. And what a failure he was turning out to be. Worse than useless! He had no idea, even if he had discovered the old cellar and the trees at the brook. It was like watching a snail in a running race.

Cain ran through the sequence of events on Earth. By the time the Heirs of Eden failed, as they were bound to, every living thing would have succumbed to the plague and died. He laughed. It was so easy: just let them be themselves. The dreamspinners would take him to the Ancient Woman, his dear mother, and he'd open up the Garden of Eden himself. He couldn't believe he hadn't thought of it before.

Then he'd have control of every living thing, every being, every cell of every being and he'd nurture the ones he wanted and put them onto a new Earth and revitalise his dear Havilah. He would create any creature he wished, just the way he wanted. And would the old man stop him? No, because he wouldn't know how.

But what if those children managed to succeed? He toyed with the absurdity of it. On the remote chance that they did manage to find the stone tablets, could he deny them passage to the Garden of Eden? No, not really. But it made no difference. The prize would still be his because he'd steal it. In any case, children of the human race would never commit murder, I mean, they could hardly bear to even dream of it.

With these happy thoughts, he summoned Asgard. 'Dreamspinner, dreamspinner, dreamspinner,' he called. Moments later the large, opaque, spidery creature appeared, his blue middle fizzing with electric light. 'Aha! There you are. How is our little plan coming along?'

Asgard's legs moved rapidly. 'Master, the particles have been mixed into the new stocks of spider web dream powders deep in the caves of Havilah.'

'Excellent!' Cain said. 'What will these dreams be like?'

'Havilarian spiders are different to those of the Garden of Eden and Earth. They are clever, brutal, manipulative and easily roused. These qualities are reflected in the action of the dream powders made from their spider webs.'

'Nightmares?'

'Bad dreams are as rewarding and enriching as the pleasant,' Asgard said, flicking his legs. 'After all, they are only dreams. Remember, creativity and enlightenment comes from the darker side of life too, Master.'

Cain was intrigued. 'Why not spider webs from Earth?'

'Earth spiders are bland and lifeless. These spider web powders do not nourish dreamspinners as deeply.'

'Why so?'

'Dream powders are as vital to us as the breathing of air is to mankind and water is to creatures of the sea. Dreamspinners will spin more dreams from Havilah from now on. I guarantee it.'

'Your band of dreamspinners has grown?'

'Now there are many,' the spidery creature signed, speaking through the vibrations of his legs. 'Each day, as the sun sets, more join. Dreamspinners cannot resist a dream.'

'Even bad ones, eh?' Cain loved this creature. 'You are most enlightening, Asgard,' he said. 'And wise,' he added.

Asgard was unsure of Cain's meaning. 'In the event of the boy returning to you,' Asgard continued, 'I have found a way of transporting you from place to place.'

If Cain had ears, they would have flapped. 'Are you suggesting there are dreamspinners who would sacrifice themselves?' he asked.

'Indeed. Some who are too old to give dreams do not wish to see the world shaping as it is. They believe a new time is coming. They are prepared to go to their deaths early.'

Cain jumped up, invisibly, and thumped the air repeatedly. 'Phenomenal news! Truly, Asgard, this is wonderful! I am delighted with you.' He lowered his voice. 'Tell me, dreamspinner, how long before the plague particles in your dream powders are ready to go?'

'The new spider web dream powders are free to use as the sun sinks over the western horizon.'

Cain gasped. 'Tonight? Already? My goodness.'

The ghost danced an invisible jig. What a turnaround! Nightmares stuffed full of plague, and a few days early at that. 'Poor, dear, little Earthlings,' he crowed. 'They have no idea what is about to hit them – and not a helping hand in sight.'

Damn the wretched Prophecy, damn the old man and damn the Heirs of Eden, he thought. Very soon there won't be a world worth saving.

# 70 LOCKDOWN

While showing footage of the hairless boy in his hospital bed, the TV screen started to flicker, soon blacking out altogether. Isabella flipped the light switch, but it wasn't working either and the buzz of the generator no longer filled the air. She shot out of the house to see if she could restart the motor.

Silence filled the kitchen. 'Was that who I think it was?' Daisy said quietly.

Archie had gone pale. 'What do you mean?' he stammered, trying to hide his face.

'That boy!' Daisy said.

Archie didn't know what to say.

'*It's Kemp*! It has to be.'

'You think so?'

'Yes. Of course. But without hair. Bald and burnt. It's Kemp, your horrible friend.'

For a moment, Archie wasn't capable of uttering a word. 'But how could it be Kemp? He'd been in the alley—'

'Where?' Daisy cut in.

Archie hesitated. 'Well, you know...'

'No, I don't know what you're talking about,' Daisy said, as she started to remove her wet clothes. 'What alley?'

Archie wondered if he should come clean and tell Daisy about the meeting with Cain, and Cain's offer. 'No, it's nothing,' he heard himself say. 'He just said he was going shopping in town, *down the alley*, that's all.'

'Strange, isn't it?' Daisy said as she removed her top. 'I saw the rescue on telly this morning and at the time I thought those big lips could only belong to one person. Do you think his burn marks are from a lightning strike or a burning building?'

'Dunno,' Archie said.

'Is that "dunno" you don't know, or are you just repeating what that dimwit Kemp said?'

'Eh? Oh, sorry, just trying to work out what he was saying.' Archie said as his brain raced. Was this Cain's doing? Even so, how on earth did he end up in a tree? Kemp could hardly swim.

Daisy felt like smacking Archie round the head. Talking to him was like chatting to a goalpost. 'Shouldn't we phone the helpline and tell them we know who it is? Don't you think that's our, duty?'

Isabella came back into the room. 'I can't seem to get it going. Arch, you'd better have a try.'

'We're going to phone the number,' Daisy said, addressing her sister.

'Phone who, about what?'

'Call the emergency number and let them know we think the boy is Kemp.'

Isabella turned on her. 'Why? Why should we do that?'

Daisy hesitated. Isabella sounded unnecessarily sharp. 'Well, he's Archie's friend—'

'And my enemy,' Isabella snapped. 'No way. If anyone wants to claim him,' she said, 'let them.' She turned away. 'Come on, Archie, the sooner we get the generator going, the better.'

---

DAISY'S HEART THUMPED. She desperately wanted to tell them about the enormous chamber, but this revelation about an unknown virus had to be the same as the images portrayed on the cave wall.

If she was going to talk about it she'd have to pick her moment carefully; Isabella was in an argumentative mood and best avoided until she'd calmed down. She headed upstairs for a shower, which drizzled cold water.

As she rinsed her hair, she thought about the huge building and, for a fleeting moment, wondered if she had simply imagined being there. Nah, that was impossible. It was as real as the water running down her back.

And what were those funny old trees that spoke to her, Daisy mused, and where did the terrible screams come from? She dressed quickly and skipped down the stairs.

When she walked in, Archie was washing his hands in the sink and Isabella was sitting in a chair with her arms folded tight across her chest, staring at the floor. Oh *well,* she thought, *better now than never*.

'Right,' she said, pulling up a chair. 'We need to talk.'

Archie sat down. 'The Prime Minister's on in ten minutes,' he said. 'We should watch him.'

'We'll do that after I've explained what happened to me earlier,' Daisy said. 'This is important.'

Isabella yawned. 'Fire away, twinkle toes.'

'OK, so this is going to sound a bit crackers,' Daisy began. 'I went to look for you this morning, Archie, and when I reached Dad's old potato patch, I found a gate with a pearl hanging from a bush.'

Isabella tutted.

'Please, Bells, let me finish. I tried to grab the pearl and, as I reached out, I fell into a ditch. When I'd dragged myself out, I was in sunshine on a small glade with three really old trees totally covered in blossom. I know it sounds impossible but these trees asked me questions—'

Isabella groaned theatrically.

Daisy shot her a look. 'At first I thought I'd died, you know swallowed some infected water or something, and ignored them – but the trees insisted and eventually pointed me towards a strange platform. After a bit of hesitation, I went on to the platform and then flew off to a ... a new kind of place.'

Isabella guffawed. 'Yes, yes, I know you disappeared, Daisy. Nice story, by the way.'

'Eh? What ...?'

'You disappeared?'

'Well, yeah.'

'And do you know how I know?'

Daisy shook her head.

'Because I saw you. I watched as you moved an object on this platform of yours and then you vanished.'

Daisy was flummoxed. 'How do you know all this?'

'I found some magic panels on Old Man Wood's bed—'

'Magic—'

'Yes, like TV monitors.'

Daisy's face had turned puce. 'What panels, Bells? You're talking bull,' she said. 'It's not possible.'

'I'm afraid it is. Happy to show you if you like.'

The children sat silently round the table. Isabella smiling.

'It's a joke, right? You're making fun, aren't you?'

But Isabella's face didn't change.

Daisy was seething. 'I knew you wouldn't believe me but it's true, it's all true. One hundred percent.' She stood up and paced around the table. 'My dreams – our dreams – are really, really happening – right now. Everything we've seen, Bells, is real, not imaginary. And we're running out of time—'

'Daisy, shut up!' Isabella snapped. 'I told you, I saw you, OK? There's really nothing more to say on the matter.'

'Anyone fancy,' Archie began diplomatically, 'a slice of Old Man Wood's starlight apple crumble? I don't know about you, but I'm starving. Nothing like a good pig-out to calm the nerves, because it's becoming perfectly clear that we're losing the plot – big time.'

Archie stood up, pulled some milk from the fridge and pushed a cake tin onto the table. Then he pressed the button that turned on the TV.

Much to their surprise, it flickered into life.

---

PRIME MINISTER KINGSFORD LOOKED TIRED. No amount of make-up could disguise this. He was flanked by senior government ministers and his COBRA team as he stood in front of an oak lectern.

*'People of the United Kingdom,'* he began, *'Never in the annals of our history has this country faced a crisis as severe as the situation that confronts us now. This afternoon, I speak to you as your leader. I also speak to you as a husband and a father and an ordinary man. I don't doubt that the words and actions that are about to follow will be met with shock. But I ask you all, before I say any more, to under-*

*stand that the measures that are about to be imposed have been thrust upon us as a very last resort. And, therefore, I urge you to listen to what I have to say with level-headed understanding.*

*'It is with a heavy heart that I tell you this. But I tell you so that together we may face the threat in front of us with the decency and common spirit that I know resides within the marrow of each and every one of you.'*

He shuffled nervously, his eyes hollow, his skin pale.

*'Following the devastating flooding of the Yorkshire area,'* he began, *'a virus known as Ebora has emerged. It is a strain that has never been seen before. It is a freak. There is no rhyme nor reason as to Ebora's aggressive nature. It is a silent enemy that we do not, as yet, understand, but rest assured, we will. As I speak to you now, top scientists from around the world are trying to identify its complex properties in order to find a vaccine. But they require more time.'*

The camera zoomed in on his face. *'Earlier today I met with the COBRA team who have been working non-stop to provide the framework necessary to protect as many lives as possible. Their work is being actioned, as I speak, on the orders of the Government following top-level consultations.*

*'In order to give ourselves the best opportunity to narrow its destructive path our first step is to limit the movement of people in and around the country,'*

The Prime Minister mopped his brow. *'By morning, our hospitals will be ready with contained areas for those showing symptoms, though you may decide, as responsible citizens, that remaining at home is the best solution.*

*'In the meantime, the following limitations are to be forced upon every person in these isles.'* The Prime Minister shuffled his notes and held a long pause. A global audience of billions reached into their sets.

*'From midnight tonight, a great safety net will be pulled over our land and drawn around our borders. Every airport in Britain, every railway and waterway will be vacated. Motorway traffic will be limited to emergency use only. Supermarkets, power companies, media organisations and their distribution partners will fall under the control of Government departments.*

*'These measures are to ensure that food and necessary supplies can be provided to everyone, at the right time, without panic and without preference so that the fundamental elements of our existence can continue.*

*'While we learn how to combat Ebora, life must go on. So, this evening, do not rush to your local stores, do not go outside for unnecessary errands or social occasions. Consider everything closed. Civil unrest will not be tolerated and the penalties for such acts will be swift and severe.'* The Prime Minister paused to sip some

water. *'Many will have noticed the presence of the military in the cities and the towns. I urge you not to be alarmed. They are there to protect you and to enforce law and order upon our nation – and for no other reason.*

*'Local travel will be possible, but ill-advised. For the benefit of safety, internet use will be limited. Updates will be posted regularly on television channels and radio stations.*

*'Until a vaccine is found, I cannot tell you how long these measures will be in place.'*

He paused again and looked directly into the camera. *'In this great country of ours we have overcome many things. Together, we shall persevere. Together, we will win this fight.'*

Tears welled in his eyes. *'Go now to your loved ones. Be safe, responsible and ever mindful. And may God bless you all. Thank you.'*

---

FOR A WHILE, the children stared open-mouthed at the screen.

It was Daisy who broke the silence. 'Bollocks!' she said.

Isabella turned on her. 'Daisy, there's no need to swear.'

Daisy was shaking. 'Yes there bloody well is!'

'No,' Isabella replied icily. 'There isn't!'

'Yes, there shitting bloody well is!' Daisy yelled.

'Daisy! Stop it!' Isabella cried. 'And anyway, there's nothing we can do about it, you heard what the PM said.'

'Isabella, how unbelievably thick are you? Don't you understand? Don't you get it yet?' She stood. 'This is our problem. This is OUR BLOODY PROBLEM.'

'No, it isn't,' Isabella replied calmly, 'and for God's sake, stop swearing. Didn't you listen to anything, *anything* on the telly? It's a national problem—'

'Yes, but it started here! Right here in Upsall—?'

Archie moved in. 'Whoa! Cool it, Daise,' he said.

'*Cool it!*' she roared. 'Have you lost your minds? Seriously — which bits don't you understand? You think you get freaky hair like that or bloody great holes in your hands or glaring red eyes *every bleeding day?* Really? You think these strange things happening to us are *normal?* Do you?'

Isabella wasn't having any of it. 'Well, it looks like I'm not the only one who's lost my mind,' she snapped back. 'This virus has nothing to do with us.'

'It has EVERYTHING to do with us, der brain,' Daisy spat. 'If you'd bothered to look at the cave paintings you would have realised it is *exactly* what was shown. It showed a plague, like in biblical times, and three stone tablets like ... like books, and they needed to be found or everyone dies.'

'Oh belt up, Daisy. You're completely overreacting.'

'Me, overreacting? You're kidding, right?' Daisy said as she stood up and swept a mass of blonde curls off her face. She faced her sister, her face puce with anger, her red eyes burning like fire. 'Take a hard look at yourself, Bells, and think of everything we've been through. Overreacting? Jeez, I really don't think so.' She gave both of her siblings a piercing look. 'Seems like you two are suffering from total memory failure.'

'Stop being so irrational and stupid—'

'Stupid? You're the daft ones, not me!' There was no reaction. 'We have to find those things that were clearly painted on the walls. This is about the three of us. It's about all of us doing whatever we've got to do, together. Why don't you get it?'

Daisy stormed out and slammed the door. Then she opened the door again and marched back in. 'And there's one more thing.'

Isabella tutted.

'Yeah,' Daisy said, 'I've worked it out.'

'Worked what out?' Archie said.

'What Kemp meant. You know, when he said those words, "dunno" and "algae". I know what he was trying to say.'

'What are you talking about?' Isabella said.

'Kemp – in the hospital bed, your holy thickness.'

'Most likely he was simply trying to alert them about the water,' Isabella said coolly.

Daisy shook her head.

Isabella smirked. 'Go on then, spit it out, Professor Stephen Hawking.'

Daisy smarted. 'Why should I?'

'Oh don't tell me – it's yet another thing that's sprung out of your fertile imagination,' Isabella said, smiling thinly.

'No. I know alright,' Daisy fired back. 'Why should I tell you when you will not open your eyes?'

'Try me?'

'Sod you, Isabella. Where the hell is Old Man—'

The door opened. Old Man Wood's head popped round the door-frame. 'Have I missed something?' he said, as he went over to the range and put the kettle on. 'Everything alright?'

'*No, everything is not alright!*' Daisy roared, fixing him with an icy stare. 'An epidemic is about to sweep the country following the worst flooding ever and, LA-DI-DAH, we're the only ones who seem to know anything about it. You're part of this, Old Man Wood, so it's time you started telling us; *what the hell is going on?!*'

# 71 LEO AND KATE

Gus was relieving himself off the end of the boat, when, all of a sudden, a shriek and a wobble very nearly made him topple overboard.

'Hey!' he shouted. 'Give me a break!'

Sue was yelling. At first Gus thought she was in trouble, but it quickly dawned on him that these were howls of joy. He zipped up and looked under the canopy. Sue was holding her phone, the back-light illuminating her face, tears rolling down her cheeks.

'They're fine,' she said. 'Look!' She handed him the phone.

*S + G, wow!!! U did it. So so happy – dancing at UR news! Survived. No idea how! scary + mad – not sure how real. At cottage. Phone works every now n then. Weird stuff happening. Any idea where u r? National catastrophe. SO pleased 4 U!!!! Hugs I, D, A*

Gus whistled. 'I knew they'd do it.'

'You did not,' Sue replied, hitting him.

'Course I did. They're tougher than you think, cleverer than you think and a lot madder than you think. Not sure which goes with who, though. Must be a few stories about how they got back. No word on the other message?'

'Nah. They must think I'm cuckoo.' She wiped a tear from her eye. 'Time for sleep, Mr Williams. It's knackering doing nothing.'

Gus looked up at the night sky which, for the first time since they had been at sea, showed a wide range of stars occasionally blotted out by a woolly cloud. 'Bit chillier tonight, and windier,' he said. He put his hand out. 'I reckon the wind's changed. Can you button down the other end if I do this one?' He pulled the sail about and jammed it into place. The boat sped forward in perfect union with the wind. He bent down under the canopy and tied off the makeshift end sections.

Then they lay on the planks, shivering a little as he studied the compass on Sue's phone. Set fair, South West.

'I could do with a warm fire,' Sue said, 'wrapped up in my furry onesie watching a good movie.'

'Drinking a cup of hot chocolate,' Gus added, 'with a pile of cream frothing on top.' He sighed as he turned the phone off, noting the two power bars.

'And marshmallows,' Sue added.

Gus wriggled closer. 'Move over. You're the worst bed hog ever—'

'Me?' Sue cried. 'Yeah right! Your snoring keeps the fish awake.'

Gus chuckled. 'At least I don't fart in my sleep!'

She hit him on the chest. 'Don't be vulgar. That smell is the skanky fish guts at the bottom of the boat.'

Gus yawned. 'Oh, sure!'

Sue pulled the two thick dust blankets up and rolled over so they were facing. They'd given up trying to do the lookout – it was simply too cold and for two nights not a light or another boat had been spotted. Their body warmth was a necessary comfort.

In the pitch black, Sue put her arms around Gus and very slowly moved her head towards his. Their noses bumped and a soft snigger came out. A moment later their lips met and this time, now that he'd relaxed, it was a far more pleasant experience. Shortly, Sue broke off and rolled over. 'Night, Gus,' she whispered. 'Hey, and Gus, if we don't make it through the night, thank you. Thank you for everything.'

He groaned.

'Sweet dreams,' she said.

---

A MURMURING CAME OUT OF GUS' mouth. He rolled one way, then the other, knocking her. Then she heard a noise. Was it Gus, or wind on the canopy?

Sue woke with a start. 'Gus?' she said, listening to the strange noises coming from him. His head rolled one way and then the other. 'You alright?'

The boat wobbled and pitched and a sense of being terribly small and insignificant, of being a tiny speck of life in a vast ocean, filled her. She reached across him for the torch, her fingers dabbing at the heavy cloth of the dust sheet. As she did so, her hair brushed across his face.

A moment later he sneezed violently, waking himself up. He sat bolt upright.

Sue flicked on the torch. 'You OK?' she said. 'I think you were having a nightmare.' She yawned and rested her head on his chest.

Gus blinked. 'Yeah. Yeah, that's all.' He said, trying to get his bearings.

Sue raised herself up and smiled. 'I think my hair tickled your nose.'

The boat pitched as it rode a larger wave and then rounded the crest and headed down again. For the first time, Sue detected a look of anxiety in Gus' eyes.

The wind thudded into the side canopy as the boat plunged into the next wave, the doffing sound of water colliding with the helm filling their small cabin.

'There's a storm coming,' he said. His blue eyes were now wide open and, in place of his usual, happy demeanour with his big toothy smile, he wore a frown. The boat lurched and spray showered the canopy. 'It could be pretty unpleasant.'

Sue spoke very calmly, trying not to betray her nerves. 'We've had it, haven't we?' she said.

'Oh, I don't know about that,' he said, regaining his bravado. '*The Joan Of* survived the worst storm since Noah, so there's no reason it can't withstand a wee North Sea gale.'

Sue shivered. 'So what you're saying, in Gus-speak, is that we're stuffed.'

Gus took too long to reply. Finally he sighed and smiling boldly said, 'Nah, not really. We beat the odds last time, who says we can't do it again. And anyway, after all we've been through, it'll be a walk in the park.' He shook his legs out, encouraging blood back into his toes and shuffled down the boat. 'I'm going to see what's happening out there, and then we need to batten down the hatches.' He opened up the makeshift canvas door and slipped outside.

Gus' over-confidence simply confirmed her worst suspicions. The boat lurched into a bigger wave and water thudded onto the canopy. Sue grabbed her phone and pressed the power button. The phone display lit up.

Moments later she was tapping away furiously. Her first message was to her entire address book:

*SOS. Sue Lowden here with Gus Williams. In small rowing boat in the North Sea. Sucked out in storm. Gale coming. No idea where we are. HELP!*

Her second was to Isabella. A thought had been niggling away at her.

*Me here. Not looking good. G being v brave me less so. Have you found clues? In your house – like pictures. You MUST find them. Sounds mad but think important. If don't speak, love you very much. Sue – n Gus. xxx*

Sue noted the bars of the battery sinking to red. One more.

*M & D, love you so much. If you get this, I'm stuck out at sea. Don't worry – never been happier. Thanks for all you have done. I love you xxx*

---

THE JOAN *Of* jolted viciously and Sue, off balance, dropped the phone. It landed in the water at the bottom of the boat with a splash.

Gus put his head back under the canopy, his head soaked. 'Do you want the good news or the bad news?'

'Uh,' Sue said as she picked up her phone.

'I said, good news, or bad news?'

Gus sat on the end of the bench and waited for her response. If he could have seen her face he'd have noticed tears trailing down her cheeks. 'Anyone there?' he asked.

Sue wiped the handset and then her eyes. 'Bad news,' Sue croaked.

Gus smiled his big toothy smile. 'Ace. Right, the bad news is that it's quite a big one.'

'Big what?'

'Bag of bananas, you monkey! Storm! What do you think?'

Sue shivered. 'And the good?'

'Lights! I can see lights!' He was shouting. 'Look ... there, can you see it? A lighthouse.'

Sue crawled down the boat and, for a moment, as she popped her head out, she caught the blink of a light way off in the distance. Her muscles tensed and her eyes widened. Was it one mile off or ten miles away? 'How far?' she shouted.

'I don't know,' he yelled back. 'I'd get a better idea if the waves weren't so big.'

For the first time, now that her eyes had fully adjusted to the murky gloom, she could see the wild seas frothing and chopping nearby. A huge, dark wave loomed up. Before she had a chance to move, it broke. She dived inside. The canopy sagged for a moment and then sprang back.

Gus immediately pulled the sail, the umbrella they used as a water holder and other odds and ends into the boat. He secured their food package with a rope, tying it against the bottom of the seat. 'Here,' he said, 'have some.' He threw her a bag of crisps and a water bottle. 'Drink.'

Sue did as she was told.

'Now,' he said, handing her an assortment of chocolates. 'Tuck these in your pockets. Just in case.'

She grabbed them and pushed two into her jeans and another lot into her jacket.

'I'm scared, Gus,' she said.

He grinned back. 'Have no fear, we'll be fine,' he replied as another wave assaulted the canopy. Quick as a flash Gus was bailing water. Sue joined in and, for the time being at least, the water in the boat took their mind off the storm.

He lay down, Sue next to him gulping in air. She was shaking. He draped an arm round her. 'Sue, believe me, everything will work out, fine and dandy,' he said softly.

She trembled. Gus knew it wasn't from the cold. He needed her to be strong. 'Look, it's like at the end of the film, *Titanic,*' he said. 'Remember? When Leonardo DiCaprio holds Kate and they're in the freezing cold water but they keep going until they get rescued—'

'*But HE dies*,' Sue shot back.

'Yeah, but he kept her alive, somehow, right to the bitter end. And you know what, I'm going to keep you alive too. Anyway, in our version, it isn't that cold, we're very close to land and you've put out an SOS – haven't you?' He held her harder and turned to her, his eyes wide. 'You have, haven't you?'

'Yes.'

'Good,' he said. 'So there you go, it's tons easier. And we're not in a hulking great boat in the middle of the North Atlantic, we're in a tiny rowing boat, somewhere off the coast of ... somewhere. So safety is pretty much guaranteed. It's a piece of cake. And, there's another thing,' he said, his grin returning, 'you're way prettier than Leo's Kate.' He kissed her forehead.

Sue snuggled into his chest as the boat groaned under the thrust of a wave which bashed the boat first one way and then the other. It lurched wretchedly, like a ride at the fair, and she felt they might suddenly tip over.

A horrible sickness swept through her.

Gus' eyes sparkled and then he started laughing. He got up and stumbled to the end of the boat, grabbed the large container that was filled with fresh water, took a deep swig and filled up his water bottle. He turned. 'You want some?'

Sue hardly dared move but she reckoned a bit of water might make her feel less queasy. She nodded and slid along the bench, not daring for a minute to let go. Sue gulped at the water, instantly regretting it. Her stomach churned.

Gus tied the rope around his wrist, pulling the plastic barrel after him. Then he pushed the barrel out and began pouring the water out into the sea.

'What the hell are you doing?' Sue screamed.

'Buoyancy aid,' he grinned. 'If we go down, and of course it's a massive "if", it would be a shame if we were to drown.'

'But we need water, Gus!'

'We've got enough,' he shrugged and tapped the water bottle as a wave threw him against the canopy. His grin grew and his eyes shone.

'We'll freeze!'

'Nah! Course we won't.'

A roller smashed the canopy and Sue cowered down, trembling.

Gus stumbled over. 'The fact is,' he said, 'we're near the coast. I can sense it. So either it's a short swim, or *The Joan Of* gets wrecked, and a boat comes along and picks us up – or a helicopter – wouldn't that be cool?'

*'No, it would not be!'*

'Aw, come on, liven up a bit. We're on the verge of getting out of the boat.'

'You're insane, Gus Williams. Totally bloody bonkers.'

Gus mocked a pained look.

Sue thumped him on the arm. 'OK – utterly gorgeous, but still bloody bonkers,' she added.

Gus tied a section of wood onto the handle of the barrel with some rope and settled into his construction mode.

Sue watched, admiring his speed and concentration.

'Oh God, I'm going to be sick,' she said, her hand moving to her mouth. Holding tightly onto the seat and using the rocking motion of the boat, she slipped towards the canopy entrance. As she leaned out a wave smashed her in the face. She reeled and put her head back in and shrieked, shaking the water out of her hair.

Gus laughed.

'Oh shut up,' she said, as she put her head back outside and let fly. Her body felt green and deathly. When she opened her eyes, she tried to figure out what she was staring at. A large, black, towering hulk right in front of her. And then it was lost behind a wall of water. Was it a boat, a cliff or something else?

She scrambled in as Gus was tying the other end of the plank onto one of the buoyancy containers. 'What is it?' she said.

'What's what?'

'The big – sodding great thing – out there.'

Gus smiled. 'Cliffs, probably.'

'Cliffs? Is that good or bad?' her attention turned to his contraption. 'What are you doing?'

Gus' eyes sparkled in the torchlight. 'This, my little vomit comet, is our life raft.'

'That?!'

Gus looked taken aback. 'Yeah. It's brilliant. You got any better ideas?' His eyes darted to the bottom of the boat where, for the first time, she noted there was a considerable body of water swishing around.

'Bail!' she cried. 'We've taken on too much water.' Immediately Sue reached for the bailing bucket, her arms flailing in the darkness. She found it but, as she bent to scoop, she was thrown to the other side of the vessel. A strong hand pulled her up. Gus looked deep into her eyes.

'Sue. The boat is leaking. There must be a small hole somewhere. No amount of bailing can save *The Joan Of.* Not now, not in this.'

After all they'd been through, she could hardly believe it. 'So we're going to sink?'

Gus pushed on the torch. 'Nah,' he said, shining the torch in his face in a mock spooky way. 'This is the part where we disembark. You just have to hold on, you understand? Do exactly as I say.'

Sue summoned her strength and nodded through her tears.

'So now you're Kate, like in *Titanic,* and I'm Leo.' He kissed her. 'OK? Whatever you do, don't let go. Promise me you won't let go.'

Sue threw herself at him and hugged him tight. Somehow, deep down, she trusted him with her whole soul. If Gus said they'd survive, they would. Everything else had worked. Why not this?

Gus noted the water was up to his knees. He slipped out of their embrace, opened his penknife and thrust it through the canvas, the blade ripping the canopy in a neat line.

In no time, the full force of the gale was upon them, blowing hard, the vessel filling with water. In the dim light they could see into the night beyond. On one side loomed a cliff and on the other ... a boat. Sue's heart soared. Did the boat even know they were there?

She turned to Gus. 'Look!'

He turned back, his face bursting with a smile and his eyes dancing like little stars in the dull night sky. 'Hold on, my Kate,' he said. 'That's all you've got to do.'

Sue smiled back. She'd hold on for Gus this day and every day henceforth.

And, before she had the chance to dwell on it, a huge wave engulfed *The Joan Of.*

Gus' big toothy smile was the last thing she remembered as her world was churned upside down and inside out.

# 72 STUCK FOR ETERNITY

She heard the noise while they were playing a game she had made up many centuries ago. The game centred on a bundle of cobweb silks the size of small peas: on the poke of a leg, she made a faint clap of her old hands or a wheezy cough and, on that signal, the little dreamspinners flicked mini balls of spider web silks towards each other's magholes. If they succeeded, a small puff of smoke burst on a very surprised little dreamspinner. So the best effect was when a multitude of pellets exploded on one maghole and as such a sophisticated game of sending secret messages about ganging-up on one another had begun.

Smaller dreamspinners never tired of this simple amusement. The powdered remains were shared out and re-manipulated into balls by the baby creatures and the game continued until fatigue overtook them or the spider web bundles ran out or an elder dreamspinner told them to quieten down.

After the Great Closing of Eden the dreamspinners discovered the Ancient Woman in the small rooms below the vast storage area of spider web dream powders. Her eyes had been gouged out and she could never leave. She was part of their family now and they looked after her with food and water as she required.

She was immortal, and the dreamspinners knew she would never die, so this nourishment prevented her body withering away to nothing. But many long years of solitude had left her physically wretched. Her skeletal frame was overhung with her own coarse, over-sized skin, her bony skull had but a few wisps of hair, her empty eye sockets were hollow, like dark holes, and the nails on her fingers long and curling like spiders' legs.

To the Ancient Woman, the dreamspinners appeared in her mind as clever, shy, solitary creatures concerned only with making and giving dreams. As the trust between them grew, and as a great passage of time crept by, she understood the immense influence of these strange, unknown, dream-giving spiders. And slowly she learnt about dreams.

She discovered how dreamspinners blended old and new spider web silks into all sorts of powerful and exotic concoctions. She was amazed to learn that these strange creatures had no interest in manipulating their power and begged them to allow her to try out new dream powder combinations in order to understand what effects they might have.

Much later, she manipulated their dream powders to give herself dreams that lasted for days, dreams where she could lose herself, free her imagination to wander and forget the perpetual darkness, the anguish and her desperate boredom. In this state she could fall in love again, dance in the fields of the Garden of Eden once more, ride the giant horses on the glorious pink Tomberlacker Plains, talk to her children ... kiss them, hug them and teach them all the things she knew ... and do it again and again.

And she did, until her heart ached like a balloon at bursting point.

In the Atrium of The Garden of Eden, the dreamspinners provided her with a degree of comfort from the solitude and darkness, while she waited and waited for the arrival of the Heirs of Eden. Yet ever at the back of her mind was the knowledge that if Eden was to open, she would never see its beauty and splendour.

She heard it again. A sound from the outside; a sound that had haunted her for thousands of years. She listened harder.

The gentle thuds both thrilled her and injected her with unimaginable dread. Someone or something walked in the dust in the great chamber above.

Her mind sparked into life. Instantly, she pulled her tiny, bony frame off the ground and made her way up the curving staircase. Her body, so ancient and pathetic, made it hard for her to move. With every step, her wasted muscles screamed out in pain. She forced herself on, her heart pumping furiously, energy flowing through each and every vein as she diligently struggled up the worn treads.

At about the halfway mark, she paused for breath, exhausted. All she could hear was her thumping heart and the rasping sound of air trying to squeeze into her withered lungs.

After recovering her poise, she listened again. Yes, she could quite clearly hear footsteps walking in the Atrium.

An Heir of Eden, perhaps? But why only one? Had they failed already?

She urged herself on, each step more painful than the last. At the top, she felt for the wooden cane. With this she could guide herself into her half of the great chamber. She leant hard on her stick, her body begging for a rest. She shuffled a few paces and stopped to listen, her lungs wheezing like wind through dry leaves. She sensed the person moving away.

'Come on! MOVE legs, MOVE body,' she cackled.

Then she heard a sound she hadn't expected. A loud—

**CRACK!**

The stick, which had supported her for so long, gave way beneath her, snapping clean in two. The old woman landed awkwardly. A strange pain ricocheted through her body.

She ran a hand down her leg. She felt something sharp and fragmented. It wasn't the stick, it was her thighbone – a shattered piece that had speared through her flesh.

When her brain realised the extent of the injury, pain coursed through her and she screamed in agony.

Moments later, as she regained consciousness, she heard another sound so haunting that it chilled her to the core. It was the unmistakable noise of a giant whirring fan, a sound she had often heard before she was abandoned; a noise that had troubled, haunted and eluded her ever since – the distinct whirr of the Great Door for those *leaving* the Garden of Eden.

Her wails that followed spoke of utter misery; of agony on a totally different scale and intensity. 'When will this wretchedness ... this cruelty end?' she cried out to the empty cavern. 'Finish this. End this. PLEASE ... please,' she implored. Her sobs trailed off unheard along the empty tunnels. 'Haven't I suffered enough?'

Lying at the top of the stairs, thoughts tumbled back. She recalled how her family had been so happy in the Garden of Eden before the punishment of immortality. She remembered their love, and, although she hadn't minded it at first, the emptiness she felt after Cain, Abel and Seth had flown the nest, left her with a sadness that grew like a cancer.

The memory of Cain's betrayal, his alliance with the serpent, his ever increasing lust for power and his embracing of darkness made her shudder, as did the shock of her capture and torture and the agony of losing her eyes. She thought of the chaos and muddle when Eden closed and the magic that had vanished.

And all that was left was cold, desperate, endless emptiness.

*WHY DID I DO IT?*

Why had she offered herself as the ultimate sacrifice? Possibly because there was no alternative. Probably because it put an end to the conflict.

In the end, though, she had spent a life in purgatory so that one day there might be a fresh start for life in a new Garden of Eden.

While she mulled over these thoughts, several dreamspinners bound her leg with tough dreamspinner silks and gave her dream powders to soothe the pain. Soon, she knew, she would spiral off into a comforting dream. The dreamspinners would take good care of her – even if her injured leg made movement impossible.

She realised that if Eden could not be woken, she would be stuck in the Atrium forever, disappearing into dust, her heart the last organ to survive in this empty world.

As she drifted off, a curious feeling of hope washed over her: whoever had worked out how to get in to the Atrium of The Garden of Eden had discovered how to get out. No one had done this since the Great Closing.

Calm swept through her like a gentle breeze. *The person who came – and went – must possess,* she thought, *truly great qualities – magical qualities that would solve the riddles to opening the Garden of Eden. Perhaps he or she would return with the other Heirs of Eden?* From the depths of her heart she felt convinced of this.

Next time, she would be better prepared and ready for them. And it wouldn't be long, she was sure of it.

Her heart began to glow like an orb of fire within her, blood pumping around her veins like molten lava. Her brain filled with a new kind of energy that brimmed with confidence, hope and desire. It was a sensation she hadn't felt in eons.

Maybe, she hoped, her sacrifice would not have been in vain.

Perhaps my story will be told after all.

# 73 UNANSWERED QUESTIONS

Mrs Pye followed Old Man Wood into the kitchen and quickly sensed there was an "atmosphere". In no time she'd delved into her fridge and larder, but her heart was heavy and her movements pained and sluggish.

Archie noticed it first. 'Mrs P, did you watch the speech?' he asked.

Mrs Pye snivelled. 'Aye. Worrying, I reckon,' she sniffed, pulled out a white handkerchief and dabbed her eyes. 'It's ... it's that poor boy I feel for. Makes me come over all strange every time I see him, everyone waiting for him to wake up.'

Archie went in for a big hug and was rewarded by a squashing from Mrs Pye's ample bosom. 'Thing is, Mrs P,' he said as he resurfaced, 'we think that boy might be my friend Kemp. What do you think?'

Mrs Pye released him and rubbed her eyes again. 'Well now, that be something.'

'It's amazing if it is,' Archie continued, 'I can't believe it. Can you? I thought he'd be dead, like all the others.'

She burst into tears.

'Oh, heck, I'm sorry,' Archie said. 'I didn't mean to upset you.'

'Never you mind,' she said, wiping her tears on her sleeve. 'Every time I see his dear little face I get an upsetting feeling in me bones, that's all.' She dusted herself off and pulled herself as upright as possible. 'I think,' she declared, 'that a special Mrs Pye sandwich is what you lot need tonight, followed by a slice of starlight apple crumble. Might have one myself too, you know – help get over this terribleness.'

And in no time, as she always did, Mrs Pye shooed everyone out of the kitchen. 'Come back in fourteen,' she said as she ushered them out of the door, and the children dispersed to different parts of the house.

---

MRS PYE TOOK her meal over the road, for she was too upset to see anyone. The three children and Old Man Wood ate their MPS sandwiches – pronounced *emps* – in virtual silence, aside from an occasional slurp or clatter of cutlery. An MPS was the abbreviation for "Mrs Pye Special". It was a slice of French bread with layers of melted cheese, ham, tomato, and crowned with a poached egg. Mrs Pye insisted that it was washed down with Old Man Wood's apple juice, which the old man had spent a lifetime perfecting, and which contained no less than nine different varieties from his very old and very gnarled apple orchard. He pressed his apples every year, always using the same, precise quantities of each apple variety.

Old Man Wood probably knew more about apples than anyone. He had a selection of twenty-seven ancient and highly prized apple trees in his orchard. Each variety was different and each tree bore fruit for a multitude of ailments and purposes: there were apples for headaches, apples for indigestion and other medicinal matters, apples for confidence, apples for energy, apples that were thought provoking and then there were apples that made the mind sharp or made it wander. Old Man Wood was besotted by apples.

When they had finished, a sense of calm filled the room. Archie, after licking his plate, broke the silence, 'So, Daisy, what *did* happen to you yesterday that makes you certain this involves us and us alone?'

Daisy took a deep breath, closed her eyes and began to tell her story. As she spoke, she tried to catch their eyes but, whenever she did, both her siblings stared at the table.

'It was huge,' she said, 'like ten Wembley Football Stadiums wide and, well, I couldn't even see the top. It just went on and on forever. In the middle I saw a tree with no leaves and smothered in dust. So, thinking I might be dead, I walked off – only to tread on a skeleton ... and the bones crunched under my feet as if I'd trodden on a pile of sticks,' she said, trying and failing not to laugh. 'It must have been there for years. Moments later, I heard this truly terrible noise piercing my eardrums. I panicked and ran round trying to find a way out. All around the edges were tunnels, thousands of them, some big, some small, but they were all blocked up. I ran and ran until I found a gateway with a couple of pictures on. I realised I'd seen the gate before – from my dreams, I think – and I figured that all I had to do was believe I could walk through it.' She stopped and tried to gauge the reactions of her brother and sister.

Isabella, Archie and Old Man Wood stared at her in complete silence.

'So that's what I did,' Daisy croaked. 'I simply walked through it and found myself in a wet ditch. And here I am.'

Old Man Wood turned on her. 'Daisy, you are a right daft fool!' he said, the colour draining from his face. 'What on earth did you think you were doing?'

The children looked at Old Man Wood, astonished. He had never, ever raised his voice at any of them. He was clearly as startled as they were, if not more so.

There was an awkward silence.

'Er ... well, it was very exciting,' Daisy replied, trying not to burst into tears. 'I rushed straight back and found this shocking news about Kemp and the plague ...'

'Daisy, don't you get it?' Old Man Wood interrupted, and he moved round to her side, putting an arm gently round her shoulders. 'You see, that person never saw the motif. He never worked out the way home. He died a horrible death all alone. That could have been you, my littlun. You're not ready for that, yet.'

'But I saw the clues,' she argued, feeling a bit confused, 'and it was easy, so parts of my dreams are true aren't they, so I know it really exists ... doesn't it? It all adds up.'

---

FOR ONCE, Isabella was quite moved. 'Right!' Isabella said. 'I think we need answers. Home from *where*, Old Man Wood? And how do you know it was a *he* who died?' she demanded.

Old Man Wood looked rattled. 'Oh, apples! I can't remember,' he answered, his face scrunched up and his deep wrinkles more pronounced than usual.

Isabella eyed him suspiciously and turned to her sister. 'Look, Daisy, first off, I owe you an apology.' She met her sister's eye and sighed. 'There are some strange wooden panels on the end of Old Man Wood's bed that follow our movements, like TV security monitors, I'll show them to you later. That's how I knew you'd disappeared.'

'Uh, really?'

'Yes. And I absolutely promise you I'm not joking,' she said and turned to Old Man Wood who waved a hand in acknowledgement.

'That's how I saw you sucked into the ground and, when you didn't return, I ran off looking for you. And I'm sorry I yelled at you earlier, but there is a part of me that simply will not accept that these strange goings on are in any way real. Do you understand?'

Daisy nodded as Isabella continued. 'You see, part of me cannot, and will not, believe all these peculiar things that are happening. That's me, Daisy. It's how I'm made, and there's nothing you or Arch can do about it. My whole life has been built around reason and fact, cause and effect, and it's very difficult for me to believe in anything else.' She smiled at Daisy, noting her disappointment. 'But if we're to explore your fantasies, then so be it.'

Daisy half smiled.

Isabella turned abruptly to Old Man Wood. 'Right, here goes. First off, Old Man Wood, we need answers because otherwise we're going to end up in a lunatic asylum and you will be the first one in.' She tapped the table with her fingertips. 'What is the story of your bed, are the images in the cave anything to do with us, and why did Sue insist the rain is *all our fault*? We need explanations, we need answers, and we need them now!'

The children gazed at the gnarled old face expecting a spectacular response. But all Old Man Wood said was:

'Mmm ... perhaps. Oh dear, my little favourites.'

'Old Man Wood, this is not helping.'

'The bed is a bit of a mystery,' he said. 'But perhaps it's time we found the riddles.'

'*Riddles! WHAT riddles?*' chorused the children.

'The riddles to finding the Tablets of Eden.'

'Like the ones Sue was yelling at us about?' Archie said. 'And the pictures in the cave?'

'Hmmm.'

'So this plague *is* something to do with us?' Daisy said, her eyes glowing like lasers.

'Well, now,' the old man said, staring at the floor, 'it's been an awful long time.' He opened his eyes wide, as if attempting to welcome the world into his mind. 'That's the problem, my dear littluns.' And he rapped his knuckles on his head. 'There's nothing in here anymore. I just don't remember.'

---

THE PROBLEM, as Old Man Wood kept telling the children, was that he really had forgotten everything.

There was nothing in his old grey cells but an empty void. But he knew he had to try, so he pulled himself together and, with Archie and Daisy in tow, headed upstairs to his room and began searching the large assortment of carvings hoping that something – anything – might jolt his memory.

The willow trees had told him that he himself had hidden the tablets a long time ago using complex magic. More importantly, he discovered that the tablets were a link to the rain and that the children were the Heirs of Eden, as he suspected.

But because the trees made the process sound so obvious and straightforward, he hadn't deepened his questioning and now he regretted it. He wondered if he shouldn't go back and talk to them again. But doing that meant he would have to think of the right questions and he didn't know what those questions were.

In due course, he announced to the disappointed faces of Archie and Daisy, who had followed his every move, that he simply couldn't find the riddles.

And, with this, he looked at the time, ordered the children to go directly to bed, dropped his shoulders and headed outside to check up on the cattle.

---

ISABELLA, fast asleep in the attic room, stirred. She rubbed her eyes and found herself staring at the old man.

'Wake up, wake up,' he whispered.

'Whososse that?' Isabella groaned.

'It's Old Man Wood, my dear,' he replied, as softly as his coarse, deep voice would allow. 'I need to talk. Come downstairs, if you don't mind.'

Isabella slipped into her dressing gown and stumbled downstairs to the living room. A steaming mug of hot chocolate was waiting for her.

They sat alone, comforted by the gentle crackle of the fire and the pitter-pattering sounds of rain on the roof tiles. Old Man Wood's face looked pained, his deep wrinkles prominent in the firelight.

'What's up, Old Man Wood?' Isabella asked. She figured she'd better come clean about finding the panels on his bed. 'Old Man Wood, um, I've got a confession to make ...'

'I know. I know all about your little ... discovery.' He glanced up, catching her eye, reassuring her. 'To be honest, I don't know how it works myself. But it's how I found you on that ledge in the storm when you were coming back home after the football match.' Old Man Wood scratched his chin and took a gulp of hot chocolate. 'Strange things, Bella ... are going on. I know you're worrying yourselves stupid about it but I'm sure all will be revealed soon.'

'But it's so confusing,' Isabella said. 'I don't know what to do – or what to believe any more. What's happening to us, Old Man Wood?'

'My dear child. You are like a blade of grass. One of many, un-trodden, fresh, pure. Hmmm. So pretty, neat and clever—'

'Stop humming, and talking in riddles and tell me WHAT is going on?'

'Things not so clear, eh. Rain. Endless ... dreams ... troubles? Have you all been ... dreaming?'

'Yes, you know we have,' she replied. 'Unbelievably vivid ones if you must know.'

'About an old woman?' Old Man Wood quizzed.

'Yes,' Isabella began. 'How did you know?' He didn't respond. 'Look, what exactly is all this about, Old Man Wood? You know, don't you?' She let the question hang and blew on her hot chocolate. 'I think we're going crazy even if the others don't. I'm not convinced anything is real anymore. And, anyway, where have you been? Archie told me you'd been talking to trees. What good is that?'

Old Man Wood harrumphed.

She continued. 'Without Mum and Dad here, we could really have done with your support. It was unfair and frankly selfish of you to abandon us.'

Isabella felt slightly foolish for letting it all spill out and an awkward silence hung in the air.

Old Man Wood's furrowed brow seemed even deeper than usual. 'Let me try and explain a little bit ... Right, well, where to begin ...' he mumbled. He hadn't expected her mini-outburst and his brain worked so slowly that he was unable to think of a response.

'Have you had them too?' Isabella asked.

'Had what, littlun?'

'Well, a dream, like ours!'

'Oh yes! Many, many wonderful, strange and exciting dreams. Some sad, some terrifying, some exhilarating and some of well ... of nothingness. Those are the worst dreams of all. Quite often I dream that I'm king of the most beautiful place you can imagine with a beautiful queen. These are fine dreams, young 'un. Then again once I was swallowed up by a large, terrifying, white spider with electric lightning bolts coming out of its middle.' He laughed and his whole face lit up with his kindly character. 'You know, little Isabella, dreams show you the things you desire or fear most in this strange life. They help you make choices.'

'But these weren't like MOST dreams, Old Man Wood, they were real. I've never felt anything like it.' Isabella's eyes lit up like candles. 'There were dreams where I felt passion swelling in my chest like never before. I tasted tears of despair and joy. I saw terrifying scenes and odd creatures, conflicting emotions ... more. And all condensed into small flashes.' She sat back and ran her fingers though her hair.

'You know, Old Man Wood, I could even feel my blood rushing through me, which was so wonderful ... but totally alien. And there's so much I can't remember – you know how it's all there, and then not there. And do you know the strangest thing,' Old Man Wood raised his eyebrows, encouraging her. 'I even had a dream about stuffing myself with banoffee pie!'

Old Man Wood chuckled and pushed a log farther into the fire. In a low voice, just louder than a whisper, he spoke, his rich tones resonating in the dark room. 'Look into the fire, Isabella. Tell me, what do you see?'

Isabella stared for a minute at the flickering flames as they danced out into the room.

'Nothing ... burning wood, I'm afraid. Why, is there something I should see?'

'Perhaps,' said the old man, sighing deeply, 'but maybe not tonight.' He uncoiled his large frame as he extracted himself from the armchair, yawned and stretched his arms out wide. 'You know, Isabella, I believe you may have been given those dreams—'

'Given them? Oh Lordy, not you as well—'

'Oh yes, Isabella. You need to pay them due attention, young lady.' He yawned. 'The universe isn't as black and white as you think it is. In the morning all will be clearer, but right now it's best if we both get some sleep.'

He followed Isabella up the stairs to the children's attic where he straightened Archie in his bed and rearranged Daisy in hers.

Old Man Wood made his way back to his room, sat on his bed and looked around at all the curious wooden panels. There, on the screens at the foot of his bed, were the children, fast asleep, their eyes shut tight. Old Man Wood ran his hand over the old wooden carvings and, as he did, they seemed to move and whisper and he felt twinges of familiarity that made his skin prickle.

He lay down, tired and worried. How on earth could he explain what was going on, and get the children to believe him, when he couldn't recall anything himself?

But the thing that concerned him the most, was that the willows had told him there was very little time.

Something about seven days. Seven days to find these tablets? Was that it? If so, time was running out fast.

# 74 NEW POWDERS, NEW DREAMS

That night, no one in Eden Cottage dreamt.

Gaia, the dreamspinner, knew Asgard had opened up a new source of spider web powders in Havilah. She was well aware that dreamspinners were flocking there. But she wanted nothing to do with these new powders.

She made sure that the dreamspinners she oversaw produced simple, staple dreams from the spider web powders made from the spider webs on Earth.

Her band of dreamspinners appeared disappointed, for the vibrations coming back indicated that these dreams weren't as bad as the nightmares Havilah normally produced. *But how could they know?* Gaia thought, and she insisted that her dreamspinners worked faster, giving dreams to as many people as they could.

She suspected Cain was behind this new dream powder source and anything involving him spelt trouble.

---

PRIME MINISTER KINGSFORD climbed into bed. His limbs were tired and his mind fizzed with information. He studied the clock. Three in the morning. Damn. He was up at six and three hours sleep was not nearly enough. He needed to be on top form tomorrow. His head hit the pillow hard as he toyed with the huge death toll of storm and plague victims. He tried to put it out of his mind and thought of his family holiday in the sun as he fell asleep, the images of feet splashing in calm, clear Mediterranean waters.

---

A SHORT WHILE LATER, a dreamspinner hovered invisibly above the Prime Minister, its long, opaque legs anchored beside the man's face. The dreamspinner extracted tiny powders from its maghole and filtered a dream which the man sucked in with long, slow breaths.

The dreamspinner wondered how this human would react to her new dream powder. She'd been told that this spider web powder was from the webs of a recently discovered arachnid found deep in the caves beneath the mountains in Havilah. And these powders gave dreams not too dissimilar to those of the Garden of Eden; stimulating and enriching, with a twist – an extraordinary twist – Asgard had claimed.

It was a pity that the spider web powders from the Atrium in the Garden of Eden had ended. She had loved these dreams, knowing what joy they'd give. Perhaps these powders would do the same. At least the dreamspinners had a decent dream to give – and the excitement had been catching on everywhere. In milliseconds she was by their child, and when she'd given the little boy a dream she sensed a dog sleeping. She checked her powder stock and there was easily enough for at least a thousand dreamers, including the canine. This dream powder stretched a long way.

She inverted herself back to the man, to see if his dream had begun.

He groaned and turned in his sleep. Then he laughed. Now he flailed his arms.

*Excellent,* thought the dreamspinner. *Their dreams are rich, just as Asgard said they would be.*

She checked the vibrations of life in the area and flicked her legs time and time again, giving dreams until her dream powders ran dry.

She'd missed several out, their sleeping patterns too erratic or their sleep too shallow, or where a dream had already been given. She would return in the next few nights, but right now her stocks needed replenishing, from Havilah, not the Garden of Eden.

As the Earth rotated on its axis, as each country slipped into darkness, she would begin afresh on the other side of the world.

# 75 CLUES

Isabella sat in bed, running through her conversation with Old Man Wood the previous night. Her phone bleeped and she read it and re-read it before rushing downstairs. She found Daisy and Archie curled up on the sofa in front of the fire.

'Look! Another message from Sue. What do you think?' She handed Archie her phone.

He read it out loud:

*Gus total hero. Now lost at sea. Have put out SOS. Supplies OK for few days. Boat holding together, just. Fish vile, but is food. U saw Kemp on TV? G saw K acting weird b4 storm with old man. Dunno how u "stop it" but stone tablets = v good, I think. Clues in pictures? Hurry. Phone dodgy. Hope near coast. Love u all S xxx*

Archie's heart skipped a beat; *Kemp acting weird with old man.* That had to be Cain. So maybe he had joined ...

Daisy interrupted his thoughts. 'So Sue thinks the clues are in the pictures.'

Archie read the text again. *Clues in pictures?* 'There's not a great deal to go on. Do you think she means in the actual image of the picture itself – or within the frame of the picture, like a piece of paper stuck behind it?'

Daisy shrugged. 'I guess we'll need to study every picture in the house. Come on, Winkle, no time to lose.'

Isabella stepped in front of her. 'If you're going to do this, do it properly. You need a process. If there's no method it'll be chaos.'

'So you're in?' Archie said.

'Only because I've got nothing better to do,' she replied. 'If you really think there's something in this madness, I might as well organise you.'

'Great, thanks, Bells.'

'I'll do upstairs and you two do downstairs.' Isabella ordered. 'Bring all the pictures into the sitting room and line them around the walls, starting from the door and working round the room. I'll go the other way. Then at least I can catalogue them and return them to their correct position later.'

Archie and Daisy hared off and before long an amazing assortment of oil paintings and watercolours lined the walls of the sitting room. Isabella flew around upstairs and emerged with several older-looking canvases and more importantly, they thought, antique-looking oil paintings on wood. They were so old the paint had cracked like a mosaic.

'Look,' Isabella said, 'I found them in the spare room.' She studied the paintings. 'These ones *must* have a secret message on them. Old Man Wood ... over here! Do these trigger *anything?*'

Together they leaned over them, trying to see if there were a series of scratches or markings that might be clues, or if the backs had writing on them.

Archie suggested that secrets were often added by invisible ink. He'd read stories where clues had been written in milk and that heat would show the markings. He tried his theory by placing the flame of a candle close to the canvas of a landscape oil painting. The others looked on in anticipation. All of a sudden Archie noticed a plume of smoke as the landscape burst in flames.

Archie squealed but Isabella reacted fast, grabbed the painting, tore outside and threw it in a puddle.

'Thanks, Bells,' a red-faced Archie said. 'I'm not sure we need to do that again.'

---

THE MAJORITY of the paintings were of ancestors who bore an uncanny resemblance, Daisy thought, to a slightly younger Old Man Wood. The rest were landscapes or seascapes.

For over an hour, they studied the pictures. Isabella decided that they ought to be moved into groups: pictures with water and pictures with trees in that corner, abstract pictures in another, still life oils on the sofa, portraits with people near the window and those with animals on the adjacent wall. But even when they'd studied them twice, there wasn't a single distinctive element that they recognised from their dreams.

'What about the carvings in Old Man Wood's room?' Archie said, his voice betraying his frustration. 'Would you mind if we have a look? You know, a fresh pair of eyes.'

'Be my guests,' said Old Man Wood, and as a group they headed up to his room.

'Look!' Archie said, jumping on the bed. 'The screens! We're still on them.'

It was the first time the twins had seen themselves on the curious panels.

'How very cool,' Daisy said as she pouted and tossed her hair. 'They are awesome.' She watched Archie admiring his spikes.

'Basically, we've got our own TV channel,' Daisy said. 'I wonder if we can record stuff?'

'Oh, grow up,' Isabella scolded. 'Stop admiring yourselves and check if there's something in here. Daisy, you start over there.'

The twins slipped reluctantly off the bed and started to inspect the carved panelling. But, although the gnarled wood and odd-looking animals and curious faces were intriguing, they once again came up with nothing.

Isabella slumped to the floor. 'This is ridiculous. How can we find what we're looking for, when we don't even have a single clue?'

'I bet you,' Daisy said as she scratched the carpet with her fingernails, 'whatever we're looking for will be right under our bums.'

'The expression,' Isabella sighed, '*is right under your nose* – not your bottom.'

'You,' Archie said, his dark eyes sparkling mischievously at Daisy, 'should know that, cos you're such a big arse!'

'Hilarious,' Daisy replied, screwing a face at him.

'Come on kiddoes. No good hanging round here,' Isabella said and she began to usher them out of the door.

But as Archie scoured the room one last time, something caught his eye. 'You know what,' he said, 'Maybe Daisy has a point. Look!' He pointed at the floor.

'Where, what do you mean?' Isabella said.

'There. The rugs.'

'Rugs?'

'Yeah ... look at them. They're old, patterned ones. Persian or something, aren't they, Old Man Wood?'

The old man squinted at them, a look of surprise on his face.

'So what?' Isabella scoffed. 'We're looking for a picture not an old, mangy carpet.'

Archie reddened a little. 'But look carefully,' Archie said, kneeling down where they'd been sitting. 'There are marks on them. They might be part of an old picture. We shouldn't write them off just because they're not on a wall.'

Isabella sighed. 'Those marks are probably stains, right, Old Man Wood?'

Old Man Wood shrugged and turned for the door.

---

BUT NOW IT was Daisy's turn to stare at the rugs. 'Archie's right. Surely it's worth a look, isn't it, Bells?'

Isabella tutted. 'They're filthy – they probably haven't been washed for—'

'Ooh, I say,' Daisy said. 'There's something on this one,' she scanned it further, 'and this one's got a kind of tree in the middle ... wow, maybe you're right, Arch. What if *these* are the pictures?'

'Oh for goodness' sakes. Fat chance,' Isabella said. 'You know as well as I do that those marks are years of ground-in mud and grime.'

Daisy picked up one of the rugs and draped it over the end of the bed. Archie copied her and, in no time, the five little rugs were folded over the end of the wooden bed-end.

The children stood back, only to find themselves admiring five grey-brown mats. But the faintest outline of a pattern where Daisy had been picking at the fibres with her fingernails had begun to show.

'They're disgusting little things,' Isabella declared.

'I'm not so sure,' Archie piped up. 'But I do know that the best way to clean a rug is to give it a massive whack.' He grabbed one, threw it over his shoulder and slung it down hard on the bed end.

A plume of dust exploded, filling the room. They ran for the door, coughing and spluttering.

'Genius,' Isabella said scathingly and she smacked Archie on top of his head. Much to her surprise and irritation a hair spike shot through the hole in her hand. 'This is quite ridiculous,' she said, ignoring Daisy's laughter as she struggled to extract her hand. 'Oh, stop it,' she said, turning on her. 'Come on, guys. Isn't this a little bit desperate? I mean we haven't even analysed all the picture frames yet.'

Isabella shook out her hand and found her hand-hole shrinking back to its original size. 'Sometimes you two really don't possess a single particle of intelligence. We clearly need to look harder.'

Old Man Wood gathered the five little rugs. 'I'll beat them outside and hang them out on the line. These little things could do with a freshen up,' he said. 'With any luck, the dirt will wash out naturally.'

---

A LITTLE WHILE LATER, Mrs Pye waddled across the courtyard, her feet splashing in the puddles. She hummed to herself and then stopped and stared at the washing line. Five rugs hung like wet towels, muddy water dripping from each one. Had she forgotten them?

She racked her brain. She was sure she'd brought them in a while back, dried them and replaced them on Old Man Wood's floor. She tutted to herself and bustled over, removed them at arm's length and placed them in a washing basket. She couldn't imagine the old man suddenly wanting to clean them, so had one of the children ...? But those children weren't exactly forthcoming in the laundry department.

Before long, she found herself scrubbing each rug in the old stone sink in the washhouse. She was amazed at the steady flow of filthy, dark water coming out but, realising the time, and without really giving it too much thought now that the generator was on, she gave up and threw all five rugs in the washing machine.

Mrs Pye had never seen a material quite so light and so tough, and yet so extraordinarily filthy.

When the wash came to its juddering conclusion, she hung the little rugs out to dry in two neat rows on the Sheila's maid above the range in the kitchen.

Mrs Pye was delighted with their spectacular colour. Each rug shone radiantly and felt soft and clean. She smacked her hands together in a moment of washing triumph and, feeling rather pleased with herself, picked up her bag and returned to her flat across the courtyard.

---

A FEW HOURS LATER, the children were in front of the fire surrounded by piles of pictures that seemed to cover almost every square inch of floor. They'd inspected the antique ones over and over again to see if a message had been left on the back or if there was mystical writing or indeed if it simply rang a bell inside their heads.

'This is hopeless,' Archie said as he stroked a stiff hair spike. 'We still don't have a clue what we're looking for and we've been at this for hours.' He picked up a modern landscape painting which had hung in their parents' bedroom. As he studied it, a sudden yearning to see them went through him and his heart stretched like the strings on a bow until his eyes watered.

'I love this picture,' he said quietly to Old Man Wood. 'A house set by a vineyard, the sun going down. A distant fire, the colours of the vines. Somehow,' he said, 'it reminds me of Mum – lovely, calm and pretty, just like her.' His bottom lip quivered. 'And what I'd do for some sunshine right now.' He sniffed and shut his eyes. 'Do you know where they bought it?'

'Hmmm,' Old Man Wood said, placing a comforting hand on Archie's shoulder. 'I'm certain that it came back from a holiday some years ago,' he said softly. 'It won't be long before they're back.'

Archie turned it round so he was now looking at the back. There, much to his surprise, he found a picture postcard stuck with tape to the top and bottom corners. The picture showed a deep, crimson-red rose set on a white background. That was all. Archie gently removed the tape and turned it over.

*A typical red rose from the vineyards of Tuscany*, was the description, and below it, in his mother's neat handwriting, was the following:

*My darling,*
*I want you to know that we love you very much, and our hearts and dreams will always be with you.*
*Best of luck, whichever direction you choose.*
*Your loving,*
*Mother and Father*

Archie massaged a spike which had gone soft. *What a weird message,* he thought. *I mean, it's lovely, but peculiar; "Best of luck in whichever direction you choose". What was that supposed to mean? And why was it addressed to just "My darling" and not "My darlings"?* It was as though it was addressed to him and him alone. Archie smiled.

Maybe it was meant for him.

Quietly and with his back turned to the girls he closed his eyes, kissed the postcard and slipped it into the back pocket of his jeans.

---

'NO TIME FOR GETTING UPSET, young 'un,' Old Man Wood said to Archie.

'I know,' he smiled bravely back. 'What do you think we're looking for?'

Old Man Wood stroked his chin. 'It must be old, really old,' he said, 'perhaps with writing you won't understand, so look for a strange script or peculiar scribbling.'

Daisy tutted. 'We have,' she replied in a bored voice.

Isabella groaned. 'Are you sure it's not on the wooden panels in your bedroom?'

'I don't believe so,' Old Man Wood replied. 'They appear to be stories, not instructions.'

'And are you *sure* there's not a wall painting behind your wooden panels —'

'No, but there were some in the church—'

'What about a ceiling painting?' Daisy added, 'like the Michael-whatshisface one?'

Isabella laughed, although Daisy felt it sounded more like a scoff. 'Michelangelo? Here in Yorkshire, by the moors?'

'Yes, even here by the moors, Bells. Why not?'

'I'll tell you what, Daisy,' Isabella sneered, imitating her voice, '*why don't you search out with your eyes, man*. Or are they not working?'

Daisy fixed her sister with a stare. '*Why don't you go feel for it, holy hands?*'

'Will you two please shut up and get back to looking for the clues,' Archie said. 'Your bickering really isn't helping. It's giving me a headache.'

---

OLD MAN WOOD slumped into his chair. He ought to return to the Bubbling Brook; the trees would know, but what would the children think? Then again, did it really matter?

He lifted himself out of his chair, when he caught the familiar sound of pots rattling from the kitchen. No doubt Mrs Pye was fishing out saucepans, preparing tea. Was it so late already? A bit of nourishment to get his brain in gear was just what he needed to help him think of the right questions for those funny old willows.

---

MRS PYE SAUNTERED into the kitchen and released the rope on the Sheila's maid. She folded each rug in half and then half again, and piled one on top of the other and placed them in the washing basket. She noted the unusually fine fabric, the lightweight, silk-like textures with delicate stitching and neat embroidery. Why oh why had they sat disregarded on Old Man Wood's floor?

She filled a saucepan and placed it on the hot plate. Then she picked up the basket and headed out of the kitchen towards the "cupboard". As she walked past the living room, she peeked through the gap in the door and gasped.

She pushed the door open. 'What in Heaven's name above have you been doing?' she cried.

The children stood up, a sure admission of guilt, and looked around them. Frames of oil paintings and portraits and sketches and watercolours lay scattered all over the room.

'We are trying, dear Mrs Pye,' Isabella said, in her smartest voice, 'to find something in a picture. The problem is, we're not sure what it is, but we do know it is vitally important.'

Archie and Daisy nodded in agreement.

Mrs Pye turned from one to the next and back, her already ruddy face getting redder.

Isabella, oblivious to the housekeeper's glare, added quietly, 'Sue said so.'

'Sue said so. *Sue said so!*' Mrs Pye cried. Her face was now bright red, as though someone had turned up a heat dial. 'Your friend Sue, who lives in Northallerton, said you should gather all the pictures in this house and leave them in one room. Because you're looking for something! AND YOU DON'T KNOW WHAT?' she tutted in disbelief. 'Now come on, Isabella, you can do better than that.'

The children instinctively turned towards Old Man Wood.

'The thing is,' the old man hesitated as he pulled himself up, 'Isabella's right. But I'll ... er ... tell you about it later. This,' and he gestured around the room, 'is all my doing, Mrs Pye. Don't worry, each and every picture will be put back in its proper place, I promise.'

'I should hope you will,' she replied, her eyes boring into each of them. 'You ought to know better, the lot of you. If you're missing something, ask me. I'd be surprised if I don't know its whereabouts. I want this room and all these pictures back where they belong by tomorrow night, even if you haven't found what you're looking for. I'm responsible for the domestics while your parents are away and they would not be happy.'

A long, embarrassing silence hung over the room. Eventually Archie piped up and said sweetly, 'What we're trying to find is a picture with some sort of old writing or marks on it, something that might be connected with this rain? Maybe you could help?'

Mrs Pye's face instantly melted into a smile. 'I'll keep my eyes open.' She exited out of the room carrying the basket. But something in the back of her mind made her stop. She opened the door. 'Any of you lot know anything about some ruggy things left out in the rain?' She looked at the blank faces of the children, '... on the washing line?'

'Ah, yes! Those are mine,' Old Man Wood said, 'thought they could do with a clean.'

'By leaving them out in the rain? Tuh. Typical!' Her small eyes lit up. 'Well, I've had a right proper go at them. You should see the difference.

Beautiful things. Come alive they have. I'll put them in the airing cupboard.' She turned smartly and marched off along the corridor, humming to herself.

*And if he doesn't want them,* she thought, *I'll have 'em for myself.* She stroked the top one and it seemed to reciprocate her touch, like the warmth of a sleeping cat.

---

'WHAT WAS Mrs Pye going on about?' Archie asked as he prised open the back of an old wooden portrait with a screwdriver.

Old Man Wood walked over and held the frame. 'She's given my old rugs a clean,' he said. 'Tickled blue about it too.'

Archie tried not to laugh. 'Why?'

'She said they'd all come alive. Don't you listen to anything she says?'

'Not really!' Archie said, staring at the next family portrait. 'How long have you had them?'

'Had what?'

'Your filthy old rugs!'

'Oh! I can't remember,' Old Man Wood scratched the back of his neck. 'It's a long time, though.'

Archie moved on to the next portrait. 'So how old are these?'

Old Man Wood walked over. 'I've no idea. Sorry, Archie.'

'The date on these portraits,' Daisy shouted from across the room, 'is on the back or on the right bottom corner. It's the same with all of them for some reason. This one's from 1638 ... and here's one from 1702.'

Archie joined in by holding up a very delicate portrait. 'Oh, I see. Look ... 1595!'

Isabella, who was in the hallway listening in, said, 'I can beat that. This shield goes back to 1382, I think that's right? It's Roman numerals.'

A sense of excitement and expectation filled the room. The notion of being surrounded by such antiquity built up a sense of awe, as if the people in the portraits had somehow gathered into the room and joined them in their search.

'Isn't it funny,' Archie said as he studied a series of individual portraits, 'how each of these have the same kind of creamy, rectangular backgrounds with pale little swirls on, while the actual images on the paintings are only slightly different?'

Daisy stared at the pictures, her concentration intense. 'My God,' she whispered. The others leaned in.

'What is it, Daise?'

Daisy's eyes were glowing. 'The backgrounds are the same, like five light ... panels.'

'Panels?' Archie said. 'I can't see anything like that, just sort of ... blurs.'

'Aha,' Isabella said, 'I knew it. I told you there were wall panels somewhere in the house.'

Old Man Wood sighed. 'Isabella, wall paintings would never last, young 'un. They simply wouldn't survive—'

'Oh, come on. What else could they be?'

Daisy looked up. 'If they're not panels, then we're missing something. What else hangs on a wall, has colour and could last the test of time?'

The children sat down in a circle, their brains working hard.

'Of course!' Archie said, a smile filling his face. 'We've been complete idiots!'

'What is it?'

'Tapestries—'

'Like those massive carpets on church walls?' Isabella said. 'Don't be ridiculous—'

Archie shot up. 'I think I've got it,' he said. And before anyone could blink he flew off down the corridor, then up the stairs, the floorboards creaking at every footstep.

# 76 KEMP AWAKES

Solomon was grateful for the shower and change of clothes. He ate his lamb chop with mashed potatoes, remembering to chew every morsel, otherwise his hungry stomach would hurt him later.

'I'm going to be honest with you, Charlie,' Solomon said, sipping a glass of water, 'there is no way my school has anything to do with this.'

'That's all very well, but the evidence suggests the storm's epicentre was directly overhead. And it's from here that this blasted pathogen started.' Stone pulled out a graphic. 'Have a look at these satellite images. The reason the meteorological geeks didn't pick it up was that it appeared like a localised storm. And, combined with the humid weather prevalent in the area, it generated its own peculiar entity and "boosh", in a matter of hours it built and built. Here.'

On the screen, Solomon viewed the weather graphic. The storm was coloured in red, its centre a much darker hue, which ballooned out until a massive area was swathed in black. There was no mistaking that it stemmed from Upsall.

'No one's ever seen anything like it.'

'But why Upsall, Charlie? We're a small community with an old school built on the foundations of a monastery just like the Abbeys at Fountains, Rievaulx and Byland nearby. Have you checked them out?'

The commissioner nodded. 'They're underwater – like Upsall – but the difference is, all the others are ruins, Upsall isn't.' Stone picked his nails. 'Something makes me think this disaster begins here and ends here. I don't know what it is, but I'm going to find out.'

Solomon wiped his lips with a paper towel. 'I'll help you all you want, my dear old friend. You know I will. But, as I said earlier, I think you're barking up the wrong tree.'

'You mentioned the girl coming to you,' Stone said, his eyes boring into the older man. 'Tell me more about this de Lowe family?'

Solomon shifted. 'Well, the mother and father are archaeologists, currently out in the Middle East on a dig and the children are popular and gifted. There's not much more to it than that.'

Charlie rubbed his chin. 'Why did that girl come to you knowing the storm was about to happen?'

'I have no idea.'

'I do,' Stone replied. 'She knew something. Something about all of this and she wanted to let you in on it.' Stone rubbed his hands. 'What else did she tell you?'

'We've been over this before,' Solomon said, smiling thinly and leaning back in his chair. 'She simply bustled in saying that her homemade barometer was indicating undue pressure. She's a scientist, and a good one. We encourage pupils to act on their instincts and she did just that.'

'But don't you think it's uncanny?'

'No, I do not,' Solomon bristled. 'We teach students to be decent, responsible citizens, and reacting to her findings is a part of that. It isn't complicated, you know.'

Stone sensed unease in the headmaster. 'When their parents are away, who looks after these kids?'

Solomon tensed. He'd hoped Stone wouldn't bring this up. 'There's an elderly uncle and a housekeeper. I saw them myself only the night before. In their circumstances, they do a terrific job.'

Stone opened up the folder in front of him, pushed on his reading glasses and scanned the document. 'There's no mention of an uncle.' He thumbed through another couple of pages. 'Ah. It mentions that a woman, named here as Mrs Pye, was taken in by the family twelve years ago. She was found with terrible injuries in the forest beneath the moors.' He looked up and said slowly, 'And has possible brain damage.'

'That's ludicrous,' Solomon snapped. 'I don't see what this has to do with your enquiries.'

Stone's lip curled. 'I'm trying to find out what the hell is going on. Just doing my job.' He smiled. 'So who is this old uncle? Why no record?' Stone pulled out some historical documents. 'After all, they're an old family in the area, right?'

Solomon stared out of the window. 'I suppose.'

'Says here there's a whole stained glass window in the church dedicated to the de Lowe family. Seems they go back a long, long way. So I repeat my question. Who is their uncle?'

'I don't know how this is relevant,' Solomon replied, feeling the heat. 'He's a loner – a hermit who lives with them. There's probably no record of him because he's never been on record for anything.'

'He was born, though,' Stone fired back. 'There's been a legal duty to record all births for more than two hundred years. Why is he not mentioned?'

'Perhaps,' said Solomon, 'you should ask the parents. I am the children's headmaster, I do not study the historical records of every child in my care.'

'But it says here that the school has given a bursary to the de Lowes for centuries,' Stone countered. 'And in fairness, the school was started by the family, was it not?'

Solomon couldn't deny it. He shrugged and scratched his head.

'Strange, isn't it,' Stone said, 'the name "*de Lowe*". Where did that come from? I mean it's not exactly common?'

Solomon pursed his lips. 'Almost certainly from French origin. Probably a Norman conquest knight, given land here by William of Normandy.'

'French, huh,' Stone said leaning back in his chair. 'I thought it might be Flemish, or Breton.'

Solomon suddenly sat bolt upright. A thought struck him like an arrow through the eye.

Stone noticed. 'Is there something you want to tell me?'

Solomon regained his composure. 'Oh, I was just thinking of those poor children. They wouldn't have stood a chance.'

'How come?'

'All three de Lowes were on the playing field when the storm broke. Little Archie was struck down by a huge lightning bolt. It was that moment that made me realise it was no ordinary storm.' Now that he remembered, it was Sue and Isabella yelling on the football field that had given him the creeps; they were having a private, though very public, screaming match about the storm as if there was something they knew. 'I gathered up a whole bunch of children and we headed to the relative safety of the school.'

Stone eyed him curiously. 'So the first part of the storm went for one of the de Lowes. I'm intrigued.'

But Solomon's thoughts were elsewhere. Why hadn't he thought of it before? It was staring them right between the eyes. The name, *de Lowe*. Stone clearly didn't know his French; de Lowe, or should it be, *de l'eau* – French for *water* – the essential ingredient of life. Was this a coincidence or part of some ancient code?

And, not for the first time, the headmaster realised there might be something a little different about those children and their old man. The stained glass window in the chapel! It had been staring him in the face for twenty-five years. A beautiful, but rather grubby, artwork with three panels showing three figures bearing gifts. And filling the background: *water*, or, *de l'eau*! He realised he had to get back to Upsall as fast as he could.

'Charlie,' Solomon said. 'I'm very tired and I am afraid it has been a shattering and overwhelming experience. Would you mind if I slipped off to bed? You know where I am, if you wish to question me further.'

Stone clasped the papers together. 'Very well. It's late and there's a hell of a day coming.' He stood up smartly. 'If there's anything you need, shout.'

Solomon knew this was his chance. 'I'd be happy to do some investigations into some of the school books if you like. Being high up in the tower, the library was relatively unscathed and there are several large old volumes which may shed some light on the history of the area. Perhaps there are plague records from the Black Death.'

Stone eyed him suspiciously before his face lightened. 'Great. That's exactly what I need. An academic with local knowledge. I'll get you back in there first thing in the morning.' He pressed his phone. 'See to it that Headmaster Solomon is returned to Upsall at first light. Give him a linked phone and full access to the site.'

The order was confirmed.

A rap at the door made both men turn. The young officer Solomon had noticed from before came in. 'sir,' he said, 'there's been a development with the boy in intensive care. He's awake.'

Solomon raised his eyebrows. 'Tell me more.'

'He's made a very quick recovery. It looks like we might be able to talk to him after all.'

Stone checked his watch. It was nearly midnight. 'Reports are due in for the next two hours and I've got to brief the PM at seven tomorrow morning. I'll get a few hours' sleep if I'm lucky.' He yawned and addressed the officer. 'Let's try and talk to the boy at nine. Make sure he has everything he needs. It'll give him more time to recover before the scientists get their hands on him.' The officer nodded and left the room.

'It's the boy they found in a tree, hanging on to life with some extraordinary injuries. Burns covering him. It's been all over the news – we've been waiting for him to come round so we can talk to him.'

'Yes, I heard,' Solomon said. 'Was he an Upsall boy?'

'I doubt it,' the commissioner replied. 'Found too far downstream to be one of yours. The strange thing is, there's no sign of the virus on him which, given his position, is quite frankly astonishing. In fact, his whole survival, in line with the injuries he sustained, doesn't add up.'

Solomon breathed a sigh of relief. He'd lost so many it hurt him to think about it. He stood up. 'Well, good luck, Charlie. I don't envy you, but I'll do my best.' He headed for the door.

'Excellent – thank you,' said the commissioner, standing up to conclude the meeting. 'Report in if there's anything unusual or suspicious, especially with regard to the de Lowe family.'

---

COMMISSIONER STONE STRETCHED his arms out as the door closed behind his cousin.

He re-ran Solomon's reaction through his mind especially the bit when he'd mentioned the de Lowe family. Something didn't stack up.

He pressed the intercom. 'Dickinson.'

Shortly, the officer strode in.

'The headmaster leaves at dawn for Upsall. Do something for me, will you? Fit him with video surveillance. From the moment he lands, I want a handpicked member of your team to monitor *exactly* what he's studying. You know the score.'

Dickinson nodded. 'And mike enabled?'

'If done without trace.'

Dickinson straightened. This kind of work was his speciality. 'Does the schoolmaster wear glasses?'

'Is there a headmaster who doesn't?'

Dickinson feigned a smile. 'Then I'll add microgram lenses to them. Consider it done.'

'Good. And keep this to yourself, Dickinson. Report back to me at lunchtime. We'll run over his findings then.'

---

OVER BREAKFAST, reports bombarded his office, while his early link-up with the Prime Minister had been dreadful. The PM sounded ill and in a foul mood, so that by nine o'clock an early-morning fatigue swept over him. He needed at least five hours sleep, not two. And the news was awful: Astonishingly awful. The plague, even at this early hour, appeared to have spread randomly across the country. Thank God the media had been shut down or the pandemonium and unrest throughout the United Kingdom would be unthinkable. But, conversely, unless they found answers soon, panic across the world was a real possibility.

His entourage swept into the confines of the hospital unit and surgical masks and gloves were put on following a spray down with a fine decontamination mist. It reminded him of the outbreak of foot and mouth disease on cattle. He pulled in a secretary. 'Is there a report on livestock? I want one in an hour.' The secretary scurried off, phone at the ear.

Kemp lay in the same bed, in the same room behind the glass. This time he was sitting up with all manner of medical equipment plugged into him: drips from his arms and patches that covered his head and upper torso where the burns had been most severe.

Commissioner Stone turned to Doctor Muller. 'What progress? Is he ready to talk?'

The doctor contemplated his answer. 'He's hardly said a word, just stares into space. Whatever he's been through has scared him terribly.'

Commissioner Stone clenched his fist. Interrogating people was a skill he prided himself on. From a young age he had had the knack of prising information out of people, whether by charm, force or by verbal intimidation. But a sick boy? He contemplated his approach.

Doctor Muller showed him into the changing cubicle. 'Sorry, Commissioner, but not a whiff of germs allowed in here. You'll need to pop these on,' he said, handing him a sterile set of overalls. 'He's doing fine in a medical sense, but we've got nothing out of him so far. Not a jot.'

'Can he speak, though?'

'Oh yes. He's been repeating the words *"Go away"* in his sleep – and various other short, garbled sentences. To be honest, nothing that makes any sense.'

Minutes later Stone, looking like a plastic yeti, entered the boy's room. He walked round the bed, nurse and doctor flanking him, and noticed the boy's eyes, wide open and, just as the doctor said, staring fixedly at a point on the wall.

---

STONE DIDN'T FEEL sorry for many people. In truth, he despised those who portrayed any form of weakness and that's why, as a rule, he disliked children. But, as he took a seat next to this boy, a sense of sadness filled him. Here was a boy who no one knew – who no one claimed – but who had clung onto life so bravely.

'Hello, my name is Commissioner Stone,' he began. 'I'm thrilled you've woken up at last.'

The boy didn't move a muscle.

'You've been on quite a journey by the looks of things,' he went on, noticing a strange shift in the boy's eyes – a small sense of panic, perhaps. 'But we're here to make you better, get you back on your feet,' he continued chirpily, 'with the best medical staff looking after you. And you're safe here, we'll make quite sure of that.' Stone looked at the nurse and doctor for encouragement. They nodded. 'We would like you to tell us what happened – as much as you can remember, OK?'

Still the boy stared into space.

'I'm going to tell you some pretty scary stuff about what's been going on, so it'll really help if you can answer some of my questions. Then we'll try and find family and friends to come and get you. How does that sound?'

The boy remained impassive, but he licked his fat lips.

A sign that his mouth works, Stone thought. 'Can you tell me your name?' he asked.

He waited for a response.

The boy closed his eyes.

'Can you tell me where you live?'

The boy opened his eyes, this time fixing the commissioner with his gaze.

*That's a start,* Stone thought. 'What do you remember about the storm – can you tell me anything about it?'

The boy stared into the distance, his eyes unwavering.

Stone sighed. He wasn't going to give anything away. He was wasting his time. Perhaps he needed a different approach. 'Look, buddy,' he began raising his voice. 'There's a disaster happening outside these walls which might affect the whole world. Somehow, and Lord only knows how, you survived with inexplicable burns all over your body. We are here to help you, but we must find out what you know.'

The boy shut his eyes again and swallowed.

The doctor, nurse and commissioner waited with bated breath for some words. The doctor made as if to speak but Stone shot him a glare. Aside from the bleeping of the monitors, silence filled the room.

'Alright, I understand,' he said. 'I understand what you've been through. But we know you can speak. You see, you've been talking in your sleep.'

The boy's eyes narrowed.

'And the longer you refuse to talk,' Commissioner Stone added, 'the more I think you're hiding something. Because experience tells me that people who don't say anything have nasty little secrets. What do you think, boy?'

The boy swallowed again but continued to stare at the wall.

'You're scared. I can tell,' Stone said, lowering his voice. 'Come on, fella or I'll be forced to fill your veins with a truth serum and you'll be singing like a bird before you know it.'

'You'll do no such thing!' Doctor Muller said.

It was exactly the response Stone had hoped for. 'Yes, I damn well will!'

he yelled. 'I have the authority to do anything to get to the bottom of this mess, so back off.'

The boy moved his eyes from the doctor to the commissioner and back again.

A tiny indication of fear. *Good,* Stone thought as he leaned in. 'And the other thing you need to know is that we've found your friends,' he lied.

The patient's eyes widened but still he uttered not a word.

But Stone was just getting going. 'Let's start again. Your name, your school and how you ended up at the top of a tree when everyone else was swept away. You've got till the count of five to answer me or I'm throwing you out of this hospital.'

Next to him, the nurse gasped. Commissioner Stone turned on her. 'You, out!' he commanded. 'Get out! Both of you.'

'Never!' the doctor replied. 'You have no right – we have a duty of care to the boy.'

'Oh really,' Stone said sarcastically. 'How frightfully honourable. For your information, I have a duty of care to the rest of the bleeding world.' His eyes were cold. 'Security!'

Within seconds, the doctor and nurse were man-handled from the room.

Now it was just him and the boy.

'Five,' he began. 'Four. Three,' he counted down, leaving longer and longer pauses.

'Two.'

'One.' Still nothing.

'Kemp,' the boy croaked.

The Commissioner thought he'd misheard. 'What?'

'My name is Kemp.'

'What else?'

The boy's face was contorting. Was he in pain? If so, he deserved it.

'What else?' he demanded.

'If,' Kemp tried to work up enough saliva to speak.

'If what, Kemp?'

'If you want to know,' the boy said, his voice shallow and faint, 'find Archie de Lowe. If he isn't dead.' Kemp's head fell back limply on his pillow.

Commissioner Stone turned and stormed out of the door, ripping at his overalls as he went.

'Damn that Solomon!' he cursed. 'He knew. He bloody well knew it was de Lowe after all. Archie bloody de Lowe!'

# 77 CLEAN RUGS

Archie appeared with the basket and the rugs.

'Where did these come from?' Isabella asked. 'They're beautiful.'

'They can't be the same rugs from Old Man Wood's floor,' Daisy said as she stroked the soft, downy material. As Mrs Pye had also noticed, they seemed to purr with pleasure. As she took in the bright patterns, her heart beat with excitement. 'Let's hang them up.'

Archie pushed the tack into the corner of the rug and, as he started to push it in, the weight of the rug forced him to drop it on the floor. He frowned. He tried again, with exactly the same result. On his third attempt, as he pushed the tack into the corner he felt it almost wriggle free. 'We're going to have to come up with another plan,' he said. 'I can't get these in.'

'I've got a better idea,' Isabella said. 'Lay them out in the hallway. Then we can examine them from the stairs. Old Man Wood, is there any chance of a bit more light? And can you make the generator run a little longer?'

While Old Man Wood strode off to find a lamp in his store and check the fuel in the generator, Isabella, Archie and Daisy laid out the five carpets neatly below the stairwell.

Isabella climbed a quarter of the way up the staircase. 'Archie, move that one along a bit. That's it. And make sure this one isn't overlapping.

Good. Where's Old Man Wood, it's too dim under the stairs? I can't see them clearly. Is it me or are they a little blurred?'

Old Man Wood returned with two lamps, which he lit and placed at the foot of the stairs. From higher up, Isabella directed Archie and Daisy to move the lights into the optimal place, and then the twins joined her in peering over the banisters. From here, the colours reflecting back were brighter and sharper

A sense of excitement filled the hall.

Daisy ran up a couple more steps, peered over and then climbed up three more, then a further four until she was almost at the top. Then down one – her head jigging backwards and forwards.

Likewise, Archie moved up two steps, then down four and up five. Old Man Wood, who was much taller, stayed on the third step, but then decided to copy the children.

Isabella moved a couple of steps down and stayed there staring at the five rugs – her lips moving but no sound coming out. It was a most peculiar sight; the four of them shuffling up and down the staircase and, apart from a bit of polite barging and the occasional muffled gasps, there wasn't a sound from them as they racked their brains.

Finally, Daisy broke the silence.

'There's writing,' she announced, tremendous excitement in her voice, 'all over them, and it changes at varying distances.'

Daisy climbed to the top of the stairs. 'OK. Archie get a pen and write this down.'

Archie scampered off and in no time was back, armed with a sheet of A4 and a pen.

'Right, it's a bit complicated. It appears to work at different levels so I'm going to scoot up and down, OK.' She skipped down a couple of risers and then up to the top as if double checking. 'We'll start with this one, the second rug along.'

Archie moved next to it.

'From up here,' she began, 'this is what it says:-

*'The first you hid in the heart of the house,*

'And now if I move down here, the same writing changes to:

*'That warms you night and day.'*

Daisy skipped down another four stairs. *'Get it out by poking me—'*

*'And singing your favourite song along the way!'* Old Man Wood finished off with her from the foot of the stairs.

---

'HOW DID YOU READ THAT?' Archie quizzed, staring at Daisy's blazing eyes. 'I can see that each rug seems to change like a kaleidoscope as we move nearer and farther away. But in pictures, NOT words.'

'Same,' Isabella said. 'I see tablets and scrolls and fire but...'

Daisy smiled. 'You know, magic eyes, remember! Did you write it down, Archie?'

Daisy ran up the steps again. 'Right Archie, let's have a go at that one. Yup, there.' She pointed at the rug adjacent to the first and he moved beside it. 'Are you ready for number two?'

He nodded.

*'For the second one you find,'* she read, before skipping down a couple of steps, *'burp it from the family belly.'*

'Are you sure?' Archie quizzed.

'Yes! That's exactly what it says. Just write it down...'

*'To do just this,'* Old Man Wood continued from the bottom step, *'you have to eat—'*

*'...Blab-ister-berry jelly!'* Daisy said.

'Blabisterberry Jelly?' Archie repeated, pulling a face as he wrote it down. 'What's Blabisterberry Jelly? Is it like *strawberry jelly*? Or more like an jellyfish? Read it again.'

Daisy did. And this time she even spelt it out.

'Blimey,' Archie said, scratching a hair spike. 'How are you supposed to burp jelly without it coming back through your nose?'

'Maybe you have to do a nose trick?' Daisy said.

'I'm quite sure ancient riddles didn't have nose tricks in mind when they were created,' Isabella said.

Daisy shrugged. 'Maybe they did, Isabella.'

'What if it's something to do with marmalade?' Isabella added.

'Nah,' Archie replied. 'I wouldn't have thought so.'

'Well, it's quite ludicrous,' Isabella said, shaking her head. 'Archie's right, none of it makes sense.'

Daisy ran upstairs again. She nodded down to Old Man Wood.

'Are you ready for the next one, Archie?' she called out. 'It's that one over there.'

Archie signalled with a thumbs-up.

'Right here we go: *The third you search,*' she began, '*is underneath your nose. It is clear, pure and cold.*'

She waved at Old Man Wood.

'*In order to draw it out,*' his deep, rich voice boomed, '*you need to send a rose.*'

'Send a rose?' Archie repeated as he scribbled on the pad. 'What the—'

'Gibberish,' Isabella said, running her hands through her hair, 'written by someone with absolutely no aptitude for poetry. It has to be ... *must be*, a red-herring. How can anyone take this seriously?'

Daisy scampered up the stairs once again. 'OK, next one coming up. Ready?'

She leant over the banister and stared hard, her red eyes glowing. '*Put them all together, then get out of the way* ...' she ran down a couple of stairs, '*what you will find will prove a guide—*'

Old Man Wood joined in, '*For all the other worlds.*'

'Have you got that Archie?' Daisy asked.

'Yeah, yeah. All down. Pretty weird, though.'

'Final one coming up. Ready?' Daisy said. 'Hang on a mo, this one's a bit faded.'

'I can't believe you can see anything,' Isabella said. 'You're making it up.'

Daisy shot her a look which, with her red eyes, wasn't something you could ignore.

'*You have but seven days and seven nights, as Earth moves in its cycle, from first lightning strike and thunderclap,*' she began, '*the world awaits your arrival.*'

---

OLD MAN WOOD sat down heavily on the step next to Archie and very quietly read the poem from Archie's sheet of paper:

*'The first you hid in the heart of the house*
*'That warms you night and day*
*'Get it out by poking me,*

*'And singing your favourite song along the way!*

*'For the second one you have to find*
*'You burp it from the family belly.*
*'To do this, you have to eat*
*'Blabisterberry jelly!*

*'The third you search for is underneath your nose.*
*'It's clear, pure and cold.*
*'In order to draw it out*
*'You need to send a rose.*

*'Put them all together,*
*'Then get out of the way*
*'What you find will prove a guide*
*'For all the other worlds.*

*'You have but seven days and seven nights*
*'As Earth moves in its cycle*
*'From first lightning strike and thunderclap*
*'The world awaits your arrival.'*

'Apples alive!' the old man exclaimed after the first verse. 'Blast!' after the second and, when Archie had finished, 'Extra double blast!' he spluttered his face ashen and twisted. He put his head in his hands and started to sob.

The children looked at each other – their eyes wide.

'Good Lord. What's the matter?' Isabella asked, taking hold of his hand. 'Is it bad ...?'

'Bad, oh yes, my dear,' the old man replied, his lips trembling. 'It is VERY BAD.' Then he looked at them earnestly, tears forming in his eyes. 'It appears that so great is the stretch of time that has passed ... since I wrote it,' he pointed at the rugs. 'The greatest length of time you can ever imagine, that I have already failed in the task that was set upon me so many, many years ago.'

There was an uncomfortable silence. The children looked at each other, and then Old Man Wood as if he had completely lost his marbles.

'I know the poems are pretty awful, but they aren't *that* bad,' Isabella said gently, playing along with him. 'The rhymes are actually quite sweet. Dear Old Man Wood, I wouldn't get too hung up on it.'

'But these *are* the clues, aren't they?' Daisy added.

Old Man Wood shook uncontrollably while muttering. 'I suppose I just never thought that this ... would ever happen. I'm so sorry. I'm afraid I may be to blame for the greatest catastrophe to befall the world.'

Old Man Wood pulled himself together with a shrug and blew his nose extremely loudly, which in any other situation would have made them howl with laughter.

'Why don't you try,' Isabella began softly 'by telling us everything that you do know? Perhaps it will make things easier.' She exchanged nervous glances with the others.

'Hmmm ... yes,' the old man sniffed. 'Good idea.'

He lifted his head and stared deeply into the eyes of each one of the children in turn. 'As you may have worked out by now, I am not who ... who ... er ... who you think I am.'

'Then, who are you?' Daisy squeaked.

'Goodness me,' Old Man Wood replied. 'It's almost impossible for you to understand, my littluns. And it's going to sound a bit barmy – well, utterly appley barmy, so you must promise you won't be afraid.'

The children nodded.

'Good, right,' he said, picking himself up off the stairs. 'I'll tell you what I can remember – and fast – for if I'm not mistaken, the sands of time are already moving against us and have been for far too long. Now, you know that bible story you read, Isabella, the one about creation and all that?' the old man began.

She nodded.

'Well it's got a little to do with all that – and more. Goes back before – a long time before. Oh dear.'

'Go on,' Isabella said.

'There's a whole history, lost and forgotten ... until now. It was my role, I think, to help out when the time came.' He began sobbing again.

The children guided him to his armchair, where he sat slumped in a sad heap with his head in his hands and tears rolling down his cheeks.

'And this history is related to the flooding and the plague isn't it?' Daisy asked.

This was met with more groaning. 'Apples, yes!'

'And we're the link, aren't we?'

Old Man Wood turned his wrinkled face and bloodshot eyes to them. 'Oh yes. Yes indeed, my littluns. You three, my favourites, are the key to the whole appley thing.'

# 78 STAINED GLASS WINDOWS

Headmaster Solomon pulled another heavy, leather-bound book from the library shelves. From Latin the book translated as "Stained Glass in the Churches of Northern England".

He carried it to the desk where it thudded down. He pushed his glasses up his nose and flicked through plates of stunning, intricate drawings page after page. Finally, he came to the end where he found one last entry:

*Upsall Church, Date: Medieval. Designer: unknown. Fabricator: Local.*

He read the description, translating the Latin out loud as best he could:

*'This is an unusual triptych, in the medieval style with adaptations of ancient symbolism, possibly pagan. It is recognised for the strong use of natural elements in its design and of curious, detailed, seated figures. One figure is similar to that of Christ, with hands showing holes from the cross, another holds a mace above his head and the third bears eyes like fire. Embracing all three is a large, disjointed emblem of the Tree of Life. Below each figure, smaller scenes tell of an apocalypse, namely flooding, disease and famine.*

*'Positioned in the laps of the figures are three books, or stones, each one bearing a repeated motif of the Tree of Life. Above, angels feed the figures from the clouds.'*

Solomon's heart nearly stopped.

He stared at the old images of flooding and disease. Wasn't that uncanny? And three of them were being fed. But fed what exactly?

*Frankly,* he thought, *they were pretty rotten images, as if drawn from memory by someone not in the least bit interested.* He needed to get in there and see it for himself. Drat. It meant he'd have to get wet.

Solomon closed the book, rummaged around the lost property for several minutes until he located a mask that he'd found at the beginning of last term, and made his way down the stairs until he reached the foul-smelling water that licked the walls and stairs.

He removed his clothes, bar his underpants and vest, adjusted the mask on his head to its maximum setting, took a deep breath, and lowered himself into the water. He swam easily on the flat surface, the noise of splashing reverberating off the vaulted ceiling in touching distance above him. At the end of the colonnade, he ducked and dived under the door arch and into the aisle of the chapel. On surfacing, he kicked off to the side and hoisted himself up onto a stone ledge.

From here he had no choice but to climb up over the stone screen that separated the aisle from the nave. He spied an opening above which he reckoned he could crawl into. But halfway through, Solomon realised this gallant approach was a tactic for a younger man. He tried to pull himself back but remained wedged. There was no alternative but to go headfirst and pray the water depth in the church was the same as in the colonnade.

He puffed out his cheeks, wiggled his bottom, wobbled his belly and slipped forward.

A moment later, with a cry, Solomon plunged through the air, belly-flopping into the water below.

---

'SIR,' came a voice from the doorway. 'I think you'd better take a look at this.'

Stone looked up to see Dickinson walking towards him.

'What is it?' he snapped.

'Your headmaster friend, sir ... I can bring the feed in here if you wish.'

Stone ushered him in. 'It'd better be worth it.'

'You won't be disappointed.' A smile crossed the officer's face.

Stone stared at the screen, trying to work out where he was. A church? High up by a window?

Dickinson filled him in. 'He's climbed the wall and looks as if he's going through the window.'

'Why?'

'He's been flicking through a load of old books on stained glass windows. I'm not sure he's found what he wants. Knows his Latin, though.'

'Of course he does. The man's a ruddy teacher—'

Suddenly, the image moved fast and filled with water. For a minute all they could make out were dark stains and a flurry of watery activity.

Dickinson could hardly suppress his laughter.

'Is the feed—'

'Yes, watertight, sir. Not sure about the mike.'

Solomon swam over to the side and found a jutting beam which he climbed on. He looked around. In front of him was the apex of the tall stained glass windows, the light splaying over him.

From the office, the two men followed his eyes. 'There,' Dickinson said. 'It's those windows he's after.'

And as Solomon stared at the top of the ancient glass pictures, trying to deduce their meaning, so too did Stone. Then, without hesitating, he took a deep breath and plunged into the cold water.

———

SOLOMON STARED through his mask in disbelief. The deluge had cleaned the panes! These weren't the grimy windows he'd seen in the book, nor the ones he'd seen every day for years, but vibrant, shining, coloured glass – bursting with life – especially with morning light beaming through them.

He surfaced, pulled himself onto the beam, removed his glasses, folded them and tucked them under the elastic of his pants. He rubbed his eyes.

While submerged, laid out like a comic, the window had told a story: three people, a flood, a plague, and even the old de Lowe castle, now a ruin. Common factors. Perhaps the three figures were ancestors of the three de Lowe children? *But who,* he thought, *were the curious angelic creatures sitting above them, giving them a substance that looked like dust?* It reminded him of Isabella's dream about the storm. A premonition perhaps?

Solomon reached for his mask, fixed it over his face and dropped in again. This time, as the outdoor light brightened, it illuminated the window further. Solomon gasped. Another layer of detail shone through.

Solomon stayed down as long as his lungs would let him before surfacing. On the beam, he reached for his glasses. 'So these are gifts, and here are challenges or, it appears ... the world ... fails,' he said out loud between shivers. 'Curious. And, unless I'm very much mistaken, lying at the foot is a long, snake-like beast with a dragon's head.' He wiped his forehead. Could this be part of the de Lowe myth that one of their ancestors had slain a dragon ... or something else?

He remembered the notches – seven. 'Seven days? Seven days of creation. Seven days of de-creation.' He stiffened at the thought. Was it a coincidence? After all, the nucleus of the storm and plague began right here.

In his bones he knew that for some strange reason this terrible event centred around the de Lowe children and that this window was somehow linked directly to those kids and a very ancient story.

---

TEMPORARILY, they lost Solomon, and then, just as Stone thought about giving up, the image came back, this time sharp and clear.

The microphone picked up every word.

Stone listened and looked. Then he leant back in his chair with his arms behind his head. 'You know, Dickinson,' he said as he stared out of the window. 'This is the only thing we have, the only damn thing we've managed to trawl up: an old stained glass window with some hocus-pocus images and a mad old headmaster banging on about the creation story.'

Stone stood up and grabbed his jacket. 'You know what? I need to see that boy again. The boy who calls himself Kemp. I need to find out what he really knows about young Archie de Lowe.'

---

KEMP STARED AT THE CEILING, bored. His recovery was speedy and now that his drips had been taken away he could move about, but to where? And why, oh why, did he tell that weasly man about Archie? What would happen to his friend if they found him? Would he too be paraded in front of the TV cameras, subjected to interviews, get put on drips and given endless blood tests?

Kemp rolled his legs off the bed. 'I need the toilet,' he yelled through the glass. 'And not in the piss pot.'

The nurse came through. 'You're feeling perkier, young man,' she said.

'Yeah. I certainly am. Any chance I can stretch my legs?'

The pretty nurse smiled and shuffled out. She rang a number, talked for less than a minute and returned. 'There's a toilet just around the corner. Why don't you pop along there? I'm sure no one will mind.'

As he walked slowly along the corridor, Kemp noted guards at every door. Were they all for him? Was he seen as a threat?

He found the toilet and opened the door. It was a large cubicle with a loo, basin, mirror and shower. He locked the door and stared at his reflection.

'Boy,' came a soft voice.

Kemp froze. It couldn't be.

'Take off your gown, so you can see me.'

Kemp removed his dressing gown and let it fall to the floor. But before it hit the ground, it was scooped up.

'Cain!' Kemp snarled. 'What are you doing here?'

The ghost put it on. 'I wanted to apologise,' Cain said, his voice just above a whisper.

'Too bloody right. Now get out—'

'In my excitement, I cared for you poorly. Despicably. But I realised my mistake just in time and managed to save you.'

'So why are you back?' Kemp whispered.

'Because I want you and I need you,' Cain implored, his voice silky.

Kemp guffawed. 'Why do you think I would ever go back to you after the way you treated me?'

'Because I made a terrible error.'

Kemp sat down on the loo seat. 'That's not enough.'

'Because, together, we can be powerful.'

'Still no! No way!'

'Because I will give you food and water. I will let you sleep. Because I know we can do this together.'

'NO!' Kemp hissed. 'Piss off!'

Cain sighed. 'Then you will remain here as a medical phenomenon, getting poked and prodded and having things pushed into you. And, eventually, you too will get the disease. Everyone will. And you will suffer a horrible, painful death—'

'It'd be better than living in you, in your hell.'

Their conversation was interrupted. 'Is everything alright in there?' a voice called out from the corridor.

'Yeah, got a bit of constipation,' Kemp replied, thinking quickly. 'I'm going to have a quick shower in a mo. I won't be long.'

'Jolly good. Shout if you need a hand. If you're really struggling, pull the emergency cord.'

Cain tried again. He had one last card. 'Join me, boy. This time it will be different. I swear it. I have made arrangements—'

'Yeah, right. You said that before.'

'This time, I swear it ... on your mother's life.'

'My *mother's* life?'

'Yes,' Cain said slowly. 'Your mother lives. I have found her.'

'It can't be true,' Kemp squealed. 'How?'

'It's a long story, boy,' Cain said, sensing his moment. 'But every single word is true. Come with me and together we will see to it that she lives with you for the rest of your life.'

Kemp put his hands over his bald head. There was nothing, ***nothing*** he wanted more in the world. The revelation left him lost for words.

'You need to come with me now,' Cain urged. 'I will not fail you. You know what to do. Put on the robe.'

Cain hovered to the door and plucked a see-through bath cap from a shelf. He put it on. 'Do it just as you did before the storm.'

Kemp switched on the shower and removed his nightshirt. 'My mother, huh?'

'You have a few seconds to decide.'

Kemp moved under the cold water. When he was fully drenched, he stepped out, shivering.

'Have you made your choice?'

'Yes.' Kemp said and he grinned through his shivers. 'But this time, cold water will ease the pain.'

---

STONE MARCHED into the sealed-off compound and went through the usual procedures of sanitation.

'He's having a shower,' the nurse said, smiling at him. 'He's feeling an awful lot better.'

'Excellent,' Stone replied.

The nurse nervously examined her watch. 'He's been in there a little while. I'll hurry him along.'

Several minutes later, she returned. 'I can't get a reply, I wonder if he's alright?'

Stone sensed worry in her tone and moved in front of the toilet door. 'It's Commissioner Stone here. You OK in there, young man?'

They listened. Just the running of the shower could be heard.

'How long?' he said to the nurse.

'Ten minutes.'

'TEN MINUTES! Rats! Dickinson – open the door.'

The officer sized up the door then ran to the fire extinguisher and pulled it off the wall. Moments later he smashed it against the lock like a battering ram.

The door swung open.

Stone ran in and searched the small cubicle. On the floor was the boy's medical gown.

'Oh, Christ alive,' Stone said as he slumped against the wall. 'He's gone.'

'What do you mean, *gone?*' the nurse said. 'It's impossible.'

But they could all see it was empty.

'What the hell is going on?' Stone yelled. 'Where is that bloody boy?'

Stone leant down and picked up the flimsy garment. As he did, and much to his astonishment, a pile of fine, grey ash fluttered to the floor.

---

CAIN DESPERATELY WANTED TO JUMP, run, thump the air, kick something, beat someone up. But he knew he needed to keep his energy level in check.

The boy was back. Ha, ha! I knew he'd come – I was right – I knew it!

He hadn't worked out quite how they might communicate, but thought it was worth a try.

'Boy, can you hear me?' he said, and then repeated it, booming out the words.

Cain listened. Nothing.

So, in his head, he thought his question very precisely. *I would like to know your name, boy!* A tingle came back. Slightly gibberish, but definitely worth developing.

He listened again. There ... just. He scrunched his face up. Yes, definitely a noise, though a bit echoey. Perhaps this wasn't going to work.

Suddenly, another absolutely brilliant idea struck him. It was risky alright, but the boy had nowhere to go and couldn't leave so it had to be worth a try.

Cain ushered their ashen body onto the floor. Then, in the same way as before when he'd left the boy in the tree, Cain pushed out of the body, trying not to do it so fast or with quite as much force. Slowly he squeezed out, as though plying himself out of a thick, tight, rubber mould. When out, he clapped his hands and looked down at the boy's naked torso sprinkled in ash.

Kemp stared back, spitting ash from his mouth. 'You let me out?'

Cain audibly sighed from beside him. 'As I said, this time it will be different. This time, I need to look after you, I have to earn your trust, boy.'

Kemp realised the ghost genuinely meant it. 'My name, by the way, is Kemp,' Kemp said.

'Ah, so you heard?'

'Yes. And please don't yell. I can hear you easily when you speak. Were you trying to think it, too? Didn't really come through.'

Cain smiled. 'Hmm. Just as I suspected.'

Kemp stood up and began to dust himself down. 'Any chance of some clothes?'

'Of course.' Cain picked up the bath cap. 'I'll put this on so you know where I am, Kemp.' A floating see- through bath cap hovered nearby. 'Schmerger!' Cain yelled.

Shortly, a tidy manservant appeared with a long, neat, pointed black beard and a strange black hat that muddled between a skull cap and a beret.

Kemp covered his privates.

'Find a robe for your new master, Schmerger. Quick, quick!'

Schmerger frowned, his long nose bending even further down. 'Sire.'

He returned with a thick, silky, burgundy red robe adorned with golden snakes. Kemp slipped it over him, and, being several sizes too large it fell over the floor.

'Now for your welcome home surprise!' Cain said.

'Surprise?'

'Yes, yes. Come along. Follow the strange hat!'

Kemp strode through an extraordinary building that looked somewhere between a vast cave and a palace. On one side jagged mountain-side rocks were inlaid with jewels and gold, and on the other, a vast chimney breast was flanked by windows and shelves filled with drawers, and all covered in dust.

'Go on, open it.'

Kemp pushed the door. As he did, the smell of roast chicken and fried bacon and all sorts of delights wafted over him. 'Food!' he cried. 'Real food. Tons of it!'

The table was crammed with an assortment of chocolates, fruit, cake, meats of all sorts. Kemp made his way over, his eyes wide. 'All this, for me?'

'Indeed. You now have a kitchen and chefs, to use as you wish.'

Kemp stuffed himself until he could eat no more.

All the while, Cain watched, intrigued. 'You know, Kemp, I think our relationship is going to be quite splendid. Tell me your hours of sleeping, your meal times and what you like doing, so that when you're not with me, you'll have that time to do as you wish – unless I require you for an emergency.'

Kemp reckoned this beat hospital a million times over. 'As long as there's a cold shower nearby before I join you.'

'Yes, good thinking. Was it easier this time?'

'Oh yeah. Miles. Hardly felt a thing.'

'Any other demands?'

Kemp licked his lips. 'The deal with my mother. She must be saved. I'm sure she'd love it here?'

'Of course,' Cain said.

'And I'd like to see my mate, Archie,' he said.

'That would be Archie de Lowe?'

'Yes.'

Cain grinned. He was liking this Kemp boy more and more. 'Perhaps we could get him to come here permanently – if we play our cards right.'

'That would be ace,' Kemp said. 'Just imagine it. We'd have a blast.'

Cain nodded. 'Wouldn't we just. But all in good time, Kemp. All in good time. I truly feared that after my terrible treatment of you, you would shun me for death. So I could not imagine a better way in which we have patched up our differences.'

The ghost was ecstatic, but there was one thing that would make this day even more perfect. He remembered the poison, the lethal Havilarian Toadstool Powder that he'd poured into the sugar bowl at Eden Cottage when he'd visited Archie in his room.

Cain had been rather surprised by his quick thinking, nipping into the kitchen and finding sugar – the perfect mask for this poison – just like that. Ha! The mark of a true genius.

Havilarian Toadstool Powder, made with tiny, microscopic, squealing little toadstools. Useless on humans, but lethal to those from the Garden of Eden.

The only substance in the universe that could reduce that Old Man Wood to little more than a shadow.

What were the chances, he wondered, that the old man would help himself to a nice, sugary drink?

# 79 THE SONG OF THE TREES

From that moment on, however hard he tried, Old Man Wood simply couldn't speak properly; words stuck in his throat or twisted in his mind.

The children looked at him with an equal sense of significant awe and worry.

'Would you like a cup of tea?' Archie asked. Wasn't that what grownups had when they needed comforting? That or alcohol. Perhaps he needed both.

The old man smiled and Archie took himself off to the kitchen. He pulled out the largest cup he could find and brewed a strong cup of tea. For good measure, he added a dash of rum, knowing that every now and then Old Man Wood enjoyed a tipple. Archie took a small sip, grimaced, and spat it out in the sink. Ugh. Repulsive, bitter.

He found the sugar bowl, stirred in a couple of heaped teaspoonfuls, sniffed it, then dipped his finger in and licked it. Finally he returned to the sitting room where he handed it to Old Man Wood who sat in his chair being comforted by the girls.

The old man beamed as he took the cup and blew on it until it was cool enough. Then he took a large gulp. 'Interesting tea, Archie,' he said as his few remaining head hairs began to curl. He winked at Archie. 'Touch of rum?'

Archie nodded.

*Clever boy,* Old Man Wood thought. And, in no time, his face had returned to its familiar woody, ruddy complexion.

'If you're feeling ready to chat,' Isabella began softly, 'tell me about the bed, and why you've taken it upon yourself to spy on us,' she said.

'Hang on! I want to know about the Glade and Atrium thing-a-me first,' Daisy butted in, irritated that Isabella had sneaked in first. Hers was easily the most important event by far. 'I mean it's a whole other world, isn't it?'

'What about the poems and the rugs?' Archie said. 'And what and where are the clearly vital tablets?'

They all seemed to talk at a hundred miles an hour, their questions getting louder and louder. Old Man Wood listened quietly to their increasingly hysterical arguing while sipping his rum tea.

Finally he spoke, very quietly and with a certain authority they had not heard before. 'First off, young'uns,' he said, 'we must find these tablets – as a matter of urgency.' The children instantly ceased their bickering. 'As we go, I'll try and piece things together for you; I'll tell you what I know as we search, because, believe me this goes back a heck of a long time, and it won't be easy.' He looked each one of them in the eye. 'Do you understand?'

They nodded.

He took a deep breath. 'Right then. As you may have suspected, I am not exactly your "Uncle". I'll tell you now that I am in fact your great, great, great, hmmm, great, great ... well, to be honest it's an awful lot of 'greats' – more than you can imagine in fact ... grandfather.'

'WHAT?!' they cried.

'DON'T be silly,' Daisy laughed. She patted him playfully on the back. 'Heard it all now—'

'You'd be dead,' Archie said.

'It's impossible!' Isabella said, standing up. 'Stop being so dramatic. Archie, how much rum did you put in—'

'Ahhh. Hmmm, now young'uns this is a great problem. What can I say?' he looked at them all lovingly. 'We are ... how can I put it ... a little bit special in this family. I have lived in this house on this hill through the ages of mankind for an awfully long time. Since way before your records like the Bible even began. As a family, we moved over the years, several times in fact, to look around and see places and there have been many, many adventures, but, on and off, I suppose I've been here on this hill in Yorkshire for thousands of years ... waiting, I believe, for this very moment.' Old Man Wood paused and his crinkly face seemed to lighten as the magnitude of what he was saying sunk in.

The children stared at him, not certain they'd heard him correctly.

'Of course,' he continued, 'I've had the very greatest pleasure in bringing up generation after generation of my family. You three are the last in the line, it would appear.' Old Man Wood cupped his mug between his large, weathered hands, took another sip and beamed at each one in turn.

'And this house alone has seen many, many re-buildings. Spent a great deal of time doing it, all by myself,' he laughed. 'And you know what, most of them are pretty similar to the original, I suppose. It's been all manner of things from a school to public house to a shop. And there used to be houses nearby, once upon a time. Now, what else? Well, not a lot at the moment, but I reckon it's coming back slowly.'

He held Isabella and Daisy's hands. 'You must realise by now that all of these strange events, like your hair and eyes and hands, have something to do with the rain and the rising water. I found that out from the trees at the Bubbling Brook; the ones I took you to see, Archie,' he said, turning to the boy who was staring at the old man with his jaw open. 'I did find them – but I'm not sure I asked the right questions. You see they're clever, those trees, they've memorised everything I've ever told them and they'll tell it back if you ask right. But as I couldn't think what's going to happen or what I'm supposed to do or who I really am ... well ...'

Isabella had had enough. 'This is madness!' she yelled, getting up. 'You're insane or sick. I can't bear it anymore.' Tears welled in her eyes. 'He's cracked, totally cracked. We need to get him urgent medical attention.'

Archie pushed her down firmly. 'Shhh, Isabella. Let him finish.' He'd noticed how Old Man Wood's eyes widened as he sipped the strong tea and hiccoughed as if it were doing something to his brain. Now was not the time to interrupt him. Madness or not, he needed to be heard.

'You see,' Old Man Wood continued, 'when I read those passages in Genesis in your Bible and laughed my head off, well, it's just that whoever wrote it must have had more than a couple of rums in 'em and I know that for sure.' He flicked a glance at Archie.

'Pl-eeee-ase,' Daisy squealed, 'what are you talking about?'

'Genesis – you know the bit about how the world was created and all that, well, hmmm, the thing is, it doesn't say that much. In fact it doesn't say anything really, just a story to start you off at a not-too-embarrassing-point. You'd think the greatest events of mankind – your creation and the creation of every other living thing here on Earth would be given a few more believable lines. But, *hic*, oh no, all you get is a story I told to some strange bloke sitting round a campfire as a bit of a joke – ha, ha – because life was more than a little complicated before – oh yes – *hic*. Very tricky. It was after a few too many jars of Walterbrew – as it happens. Cor, now there's a drink.'

He slurped on his tea, which had the effect of sending his hair curling outwards and his eyes bulged even more. 'Can't believe I remembered that.'

'Old Man Wood, I don't think you're well,' Isabella said, before addressing her siblings. She pointed at her head and twirled a finger. '*Seriously, we need to do something – he has totally lost it.*'

The old man ignored her and carried on rambling. 'This bloke, you see, quite a clever fellow – terribly serious and, hmmm, well, it just seemed a good idea at the time – couldn't resist it I suppose, fantastically entertaining.' He hiccoughed again. 'There is truth in that passage, though; Havilah is full of treasure and things beyond your wildest imagination. And Cain and that serpent of his are wretched,' he spat, 'and the other thing is the flood ...'

On the word "flood" he slurred quite badly, and Old Man Wood checked himself before hiccoughing very loudly. But, now he was on a roll, a mere hiccough wasn't going to stop him.

'Oh yes, I do feel a little guilty, if you know what I mean. Well, you may say it's not possible but I tell you it's true. I was there. Amazing isn't it? I wrote those poems, did I say that? Such a long ... what actually happened is quite different because, well ... hmmm ... all those places exist or used to, rather like here. Otherwise you might get ... now what was I talking about?' he continued, forgetting himself.

A blink of lightning followed by a ripple of thunder sent a message that another storm was close by. It seemed to intensify the situation.

'Stop rambling and tell us, in plain English, what on earth you're talking about,' Isabella demanded.

Daisy, however, giggled and leaned in on him. 'Go on, tell us Old Man Wood. Tell us your story ...'

But, unfortunately, Old Man Wood, whose few head-hairs were standing erect like the threads of a worn brush, started to hum a strange tune which sounded as if the wind was rushing through trees, its rhythm building all the time.

He clambered out of his chair and stood tall in the room, his big trunk filling the space in front of the fire as strange whoooshing and swissssshing sounds came out of his mouth and vibrated round the room.

Moments later, his hands and body moved in a slow, graceful way as a breeze appeared to blow through the house.

The children sat down and watched as the old man hummed the song of the trees.

---

SUDDENLY ARCHIE HAD AN IDEA.

He slipped out of his chair, and while the two girls listened, mesmerised by Old Man Wood's extraordinary movements and the swishing, whooshing noises of his song, he crawled on all fours behind the back of the armchair to the fireplace. He found a poker and thrust it into the fire, shifting the logs in the embers. There was nothing and, for a brief moment, he felt rather foolish.

Under his breath he recited the words of the poem.

*'THE FIRST YOU* ***hid in the heart of the house***
***'That warms you night and day***
***'Get it out by poking me,***
***'And singing your favourite song along the way!'***

ARCHIE LOOKED up to see Daisy standing, copying Old Man Wood, humming away and moving her arms in slow, controlled waves, somewhat, but not exactly, mimicking the old man's motions.

She wore a huge smile on her face.

On the contrary, Isabella lay on the sofa, her knees up to her chest and her head between her hands.

Archie picked up the rhythm and began to hum along, and as he got the hang of it, he decided to bolster the fire up anyway and thrust the poker in once again.

With a tiny flash, a strange flicker came out at him. Archie's heart skipped a beat.

He poked with a little more urgency and the light intensified.

He looked about. Had anyone else seen it? Daisy and Old Man Wood were singing as if in a trance; Isabella cowered on the sofa.

He turned his eyes back to the fire and found that, right before his eyes, an object very slowly approached. He could hardly breathe. But Old Man Wood had come to the end of his song and, the moment he finished, the "thing" receded back into the orange glow.

---

SEEING Old Man Wood like this made Isabella feel as unhappy as she could ever remember. As his song ended, she slipped off to the kitchen where she heard the gentle drone of the generator. She worked out that it might run for another fifteen minutes or so if they were lucky.

For a while, she thought she might slope off to bed; leave them to it. Perhaps, first, she ought to check the TV for any up-to-date news.

She flicked on the remote control and, as the telly warmed up, she opened the fridge to see if Mrs Pye had left anything worth snacking on. She peered inside. Nothing she fancied, so she grabbed an apple and sat down on the chair and took a large bite.

For a minute or two she watched the news repeats that had been going round and round in a loop.

She bit in hard again, wiping the juice off her chin as a message ran along the bottom in bold red letters. *"Important announcement coming up."*

*What was so important that it had to be flagged?*

Daisy and Archie came in just as the picture changed. It now showed a live feed from the same press office with oak-panelled walls, but this time full of weary-looking officials.

A tall man, with grey hair and a pointed nose, made his way to the lectern. An elegant, smart lady, the Deputy Prime Minister, introduced this man as the chief coordinator of the flood crisis, Commissioner Stone.

*'First of all,'* he began, a subtle Yorkshire trace in his voice, *'I speak on behalf of the COBRA team to offer my thanks to all of those who have dug deep in protecting and keeping the citizens of our island safe at this terrible time. The help and resolve given by so many continues to touch the lives of millions.*

*'I will be frank,'* he said, looking directly into the camera, *'the epidemic, the so called Yorkshire Plague or Ebora, reached all parts of the country overnight. It strikes at will. There is no logic to its method nor is there a cure for those affected. Not yet. Medical centres are overwhelmed as our few doctors who do not have symptoms themselves, struggle to keep up. If you think you may have symptoms, please ring our helpline number at the bottom of the screen. Our advice is, be patient, drink plenty of fresh water and keep warm. And please, stay at home.'*

He shifted and smiled. *'While many are suffering, we have heard stories of incredible bravery and heroism. We're going to share some real life situations from the flooding. These are tales of extreme courage and dogged resilience. Above all,'* he said, his voice quivering, *'they are stories of hope.'*

The screen cut from the press conference to a scene on a beach, waves crashing someway behind the sand. On it, a reporter with his microphone at the ready waited for the link up.

*'Here I am near the beautiful Suffolk coastal town of Southwold.'* The camera panned to a lighthouse and then away to colourful beach huts. *'Famous for its beer and as an upmarket holiday resort, last night it was the scene of an extraordinary rescue off the coast, where two names will surely be remembered for an awfully long time. I'm handing you over to Serena Strutt who continues the story.'*

*'Thank you, Bill,'* said Serena, her perfect smile beaming at the camera. *'On the day of the storm, two children from the village of Upsall in North Yorkshire found a rickety old rowing boat, built a canopy in a manner of minutes from odds and ends found in a shed, and then, miraculously, they survived what is now understood to be the most vicious storm of all time before being sucked out into the North Sea.*

*'Against quite incredible odds, they survived. Last night, their boat sank in a fierce gale last night off this very coast. The coastguard spotted them and these, frankly, remarkable children were rescued.'*

The children watched in silence, mesmerised by the images, huddled together, their arms locked around one another.

*'I have with me here, one of the survivors, Sue Lowden.'*

The moment the words were out of the reporter's mouth the kitchen erupted. Daisy and Archie leapt up and down, screaming their heads off. Isabella sank to the floor, tears falling freely down her cheeks.

*'Sue,'* Serena said, *'what an amazing story. I know you're still quite numb from your experience, especially as Gus Williams, your partner on the boat, has gone to hospital, but please tell us more.'*

The camera moved and Sue came into shot. She'd lost weight but her eyes sparkled. *'I just want to thank Gus,'* her eyes began welling up, *'he was amazing.'*

'At snogging,' Archie quipped.

'Oh shut up,' said the girls in unison.

Back on the screen, Sue recalled some of their adventures, how they'd built the canopy and caught fish to eat.

Serena Strutt shook her head. '*Sue, what a truly astonishing story and, of course, our thoughts are with Gus. Is there anything else you'd like to say?*'

Sue looked down at her feet as if trying to rein in her emotions. Then, very slowly and as the camera zoomed in on her face, she looked directly into the lens and very sadly said. '*Infected now*,' before adding, '*lush*.'

For a second, Serena looked confused, but being a professional she draped an arm around the girl. '*Thank you Sue – I know this is a very emotional time, and we really do wish Gus a speedy recovery. Back to you in the studio.*'

---

THE SENSE of relief in the kitchen was extraordinary. But while Archie and Daisy danced around, Isabella sat down at the kitchen table with a pen and paper. She was instantly struck by the oddness of Sue's response. Sue never, ever used words like "lush". That was a Daisy kind of word. Not a Sue word.

Daisy pulled a chair up. 'What's up, sis? Thought you be jumping over the moon.'

Isabella shook her head. 'Inside, I am, believe me. But there's something wrong, that sentence wasn't right in any way.'

'Know what you mean,' Daisy said. 'Sounded like something she'd planned, if you ask me.'

Isabella pushed the pencil through the hole in her hand and spun it round. 'Yes. You're right. But what did it mean? I thought "lush" meant, kind of cool.'

'Yeah, that's right. Gorgeous – lush.'

Isabella twiddled her hand in the air, the pencil making a strange starry shadow on the paper. 'Maybe you're right. Perhaps she had planned it.' Isabella wrote down the sentence on the paper and looked at it.

She rearranged the letters in a circle and tried to see if there was a pattern or some obvious code. As she pondered the letters she asked: 'Is Old Man Wood alright? It might be an idea to check on him.'

Archie slipped out of the kitchen and returned a couple of minutes later. 'He's wandering around with his hair sticking out on end. I think he's, sort of, OK.' He hesitated. 'Look, while you were singing that hummy song, a weird object came out of the fire—'

'Holy moly! I think I've got it,' Isabella exclaimed, ignoring him.

Daisy and Archie crowded round.

'Look. Take the word, '*Infected*'. In it is the word, '*find*'. She crossed out the letters. Now what's left? '*The*'. She crossed that out as well.

They stared at the paper. Daisy clapped her hands. 'Look – the word, '*uncle*'.'

'Excellent,' Isabella said, surprised by her sister's grasp. 'Which leaves', she continued, '*S, O, W*.'

'*Find the uncle sow*,' Archie said, 'or, '*wos*'. You think she means Old Man Wood?'

'Possibly,' Isabella replied, pulling the pen in and out of her hand-hole. 'But it's not like her to make a glaring error like that. She knows perfectly well what his name is. Hang on, what if it's '*clown*' and then you've got, *E, U, S*.'

'*Sue*.' Daisy said. 'That's it! *Find the clown, Sue*.'

Isabella shook her head. 'No. It just doesn't stack up.' She stood up and began pacing the room. 'I mean what could she possibly be referring to?'

Daisy sat down and played with the letters, her eyes glowing, a gentle pink light forming over the paper.

She rearranged the final letters and clapped her hands.

Isabella ran over. She studied the paper, squeezed Daisy's shoulders and took a deep breath.

'Archie,' she ordered, 'make another cup of tea for Old Man Wood, exactly like before.'

'You sure?'

'Yes! Just do it, now!'

'God. OK – why? You saw what happened to him. He'll go properly bonkers.'

'Sue's message.'

Archie skipped over and read it out loud.

*'FIND THE CLUES, NOW.'*

# 80 RUM TEA

'What were you saying about the fire, Archie?' Isabella asked.

Archie grabbed the bottle of rum and poured in a generous measure. 'Oh, yeah. An object appeared to be coming out of it,' he said, 'but when Daisy and Old Man Wood stopped singing, it retreated.'

'Have you finished with that?' Isabella asked, sniffing the tea. 'It smells gross.'

'Not quite, it needs some sugar to sweeten it up,' Archie said. 'Pass it over.'

Daisy picked up the sugar bowl, took a long, hard look inside and handed it over. 'Are you sure that's sugar?' she said.

'It was the last time I looked.'

Daisy shuffled on the spot. 'Just curious. Looks like something else, bit weird, that's all. Sounds like it's wailing.'

'Wailing?'

'Yup – like it's crying.'

Archie heaped a couple of teaspoons into the cup and stirred it round. Daisy peered into it and shook her head. 'What is sugar, anyway?' she said. 'Is it, mushroomy?'

'Oh, for goodness' sake, Daisy.' Isabella said. 'Now is not the time to start learning about sugar and mushrooms. Now,' she said, addressing the twins, 'here is the plan.'

---

JUST AS THEY were about to head back into the sitting room with the tea, Daisy's ears tuned into the TV. She turned and faced the screen.

Commissioner Stone was thanking the various officers around him and trying to placate viewers that the nation shouldn't be too worried. He sounded confident. '*One final thing,*' he said, a crooked smile crossing his face, '*we now know that the epicentre of the storm centred on the small moor-side village of Upsall.*'

'Archie, Bells,' Daisy called out. 'You dudes should watch this.'

The Commissioner continued as Archie and Isabella returned through the door. '*We'd particularly like to speak to anyone who was in the area of Upsall the day the storm broke. We know that most were tragically lost and almost certainly swept away, like the brave Gus Williams and Sue Lowden who we heard from earlier.*'

Another camera homed in on the lean, moustachioed face of Commissioner Stone. Clumsily, Stone turned towards it.

'*There is one family we know of, whose three children were on the football pitch at that time. There's little doubt the water took them, but if anyone has seen or heard from any of them, particularly this young man on your screen now, Archie de Lowe, then please get in touch with your local authority representative.*'

A picture of Archie, a couple of years younger, filled the screen.

Archie put the tea down on the table. 'Jeez,' he said. 'Why me?'

'Who is the only person,' Isabella said, 'who they know, who knows you?'

Archie squinted. He could feel his hair hardening.

'Kemp. That's who,' Isabella said as she wheeled away. 'You're a fool Archie. I told you not to trust him.'

'My God,' said Daisy. 'I forgot to tell you. You know when he said those words in the hospital—'

'*Dunno* and, er ... *Algae*, wasn't it?' Archie said.

'Those exactly. I think he was trying to contact you.'

'What do you mean?'

'For *Algae,* read, *Archie,*' Daisy said. 'And for *Dunno*, read—'

'*de Lowe,*' Archie finished.

They looked at each other. 'Do you think he was trying to warn me?'

'Almost certainly,' Daisy said.

Isabella shrugged. 'Looks like we'll never know. But what we do know is that, because of him, they're now hot on our case.'

---

THE NEWS that they were being searched for felt like a body blow to Archie. He'd slightly hoped that his first appearance on national television might be as goalkeeper for Leeds United, not as someone wanted by the authorities. What had Kemp said to the police? Had he spilled the beans and told them about Cain and the coat? Even if he had, though, they couldn't possibly have believed him, could they? They'd have thought he'd lost his mind.

He sank down in his chair, trying not to worry about it, conscious that his hair was as hard as steel, while his blood coursed through his veins. He had that angry feeling that pricked him every time he thought about Cain.

Daisy sat on the arm of Old Man Wood's chair. 'Tell us more about your song,' she began. 'It's beautiful.'

Old Man Wood smiled a little drunkenly and sipped his tea. 'I don't know where it comes from,' he said. 'Reminds me of this whole other place. A time long ago. Feels apple-marvellous, though, doesn't it?'

'Teach it to us,' said Isabella, who was sitting on his other side.

'Really?'

'Oh yes,' the girls said at once, smiling sweetly.

'Liked it, did you?'

'Absolutely,' Isabella lied.

Old Man Wood beamed. He couldn't refuse smiles like these and, after taking another large swallow of tea he climbed out of his chair.

'Whoooosh, swissshshhh, swissshy, swoosh,' he began, his eyes closed in concentration, his arms pulling slowly around like a gentle breast-stoke motion.

The girls stood up and copied him. Daisy was immediately right on track with Old Man Wood, as if she absolutely understood it.

Isabella, on the other hand, found it rather embarrassing. Try as she might, the song and movements didn't register.

The pace built up.

As before, the deep vibrations of Old Man Wood's voice made the whole room tremble and, when the music reached its climax, a curious wind curled around them and through them and up their spines.

Archie crawled over to the fire and, as planned, began poking around, but his thoughts weren't with the song, they were still fixed solely on Kemp and Cain and he hadn't hummed or sung a word.

Nothing happened. No bright light emerged from the fire.

The children looked from one to the other and then back again, confused. Why hadn't it worked? Had Archie lied?

'Encore, encore – more, more!' Isabella clapped as she danced over to Archie and whispered into his ear. 'This time, Arch, you've got to sing it too. It's all or nothing. Understand?'

As the lights failed and the noise of the generator departed, they heard only the sounds of their breathing and the distant cracks and rumbles of the storm overhead. Archie ran off and found the lamps Old Man Wood had used to highlight the rugs. He lit them, and positioned them either side of the room, where they cast a deep orange glow.

Old Man Wood's face, now greatly accentuated by the soft rays, beamed from ear to ear.

Daisy, who hadn't noticed Archie's lack of vocal involvement, clapped encouragement. 'That was utterly lush,' she said, winking at Isabella. 'Encore, encore, Old Man Wood. More, more!'

Old Man Wood remained standing, drained the rest of his tea and put the mug down with a clatter on the mantelpiece. He breathed in deeply and smacked his chest. 'This time,' he said, 'you go a wee bit higher, girls. You'll feel it in your blood. The song will take you there, if you believe in it.'

'Can I start?' Daisy said. 'It's so beautiful and moving. Rather like being in paradise.'

Old Man Wood's booming laugh rebounded off the walls. 'That's exactly what it is. Clever littlun. Well of course you can. I'll take it up as you begin.'

Daisy began. She closed her eyes and extended her arms. 'Whoooosh, swishes, swiffy swissh whoooosh,' she hummed.

Old Man Wood smiled. Even if the children didn't have a clue what the song meant, it thrilled him that the song resonated well with them. He couldn't think how it had come to him, but it reminded him of a time when things in his head weren't quite so foggy, as if the song unlocked a hidden door to a room full of secrets.

He joined in, this time even more enthusiastically, whirring the strange noises in and out of his mouth and gesticulating, slowly at first, with his strong arms and hands, building up his movements as the song increased in tempo, so that before long it sounded exactly like wind rushing through leaves in a big tree.

Isabella stood up and shut her eyes. 'Swiffy swissh whoooosh.' Goose-bumps ran up her back.

Archie, poker in hand, sensing the power of the song, stood up and began as well and in no time was consumed by the mesmeric, chanting tones.

Suddenly, from rather sad embers, the fire burst into life.

Isabella and Daisy, without even realising, raised the tune up an octave with the hummy, swishy and whooshy noises, and the momentum grew.

'Swiffy, hummm swish sshshh. Swiffy swissh whoooosh, swissshshhh hmmm ...' Louder and louder it grew, the four of them consumed by the music.

Old Man Wood suddenly took the piece to a whole new level, roaring the song out. Daisy and Isabella climbed an octave higher and as they did wind gushed over them like a tornado.

Archie opened his eyes. Old Man Wood's hair stood fully erect on his head and his face had the look of a wild, sea-worn pirate; his ruddy complexion setting off his thick frown-lines, his face flickering in the fire-light, his concentration intense. His dark eyes, unblinking, fixed stonily to a point on the wall as if he wasn't looking at the wall at all; but looking back through time at another world.

The storm outside now crashed about the cottage. Rain lashed violently down onto the tiles of the old building and flashes of lightning illuminated the room as a massive crack of thunder shook the building.

Old Man Wood's movements with his long arms now became more expansive, flailing around like a mad conductor who had lost control of his orchestra and was trying wildly to get them playing together.

'Has anyone opened a window?' Daisy shouted over the din, trembling a little in awe as wind started to whirl around her. But her voice was drowned out by the music and the bangs and cracks of thunder. She rejoined the singing. Suddenly an extended gust of wind picked up a bundle of papers and scattered them around the room, like confetti.

Now, noise, air and paper whirled wildly about as if a thousand ghosts had suddenly flown into the room at once. Every hair on the children's bodies stood to attention as Old Man Wood stared crazily at the wall, his brow furrowed, his body upright and his face majestic.

As the song mellowed, bits of paper floated gently to floor.

Daisy and Isabella, soaked in sweat, looked over to Archie, lost amidst the muddle of paper and debris.

From out of nowhere they saw a fabulous smile spread across his face. And they could hardly believe what they saw; for in his hand was a tablet; a dusty, stone tablet which was very, very old. On the top, etched in gold, was the emblem of the Tree of Life – a tree with roots that joined with the branches, like a globe.

'Oh my ... oh my,' Daisy cried. 'Look! Bells! Look at Archie! *It's true*! The tablets from the clue in that silly rhyme.'

They said it together:

*'The first you hid in the heart of the house*
*'That warms you night and day*
*'Get it out by poking me*
*'And singing your favourite song along the way.'*

Archie thumped the air as they hugged. 'One down, two to go, what a result! Old Man Wood, you aren't so hopeless after all!'

They turned their attention back to the old man, but the combination of the song and Archie's brew had got the better of Old Man Wood. He lay collapsed in his armchair, snoring heavily, sweat sheening his gnarled face, a few strands of hair still erect on his old head.

'I hope he's OK.' Daisy said.

'Sure he is,' Isabella replied. 'He just needs a good sleep, that's all.'

# 81 A NEW BELIEF

Golden brown in colour, hard as steel and inlaid with beautiful scrollwork, the tablet from the fire was roughly the size and weight of a small paperback book. As Archie touched it, a cosy tingle, like the warmth of love, enveloped him.

He traced the engraved surfaces, running his fingers along the lines of the symbol of the Tree of Life, its characteristic swirls mirrored up and down, and he noted that it was the same artwork as they had seen on the walls of the cave.

They passed it round, marvelling at its beauty.

'Look, guys,' Isabella said as she handed it over to Archie. 'I don't know what to say.'

'Well, you should be thrilled to bits that Sue's alive—'

'And Gus,' Daisy added. 'He's a hero.'

'Yes, of course, Gus too,' Isabella said, beaming. 'But what I meant to say,' and she stuttered, trying to find the right words, 'what I really meant to say, was, thanks.'

'Thanks? For what?' Daisy replied.

'For not believing a word I was talking about,' Isabella said.

'We never do, anyway,' Daisy responded, raising her eyebrows. 'Here, your turn, Bells.' Daisy handed her the tablet and rose from the kitchen table.

Isabella pulled it to her lips. Like with Archie, a glow, a rush, a joyful sensation shot into her like a fizz of confidence that pushed her fear and worries sideways. Isabella smiled and pulled it to her chest. 'Look, I'm sorry I didn't believe you, I just couldn't. Now, I can see how massively wrong I've been. By the way, where's the paper you wrote the poems on?'

Archie pulled it out of his pocket and handed it over.

Isabella read it and frowned as Daisy returned to the table.

'Problem?'

'Just a bit,' Isabella said and she proceeded to read:

*'You have but seven days and nights*
*'As Earth moves in its cycle.*
*'From first lightning strike and thunderclap*
*'The world waits your arrival.'*

'I was right,' Daisy said. 'Remember, Archie? I told you I thought we had seven days—'

Isabella put her hands up. 'I've been holding this whole thing up, haven't I?' She bit her lip. 'And we've got to find two more of these little beauties in three days.'

'What's the problem?' Daisy said.

'It took us three days just to find this one.'

'Only because you were poncing about, being all sciencey and dull.'

On any other occasion Isabella would have punched her. But not today. 'I know, and I'm sorry.'

Daisy smiled and pulled out a bag. 'We'll find the next one in the morning. The Blab-is-ter-berry Jelly one, or whatever it's called. Right now, it's about time we started to look the part.'

Daisy reached in and slipped on her metal-rimmed, pink-lens spectacles.

She tossed the bag to Archie who pulled out a hat and he passed it on to Isabella.

'What is it?' Isabella asked.

'Just put it on. You too, Archie.'

'Seriously?' he said. 'Do I have to?'

Isabella opened the bag, her face full of questions, and removed the contents.

'Go on,' Daisy insisted.

'Studded, fingerless, black leather gloves?'

'Absolutely!' Daisy clapped. 'Mrs Pye and I have made some adjustments. Same with yours, Archie. Hope they fit.'

Isabella slipped them on and was amazed to find how comfortable they were. 'What's with the stud popper thing in the middle?'

'Oh, that's a trouser popper. Mrs Pye's idea, so your gloves don't slip off.'

Isabella didn't know whether to laugh or cry. 'Oh, Daisy, I don't know—'

Daisy leaned over the table and put a finger to her sister's lips. 'Sshh. No more excuses, Bells. If we're going to save the world we may as well try and look the part. In any case, it's way time you got a bit more bling, sister.'

She turned. Mrs Pye had reinforced Archie's beret with leather patches for his spike-ends and added three studs around the rim. 'You do look handsome, my dear Archie, in a rugged, French kind of way,' she joked.

Isabella was impressed. 'That, Daisy, is a very good idea.'

'Yup,' she agreed. 'No more getting poked by those silly spikes, right?' Daisy shot off next-door and came back holding Isabella's phone.

Isabella knew exactly what she was thinking and burst out laughing.

Archie protested, 'Please, Daise. What now?'

'I think,' Daisy said, mischievously, 'that it's time for a very special selfie!'

---

AS THE SHUTTER clicked on the camera, they heard a deep groan. The children turned towards the door.

'Old Man Wood?' Archie said. 'He was fine a minute ago.'

'Oh heck!' Daisy said. 'He's probably drunk on your rum-based tea and crashed out.'

The children smiled at one another.

'The least we can do is make sure he's comfortable.'

They trooped back into the living room, a room they barely recognised as paper, canvas and pictures littered every inch of the floor.

'Lord above,' Isabella whispered. 'If Mrs Pye sees this, she's going to go utterly mental.'

'It's a warzone—'

'Chill, guys,' Daisy cut in. 'If we don't find the tablets, then there won't be a world left in which she can offload her tidiness anger. We'll deal with it later. Hey, there he is.'

Archie re-lit a couple of candles and joined the girls next to Old Man Wood on the sofa.

'He's fast asleep,' Bells said.

Daisy wasn't so sure. 'Old Man Wood, you there?'

He groaned.

'Hi,' she said, resting a hand on his forehead, 'you should go to bed. Busy day coming up.'

A flicker at the corner of his mouth. 'I ... I think—' he whispered before slumping back.

'What?' Daisy said. 'You think you're a bit tiddly, eh, Old Man Wood?'

The old man suddenly looked grey and withered and terribly old as he tried to sit up. The children gasped.

'Poison,' he spat. 'You've got to—'

'Poison?' Isabella exclaimed. 'What poison?'

Old Man Wood tried to speak but the words wouldn't form. His bony hand grabbed Isabella's wrist and she squealed as he gripped it hard and levered his head off the pillow. He stared at her with watery, scared eyes, 'Y-o-u ... y-o-u-r ... p-o-w-errrr—'

And then his grip loosened and his head fell back slowly onto the pillow, like a rock falling through water, and his eyes shut.

A look of peace descended over him.

The stillness in the room was deafening.

Stunned, the children instinctively stepped back as a huge rumble of thunder rolled out over the cottage rattling the glass in the windows.

'Holy crap,' Archie trembled. He fell to his knees and wiped a tear from his eye. 'I think we've just killed Old Man Wood.'

***To be continued ...***

## BOOK 3 - THE CHAMBER OF TRUTH

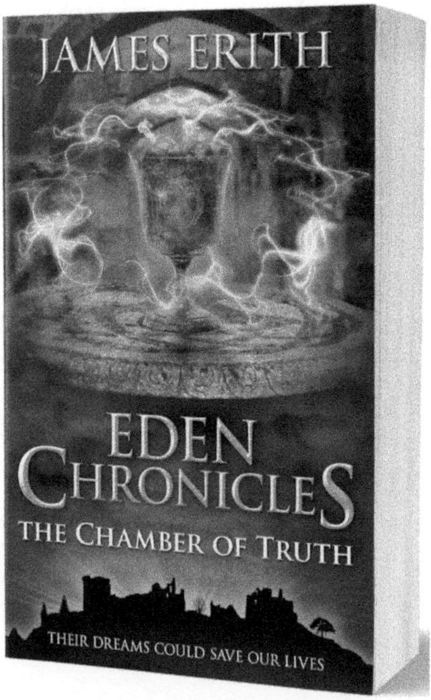

## *The Riddles*

'The first you hid in the heart of the house
'That warms you night and day
'Get it out by poking me,
'And singing your favourite song along the way!

'For the second one you have to find
'You burp it from the family belly.
'To do this, you have to eat
'Blabisterberry jelly!

'The third you search for is underneath your nose.
'It's clear, pure and cold.
'In order to draw it out
'You need to send a rose.

'Put them all together,
'Then get out of the way
'What you find will prove a guide
'For all the other worlds.

'You have but seven days and seven nights
'As Earth moves in its cycle
'From first lightning strike and thunderclap
'The world awaits your arrival.'

# 82 DEAD, OR ALIVE

From all the paper and card and canvasses and various other artworks that had been stripped from their frames and scattered about the floor, it looked as if a tornado had swept through the sitting room.

In front of them, lying on the sofa opposite the fire, Old Man Wood was as still and as white as a stone sculpture. The gentle embers from the fire glowed red and orange, lighting the hearth and accentuating the old man's pale, drawn features.

The children peered over him in shock, their lips trembling.

Tears rolled freely down Archie's cheeks. 'I killed him,' he said. 'The only person who had a hope in hell of figuring out what's going on, and I murdered him.' His lip wobbled. 'It was only tea with sugar and a shot of rum...'

Daisy shook her head. 'He's not dead, Winkle.'

'Of course he is! He hasn't moved or breathed or groaned for ages—'

'Didn't you listen to a word he said? *He can't die*. That's what he told us. He said that he was our great, great you-know, loads of great Grandfathers or whatever it was. So he can't be dead, can he?'

Archie looked at her, confused. 'He's not breathing.'

Isabella reached in and placed two fingers on his neck. 'There is a pulse, Archie. It's weak but it's definitely there. Have a feel.'

Archie replaced her fingers with his, scrunched his face but shook his head. 'I can't feel anything.'

For some time there was an awkward silence.

Finally, Daisy couldn't bear it any longer. 'What do you think we should do?' she said. 'Let him sleep it off?'

'He's got to wake up,' Archie replied, 'to help us find the other tablets.' He sat down on the arm of the armchair and gently slapped the old man's face trying to rouse him. Then he pinched his cheek.

'Come on, wakey-wakey,' he said gently. 'Please, Old Man Wood, you've got to wake up—'

'Water!' Daisy said. 'Let's shock him with a bucket of ice-cold water. That's what they do in films – or we could give him a shot of whisky.'

'NOT alcohol,' Archie said. 'He's had far, far too much of that—'

Without listening, Daisy whizzed off and returned with a bucket half-full of cold water. She thrust it in Archie's direction. 'You killed him, so you do it.'

Archie took the bucket but stood still, utterly appalled. 'I only did it because Isabella told me to. It was her idea, so she should do it.'

They turned to their elder sister.

'Absolutely no way,' Isabella said firmly. 'If you think water shock is the best idea, then I suggest you both do it.'

The twins looked at one another.

'What if he wakes up and properly freaks out?' Archie said.

'Old Man Wood would never do such a thing—'

'Daisy, didn't you notice what happened before? He totally lost the plot. What if he's now permanently unhinged?'

'Unhinged?'

'Well, yeah, damaged beyond repair. You know, like a crazed lunatic psychopath – or worse.'

'Archie, if you haven't cottoned on by now, the whole world has gone crazy, and we're caught in the middle of it.' Daisy said. 'Here, give it to me.'

In one movement, Daisy grabbed the bucket and emptied the contents in a long stream directly over Old Man Wood's head, the water flowing over his nose and down the deep lines of his face and onto his chest.

Instinctively, the twins took a step or two backwards, in case Old Man Wood suddenly stood up and flailed his thick arms.

But Old Man Wood's deathly face-mask didn't budge.

The twins turned to each other, laughing nervously, slightly in awe at the volume of water soaking the sofa and carpet.

Daisy's eyes were wide open. 'Still nothing?'

'I told you he was dead,' Archie said.

Daisy shook her head. 'But why would Old Man Wood lie about death like that? He would *never* do such a thing – it doesn't add up.'

'Look, you morons,' Isabella said, standing up impatiently, 'we can do one simple test to find out. It'll prove his mortality beyond doubt.' She hared upstairs and returned moments later holding a small compact mirror, which she placed just under his nose.

'This is a classic check used by paramedics globally,' she continued. 'If he's alive, the mirror will fog up due to condensation.'

A roll of thunder boomed around the cottage, shaking the foundations of the building and heightening the seriousness of the situation. Isabella held her hand steady.

'Look, just there.' Daisy said, staring at it deeply, 'a tiny coating.'

Isabella frowned. 'There's nothing.'

'Yes, there is! He's definitely alive.'

Isabella shook her head. But how could she query Daisy when her sister could see extraordinary detail and she couldn't?

'Are you sure?'

'Absolutely,' Daisy said, and she stepped forward and prodded one of his arms. 'He's probably in some sort of coma and needs to sleep it off. Let's get him to bed.'

'But he weighs a ton,' Archie complained.

'Dur! And you're the strongest boy in the world, or had you forgotten?'

Archie shook his head and turned red.

'For crying out loud, Archie, you pulled that tree out and carried me miles, and pushed an enormous ten-ton boulder out of a cave.' She rolled her eyes. 'Come on, get with the programme.'

Archie groaned. 'But I can't do it *all* the time, Daisy. I'm not super-strong now. It's only when I'm angry or really need it.'

'Then I'm going to make you angry, Winkle,' she said his nickname very slowly and deliberately. Very, very angry indeed.'

'Don't, I'm not in the mood.'

Daisy ignored him. 'Winkle, Winkle, Winkle—'

'Stop it!'

Daisy grinned maliciously. 'Where's Isabella? She's usually pretty good at helping me with this kind of thing.'

Isabella yawned and stood up. 'Here, watching you both.' She kicked at a bundle of debris on the floor. 'I hate to be the bearer of obvious news, but if Mrs. Pye walks in here, she is going to have a heart attack.'

'Big deal,' Daisy said. 'She could help us move Old Man Wood if superman-boy here refuses to co-operate.'

Isabella laughed. '"Superman-boy"? That has to be the worst hero-label of all time,' she crowed. 'Logically, shouldn't it be "Super-boy".'

'Oh, Bells. Really?' Daisy said. 'That is so, so ... lame.' She studied her watch. 'Anyway, Mrs. Pye won't be over until supper. So either we go to her now and explain what's been going on and how Old Man Wood ended up dead or comatose – or we have an hour to get Old Man Wood into his bed and back to normal.'

The children looked at one another.

'Well, come on brain box,' Daisy said to Isabella. 'Stop thinking and give us a hand.'

Isabella grabbed some matches and lit several candles en-route to Old Man Wood's bedroom.

Then, with a terrible struggle, the children managed, huffing and puffing, to drag the huge figure of Old Man Wood to the foot of the stairs.

'Archie, it is incredibly inconsiderate of you not to find your strength when we could really do with it,' Isabella stormed.

'Yeah, isn't it just,' Archie said, struggling under the dead-weight of the old man's shoulders. 'Can you please grab him – I can't hold him here forever.'

'No.'

Archie summoned his strength. 'Look, guys, I don't know how my muscle thing works, OK?'

Daisy marched up to him and slapped him hard around the face, the noise cracking like a whip.

'Bloody hell! What was that for?'

'Because you need to focus and start controlling this gift of yours—'

'But there's no need to hit me.'

'Yes, of course there is! Get a grip.'

Archie reddened and his mace-like hair visibly tightened. 'Daisy, I'll get you back for this.' He took a deep breath. 'You two hold a leg each.'

Archie lifted and, almost as if he wasn't trying, he started up the stairs bearing almost the entire weight of Old Man Wood.

In no time, Old Man Wood lay in his bed. The flicker of light from a lone candle emphasised the deep wooden carvings on his bed, and the soft glow of the panels at the foot of his bed highlighted the lines on his face.

'I hope he'll be alright,' Isabella said as she pulled the duvet up over his body. 'It can't be good for a man his age to be ill like this.' She laid a hand on his forehead.

'What if he's been poisoned? That's what *he* thought it was – he definitely said something about poison,' she said, as if thinking her thoughts out loud. 'But where would it have come from? And why aren't we all infected?'

'Maybe he caught the virus we heard about on the telly?' Daisy said, as she also rested a hand on Old Man Wood's brow. 'What if he caught it from visiting those trees he told us about – you know the ones, Archie.'

'You're right,' he said. 'He went right underwater – whereas I didn't.'

'But *I* did,' Daisy said.

'Did what?'

'Got drenched when I fell in the ditch on the way to that weird atrium place. And I'm alright, I think.' She randomly sniffed her armpit as if that was an indicator of health.

Isabella squeezed her shoulder. 'I'm afraid there's not much we can do about it – but pray,' she said softly. 'He needs to rest, that's all – there's nothing more we can do to help.' She moved a pillow out of the way so that the old man's head lay flat.

'Archie,' Daisy asked, cocking her head, 'what did you put in his tea?'

He raised an eyebrow. 'Two measures of rum and a spoonful of sugar. I dipped my finger in it and licked it – utterly disgusting.'

'But there was also something really random about it,' Daisy said. 'Like toadstools and squealing.'

Archie shook his head. 'Daisy, you do come up with some rubbish.'

'No, I don't.'

'Well, it did the trick; we found the first tablet, didn't we?' he said.

'All I'm saying is that I definitely thought there was something in it.'

'Uh-oh, here we go – your magic eyes again, eh?' Isabella quipped.

'Well, I won't be having any tea from you, Archie. Poor, dear Old Man Wood.'

'If you ask me, that tea had magic mushrooms in it,' Daisy said. 'Don't they kill you?'

Isabella shrugged. 'I don't know. What gets me is this: we only found the tablet because of the song which came from the clues on the five ancient rugs, so does this mean Old Man Wood has been around for as long as he claimed? You know, since the beginning ...'

'But the beginning of what?' Daisy added.

'I don't know,' she said. 'But how would he know about the song and the storm and everything else if he wasn't telling the truth?'

Archie nodded. 'And remember his despair that *he* was somehow to blame—'

'And, of course, there's this weird bed with its wooden telly panels,' Daisy added.

'And spying on us too,' Archie said, taking off his beanie and stroking his foremost hair spike.

'The one thing we do know is that we have to solve the riddles – so we might as well try and figure out where the next tablet is as fast as possible. Something about jelly—'

'Blab—' Archie tried. 'Or blisters—'

'Heck,' Isabella blurted out.

'What is it?'

'Oh, nothing,' Isabella said, but her face told a different story. 'Really, it's nothing,' she said.

'You sure?' Daisy said, sensing her discomfort.

Isabella groaned. 'I forgot to tell Old Man Wood about his cattle.'

Archie and Daisy looked confused. 'What about them?' Daisy said.

'When I ran off to find you, I went up to the corral in the ruin and counted the cows and the sheep – two were missing. I was going to say something but we got caught up in all ... this.'

'He'll be gutted if it's true,' Archie said. 'Especially his cows. But they can't exactly go anywhere—'

'Unless they're stuck in the mud,' Daisy said.

'Or they've been struck by lightning and gone A.W.O.L.'

'Or washed away in a mudslide.'

'We'd better check – it's the least we can do.'

'You two go,' Isabella said, a little too quickly, 'while I look after Old Man Wood.'

'Why?' Daisy snapped back. 'Are you afraid of the dark?'

'No, of course not,' she said. 'It's just that I've already been, and you haven't.' But Isabella wasn't telling the half of it. She'd been scared out of her wits by a strong sensation that invisible eyes had bored into her and somehow talked to her brain.

Archie grabbed her arm and pulled her up. 'Come on. We could do with some fresh air, and that includes you, Bells,' he said. 'We won't be long and besides, he needs quiet and rest.'

Old Man Wood's chest moved slightly and the briefest sigh passed his lips. The children looked at one another and smiled.

Archie studied Old Man Wood's unmoving face. 'By the looks of things, he'll be out for hours. With any luck, in the morning he'll be able to help us with the next riddle. And anyway,' he said, as another thought struck him, 'if any of the animals are stuck it'll take all three of us to pull them free,' and he smiled at his sisters, 'Superman-boy or not.'

---

ABOVE THEM, a large moon emerged low in the young night sky, chasing away the remnants of the storm. It cast a thin light over the sodden ground, the starlit sky mirrored in large, overflowing puddles. The children picked their way carefully up the hill towards the cattle, avoiding fallen trees and deeper pools, using torch and moonlight to guide them.

By the edge of the ruin they stopped and sat down on a low stone wall – part of the old escarpment – and looked out across the valley at the immense, grey, moving mass of water reflecting the crisp moonlight.

The whirl of helicopter blades in the distance cut across the silent night.

'I hope the Talbots are OK. Their house has probably been submerged,' Isabella said, brushing away a strand of hair with her gloved hand.

'What about old Granny Baker?' Daisy added. 'She's not moved in years. I wonder if anyone managed to get her onto a rooftop.'

'What, in her wheelchair?' Isabella scoffed. 'Poor thing, she's probably floating towards York with all the rest of them.'

'You are unbelievable sometimes,' Daisy remonstrated. 'There's suffering down there in the valley on a scale we simply can't appreciate. People are hurting, their loved ones are missing and, just because we survived and Sue and Gus survived, it doesn't make it OK. Think of those messages on your phone, Bells! Houses ruined, possessions gone. Death, everywhere. Don't you get it?'

'Of course I do,' she fired back.

They looked forlornly over the mass of water until Archie broke the silence. 'They're looking for us, you know. We're wanted like ... like murderers, like escaped convicts. Maybe we should turn ourselves in and tell the authorities everything we know—

'Seriously?' Daisy said, appalled.

'Yeah?! Why not?'

'Because they simply won't believe us, that's why.'

Isabella nodded. 'The mere fact that Sue was telling us to get on with finding these tablets and went so far as to stand in front of TV cameras and come up with an appalling anagram means that she has to be deadly serious. If she thought it was a better idea for us to come in, she'd have probably turned to the camera and said, simply, "Come on in, de Lowes, you have nothing to fear". The fact that she didn't, and then had to shroud it behind some dodgy word-play, means, in my humble opinion, that we have *everything* to fear.'

Isabella grabbed hold of Archie's hand and looked into his eyes, as though in reassurance. 'Archie, whatever Kemp may have told them, it's more than likely that we are presumed dead. I mean, just look at the destruction out there and the list of lost and missing people on the texts on my phone.' She swept her hand over the wreck of the Vale of York in front of them. 'Sue won't have told them anything. Solomon might have, but there's every chance he's been struck down with this disease. After all, he was bang in the middle of it. So the mere fact that they had to put out a wanted notice on national telly after a monumental announcement means that they're grasping at thin air.'

Archie wasn't so sure. 'Do you think they'll come after us?'

'I'm afraid I don't know what to think, bro,' Isabella replied. 'But don't you think they'll have other things to worry about? There must be over a million people displaced, or dead – and that alone is going to keep them pretty preoccupied.'

'Yeah, of course,' Archie agreed. 'But what if they've figured it out?'

They fell silent again, none of them volunteering a response.

Archie thought it might be the right time to bring up the extraordinary revelations of Old Man Wood. 'Where do you think Old Man Wood comes from? He ... he's ... he's ... do you think he's an alien?'

'Alien!' Daisy said. 'What deranged alien planet would have an old bodger like him? Planet "Apple"?'

Archie chuckled. 'So you think he's human; human-ish, like us?'

'Yeah, of course he is,' Daisy said. 'He's just a bit of a stir-fry, slightly bonkers, kinda random, super-old, wizardy-person.'

Archie and Isabella exchanged sideways looks.

'Then how do you explain how he fits in?' he said.

'Some deep, ancient magic he knows about – or it's a bloody good illusion,' Daisy replied. 'He's probably been practising since he was a little boy—'

Isabella guffawed. 'The only thing Old Man Wood practises is making apple juice and growing weird-shaped carrots,' she said. 'Of course he's an alien,' she said. 'As everybody knows, producing apple juice from sixteen varieties of apple tree is a well-known alien trait.' She smiled at her sarcasm. 'Seriously, if his bed and the rugs are not of this Earth, what other conclusion can there be?'

Daisy took off her pink glasses and rubbed her eyes. 'What if,' she started, 'an alien took over Old Man Wood's form—?'

Isabella spluttered.

'No, really. I mean, how else can we explain his weird songs and strange rugs with moving poems? He might be part of an advanced alien race from space—'

'Advanced?'

'OK, maybe not so advanced—'

'Daisy,' Isabella said, 'if you were an alien, would you really choose Old Man Wood as your representative on Earth over five billion other possible candidates?'

Daisy looked offended. 'Why not?' she said. 'He's the kindest, sweetest man in the universe and he wouldn't harm a fly. If you were an alien wouldn't you go for the kindest, nicest person?'

'I don't know,' she said, frowning. 'Probably not—'

'Well, I would. It's stereotypical nonsense stirred up by Hollywood that aliens are always bad, apart from, of course, ET.'

Isabella shook her head. 'There's a perfectly logical reason for this though: bad people are generally manipulative and don't care about anyone or anything aside from their own circle. Therefore, they crush good people and win—'

'No, they don't. Good people have a habit of coming out on top. That's why the human race has been so successful—'

'Nonsense,' Isabella said. 'Humans are only winners because their brains are more advanced than anything else's. We can think things through – unlike someone sitting pretty close to me. It doesn't make a spot of difference if people are nice or decent or—'

'Stop it, Bells,' Archie interjected. 'Daisy was only offering a theory on the back of inexplicable evidence. Have you got a better explanation?'

Isabella poked at the see-through hole in her hand, her hair over her face like a veil, and held her silence.

Archie rubbed a hair spike through the cloth of his beanie. 'What if he's actually telling the truth?' he said. 'What if he really has been around for all this time and he simply forgot everything – like he said?'

Isabella guffawed again.

'I mean, they used to live to a great age in the Bible didn't they – so maybe he's from Old Testament times and got stuck in a time-warp ...?'

'Oh, shut up, Archie,' the two girls said in unison.

'No, no,' he countered, refusing to give in. 'I'm betting Old Man Wood was the exact same person he is today when Dad was a little boy. And I bet you he's the same person in all those oil paintings we collected from around the house.'

'Thank you, Winkle—'

'I just don't believe he's capable of making up such a tall story.'

Archie paused, allowing the girls a moment to respond. They didn't. 'So, maybe he's a wizard. We've seen the moving bed panels, so we know he's full of magic tricks, and he's full of pain about forgetting his "life mission" which, as far as I can tell, involves saving this place called the Garden of Eden. And we all know Eden existed in biblical times, either as a real place or as part of the creation story.

'Maybe,' he continued, 'it's not only an allegory for early man, but a story about an entirely different planet? Maybe the whole story at the beginning of Genesis is a kind of code, a cleverly plotted fable full of clues, before it delves into the history of the early Israelites?'

Isabella flicked the hair off her face, her eyes glowing with wonder. 'I'm quite amazed,' she said, 'that you were actually paying attention to my lecture.'

Archie grinned. 'Yes, of course I was. The thing is, there are too many oddities. He talks to trees and grows star shaped carrots and is fixated by apples. And the tablet only came out after we all sang his weird song which blew the house apart and in so doing proves that the riddles on the rugs are true.'

The girls nodded in agreement.

'More importantly, he featured vividly in our dreams as a great, old, wise, mystical man who may well be part of time eternal and who is actually trying to help us.'

They sat silently on the cold stone. A chill grey wind blew gently across them, smelling of damp, matching the girls' mood. What he'd said rang true; they just didn't want to believe it.

'OK, Mr. Know-it-all,' Isabella said. 'Explain why it happens to be us and not anyone else.'

Archie shrugged. 'Perhaps it's because we just happen to be the poor sods who live in Eden Cottage, who he looks after,' he said. 'Think about it. The cottage is full of curiosities, like the rugs and your atrium-y place, Daisy—'

'But why can't he remember anything?' Isabella said bluntly. 'He's no help whatsoever. Every time we want to know something, he dithers, or goes off on one of his walks, or gets giddy, or drunk or ... or he dies.'

'Isabella!'

She put her hands in the air. 'What I'm trying to say is that he hasn't actually helped us with anything—'

'Don't you think there's a reason for that?' Archie said.

'What do you mean?'

'The reason he can't tell us is because he doesn't know. He sort of knew it once but doesn't anymore.' Archie removed his beanie and scratched first one, and then another hair spike. 'Anyway, if he is as old as he says he is, no wonder he's forgotten everything.'

'What are you talking about?'

Archie shook his head. 'Seriously, can you remember things from when you were three or four years old?'

Both girls shook their heads.

'Exactly! You can't. If Old Man Wood's as old as he says he is, it's going to be a pretty big struggle to get him to recall detail from hundreds, if not thousands, of years ago. When the tablet came out of the fire, he knew about it in a vague, roundabout way – like with the song – and he needed us to prompt him and vice versa—'

'Problem is, Winkle,' Daisy said, 'we still have to solve the riddles.'

Isabella nodded.

'And we're running out of time.'

Isabella looked sheepish. 'I know, and it's my fault,' she said quietly.

'That's irrelevant now,' Archie said, warmly. 'Deep down, Old Man Wood knows everything – we need to coax it out of him, show us how to do it.'

'Certainly won't be easy if he's dead,' Daisy added.

'Even if he's alive,' Isabella added, 'he's going to slow us down.'

Spitting rain now fell. They screwed up their faces as larger drops began to fall. The children stood up ready to move.

'Tomorrow we have to find the remaining tablets,' Archie continued, adjusting his beanie. 'They hold the key to finding this 'Eden' world – whatever it is – even if we don't know why it involves us.'

Daisy draped her arms around Isabella and Archie's shoulders. 'Don't get me wrong, guys, but let's be honest. Without Old Man Wood, I don't think we've got a chance of finding anything.'

# 83 PRESSURE MOUNTS

Commissioner Stone yawned. He stared at himself in the mirror, noting dark purple bags under his eyes – even darker than the last time he'd looked. As he dragged a razor across his face, even his stubble felt harder than usual.

Another fitful sleep – four hours tops. He needed twice that.

'Good morning, sir,' came a muffled cry from outside the hotel suite door. 'We have the deputy PM and the Head of the European Commission waiting for you.'

Stone nicked his narrow, bony chin and a bubble of blood dropped into the basin. He swore. 'Tell them I'll call back – give me ten minutes.' He cupped his hands and splashed cold water on his face, the shock running through his body. Exactly what he needed.

He towelled his face, hoping the cut would start to congeal, and applied a generous splash of cologne. The liquid stung. *But it was nothing*, he thought, *to what lay ahead.*

He opened the bathroom door, his dressing gown fastened around his midriff, to find his room packed with people. On seeing him, they all spoke simultaneously.

Stone stared open-mouthed.

'Sir, you need to see this,' said a large lady with short red hair, thrusting a file at him. He brushed it aside.

'We need to speak, urgently,' a small, squat, dark haired man with a bushy beard demanded.

Stone ignored all of them and made his way through the throng to the bed. 'What the hell is going on?' he yelled as he spotted Dickinson remonstrating with a man in a white coat. 'Dickinson,' he roared. 'What is the meaning of all this?'

The officer extracted himself. 'Bedlam, sir,' Dickinson said, calmly. 'I've kept them at bay for the last half an hour but couldn't keep them out. We've got trouble from just about every department in this country. Actually, more like the world.' He cocked his head. 'Best if we head back to the bathroom.'

Stone grabbed his trousers and looked around at faces he'd previously noted from the newspapers or television.

'Why in hell are they here?'

'All the Government facilities are overwhelmed, sir, or unobtainable. The PM has vanished.' He locked the door. A strange silence filled the cubicle.

Commissioner Stone dressed, then closed the lid and sat down on the toilet. Dickinson settled on the edge of the bath.

'The Ebora virus has spread overnight, massively,' Dickinson began. 'Apparently, you're the only person with any real authority – that's what they're saying – and this is according to the PM's office. Most of that lot arrived in the last hour – it's like a helicopter park out there. One hundred and five at the last count. Amazing no one's been killed if I'm honest.'

Stone swore under his breath. 'Right, here's the plan. Set up three secretaries with desks in the hall and we'll process this lot like a post office queue. While they're doing this, I want you to go and find Doctor Muller and my cousin, the headmaster, Solomon. Bring them in straightaway.'

Dickinson unlocked the door, fought his way across the room and stood up on the bed. 'Your attention!' he shouted. The noise level abated. 'Commissioner Stone will come out and address you if you give him some room. So please, let's have a little decency and order in here.'

He slipped off the bed and wormed his way out of the room.

Stone made his way over, clambered onto the bed and addressed the room.

'Thank you for barging your way in,' he said, his Yorkshire accent heavy with sarcasm. 'Having woken up barely fifteen minutes ago, I must inform you that I am not as yet up to speed with developments. As you can see, I am not even fully dressed.'

He smiled and scoured the room, reading their faces. *They're on edge, scared witless,* he thought, *the whole damn lot*. Time to be friendly, reassuring. If they want leadership, they're going to have to wait for it, not swamp me.

Dickinson poked his head around the door and nodded.

Stone cleared his throat. 'Now, please. In order that we can deal which each one of you, I would like you all to give your details to my secretaries who are waiting in the main hall. I will then be able to get round to seeing you as soon as I can, in an orderly, civilised manner.' He sounded like a customer relations officer.

'And if your query cannot be met by me, then you will be referred to the correct department—'

'But this is urgent, it cannot wait—' a suited gentleman with a foreign accent shouted.

Stone's pale blue eyes bored into him. 'I don't care who the hell you are, sir. Understand? We do this my way or I'll toss you back out into the flooding. Get it?'

The tall man's dark eyes met Stone's, before turning away.

Stone grabbed his jacket and made his way into the bathroom while the melee departed.

*In just five hours, the world has gone mad*, he thought. *And I'm the one expected to supply the answers.* He swore.

Stone adjusted his tie and studied his reflection in the mirror. *I don't even know the bleeding questions,* he thought, *let alone the answers.*

---

DR. MULLER MOVED his jaw from side to side and nestled his spectacles on the arch of his nose. 'We have a pandemic, as I suspected.'

'You're suggesting the disease is out of control?'

'I'm not suggesting, sir—'

Stone swallowed. 'Has anyone reported in – the geneticists, the scientific fraternity – has Dr. Harries called?'

The doctor shook his head. 'There's been too little time. The spread is unprecedented—'

'What of the boy? Has he been found?'

Dickinson stared at the floor. 'We've searched everywhere. Not a trace, I'm afraid, aside from the ash we found in the toilet.'

'Have forensics tested it, carbon tested or whatever they do?'

'It is just ash, sir.'

Stone thumped the desk. 'I don't care if it's shit! Is there any good news? What the hell are we going to tell everyone? They're clamouring for information. What do you suggest? Tell them we don't know a bloody thing? Tell them that our one hope – our one pinprick of light – has simply vanished into thin air? How's that going to sound?'

The others shifted nervously.

'Does the Prime Minister know?'

The doctor took a deep breath. 'Half of the cabinet have Ebora. The rest are involved with the containment process with the military chiefs and others.'

Stone gathered himself. 'Doctor, what other cheery news?' he began sarcastically. 'Has it spread out of the containment zone? Out of Yorkshire? Don't tell me it's reached Manchester and Leeds?'

The silence said it all.

'Oh, Christ,' Stone said. 'It has, hasn't it?'

Dr. Muller's face remained impassive. 'I'm not sure how to tell you this, but reports are coming in from across the pond. As people are waking up, they're reporting the same signs. And we know how fast it incubates—'

Stone eyed him curiously. 'The pond? What – the English Channel? It's reached Europe?!'

'Plenty of cases in Europe have also been reported, Commissioner. But I meant America. Across *that* pond – the Atlantic.'

Stone's eyes nearly popped out of his head. '*America*! *America ... are you bleedin' sure?!*'

Dickinson marched in. 'The US Secretary of State would like to speak to you.'

Stone uncurled his fingers, pulled out a handkerchief and dabbed his brow. 'Can't he speak to the PM – one of the Cabinet?'

'Here's the problem. The PM is indisposed—'

'Indisposed?'

'Yes, unavailable, sir—'

'Yes, I know what indisposed means.'

Dickinson whispered in his ear. 'According to the Prime Minister's wife, he has Ebora symptoms.'

'Christ alive!' roared Stone, kneading his temples. 'What next?'

'Well I was coming to it, but the Home Secretary instructed me to let you know that as of 07:00 hours this morning, you have been granted full powers to do whatever is necessary and with any means known to humankind to get to the bottom of this, sir. She's waiting for your call.' Dickinson raised his eyebrows. 'May I suggest you call her before you talk to our American cousins?'

---

SOLOMON BUSTLED IN, shutting the door firmly. He exhaled. 'Who on earth are all those people in the hall?'

Stone lifted his eyes at the sound of Solomon's voice and removed his glasses. 'A spokesman for the President of the European Union, the Secretaries of State for four of our near neighbours, the First Minister of Scotland, the head of OPEC, a couple of major global industrialists, a supermarket chief executive or two, the supreme commander of European forces, Field Marshall Allen and the Chairman of the London Stock Exchange. And that's just for starters. Even Lord "bleedin'" Sugar and Sir Richard "blast-off" Branson are apparently en-route. And then there's Bono on the phone every fifteen minutes. Anything else you want to know?'

Solomon wiped his brow. 'Good Lord. I'm sorry, cousin, I had no idea— '

Stone leaned back in his chair and clenched his hands. 'What did you discover at Upsall, headmaster?'

Solomon knew this wasn't an informal chat.

'Plenty – I'd like to think – though a little more time would be beneficial – if at all possible.'

Deep down, Solomon knew a lot more time was needed. He'd looked upon the stained glass windows in a totally new light and in it he'd recognised the de Lowe children, the flooding, the pestilence and he'd touched on something – a message maybe, that he felt the de Lowe's knew.

The question was, how much should he tell Stone on the basis that this "feeling" was entirely conjecture?

Stone raised his eyebrows and smiled back, but his eyes were hard. He'd recorded Solomon's movements on a hidden camera. He knew Solomon's every move. 'Tell me,' he said, 'what you discovered.'

Taking a deep breath, the Headmaster began. 'As you know there is an extensive library in the tower at Upsall. I tried to find some connection to this plague and, given the shortness of time and the large selection of tomes therein, I struggled to come up with anything of note. However, I was drawn to the stained glass that fronts the chapel. You know of it?'

Stone flicked his eyes at Dickinson. *So far, so good. Exactly right.* 'Yes, a murky thing—'

'It is a triptych,' he continued. 'Three stained glass paintings as one that show the Father, Son and Holy Ghost. On them are references to water, pestilence and one other curious-looking event. The first two are, of course, relevant to the situation we have at present.

Solomon wiped his lips. 'Before you jump to any conclusions this is standard imagery commonly found in medieval artworks. However, if you're searching for an easy connection, a soft target if you like, it's right there on the glass.'

'What about the de Lowes? Is the stained glass related to their ancestry in any way?'

Solomon nudged his glasses and moistened his lips. 'Almost certainly,' he began. 'I believe the family would have been involved in the building of the monastery and, thereafter, in the formation of the window. Records I unearthed tell of a family here under the name of "De L'eau" at Domesday. Then, I discovered one even earlier name.'

He paused and looked at his cousin. '"Aquataine".'

Solomon smiled in his head-masterly way as he noted the confused look on Stone's face. 'The link? Well, clearly it's in the commonality of the word for water: De l'eau is the French for "water" and, the Latin for "water" is Aqua – as in this name of, Aquataine—'

'Shouldn't it be Aquitaine,' Stone said, 'you know, with an "I"?'

'My thoughts exactly,' Solomon said. 'But I've seen the name spelt this way on several parchments, so I don't think so. Perhaps it is trying to tell us that there is some connection between the water of the surnames and the water that surrounds us.'

The Commissioner rubbed his face, touching the shaving cut on his chin. This was exactly what he'd hoped for, just the sort of information he needed. 'So, we have a flood that begins in Upsall. And we have a pandemic that begins in Upsall. We have a girl who predicts the flooding whose ancient family name means "water", and we have an eccentric old man — a hermit — who lives with them, who is of unknown origin. We have a stained glass window in Upsall with three figures surrounded by flood and disease. *Uncanny, isn't it?*' he said, cocking his head to the side. 'So what, or perhaps, *who* connects these things?'

Solomon smiled back his most practiced teacherly-smile. 'Am I getting a sniff, Charlie, that you're attempting to link the de Lowe family to the disaster?' He raised his eyebrows. 'If you are, then my question is this: what could those three possibly know? They're school children, how can they possibly be involved?'

Stone smirked. 'There! The conundrum, in a nutshell. You tell me?' he said, throwing the question back. 'What dirty little secrets might an old family like the de Lowes harbour, huh?'

The headmaster shrugged. *Whatever happens, don't rise to his taunts*, he told himself. 'I'm not sure I quite understand.'

Stone's manner changed. For a brief moment he trailed a finger over some papers and then looked up. 'By the way, I thought you might like to know that we've found two more of your pupils.'

'Goodness me, who?'

'A girl by the name of...' Stone looked over at Dickinson.

'Sue Lowden,' Dickinson added, reading a clipboard. 'And, a chap by the name of Gus Williams. He's in hospital.'

Solomon peered over his glasses. 'That's terrific news! Yes, they're mine alright. Lovely kids,' he said, enthusiastically. 'So much anguish and darkness and now two survivors. Amazing isn't it?'

Stone cocked his head. 'She was interviewed on the telly. Said she owed it all to Williams – saved her life by making a canopy over a small rowing boat. A right hero.'

'She's a fine student and he's a decent lad.'

Stone drummed his fingers on the desk. 'The thing is, when my man interviewed her she mentioned she was a very close friend of Isabella de Lowe,' he said, his voice barely above a whisper and soaked with irony. 'Now, isn't that a surprise?'

Solomon didn't like the way this was going. 'Not at all,' he said, trying hard not to show any feelings. 'Those two were almost inseparable.'

'Is that so?' Stone said, glaring at the headmaster. 'Apparently, Isabella de Lowe gave her the idea to find the boat. Now that's pretty sharp thinking, don't you reckon?'

'Yes, as I said, they're smart kids.'

'So smart that she even managed to tell her about it before the storm struck.'

Solomon's face dropped. 'She's no fool, Charlie. She's a brilliant student—'

'As you keep telling me. Let's go again. This is the same student who went out of her way to ask you to call off the match and your celebrations, because she knew that vast storm was heading your way? The same girl who made a "storm glass" to prove it.'

Solomon didn't know what to say. 'I've told you all I know,' he said examining his watch. 'I take it you're getting Sue and Gus transferred back here.'

'Yes, of course,' Stone said, rubbing his hands. 'For some proper interrogation.'

Solomon's eyes hardened. 'You'll do no such thing.'

Stone slammed his palms on the table. 'I'll do whatever it takes. And I don't care if it's the Pope, the President or Her Majesty, the Queen. My job is to find out what the hell is going on here—'

'But torture, Charlie? She's a child—'

'*I need her to talk,*' Stone said coldly, his eyes boring into Solomon. 'And I'm running out of time.'

'I will not let you do that with my pupils,' Solomon said standing up.

Stone grinned. '*Especially* with your pupils, it seems.'

'You always were hard, Charlie, and I don't begrudge you your situation, but these children are in my care. You'll interrogate her over my dead body—'

'That can easily be arranged,' Stone said. 'Sit down old man.' He nodded at Dickinson who pushed the Headmaster down. 'Count yourself lucky you're not going to feel a few volts up your arse as well. And one more thing, before I discuss our progress with the Deputy Prime Minister and the US Secretary of State. That boy, you know, the one found up a tree, burnt like he'd been sprayed by some flammable liquid. We found out his name. A bit of a tip off.'

Solomon tensed. 'Who was it?'

'Kemp. The boy's name was Kemp.'

'Kemp? My goodness—'

'Yeah. Ring any bells?'

'Yes, golly-gosh. Indeed. Well, well. How remarkable.'

'Isn't it? Funny how your pupils keep popping up from the dead in the most unexpected places.'

Solomon shook his head. *It was impossible. Kemp's coat had been found.* Besides, Kemp was renowned for being a poor swimmer.

'Do you want to know who Kemp called for?' Stone said. 'The one and only person he named – the person who he implied might have the tiniest inkling about what's going on out there?'

Stone stood up and moved in close to his older, portlier cousin and whispered in his ear. '*Archie de Lowe.*'

Solomon's jaw dropped.

Stone walked round to his chair behind the desk, sat down and leaned in. 'I thought you were here to help me headmaster, not get in my way. So, do you now understand why I need to know what these kids know? *Comprenez-vous?*'

'Yes, of course. Very well,' Solomon croaked. 'But let me do it, Charlie. All you'll do is scare them. They trust me, I promise you.' Solomon raised his eyebrows, his heart thumping wildly as he mopped his brow. 'Let *me* ask the questions, my way. I know how these children work. I'll get the results you need.'

Stone eyed him for a while. 'Fine,' he said. 'A helicopter with thermal imaging is on its way to their cottage as we speak. If any of the kids are there, we're going to pick them up. So, believe me, headmaster, if you don't get everything I need – full co-operation – I'm going to be hot on their heels and no-one's going to like it. I can absolutely assure you of that.'

# 84 AT THE RUIN

The courtyard by the ruin was surrounded by the last few remains of a wall which had, over time, disappeared under mud and moss and bushes and the odd straggly tree. As they approached, a thick silence filled the air, broken only by an occasional grunt or gloop of feet swilling about in the mud near the old corrugated iron-roofed corral.

On hearing footsteps, the livestock groaned and mooed and baaed before tentatively emerging from the tin shelter. For several minutes Isabella, Archie and Daisy counted and then re-counted the animals while speaking in soothing, calming voices.

Archie shook his head. 'Three out of nine cattle and one sheep missing. Bella, is that right? Have you guys checked right at the back?'

The children walked slowly into the body of the metal-roofed shelter, their boots sticking in the ankle-high sludge, slurping at every movement, making sure each step counted so they wouldn't slip or slide, occasionally leaning on animals that refused to budge.

Suddenly, a terrible whirring noise rattled overhead, making the structure rumble. The children automatically folded their torches in their tummies and held their breath, and Daisy plugged her ears too. In no time, the helicopter had passed.

'Let's go!' Isabella cried, turning. 'We can be saved!'

Archie grabbed her arm. '*From what, Bells? Saved from what, exactly?* It's just like Sue said. They're onto us – best if we stay hidden until we've found these tablets.'

Whirring sounds filled the night sky as the helicopter appeared to linger over the cottage before flying off.

By the time they'd waded out of the corral the helicopter was a distant speck in the night sky.

'Do you think they knew we were in there?' Daisy said rather breathlessly.

Archie shook his head. 'It shot up from under the cliff face, so I doubt it. Anyone find the missing animals?'

'No, and I counted twice,' Daisy said, her voice muffled as she held her nose.

Isabella groaned. 'That means that two more have gone since I was last here – although I could have been wrong with the sheep. They looked terrified enough at the time. Did you notice how their eyes are glazed over. Three look sick, diseased, even.'

The thought that somehow the disease had spread to the animals was not welcome.

'Let's go home,' said Daisy, shivering.

'Right away,' Isabella agreed, but almost immediately, a strange, slithering noise could be heard from nearby. She looked around, her eyes bulging, her face as white as snow.

Out on the grassed area of the old ruin they shone their torches over the rocks and bushes and, as they did, a cold chill crawled over the three children – as if they were being watched.

Daisy's teeth began to chatter. 'We need to get out of here,' she said, flinching. 'There's some weird thing hanging about 'round here.'

'What is it?' Archie asked.

'I dunno,' she whispered.

With their senses now on high alert, the children started through the rock-dotted courtyard towards the track, hairs erect on the backs of their necks. A low rumble rolled out through the evening sky. Collectively, their pace quickened.

Soon they were running.

Without knowing how it had happened, Isabella found herself sprinting, skimming over fallen trees and dashing past piles of rock, hurdling huge puddles and suddenly she was at the end of the field near the cottage.

She turned to check on the other two, but saw nothing except the night gloom. *Perhaps,* she thought, *they'd gone another way.* But where? They weren't that stupid. She smiled. *It's these feet again, making me run like the wind. They'll be back soon enough*, she thought, and she let herself in, conscious that she was barely out of breath.

---

DAISY AND ARCHIE watched Isabella accelerate away from them into the murky darkness. They stopped to catch their breath and looked at each other quizzically.

'When did Bells learn to run like that?' Daisy panted.

Archie shrugged. 'Don't know. But that was utterly ludicrous,' he said, leaning on a smooth, grey boulder. 'Actually, if you think about it, she tore around the property in about twenty minutes yesterday—'

'And she must have bounded up the two hundred and twenty-two stairs to escape the collapsing cave like some kind of super-leopard,' Daisy said.

'Did you notice another thing?' Archie said, as he rubbed his chin. 'She hates it up here. She was shaking like a jelly.'

'Yup. I noticed that too. Sweating too, and as white as a sheet.'

Archie peered into the gloom. 'Daisy, I think we owe it to Old Man Wood to find the other animals. What do you think?'

'We can try.'

'Cool. Let's check if there's anyone or anything about who shouldn't be.'

Daisy moved her head from side to side as though examining the area. 'Something's hanging about. I can't tell what it is though. Sounds a bit like a ... do you think it might be a bloke stealing them? Making creepy noises to scare us off?'

'I don't know,' he said quietly. 'But it isn't right. I think we should find out.'

'What if it's a lunatic, with a gun?'

Archie frowned. 'Then we should find out.'

'Can't we wait till morning?'

'We won't have time. Come on.'

Daisy eyed him curiously. 'Very well, brave brother – ye with the spiky hair. Lead on.'

Archie smiled. 'Do you want to go first?'

'Oh, get a move on,' she said, taking the lead and marching back the way they'd come. 'Let's see what's lurking yonder, huh?'

In silence, the only noise being the squelching and squishing of their boots in the mud, they doubled back to their original position and then headed further in towards the fallen-down castle keep, strewn with boulders.

'To be honest with you, Archie,' Daisy said as she went, 'I could hear something moving about after we'd counted the animals. But the thing is, it wasn't a sound I've ever heard before.'

Daisy picked her way through the old walls and slabs of stone of the ruin with ease, despite the thick cloud that obscured the moonbeams. The harder she concentrated the easier it became.

Soon she was manoeuvring as if it were light, skipping over rocks and jumping across gullies as though it were daytime, her senses on high alert.

Carefully, she crept up to a shaft of rock and leaned into it, remaining quite still, listening. There – again, the exact same noise as before; a curious mix of heavy, syrupy breathing, like large, wheezy bellows. 'You must be able to hear it now?' she whispered.

There was no response.

'Winkle?' she whispered into the cold night air. She turned. 'Archie! Where are you?'

It hadn't even registered that Archie wasn't right behind her. She retraced her steps, weaving back through the low ruins, her eyes following her footprints.

Without warning, her legs disappeared from under her and a heavy, hard object struck her sharply on the back of her head. Disorientated she fell forward, her arms pulled hard behind her back. She tried to wriggle free.

'REVEAL YOURSELF,' said a familiar voice.

'Let go of me!'

'Who are you?!' he hissed.

Daisy couldn't believe it. 'Your sister, you bloody numpty!'

'Whoever you are, YOU are not my sister.'

'Unfortunately, I am, Archie, you stupid, spiky, knob-end.'

There was a pause while Archie, baffled by the response, wondered what to do next.

'OK! What's my nickname?'

'Winkle. I alone call you Winkle. I don't know why, but it just suited you when you were little and it stuck because it really, really irritated the hell out of you.'

Archie loosened his grip. "Winkle" was her private name for him. Slowly he turned her round to face him, not loosening his grip on her too much.

'What the hell was that all about—?'

'Your ... your eyes, Daise!' he said, 'what's happened to your eyes? Are you ... alright?'

Daisy pushed him away. 'What *are* you talking about, there's nothing wrong with my eyes,' she said crossly, 'apart from being red, like traffic lights on stop.'

She rubbed her skull, more concerned with the blow to the back of her head. 'That really hurt, Archie – what's up with you?'

'No seriously, Daisy. You're lucky I didn't smack you harder. Look, are you sure you're alright? I mean ... look, I don't know how to tell you this but they're glowing, like dishes. It's like you're an alien! Your eyes are burning like torches. I thought YOU were the monster.'

A chilly wind blew over them. They shivered.

'I'm really sorry, Daisy. I didn't realise—'

Daisy hoped Archie couldn't see her tears. 'I don't know what's happening to me, Arch,' she whispered. 'I've got these weirdo eyes which kind of go into overdrive when I concentrate. You won't believe what I can see – things in incredible detail – like individual particles in the storm glass – or objects miles away, or seeing stuff in the dark. And every time I use them, it gets stronger and I discover more. It's like a game, going up levels all the time.'

She wiped her cheek and continued. 'Remember when we came up here and looked out over the flooding? I got a bit caught up wondering if I could actually see people sitting on their rooftops waiting for help. Well, I could! I really could see water flowing through the streets. And running up here tonight – it was as clear as it would be on a sunny day, apart from ... well, it wasn't, was it?'

Archie couldn't think of anything to say.

'Archie, it's not the only thing; I can hear amazing stuff, too. When the rain stopped at home, all you lot could hear was the sudden quiet but I heard drips of water splashing directly under the house.'

'So, what do you think it is?'

Daisy rubbed her eyes. 'If I'm right, I think it's got something to do with the water in the third poem. The "clear" and "pure" bit.'

Archie repeated as much as he could remember.

'The third you search is under your nose.
'It's clear, pure and warm (I think).
'In order to ... something or other
'You need to send ... hmm, can't quite remember.'

'At first I thought it was to do with bogeys – you know, being underneath your nose. You think there's a stream under the house?'

Archie looked at her with renewed wonder and, instinctively, even though Daisy's eyes were still glowing, but not as brightly, he moved in and hugged her.

'Does it hurt?' he asked, his voice hushed.

'What? My head?'

'No, you daft cow. Your eyes.'

Daisy shook her head. 'No. Just a bit tingly, that's all.'

They both sat quietly. 'Can I ask,' Archie said cautiously, 'what was it *really* like in this atrium place you went to? Did you use your mega-eyes in there? Did you hear anything else apart from a great blood-curdling scream? And did you really get out just by looking at a door—?'

'Simmer down, Winkle,' she whispered. 'The atrium was terrifying ... it's hard to remember anything in detail. I was lucky—'

Suddenly, a snorting sound, like a wave blasting through a blow-hole, burst out from the other side of the rock.

Archie crouched down.

Hooves clattered on the flattened rocks nearby and pounded the wet ground. Cattle and sheep ran quickly. A crisp bark, cracked the air, slicing through the silence followed by a low, hissing sound.

'What the—'

Daisy pushed a finger over his lips. She could hear his heart thumping.

'What is it?' Archie whispered, as they slipped down the cold slab of rock.

'Sshh. Let me listen.'

Shortly, another strange bark was followed by a hiss, this time much closer.

'It isn't a fox, or any kind of dog,' Daisy said, under her breath, her brow furrowed in concentration. 'It definitely isn't a bird call, or a ferret and it's not a cow, or a goat, or anything from the deer family. I don't think it's a cat – you know, like a lion or leopard or panther. It's certainly not a chicken, or a sheep, or any of the rodent family. It's not a hyena because they laugh ... and I doubt it's a crocodile, because I've never heard one, and they go "snap", but it could be a bison or rhino from Africa, so —'

'Daisy!' Archie hissed, 'stop! You don't have to go through the entire animal kingdom.'

'Oh. Sorry,' she said.

'So, what is it?'

'I don't know! But it's definitely not an elephant or a bear or a llama ...'

Archie glared at her.

For a few moments they sat stone-still behind the large, weathered slab of rock. Smeared across the dark sky ran the wavy form of a rain cloud.

'What are we going to do?' Daisy whispered, trying not to appear too cowardly. 'We can't stay here shivering all night only to get eaten.'

Archie nodded. 'Any ideas?'

'How should I know? What do *you* think we should do?'

'*I don't know*.'

'Well, it was your idea!'

'Sshhhhh,' Archie squealed, 'it's really close!'

The slither of something snake-like moved just out of eye-shot. The twins hugged the rock. Then it grunted loudly, and barked.

Daisy squirmed and her ears filled with pain. Tears flowed down her cheeks. She smothered her ears.

'Daisy!' Archie said. 'What is it?'

'A noise! Incredibly high-pitched. It's killing me.'

For some strange reason he couldn't quite understand, Archie stood up, ricked his neck from side to side and jumped out onto the grass to the side of the rock ready to face whatever it was head on.

'... NO!' Daisy cried.

But almost immediately the farm bell rang, its toll echoing eerily up the hillside.

In a flash and a slither, whatever had been there, vanished.

Daisy shook her head and stepped out to join Archie. The painful shrilling noise had evaporated, like the strange beast.

Holding their breath, the twins moved around to the other side of the rock. Nothing. Just the same, curious, track-marks.

They listened and waited, exchanging looks, wondering if it was safe to run for their lives. With Daisy's eyes on full beam, they simultaneously sprang off and sprinted through the mud and over branches and rocks towards the track.

As they stopped to catch their breath by the old rutted path, a voice came out of the dark below.

Instinctively they crouched down.

'Yoo-hoo!'

'Who ... who's there?' Daisy called out.

'Only me!'

Archie and Daisy exhaled audibly and smiled.

'What are you doing up here, Mrs P, scaring us to death?'

'Well, little ones, I came to find you. And I thought I might see a heli-doctor, rescuing all them poor folk and that. But I might ask you the same; what you doing, you two, out here in the dark at this time?'

Archie caught Daisy's now back-to-normal eyes. 'We were looking for, er, for ... for Blabisterberry Jelly,' he said, at which they both burst out laughing.

'For, eh ... what?!' Mrs. Pye shrieked, her voice sounding a little more shrill than normal. 'Jelly? At this time of night?'

'No, Mrs P – it's a kind of joke,' Archie said. 'It's something we've got to find – apparently. But don't worry – it's not important right now.

'Did you find any "helidoctors"?' Daisy asked.

'I didn't, no. Got a little waylaid I'm afraid to say. But I heard one right bang overhead while I was lying in me bath. Stayed there some time, too, till me water went all chilly and I ended up with granny-fingers.'

For the rest of the walk they moved in silence, their boots squelching in the mud. When they arrived near the cottage, Mrs. Pye coughed, very lightly, but just enough to send a shiver down their spines.

Mrs. Pye, aware that she was being looked at, started coughing more until Archie felt compelled to give her a pat on her back.

Could Mrs. Pye's cough be linked with the bark they'd heard at the ruin? No, not Mrs. Pye.

Perhaps all the strange events of the past day had simply stretched his mind so that now he was over-alert to every squeak, splutter and cough.

# 85 CAIN AND KEMP

For Kemp, the euphoria of being alive, and not in hospital, remained. No interrogations by that dreadful man, Stone; no being stuffed full of tubes and wires; no nurses covered in protective clothing padding and prodding him and filling him with disgusting medicines or sharp needles. No worries about anything.

Much to his astonishment, Cain had delivered on all his promises – food coming out of his ears, a palace to run about in, servants at his disposal, and jewels and treasure everywhere. The place was smothered in riches and Kemp was dazzled by it all.

Cain's demands on him were minimal. Schmerger, the strange, bearded, unsmiling servant, had given him a salve for his burns which healed in record time and Kemp soon felt better than he had for an awfully long time.

For the moment at least, Cain's mood bordered on delirious. He sang and laughed and showed Kemp around the palace, telling stories – all of which sounded ludicrous – and repeatedly told Kemp that it was all his. Not only that, but it was his to do with as he wished.

His to enjoy, his to destroy – if he so wished.

Overshadowing this, Kemp wondered whether Cain would deliver his mother as he had sworn he would.

Festering at the back of his mind, he wondered if Cain had fabricated the truth about his mother. After all, evidence suggested that she had died a long time ago.

It didn't help that he didn't entirely trust Cain. Cain was dangerous, he sensed, and Kemp couldn't help asking himself why Cain wanted him so badly? *What, exactly, was the ghost's grand plan?* he thought.

Cain hadn't avoided the subject, since Kemp hadn't asked, but Cain's demeanour compelled him to require some answers.

That time came at supper.

Kemp grabbed a spoon and helped himself to a bowl of beef stew. He couldn't remember eating anything quite so tasty in years. Cain's overcoat floated across and parked up next to him.

'Why?' Kemp asked.

'Why, *what*, boy?'

'Why do you need me?' Kemp asked bluntly. 'What's this Prophecy of Eden thing-a-me-jig you told me and Arch about? What's it got to do with you?'

'I wondered when you'd ask,' the gap between Cain's hat and collar said. 'The universe is exceedingly old, boy. Every now and then there's a shift, a repositioning in how it aligns itself.' He appeared to sniff the air. 'It is doing so right at this precise moment and your friends the de Lowes, by way of a long, ancient and rather tedious selection process, have received dreams in which they have been given instructions on how to open the Garden of Eden. If you must, it is the ultimate test for your entire species. If they fail, then mankind will be seen to have failed and life on Earth will be erased. Earth will begin afresh, with different, new beings.'

Kemp looked incredulous. 'So, Archie has to save the world. Ha-ha, that is bloody hilarious.'

He grabbed a chicken leg and licked it before biting deep into the flesh. 'Fat chance he's got. In any case,' he said with his mouth full again, 'it doesn't make sense. Humans are doing alright, aren't they? We're civilised an' all that – we've got TV and the internet, satellites, fast-food, nuclear stuff and massive football stadiums. What's not to have?'

The ghost sighed. 'Running a planet is far more than those things, my dear fellow. I know it'll be difficult, but you're going to have to stop thinking like a ridiculous Earth human. There's really no use for it here. You see, the energy of the universe is made by zillions of things and, when something happens in one area of the universe, it almost certainly has a knock-on effect elsewhere. Humans were given a time in charge but, in all honesty, they haven't really cared for the others particularly well, have they? I've heard that it's gone a little lop-sided.'

'Others? Lop-sided? *What others?*'

Cain coughed gently. 'The other animals, plants, soils and living things that they were meant to care for. All organisms have a purpose and neglecting one puts tremendous pressure on the others. The knock-on effect, if you will.'

Kemp sneered, but nodded almost knowingly.

Cain interpreted this as a green light to continue. 'If your friends succeed then there is hope for the planet that the present incumbents might turn it around, though it is highly unlikely. If not, then new inhabitants will be made in the Garden of Eden and filtered in to what will essentially be a brand new Earth. With any luck, we should be able to control that filter.'

Kemp crammed a parcel of cheese wrapped in bacon into his mouth and chewed it thoughtfully. 'So what you're saying is that humans have massively screwed it up, right?'

'The long and the short of it is this: if mankind hasn't evolved and matured enough to survive a few simple tasks, then it simply doesn't deserve stewardship of the blue planet – Earth. Your type of mankind will come to an end. Another will begin. It's happened before and it will happen again.'

'Blimey. And everything you've just said,' Kemp said in between wiping his mouth on his sleeve, 'was given in dreams to those de Lowes.'

'Indeed. This shift in the universe sparked a series of dreams sent out by the dreamspinners. That's the name for the ugly spidery things we travel through.'

'I wondered how they fitted in.'

'They are the most ancient of all creatures that belong to the universe – if they are creatures.'

'Those things with the electricity-filled abdomens belong to the universe?'

'Absolutely.'

Kemp cupped the back of his head in his hands and leaned back. 'You know what, Cain, I think that is the biggest loads of bollocks I've ever heard.'

Cain eyed him curiously. 'I don't understand.'

'What I mean,' Kemp said, 'is that it doesn't make any sense.'

'It makes perfect sense,' Cain said. 'Nothing could be clearer.'

Kemp scrunched his face up. 'You're saying that Archie, Isabella and Daisy have been chosen to survive some massive challenges and if they don't, several billions of humans and everything else on the planet will get trashed.'

Cain sounded undeterred. 'Some trees will probably survive and much of the sea-life made it through last time. But yes, everything else will be destroyed.'

Kemp helped himself to a large slice of chocolate cake. 'It's not very fair, is it?' he said. 'I mean, what kind of universe comes up with stupid stuff like that? For school kids?' A drizzle of chocolate slipped out from between his large, plump lips. 'Anyway, you don't reckon they'll do it, do you?'

'That, my boy, is why I wanted to save you. The challenges were designed for strong, wise men, versed in nature and in magic and in war. You're right, they were never designed for children.'

'But, you didn't want me, you wanted Archie,' Kemp said, his voice hardening.

'Of course. But Archie's folly is your opportunity,' Cain replied, his deep voice smooth and syrupy. 'Archie is an Heir of Eden who has been given a strong ancient gift – why shouldn't I have desired a union with him?'

Kemp felt slighted, but it was true. 'What are these gift things that make them so important, then?'

'Physical attributes mainly,' Cain said, 'extended uses of the senses; heightened vision, hearing, smell and increased strength – that sort of thing. Nothing too dramatic.'

'Wow. Cool,' Kemp said thickly. 'And this Garden of Eden – what's that all about? Why does it have to be opened? Why doesn't everything stay the same?'

'You really are full of questions. Perhaps it is all this food.' Cain smiled. 'The answer, my boy, is many-fold. You see, the Garden of Eden is where new species were created and developed. If a species proved successful it was placed upon a planet to develop and evolve and primarily have some sort of useful function.'

Cain paused and wondered how much he should tell. 'For a long while, the Garden was closed. You see, there was a ... how should I put it ... a disagreement about how it functioned, about the legitimacy of what was being created.'

'Sounds like a right load of tosh.'

'Indeed,' Cain said, 'whatever tosh means. But it was certainly complicated.'

Kemp bit into an apple. 'But if the Garden of Eden is miraculously opened, won't everyone survive?'

Cain chuckled throatily. 'The chances of Eden opening is so utterly remote that it is almost not worth considering, but I have in place my own safety net of sorts, just in case.

'You see, after the flooding, comes pestilence, which is out there causing bedlam. All the clues are written down at the beginning of those old historical books you Earth humans seem to get so much pleasure from. Anyway, I thought I might speed the process up.'

'Don't tell me,' Kemp said, 'you've given the disease to the de Lowes?'

Cain suddenly realised the boy was smarter than he looked. 'Not a bad idea, but unfortunately, the Heirs are protected. Now, here's a clue. Those ugly dreamspinners came to me with the news that there are no more dream powders remaining from their main stores. So, in return for a bit of help from them, I have allowed them to create some dream powders here, subject to a few modifications. Do you understand?'

Kemp rubbed his greasy chin thoughtfully. 'Yeah, I think so.'

'Very well. Try again.'

'OK,' Kemp grinned and rubbed his chin. 'How about you've given the disease to all the world leaders through your dreamspinner mates, and as they get ill, each country blames it on the other and then they blow the shit out of each other.'

'Bravo. Another fine suggestion, but no, I'll tell you. All I've done, my friend, is slip a little of the disease into my brand new store of dream powders.'

Kemp smiled. 'And these dreamspinners dish out dreams every night – around the world?'

'Precisely.'

Kemp wiped his mouth with his sleeve. 'You're spreading this disease as people sleep. That, my ghostly buddy, is blooming genius.'

Cain was delighted. 'You see, I'm not just a pretty face.'

Kemp banged the table as he laughed. 'They won't know what's hit them. And so fast and un-warned and utterly brilliant – they'll never work it out because no one really knows how dreams work, right?'

'Absolutely. My thoughts too,' Cain said. 'Superb little plan, isn't it?'

However, a thought struck Kemp and his face darkened. 'You promised to bring my mother here, didn't you? That was our deal.'

'And I will,' the ghost said, purring. 'I'm glad you mentioned this because I wanted to talk to you about your mother. It's important that our relationship is based on the truth. Don't you think?'

'Truth?' Kemp said nervously, 'What is it – is she dead? She is, isn't she?'

Cain remained silent.

'Or ... she's in a mad-house or something?' Kemp's voice creaked.

*Closer than you think*, Cain thought. 'Do you know how your parents died?'

Kemp nodded. 'Car crash, in the hills.'

'Correct. Before I returned you to Earth, I met up with your father's ghost.'

Kemp looked astonished. 'You can do that?'

'Why, of course. After all, I too am a kind of spirit, though I have considerably more substance than the truly dead. Spirits are easy to find if you know how, but frightfully airy and irritable. Your father told me about your mother, about the accident when you were just a babe. He told me many things.' His voice dropped. 'But the most fascinating thing is that your mother never died. She was found. She survived.'

Kemp's brain slowed to a halt as he computed Cain's story. The apple in his hand dropped to the floor.

'She lives, truly. Your mother is as alive as the next person.'

Kemp swallowed. 'You're having me on,' he said very quietly.

The ghost made a sound as if it were sucking in a mouthful of air. 'No, boy.' The ghost removed the hat and placed it on the table.

Kemp shook his head. 'I thought you'd bring her to me as, you know, as a ghost, a spirit or something.'

'My thoughts, exactly. I too am most surprised by this turn of events—'

Kemp eyed the top of the coat curiously. 'You're sure this isn't a joke, right?'

'I swear, on my death, that I am telling you the truth. However, the news isn't as good as you might wish. You must be prepared that, if I bring her to you, she will reject you. There is a strong chance that she will not want to know you.'

Kemp looked confused. 'That's not true, Cain. Of course she would. I'm her son.'

'I understand how you feel,' Cain said, sighing. 'However, she remembers nothing of you. She suffered damage to the brain—'

'Brain damage?' Kemp looked wounded. 'But mothers always, always know their children,' Kemp said defensively, 'no matter what. She'd know me, I'm sure of it. What's her name?'

Cain's overcoat stood up so that he was standing in front of the boy. 'I didn't think you'd believe me, but I do not lie. And the terrible part of this is that there is a strong likelihood that you too will reject the woman.'

'As if I would do such a thing,' Kemp stormed. 'Never! Who is she?'

'Very well,' Cain said. 'But don't tell me I didn't warn you.'

Kemp levelled with the ghost. 'Tell me who she is.'

'Your mother,' Cain said slowly, 'is the exact same woman who looks after the de Lowe children—'

Kemp's eyes hardened as he worked out exactly who the ghost was talking about. Then he burst out laughing. 'You're having me on, aren't you? Mrs. Pye ... Mrs. bleeding Pye? Is that the best you can do? Mrs. Pye, that big, ugly, old hag.' Kemp slapped his thighs and bent over double, great guffaws spilling out of him. After a while, he straightened and then sat down. Only now, his eyes watered.

The overcoat sat down beside him. 'I told you this wouldn't be easy. Often, young man, things are best left exactly as they are.'

Kemp's mood changed fast. In no time his face raged with anger. 'Listen here, Cain,' he roared, 'I'm telling you, Mrs. Pye is NOT and *cannot be* my mother. Do you understand?' Kemp stood up, tears flowing. 'She can't be. It's impossible.'

Cain hovered next to him and whispered in his ear, 'Thing is, boy, it is the truth. She really is.'

# 86 HAVILARIAN TOADSTOOL POWDER

Isabella let herself in, stripped off her waterproofs and entered the kitchen. She added a couple of logs to the belly of the stove, grabbed a clean tea towel and dried herself off.

She popped the kettle on the range and, while she waited for it to boil, she shook as she remembered the sensation that had entered her mind and filled her with dread. *Those eyes,* she thought, *and that noise,* which had washed through her head like a mass of incomprehensible, jumbled words and sentences.

She poured the boiling water. A cup of tea for herself and an apple tea for Old Man Wood, in case he was feeling better.

On the table were two candles and she searched around for a match. She looked in all the obvious places but either they'd run out or they'd been taken next door. She felt heat building in the tips of her fingers and, thinking of a flame, she clicked the end of her thumb and forefinger. To her amazement, a tiny spark flew out. She laughed, nervously, and inspected the end of her thumb and her digit. *Static?*

She tried again and this time another spark fizzed out, fading in the air. *But it doesn't make sense.* Something had to make it spark. She clicked her fingers again and this time a tiny flame shot out of the end of her thumb. Isabella didn't know whether to jump for joy or scream in terror.

But the strange thing was that it didn't hurt and, if anything, felt entirely natural. She sat down and studied her fingers in more detail, a surge of euphoria rushing through her. She placed a flame below her fingers, but they didn't discolour or burn or singe. It was as if her hands had become impervious to heat and pain.

Isabella lit the candles, knocked on Old Man Wood's door and entered, placing the candles on the tables. Then, she went back for the tea, which she set beside the still outline of the old man lying in his bed.

'We heard noises at the ruin!' she said softly as she busied herself about the room. 'I left Daisy and Archie out there,' she said, leaning briefly over him, his face obscured by the dim light and the folds of a blanket. 'I'm afraid there's bad news with the cattle: three cows missing and one sheep. Too dark to tell which ones though.'

She lit another candle on his table then returned and jumped up onto the bed, which wobbled and creaked a little. Then she lay back on the soft downy pillows at the side of the old man.

Old Man Wood lay perfectly still and she very carefully reached over and read his pulse. She squinted. Faint, but definitely something. She propped herself up and turned her gaze towards the wooden panels at the foot of the bed.

'You'd have seen us, if you'd watched the panels,' she said.

No response at all.

Isabella sighed, 'There's some tea for you – apple tea, to make you strong,' she said, remembering his tea-mantra.

As she sipped hers, she turned her attention to the images on the wooden panels.

There was Archie, crouching down as if waiting for something. In Daisy's panel she could make out a running human figure, similar to her sister, but with glowing eyes, like car headlamps.

Why was Daisy's panel doing strange things?

A strange slurping sound emanated from Old Man Wood. 'I think her panel's gone a bit funny, Old Man Wood,' she said, nudging his arm. 'There's tea on your bedside table,' she repeated, 'if you'd like it.'

Suddenly Archie attacked the figure with the bright eyes and threw it violently to the ground.

Isabella sat bolt upright. 'Archie's beating it up! He's pinning it down!' she cried, leaning towards the panels. 'Go Archie! No one messes with Superman-boy!'

She chuckled at the thought, and stared at Daisy's panel. 'Oh! Hang on!'

*Archie's beating Daisy up?* she thought. *Are they messing about?* 'Hey, Old Man Wood, did you see what led up to this?'

For a moment she wondered if she should dash up there and sort them out but, as she viewed, they seemed to slump down behind a rock, chatting.

She checked her watch. Typically, delicious smells would drift out of the kitchen at this time, at which point Old Man Wood would nearly always comment on what it might be and rub his tummy in anticipation. But there were no fabulous smells and still he didn't stir a muscle. 'I wonder where Mrs. Pye is?' she said. 'I'm starving.'

Isabella leant over to his side of the bed and called out, sweetly, 'Old Man Wood?'

No reaction.

'Can I get you anything?'

His face, in the dim candlelight, looked milky-white and a terrible fear swept through her that he might have passed away while she was talking to him.

She slid off, grabbed a candle and walked around the large bed to the other side and set it down on the bedside table. Old Man Wood's face was mostly hidden by the folds of a thick pillow and his body was covered by a duvet. She perched on the edge of the bed and gently levered the pillow out of the way.

Isabella's heart began to race. Something about him didn't look right.

'Come on, Old Man Wood, wakey-wakey,' she teased. Nothing, again. A terrible panic began building in her mind. 'Please. Wake up. Please.'

She moved in to inspect his face, lifting the candle up to offer more light.

She cupped a hand over her mouth as her stomach lurched. 'OH-MY-GOD!' she said standing up quickly but with the presence of mind to put the candle down first.

Old Man Wood lay motionless, his eyes shut, his skin as white as snow. Dotted over his face in tiny clusters were tiny white toadstools which she traced all the way down his neck.

She folded back the duvet and unbuttoned the top three of his shirt buttons. As she folded back the lapels, she stepped back from the bed stunned.

Before she could help herself, she retched.

*WHAT ARE THEY?*

In the candlelight tiny, pulsing, toadstools poked out of his chest like minute pins holding weenie umbrellas.

Instinctively, Isabella reached for his wrist and held it, counting. A murmur, the faintest, faintest dimmest of beats, that's all.

*Get an ambulance. No, it won't get here – the air ambulance – they're rescuing people from the flooding. What about phoning the hospital, they'd know what to do?*

She clenched her fist. With no power, they had nothing. No phone, no communication.

*In any case*, she thought, *the hospital probably didn't even exist anymore.*

*COME ON. Think! THINK!*

She slapped her forehead as if it might trigger an idea; there must be some way of making him better! Resplendix Mix! Old Man Wood's potion he'd used on them. *But where was it?*

She tore round the room searching for the strange bottle without a lid.

She rummaged through his coat and trouser pockets, through his chest of drawers and then ran downstairs and scoured the sitting room.

She returned up the stairs, entered Old Man Wood's room and leaned against the wall. Reality was hitting her hard. *We're lost if he doesn't survive*, she thought.

Then, without knowing why, she moved towards him and placed a hand on his brow. Pinpricks of heat, like mini, red-hot needles emanated from the toadstools. She kept her hand there, her palms crossed on his forehead.

Now the temperature built. Her hands were tingling, sucking out heat. The longer she did it the more disgusted and furious she became until a rage began to bubble up inside. And the angrier she became, the hotter the heat pouring into her hands. Soon the heat was almost too much to bear.

She removed her hands and quickly turned down the duvet covering his body. Suddenly a large, vile green toadstool the size of a hammer sprouted out of his belly and sliced through his shirt. Isabella squealed.

She rocked backwards, holding her mouth. '*NO*!' she cried. '*NO*!'

Now that his shirt had slipped off his chest, she could see hundreds of multi-coloured fungi littering his body, like bits of confetti, *eating* him.

Old Man Wood's last words, she realised, weren't about the poison *in the water* – they were concerning the poison *he'd taken*.

Isabella backed away towards the door. *Someone, give me the strength to do something. Anything.*

She stared and the longer she did the more frustrated and cross she became. Fury filled her growing like a furnace.

Another large, green and red toadstool sliced out of his chest, the noise like tearing metal foil.

Without warning, her whole body burned as though on fire. The surge consumed her, the heat inside her body roaring until her blood boiled and her temples throbbed as if her arteries might burst.

Her eyes blazed as if they were made of lava. She clenched her teeth, but the intensity deepened, hotter, faster – until her entire body was set to explode.

She extended her hands and pointed them at the two main, menacing toadstools, thriving, it seemed, with each flashing pulse, growing taller and fatter.

A strand of hair blew over her face as a wind picked up around her. From her hands an orangey-pink mist radiated, wrapping Old Man Wood in a wispy pink cocoon. Soon, it looked as though he was surrounded by fire.

Isabella let out a long piercing cry of anger and pain.

A second later, the body of Old Man Wood rose above the bed, the pink glow encircling and rotating like candy floss.

A high-pitched whirring noise built up and up until the intensity was almost unbearable, the cocoon swirling faster and faster.

The toadstools on the old man's body began to quiver, like birthday candles on a bowl of jelly.

All of a sudden a toadstool exploded off Old Man Wood's body, smashing into the ceiling. Then another – shattering the mirror – and another through the windows.

Toadstools from every part of his body rapidly discharged, peppering the walls, ceiling and bed. The noise was like a gun fight, fires starting on the wooden panelling surrounding the room.

All the while Isabella stood still, her hands extended, her concentration absolute as the swirling glow over Old Man Wood forced the toadstools out.

Soon, her energy wavered and the cocoon around the old man weakened. Only one remained. The large, lime green toadstool on his chest.

Exhausted, her strength gone, her body spent, Isabella had nothing more to give. She dropped her hands. The pink energy fizzling away.

Dizzy, her head as heavy as lead, Isabella stumbled into the wall and fell to her knees.

'I can't,' she cried. 'I'm so, so sorry, Old Man Wood ... I'm so terribly sorry.'

And she collapsed on to the floor.

# 87 THE RING OF BABYLON

Gaia reached out a long, silvery claw. So, Asgard had sided with Cain and the news coming back through the ether painted a bleak picture.

Cain had added the plague to their dream powders to make lethal dreams. The spread was unimagined, unaccountable, swift and devastating. *It was the perfect mass-murder weapon.*

'How many dreamspinners are using Cain's spider web powders?'

'Hundreds,' a smaller dreamspinner vibrated, 'maybe thousands. More go every minute.'

'And each one uses his powder?' She already knew the answer.

*I need Genesis,* she thought. *She'll know what to do.*

She reached out for the vibration of the old dreamspinner, channelling her energy into the universe. A wavy, strange vibration tickle returned – slight and distant.

In a flash, Gaia inverted through the electric middle of her body, flashing through the universe to the spot where she desperately hoped Genesis would be.

She arrived moments later in a cave. A cave as tall as a mountain and half as wide. Was there such a place on Earth, or Havilah?

Gaia's opaque, silvery legs walked on the air towards the middle as though on an invisible grid.

*Genesis would not be invisible here,* Gaia thought, and she altered herself so she might also be seen. By doing so, she would see any dreamspinners that had themselves turned visible.

As she suspected, Genesis was waiting for her. 'You have come. Good. At least there is one of the ancient order still in possession of their faculties.'

Gaia had almost forgotten what a large, intimidating dreamspinner Genesis could be. Around her neck, and down the length of her shimmering silvery body, grey hoops gave her a formidable appearance. And far from the broken creature that had departed to die after giving the boy his Gifts, she looked menacing.

Her three black eyes pierced into Gaia. 'You know?'

'I do, mother. Our order, our traditions, are being dismantled, our purpose lost, dreamspinners corrupted. Asgard has aligned with Cain. Disease spreads from powders made from the spider webs in Havilah. As the sun goes down while Earth rotates, he spreads dreams of fear and failure. Death extends across the planet.'

Genesis tilted her head. 'Cain should *never* be trusted. Asgard has showed him our secret and he has grasped it in his ghostly hands. Dreamspinners have been led to believe that the Heirs of Eden cannot open the Garden of Eden, so Asgard makes it his business to determine our future. He sees no hope in the Heirs of Eden.'

Genesis raised herself up. 'But the Heirs have *every* chance. That is why the universe selected them. Furthermore, there are ancient mysticisms that Asgard does not know.'

The great dreamspinner's posture fell a little and her vibrations quietened. 'I should have shared these with you many suns and moons ago, Gaia. And when I do, I will make a calling to stop this madness.'

'A calling, mother?'

'Yes. You will see. I alone know of it. There is a power to recall dreamspinners from every corner of the universe. But first, let me inform you of the ancient ways, for my time is not long now, and you, Gaia, will take my place. One mother of the universe to another.'

Genesis rose up again. 'The prophecy is far from failing. Even now, as the old man suffers from Cain's poison, there is hope. For he is protected by a charm the Heirs possess and which Cain long ago abandoned. It is the magic of love. Besides, these Heirs are not so weak or so frail as Asgard imagines, nor are they so stupid or so slow. It is a clever choice to use children as the Heirs; they are neither too cowardly nor too proud, as Asgard assumes. And they learn fast. And, moreover, it contains the element of surprise. Cain and the Mother Serpent will underestimate them.'

Genesis dipped one long, bony leg after another into the electric blue fire of her maghole, which raged harder than Gaia had seen for some time.

'You helped the old man find his Resplendix Mix, did you not?'

Gaia was astonished. 'Indeed. I wanted balance—'

'Balance. Good.' Genesis hummed. 'Now you will need to go further. The old man once possessed a branchwand. Find it and deliver it before the third tablet is found. Discover the dreams for informing him of its purpose. I will show you how to do this.

'And know this: Cain's twin, Abel, is not so crazed anymore. Time has banished his anger and he seeks his revenge. Like Cain, his shadow grows. And even though Seth, the little brother, will not come out of his place of hiding, he has promised a great gift.'

'But what of us? Is Asgard truthful? Is our time at an end?'

Genesis flicked her legs into her maghole. 'Tell me, Gaia, what do you know of the Prophecy?'

'Three tablets lead the way to the Key of Eden,' Gaia replied. 'The lock must be released to open the Garden and then life will begin anew, the Garden reborn. New species will come unto Earth and Havilah. But one failure will prove mankind's failing, and the Earth will be cleansed.'

'And, tell me, what if the Heirs have the three Tablets but do not find the key? Do you know what happens then?' Genesis asked.

'They die—?'

'No, not necessarily. Opening the Garden requires that a great power be unleashed. We dreamspinners have the means to create this, when there is no more. These things have been long forgotten.'

'Create? Create what, mother?'

'Here.' Genesis passed over a polished white ring made of a glass-like stone.

'What is it? I know of no such things.'

Genesis' dark eyes sparkled. 'This is the Ring of Babylon, hidden on the walls of the cave and shrouded from common knowledge. But Adam will know, deep in his lost mind.'

Genesis ruffled her body so that she appeared, for a moment, larger, like a huge angel, her silvery, almost see-through body cloaking her strange spidery frame. 'If the Heirs succeed, there is a choice even if they cannot open the lock.'

'I do not know of it, mother.'

'If the children survive, a new world will arrive.'

'If that time happens there is one thing the Heirs must do. Point the ring at the red planet. One of the Heirs must push their breath through it. That is all. But it must be done before the sun goes down on the eighth day.'

'For what purpose?'

'The Garden of Eden is dead. One breath of life through the Ring of Babylon will create holes in space through which will be sucked life-givers.'

'For life-giver, you talk of comets?'

'Yes. When one life-giver collides with Earth and another with Havilah and The Garden of Eden and Assyria and Cush, five new places of habitation will be formed. This will signal the end of the ancient order and the beginning of the new.'

'So, Eve and the old man, Cain, Abel and Seth will die?' Gaia said. 'I had no idea. Then a new time really will begin. A new time for us all, even dreamspinners...' Gaia flickered her legs out. 'Then Cain cannot prevail. He fails.'

Genesis dipped a couple of legs in her maghole. 'After a great sleep, the Heirs of Eden shall be the stewards.'

'The Heirs? But there are only three. How are they to reproduce and populate?"

'There are others, Gaia. More than you realise. When the time is right, the process of populating the worlds will be quick enough. But when they are of an age they will die, as it always should have been. The mistake of endless life will never be repeated. Remember, Gaia, this may only happen if they are alive at the end of the seven days and if they have the tablets.'

'After defeating Gorialla Yingarna, the mother serpent—'

'Yes, and if they overcome Blabisterberry Jelly.'

Gaia shuffled and cleaned two legs in her maghole simultaneously. 'One failure—'

'Is all it takes,' Genesis interrupted.

'I understand.'

'Good. Remember it well. And Gaia.'

'Yes, mother?'

'Cain and Asgard and his band of deserters must never know of the Ring of Babylon. There. You know all that I know. Now I must summon dreamspinners and put a halt to the error of their ways. And while they come to me, they are not spinning dreams filled with poison.'

Genesis produced a thin, shiny stick the size of a small piece of wire, glittering as if it were made of one piece of elasticised diamond. She tapped on it quickly as if it were a drum, creating reverberations that hummed high and low, deep and soft, loud and searching.

'Stand with me, my daughter of the universe, and watch.'

Back in their invisible state, the two dreamspinners waited as the humming continued wailing, its sound at once both harmonious and haunting, singing into the expansive universes.

It didn't take long.

Moments later, as if by magic, dreamspinners started popping out of the sky into the huge cavern in tiny flashes, pinpricks of light, until the huge chamber was packed with thousands of opaque, spidery-looking creatures with fiery, blue middles.

# 88 SOLOMON'S INTERROGATION

'Headmaster!' Sue rushed up to him and gave him a hug.

The headmaster hadn't anticipated it and only after a moment reciprocated.

'You survived!' she said, 'I can't believe how lucky we are.'

The words filled Solomon with a pang of guilt; *how had he lived, when so many had died?* he thought. 'And you are well?' he asked. 'How is our hero, Gus?'

'Oh, he's doing really well, thanks,' she said, smiling back at the familiar, yet slightly less rotund face of the headmaster. 'In fact, he's bored and itching to get out of his bed. Seems like all he had was a sort of mini-flu.'

'What a great relief,' Solomon said, and he meant it.

Sue looked around. 'Cool place, isn't it? What's it called, Swinton Park? I heard it was once a beautiful hotel.' Another helicopter buzzed overhead and settled down just behind a large cluster of bare trees just out of sight through the windows. 'I've never seen so many helicopters in one place,' Sue said, almost in awe. 'Have you met the Commissioner? He's a bit of a creep if you ask me. I've got a "debriefing" with him in half an hour.'

The headmaster had forgotten what a lively, pretty girl she was – and clearly desperate to talk. 'Sue, I wouldn't mind a brief catch up before you see him. Find out all about your extraordinary adventure. Can you spare a moment – outside? Have you got a coat?'

Sue caught his eye. 'Sure.'

They pushed open the double doors that led from the reception and rounded the thick stone walls heading up the path in the darkness. Solomon continued on around the lake towards the gardens.

'Headmaster, where are we going?'

'Please, call me Solomon, won't you, Sue? We're not at school now so you can leave the airs and graces behind, don't you think?' He smiled his head-masterly smile, his small, tea-stained teeth a little too evident. 'A little bit further, if you don't mind stretching your legs.'

He stopped for a minute and turned to face the vale behind them. 'Such a beautiful place isn't it, perched here on the Daleside of the Vale? Did you realise that Upsall is almost exactly opposite on the edge of the Moors, right over there?' he said, pointing into the distance. 'And have you seen the lake? It's well worth a visit in the morning. Dug by hand, so I'm told, and now overflowing like a mini Niagara Falls. A most impressive sight.'

Sue thought this commentary was rather odd but, as they walked around a clump of dense yew trees, she spotted a bench lit by an old street light. Solomon beckoned her to sit down.

He pulled out a notepad and a pen.

*We're being monitored*, he wrote. *You are in terrible danger.*

'Can you hear the geese over there?' he said. 'They're Canadian, you can tell by their distinct call.'

*I'm bugged. You are too.*

'Er ... Gosh – wow!' she said, the colour draining from her face. She shook her head and felt a hard nodule on her lapel. 'You're very knowledgeable,' she stuttered, her brain fizzing. 'Are they, er, related to Iberian Geese?' she said, racking her brain about birds.

He nodded encouragement.

*Why?* she wrote.

'Perhaps,' he said peering at the pad. 'You may well be right, I'm no expert. There used to be a famous deer herd here, but I believe all the animals have been put down,' he continued. 'A very ancient breed, by all accounts.'

*They're on to the de Lowes.*

'Oh! I like deer,' she said, rather thickly.

*Crap,* she wrote, before scribbling it out.

Solomon was a little taken aback and gave her one of his most knowing looks. 'I can't begin to tell you how thrilled I am to see you again,' he said. 'Tell me, how did you find that old rowing boat? I'm rather astonished it held together. Was that Isabella's idea?'

He scribbled fast. *I have to ask.* He pointed at her lapel again and gave her an encouraging look.

She grabbed the notebook and coughed as she turned the page. 'Well, yes! I suppose it was. Isabella realised the huge storm cloud might blow at any time. It was pretty obvious really. I mean, there was lightning shooting out everywhere, and all they had to do was run up the track home. She probably reckoned I wouldn't get home so, just in case, she suggested the boat. In hindsight, it was totally inspired. Then, luckily, I bumped into Gus.'

*Sorry, don't normally swear.*

'Sue, can I ask? What made Isabella so infatuated with the storm cloud? I know you both came to see me with a home-made barometer, was it something to do with this – were you just playing "scientists"?'

Sue shot him a curious look, trying to ascertain what sort of reply he was fishing for. 'Yeah, I suppose so. Isabella went a bit crazy on weather forecasting and...'

She stalled and stared at the ground.

'My dear,' Solomon said. 'Is there something you'd like to tell me?'

'Well, yeah, there is one more thing – but it's a bit weird. Actually no, don't worry about it – it's probably irrelevant.'

Solomon pressed her. 'Tell me everything,' he encouraged. 'I'm intrigued that Isabella knew enough to think of getting you a boat, but why didn't you simply head up into the tower – like many of the children and me?'

'We did calculations, sir.'

'Calculations? Whatever for?' Solomon raised his eyebrows in anticipation.

'OK – this will sound ridiculous.' Sue took a deep breath. 'I'd had a dream about a storm. Actually, it was more like a nightmare. Thing is, it felt so clear I thought it might be a premonition, you know, when you see something before it actually happens.'

Solomon nodded.

'Anyway, I told Isabella about it. You see, I always try and write my dreams down the moment I wake up. Amazingly, she believed me.'

'So it's happened before?'

'Yes. A couple of times. Anyway she then got all excited about it – in a scientific, meteorological way, you understand—'

Solomon smiled encouragement and mouthed: '*good*'.

'—and then she started looking at storm data on websites and she got more and more carried away until she made a barometer which kept bottoming out and all the while, much to our astonishment, the cloud kept growing until she came to the conclusion that this one was going to be the biggest of the lot. From her calculations, I don't think she thought the school tower would make it.'

'And all this came from a dream?' Solomon said, almost to himself. 'Fascinating.'

He handed Sue a note, with a finger over his lips.

*No more!*

Sue smiled back at the headmaster. It was nice to have someone to talk to.

*There's more,* she wrote, *much more*.

'Getting a bit chilly, isn't it?' Solomon said, rubbing his hands together. 'Let's go back inside shall we?' They linked arms. 'I am so terribly sorry about your losses. I am afraid our whole community has suffered dreadful personal tragedy. We are very much the lucky ones – I doubt if the populace will ever really recover. Life has a habit of bouncing back, though, so let's hope that maybe one day things will return to something near normal.'

Sue looked pensive. 'Why are there so many people rushing around with protective kit on?'

'You mean you don't know?'

Sue shook her head. 'I've heard there's some kind of virus out there. Is it true?'

Solomon pushed his glasses back on. 'My dear, absolutely. The country is in quarantine, everything – and I mean *everything* – has ground to a halt. According to a military chap I sat next to at lunch, half the towns and cities are up in flames. Mass looting – general pandemonium. By a total fluke, Swinton Park is possibly the safest place in the world, right now.

'You look a little pale, Sue, let's sit down by the fire. I thought they might have told you.' They walked inside, took off their coats, nodded at a couple of uniformed men who rushed by and sat down by the fire. 'But I guess there have been other things to worry about.'

Sue's face had gone white. 'Seriously? Is it the truth?'

'Indeed. Never more so. Why do you think Gus is in his little room? I believe it has been named *Ebora*, a rather crude blend of the Roman word for *York* – Ebor, and the *Ebola* outbreak in Africa. The problem is, these scientists have absolutely no idea how to contain it.'

'None at all?'

'Not only does it spread by touch and by bodily fluids, but it appears to fly through the air. And the strange thing is that, quite suddenly, it turned up the length of America, as though it flew west with the night. Maybe it did, who knows?'

'America?' Sue said. 'That's impossible.'

'Yes, both sides of North America and South America too, apparently.' He exhaled loudly and smiled. 'In a way it's a miracle neither of us has caught it. But, since they have no idea how it operates, there's no preventative advice that they can give to those who haven't been affected.'

Sue screwed her eyes shut and clenched her hands as the magnitude of what he was saying sunk in.

Solomon noticed, reached over and patted her arm lightly. 'As you know, it all began right here in Yorkshire. Upsall is the epicentre, they say. On the meteorological charts, the storm mushroomed out of Upsall and covered a good part of the United Kingdom. The animations are most impressive. We're here because we're about the only people known to have survived. Our dear friend, the Commissioner, seems to think that there is something, or someone, in Upsall that can tell us more.'

Sue scribbled on the pad. *There is.*

'Sue,' the headmaster continued, alarm in his face, 'do you know of anything that might somehow link this storm or the Ebora with Upsall School or with any of your friends?'

Sue's eyes met the headmaster's. *Do I trust him? I have to – who else is there?*

She pulled her pen out.

*It's the de Lowes,* she wrote, allowing him to read the page.

She carried on writing and very calmly said, 'No, not that I'm aware of.'

The headmaster smiled and gave her a very faint wink out of his right eye. 'And does Gus know of anything, anything at all, Sue?'

'I don't think so,' she said handing over the notebook.

He read it.

*They have to find three tablets. Then kill an old woman – I think.*

'—Murder?' he coughed, before realising his mistake. 'In the village?' he added, too late. He passed the notebook back as he waffled on about a rather curious death claim in the village, hoping to mask his slip-up.

Sue cringed. She scribbled again.

*If they fail, we die. They're running out of time*

Solomon looked up, his face red from his gaff. 'Exactly as I thought,' he said. 'I never suspected anything else from you other than complete honesty.'

*How do you know?* he wrote.

She took back the pad. *I dreamt about it. So far, everything true.*

She handed the book back to the headmaster. He smiled at her and tossed it onto the fire. 'Thank you, my dear. Now, I think it's time we'd paid a visit to the dear Commissioner. He's been looking forward to meeting you.'

As they stood up, a crowd of people arguing loudly walked into the room. Solomon leant in very quickly and whispered into her ear. 'Sue, whatever happens, you absolutely *must* trust me.'

---

SOLOMON AND SUE waited for half an hour in the ante-room outside his office as a stream of people filed in and out. Every so often they caught a few words or exclamations from Stone as the door opened and closed.

Dickinson, smart as usual, his hair neatly combed to one side, ushered them in and remained with them, sitting to the side of the desk, his tablet switched on ready for note-taking.

Stone rubbed his eyes, leaned back in his chair and drew a hand through his thick silver hair. He fixed Sue with a crooked smile. 'So, I'll tell you what we know,' he began, talking directly to her. 'And as I go, why don't you fill in the blanks. And please, don't muck me about, girl. We're fighting a losing battle here and if I don't think you're co-operating, I have the means and the methods to make you talk, understand?'

Sue gulped and nodded.

'Firstly, this storm and Ebora have both got something to do with Upsall.' He lifted his eyes to meet hers. 'Secondly, there's a connection with the de Lowe family.'

Sue gasped. 'How do you know that?'

'So you agree, do you?' Stone shot back.

'No, I ... er, I never said that.' She flashed a look at Solomon.

Stone knew he'd struck gold. 'We know – don't we, headmaster – that there's something a bit quirky with this family? You see, your friend Kemp told us.' Stone said, going straight for the jugular.

'Kemp? He's alive?' she stammered before controlling herself. 'What would Kemp know?'

Stone smiled shiftily. 'Oh, he appeared to know all about it.'

'About what?'

'You tell me.'

For a moment there was silence. Stone leaned forward. 'Tell me about your dream, Sue?'

'Dream?'

'Yes, those things you have at night, you know, while you sleep – I'm told you had one all about the de Lowes. A kind of premonition? Am I right?'

Sue nodded.

'Why do you think that was?'

'I don't know. I dream quite a bit and I write them down. I like trying to work out their meanings.'

'How very interesting. I used to write a diary at night when I was your age until my mother found ink smudges all over my pillow.'

Sue smiled. 'Oh, I use a Biro or a pencil so it doesn't make such a mess.'

Stone pressed his intercom. 'Has it arrived yet? Good. Send it up when you're ready.' He turned back to her. 'Excellent. That means your diary won't have deteriorated in the floodwaters too much.'

'You can't do that,' Solomon stormed. 'They're a girl's private thoughts—'

Stone slammed his hand down on the desk. 'Screw her thoughts, Headmaster. I can do what I damn well like.' They glared at one another. 'Where are the de Lowes, Sue? Where are they right now?'

'I have no idea,' Sue stammered. 'We last made contact on the rowing boat a couple of days ago. I think they were at home, although the text didn't say.'

'You're lying again,' Stone said. He turned. 'Dickinson. Was anyone at the property when you flew over?'

'Our thermal-imaging camera found the outline of one female adult. More than likely that of their housekeeper, Mrs. Pye. No others, sir. We circled the remains of the house twice, sir. No other bodies in sight.'

Sue felt sick. 'I don't know. Really I don't.' She fought back her tears.

'First Kemp vanishes, now the entire de Lowe family go absent,' he yelled. 'Dickinson, has anyone found the parents yet?'

'Negative, sir. We have a team scouring their last known locations.'

'Tomorrow, at the crack of dawn, I'm sending in a little expeditionary team to check out their little hovel on top of the hill. You better be certain they're not there, Miss Lowden.'

A knuckle rapped at the door. A man with a protective facial mask entered and handed a plastic bag to Dickinson. 'I've given it a bit of a dry, but it was pretty well protected by the bag,' he said, before exiting.

Sue recognised it immediately. 'That's mine—'

'Actually, I think you'll find it's Government property,' Stone smiled as he opened up the pink hardback diary. 'Tell me, what date did you say you had this epiphany?'

Sue face turned to thunder. 'About two weeks ago.'

Stone flicked through, eyebrow raised. 'Gosh. What drivel, all these feeble girlie thoughts. Ah. Here we are. Entry for Tuesday 28th October.

*'Another nightmare,'* he read.

Stone looked up, his face puce with anger. 'Is that it?' He flicked through several other pages. '*Another nightmare*? Is that all you wrote? What about all this "recording your bleeding dreams"?'

'I did,' Sue exclaimed. 'It's all there.'

Stone hurled the book at her. 'Find it! NOW!'

Sue nervously flicked through.

Next to her, Solomon burst out laughing, stood up and reached into his pocket.

'What's so damned funny?'

'It's just that, oh dear,' Solomon mopped his eyes with a handkerchief.

'Are you, my dear cousin, trying to ascertain what her dreams were all about?'

'Of course I ruddy well am.'

'Well, why don't you simply ask? Sue told me and I have to say that, when she told me, they were so ludicrous I didn't feel it was worth mentioning.'

Stone puckered his mouth. 'So tell me what she told you, Solomon. I'll be the judge of that.'

Sue shot the headmaster a worried look. *I have to trust him*, she thought.

'Sue's dreams were about the de Lowes finding three tablets that had code or whatever it is on them to save the world.'

Her heart sank.

'Tablets?' the commissioner said. 'What kind of tablets?'

'Computer tablets, I imagine – you know, iPads or the like – such as Dickinson's holding. Isn't that right, Sue?'

Sue's eyes almost popped out of her head. She laughed nervously. 'Er, yeah. I told you it was a bit weird.'

Stone eyed them both. 'Well, why isn't it on the recordings then?'

'Because, my dear old fellow, Sue was so embarrassed about telling me that I asked her if it might be easier to write it all down. So she did, on condition that I burned it afterwards. If you seriously believe there is anything worth following up concerning Sue's dream you'll probably find that the de Lowes have long departed Eden Cottage in search of these electronic devices. They're probably looting the High Street as we speak. Otherwise I think you might have to consider that Sue simply had a premonition about a very great storm. People do, you know.'

Stone swivelled on his chair and clenched his fists. It didn't add up.

'You dreamt about a storm, Sue, and in particular its violent nature. You also dreamt of the de Lowes, correct? So what's to say there isn't some fragment of truth to all of it?'

He stood and paced the room, shaking his head. 'Let's consider what we have. One ancient family who live by a ruin next to an ancient monastery, a biblical storm and a biblical plague, and you think electronic iPad tablet devices are involved?'

'That's what I saw,' Sue lied.

Stone moved right up to her, almost sniffing her. 'We'll find out tomorrow then, won't we?' he whispered quietly into her ear. 'If the de Lowes are home then I'm going to squeeze them until they squeak – for a bloody month if need be. If they're not, then believe me, I'll track them down.'

Stone returned to his seat and took a deliberately deep breath. 'Now, where do you think they would they go for these things? York? Leeds?'

Sue thought quickly. 'Perhaps, if there's any truth in the matter, you might be looking at this the wrong way. In my experience, Commissioner, dreams often highlight things that hint of something else. Dreams detect signals of worry or stress in the brain. So if you look at it like that, the key question isn't *where do you find the tablets*, but, perhaps *what you might use them for*. In which case, sir, there's every likelihood they may already have them.'

Stone stared at her and then the headmaster. 'Do you get this kind of shit all the time, Solomon?'

He turned his gaze to Sue. 'So, what you're suggesting is that they're after some kind of digital ... code?'

Sue shrugged. 'I don't know. A code or a sequence or something.'

'Do they own iPads or similar tablets?'

'Not as far as I'm aware.'

Stone nodded and checked his watch. 'Right. Thank you, both. Sue you may go.'

A rush of relief swept over her. 'I'm here to help, sir,' she said. 'Please – if there's anything I can do to assist—'

'Thank you, I'll bear it in mind,' he said, smiling badly. 'Right now, Miss Lowden, I have other business to attend to. I've noted your offer and I'll let you know.'

# 89 SOLOMON'S THEORY

Stone sat down heavily and yawned. 'Still getting bloody nowhere,' he said to Solomon, irritably.

'I've had everyone screaming at me all day. Do you have the faintest idea what kind of huge turd is hitting this continent-sized fan? Well, I'll tell you. This place should be called Turdistan. No one has a bleedin' clue how this Ebora is getting around. It's a total bloody mystery.'

He rubbed his eyes as a wave of fatigue swept over him. 'And now the scientists say they need at least six weeks before they can crack it. Current estimates tell us we don't have six days, let alone six weeks!'

Solomon frowned as an idea popped into his head. He looked up as he accepted a cup of tea from Dickinson.

'Charlie. Something has struck me. Do you have a world map – even better, do you have a world map where the known outbreaks are marked?'

Dickinson nodded. 'Yes, it's on the global updater, sophisticated software developed in Estonia – I can hook it up to the projector if that's of any help.'

'Yes, it would be. And Dickinson, would you be able to play the recording back of me and Sue? There's something I said which may have a little more truth in it than I realised. About a third of the way through, I'd say.'

He sipped his tea while Dickinson played with his gadgets.

'This better be good, Solomon,' Stone said, eyeing him cautiously.

'It's a ruse, Charlie. And you may well throw it back in my face, but I think we're going to need to search a little more 'out of the box' as those young management fellows say.'

Dickinson pressed play. Their voices came across remarkably clearly.

Solomon perked up. 'A little further along. Not much. Yes – here.' They listened.

*'... not only does it spread by touch and by bodily fluids, but it would appear to fly through the air ...*

*'And the strange thing is that, quite suddenly, it turned up the length of America, as though it flew west with the night. Maybe it did, who knows?'*

*'America? That's impossible.'*

*'Yes, both sides of North America and South America too, apparently. In a way it's a miracle neither of us has caught it—'*

'Stop,' Solomon said and bit his lip. 'Play it again.'

When the passage finished for the second time, Stone piped-up. 'Headmaster, are you suggesting that this virus can fly?'

'No, not exactly.' He turned to Dickinson again. 'Can you spark your projector into life? Jolly good. Now, is there a kind of electronic gizmo which displays a time-line for when these occurrences took place?'

'By "occurrences",' Dickinson said, 'I take it you mean the approximate recorded times of Ebora infection?'

'Absolutely, I'm keen to see if there's a link to the disease being reported in relation to the time of day.'

'OK,' Dickinson said, 'I think I know what you mean.' Dickinson tapped away for a little while.

Soon, a large map of Yorkshire and the Northern half of England filled the screen covering the white wall. At the top was the date and time.

'Right, with any luck, this graphic should play the sequence from the very first engagement with the disease right up to the current minute.'

Dickinson dimmed the lights. 'The map should zoom out as the virus' spread increases,' he said, as he hit a key and the sequence began.

They stared in silence as the map stayed put while the time-clock flickered through the motions. 'OK, now it's midday on Friday – this is when the storm struck,' Dickinson said. 'Would you like me to super-impose the meteorological map as well?' He tapped away, reversed the time and then pressed play.

On the screen, a huge storm-cloud in purple, yellow and red colouring mushroomed out of Upsall moving at an amazing speed until it covered a circular area reaching from Northumberland to Nottingham to the north and south and Scarborough to Manchester on the east and west axis.

'As you can see,' Dickinson said, 'at about five p.m. the bulk of the storm suddenly dissolves into ordinary rain clouds.'

'Dickinson. Pause it there, if you will,' Solomon said. 'Thank you. Is there any way you can overlay a night and day shadow map on top—'

'Showing the sun's passage around the globe? No problem.'

Solomon shook his head. 'Amazing what these little tablet things can do, isn't it?'

The adjustment took a little longer. 'Right,' Dickinson said. 'By the way, just an observation, but notice how the torrential rain cloud dissipates at the exact moment the sun goes down?' He returned to the current graphic. 'Anyway, let's see how this works.'

The map continued on its time-led journey. As the clock ticked through Saturday, a few specks in red, denoting the virus, began to appear, growing in number but generally spanning out only across the immediate area of the Vale of York.

The map then went darker, showing night.

The red dots began increasing in number though the night and the map zoomed out a little to include reports of infection from London and the South of England. Through Sunday, the red on the map widened a little but mainly intensified in Yorkshire, the north and midlands. As Sunday night came around this pattern was repeated.

On Monday, three days after the event, the general increase continued overnight when suddenly the map zoomed out. As morning extended, a vertical line of red dotted the atlas, spanning an area in the northern hemisphere from Reykjavik in Iceland to Lisbon in Portugal and Marrakesh in Morocco.

Then, quite unexpectedly, the globe spun on its head, showing a less orderly but unmistakable colouring of red dots weaving through the heart of Africa all the way down to South Africa.

Now the globe spun again as day broke across the Eastern shore of America.

All three men stood up.

'Pause it there!' Solomon said, his voice quivering. 'Thank you, Dickinson.' He faced his cousin. 'Now, if my theory is correct and the infection has spread at night, as we sleep,' he said, his brow furrowed, 'the next bit should be rather interesting.'

As the line of darkness gave in to the light of morning, following behind, like a red wave, came thousands of tiny dots. And as they watched, Ebora quietly swept across the Americas, North and South, quite literally as day follows night.

When the animation finished the three men remained in silence for a considerable time.

'So, Ebora comes at night?' Stone said.

'In waves,' Solomon agreed, mopping his brow.

'Maybe it's a biological agent, triggered by the dark?' Dickinson added.

Solomon hummed. 'I see where you're coming from, but does it really add up? Ebora originates from Upsall, spreads around as you'd expect with no particular order to it and then, two days later, it follows a strict pattern. As though something has taken it on—'

'Maybe there's a night particle—?' Dickinson added.

'A night particle?' Stone coughed. 'Come on, lad. Even I know there is no such a thing. More likely, someone's taken a flight from here to New York and it's spread hand to mouth—'

'In a day? It's impossible, Charlie. You know that.' The headmaster said, sitting down. He removed his glasses and dabbed his eyes.

'Now, who would like to hear my theory?' he asked.

'I'm all ears,' Stone replied with a heavy drip of sarcasm.

'You're going to find it hard to believe, Charlie, but hear me out. First of all though, here's a riddle for both of you. *What goes by night, has many forms and is given to all people?*'

'This is no time for riddles, Solomon.'

'Actually, yes, I think it jolly well is.'

'Ghosts, spirits?' Dickinson volunteered.

'No. Nice idea. You're in the right kind of area.'

'This is ridiculous—'

'Rain!' Dickinson said.

'Wrong! ... although in one sense you are, I suppose, absolutely spot on. Here's a clue. What does the riddle have in common with Sue?'

'Are all your classes like this?' Stone said, flatly.

'She had a dream about the storm?' Dickinson said.

Solomon clapped his hands. 'Now we're getting somewhere. Yes, she *dreamt* about the storm. The answer to the riddle is, "*Dreams*".'

Stone clapped slowly. 'Bravo. Where the hell is this going, Solomon?'

The headmaster was on a roll. 'We know that Sue had a premonition. And it was so clear and so frightening that it even made her friend scared out of her wits – scared enough to chart weather sequences from around the world. And then, lo and behold, her dream came true. In fact, everything about it came true! So what I'm saying is this: either she has some kind of psychic powers or, perhaps, she was given that dream.'

'Oh, bloody hell,' Stone tutted. 'What – by freaking aliens?'

Solomon shrugged. 'I don't know! But what I do know is that throughout the world, come nightfall, the one common factor irrespective of creed and gender and race and animal type ... and anything else that sets us apart from one another, is that we sleep and therefore we ... dream.'

Stone took his feet off his desk, stood up and paced around the room, scratching his chin. 'Am I right in thinking that you're saying little alien bugs are flying about dishing out dreams?'

Solomon shrugged. 'I don't know. It is simply a theory. But we haven't got anything else, have we? And Ebora isn't caused by a lack of hygiene or spread by vermin. It is something else, Charlie. We may have to contemplate running with some distinctly unsettling propositions if we're to get to the bottom of this.'

Stone harrumphed. 'Dickinson, what do you think?'

The young officer had gone a little pale. 'I think it's utterly brilliant, sir.'

Stone rolled his eyes. 'Brilliant? Bollocks to that. Brilliant? So, what do you think I should do? Ring up the President of the United States of America and tell him to order his people not to go to sleep, in case they bloody well dream?'

He stood up. 'I can just imagine the scene at the White House. *The Brits have a plan for the Ebora,* he'll say, *this deadly virus they've unleashed on the world. It's called "Stay Awake". Gee, why didn't we think of that?*'

Stone's cold eyes bore into the headmaster. 'In my humble opinion, Solomon, that has to be the most unhelpful crappy piece of advice I've ever heard.'

Solomon eyed him curiously for a while and pushed his glasses up the bridge of his nose. 'Charlie, you're an excellent police officer with outstanding qualities, but sometimes I do think you really are one of the stupidest people I have ever had the misfortune of stumbling upon.'

Stone glared at him.

Solomon continued. 'You must realise that if what I'm saying is anywhere close to the mark, then what we're witnessing, right now, is some kind of alien or extra-terrestrial threat to us as a race. We may well be being led into extermination.'

Stone chortled. 'Wiped out? Don't be silly. Humans always find a way.'

'Hear me out, Charlie. You just said we haven't got an answer. Face it, our brain functionality does not allow us to think of anything outside of our general programming. If you ask me, my dear chap, something sinister and world threatening was opened up in Upsall. This power – or whatever you want to call it – is not only lethal, but without precedent. And, like it or not, it would appear to me that there are only three people in the world who know anything about it. My guess is that those three just happen to be the de Lowe children.'

Stone shook his head. 'They're bloody kids. Kids causing trouble with something they don't understand. That's my guess.'

'But so what if they're kids, Charlie? It makes perfect sense. Their minds are open and not closed – like yours, mine and most of the human race. Take a look at the boy, Kemp. What happened to him wasn't an accident of the storm: those burns, his malnutrition. They weren't the result of Ebora. And then, quite suddenly, he disappears off the face of the planet, leaving a puff of ash. In my opinion, he's a part of this too, Charlie. And it's something we cannot fathom.'

Solomon paced the room like a lecturer. 'Remember the stained glass windows of Upsall church? They clearly showed that after rain, comes pestilence. And Dickinson neatly pointed out that the terrifying storm cloud evaporated at the exact moment the sun went down. The question is, why didn't it continue on to pulverise the rest of the country? Something made it stop, which is why it moved on to the disease. We are being beaten and battered by something brilliantly clever, Charlie. And, it is utterly ruthless.' Solomon sat down. He needed a drink.

'Have you quite finished?' Stone said, as he chewed a fingernail and spat it out over the floor. 'Thank you for that huge load of complete shite. Let me remind you of a couple of things. Firstly, that I run the show round here, and secondly, I do not need any jumped-up loony theories about aliens and dreams. Do you understand, headmaster? What I need is proper, logical solutions and I need them now.'

The headmaster smiled at him wearily. 'As I said, it is a theory, that's all. Please don't forget that all I am trying to do is help you. I lost most of my students in this disaster and I, too, intend to get to the bottom of this one way or another.'

Stone acknowledged him with a wave of his hand. 'Dickinson, did you get the results of the ash from Kemp's disappearance?'

Dickinson sorted through some emails on his computer. 'Ah, here. Inconclusive, I'm afraid,' he said, looking up. 'The carbon dating machine appears to have broken down.'

Stone swore. 'What does it say?'

Dickinson read on. 'Well, the results that came back said that the ash was over a million years old. That the boy somehow – combusted—'

'Kemp burnt himself to death?' Stone spat. 'Incinerated into a small pile of ash in the toilet?'

Dickinson smiled. 'Hence why they think the machine is faulty.'

Solomon sensed his moment. 'Look, if I can get into that house of theirs, maybe I can find out if there's anything that might match what I found in the church. Surely it's worth a try?'

Stone eyed him curiously. 'Yeah, alright. Take the girl with you. She knows them well enough. But on one condition: you only go if they're not there. I don't want you interfering if and when we find them. Is that clear? Our team will be there shortly after dawn. They'll be back by midday. You'll know by then.'

'Good,' Solomon said. He stood up, thanked Stone and Dickinson, and let himself out.

Outside the door, he exhaled loudly.

If the children were there, as Stone suspected, then there was no way he could get the de Lowe's away from the cottage before the soldiers arrived at dawn. And if his theory had any weight, well, then what?

---

DICKINSON SAT DOWN. 'Persuasive – your cousin. I like him. I wish my teachers had had his charisma.'

'But not very useful on a practical level, I'm afraid,' Stone said. 'Bloody lunatic if you ask me.' He scratched his creased brow. 'Play that recording again. There's a bit towards the end that I didn't quite understand – it's been nagging at me. Something he says doesn't add up.'

*Two can play at this game,* Stone thought.

Dickinson clicked back towards the end. Then back a little.

'Yes. That's probably about right. OK, let it roll.'

The recording came to life, filling the room.

*'Sue, do you know of anything that might somehow link this storm or the Ebora with Upsall School or with any of your friends?'*

*'No, not that I'm aware of.'*

*'And does Gus know of anything, anything at all, Sue?'*

*'I don't think so.'*

*- long pause -*

Then, not so loudly:

*'Murder? ... In the village ...?'*

Stone leant in. 'What's going on there, Dickinson? Did she mouth something to him?'

Dickinson ran it back and they listened again. 'It's like they're sort of having another conversation, separately.'

Stone put his hands behind his head and exhaled. 'Is there a chance, Dickinson, that Solomon and Sue are taking us for one BLOODY great big ride? Why do I have a very deep suspicion that underneath this Ebora disaster lies some kind of murky secret?'

'What do you want me to do, sir?'

'Go with the crew at dawn. Watch, listen – find out all you can. And believe you me, when we get those kids I'm going to shove so much electricity up Archie-bleeding-de Lowe's backside that his hair will be standing erect for the rest of his life.'

His COBRA hotline buzzed.

'Mark my words,' he continued. 'Sometime soon they're going to have to come running out of their burrow and when they do, I'll be there.'

Dickinson strode towards the door.

'One more thing, Dickinson: I want you to personally radio me when you get to that cottage at first light, understand? I want you to be my eyes and ears.'

Stone picked up the receiver. 'Stone,' he said. He listened for a minute, cringing at the sharp tones cutting down the phone.

'Secretary of State,' he said, trying not to express his irritation. 'No, I didn't realise you've had the Americans demanding to send in their troops, nor coming here to find the cause of Ebora. Please remind them that the best help they can give us is in areas such as forensics and molecular science—'

He listened to the shrill voice on the other end.

'Then it seems to me,' he said, 'that we could do with them helping to keep the peace, not in threatening to blow the hell out of Yorkshire, or any place else they suspect.'

The Secretary of State spoke at length again.

Stone responded. 'On that matter,' he said, 'I have a lead in regard to Archie de Lowe and his sisters. Nothing certain, but I'll know more in the morning when my team have swept through their cottage. I'll call you at eleven with an update.'

Stone replaced the phone and mopped his brow.

It was out of control. The world was in crisis. The Americans now blamed Middle Eastern terrorist groups for planting Ebora and destroying the west, the Chinese were blaming the Russians and the Europeans were blaming the Americans who were ready to decimate the North of England with a very, very big bomb in order to stop its spread at source.

Stone shook his head. *It was already too late for all that.*

He thumped the table. Everything would be a good deal easier if they could just find Archie de Lowe.

# 90 ISABELLA'S POWER

The twins were by the track, near to the courtyard, when they heard Isabella screaming.

Daisy and Archie looked at each other, then Mrs. Pye.

'It's Bells,' Daisy said. 'Something has happened.' They rushed inside following the noise up the stairs. As they turned into Old Man Wood's room their eyes met a quite extraordinary sight.

For from the crack in the door they saw Old Man Wood's mushroom-littered body levitating in a cocoon of swirling pink light coming from Isabella's hands.

As they stepped inside, the fungi began to detonate. Daisy and Archie threw themselves behind the door as toadstools thudded into the panels and wall and door like rifle bullets. As the noise died down they poked their heads inside. Isabella, on her last reserves, stumbled and fell against the wall.

Archie rushed to her, holding her up.

Daisy followed. 'What is it?'

Archie glanced at Old Man Wood's chest, where the last remaining toadstool glowed from green to white. 'I think he's dying,' he said.

Suddenly, it grew.

Archie ran forward and attempted to rip it off but only succeeded in burning his hands.

Then, without knowing why, he moved behind his sister, extended his arms around her body and directed her wrists aloft. Daisy instinctively did the same so that Archie was sandwiched in the middle, their arms pushed forwards.

He shut his eyes.

'Be strong, Bells,' he said. 'Reach inside and draw out every sinew and fibre – and then go a little bit further.'

The lagging pink cocoon suddenly fizzled into life.

With one last, deep breath she screamed:

'OUT ... **OUT!**'

She thrust her hands at the fungi and slammed everything she had at it. Archie and Daisy shut their eyes.

The toadstool quivered and swayed, but stuck.

'More, everyone,' Archie yelled, 'Together, all of us. Bells, ONCE MORE ... on the count of three.

'One, two ...

**NOW!**'

A huge volley of power rocketed out from the children's extended arms, the recoil throwing them against the wall. The toadstool flinched, then swayed and shook, before blasting off Old Man Wood's chest, circling the room twice like an out of control firework and smashing into the bed panels at the foot of his bed, spraying the room with wood and splinters.

As the pink cocoon faded, Old Man Wood's body floated down.

Archie and Daisy untangled themselves and picked themselves up off the floor.

Darkness filled the room save for the crackle of fire on the panelling spreading quickly towards Old Man Wood's bed.

Isabella lay on the floor, motionless.

Archie acted fast. 'Daisy, get Isabella out of here!'

He ran to the bed and, in two deft movements, lifted the torso of the old man and then hoisted him effortlessly over his shoulder, his body swamping him like a bear.

Outside, Archie laid Old Man Wood next to Isabella. He looked over her pale sweaty face, brushed her hair away and gently kissed her forehead. Soft breaths came out over long intervals, her face ashen and her eyes closed but ringed with dark patches, like a panda.

'Hey, Bells,' he whispered. 'You did it. You saved him, I'm sure of it.' He detected the faintest glimmer of a smile. A tear rolled down her cheek. He smiled back and wiped it off. 'Back in a minute.' Without hesitating, Archie rushed back in and, wielding a carpet, smothered the flames.

He ran down the corridor to the bathroom, emptied the contents of the bin on the floor, filled it with water and returned to extinguish the glowing embers. Finally, coughing lightly, he rejoined Daisy, who was dabbing Isabella's brow with a wet cloth.

'What were those things?' Daisy whispered.

'No idea,' he replied. 'What she did was ... astonishing, utterly amazing! She's got wicked powers!' Archie said, staring proudly at his big sister. 'Awesome.'

Isabella stirred.

Daisy offered her a cup of water. 'Did you know you could do that, Bells?' she asked.

Isabella smiled.

The twins grinned but a groan moved their attention to Old Man Wood.

Archie felt for the old man's pulse.

'Nothing,' he said. 'It's like it's vanished.'

Archie wiped his nose, holding back his tears. 'We're too late.'

Daisy reached out and took the old man's hand. 'I'm so, so sorry, Old Man Wood.'

For several minutes, Archie and Daisy sat by the old man's still body.

Finally Archie spoke. 'What happens now?' he whispered. 'How do we find the tablets without Old Man Wood?'

Daisy shook her head. 'I don't know. We've had it, haven't we?'

A strange groan came from the floor, like a whiny floorboard. Archie and Daisy looked at one another, then moved their gazes downwards.

'Well, I'm not bloomin' dead yet,' a deep, croaky voice said.

'Old Man Wood!' Daisy cried, giving him a hug.

'Aw, ow! Gently now,' he said, as he opened his eyes.

His accentuated wrinkles formed a smile and his eyes shone like jewels in the candlelight. 'Apple juice,' he said. 'And a little bit of Resplendix Mix, if you don't mind.'

'Yes! Of course,' Archie said. 'Where is it?'

Old Man Wood forced saliva into his mouth. 'Coat,' he said. 'In the boot room.'

Archie switched on his torch and tore off downstairs, returning with the strange medicine and a bottle of Old Man Wood's apple juice.

'Here,' he said, offering the golden liquid of the Resplendix Mix to Old Man Wood's lips. The moment it touched them, colour began to return to his cheeks. Old Man Wood blinked and sighed and then ooh-ed and ah-ed and grimaced as the healing medicine went to work.

Archie took it over to Isabella and did the same. Just a drop, like Old Man Wood said. The bottle opened for her and, before long, Isabella's eyes were wide open.

Then Old Man Wood smiled, a look of intense happiness on his face. But, as footsteps creaked up the stairs his expression quickly turned to alarm.

The children froze. Then slowly they turned to face whatever was coming up.

A voice rang out from the dark beyond them. 'What, in the Devil's name is going on?' it said. 'I don't know what's got into you lot. Making every effort to totally destroy the house, huh! What a terrible din, the likes of which I can't remember.'

Mrs. Pye peered into the dark. 'Been lighting fires have you? Well I hope there's a good reason for all this queer behaviour.' She shook her head. 'Your tea's on the table, or had you forgotten?'

She trudged slowly back down the stairs, tutting.

The four of them sat on the landing, chuckling like naughty schoolchildren.

Archie was the first to speak. 'What happened? What were those toadstool things?'

The old man sat up and slowly stretched his arms out wide. 'All I can say is that it's not every day you get poisoned with Havilarian Toadstool Powder. It's the most deadly powder known to ... well ... certain things. If I am in fact alive, which I suppose I must be, then I'm probably one of the few that has ever survived. So how did that happen? Who or what do I have to thank for saving my flesh?'

'You'd better thank Isabella,' Daisy said, clapping her hands. 'She did it and I have to say, it was wicked!'

'Well, I never,' Old Man Wood croaked. 'And how—?'

'Using a cocoon of pink light and energy,' Archie said. 'But your cool wooden TV panels got smashed to bits.'

Old Man Wood seemed unconcerned. 'We needn't worry about that now. What's important is that we're here and I reckon we'll be a good deal stronger for it.'

He shuffled over to Isabella and helped her up into a sitting position, and then wrapped his arms around her. 'Thank you, littlun,' he said into her ear. 'I owe you.' Then he picked himself up off the floor, stood up and ran his arms high above his head. 'Right, as Mrs. Pye said, tea is on the table and I for one am *famished*.'

---

OLD MAN WOOD'S body tingled as though it had been crammed full of electric-tipped feathers and his head fizzed with excitement.

Right now, his secrets, his magic and even his purpose were pouring back to him as though a chain had broken and unlocked the gates of his mind.

The time had arrived, no doubt about it. The opportunity to help the Heirs of Eden plot a return to the Garden of Eden had come at last. Finally, just as he'd quietly suspected, the chance had come to re-ignite the sparks of creation.

The children *had* been given the Great Dream and, it appeared, the legendary Gifts of Eden. Old Man Wood shut his eyes and smiled; that was enough thinking for now.

First, he needed nourishment. Then he would let the memories fill his head.

# 91 A LESSON FROM THE PAST

'Why did those toadstools make you so nearly die Old Man Wood?' Daisy asked as she scraped her fork around her plate. 'You said something about Havilarian Toadstool Powder but we've never heard of it before. Did you poison yourself?'

Old Man Wood chuckled, his chest heaving up and down. 'It is no mystery, my littluns,' he said, 'and, no I didn't. You see—'

'But what exactly was it?'

'A terrible substance, no doubting it,' he said, studying their blank faces. 'Must be something close by, but ***how it got there*** is indeed a mystery. In any case, whoever did it must have tried to put us off – to stop you lot making it to the other worlds—'

Archie dropped his fork and it clattered over his plate. 'What other worlds?' he said. 'I didn't know there were other worlds. I thought all we had to do was find three tablets. How many worlds are there?'

'Three,' Old Man Wood replied calmly and without pausing. 'There were five, but two of them blew themselves to pieces. Now, if I remember rightly, those ones were called Cush and Assyria – though I don't reckon there's much there any longer. They got a little too clever for their own good and forgot what Nature was all about.'

He leaned back in his chair and rubbed his chin. 'Without sounding too miserable, it might be that Earth is heading the same way. But anyway, where was I? Ah, yes. The other two planets are Earth and Havilah. Yes,' he said, thoughtfully, 'those two are the last remaining ones. Of course, there's also the Garden of Eden, but no one knows what's happened there. It's been closed an awful long time, since the great flood—'

'*The Garden of Eden*?' Isabella interrupted, suddenly wide-awake. '*The Garden of Eden,*' she repeated, '*with the flood*? *That* Garden of Eden?' she leaned across the table. 'You're talking about the Biblical place, with Adam and Eve, the serpent, Cain and Abel, Noah ... you know, Genesis ... animals going in two by two?' She fixed the old man with her hardest stare. 'It isn't a real place, you know. Everyone knows that!'

Old Man Wood frowned. 'Well, er ... no. I mean, yes. Oh appley-deary me. In the books, it's not quite the same thing ... only a smidgen of it—'

'Look,' Isabella said. 'Those Bible stories succinctly explain life before the records that come after it. If you carry on like this, Old Man Wood, we're going to have to think again about putting you in an old people's home.'

Daisy rolled her eyes. 'Bells, I thought you'd left all that behind?'

'There's no way in the world that Genesis and Creation could have physically happened.'

'It's w*orlds*,' Archie corrected her.

Isabella glowered at him. 'Life on this planet *evolved*, everyone knows that.'

'Ah,' Old Man Wood said. 'I was getting to that bit—'

'There's more?' she said.

'Oh yes, littlun. You see, once upon a time, there really was a great flood on the Earth – like the one we've got now I suppose—'

Isabella slumped back in her chair. 'And now, it's a nursery story.'

'Back then,' the old man continued, 'the "Rivers" flooded and remained flooded so nothing could travel from one world to another—'

'Rivers?'

'Oh yes. The Garden of Eden and Havilah are like Earth in a geographical, roundabout kind of way.'

Isabella massaged her temples. 'This is completely and utterly crackers,' she said. 'No known life forms in the universe have ever been found. And, furthermore, you're damning a whole civilisation of believers.'

Old Man Wood laughed, 'Bella, this isn't going to be easy—'

'Easy—?! The Bible and those other religious texts are sacred books, worshipped globally—'

'But the beginning holds the clues to what's going on NOW,' Old Man Wood argued. 'How else were they going to pass on the knowledge, the special secrets—?'

She glared at him. 'Entire cultures begin with this story!'

Old Man Wood shrugged. 'Well, no-one knew it'd be quite such a popular story at the time. And, anyway, it seemed like a good place to start—'

'Oh my God,' Isabella said, slowly. 'This is deeply, deeply flawed,' she said, shaking her head.

'What are *Rivers*?' Archie interrupted. 'I take it these aren't *real* rivers are they? And anyway, isn't Assyria somewhere in Africa? I'm sure Mum and Dad mentioned it last time they were back.'

Mentioning their parents made the children suddenly a little reflective and an uneasy silence hung in the air.

Old Man Wood turned to Archie. 'I haven't explained it properly, have I?' he said, relieved to move away from Isabella's grilling. 'But you're absolutely appley-right about one thing! *Rivers* are the connections between worlds—'

'Like wormholes?' Daisy said, as though a little spark had burst into a flame. 'Portals that transcend space, and all that stuff.'

The old man clapped his big hands together. 'Why, that exactly!' he said. 'Wormholes, portals, *Rivers* – they're one and the same thing. And yes, those places here on earth, Assyria, the Garden of Eden, Cush and Havilah, many others – were named in memory of their own worlds far, far away in other universes a long, long time ago.'

Daisy continued, intrigued. 'So, you said that people stopped travelling from planet to planet through these "Rivers". Why did these worm-holey things close down?'

'Hmm. Now, that's a good question,' Old Man Wood said, his face deeply lined in thought. 'War and a difference of opinion, I suppose. You see, those stories, like that Genesis one, were nearly right,' he said, his face darkening. 'But, oh, what a terrible time, even if it did save Earth and Havilah.'

'I don't understand. How could a massive flood *save* Earth?' Daisy asked, confused. 'Didn't everyone die apart from Noah? And anyway, what happened to this Garden of Eden place?'

Old Man Wood hummed as he thought about his answer. 'As far as I can remember, hordes of bad folk found a way of going back through the *Rivers* and into the Garden of Eden because, up until then, you could only go out of the Garden and not in. As a result, the Garden found itself being poisoned; its structure eroded and destroyed, and then ... war.'

Old Man Wood's eyes filled with tears, his brow deep and furrowed. 'A terrible war. People tried to make a claim on the Garden of Eden, and when the fighting finally stopped, blood covered the worlds, rivers ran red, flames singed the land, bitterness ran through veins, treachery mastered minds. Hatred and anger everywhere. A horrible time.'

Old Man Wood wiped his eyes and pulled himself together a little. 'To put it to an end, there was a moment of extraordinary sacrifice, one moment that alone is worth the Garden of Eden coming back to life.'

For a while, silence reigned as Old Man Wood stared into the distance. The children hardly dared to breathe.

Isabella took a deep breath. 'OK – so if what you're saying has some truth to it, what made this Garden of Eden so special?' she asked quietly. 'Why did it matter?'

Old Man Wood regarded her, his face deadly serious. 'Because, my dear little Bells,' he said, 'it's where everything began. That's why—'

'Everything?'

'Yes, everything. How do you think all these billions of things that make up the world around you actually started?' He studied their puzzled faces. 'Everything – dinosaurs, people, trees, fish, bugs, flowers, bacteria, clouds, particles, atoms, matter, energy – even your dreams – were all started in the Garden of Eden. From there, each creation began to grow and mature or die, or, as you lot say, evolve.'

Isabella shook her head. 'But I thought life began on Earth from a collision involving a meteor or a comet?'

The old man leant back in his chair and roared with laughter. 'Big-bangs, lumps of rock in space colliding with each other,' the old man said. 'Oh, yes, those life-givers did happen, but a long time before the living things came about. And it took an awful lot of knocking and banging them together to make the right kind of place. And who says they won't come again?'

Isabella's face had turned the colour of milk, Archie glumly stroked his foremost hair spike and Daisy massaged her temples.

Old Man Wood clapped his hands. 'But enough of all that. It's complicated – and anyway, weren't we talking about Havilarian Toadstool Powder?'

The children nodded.

'Well, young 'un's,' he continued, 'Havilarian Toadstool Powder is a very rare powder that blends itself to look like anything it's mixed with: liquid or solid – so it's hard to know how I digested it. It's so deadly that it's the only thing that can nearly kill me ...'

'What do you mean?' Isabella queried, her voice barely above a whisper. *'Nearly kill you.* Does that make you ... I mean ... are you ... please, don't tell me you can't ... actually ... die?'

'I'll die if I return to the Garden of Eden, one day,' Old Man Wood said slowly. 'But if I don't, then I suppose I'll carry on like I have done, indefinitely.'

Isabella coughed and looked as if she were about to vomit all over the floor.

Daisy, on the other hand, shut one eye and ruffled her hair deep in thought. 'You're saying you've been alive ... *forever?'*

Old Man Wood smiled back a little warily. 'Yes, littlun.'

'Blimey,' and then she swore, '... sorry, WOW!' Daisy squealed. 'You've really lived ... that long? Forever, and ever, amen?'

Old Man Wood shifted, turning pink.

'Then, that makes you ... you're ... you're immoral?' Daisy squealed.

'It's *immortal*, not immoral, you numpty,' Isabella snapped.

'Yeah, yeah. Whatever,' Daisy said, nodding. 'Pretty awesome.'

Archie was visibly trembling. 'But you can't be—'

'Look carefully,' Old Man Wood said. 'That's me in all those pictures you've pulled off the walls.'

'I told you so, I told you so,' Daisy said, squealing with delight. 'Does that make you, like ... God?' she asked. 'Please say yes!'

Old Man Wood smiled. 'I promise you,' he said 'my situation is nothing more than a terrible curse. A burden that is heavier than you can possibly imagine. I was telling you about the poison...'

But now that he studied the children's expressions, Old Man Wood realised they deserved more of an explanation. 'If you must know, I've watched you humans develop for an awfully long time.'

The children looked at each other and then at Old Man Wood with their mouths ajar, the enormity of these words not lost on them in spite of their young years.

After a long and very awkward silence, Isabella spoke. 'Look, this is a bit of a head-fry, and I'm still not sure I really, truly grasp what you're saying. So let me recap: You're saying that *Rivers* are connections between worlds? Yes?'

'Indeed,' Old Man Wood replied. 'They are the routes between Earth and other planets. Daisy has already experienced one when she visited the atrium.' He smiled warmly at Daisy.

'And you're saying that the Garden of Eden really did exist, right, like a huge laboratory?'

Old Man Wood agreed.

'And the Garden of Eden is a planet, and not actually a garden – with flowers and berries and veg?'

'That's right.'

'And that every living thing came from there?'

He raised his eyebrows.

'And then these other places went to war, and in so doing shut it down. And you've been around for the whole time since?'

The old man nodded.

'And now, we've got to discover three tablets by way of five random poems on five mangy old rugs to get to these other worlds – particularly the Garden of Eden?'

'Hmm, well, yes, I suppose.'

Isabella screwed up her face as though she was on the verge of bursting into tears. 'You've got to agree it is utterly irrational,' she muttered. 'Why?'

'To open the Garden of Eden, of course,' Old Man Wood said. 'It's a source of incredible power. The power of creation is something you here on Earth can barely imagine.'

'But why *now* and, more importantly, *why us*?'

Old Man Wood stretched his arms out wide. 'Something has shifted in the universe and, as a result, you have been given the Great Dream. And it's you lot, because your direct family line happens to have been under my care for thousands of years. It is a test, I believe, like those examinations you have at school, only a little bit more important.'

He rubbed his chin, thinking. 'Not all my brains have returned inside here,' and he pointed at his skull, 'but as far as I remember, this test was put in place to see whether those chosen on the planet were ready.'

'Ready for what?'

'To survive and move mankind on to its next stage.'

Isabella didn't like the sound of this. 'And if they aren't ready and fail, then what?'

'Hmm, good question,' Old Man Wood said. 'Let me think. I believe the species on the planet will be done away with.'

'Done away with?' Isabella said. 'You mean killed?'

Old Man Wood shrugged.

'Like the dinosaurs?'

The old man hummed. 'Yes, I suppose you're right. Those horrid scaly things were a terrible nuisance. But you see, when the universe had something better planned it got rid of almost all of them except crocodiles and birds and a few others. The universe changes – it just does that, you know. A new time is upon us and it's going to try and do it again.'

'Didn't an asteroid hit the earth and wipe them out?' Daisy said, quietly. Her bones ached, and her head throbbed. She remembered the cave paintings, and the final panel. Now, the puzzle was coming together.

Old Man Wood continued. 'It's not the first time, and it certainly won't be the last. There have been all sorts of new types of mankind—'

Isabella butted in: 'Homo habilis, homo erectus, Neolithic man and now us, homo sapiens,' she rattled out. 'Dad taught me. But I thought they came one after the other, in some kind of order?'

'Clever of you to know all that,' Old Man Wood said, encouragingly. 'Then, perhaps it's time for another one—'

'If we don't fail,' Archie added.

'Yes. Something like that,' Old Man Wood said. He stood up and piled the plates together, the candlelight accentuating the grim reality and faces of the siblings. Then he opened the door to the range cooker where the embers sat like small duvets of ash over glowing bodies and added a couple of logs. The children's eyes followed him as he went about his business as though he were a kind of pet alien; freaky, yet all theirs.

'Well now,' the old man said as he sat down again and looked up at the kitchen clock. 'Best get off to bed. There's a busy day ahead finding these tablets and it's already near enough eleven.'

'Shouldn't we be searching for them right now? Archie said. 'If it's so important, we don't have a moment to lose. Daisy, you thought there were seven days in which to do this ... I think I can remember the poem:

*'You have but seven days and seven nights*
*'As Earth moves in its cycle*
*'From first lightning strike and thunderclap*
*'A world awaits your arrival.*

'How long is it since that first lightning bolt?' He rubbed his strange hair in recollection of the event which birthed his spikes. 'Three days ... four?'

Daisy screwed up her face as she attempted to recall the days and nights, counting them off on her fingers. 'After tonight, I reckon there are three days left.'

'Over half way already,' Archie said, flatly. 'And, so far, all we've managed to do is pretty much destroy the house, get on the "international missing persons" list, start a Biblical storm, lose three of the animals and set off a global plague—'

'And we only have one tablet.'

'Yes. Is that good, or bad?'

'Shocking,' Daisy said. 'And we don't even know what the other riddles mean.'

Old Man Wood pointed towards Isabella whose forehead lay neatly perched on the table, her hair folding down in front. 'You won't be getting much joy from clever-clogs over there.'

As he said it, Isabella stirred, yawned and moved her head so that it lay on her forearm. 'I'm still awake,' she murmured, 'listening to your incredibly interesting conversation.' She yawned. 'And by the way, if there are any tablets that need finding up by the ruin, count me out. I would rather the world slips to a miserable end than scout around up there again.'

'Thanks for your huge support, as always, Bells,' Daisy said, yawning. 'I'm going to bed. Coming?'

The other two stood up.

Daisy hugged Old Man Wood. 'Are you going to bed too?'

'No, my dear littluns.' he said, 'there are a few things I still need to find out.'

'Like what?' Archie said.

'Like what the poems on the rugs are all about. Since I have no idea what Blabisterberry Jelly means, or where we'll find it, I guess I'm going to have to do some rooting around.' He smiled broadly. 'Before you head upstairs, does anyone know what happened to those poems Archie wrote down?'

Archie sighed. 'They're somewhere next door, probably ripped to bits when we found the tablet. I'll go and find them.'

Daisy laughed, thinking what a terrible state the room was in. 'Wait for me, Arch,' she said. 'I'll lend you a hand, they could be anywhere.'

# 92 MEMORIES RETURN

Isabella reluctantly stood up and, with leaden feet, followed Archie, Daisy and Old Man Wood into the dark living room where the embers of the fire glowed like dulled molten gold. After watching them poke and prod at the debris in the candlelight, turning over bits of paper here, shuffling others there, Isabella's impatience got the better of her. 'Oh, come on! You're all being completely hopeless,' she roared. 'Stand back, please, and leave it to the pro.'

They backed away and in a matter of moments Isabella's body flashed from one side to the other, up and down the room, her hands shooting here and there collecting up sheets of paper, her feet moving like a blur, her fingers shuffling through the slips of torn paper. When she slowed, she held a large, stacked pile of paper with, at the very top, the sections that made up the strange poems.

'How-the-hell-did-you-do-that?!' Archie said, wide-eyed in shock.

'Easy,' she replied.

Daisy shook her head. 'You know, Isabella, you're really taking organisation to a scary level.'

Isabella cuffed her on the arm. 'On the day of the storm,' she began, 'when I woke up, my feet and hands ached for hours.' She held them up. 'I know I can heal and protect with my hands, like I did with Old Man Wood, but sometimes my feet move as if they're jet-propelled, I've been zooming about – when I ran back from the ruin I wasn't even out of breath.'

'We noticed,' Archie said drolly. 'Daisy has always been faster than you.'

'Well, not anymore!' Isabella said, her eyes twinkling. 'And the rest you know about.' She drew in a large, satisfied breath. 'It does seem to work better when I concentrate—'

'Same with mine,' Daisy said. 'Though my things are not only seeing kind of weird stuff but hearing it too. You won't believe the odd sounds I hear.'

She caught Archie's eye. 'For example, there's some kind of water-course underneath the house. I bet you didn't know there's a noise dripping away, did you? And mice all over the place nattering away all the time. They are sooo dull—'

Isabella, Archie and Old Man Wood looked at Daisy with increased fascination.

Archie looked her hard in the eye. 'You mentioned it at the ruin. Read the poem, Bells!' he demanded. 'It's the third one, I think.'

Isabella obliged.

'The third you search is underneath your nose.
'It's clear, pure and cold.
'In order to draw it out
'You need to send a rose.'

'I thought it was: *clear, pure and warm,* like snot,' Archie said. *'Clear, pure and cold* has to be water.'

'It's coming from under the house,' Daisy said. 'Drip, drip, dripping-away.'

Old Man Wood suddenly became agitated. 'By all the apples!' he said springing out of his chair.

**DOFF!**

Old Man Wood's bald head walloped a low beam and the noise echoed around the room.

**'OW!'** Old Man Wood howled. 'OW, damnable beams!' he rubbed his bald, moon-scaped pate. 'Always thought I'd built the bleedin' house too low!'

He sank down cautiously into the armchair, blinking and screwing up his face and rubbing his head like mad.

'I hope it won't muddle him up again,' Isabella whispered to Archie.

'Hmmm,' Old Man Wood eventually muttered and the children collectively breathed a sigh of relief. 'I'm sure there was once a well in the middle of the house, and if I'm not mistaken there was also, secretly, a tunnel connecting the ruin to this house, which many, many moons ago was a popular inn. You wouldn't believe how different it was...'

'Do you have architectural plans tucked away in your cellar?' Archie asked. 'I mean, you said you'd rebuilt it about thirty times. You must know the layouts like the back of your hand.'

Old Man Wood thought for a while. 'I can't remember ... oooh ... no. It's been so long, you can't conceive how long, that I've been waiting for all this to happen. So even though I now remember where I come from, which, I suppose, is soldered into my brain, there's an awful lot in-between which is a blur.'

He noted their disappointed faces.

'There was a time, several hundred years ago, when I thought it was time to return to the Garden, but it was a false alarm – even the Universe gets it wrong from time to time,' he smiled at the thought. 'Thinking that my reason for being had passed, memories started to ebb away, like the tide, I suppose. There's a massive amount that I don't think I'll ever get back, but the tide is rushing in again, faster than a galloping horse.'

Old Man Wood smiled kindly. 'We're just going to have to work it out together. If it's any help, I'm sure there was a network of cellar rooms underneath the ruin – like a labyrinth, I suppose. I got lost there for a couple of weeks once upon a time. Most unpleasant it was too, so I haven't been there much recently.'

'When was that?' Archie asked.

'Oooh now. Let me think. Probably a few centuries ago. Back in the ...' He counted several hundred on his hand. 'About the mid seventeen-hundreds.'

The children looked at each other, dumbfounded, trying to get their heads around this vast stretch of time. A couple of days with Auntie Spoon felt like a few hundred years, so goodness knows how it must feel to be so old.

'Before Australia was discovered?' Isabella pressed.

'Hmmm, well, yes I suppose it is rather a long time for you little things to contemplate. Now, you must have heard about them Aboriginal peoples. Most interesting bunch and they've been there a long time—'

'I know we need to find the well and the tablets and all that stuff,' Daisy interrupted, 'but is the Q'ash Warshbit a real thing, did it *actually* exist?' she asked. 'Were those stories about Iso that you told us in front of the fire, actually true?'

'Oh yes! Most definitely, all those stories really happened. One day you might actually meet Iso – she's out there somewhere, I'm sure of it. You never know—'

'Please!' Isabella roared, giving Daisy a hard stare. 'Would you two be quiet for a moment! How are we going to find the dripping water?'

Old Man Wood paced around the room for a few minutes, alternatively rubbing his chin and his head, and humming to himself. Finally he sat down in his armchair and sighed.

'I think, my little ones, we may have to go up to the ruin and find those old cellars.'

Isabella groaned. 'But what about the "thing" we heard at the ruin?'

'Well, you and your MAGIC powers should be able to sort it out,' Archie said, sarcastically. He appeared disappointed that he seemed to have missed out on the wider, perhaps cooler, distribution of gifts.

The girls looked away, embarrassed.

Old Man Wood leaned in, his brow deeply ridged. 'What kind of *thing* are you talking about?' he asked.

Daisy started to recall how they had heard a strange cough and an evil bark and how, just as the bell had rung, Archie had idiotically jumped out and found nothing there. 'And on the way back we bumped into Mrs. Pye.'

'Are you quite sure the noise wasn't Mrs. Pye?' Isabella said.

Archie burst out laughing. 'Mrs. Pye it definitely wasn't. She's more like a strange looking angel than a monster – isn't that right, Old Man Wood?'

Old Man Wood looked shaken, his face pale and withdrawn. He waved a hand in the air.

Isabella rolled her eyes. 'You know perfectly well that monsters don't exist here in Yorkshire.'

'Are you absolutely sure about that, sis?' Archie said. 'Coz the panels on the bed didn't really exist, did they?'

Daisy caught his eye. 'Nor the exploding toadstools,' Daisy added, 'and the tablet coming out of the fire was pretty imaginary.'

Archie clapped her on the back. 'Come on Bells! *Anything* is possible. Don't you understand; our dreams – these strange events – are leading us to this Garden of Eden place. We're inexplicably linked to it, and nothing can stop it.'

Isabella looked crestfallen. 'Look, I know, alright. But if we have to find one of the tablets at the ruin, I'm not going.'

Old Man Wood noticed her anxiety and draped an arm around her shoulders. 'Bells, together we'll be fine, I'm reckoning. Nothing like a good night's sleep to stamp out your worries.'

'Are you sure we shouldn't start right away?' Archie said, persisting.

'No. We have to find Blabisterberry Jelly next,' Old Man Wood began. 'My friends, the willows, may just have the information we need. I'll head down there shortly. Tomorrow will be quite a day so I suggest you grab every moment of sleep you can.'

Archie nodded. 'So that's it then,' he said firmly. 'Tomorrow, at dawn, we find Blabisterberry Jelly,' he said, looking at the poem as though it would be dead easy. 'Let's meet at six for breakfast.'

# 93 THE TRUTH OF KEMP'S MOTHER

'As I said,' Cain began, 'I am simply telling you the truth. That woman is your mother.'

'Then take me to her,' Kemp demanded, 'this minute. We'll settle it once and for all.'

Cain was beginning to regret ever having mentioned the boy's mother. The ghost hovered away and let the overcoat slip to the floor. A body of dust puffed up and the specks played briefly in the light as tiny particles of glitter.

'What benefit will it be for anyone?' Cain said. 'The woman will not see you as her son as much as you do not wish to take her as your mother. Why complicate? Why muddy the waters? What can you possibly gain?'

'If you're saying Mrs. Pye's my mother, fine, let's go and ask her. If she denies it then I know you've been lying,' Kemp said. 'If she says that she is, then so be it. But if you're telling me lies, I will never go with you again.'

'You are not listening,' Cain responded, angrily. 'Of course she will deny it. She will deny ever knowing you because she doesn't know you exist, boy. Then what? Would you like me to present a fake, to make you *feel* better? So you can live out your fantasy of having a mother?'

Kemp didn't have an answer, but something troubled him. 'Why won't she remember me?' he said, staring at the floor.

'When your father died,' Cain said, as a brilliant idea popped into his mind, 'your mother escaped the accident, but not without terrible injuries. Because of them, she has no recollection of anything before that time. What I am about to tell you may be hard to stomach.'

'Go on,' Kemp said.

'You might think this is not possible, but it is,' Cain began earnestly, 'the old de Lowe helper—'

'Old Man Wood?'

Invisible to the boy, Cain beamed. 'Yes, I believe that is what they call him. He found her and seeing her broken took her back to the de Lowe cottage to care for her. But as he attempted to heal her, that old man did a terrible thing. I'm afraid, boy, that what you're about to hear won't be easy to digest.'

'How do you know this?'

'Your father's ghost told me this, so it must be true.' Cain grinned and thumped the air.

Kemp prickled. 'What did my father tell you?' he said, quietly.

'That Old Man Wood, for reasons I expect of pure bloodiness, cut into her head with a large, sharp knife and removed a section of her brain, a piece of her memory.'

Kemp's eyes bulged. Then a shadow of doubt passed over his face. 'I never thought the old man was the blood-thirsty type,' he said. 'Always seemed as soft as putty to me.'

Cain responded swiftly. 'One of the biggest lessons I can give you is that there's always, always, more to people than meets the eye. Take me, for example. At first you found me reprehensible and vile, didn't you? And with good reason.'

Kemp nodded, slowly.

'And now we're quite the best of friends, aren't we? You're learning fast, boy. I've heard stories about that old man from various ghostly friends of mine and I'm told that he harbours a terrible past—'

'Really?'

'Absolutely! Of bloodletting and gore. Unmentionable cruelty. There's little doubt that the old man thinks nothing of cold-blooded murder.'

'Old man whatshisface? Are you sure?'

'When I heard he was in charge of the Heirs of Eden, I wondered for the safety of those poor de Lowe children.' Cain wondered if he'd gone too far.

'Have no fear though, boy. You are with me now, and safe enough. I will take you to your mother. But do not say later that you did not heed my warnings.'

Kemp sat deep in thought, twisting a knife around his fingers. 'I think I need to get it over with,' he said at length. 'I need to know, one way or another.'

'Very well,' Cain said. 'In the morning, at first light on Earth, I will summon Asgard. He must sacrifice two of his dreamspinners for us to travel there and back. They will need forewarning.'

Cain called into the air, 'Dreamspinner, dreamspinner, dreamspinner.'

Seconds later a tiny flash was followed by an opaque, white, almost arachnid creature, standing in mid air.

'Asgard, tomorrow at first light I must honour my promise to the boy. We go to find his mother at Eden Cottage. Can you give us transport within your brethren?'

Asgard tapped the air beneath him. 'There are many who are old and would rather die than see the demise of the dreamspinners. They are yours, for now. But be warned, Cain. Genesis, our mother, has returned from her self-imposed exile. She draws many dreamspinners to her. Even those who are old.'

Cain smiled. 'But as we know, Asgard, there are but three days left to open the Garden of Eden. The Heirs have but one tablet. The task is beyond them and all the while the Earth cries out of its own accord.'

Asgard stared at Cain, the dreamspinner's three black eyes boring into the ghost. 'I will be here just before dawn for your trip to Earth.' And in the next moment, he had vanished.

Cain turned to Kemp, who was cramming a chocolate-coated strawberry tartlet into his mouth. 'Now, rest, boy. Tomorrow you will discover the truth and it may not taste quite as sweet.'

# 94 GUS ESCAPES

Gus beamed his biggest, toothiest grin at Sue as she walked through the door, a big suit covering her from head to foot like a spaceman. She ran over and, without thinking, jumped up into his arms.

'Missed you,' she said, as tears formed in her eyes.

'Me, same,' he replied. 'Though it's not quite the same kissing a plastic helmet.' He put her down and stepped back. 'Cor! I'm digging the sexy outfit,' he joked.

Sue hit him playfully on the arm.

'I'll leave you two to it, then,' said the nurse who'd accompanied Sue in. 'To be perfectly honest with you, there's nothing wrong with you, is there, Gus?' The nurse looked her up and down. 'I have a strong feeling, young lady, that you'll survive without the suit,' she added, winking.

The door snapped shut.

'When are they letting you out?' Sue said through the protective helmet.

'Don't know. No one knows anything round here. They're all shit scared, apart from that nurse. She's totally chilled, but if I go "BOO" to the others they shriek and run away!'

Sue held his hand.

'Thing is, I'm fine, one hundred percent. All I had was a twenty-four hour bug, nothing serious. Certainly not this Ebora, otherwise, by the sounds of it, I'd already be dead.'

'Thing is,' she said, 'you're a survivor. So they'll want to know what makes you so special.'

'You don't know?'

'Course *I* do,' she smiled. 'Just the other numpties round here.'

Even though her surveillance bug was pinned to her clothes in the changing room she knew she should keep her voice down. 'Gus. Do guards watch over you?'

'Not really,' he shrugged.

'What about doctors?'

'Nah. The nurses are alright. There's a camera over there and someone outside, but I'm pretty sure they're asleep half the time. Last night whoever it was slipped off at about ten o'clock. When I popped off to the toilet there was no one around. But they do the rounds in roughly four-hour cycles. Yesterday they came in to take blood three times, urine twice and ... it's a wonder there's anything left. Do I look a bit pale?'

Sue laughed. 'Very—'

'Anyway, for the last twelve hours I've been the last thing on their minds. They're trying to make a serum or something. They're really not interested in me.'

'Good,' Sue replied, moving close. 'That creepy Commissioner is close to finding out about Archie and the others. We've got to help them. So I'm getting you out.'

'Cool,' Gus said. 'How?'

'I don't know.'

'What you've come here without a plan?' Gus said feigning shock. 'How very un-Sue like.'

'Actually,' she said as an idea rocketed into her head, 'I have. Where are your clothes?' He pointed at the cupboard. Sue marched across, took them out and, as subtly as possible, placed them on the bed.

Sue searched the small room and pulled up a privacy screen at the far end spreading it around the bed as far as it would go. She sat down on the bed and beckoned Gus to do the same. She unzipped her headpiece, detached the poppers and pulled it over her head. Her hair tumbled out.

In the confines of the small bed, she began to slip the remaining part of the protective suit down her body. 'Give me a hand, please.' Her eyes twinkled.

Gus' smile spread across his face, a mix of glee and nervousness. In a short while, Sue lay naked on the bed save for her underwear. She looked up at Gus beside her who was painfully trying not to look.

She giggled. 'Kiss me.'

Gus hesitated, stunned by Sue's directness. 'You're kidding!'

'Go on,' she whispered.

Gus hesitated.

'Don't worry – it's all part of the plan.'

'This is your plan?'

'Yes, and you're on camera, so it had better be good!'

Gus didn't need to be asked again.

---

IN THE CORRIDOR OUTSIDE, the nurse hurried down to the desk outside Gus Williams' door and checked the clipboard.

Time to get the girl out. She looked up at the screen and for a moment couldn't think what she was looking at. Then it dawned on her.

She readied herself to march in but then she remembered being fourteen and the feeling of being kissed. She smiled. If the news was as bad as everyone said, how many more youths would miss out on this simple pleasure?

Better to gently warn them.

The nurse knocked on the door. 'Miss Lowden. Time to go! And don't think I don't know what you two are up to!'

From behind the door she could hear giggling followed by hysterical laughter.

*Oh, to be young and in love*, the nurse thought. 'I'll be back in five minutes,' she said and then called out. 'And when I come back, I want you out of there.'

The nurse smiled. There's absolutely nothing wrong with that boy. Cheeky lad and all. She'd give them their last few minutes alone. She sighed. There were more important things to be getting on with than peeping at them on the monitor.

---

SUE LISTENED as the nurse's footsteps tapered off down the corridor. 'Right, Gus. Get in the protective suit.'

Gus leaned in again. She moved away.

'Uh?'

'Get in that suit, NOW!'

Gus looked confused.

'It's your way out, silly,' she said, her eyes sparkling. 'People round here know who I am, but we can't have you just wandering about. If you put the suit on, no one will know any better.' She pulled his t-shirt on. It smelt entirely of him and it felt strangely reassuring.

'I'm going to make a run for the toilet while you get changed. You'll need to make a dummy in the bed with the pillows – make it look as realistic as you can. As soon as you hear the nurse return, open the door in your protective suit, turn to the bed and blow a kiss, switch off the light, pretend to snivel like a girl and head down the corridor.' Sue smiled at the thought of it.

'Go directly outside and walk to the right. I'll join you. There are loads of people milling about and tents dotted here and there. Just walk like you mean it.'

'You're mad!' he said.

'I'm not, Gus. We need to help Archie and his sisters and I need you. And besides,' Sue said with a sparkle in her eye. 'If you ever want to see me nearly naked again, you'd better do exactly as I say.'

# 95 OLD MAN WOOD'S PROBLEM

*The willows,* Old Man Wood thought, *may not know about the water under the house but they are sure to know how to eat Blabisterberry Jelly.*

As the children headed up the stairs to their attic room, the old man donned his coat and boots and slipped quietly out of the back door, down the path to the potting shed, selected a clean, plastic, water-tight bucket and, using his torch to help him find his way, he trudged down the steep, treacherous terrain past the decimated remains of vegetables and ruined fruit trees. When he found the brown water line, he followed it, just as he had with Archie, until he came to the impenetrable willow barrier – the Bubbling Brook.

'Bethedi,' he whispered. 'You awake?'

'Uh! Eh! What time d'you call this?'

'Who's there?' said another voice. More voices joined in and shortly Old Man Wood found he could see the figures of sleepy elf-like tree-spirits rubbing sleep out of their tiny eyes and leaning out from their respective boughs or dangling from branches like bats.

'It's me,' Old Man Wood said, shining his torch around. 'I need to ask about a few things.'

Bethedi's gnarly old tree spirit bounded down the tree and perched near his head. The tree-elf stretched his arms wide and yawned. 'For sure, my old friend. We've all got good memories, hum-hum. Ask away.'

'I've discovered many things,' Old Man Wood began, 'like those little rugs with verses written on them. And you're right, time is running out on us.'

The wind picked up and blew heavy drops of water off the branches where they sprinkled down into the pool. In the torch light, Old Man Wood watched the water rings spreading out and beyond. In the corner of his eye, he noted that, attached to each tree, little elves moved along branches and stems to listen.

'Now before you start, hum-hum, make yourself comfortable,' Bethedi said. The old man wiggled his bottom onto a stump and leaned back on a tree trunk. 'You have questions? Well, good. I am pleased to hear it.'

'Tell me,' the old man said, 'what in the apples is Blabisterberry Jelly? Where would I find it and what do we do with the three tablets if we find them?'

Bethedi roared with laughter.

'Oi – you – cut it out!' sang a thrush from higher up. 'We're sleeping. You know the rules: no talking after nightfall.'

'Hum-hum. You are a right one,' whispered Bethedi. 'It's lucky that in the deep roots and folds of our bark we hold your secrets close. You told us Willows about three tablets and a very cunning plan, hum-hum. Well, do not be a-worrying; we remember. Your secrets are safe, even from those a-blasted birds, hum-hum. You want to know about Blabisterberry Jelly.' Bethedi took a deep breath.

'Blabisterberry Jelly, my old friend, is the most amazing, cunning, hilarious and terrifying potion ever created. Made from about three hundred ingredients – each one doused in magic – so that even the great wizard, Merlin, your old friend, didn't like to use it, hum-hum. Remember how you told us that he never really understood it, or how to control it?'

For some time, Bethedi told a few stories about Blabisterberry Jelly and, as he spoke, the nature of the mixture began to come back to Old Man Wood.

'But why is it dangerous?' he asked. 'And how does one of the stone tablets come from it?'

Bethedi hum-hummed. 'Now here's the thing, hum-hum,' the little elf began. 'If used in the wrong way, Blabisterberry Jelly is lethal. Too many grew frightened of it because they couldn't trust it. This was the reason you used it to protect the stone tablet. The riddle you found will reveal the tablet, but only to those who truly believe, hum-hum.'

And so, as the night drew on and the rain came and went, Old Man Wood rediscovered some of the mysteries of Blabisterberry Jelly, and bits and pieces of his long life and adventures. Finally, he asked about the water source under the house that Daisy had mentioned. 'Did I ever tell you of a well under the house?'

Bethedi thought for a while and hum-hummed, knowing what to say, but not quite knowing how to say it. 'Yes, dear old friend,' the tree-elf said at long last, rubbing his tiny, long beard. 'Once you talked of a well, deep in the hillside. The only route to it was through a labyrinth beneath the old castle. It was guarded by a fearsome beast you saved from execution when the Garden of Eden closed.'

'Why would I do a thing like this?'

'When the tablets and their riddles were put in place for the new time, the beast would have suffered an eon of sleep and, on awakening, either it would die or the new Heirs of Eden would prevail. Never was there a better test of bravery and cunning than to outmatch and outwit the monster.'

'Apples-alive!' Old Man Wood said, shocked.

'Oh yes, hum-hum,' Bethedi said, leaning back and gauging Old Man Wood's reaction. Then he continued, selecting his words carefully.

'When you put these spells in place many thousands of years ago, you did it to deter impostors who might stumble upon the secrets, but no one wanted you to go so far, hum-hum. The clues were too difficult and we knew you would never be the same person as the energetic youth you were then.' Bethedi's voice was deep and sincere.

'And now, my dear friend, you are old, humanised and soft. You have lost your magic and your youth. You fooled yourself that you would be young forever. You see, we trees understand the ageing process better than most things borne of Mother Nature. With great age comes wisdom and understanding, but also a loss of skill, courage and clarity.' Bethedi ducked behind a leaf and momentarily rubbed the corner of his mouth with it.

'I know the water is up and you have to find the tablets and try and get into the Garden of Eden – everything is talking about it – but you will struggle, if indeed your Heirs conquer Blabisterberry Jelly. You told us it was your finest riddle – and your hardest. And you were quick to tell us

Willows how clever you'd been, but, hum-hum, unfortunately you kept it from us. Sorry, dear friend, but we cannot help you further. For this, you are on your own.'

Old Man Wood slumped further down the trunk. He, more than anyone, should have known better. Living things never remain the same, they change and evolve. Why would he be any different?

Old Man Wood thanked them and, feeling quite stiff from leaning so long on the tree, bade them goodnight.

He lowered the plastic bucket into the Bubbling Brook and watched as the water filled it. And with his mood as dark as the night surrounding him, the old man started home, slipping up the wet, muddy slope careful to keep as much water in the bucket as possible.

Deep, troubling thoughts filled his mind. From what he'd heard, he was almost certainly leading them to a violent, terrible death. He needed his wits, and a bit of magic wouldn't go amiss, he thought. B*ut where the apples would that come from?*

He heaved the bucket up, feeling the weight in his arms. And how would he explain the secrets of the Beast – or whatever it was – when he didn't have a clue?

# 96 KEMP GOES HOME

'Now when we arrive with the woman,' Cain said, 'her reaction may be one of profound shock. She will not understand what she sees and nor should she. Together, our appearance is that of an ash-covered human, as if we have climbed out from a foul, sooty chimney.'

Cain mused on his description and wondered whether this was the right approach. 'Perhaps I should let you talk to her alone,' he mused. 'Seeing an ashen man will almost certainly make her nervy.'

Cain lunged athletically and jogged up and down on the spot as if to remind the boy who was in control. 'If I do this, under no circumstances must you make her scream or wake the others. Understand? We do not want to be found. Furthermore, these dreamspinners are a cautious breed, my friend, and we would not want to be accused of being caught meddling with the prophecy. Goodness knows what might happen. I would be stranded and you, dear child, would more than likely lose your life.'

"Yes, yes, yes,' Kemp said impatiently and he pushed his wet arms up and through the arm-holes of the overcoat that hovered in front of him. Then, as before, he donned the trilby hat that the ghost preferred. Pain prickled through him but, in comparison with the first time, it was like a mild case of pins and needles.

Cain sensed the boy had settled and called out into the dark sky. 'Dreamspinner, dreamspinner, dreamspinner.'

Seconds later, two tiny flashes appeared. Asgard, along with another, even more grey-ringed dreamspinner hovered above them, their flashing magholes reflecting blue light on Cain's ashen body.

Cain clapped his hands and a puff of ash exploded into the sky. 'Excellent. As quick as ever, Asgard. Good, good.'

Asgard floated upon the air as though standing on an invisible cloud. 'This is Avantis. She travels one last time.'

An ashen Cain bowed low in front of the dreamspinner. 'We are humbled by your sacrifice,' the ghost crowed.

'My sacrifice is nothing in comparison to yours, Master of Havilah.'

'Time to go. Light breaks on Earth shortly,' Asgard said.

Avantis moved in front of Cain. 'I am ready, when you are.'

'Good,' Cain replied. And without further ado he dived through the extended maghole.

In the blink of an eye, Cain and Kemp lay on a cream carpeted floor.

Slowly they picked themselves up and Cain looked around, noting how the woman slept soundly in her bed.

The room, Kemp noticed, was simple, uncluttered and painted in a soft pink. Photo frames of the de Lowe children in various holders and old wedding pictures of their parents crowded the table and dresser tops. A scrap book on her desk stuffed with local newspaper mentions of the children, and a recent picture of Daisy and Archie in the football team lay on an open page ready to be glued in. On another table sat a couple of trinkets, a small silver cup, a necklace and a glass jar with an ornate silver top.

At the far end of the room, in the corner, was the television facing a comfortable armchair with floral pink cushions and a matching blue cover-throw.

Cain stood up as the woman stirred – this was his chance. He moved towards her and sat down almost weightlessly on the bed, close enough to place a hand over her mouth if she were to scream.

Then, true to his word, Cain removed himself from Kemp, his spirit flying freely into the room. 'Take your hat off, boy. It doesn't really suit you. And the coat. I'll hang them up outside the room and wait there for you when the hand on that timepiece moves to here,' he said, pointing at the clock.

'Good luck, boy. And if it's any help,' he whispered, 'you are the son of Tobias and Lucy Kemp.'

'Forty minutes?' Kemp said.

'You are on your own now. I need to pay someone a visit.'

---

DICKINSON KILLED the engine and let the RIB drift in towards the makeshift shoreline. A huge beam of light scoured the scrub for a suitable landing area and within a few moments one of the men, a compact, shaven-headed man with a crooked nose, named Geddis, thrust an oar in so that the boat swung round and beached perfectly. Four of the five jumped out and, water up to their knees, pulled the boat until it slid noiselessly onto the bank.

'It's mud, sir,' Geddis announced. 'Damn hellish amount.' He sniffed the air. 'And fog closing in fast. Might take some while to get up that hillside, sir.'

Dickinson stared through the misty early morning darkness, a hint of light growing in the east across the hills. 'You two head right. Two left. Back here in five minutes,' Dickinson said. 'Look for tracks – signs of anyone coming or going. And if you spot anyone, take them. Under no circumstances maim or kill. I need these people alive.' He clicked his radio, snapped his headphones open and pushed them over his ears. 'Dickinson reporting in. We have touched land.'

Dickinson listened, then replied. 'Thick fog, sir. Visibility approximately ten metres. Not sure how much use the camera will be until we get close to the house. Scouting the perimeter area at this moment.'

Shortly, Dickinson's radio burst into life. 'Sir,' came the metallic tone of one of the soldiers through the radio. 'Footprints. One, two days old. Hard to tell – prints saturated by mud and water.'

'What sizes?'

'Some big, some small, sir.'

'Can you tell where they lead?'

'No, sir. Looks like they lead into the flooding. Impossible to tell, sir.'

Dickinson rubbed his chin. *Maybe they've already gone,* he thought, *exactly as that girl Sue said.* Perhaps they really had gone to find an electronic tablet. There was only one way to find out.

Dickinson buzzed his radio. 'I'm coming over. We'll wait for more light before we begin the ascent. No-one will see us in this stew.' He paused and pressed the button again. 'Reconvene at the boat in five minutes.'

---

ARCHIE WOKE UP SWEATING.

He'd dreamt of Cain. Cain laughing from under a cloak with such bitterness that his blood boiled and pulsed in waves around his body. Then, Cain merged into Kemp, becoming a monster before spitting ash in his face like a fire-breathing dragon. Archie's head throbbed. He sat up and wiped his brow, then opened his eyes and stared out from under the huge drape at the dark, silent room. His chin stung, from where the ghost had nicked him with the dagger only three nights before.

He rubbed the newest cut, a thin clear liquid moistening his fingers.

Archie checked his watch, then climbed out of bed and, treading lightly on the creaking floorboards, found his way to the table where he lit a candle and slipped down the stairs. In the bathroom, he held the candle up to the mirror and inspected the cuts. There they were – not more than a centimetre long, open, hot, angry and sore, and in exactly the same position either side of his chin. Cain's doing – to remind him, perhaps?

And anyway, why, hadn't Resplendix Mix cleaned it up, like it had with everything else?

Archie tried to forget about Cain but this was easier said than done. Those haunting words of his kept reverberating round his brain. '*Courage, young man, so you are feared and respected,*' and '*Your strength will be without doubt. I assure you these rewards will be genuine.*'

The iciness in that cold, deep voice swished around his head. Archie needed to wake up. He splashed cool tap water over his face and looked back at his curious reflection. His crazy hair, gelled into wire-like points, was tight and strong and he realised that his follicles somehow reflected his mood. When he relaxed, a softness came to his spikes which might, in a very tiny way, be shaped or sculpted.

He prised open the most recent cut with his fingers, and then picking up a nail brush on the side of the bath, scrubbed the gash hard, as if it were an ink mark. He winced as the wound opened and blood dripped out, decorating the white ceramic basin with deep crimson drops, each one splashing over such a large area, fixating him.

He was snapped out of his daze by Daisy calling down the passageway. 'Winkle, get a move on! I need to go!'

Archie grabbed a handful of toilet roll and pressed it firmly to the cut, hoping the wound would congeal. Daisy walked in, her hair stuck to her face in a gigantic mess.

'What are you doing?' she said, moving a clump of curly blonde strands from her forehead.

'Random cut that needed a bit of a clean,' he said.

Daisy screwed her face up and grunted. 'Your hair's still crap,' she said, as she stared at her face in the mirror, moving closer and closer so that in the candlelight her eyes looked particularly ruddy.

'Awesome. Wonder what else they'll do today?' she said, as she opened her eyes as wide as possible and pretended she was a vampire, snarling and clawing randomly at her reflection.

Archie laughed. 'Don't be a fool. And hurry up. We've got Blabisterberry Jelly to find – or had you forgotten?'

'Forgotten? Nah. I can hardly wait,' she said. 'Off you go.'

---

A COLD CHILL hung about them in the dark kitchen. Isabella lit three further candles to offer a bit more light and Archie scrambled around for some newspaper and kindling which smouldered before igniting on the old embers of the fire in the belly of the old range cooker.

Daisy sat in a heap next to the table. 'What do you reckon it is?' she said.

'What is?'

'Blab-ista-stuff, or whatever it's called?'

'Blabisterberry Jelly?' Isabella said smartly. She turned her head skyward as if deep in thought. 'By the sound of it, it may well be some kind of fungus or tree-growth or pus-filled plant. Or perhaps the "jelly" refers to a kind of gelatine mineral deposit, like oil.'

Archie lowered four plates onto the table. 'What if it's some kind of jelly fish? A weird creature from out there in the flooding.'

Daisy looked horrified. 'Oh God, I hope not. I hate jelly fish. It'll be full of disease and dead stuff. Bells, can I have an extra helping of cheese on my Mrs Pye Special sandwich and a double egg? I'm starving.'

'Give me a chance,' Isabella shot back. 'The oven's not hot enough. Anyway, stop being a slob – get some apple juice out and lay up,' she ordered. 'Has anyone seen Old Man Wood?'

'I heard him snoring from Mum and Dad's room earlier,' Archie said. 'He's moved in.'

Isabella sliced the thin loaf of crusty bread that Mrs. Pye had left out, added ham and several slices of cheese to each, followed by a chunky wedge of tomato on top. 'You'd better go and get him. Make sure he hasn't gone mad or died again.' She dripped three drops of sauce on top. 'Anyone know where Mrs P is? Very odd that she's not put in an appearance.'

Daisy smiled wickedly. 'I'll go and kick a ball around in the courtyard. If that doesn't wake her up, nothing will.'

Archie tore off up the stairs in one direction as Daisy shot out of the back of the house and on to the courtyard where she found a ball and began to kick it against the wall right beneath Mrs. Pye's apartment.

As the water boiled, Isabella turned into the kitchen where she realised the quiet wasn't in her imagination. She was on her own, so she opened the oven door and slipped the first of the Mrs. Pye Specials onto the top shelf, and soon the smell of melting cheese made her mouth water like crazy.

---

BENEATH THEM, in the courtyard, Kemp could hear a ball being kicked; its thudding reverberating annoyingly through the window panes.

Kemp stared at the plump woman waking in front of him. She tossed from side to side and groaned. Could this odd looking woman really be his mother? He didn't know whether to laugh or cry, to scream with annoyance or with delight, as a horrible doubt lingered. No – impossible. She couldn't be. Suddenly Kemp wanted to be as far away as possible, not in this room, not even within a hundred miles of here. Kemp stood up and gingerly crept towards the door.

He turned his head back to the woman, just as she stretched her hands out, drew them together and fanned them out, flexing her pink digits in front of her face. A snapping, cracking, popping sound came out of each little joint, but one thing caught Kemp's eye.

He stared hard at Mrs. Pye's hands. There, again. As she did it, now he did the same.

One odd, strange movement.

He pushed his arms out and flexed his fingers and then pushed his thumbs together, which, just like Mrs. Pye's, bent back at a quite extraordinary angle.

He'd never met anyone who could get even close to this level of dexterity, this bendiness, the way the thumbs pushed flat on their pads at ninety degrees.

Mrs. Pye opened her eyes, stared at his thumbs, then at her hands, doing the same motion. Slowly, she fixed her gaze at him, her initial reaction betraying shock and fear and now curiosity.

Kemp stared back, mid stretch, his thumbs bent back and for what seemed like an eternity, the room filled with silence.

'Please, don't scream,' Kemp implored.

Mrs. Pye scrunched up her face and eyed him curiously.

Kemp stood stone still, not sure what to do next.

'What do you want?' Mrs. Pye forced out.

'I just wanted to see you.'

'You're Archie's friend, now, aren't you?' Mrs. Pye finally said, and she shifted up the bed to see him better.

Kemp nodded.

Mrs. Pye tutted. 'And you've lost your lovely hair. If I remember, it was bright—'

'Ginger,' Kemp butted in. 'Just like—'

'Mine,' she said and, as she did, she smiled, although it looked every bit like a scowl to Kemp.

'Yeah,' he said.

The long silence returned. Kemp stared at the woman, her funny scars, her fat lips and her slightly long nose and, in particular, those sharp, light blue eyes. It was like looking at a distorted mirror.

Maybe Cain was right.

'I need to get up, young man,' Mrs. Pye said. 'So unless you've other business ...'

Kemp hesitated. 'Yes. I mean, no. I mean—'

'What's the matter? You got a problem with one of my lot?' She shot a look towards the desk with the scrapbook and photos of the de Lowe children.

'No, no. Not them,' Kemp said.

'Well then, be off with you. Don't know what you're thinking, creeping into people's houses. I've a good mind to telephone them police.'

But Kemp's feet remained glued to the floor. 'Mrs. Pye,' Kemp stuttered, trying to find the right words and then, summoning every ounce from a place deep within him, he said: 'How did you, er, how did you get those scars?'

Mrs. Pye shot him her most dastardly look. 'None of your business.'

'The thing is,' he replied, as tears filled his eyes. 'I do believe it is.'

# 97 A SIP OF WATER

If his theory was correct, and the virus was being spread by something in dreams, Solomon thought his chances of survival were probably greater than most. After all, he'd been a light sleeper for years and he rarely, if ever, dreamt.

He woke before dawn, dressed and headed outside to find Dickinson with his team preparing to take a Land Rover down to the water. From there they would motor across the Vale of York to the edge of the Yorkshire Moors and then climb up to Eden Cottage.

They exchanged pleasantries.

'Dickinson,' Solomon began. 'Please keep me updated. If they're not around, I'd like to drop in as soon as I can to tie up some of my research.'

The officer nodded. 'We should be in and out in no time. With any luck we'll be back at lunchtime.'

'I've been given a radio. What frequency are you on?'

Dickinson gave him the information and gathered his protective helmet.

Solomon smiled. 'Good luck. Let's hope they haven't caught the Ebora virus, huh?'

As they departed, Solomon went back to his lodgings and then on to find Sue in the room above his. He knocked on the door. When he knocked again, the noise told him a good deal of scrambling was going on. Sue wasn't alone.

'It's Solomon, Sue. Can you let me in?'

More scrambling from inside. Finally the door opened. Sue's head peeped round the door. 'Morning, sir,' she said gaily, a twinkle in her eye.

Solomon moved in and shut the door behind him. 'Stone's obedient dog has gone to sniff out Eden Cottage,' he began. 'He reckons he'll be back by lunchtime, so we'll need to be ready to go.'

Sue looked up from her perch on the bed. 'OK,' she said. 'What do we need to do?'

'First get your hands on some of the protective suits. Three of them.'

'Three?'

'Yes. One for you, one for me and one for Gus.'

'Gus?'

'Yes. Gus who is hiding in the cupboard.'

Sue reddened. 'Sir?'

Solomon smiled at her. 'You must think I was born yesterday,' he said. 'Besides, I'm a schoolmaster. Come on out of there, Mr. Williams.'

The door swung open and the large figure of Gus tumbled out over the floor in a muddle of arms and legs.

Solomon helped pick him up. 'Right now, I am your friend, not your headmaster,' Solomon said. 'So let's be grown up about this.' Gus sat down beside Sue and stared, red-faced, at the floor. Solomon moved over to the radio and turned up the volume. Then he sat down next to them on the bed.

'We know,' he began quietly as the song crashed into the chorus, 'that the de Lowes are on to something quite astonishingly important. There are clues littered everywhere; in the old books in the library, the stained glass and, I'm sure, in their house, but what it is they have to find, I don't know.'

Solomon rubbed his hands. 'However, the world is falling apart at an alarming pace and until they get hold of this thing, I have a terrible feeling that this deterioration will continue swiftly and without mercy.' Solomon looked from Sue to Gus and back again. 'From the chaos out there, they may already be running out of time.'

The headmaster raised his eyebrows. 'I am increasingly certain that we must keep Archie and his sisters away from Commissioner Stone and his cronies. Officialdom will only hinder the children, and my instinct tells me is that it is up to the de Lowes, and only the de Lowes to find what they have to find. If not, then I am quite sure Isabella would somehow have managed to bring this to the authorities' attention.' The headmaster removed his spectacles and rubbed his eyes.

'I cannot begin to tell you how much pressure Stone is under. I'm talking pressure on a massive, global, governmental scale. And the problem is that he thinks finding Archie de Lowe is the answer to all his woes. As such, that man will stop at nothing to find them. He will want to extract every grain of information out of Archie and indeed his sisters.'

The music went quiet as the song ended, and Solomon did the same.

'Here's what I think,' he said as the next song burst into life. 'We need to be ready for two situations.'

'Two?' Gus queried.

'Indeed. The first is the eventuality that the children are at the cottage and are brought back here, in which case we'll need to set them free, at all costs. The second option applies if they are not at home. If that is the case, then we need to get into Eden Cottage and find out whatever we can in order to protect them. But it is vital that we keep this from Stone and send him and his boys on a wild goose chase.' He smiled at Gus and Sue. 'And to that effect, to get you both to Eden Cottage with me, I have a plan.'

---

OLD MAN WOOD came downstairs holding a large bucket filled with water. He placed it in the hallway and made his way into the kitchen. '*Stop eating*!' he shouted, waving his arms in the air. '*Please! STOP, NOW*!'

'Why?' Isabella said. 'Is it the Havilarian Toadstool Powder?'

'No, no. You must be ravenously hungry for Blabisterberry Jelly—'

'You *eat* Blabisterberry Jelly?' Archie said as he chewed on a combination of ham, egg and cheese. 'Are you sure?'

'*YES!*'

'I hope it's as good as this,' Daisy said, forking in a huge mouthful.

'*NO*!' the old man begged. 'Daisy ... please don't.'

Daisy lowered her fork and fixed him with her red eyes. 'So what does this jelly look like?'

'That's the thing. I don't know,' he began, 'but you'll find out, I can assure you. Believe me – but it really is vital you're starving.'

'I'm always starving!' Archie said, as he made to help himself to more.

'NO!' the old man roared and he reached onto the table and tossed Archie's plate into the corner of the room where it smashed into fragments.

'Archie,' the old man said firmly, 'I am deadly serious. This is no game, it is not a joke. Blabisterberry Jelly is lethal, it will kill you.' He turned towards the plate in the corner. 'I am sorry about your wasted Mrs. Pye Special, though.'

Daisy stared at her plate, desperate for another mouthful, but instead she stood up and tossed her plate across the room where it too smashed into little pieces.

'Daisy!' Isabella cried.

Daisy shrugged.

'Why couldn't you put it in the bin like an ordinary human being?'

'Bells,' Daisy said, flipping her pink glasses from her forehead to the brow of her nose, 'this is no time for rubbish bins. And besides, we aren't ordinary human beings.'

'Clear it up,' Isabella demanded.

Daisy snarled. 'Don't you ever listen? We are about to go and eat Blabisterberry Jam or whatever it's called and we may well die and you want me to clear up a plate?'

She grabbed Isabella's plate and threw it like a Frisbee across the room, where it too smashed into tiny pieces.

Isabella's face turned puce and she stamped her foot.

*'Enough,'* Old Man Wood roared.

The girls sat down, a little bit in awe of his raised voice.

'I learnt about Blabisterberry Jelly from the Willows at the Bubbling Brook last night. It's a good deal easier if you're hungry, but impossible if you're not.'

The children looked at him with concerned faces. 'Now, my littluns, first things first, we need to find it.'

'Find it?' Isabella said. 'Where? In the house, outside the house, by the ruin?'

'Why,' the old man began with a smile, 'somewhere round here I'm reckoning. But first,' and his face grew into a smile, 'follow me. I've got a little something you'll all be needing.'

They followed him out of the kitchen and into the hallway.

Old Man Wood produced a mug, bent down and filled it with the not entirely clean water from the plastic bucket. 'Now, drink some of this. It's a wee bit special.'

Isabella knelt down and sniffed it. 'Smells funny. Slightly sulphuric. Are you sure it hasn't been infected? If it comes from the flooding, you do realise it's almost certain to kill us.'

'My dear Bells,' the old man said, 'it's from the Bubbling Brook—'

'But your Bubbling Brook place is within the vicinity of the flooding, is it not?' Isabella said, knowingly. She stood up. 'This sample needs testing and at the very least boiling before anyone touches it—'

'It is *special water*, Isabella,' Old Man Wood said, his tone exasperated.

'But why is it so special that it doesn't require treating?' Isabella insisted.

Old Man Wood looked at her stunned. Then he turned to the other two for support.

Isabella noticed. 'All I'm trying to say is, why should this sample be absolutely fine in contrast to a sample taken from anywhere else in the floodwater because, to all intents and purposes, they must be from the same source and therefore infected?'

He shook his head. 'Because this water will enable you to speak, read and write in any language,' the old man said. 'Don't ask me how it works. It's an appley-funny-peculiar sensation at first, but you'll get used to it.'

Daisy shrieked. 'Ooh! I get it. I had some when I went into the glade – remember?' she said. 'I've had the coolest conversations with things. Did you know, this house is full of little notes from lovey-dovey mice?'

'Those are droppings, Daisy,' Isabella said.

'Depends on how you read them, Isabella,' Daisy said. 'All they go on about is food and sex. They're at it all the time and they go on and on and on ...'

'Like someone else we know?' Archie said.

Daisy hit him. 'Here, give it to me.' She grabbed the glass of water from out of Old Man Wood's hand, raised it to her lips, sniffed it and then, as she stared Isabella in the eye, downed it in one. 'Ah,' she said, and she belched and sat down with her eyes shut tight.

'You are quite disgusting,' Isabella said, wafting her hand in front of her.

Old Man Wood passed the mug to Archie. 'A couple of mouthfuls should do it,' he said, his eyes raised in earnest. Archie did as the old man recommended and passed it on to Isabella, who very reluctantly and only after popping in a finger and licking it, took a couple of small sips.

'Come on, Bells,' Daisy said. 'That's hardly going to work.'

'Just because I'm not as greedy as you,' Isabella said. She fixed her sister's eye and drained the glass. 'Urrrggh!' she cried, pulling a face as Daisy laughed.

'Disgusting ... pheteucx!' Her eyes watered and instantly it felt as if her eyeballs were walloping about her head like pinballs.

As their brains fizzed and their ears crackled and eyes spun, Old Man Wood explained how it worked. 'When you concentrate on something you'll find there's a difference. But when you concentrate *an awful lot,* that's when it starts happening; you'll see and hear things ... well, you'll find out soon enough. Don't worry,' he reassured them, 'you won't whoosh up into the air or grow a moustache or anything like that.'

He led them out into the courtyard where sunlight was attempting, rather sadly, to break through the thick white fog coming up from the valley. 'Now, littluns,' he said, smiling, 'somewhere around this courtyard, according to my old friend, Bethedi, there's a sign on a wall or a stone on the floor. It'll tell us what to do.'

'What sort of sign?' Archie asked.

Old Man Wood shook his head. 'If I knew, young man, I reckon I would tell you. Perhaps it's like peculiar writing you find on walls in the towns ...?'

'Graffiti?'

Old Man Wood appeared confused. 'I suppose,' he said, 'it could be graff ... whatever that is. But you'll need to look carefully – it could be anywhere. Now, for apples' sake concentrate, the lot of you.'

# 98 DAISY'S DISCOVERY

Daisy's search faltered immediately. Instead of looking for the writing or the sign outside, she had been distracted by a peculiar, strange, high-pitched squeaking sound coming from somewhere inside the house, which had been bothering her for a couple of days. She went back in to the house to investigate and ended up back in the kitchen, rooting through the condiment jars and flour pots and herbs. Eventually she honed it down to one particular area and, now concentrating at her utmost, she could see the offenders through the cupboard door.

She ran back outside. 'Old Man Wood, you'd better come and check this out.'

Soon the others joined her. And even though Daisy's hearing was a hundred times greater than theirs, Archie and Isabella also heard a strange noise coming from within the cupboard.

'It's a trapped mouse,' Archie volunteered.

Daisy shook her head. 'Nah. Too many. Sounds like a whole load of them—'

'An infestation?' Archie said.

Daisy nodded knowingly as Isabella took two steps back. 'Actually, by that scurrying noise, I wouldn't be surprised if it's a whole load of rats trapped behind the door waiting to rush out.' She caught Archie's eye and winked, trying not to laugh.

'Yeah, definitely rats,' Archie said, waiting for the explosion. 'I hope they don't bite too much.'

'Oh, shut up, you two,' Isabella said from behind the door. 'Stop it! Stop being so childish. You know I hate them.'

The twins thought this was brilliantly funny. Daisy opened the door and both of them started shrieking, and then they howled with laughter at Isabella's terrified reaction. 'Oh chill your pants, Bells,' Daisy said, pulling the sugar bowl out. 'The noise is coming from here. I promise you there are no rats.'

Now that they were concentrating on the bowl, the high-pitched commotion grew. Daisy placed the bowl on the work surface as four pairs of eyes peered into it, baffled. For a while, all they could see were the granules of sugar. But it quickly became clear to Daisy that this wasn't entirely sugar. She found herself looking at a mixture of microscopic toadstools that kept on morphing into granules like miniature Christmas lights in a random flashing sequence.

She stood up and took a step backwards. 'These are microscopic mushrooms,' she said.

'Are you sure?' Isabella said. 'Not sugar?'

'Definitely not. Try one. I dare you.'

Isabella shook her head. 'Fungi? Here?' Isabella's expression dropped. 'What if this is the Havilarian Toadstool Powder?!' she cried.

'The stuff that nearly killed you, Old Man Wood.' Daisy added. 'What do you think?'

Old Man Wood studied it, but it was hard to tell from his expression if he could even see the fungi let alone hear them. 'If it is,' he began, 'it's lethal stuff, especially to me.' The children backed away as Old Man Wood shot off out of the room.

'What's it doing here?' Daisy said. 'It's a very odd place to live—'

'No, it isn't,' Archie cried. 'It makes total sense.'

Daisy looked confused. 'Go on, Sherlock. Reveal all.'

'I added a spoon of sugar into the tea full of rum that sent Old Man Wood bonkers,' he said. 'At the time you two thought it was a bit funny.'

Old Man Wood returned wearing a pair of rubber gloves and holding a small glass jar.

'Havilarian Toadstool Powder can't escape from this old thing,' Old

Man Wood said. 'Would one of you mind pouring it in? If it touches me, I might end up a bit like last time.'

Isabella carefully jigged the sugar and slowly the powder emptied from one container to the other. As Old Man Wood sealed the latch, the screeching howls from the tiny toadstools ceased.

The children exchanged glances. 'But why only you, Old Man Wood?' Archie asked.

'Because the toadstools only poison those from the Garden of Eden, that's why,' the old man replied. 'Which reminds me – if we ever get there, the only way to dispose of these horrible things is in the River of Life.'

Old Man Wood slipped the jar into his coat pocket.

'You sure you don't want me to take it?' Archie said. 'What if you fall and it breaks?'

Old Man Wood smiled. 'Need to be some strength for this to break. In any case, it'll remind me to be a little bit more careful.' He ushered the children out. 'Come on, come on. We have the urgent matter of finding Blabisterberry Jelly.'

---

AFTER A FEW MINUTES, it became clear that what they were searching for was akin to finding a needle in a haystack. Hundreds of stones from the cobbles on the floor to those in the walls, and even the roof, bore some kind of writing or message. And worse still, many had messages on that were so old and scuffed that they took considerable deciphering.

"... NOT HERE. SORRY," said a weathered grey stone that Daisy found. And then, as she neared Mrs. Pye's flat, she found another three similar messages. Irritated, she opened the door of one of the shed doors beneath Mrs. Pye's flat, let herself in and lay on the floor.

This old stable, used mainly by Old Man Wood, was crammed full of things to mend. Dotted on the floor and hanging off the walls were an assortment of old chairs and picture frames and lamps and parts of old bicycles and even an old piano, its ivories removed. To Daisy's left sat a colourful carpet with a big hole in the middle and, to her right, a doll she recognised from her childhood that was missing an arm, a leg, and an eye.

Daisy rather liked it in here and sat down among the odds and ends as the dappled daylight filtered in through the dirty, cobweb-filled windows. For a minute the quiet allowed her to empty her mind. She closed her eyes, oblivious to the cacophony of new sounds and images around her. She breathed deeply and for a while sleep called her.

Suddenly she heard a familiar kind of noise, which was neither a squeak nor anything unusual. She roused herself. Perhaps the wind had pushed the door, making it groan. But as she thought about it, she realised there was no wind only the gently swirling cloud down in the valley swamping the vale.

She listened again and heard a voice. A boy's voice talking slowly, whispering and ... weeping. It wasn't Archie and it certainly wasn't Old Man Wood. She listened harder and realised the words were coming from Mrs. Pye's flat directly above her.

Then she heard, unmistakably, Mrs. Pye's distinctive tones.

*Who the heck was it?*

Quietly, Daisy slipped out of the mending room, ran down the courtyard and bounded up the stone stairs on her toes, barely making a sound. At the top, she prised open the door to Mrs. Pye's apartment, slipped inside, tiptoed down the narrow, dark corridor and stopped outside Mrs. Pye's bedroom door.

She caught her breath, her senses on high alert. She listened. Nothing. Just muffled sounds, like ... sobs, crying. Daisy desperately wanted to look inside but something told her not to. She stared hard at the door as if willing it to move aside. Then, much to her astonishment, she found herself seeing right through the wooden door, as though she had somehow opened up a large porthole of glass. And the harder she stared, the clearer the image.

There, in front of her, was the large figure of Mrs. Pye sitting on the bed with her eyes closed and a wide grimacey-smile traced across her face, a smaller figure folded into her bosom.

Astonished, yet intrigued, and nervous that she was seeing things, Daisy tip-toed down the passageway and, as her concentration moved from seeing to keeping quiet, she found herself staring at the dark magnolia-coloured wall. When she regained her concentration, the see-through portal reappeared and she found herself looking at a boy. A boy she'd definitely seen before. But who was it?

Suddenly it came to her, though it made no sense. It looked like the boy from the TV, the boy who survived the storm, the miracle child, the boy otherwise known as ... Kemp.

KEMP!

She swore, under her breath. What was he doing here! Isabella's greatest enemy ... here ... with Mrs. Pye ... how? Had the world ended already? Was she in a parallel universe or something?

She watched. For ages, they didn't say anything, just held each other as though *they had just found each other and didn't want to ever let go,* she thought. Daisy noticed tears streaming down Kemp's face and then she began to see the similarities.

The hair, the lips, the piggy blue eyes.

Daisy was filled with a strange prickly sensation. She shuddered as she remembered what Archie had told her about Kemp losing his mother when he was a baby. And she recalled Old Man Wood's story of how he had found Mrs. Pye in the hills, as near to dead as you could get, mangled and scarred with no memory.

The whole truth of the matter came to her: Kemp and Kemp's mother, Mrs. Pye. And at that moment, as she watched the boy through the wall, her heart pinched and ached for him.

And for the first time in her life, Daisy de Lowe felt ashamed of her behaviour towards Kemp. This sad boy, who hadn't had the best of luck in life, a boy who'd never known his mother or father, a boy they'd pushed aside and turned into a monster.

Daisy shook her head and moved down the corridor. How did Kemp get here? After all Eden Cottage was stuck out in the middle of nowhere. Furthermore, wasn't Kemp in hospital? He had to be, unless the TV interview had been pre-recorded. Maybe he found out and escaped? But it was miles and miles over terrible flooding.

It didn't make sense. But, then again, nothing made sense any more.

Daisy crept along, deep in thought. A shiver worked up her spine, a feeling as if something was watching her. She shook it out.

At the top of the stone staircase she noticed a strange overcoat hanging on the wall.

She looked back down the corridor. Kemp's coat? No, too big, but then again, too small for the voluptuous figure of Mrs. Pye. Perhaps it had been there all along, for years? Perhaps, Mrs. Pye had left it there as a reminder that she might one day find a man in her life?

Daisy lent in and smelled the fabric. Old, like moths and soot and peat combined, she thought. She sniffed again. More like the ash that drifted about when Dad cleaned the fires. She fingered the fabric, noting how intricately the patterns ran together, and as she did she heard a soft, deep voice, almost purring. Her arms freckled with goose bumps.

Daisy wondered if she should put it on, to warm her up. All she had to do was reverse into it.

She turned around and put her right arm behind her, searching for the hole that led down the arm of the coat. There. She thrust her arm quickly down into the coat and, as she did, she gasped.

An intense, cold rush sped into her arm, like icy treacle. She moaned. It felt so cold, but yet so warm and electrifying.

She twisted her body around as if to push her other arm in when the door flew open.

In front of her stood Kemp. His mouth open.

Daisy, in shock, let the left arm of the coat swing.

'Daisy,' he said, moving quickly towards her. 'I know you generally do the opposite of anything I say, but I absolutely urge you, in fact I'm begging you, not to put that coat on.'

Daisy shrugged and looked him up and down. Kemp had lost weight and his baldness made him different; less childish, she thought, as a curious tingle ran through her. 'Give me two good reasons,' she said.

'Please don't,' Kemp said. 'For once in your life, just believe me,' he said. 'You really don't want to do it.'

Daisy felt for the other arm-hole. 'That's not even one reason,' she said, as she slid her arm into the coat. She closed her eyes as the freezing syrupy feeling swam through her arms and into her chest.

'Don't do it,' Kemp said, his voice betraying his worry. 'Get out of there, Daisy. *Get out of there NOW*!'

But already Daisy's eyes were shutting, and the sound of a man's laughter filled her ears.

# 99 BAD NEWS FROM AMERICA

'It's impossible, sir,' Dickinson said. 'Visibility is down to no more than a couple of metres.'

The radio crackled back. 'I don't bleedin' care if you can't see your effing noses, you're going to get up there and then back here, with or without those children.' Stone's voice calmed down. 'Dickinson, I need to know. And fast. We can't risk the helicopters. You're on your own. Do you copy?'

Dickinson shrugged. 'All I was saying, sir, is that we will not be able to proceed at the speed we anticipated.'

'What the hell do they train you for?' Stone yelled down the radio. 'Sunning yourselves? It's not a bloody holiday.'

Dickinson turned to the unit. 'You heard the man.' He pulled out some instruments from his rucksack. 'We need to move.' He delved into his bag. 'Compass, map, heat sensors. Everyone should have the same, if you haven't, I need to know. Understand? It's like semolina out there and if you get lost don't expect us to come looking for you.'

Dickinson had served in four tours: Afghanistan, Syria, the Balkans and Iraq. But never had he encountered conditions like this. A white-out as thick as custard spread out over a wasted, destroyed landscape. It gave him the collywobbles just thinking about it. Going in blind. Utterly devoid of sight. At least, he reasoned, there wouldn't be land-mines or IEDs or sniper fire to worry about, only bogs and brambles and random pools.

He never imagined he'd be plucking three children out of a remote hillside cottage in the midst of a global meltdown.

The country was already out of control. In places, reports said that the army were shooting anyone suspected of having Ebora. Elsewhere, the dead were being laid out on the doorsteps, exactly as they'd done at the time of the Black Death.

The difference being that this was viral, and back then it was bacterial. Both were horrible, nasty, silent killers. Both terrifying, unknown enemies.

They'd had the best of it tucked away at Swinton Park, trying to hold things together. But that would change and Dickinson knew it wouldn't take long. And he had half a mind to see if he could engineer a way of staying.

He shone his torch into the white wall of cloud and the light bounced back. The bottom line, according to Stone, was that they were doomed unless these kids came up with the answer.

That's how Stone operated, he supposed. As a predator sniffs out a weakness or a flaw, he'd chase and chase until he pulled his prey down, extracting whatever information he needed. And nearly always he was proven correct. He'd done it time after time, over and over again.

*But,* Dickinson thought, *kids on the search for tablets – electronic or otherwise – to stop the world's greatest catastrophe?* It just didn't stack up.

Unless you added in the Headmaster's idea that the disease was being spread by dream-giving aliens, then they had nothing to work on. Nothing whatsoever aside from the suspicions of every nation that it was some kind of hideous biological weapon attack.

*Maybe they should bomb the hell out of Upsall and be done with it,* he thought.

They had barely started before Simonet, operating the tracking system, came bustling over. 'Bad news, sir.'

Dickinson halted. 'What now?'

'The tracking device has frozen, sir. Satellite down. We can wait for them to come on-line again, but no guarantees.'

Dickinson kneaded his temple. 'No. We need to keep moving. Let's get up this hill and work it out from there.' He turned to the four others. 'Keep tight and don't wander off. If you do, you'll get lost. If by a miracle you manage to spot a significant feature, like a waterfall or cliff face, call a halt and we'll see if we can locate it on the map.' Dickinson stared at the Ordnance Survey map.

'If we head directly up from our landing point, we should be there in twenty to thirty minutes. Any deviation by the smallest degree and it'll take significantly longer.'

Dickinson's radio buzzed into life.

'Corporal,' crackled Stone's voice from the command centre. 'You may have noticed a satellite failure.'

'Affirmative, Commissioner. The imagery disappeared less than a minute ago.'

Dickinson could have sworn he heard the Commissioner sigh. 'Good. Well, you should know where you are.' The crackle of the radio cut out and then came on again. 'I, er, have news just in.'

'I take it this is not good news, Commissioner.'

The radio went silent for a while.

Dickinson didn't like the sound of this one bit.

Stone's voice was softer. 'I mentioned before,' he began, 'that various nation states believe that this area of Yorkshire is the originator of this global catastrophe. Well, the United States tabled an emergency proposal to destroy the entire area.' The radio went silent. 'I'm talking pretty much the entire northern half of the country in what they are calling, *a global action of absolute last resort.'*

'When?' Dickinson said.

Stone's voice betrayed his emotion. 'They wanted to detonate at midnight tonight, leaving a chance for the top brass to get out. But we told them our situation and, to my surprise, we managed to get an extension. So, gentlemen, we have approximately three days to find out what the hell is going on. I need you in and out of there, like yesterday, fog or no fog. If the children aren't there, let me know ... in fact I think I'm going to send the headmaster towards you as fast as possible to see if any of his findings from the church at Upsall match up. Might be worth having you lot about to help him up to the cottage. Then I need you back. There's trouble kicking off everywhere. I think the news leaked.'

The soldiers stared at one another, stunned.

'For Queen and country,' Dickinson said quietly, 'and for this entire planet. Lads, you're now on the world's most important mission: to find these kids. Fail, gents, and we've all had it.' He patted a couple on their backs. 'Time to get a move on.'

# 100 A STRANGE NEW LANGUAGE

To the common eye the insignificant scratches or scuffs littering the walls were scribbles of one sort or another; love notes, bits of information, travel updates, even stories. Some had been added years and years ago and said things like: 'PLAGUE, KEEP OUT!'

Other inscriptions had been painstakingly crafted. Many were recent, and where it was dry, like under the extensively wide eaves, considerable bird scribblings made for compulsive reading.

Archie felt faint, and starving. He climbed the stepladder and sat reading the graffiti, mesmerised and slightly forgetting that he was looking for clues as to how to find Blabisterberry Jelly. A small part of him wished that his eyes and brain would stop and, when that happened, his concentration withdrew so he saw nothing bar scuffs and scratches.

Old Man Wood had been searching the house around the front and came back to see how they were getting along. 'Any luck, Archie?'

Archie buried his face in his hands. 'I never knew other THINGS could write!'

The old man chuckled. 'You lot don't know much, I suppose,' Old Man Wood said. 'It's a secret that's been kept back from human types. You see, humans have one way of communicating, everything else another. That's just the way of it.' He clapped Archie on the back. 'It happened a long time ago, part of the Great Deal. I'm sure you'll learn about it one day.'

Archie's eyes rested on a message on the dry windowsill which otherwise would have looked like a series of distorted birds' messes. He concentrated hard and shortly a message came out. He read it out to Old Man Wood.

*WANTED: SINGLE GEESE FOR LOVING HOLIDAY CRUISE TO SOUTHERN HEMISPHERE. SEE ORAVIO AT THE GRAVEL PITS – TWENTY FLAPS SOUTH-WEST WITH THE WIND. IF IT TAKES YOU MORE THAN THIRTY, I'M TOTALLY NOT INTERESTED.*

Archie rubbed his foremost hair spike whose texture was comfortingly smooth. 'That wouldn't be the fat goose that waddles around out here looking a little bit pleased with himself?' he asked.

Old Man Wood shrugged. 'Suppose it could well be.'

'That Goose calls himself Oravio?' Archie said.

Old Man Wood nodded.

'And he comes up here, to ... to find a date?' Archie sounded put-out. 'Like all the other animals in the area. Our house is like an enormous dating magazine. It's animal "Tinder",' he laughed, 'a giant community notice board.'

'What did you expect?' Old Man Wood said, putting a comforting arm around his shoulders, 'that other living things don't communicate?'

'But what do you mean by *communicate?*' Archie said. 'Animals don't talk like we do – all they do is sniff each other's bums or twitter or quack or baa or moo. They aren't smart, like us.'

Old Man Wood's deep laugh boomed out. 'Ooh, you're right there, they're not clever – like humans! Clever at putting themselves first at the expense of everyone else and all that, but it doesn't mean other living things can't and don't talk.'

The old man scratched his chin as he gathered his thoughts. 'You see, Archie, one of the flaws of the human race was to fail to recognise that living things do actually converse with one another. All these animals, these creatures and trees and insects and plants, *they know*. It's just that, after a while, the humans couldn't be bothered. Which is hardly surprising, I suppose, because the population of man grew and grew and there were other things to worry about, I'm sure. But it's a shame, nonetheless. Some of those birds are mightily entertaining. Look at those pigeons ducking out the way of cars. To them, it's a mighty fine entertainment—'

'Except when they get hit.' Archie added.

Isabella had wandered over and was listening intently to the old man. 'Don't tell me that trees actually talk?' she scoffed. 'Creatures, TREES actually chatting away to each other. You'll be telling me they watch TV next. You are joking, right?' Isabella said.

Old Man Wood raised his wrinkly brow and shook his head.

'See, Archie?' she said. 'He's making it up.'

'No I am not, Bells,' Old Man Wood said. 'Take your cat, Psycho-cat. Look at the way he moves, swishes his tail, paws his face, rubs against you and opens his eyes when he's cross. He's talking away to you – but you have no idea what he's really saying. You call it "body language" and that's what creatures do to give you clues. The next time you see Psycho-cat, just remember that.' The old man raised his dark eyes to the sky as if remembering things from a long time ago. Then he exhaled slowly. 'The great divide in communication is something that took me hundreds of years to get used to, especially with trees—'

'With trees?' Archie said.

'Yes, Archie, like those Willows which I wanted to show you.'

'But they don't *really* talk, do they?' Isabella said.

'Of course they do,' Old Man Wood replied, his tone a little more upset than usual. 'Trees are the greatest living things on the planet. They are way older than humans and far cleverer. Their roots stretch deep into the earth, their branches high into the sky. They listen out for every season; they play with the winds, with the air and the birds. They clean the waters and filter the air and they sing songs when they swish and they sway and they are funny and sad and beautiful.'

The children listened silently as Old Man Wood continued. 'Each living thing has energy and this is otherwise known as *spirit*. It's strong in some and dim in others and it is this spirit, this energy, which binds us all together. It is the energy we get when we love and when we care and when we feel. It is this energy that allows us to be.'

The old man sighed as he remembered. 'But the trees had a terrible time, especially after everything they had given up.'

'You're talking in riddles again, Old Man Wood,' Isabella said. 'What do you mean, "given up"?'

'Now let me think,' he said as he rubbed his chin. 'In the Garden of Eden, most of the trees moved, some faster than others. But when they came to Earth they had to give up their mobility. There wasn't really room for them all to be running around. So they found a suitable place and dug in their roots – like anchors I suppose – to support the planet, hold it together, help us breathe.'

Isabella shook her head. Her belief system was being mightily challenged. Unless she remained calm, she could see herself slipping into madness.

'So you're saying humans are rubbish?' Archie quizzed.

Old Man Wood laughed his booming laugh. 'No. Humans are wonderful. Smart, clever, resourceful. But they look after themselves first at the sake of every other thing, even though they tell themselves they don't. They always have and that, my boy, is why they've been so successful. And it's why you must succeed,' he said turning to them.

Old Man Wood noticed their perplexed looks.

'I'm afraid the water from the Bubbling Brook will shock you,' he said sweetly. 'But from now on, it is essential that you open your eyes, your ears – and your minds!'

# 101 DAISY AND CAIN

Daisy closed her eyes and groaned as an immense feeling of power grew inside her.

She could trace where the sensations of the cold, an almost painful icy flow, ran through her sinews like thick oil. A powerful, strange, exotic feeling began to build as a wave slowly swept over her, through every little vein, down every artery, into her hands, teasing the nerves in her elbows, her breasts, her genitals and into her knees and then to the end of each toe. The sensation tingled parts of her she never knew even existed. She gasped and cried out.

She could hear a low, silky voice talking directly into her brain. 'There is so much more,' was all it said.

Daisy moaned, but something wasn't right. She forced her eyes open and saw Kemp. 'What ... what's happening to me?'

Now the voice came back at her and the feelings intensified. 'Come with me,' it said, 'willingly, like the boy and you will have everything. Say "Yes" and it will be done.'

Daisy almost gave in then and there as a slither of cold ran through her body and circled her midriff before plunging into her groin. A blinding flash blew through her brain and the feeling grew and grew before rocketing through her body.

She breathed deeply, trying to regain control. *Too much.* She opened her eyes. Kemp, again, a look of deep concern plastered on his face, pulling at her arm, pleading, yelling. Had he noticed?

Daisy gathered herself but her arm was stuck. Something in the coat held it.

She thrashed one way, then the next, but the more she did so, the more a curious sensation built in the fingers of the trapped arm. At first it felt like pricks from small, sharp pins but soon these joined together until collectively they hurt more and more as if thousands of pins were thrust in. Soon it burned. She gritted her teeth. Her hair was singeing.

'Let go of me!' she seethed.

She tugged, but it stuck, as if caught in a vice. 'Let go of me, now!' she cried.

'Let her go!' Kemp said, his voice firm. 'She does not go willingly.'

The pain receded.

'Let her go now, or I will never go with you again.'

Suddenly, Daisy lay on the floor, her arm red and tender halfway to her elbow. The delicate hairs on the backs of her fingers were singed.

Instantly, she knew that Kemp had suffered the same fate.

'Please, go ... now,' said a soft voice above her – Kemp's voice. A voice so gentle, she'd never have believed him possible of uttering it.

In a millisecond, Kemp had taken her place and his arms pushed into the sleeves of the grey coat. From out of the coat pocket he pulled out a curious-looking trilby hat. He boxed it out and, with a tiny smile on his face, slipped it over his head. As he did this, not once did he take his eyes off her. Not once did his expression alter.

Then, as if by magic, underneath the long coat, Kemp suddenly morphed into a human figure of ash. But the person the ashen features revealed was an older-looking human with sweptback hair and scabbed skin marks. Daisy scampered backwards as the figure loomed over her and then pounced towards her face, ash falling from it.

'Come with me,' it demanded. 'Come. You know you want to.' Ash fizzed out of its mouth showering her like a fountain. And then, with a windy chuckle, the grey-coated ash-man stood up and dived headfirst down the stairwell, vanishing in a tiny blue flash.

Daisy's heartbeat raced and she looked down at nothing but a tiny pile of ash on the stone stairs below.

# 102 DECIPHERING THE CODE

Daisy sat in stunned silence. Her red eyes shone brightly, like the depressed brake lights of a car. Her heart thumped. That, she thought, was weirder than when she'd landed in the Atrium or whatever place that was.

What sort of monster lived in a coat? Was it a ghost? She shook as she thought about it, her whole body resonating at the memory. Those feelings – so cold and painful and yet hot and exhilarating – at the same time. Like her dreams.

And how come Kemp was with it? In fact, was Kemp actually dead, or alive, or now some kind of spirit? But she'd felt the flesh and blood of his arm pulling at her, trying to release her from the creature and thinking of that, she'd sniffed the sharp smell, the distinctive pungent tang of his burned hair.

Kemp had warned her, so why didn't she listen? Was she simply so bloody against him she wasn't prepared to give him a chance? And then she thought of Kemp talking to Mrs. Pye. His tears and their soft, loving words. Inside, Daisy felt terrible and her heart wanted to reach out and tell him that he was OK, and that she understood.

'Mrs. Pye,' she said as she leapt up and ran along the corridor. She stood outside Mrs. Pye's bedroom door and swallowed. *What should she say? What words would be comforting enough for Mrs. Pye or ... simply, right?*

She knocked on the door and, with a deep breath, walked in. Mrs. Pye sat on the bed, her body swaying from side to side, tears rolling down her cheeks.

Daisy ran up and threw her arms around her. But although Mrs. Pye reacted by closing her eyes, she continued swaying, murmuring incoherently.

When Daisy pulled out of her embrace and took a step back, Mrs. Pye carried on doing the same thing, her eyes staring, lost across the room, her voice like a slow chant, her body rocking back and forth, to and fro.

Daisy waved her arms in front of her face.

*Oh no,* she thought. *Mrs. Pye has slipped into a mental state of shock.*

---

FOR A LITTLE WHILE, Daisy did everything she could think of to try and snap Mrs. Pye out of her state. She tried yelling 'BOO' suddenly and very loudly in her ear, she pinched her cheek and gave her a mild Chinese burn, but Mrs. Pye was immovable. Daisy then did a dance right in front of her, which in normal circumstances would have had Mrs. Pye chortling and telling her to "stop it, you daft brush".

Finally, Archie appeared. 'What are you doing?' he said, as he popped his head around the door.

Daisy shrugged. 'It's Mrs. Pye. She's away with the with the bleeding fairies. Watch this.' Daisy then proceeded to swirl like a Spanish dancer right in front of Mrs. Pye before clapping her hands loudly right in front of her face.

'I see what you mean,' Archie said, a frown ridging his forehead. 'Any idea what's set her off? Something must have happened.' He frowned. 'Maybe she saw that the authorities were looking for us on TV, that we're wanted. Or maybe it's because we've smashed up the house—'

"Nah. I found her like this. And we do look a bit weird,' Daisy said.

Right now, she needed to get her head together about what had happened with Kemp, and how he'd discovered that Mrs. Pye was Kemp's mother, and how she'd been manhandled by a ghost let alone explain it all to Archie. She shook her head.

Archie put a hand on her shoulder. 'Sorry to drag you away, Daisy, but we could do with a hand out there ... it's a bit complicated and we're getting nowhere. We'll check up on Mrs. P later, OK?'

Archie first of all gave Mrs. Pye a hug and then Daisy moved over to Mrs. Pye and, looking into her eyes, planted a small kiss on her forehead and said, 'we'll be back shortly to make sure you're alright, I promise.'

---

'SO, HERE'S THE PROBLEM,' Archie said. 'When you concentrate the whole place turns into of a nightmare of notes and letters.'

'I know. Irritating, isn't it?'

They met up with Isabella and Old Man Wood in the middle of the courtyard.

'You know something,' Daisy said dreamily as she stared at the wall next to the front door, 'it's probably a good thing that humans don't understand any of this. Listen to this classic.' She moved in and pointed to the windowsill.

*'NEST VACANT,'* she read raising her eyebrows.

*'FAMILY EATEN. NEST WILL ROT IF NOT OCCUPIED. LOOK IN THE HAWTHORN BY THE BUBBLING BROOK. ASK FOR SPRINKLE THE THRUSH.'*

Daisy shook her head. 'And there's more. Listen to this one.

*'PREDATOR EVASION COURSES: PROTECT YOURSELF AND YOUR FAMILY. BASED ON GROUND BREAKING RESEARCH BY DR. ROB ROBIN, GUARANTEED 35 PERCENT SURVIVAL INCREASE.*

'And then, in smaller writing, it says; *Conditions apply.'*

Isabella burst out laughing. 'They're adverts!'

Archie kicked a loose stone, which flew out of the courtyard towards the path. 'But it isn't helping us find Blaster-whatever-it-is Jelly. And I'm starving. Are you sure we can't eat something?'

'Certainly not,' Old Man Wood replied, groaning as he attempted to move some loose stone slabs from the corner of the yard.

Daisy shook her head. 'What did the willow trees say? Are you sure they meant this courtyard, not the ruin?'

'Oh yes, this is the right place alright.'

Daisy sat down. 'Have we checked everywhere?'

'Twice,' Archie said, settling beside her. 'Can't your eyes find it?'

Daisy looked incredulous. 'No, Archie, apparently they can't,' she said flatly.

Archie's stomach rumbled. It he wasn't allowed to eat any food at least he could look at it. He decided to nip inside and sneak a peek inside the fridge.

He stood up, walked across the steps and, just as he opened the front door, he looked down at the metal foot-grate. Bending down, he moved it aside and there, in large letters, were the words:

'BLABISTERBERRY JELLY'

'Over here! I think I've found it!' he said. In no time four faces were peering over the stone.

'There's small writing beneath it,' Daisy said. 'Bit worn out – looks like instructions.'

Archie sniffed. 'I'll pull up the slab? It'll be underneath.'

'I don't think so—' she said, but already Archie was on his hands and knees trying to squeeze his fingers into the gap on one side. He groaned and pulled and heaved until his face started to sweat.

Daisy watched Archie straining. 'You haven't lost your strength, have you?'

Archie bristled and he made an even greater effort.

Eventually he relented.

Daisy smiled. 'Now, let me read the instructions to you,' she said, in a very irritating kind of school-mistressey manner. She adjusted the pink glasses on the bridge of her nose and cleared her throat.

'*TO OPEN ME,*' she read, '*KNOCK THREE TIMES* AND *PRESS ON EDEN'S* ... and the final word is scuffed. It goes something like, blank, blank, blank, maybe blank, then a P, blank, blank. I think.'

*_ _ _ ? P _ _*

They all looked at each other quizzically.

'Gatepost?' Isabella said, getting excited. 'It could be a ... gatepost?

'We don't have a gatepost, we have a rock,' Daisy said.

Archie rubbed a hair spike. 'The rock does look like a gatepost,' he said hopefully. 'But it's missing a "T".'

'It's a massive grey rock, or obelisk, with *"Eden Cottage"* etched into it.'

Daisy said. She ran to the top of the yard and concentrated hard on the gate-rock and just as before all sorts of writing started to appear.

A fresh one, not yet blurred from the rain read:

"NOPPY LOVES SCROPPY. BUNNY KISSES."

Further up were watered down names from a deer called Lush, a fox called Sand and a badger called Leaf. Perhaps they lived here too. Then one caught her eye, nestled under the dry overhang of the stone.

"RED TO THE RABBITY FAMILY. SORRY ABOUT FLOPPY BUT I AM A FOX. THE FLOODS HAVE MADE IT VERY DIFFICULT TO EAT ANYWHERE ELSE. DON'T HOLD IT AGAINST ME."

'Wow!' Daisy said under her breath. 'Incredible.' And then she just made out a very recent addition beneath it:

"BEWARE. EVIL SURROUNDS THE OLD RUIN FOR ALL."

Daisy swallowed. 'There's nothing!' she shouted.

'Nothing?' said Archie. 'Are you sure? I mean magic eyes or not, were you concentrating hard enough?' he said sarcastically.

'Shut up, Arch – what's got into you?' Isabella said. 'You're getting really nauseating.'

'If it's that irritating, zap me with your hands?'

'I'm very tempted, Archie.'

Archie didn't react. He stood dead still. A brilliant idea had suddenly leapt into his head.

'I think I've got it!' he cried. 'Listen. It's got nothing to do with the gatepost. It's *carpet* – you know: blank, blank, blank, P, blank, blank.'

'*The hand-mark on one of the rugs*,' Isabella cried. 'Archie's right!' She ran inside and, moments later, returned with the carpet rolled under her arm.

She re-read the riddle: '*TO OPEN ME, KNOCK THREE TIMES* AND *PRESS ON EDEN'S CARPET.*' Isabella looked delightedly at her siblings. 'Well, there's only one way to find out. Who's going to press and who's going to knock?'

'I'll press on the hand mark. Archie knocks,' Daisy said. 'Are you ready? On the count of three.'

'One, two, THREE'

Daisy moved her hand in alignment with the smaller outline of the hand on the carpet.

*KNOCK, KNOCK, KNOCK.*

They held their breath.

Then, ever so slowly, the paving slab with *'Blabisterberry Jelly'* written on it started to fade away and in its place appeared a stone stairway.

The children and Old Man Wood exchanged glances. 'We did it,' Isabella said, nervously.

From the bottom of the steps a sweet perfume wafted up to them. They stared down. Then a lovely, sweet voice came up to them.

'Hello there!' it said. 'Well, now, there's no time to dally. Come along, come along.'

Isabella cringed, her body filled with trepidation. 'Oh hells-bells,' she whispered. 'We've really got to go down there, haven't we?'

# 103 TROOPS ARRIVE AT EDEN COTTAGE

'Look, sir, buildings,' Geddis said, relieved. 'The fog's a little thinner up here.'

The stony corner of a building, like a ship, quickly emerged out of the white, creamy soup.

'OK, quiet. Protective clothing on, please.' Dickinson said.

Without hesitating, the troops donned the white protective helmets and gloves.

'Call in on your MICs please.' The troops responded. 'Geddis, anything on the sensors?'

Geddis shook his head. 'Nothing, here, sir.'

Dickinson waved them forward. 'Remember, if you see them, do not shoot – is that perfectly clear? Shoot as a very last resort and not to kill. Did you get that, Talbot?'

The four soldiers responded to their commander in the affirmative. At least there were no problems with the microphones and earpieces.

By now the fog had caught them up and, in order not to get swamped by the huge blanket of white cloud, the troops moved silently, hugging the wall, moving in a line of five.

Dickinson stopped near the front door. 'Geddis, do you read anything?'

'Negative. Nothing in the courtyard area. And as far as I can tell nothing through these three windows on this side of the house.'

'Inside,' Dickinson commanded, tipping his head.

The men moved fast, opened the door and entered the hallway.

'Looks like someone's been in here already, sir,' said Pearce, the tall, wiry commando, as he inspected the mess of frames, canvasses and pictures lying in heaps all over the floor. 'Someone's given the place a good going over. I reckon they've already been and gone.'

Dickinson sucked in a breath as he inspected the pictures. 'Maybe they searched the house and took the kids.' *After all,* he thought, *the helicopter hadn't reported any sign of life during its reconnaissance mission.*

His earpiece crackled. Geddis' voice came through, breathing hard. 'Better make your way upstairs, sir. There's been one hell of a struggle up here. It's riddled with bullet holes.'

Dickinson instructed Talbot to come with him, leaving Pearce and Mills downstairs to search the remainder of the downstairs.

At the top of the stairs, signs of a battle could be seen on the landing where a burned rug lay on the floor.

Dickinson inspected it. 'Over a day old, maybe they've been gone longer than we thought.'

'In here, sir.'

Dickinson moved in and looked around. The room, as Geddis said, was a wreck. Small holes littered the wooden panels on the walls; the four-poster bed lay in a heap, the bottom end in bits, splinters scattered over the floor. 'Jeez, what happened here?'

'First impressions would be a gunfight. By the look of it, a hell of a lot of rounds. Machine gun, possibly a grenade or two.'

Dickinson ran his hand over the carvings on the bed. 'Any ideas who was involved?'

The pair searched the room.

'Have you noticed something?' Dickinson remarked. 'It doesn't really stack up. Masses of bullet holes but no—'

'Shells.'

'Precisely.'

Geddis whistled. 'You're right. There are no shells, sir, anywhere,' he said, scouring the floor. 'And, if I'm not mistaken, looking at the holes, they've used one helluva strange gun.'

Dickinson took out a tiny camera and began filming.

The headphones in his helmet crackled. 'Sir, Pearce here. We're going across to the other buildings. No sign of life in the main building. A few smashed plates, but the oven is warm. Did you say there was a housekeeper, sir?'

'Affirmative. Apparently she lives on site, in one of the outbuildings. Call me when you find her.'

Dickinson checked his phone and wondered whether to call Stone. No, perhaps he'd do it when he had a proper feel for what had gone on.

He shook his head. Clearly there had been a terrible struggle, but there had to be a clue – something – that gave them a chance to find out where they may have gone. Surely, they would have left a message somewhere?

'Commander,' the radio blared.

'Dickinson here.'

'You'd better come over. We've found someone. I think it's the woman you were talking about.'

Dickinson clenched his fist. 'Excellent. Coming over.'

'Follow the building. You'll eventually bump into Mills. Doesn't look as if she's got plans to go anywhere,' Pearce replied.

Dickinson reeled. 'What do you mean? Is she dead?'

'Negative, sir. You'll have to see for yourself. Looks like shock.'

Dickinson left Geddis to check out the other rooms, slipped out of the front door, and was immediately swallowed up by the dense fog. He moved around the courtyard until he saw Mills standing beside a stone flight of stairs.

Pearce met him at the top. 'I don't think she knows we're here,' he said.

When the commander walked into the bedroom, there, sitting on the bed and staring at the wall, was a large woman dressed in a pink, woollen dressing gown. Her piggy eyes were red from crying, and red hair hung loosely across her face and down her neck. Her forehead bore the deep traces of scarring and her plump, full lips were parted as a strange humming noise emanated from her. She rocked to and fro every so often, her arms across her chest as though protecting herself from cold.

Dickinson stepped in front of her and, when her reaction didn't alter, he squatted down and moved his palm a couple of inches from her face as though cleaning an invisible window.

'Hello?'

Not a flicker. He tried again with the same result before rejoining the other commandos outside the room.

'You're right. It's shock,' he said.

Mills agreed. 'I've seen this type of behaviour before. Might be best, sir, if you take off your protective garments and go in and start talking normally. She doesn't appear to have any Ebora symptoms.'

Dickinson nodded, removed his gear and re-entered the room. He knelt down before Mrs. Pye.

'Hello,' he said, awkwardly. 'I'm from the national rescue centre which is currently based at Swinton Park, near Masham. Do you know where that is? We're trying to find the cause of all this misery,' he said softly. 'You know, the storm and the rainwater and now there's been an outbreak of a terrible disease which is spreading. We have a feeling that Archie and Isabella and Daisy might know something that could really help us get to the bottom of it. That's why we're here, so please don't be alarmed.' He ran a hand through his sandy hair, turned towards Mills and shrugged.

Mills gestured for him to keep going.

'Can you tell me where they are – the children?'

Mrs. Pye remained staring at the wall.

'Can you tell me your name?' he tried. 'Do you know what happened in the house?'

The woman continued to stare at the wall.

Dickinson waited patiently, before standing up and heading outside. This wasn't going to be easy. She needed medical help, and it wasn't going to be forthcoming from them. Perhaps he should call Stone, see if he had any ideas.

Dickinson unclipped his phone.

Stone picked up straight away. 'Well? Any luck?'

'It looks like someone's beaten us to it,' Dickinson said.

'Hell!' Stone swore. 'Any sign of the children?'

'Nowhere to be seen, sir. The place is a mess. There's been some kind of battle upstairs, odd gunfire marks in the wooden panelling, and a couple of fires have started.'

Stone sucked in a breath. 'Weapons? That's not good. What kind of shells?'

'That's the strange bit. There aren't any. It's as if they cleared up after themselves.'

Stone's silence spoke volumes. 'Are you quite sure?' he said at length.

'Affirmative. I've taken footage,' Dickinson said. 'And it would appear that someone has rifled through all the pictures—'

'Pictures?'

'Yes, sir. Framed pictures, canvasses, oils. They litter the downstairs rooms.'

'Anything else?'

'We've found the housekeeper, sir.'

Stone's tone lightened. 'What did she have to say?'

'Nothing yet, sir. She's in shock – scared out of her mind. Mills said he'd seen something like it before, in the Middle East – a girl who'd seen her entire family tortured to death in front of her.'

'Can you get *anything* out of her?'

'We're trying but it's negative at the moment. She hums and stares at the wall, shaking.'

'Try again, Dickinson,' Stone ordered. 'Use electricity to jar her or water-board if necessary ... we need answers—'

'But torture, on a woman?'

'It's called *interrogation*, Dickinson,' Stone snapped, 'and I don't care how you do it. I just need results.' He slammed down the phone.

Dickinson went back into the room and knelt down in front of Mrs. Pye.

'Hello,' he said. 'It's me again. We really need to know what's happened and you're the only person we can find. You see, if we don't find the answers, the whole area around here will be destroyed by a very big bomb. So in order to prevent this, and the loss of hundreds of thousands of lives, we could do with your help.'

Still the woman rocked and stared at the wall.

Dickinson's patience began to desert him. 'Please,' he begged. 'Everyone is going die if we don't get some answers.'

A tiny flicker flashed in Mrs. Pye's eye and Dickinson wondered if she could hear him after all.

'All we need are a few simple answers,' he urged.

The woman resumed her staring and humming.

Dickinson hated this. He didn't have Stone's cold-hearted approach to interrogation, the iciness needed to extract answers. Maybe they should take her back with them so Stone could work on her? Then again, perhaps he should try a different approach. If he wasn't mistaken, she cared for the children. She must have feelings for them.

'Archie and the girls will die if you don't help them,' he began. 'Do you understand? Your children will be killed by this terrible thing if you don't help us find them.'

The woman suddenly turned to him. Her eyes moist again and tears ran down her cheeks as her shoulders heaved. 'Taken,' she said, her vocal chords straining. 'From me.'

And then she resumed her rocking and staring at the wall.

# 104 CAIN'S NEW IDEA

'Who cares what I did?' the ghost crowed.

'I do,' Kemp said angrily.

'You? But, my boy, you loathe them. That's what I rather liked about you. And now, suddenly because I, a mere spirit, go and give Daisy de Lowe a little tickle, you get all upset.'

'Tickle? That wasn't a tickle, you violated her—'

'Oh come now. I wasn't harming her, quite the opposite,' Cain said, 'and she is rather exquisite, if you ask me.'

Kemp's face looked ready to explode.

'You're not jealous, are you?' Cain asked. 'Or worried that I'd take her instead of you?'

Kemp shook his head. 'Of course not,' he said thickly. 'What you did was plain stupid.'

'Why? Surely you must see by now that the de Lowes are going to die. Those pathetic Heirs of Eden still haven't got a clue what's going on, although I'll grant you, by the amount of debris downstairs, they are trying.'

'But now Daisy knows I'm alive,' Kemp said.

'So what, boy?' Cain snapped. 'It doesn't matter. Why not have a bit of fun with them? If I was allowed to kill her, I would.' He paused. 'Then all of this would be over.'

'So why didn't you?'

'Because if I, or anyone else for that matter, interferes directly with the Heirs of Eden's quest, they will have succeeded.'

'Then you nearly gave it to them on a plate,' he said. 'How stupid can you get?' Kemp scratched his head; he needed to change the subject. 'Anyway, thanks for taking me to my mother,' he said. 'You were right.'

Cain drifted closer. 'My pleasure, boy. How did it go?'

'She knew,' Kemp said. 'We share the same thumbs; they bend right back like this.' He manipulated his digits.

'Fascinating,' Cain said, drily.

'When I looked closer, I was just like her. You know, hair, lips, even our noses are the same. She's bloody ugly though, unlike me.'

Cain laughed. 'So now we share our secrets.'

'Yeah,' Kemp said. 'And mum's coming here when the world gets destroyed, just as you promised, right? And please, don't do what you did with Daisy again, OK. It's freaky and a little bit pervy.'

Cain smiled. 'Ah, yes, yes. Of course,' Cain replied. Cain wondered if having the boy's mother around wouldn't be such a bad thing. Keep him under control; guide him in other ways, someone to play him off against.

Another thought had been niggling away at him. If Earth was to finish, as was increasingly likely, and Kemp was the sole survivor, then the boy would need a companion or two. Ghosts were hardly ideal playmates.

In due course, the boy would wish to reproduce and raise a family. But Havilah's human population were stuck, frozen in time like small, glass, upside down dishes littered upon the ground.

'You rather like her, don't you?'

'What?' Kemp said. 'My mum? Yeah, of course—'

'I meant the girl.'

'Daisy?' Kemp immediately went defensive. 'She's annoying and a show off and stupid, but she is pretty—'

'So you do like her!'

Kemp smiled. 'You're a horrible ghost, aren't you?'

'Perhaps,' he whispered into Kemp's ear.

'Stop doing that,' Kemp said, swishing at the air with his hand.

Cain moved through Kemp to the other ear. 'Or is there another girl?' he said.

'Stop that!'

Cain laughed with the boy. 'Come on, tell me.'

'No! Go away. Who I fancy is none of your business.'

'It's every bit my business,' Cain said, pretending to sound a little offended. 'Anyway, to find out all I have to do is look into your mind.'

'You wouldn't—'

'I already have.'

Kemp smiled and tried to think if there really was anyone else. 'Well if you must know, before you go rummaging through my head, there's a girl called Sue who is pretty hot.'

'Hot?' Cain chuckled. 'You don't mean that in a literal sense, do you? She doesn't actually feel hot, does she?'

'No! It means she's a bit of a babe, like Daisy, but with brains.'

'How interesting,' Cain mused.

Kemp sighed. 'Thing is, Daisy *hates* me. Sue, on the other hand, is properly gorgeous, and *really* hates me. The crap thing is she's the best friend of Isabella and Isabella hates me more than anyone or anything in the world, so basically it would never happen.'

'Why not? Strange things happen all the time,' said Cain, who hummed a strange, wispy tune, a trait which Kemp knew as his way of thinking. 'Why does Isabella detest you so, boy?'

'Well it started when I put a dead rat in her gym bag, which rotted and filled with maggots. When she found it, it made her so ill she ended up in hospital.' Kemp grinned. 'She's never forgiven me.'

Cain laughed. 'I tell you what,' he said at length, 'why don't we go and find her?'

'Isabella?'

'No, you fool. The girl who you say is the "hot" one?'

'Sue? She's probably dead like all the others—'

'I'll ask her spirits to find out, or better still, let me have a word with Asgard. The dreamspinner will find out in no time. Ghosts can get a little touchy, especially those related to the recently deceased—'

Kemp felt a little uneasy. 'Look, it's very nice of you to help me, but I'll save you the hassle. I promise you, she'll never, ever go with me, dead or alive. And anyway, what would I say to her? She's like, really clever and smart.'

'And you're not, boy?' Cain sighed. 'You're switched on enough to have joined me. In any case, you can give her a choice. Tell her it's you, or death.'

'That's not a great chat up line.'

'It worked for me.'

'Well, you're a ghost—'

'Indeed, but I wasn't always like this, you know. A long time ago I was extremely powerful and I intend, with your help, to reacquaint myself with that position.'

'So, why are you so interested in my love life, or lack of it?'

Cain appeared to sigh. 'As you know, I live forever,' he said wearily. 'You, however, will not. When Earth is no more, I can assure you that at some point you will wish to raise children.'

Kemp looked repulsed. 'OMG!'

'Whatever "OMG" means, I note the horror on your face. Don't be naive, boy. It is a perfectly natural development in the cycle of a living thing to procreate, to keep the wheels of life turning. For some species it is their sole purpose. It is said that with the failure of the Heirs of Eden, the humans on Havilah will awaken.' He shrugged, invisibly. 'But who knows if and when this will happen. With my help, you and your offspring will rule Havilah and Earth and the Garden of Eden. If this is to happen, you will need a woman with whom you can procreate.'

Kemp looked blank.

Cain spelt out. 'You'll need to make babies.'

It took Kemp a while to register. 'Blimey,' he said as the penny dropped. 'I'll be like the first guy in the world. Everyone will be based ... on me!' he said at length.

Cain agreed. 'Lucky worlds, huh?'

'Blimey. Like Adam and Eve ... you're a bloomin' genius.'

'Yes, I know,' Cain said, sounding rather smug. 'So, tell me,' he added, 'who is the superior, Daisy or Sue?'

Kemp weighed it up. 'Daisy is bottom of the lowest class, but she's smarter than she makes out and she's an athletic goddess. Sue, on the other hand is top of everything but shocking at games.'

'Then we must entice Sue into our little family, to complement your strength and athleticism.'

Kemp beamed. 'You'll do that for me? How?'

Cain, though completely invisible to Kemp, sat down and thought.

'We'll steal her,' he said at length.

'Steal?'

'Indeed. Though you must ask her first, so that we can gauge her reaction. Then, if she won't come willingly, we'll simply take her.'

'You can't do that!'

'My dear boy, of course I can. I'm Cain, and in a couple of days we'll be the most powerful person in the universe. Your Earth is about to end. Everything will die.'

'I still don't think she'll come. You haven't met her.'

'She'll come,' Cain croaked. 'There's one thing that divides living things from dead things. Living things will do anything in their power to actually live, boy, and not die. You're a testament to that, aren't you?'

Kemp nodded thoughtfully. 'She's pretty stubborn though.'

'Tell me, truthfully. Will she really refuse life for death?' Cain sighed. 'Never. Humans always say honourable, noble things like that, but they don't mean it. Sue will not get a better option. And when she understands the situation and her frankly perilous position she'll come over to us boy, with reluctance. Then time will do its healing. It will be significantly easier if she comes without making a fuss.'

# 105 BLABISTERBERRY JELLY

Daisy heard a mechanical buzz, then a muffled voice. 'Someone's here!' she said, as the sound reached her again. She froze at the top of the steps.

'What is it?' Isabella said.

Daisy concentrated hard. 'Footsteps, boots.'

'The army?' Isabella replied.

'Two people with walkie-talkies. Men's voices, I think. They're close. I think the fog has heightened the sound.'

Isabella ushered Old Man Wood down the stairs. 'Come on, Daisy.'

Daisy peered into the fog at the direction of the noise. Then she took off into the thick cloud and disappeared into the yard.

Isabella swore. *That idiotic, stupid girl.*

Moments later, Daisy reappeared and raced down the steps. 'Come on!' she said. 'Quick.'

'What do you mean, *quick*?' Isabella hissed. 'I've been waiting for *you*.'

'Either of you have any idea how to shut the stairwell?' Daisy said, urgently.

'Who is it?' said Archie, eagerly.

'Soldiers,' Daisy said, 'in protective helmets. They've got guns.'

'Oh terrific,' Isabella whispered.

Voices and the sound of boots scuffing the flagstones could be heard near the corner of the courtyard.

The children stared at each other and then, with a curious *whoosh,* air swept around them and sealed the trapdoor at the top of the stairs shut, leaving a small echo reverberating around the room.

Now, no exterior sounds could be heard and the three children and Old Man Wood collectively exhaled and turned towards a simple, round, stone table and four stone stools. On the walls were torchlights, which, much to Isabella's annoyance appeared to run brightly, but off neither electricity nor any type of fossil fuel she'd ever seen.

In the middle of the stone slab sat a large, shining, golden goblet containing a substance rising above its rim, like ice-cream above a cone.

'So this is Blabisterberry Jelly,' Old Man Wood said, expressing the general look of surprise on their faces as they stared at the cup filled of golden brown, toffee-looking, apricot-coloured goo.

A whooshing, rushing, firework sound came from the goblet, and while Daisy and Archie leaned in, Isabella instinctively ducked under the table and then pretended she hadn't.

'OOOh! Hello, my dears! Who do we have here today?' the voice was that of a sweet old woman, not too dissimilar to their great-grandmother, and certainly in no way menacing or frightening. Her words were delivered as though it was an everyday occurrence to have visitors.

The children looked at one another.

'Is it a ghost?' Archie whispered.

'I don't know. I can't see it.' Daisy stared back at him, her eyes wide.

They scanned the room.

'Now, don't be shy,' the sweet, elderly voice continued. 'I want to hear all about you.'

The children stared at one another and then at Old Man Wood, who simply shrugged.

'Well, my darlings,' it continued, 'let me see if we can break the ice on this fine little gathering.'

Daisy pointed towards the goo. 'I think it's coming from there,' she whispered.

The goblet of goo continued. 'I see that we have two beautiful girls, a lovely, handsome, young man, and, aha, you've brought along Grandpa. Now, let's have a look at all of you. Goodness, so very fit and healthy and may I say how terribly youthful you three are. Isn't that a surprise?' The tone sounded almost mocking.

'If you don't mind, I need to do a bit of an inspection, to make sure I know *exactly* who you are.'

Before any of them had the chance to react, a vapour drifted up from out of the bowl, and began to swirl around them like the tendrils of a climbing plant encircling a tree-trunk, each member of the family ensnared within, as if bound by a rope.

Then the smoke disappeared into their ear, mouth and nose cavities and, as it rushed inside, more followed until the children could feel it inside them, tickling their minds, chilling their lungs and freezing their guts.

Just as they were getting used to it, smoke drifted back out of their orifices and back into the goo once more.

All four breathed deeply as if their internal organs had received a smart little tidy-up.

'Bless you all, my dears,' the voice said. 'So you've found me at long last. Goodness, you've taken your time though, haven't you? Well, not to worry. I believe your search for the tablets is well under way. How do you think you're doing?'

The children scuffed their shoes over the floor awkwardly.

'Er ... not too bad,' Daisy said, reddening.

'You're talking to pot of marmalade, Daisy,' Isabella whispered.

'I don't care,' Daisy said from out of the corner of her mouth. 'At least it's polite marmalade.'

The strange, pleasant, old woman's voice piped up again. 'I can't begin to tell you how excited I am. I'd offer you a cup of tea or the like but, my sweets, that isn't possible ... so, tell me, what are your names? You look like a right little lamb. Yes, you with the lovely blonde locks.'

'Er ... Daisy,' Daisy said, looking straight at the goblet of goo.

'So,' the sweet voice said, 'Daisy, my darling, do *you* think you can do it? You look plucky enough to me.'

Daisy's face contorted. 'Do what?'

'Eat me,' the voice said.

Daisy laughed awkwardly. 'Ah-ha ... *eat ... you? What exactly do you mean* – if you don't mind me asking?'

'As I said. *You must eat me*, my dear.'

Daisy snorted and a small bogey blew out of her nose and landed on the rim of the cup where it immediately burned up.

'Seriously?' she said, a little embarrassed.

From the silence that filled the small chamber, Daisy realised the goo was being deadly serious. 'Oh, right. Well, yeah, of course ... I knew that,' she said, cringing, and staring wide-eyed at her siblings.

The voice from the goo sensed her discomfort. 'I do not wish to be disrespectful sweetheart, but you *did* find the riddles?'

'Yup, of course we did.'

'Then, tell me, little darlings, that you studied them?'

Daisy's face had turned from pink to red and Archie noted Daisy's unease. He coughed and recited the second verse of the riddle.

*'For the second one you have to find*
*'You burp it from the family belly.*
*'To do this, you have to eat*
*'Blabisterberry Jelly!'*

'Very good,' said the voice, displaying a hint of sarcasm. 'You see, *I* am Blabisterberry Jelly and all you have to do is eat me. Clear, so far?'

The children nodded, dumbly.

'Well, come on then,' Archie said as he made a lunge for the goblet.

'Not so fast, young man,' the voice said, as a small cloud of smoke puffed out of the goblet in his general direction.

Archie reeled and fanned the billow with his arm.

The sweet voice turned a little sterner. 'It isn't quite as simple as that. In order to succeed, you have to believe that I am, quite simply, the most delicious food you have ever tasted. It really is incredibly easy.'

Old Man Wood groaned. 'And what if we can't?' he asked.

'If you don't *believe*, you don't belch. And if you don't belch, you don't get the tablet, and if you don't get the tablet ... you die.' The voice softened. 'Isn't that right, young man?'

Archie smiled as the cogs of the puzzle slipped into place. 'My name is Archie, ma'am,' he said politely. He licked his lips ready to tuck in.

'Know this, handsome Archie,' the kindly voice of Blabisterberry Jelly continued. 'If you think about my form and eat me as you see me, you will taste the thing you see, and not the food you desire. Do you all understand?'

Archie nodded. *What a doddle,* he thought.

Daisy was feeling increasingly thankful that she'd hardly touched her breakfast.

'It is important you are clear about this,' said the voice.

'What a result,' Archie whispered. 'I hope it's gonna be good, 'cos I am starving.'

But Isabella's hands trembled. 'I don't like the sound of this,' she whispered. 'Not one little bit.'

The goblet heard her. 'My dear, which bit in particular do you not like?'

Isabella hesitated. 'Well, what if it isn't possible to eat whatever it is? What if it's so disgusting – I mean, does it matter?' she asked, her voice cracking.

'Aha! A very good question pretty young lady, whose name is ...?'

'Isabella.'

'Isabella, such a pretty name for such a delicate face. I will be honest with you, if you don't eat your platefuls you will never leave. Is that perfectly clear?'

Isabella swallowed.

'And, another word of advice,' the voice continued, 'the longer it takes, the larger the portion sizes become?'

The children nodded, not entirely clear about where this was leading.

'Good,' the Blabisterberry Jelly said. 'You're a smart bunch, aren't you? Grandpa must be so proud.'

'But what if I really can't eat—'

'Then, my dear, you'll get a little ... overwhelmed.' A high-pitched cackle echoed around them, and then, as before, the sweet tones resumed. 'This is why my portions always start so small. It's terribly easy. Just believe what you want to believe. You have only yourself to fear.'

Isabella's stomach churned. *Portions? Portions of what, exactly?*

In the marrow of her bones something told her that this absolutely, definitely, wasn't going to be a piece of Mrs. Pye's cake.

# 106 TO THE COTTAGE

Dickinson had seen enough.

*Taken from her*. That's all she'd said – three times. When pressed about where they had gone, she'd stared at him with sadness in her eyes and returned to staring at the wall.

He waited for Stone to pick up.

'Sir,' Dickinson said, as his phone clicked. 'We've searched everywhere. The woman told us the children have been taken and I'm afraid we can't get any more out of her. To be honest, I doubt if she knows any more – she's in a terrible state.'

'Did you use other methods?' Stone asked.

'Absolutely,' Dickinson lied. 'If anything, it made her worse.'

For a moment the line remained quiet as Stone thought it through. 'You reckon the house has been ransacked and the children abducted?'

'That's one theory,' Dickinson replied. 'We've been round the house and buildings twice and not a squeak of life. All I can tell you is one hell of a struggle took place upstairs and downstairs. Some of the children's clothes we found were covered with bloodstains and torn to bits. Even the generator hasn't been on for a while. I hate to say it, sir, but there's a strong chance they're already dead.'

Stone cussed into the radio. 'I've got Solomon and Sue here. Is there anything they can salvage?'

Dickinson rubbed his chin. 'Whoever it is must be a step ahead of us. If Solomon can find any links to the chapel that'll be something. You've got nothing to lose, and it might not be a bad idea to have Sue look after the woman. She might loosen-up if she sees a friendly face. I'll fix up a camera in her room so we can see if she's faking it or not.'

'Nice idea,' Stone replied. 'When you've done that, get down to where you left your boat. Meet the RIB coming over from our side with the headmaster and girl. You'll need to guide them in.'

'Heading down now, sir. Thickest fog you've ever seen.'

'Fine, but I need you back here. We had a perimeter break last night. This place must be secure while we begin the evacuation. I think word about the Americans' intention has sneaked out.'

'OK, Roger that,' Dickinson said. 'We'll be there as soon as we can.'

---

STONE TURNED TO SOLOMON. 'Eden Cottage is empty. From what Dickinson said, the children have been abducted, so you're on, cousin. Find out all you can. Take Sue, she can look after that caretaker woman and we'll ask her to see if she can figure out what happened. The RIB leaves as soon as you've got your things together. You'll find supplies for several days and I'm giving you a radio. Touch base the moment you're in the house, and then at four hourly intervals during daylight hours. Is that clear? I'll also give you some fuel – see if you can't start up that generator.'

'Good, thank you,' Solomon said. 'What if there's nothing after a day or so?'

Stone understood what he meant. 'I'll do what I can to get you out of there,' he said. He stood up and looked his elder cousin in the eye. 'If we've not got you out after three days, take provisions and seal yourselves in the cellar. Understand? Go deep and you should be alright.'

Solomon nodded.

'The clock is ticking and we need results.'

'Indeed, Charlie. You know I'll do my utmost to get to the bottom of this.'

---

SUE STRODE DOWN THE PATH, hoping like mad Gus had managed to get down there before her. In no time, she was swallowed up by a blanket of fog and, had it not been for the familiarity of where to go and the hard tarmac beneath her feet, she wondered if she would have got lost. Her fears were short lived. Despite the protective suite, she recognised Gus before he noticed her for, even though Gus was tall for his age, he was undoubtedly smaller in build than the other men and women who scurried around the small RIB.

Sue slipped on the protective helmet. She moved in closer.

'Hi,' she said, winking at Gus through the plastic mask. 'I'm Sue. Is Mr. Solomon here yet?'

Gus raised his hand. 'He's over there,' he said, his voice a little lower than usual.

Sue followed his gaze and just managed to make out the headmaster heading towards them.

'Hello, sir,' Sue said, as he approached.

'Ah. There you are Sue. Jolly good. Have you got everything you need?' He turned to the man next to him. 'These two are with me.'

The man, squat, with jet black hair and a matching bushy beard, eyed them up. 'I was told only one.' He checked his pad.

'No, both are coming,' Solomon said. 'Top level researchers. And we need to get a move on.'

The man scratched his beard. 'Better check with security,' he said, and he reached wearily into his pocket.

'Can I ask your name?' Solomon asked directly.

'Corporal Lambert.'

'You are aware, Corporal, that I have been given *carte blanche* on this operation by Commissioner Stone? I also happen to be his cousin and head of this investigation.'

Lambert stiffened. Solomon noted his hollow eyes and scarred face. He probably wasn't someone to mess with. 'Perhaps I can persuade you otherwise – we're in such a terrible hurry. Perhaps this might help a little...'

He reached into his pocket and withdrew a few notes. They shook, Lambert accepting the money with a sly smile.

'Alright,' Lambert said, slipping the cash into his back pocket, 'you've paid the ferryman, but I'll still need names. There were two incidents last night, one involving people breaking out, the other with people breaking in. One of them was the kid who survived in a boat. Apparently he's got the disease – that's what they're saying. If security's breached apparently we've 'ad it.'

'Very good, Corporal,' Solomon said, hardly daring to catch Sue or Gus' eye. 'Can I suggest we get going – I'll fill you in as we go? It's quite a distance in these conditions and Dickinson is needed back here pronto.'

Lambert weighed up the suggestion before helping each of them into the twelve-foot RIB and pointing to where he wanted them to perch on the thick, air-filled sides.

Solomon sat on one side, Sue and Gus, the other.

After balancing out the additional weight of fuel and provisions, Lambert gave the boat a shove and hoisted himself up and over the side.

Moments later the engine throbbed into life.

'How can you tell where to go?' Sue asked, looking around. 'It's a total white-out.'

Lambert smiled, showing off a silver capped tooth. He then produced a small electronic device from the inside pocket of his coat. 'This clever navigation system, darlin',' he said. 'Links up to a tracer on the other side. That's them – the red dot.' He showed her, clearly pleased with himself. 'We're the green flashing one. All we've got to do is aim for it. So long as we don't smash into anything too chunky or the light disappears, we'll be there in a couple of hours. Slow goin' in this stuff.'

Sue shivered as the cold, damp, fog leached into her. Apart from the mechanical throb of the engine and the gentle thump of water on the prow, the eeriness and quiet of the water filled her with unease.

Every so often the boat clunked or biffed on something and, holding on extra tight to the safety rope around the edge, she peeked out into the endless, still, white veil. Before long, she slid down the inflated rubber edge and leant on Gus' leg. More than anything, all she wanted to do was snuggle up next to him, just as they had done on "The Joan Of".

Soon, every hair on her body stood to attention. She imagined hands reaching out and grappling at the boat, grotesque, zombie-like bodies hauling themselves in, or pulling them overboard. They were in a corridor of death, and a dark, terror filled her.

Eventually, she shrank down and lowered her head to her chest so that she couldn't see, grateful for the throbbing heartbeat of the engine. The fog's stench was a heady combination of stale water and devastation and it permeated every particle of air.

Lambert peered into the gloom, adjusting the rudder every once in a while and slowing if he saw larger objects looming out of the fog at them. 'Who's the lad then?' he said at long last, pulling out a pad and pen.

Solomon coughed, relieved someone had broken the silence. 'My technical assistant, you mean?'

'Don't he speak?'

Solomon flashed a look towards Gus. 'His name, if that's what you mean, is—'

'Kemp,' Gus answered.

'Absolutely,' Solomon added, raising his eyebrows at the boy. 'Kemp,' he repeated.

'University of Durham, PhD student studying religious artefacts,' Gus continued. 'Specialising in the stained glass windows of the churches of Northern Britain.'

It took all her concentration for Sue not to explode with laughter. Was his voice lower *and slightly posher*?

Lambert nodded, impressed. 'You reckon there's some kinda link then, do ya? That's what I've been hearing, Kemp. Some spooky thing from hundreds of years back, come back to punish us. You know, like in them old times, when the Gods sent plagues and stuff to kill everyone.'

Gus turned towards Sue, his huge, toothy smile evident through the clear plastic hood. 'Um ...'

'That's exactly the sort of thing we're going to see if we can find out, Sergeant,' Solomon butted in. 'You see, Kemp has an almost unique perspective on these matters. He was born in a house bang next to York Minster, where he was fortunate to have access to some of the rarest forms of ecclesiastical artworks in the world, weren't you, Kemp?'

Gus stared at the headmaster for a while. 'Indeed,' he said coolly. 'A very unique ... childhood.'

Solomon was enjoying himself. 'Didn't you write a thesis on it?'

Gus spluttered. 'Yeah. Er ... about triptych stained glass window arrangements and other things,' he said hurriedly.

'Gothic?' Solomon said.

'Absolutely,' Gus replied, wondering what had got into the man. '90's Gothic-revival kind-of-thing.'

'90's Gothic revival?' Lambert said. 'You're pulling my leg.'

Solomon chuckled. 'My dear old thing we're talking about the Thirteenth century—

'1290's, to be precise,' Gus added. 'An important time in—'

Sue shrieked, 'How long before we arrive?'

Lambert looked down at the screen. 'About fifteen minutes. You lot had better keep look out. I'm told there's loads of stuff lying round the edges – you know, cars, trees – maybe a rotting cat or two.' He smiled. 'Maybe a few human corpses.'

When the RIB brushed on the bare tops of willow tree clumps submerged beneath the water, they knew they must be close. Lambert negotiated through piles of metal, plastic and wooden debris until, eventually, Gus spotted a faint circular ring of bright light glowing out of the fog not too far away.

Lambert aimed for it, cut the engine, and let the boat drift in.

Shortly, instructions came from the bank, and while Lambert guided the rudder, Gus grabbed the nylon painter and tossed it to one of the talking figures on the side of the water who pulled the boat further in. Then he jumped off the prow into the mud, where a blond-haired man helped him regain his legs.

As Sue did the same, Gus moved to the fringes, tested the weight of a rucksack and hauled it up onto his back. With his head kept low, he waited while the others gathered their provisions and, in no time, they began the tricky, slippery climb up the hillside towards Eden Cottage.

# 107 STARLIGHT APPLE CRUMBLE

Without warning, a fountain of sparkling dust blew out of the goblet of goo, like a firework. Streams of bright, vibrant colours creating a dazzling, glittery cloud that soon hovered over the table.

The children and Old Man Wood smiled at one other, wide-eyed in amazement. Then, the dust parted and formed swirling circles above them, like coloured halos.

These halos descended down over their heads, spinning in front of their eyes and over their ears, a noise tingling like miniature bells.

The children instinctively shut their eyes, as the strange particles swept into their heads through all available holes and tickled their brains.

When the noise reappeared, they opened their eyes to find the halos in front of them, each one moving towards the middle of the table like fat bagels flying in slow-motion.

As they met, another explosion of glitter spewed into the air with the sound of broken glass.

In front of the children's astonished eyes the dust divided and descended in equal parts onto their plates.

When the children and Old Man Wood looked down, the colourful glitter had gone. They stared at their stone plates with mouths open, their eyes on stalks.

A second later, screams of horror and shouts of absolute disgust erupted in the small chamber.

---

OLD MAN WOOD REELED.

On his plate a miniature dreamspinner crawled on long, opaque legs around the rim of the stone platter, it's translucent, jellyfish-like body with a hole where its abdomen should have been, pulsating with mini forks of blue lightning.

Old Man Wood sat quite still with his mouth open, staring at the creature, while all around him the children screamed and hollered and wailed and gagged at the sights in front of them.

*Apples alive, I did this,* he thought. *These things are our worst fears. It is a trial of will.* At least that's what the Willows said. It had to be true, but how in all the apples on all the planets in all the universes had he done it?

Shocked, he stared at the creature moving around the plate, trying to think. But the longer he stared and the children screamed, the larger the strange, spidery creature grew.

When Daisy came over and threw her arm round him wailing, he snapped out of it, and remembered where he was and what he had to do.

'SILENCE!' he roared. 'Listen to me, and listen hard. Look at me, Isabella – you too Daisy. Look me right in the eye.' The children did as he asked. 'Whatever you do, DO NOT look at your plates until I tell you. Right, good.'

Old Man Wood took a deep breath. 'All of this is not real, my littluns,' he said, his tone softer. 'What you have to imagine is that this plateful is your favourite food, your most favourite meal in the world.'

'That's impossible—'

'No, little Bells, it is not,' he said. 'WE HAVE TO DO THIS or Blabisterberry Jelly will overwhelm us. Keep looking at me, girls, and you, Archie.' He held each pair of the children's terrified eyes.

'You have to believe me,' he said, as he picked up a spoon and fork.

'Keep looking at me. Good. Now, I'm going to prove how easy this is. I'm imagining, with all my heart and soul, that this is my favourite food...'

'Starlight apple crumble?' Archie said.

'Exactly!' Old Man Wood said. 'It's a thick slice of warm, yumptious, starlight apple crumble on my plate where the apple is sweet and juicy and the crumble crunches. How it melts in the mouth.'

The Old Man shut his eyes and concentrated hard on a mouthful of starlight apple crumble helped along with a huge dollop of thick, creamy custard.

He opened his eyes and looked down. For him, the strange, thin, spidery creature began to recede into apple crumble covered in yummy custard. The others looked on, riveted by the repulsive scene of Old Man Wood about to eat an alien-like spider.

'You see,' he said, cutting into the dreamspinner, 'you have to believe that what you are about to eat is what you *truly* want to eat. It doesn't have to be big or clever, but Blabisterberry Jelly will know if you mean it. I promise you this, my littluns, you must not be found wanting.'

Old Man Wood shut his eyes and helped himself to the mouthful, pushing the pulsating spoonful with a long leg hanging out into his open mouth.

All the children could see was the quivering electrical abdomen of the dreamspinner flashing, electrifying his stubby teeth as he bit down.

'Cor! That is utterly fan-tab-ulistic!' Old Man Wood spluttered, helping himself to another spoonful. 'This has ... mmm ... to be the greatest ... yummiest ... sweetest, starlight apple crumble I've ever had in all my life.'

He piled in again. 'And I should know,' he enthused as he chewed, electric blue crackles of lightning washing round his mouth, 'Coz I've been making it for an awfully long time.'

# 108 A DISGUSTING WAY TO DIE

Daisy shook with fear.

She simply couldn't believe Old Man Wood was eating the most horrific, weird, spidery-alien-thing she'd ever seen. The sight filled her with dread and she noted how Isabella and Archie's faces were pale and green.

No books, no schooling, ***nothing*** could prepare them for this kind of experience. Daisy shut her eyes and took a deep breath. Holding onto her nose she sucked in a huge lungful of air, exhaling slowly before repeating the process two or three times.

How did the goo know?

The *incident* had happened three years ago. They'd been playing football and some of the boys started getting rough, kicking her and tripping and making dangerous tackles. She smiled now she thought about it, how similar it had been to the match against Chitbury.

She'd tried hard, desperately hard not to cry. But her legs hurt and it was so unfair! When the tears rolled, the boys made it worse, calling her names – one even spat on her. And, even worse was the way they enjoyed her discomfort.

On their way home, Daisy hardly spoke. When she did, she'd told Archie that she'd never cry again. No one had a right to make her so upset and, from that day forward, she vowed she would never shed another tear.

Instantly, Archie turned to her and offered her a bet, partially as a bit of fun, and partially because he argued that crying wasn't a bad thing to do. Three weeks' worth of school sweet-tuck if he made her cry within a week.

She'd laughed at him.

Three days went by and Daisy had all but forgotten the incident of Archie's bet. But then, after school one day, they passed a young man walking down the lane from the ruin with a large black Labrador. He was a rambling type often seen walking from village to village across the moors.

As they played in the ruin, Archie spotted it. That evening just before supper, Archie ran up with a garden trowel, found the juicy dog mess, cut it in two, and carefully placed a dollop in each of her woolly boot slippers, before leaving them out by the back door.

They played football until the sun down went down and as an evening chill came over the moors they'd warmed up by the fire. Daisy asked if anyone knew where her woolly boot slippers were. When Archie told her they were by the back door, she marched off and found them.

Without thinking, she pushed her feet in.

Seconds later, the entire family rushed out to find Daisy shrieking hysterically then screaming. Then vomiting and retching. The tears flowed.

She remembered that turgid smell and the way it stuck like glue between her toes, got under her toenails and then, amazingly, transported itself all over her during her tragic attempt to remove it.

She lay in bed for a whole day, and for several weeks spent hours cleaning her feet, scrubbing them almost obsessively.

Now that she thought of it, she'd never paid out the bet. He'd been in way too much trouble.

Daisy took a deep breath.

Sitting proudly on Daisy's plate lay a well-formed steaming, brown dog-turd, gleaming with a sheen as though freshly laid. Daisy prodded it in stunned amazement and for a second wondered if it could be fake, or a type of joke chocolate. But when she caught a whiff of its distinctive odour, she instinctively retched.

Then, holding her mouth and stomach, she vomited behind her.

Daisy returned to stare at the smelly, sweating, stinking turd. 'Dog shit!' she whispered. 'And I've got to eat it.'

Her guts contorted involuntarily and looked up at Isabella, who had climbed on her stool, petrified. Things were clearly not going well for her either.

They all screamed again and, as they did, the turd grew a little larger.

'*NO!*' she yelled, but on that, it expanded a fraction more. She closed her eyes and tried to calm down.

Why? Every time she'd seen a dog poo from that moment on, she'd given it a wide berth and if anyone trod in one and her nose caught that certain whiff, her stomach twisted and her face turned white, then green, and she had to lie down or throw-up.

And now, somehow, like it or not she was going to have to tuck into it with a knife and fork. She wanted to retch but, instead, she stretched her arms out wide to allow for more oxygen. She clenched her eyes tight.

Old Man Wood had to be right. He'd done it – right in front of their eyes and if he could, so could she.

Daisy thought hard. If the turd was an illusion she had to replace the grotesque with something totally amazing. But what? Thank God she'd missed out on breakfast.

*OK*, she thought, *which meal stood out head and shoulders above any other she'd ever had?* Nothing sprang to mind until the aroma of the Chinese meal they'd had for her last birthday treat in Southallerton tickled the sensors in her brain. Yes! That Peking crispy duck all flaked and rolled up in pancakes with cucumber, spring onions and a dab of plum sauce. Nothing had ever tasted quite so wonderful.

But ever present, in a corner of her mind, she could sense it; stinking, vile, slimy. She opened her eyes and stared and, as if the turd understood, it grew. Daisy's stomach leapt again.

She shut her eyes again. *Crispy, shredded, aromatic duck,* she thought, *with extra plum sauce, wrapped up in a pancake.*

*Come on, Daisy,* she urged, *it is utterly delicious – and it has to work.*

---

ARCHIE STARED at Old Man Wood.

Why did the creature creeping around the plate make him feel so uneasy? Why was it so familiar? Archie racked his brain. Then suddenly it hit him: this was the same creature that had sat above Daisy while she slept – the night he'd woken, the night of their final nightmare – before it started, before everything went mad and the rain came down and before the destruction and the plague and the riddles. Before they had any inkling that they were linked to these strange goings on.

His pulse quickened. This spidery-creature looked like a smaller version of that one and, now that the memories returned, he remembered how, at first, he thought the creature might be taking something from Daisy but soon came to the conclusion that it was actually *giving her something*. Yes, that was it. Giving her a powder from the ends of its long legs. And he'd wondered then if this strange creature had been supplying them with their weird dreams.

He scratched his hard front hair spike. The objects on their plates represented their worst fears – he could see that: Daisy with her terror of dog poo, Isabella with her revulsion to dead rats.

On his plate, four round, human eyeballs like marbles twitched, their muscles and tendons attached to each side like the ectoplasm of a bloody jellyfish.

As he inspected them, he noticed how much larger were the ones which bore pale-blue irises in comparison to the other two that had dark, nutty-brown colouring.

Each eye dripped with blood and stared back at him as if they were watching him – *staring madly at him – following him*, Archie thought.

A strand of a nerve twitched, rolling one of the eyeballs over. Then another did the same.

Isabella screamed again, so too, Daisy.

He joined in.

*Who could do such a totally horrendous thing? This wasn't a trial, it was torture.*

He shuddered. Were these the eyes of the Ancient Woman, sucked out and now for his consumption? They had to be. That horrific dream-image never went far away: the extreme violence of his actions, the peculiar sensation of murdering someone and how it had felt so natural, so right.

Every time he'd woken up, he'd been consumed by guilt until he found this feeling replaced by an anger that he found hard to control.

He examined his plate. *Two sets of eyes? Why? The ancient woman ... who else?*

A terrible chill swept through him, as the realization hit him. The other set must belong to Cain. Cain the ghost, who'd told him his eyes had been removed when he'd sat in his room, scaring him witless.

On his plate lay the missing body parts of the two people he feared the most; a spook and an imaginary figure from his dream?

*Jeez, his head must be screwed.*

But if Old Man Wood's strange spider was real, then maybe the Ancient Woman was also real? And maybe, if he was going to kill her – perhaps his dreams stood as a warning?

Archie liked this thought. It made some sort of sense.

He remembered what Cain had said about protecting this Ancient Woman – Cain's mother –against those that might harm her.

So, perhaps his job was to shield her.

Thinking about Cain's concern for his mother, he thought of his own. Why wasn't she here, helping them? Did they have any idea what had happened to them, what they were going through? There hadn't been a word, nothing.

*Maybe*, he thought, *they had been abandoned.* Left to get on with it.

Archie's gloom was punctured by the scraping of a fork on the stone platter in front of Old Man Wood. He looked up to see a portion of electricity-filled jellyfish with thin, almost translucent bones heading towards the old man's mouth.

Archie watched, dumbfounded, as Old Man Wood devoured the curious ghost-like spider.

*So why,* Archie thought, *do spidery-alien creatures give Old Man Wood such fear?* If the creature had been dishing out dreams, as he suspected, then what did it say about Old Man Wood?

Maybe, it showed an uncertain future, or was Old Man Wood in denial about something ... something about this Ancient Woman and Cain?

Watching the old man tackling his plateful with relish, his eyes shut in bliss, loaded Archie with courage.

*If Old Man Wood can do it*, he thought, *then so can I.*

Without knowing why, Archie shut his eyes as he imagined the eyes to be everlasting gob-stoppers. He felt for his plate, picked one of the eyeballs up in his fingers and popped it straight into his mouth. A moment of bliss swept over his face.

'Wow, this is the bes' gosoppa I've eva ha,' he said, as he swirled it round his mouth.

'Keep going, Arch,' Daisy said, clapping wildly.

'Those eyes will soon disappear from your plate...' Old Man Wood said, egging him on.

Only, this comment made Archie open his eyes and look down at his plate to see the vile assortment of eyes and their tendrils. He lost his concentration and went very pale.

*Uh oh*, he thought, as he felt a movement from the eyeball tickling the roof of his mouth and the trail of nerves flickered the back of his throat. Worst of all he was sure he could feel the eye growing. It felt the size of a ping-pong ball.

He wretched violently and the eyeball popped out bouncing rather dramatically a couple of times on the table.

Archie shook his head. 'Idiot,' he mumbled.

'Sorry about that, Arch,' Old Man Wood said, wincing. 'For a moment, I thought you had it.'

Archie head-butted the table. '*I'm* the idiot, not you! I thought of an everlasting gob-stopper. By its very nature, it's an incredibly dumb thing to do.'

Archie wracked his brain. There had to be an easier way of doing this. He stared at the eyeballs on his plate, which stared straight back, as though testing him. Then they grew a fraction. *Oh please*, Archie thought. They were about the size of normal eyes now. Any larger and this was going to get messy.

Not eating their platefuls was going to be a horrible way to die.

# 109 GUS IN THE ATTIC

Sue found it strange being de-briefed by Dickinson in the de Lowes' house with Gus, the headmaster and not a de Lowe in sight.

She sighed. A week ago, who could have possibly imagined that they were on the cusp of Armageddon? And a week ago, she would never have believed she could be so madly in love with anyone, let alone odd, hilarious, brilliant, gorgeous Gus.

The dense fog that lay over the fields and forests in the great Vale of York made for a quiet, empty, alien atmosphere. And an expectation lingered that something unpleasant might be about to interrupt it.

Dickinson had stopped the group to rest three times and Sue had been grateful for the breaks. On the first, Dickinson instructed the party to thread rope between them so that no one might wander off in the wrong direction.

When the stone walls came into view, they had collectively breathed a sigh a relief. Inside the building, where she'd spent so much time playing, it felt cold and uninviting. Even the normally toasty sitting room with its warming flames and low beams struck them as being mysteriously empty and unwelcoming. Sue feared the worst.

Solomon set to work laying a fire as Dickinson began. 'Sue, in a moment I'm going to take you over to the woman we found—'

'Mrs. Pye?'

'Yes,' he said. 'You know her, don't you?'

'She's lovely.'

'Good,' Dickinson said. 'She's suffering from shock. You're to look after her, make sure she's fed and watered and if she lets on about anything, names, where the children might have gone, that sort of thing, let us know immediately. Write it down so you don't forget.' He winked at her.

His radio crackled. 'I'm going to leave you both one of these,' he said, putting a handset on the arm of the sofa. 'Call in if and when you get a sniff of progress. I'm guessing Stone briefed you.' He looked knowingly at the headmaster who nodded and turned away.

Dickinson addressed the noise. 'I've just got to introduce the woman to Sue, and then we'll be off.'

'Still no signs?' Stone's voice crackled back.

'Dead as a dodo, sir.'

'I've sent units in to the local town centres – anywhere where electrical tablets and the devices are sold. Though I'll be surprised if there are any left. Looting like you'd never believe.'

'OK, Roger that. Anything else you need from here, sir?'

'Just a quick word with Solomon, if he's about.'

Dickinson handed over the radio.

The headmaster pressed the button. 'Solomon here.'

'Good. You know what the score is. Don't sleep until you've combed through everything, understand? We don't have time. And remember what I said.'

Solomon handed back the radio.

'Right, Sue,' Dickinson said. 'Let's find Mrs. Pye, then I'll leave her in your hands.' Dickinson looked around. 'Anyone seen that understudy of yours?'

Solomon picked a matchbox up from the top of the wooden mantelpiece, opened it, and struck a match. 'I've sent him upstairs to begin logging everything up there. As the Commissioner said, there's no time to waste, is there.'

Dickinson smiled back. 'Yes. Quite.' He turned for the door. 'Good luck – keep us posted.' And with that their boots scuffed on the floor as they headed out of the front door, across the paving slabs and into the fog.

---

WHILE SUE NURSED MRS. PYE, the headmaster and Gus listened from the edge of the building to the sludging and slurping sounds of boots and the chatter of the men as they departed down the slope. When the noise petered out, they made their way back to the living room.

'Gus, I really do think you ought to remove that helmet and the rest of that gear,' Solomon said. 'I must say, I very nearly laughed out loud when you said you were Kemp.'

Gus smiled toothily back at him. 'Anything to liven things up a little. Strange how his name popped into my head.' Gus began looking at the clutter, made up predominantly of pictures dotted around the room. 'What *have* they been up to?'

'That's what we need to work out, my boy.'

'It's as though they were looking for something in the pictures and then left in a bit of a hurry—'

'You're telling me,' Solomon said, picking up one of the old portraits. 'I'll inspect the kitchen. If they left in the middle of the night there may be traces of a meal. After that we need to try and figure out what on earth they've been looking for with all of these.'

'It's quite a mess,' Gus said. 'I'll go and check their room, see if there's anything that might give us some idea of timing.'

Solomon smiled. 'Well, at least I know where Archie gets it from. All of this could very well be his doing.'

Gus headed up the stairs. When he reached Old Man Wood's room he called for Solomon and together they inspected the remnants of the room in silence.

Gus whistled. 'It's like a nail bomb's been detonated in here—'

'Yes, but without the nails,' Solomon said as he inspected the strange, irregularly-sized holes dotted around the wooden panelled walls. 'And no shell cases or cartridges – that's what the soldiers were saying. There's no metal here at all.'

'Are you suggesting,' Gus said, 'that something organic made this mess?'

Solomon stroked his chin. 'I don't know. But it is most unusual.'

Gus took off up to the attic room where he searched each of the children's areas. He tried to see if there was a tell-tale article of clothing that might give away their whereabouts or a book or a slip of paper or a note. He searched Archie's mess first, then Daisy's area and finally, Isabella's immaculate section: bed made, books put away, everything in its place. He turned to go when he noted a drawer below her bedside table. Gus stared at it and tried to pull it open, but found it jammed tight. There wasn't a keyhole, so how could it be locked? He traced his fingers around the bedside table, feeling only solid sides. Then he placed his hand underneath and rocked the base one way, then another. Gus smiled. The drawer slid open the other way. A hidden drawer, *neat*. He peered inside. Her diary lay there with a pen clamped underneath an elastic strap.

Gus picked it out and opened the thick, pink, bound book. He noted the dates and flicked through, catching snippets of familiar names as he went until he reached more recent entries. He skimmed the extract of her trying to work out who and what the people in her dreams meant. He turned the page over and read about their adventures, their odd magical gifts, about Old Man Wood being the oldest man ever and how much she missed Sue.

A terrible thought hit him. Sue and Isabella were close, like twins. How would Sue react if Isabella had been killed? Nervously he turned another page. Now the entry was smaller, and here he saw a five-verse poem. Nothing more, no explanation, but it appeared to be about finding three tablets and another world called Eden. Was this what it was all about?

He heard the groan of a floorboard. Instinctively he froze and crammed the diary into his pocket.

The noise deepened. Footsteps. He noted that while the tread was silent the creak of the floorboards gave whoever it was away.

It had to be Sue coming to sneak up on him. He smiled. He could pretend he hadn't heard her and surprise her with a kiss. OK, she might get really cross or pretend to be annoyed – but only for a moment, then she'd melt and laugh, and then kiss him.

Why not give her a happy surprise?

Gus grinned as he waited by the drawn curtain, until he could almost hear her breath through the other side of the velvet. Then, in one sharp movement, Gus whipped the curtain to the side.

'TA-DAH!' he said, moving in for the kiss.

'Hello, Williams,' said a curiously familiar voice.

Gus stopped just in the nick of time, his lips still puckered.

Then he stumbled and collapsed down on the bed.

'Y ... YOU? HOW?!'

# 110 THE ILLUSION CRUMBLES

Every time Daisy stared at her plateful her stomach churned. 'It's the smell, Old Man Wood, I can't do the stink, you know that!' she looked exasperated. 'We don't have a dog, because I can't handle the whiff! *I don't do it!*' Her lips quivered and her eyes began to water. 'I can't—'

'Look at me, Daisy. Now,' Old Man Wood ordered. 'You must overcome your fears. That's what this is about. Push fear out of your mind and draw in the things you love.' He looked deep into her eyes. 'You can do this, no sweats, but you ***must*** concentrate, littlun. So, close your eyes, sweet Daisy – there, that's it – and imagine something apple-tastically delicious. Imagine it exactly, imagine every last little piece. Imagine how yummy that first bite is – the texture, the aroma, that apple-crunchiness, the smoothness. And remember, that thing in front of you is only an illusion.

'You saw me do it, didn't you?' Old Man Wood continued, 'so you must believe me when I tell you that the reward is well worth the trouble.' An idea popped into his head. 'Daisy, I want you to keep your eyes shut, understand?'

She nodded.

'Would you like me to give you a spoonful of your... your...'

'Duck. Crispy, aromatic, Peking duck,' Daisy said, quickly.

'Yes. A great choice,' he said. 'With cucumbers, spring onions and a blob of plum sauce?'

'Ooh yeah. Exactly,' she said and a flicker of a smile briefly turned up the corners of her mouth.

Daisy took a deep breath, clenched her eyes tight and licked her lips.

'Good. Now imagine the scene. It's your birthday party at that Chinese restaurant,' Old Man Wood said. 'Everyone is smiling, laughing – there's music and the waiters show you over to an immaculate white tablecloth where you take a seat. You're wearing your new red dress. Mum and Dad are squabbling over the wine list. Mrs. Pye is tidying Archie. Then it arrives; your fabulous crispy duck on a large platter. Everyone stops and stares, jealous of your excellent choice ... and it's all yours. Your face lights up when you see it. Doesn't it smell wonderful?'

'Yes. Oh yes!' Daisy said. 'That's lush. Keep going, please.'

'Now, concentrate on the smells of the aromatic duck. It's been stripped off the bone and you've added a spoonful of plum sauce and sprinkled spring onions and cucumber on top. Now I'm rolling one up for you.'

Old Man Wood cut off a portion of the steaming dog turd from Daisy's plate.

'By goodness this is the finest pancake I've ever seen,' he said. 'Would you like to try it?'

Daisy nodded, her eyes closed tight.

'Open your mouth. I'll pop in your first delicious mouthful.'

Archie's eyes were bulging out of his head as he watched Daisy and his cheeks began puffing in and out. He pulled his hands up over his eyes and stared through the cracks of his fingers. A small squeal escaped from his lips but Old Man Wood flashed him an icy stare.

Daisy opened her mouth and took in the first mouthful, and it really was the most delicious mouthful of crispy aromatic duck she had ever tasted.

'Another bite, Daisy?' asked Old Man Wood gently.

'Oh my God, YES! It's AMAZING!'

Old Man Wood sliced another chunk off the large pile of canine excrement and raised it to her lips.

She opened her mouth wide as a tiny maggot crawled out of the poo. 'Mmm mmmmm. Guys, this is absolutely, divinely, scrumptilious,' she said. She took the whole mouthful in one go, licking her lips.

But suddenly, from the other side of the table came a loud

**GA-DONK!**

Followed by a crash.

---

ISABELLA LAY MOTIONLESS on the filthy floor. A thin trail of blood extended from the side of her head where she had clipped the stone table.

'Ah! No. Deary me,' Old Man Wood said, as he rushed over to her side. 'Are you there, littlun? Come along, wakey-uppy.'

He dabbed the cut with a handkerchief. She stirred and groaned and then wretched loudly, the noise reverberating around the room.

With Old Man Wood's help, she sat upright and felt for her head. 'OW!'

He kissed her forehead. 'Apples alive! Oh my! Oh my!' he said solemnly. 'This is harder than I ever would have thought, my specials,' he said, as if in private to Isabella.

'I don't think I can do this, Old Man Wood,' she said groggily.

'OH GOD! Get it off! GET IT OFF!' Isabella screamed. 'NO! NO! NOOO!'

She jumped off her stool and pointed at it accusingly, all the while backing away. 'I CAN'T EAT THAT,' she yelled. 'NO WAY!'

On Isabella's plate lay a decaying rat. Its inners crawled with hundreds of maggots that seemed to move as one body. Suddenly the rat with the maggots crawling inside it grew.

Isabella screamed and she shut her eyes, trembling. Then she curled up in a ball on the floor.

'But I think you can,' Old Man Wood said firmly. 'It's about what's going on in here.' He tapped his head.

'But it's impossible. You don't understand.'

Old Man Wood sighed and, while making a fuss of her and checking there were no obvious signs of concussion, he helped her up.

He turned to the table. For a moment he wondered if his eyes had deceived him.

'What in all the apples?! How ... how did you manage that?'

Daisy's plate sat empty. Archie's too.

'Daisy licked her plate clean,' Archie said, squirming. 'It was quite easily the most repulsive thing I have ever seen. Anyway, everlasting gobstoppers are the dumbest things to choose, so I thought I'd shut my eyes and swallow them whole. They actually weren't that bad. Could have done with a glass of water to wash them down.'

Without warning, much to his and the others' surprise, Archie belched long and loud, the sound reverberating around the stone chamber rather eerily like a huge frog-croak.

In any other circumstance, it would have propelled the twins into uncontrollable hysterics, but this burp carried on and on and, as it did, a peculiar balloon grew from his mouth, expanding as he expelled the air. When he'd finished, he peeled it off his face, and left it to hang in mid-air, as if it were a helium balloon on a string.

'Bloody hell,' Daisy whispered.

'Fab-tab-e-dozey!' Archie cried, delighted with himself. 'It's the *belching from the family belly*! If we all do one – and join them up, then surely that's the way to get the second tablet!'

Daisy turned to Archie rather seriously. 'Archie. Girls like Isabella do not go round burping, and certainly not blowing out sticky bubbles,' she looked at him rather seriously. 'And for your information, neither do I.'

Unfortunately for Daisy a long, trumpet-like noise blasted out of her throat for the best part of several seconds. Out popped out a similar, sticky, golden balloon.

Stunned, she peeled hers off and joined the balloon to Archie's.

Almost immediately, an enormous deep croak, like a tree crashing down, grumbled out of Old Man Wood's mouth that went on and on and ended with another bubble. He instantly turned red and apologised profusely.

Archie could barely control himself. He convulsed until tears rolled down his cheeks. But his laughter ceased when they turned towards Isabella, who sat shaking in her chair, her face pale and sweaty.

Then their stares turned towards her plateful and collectively they gasped.

The size of the dead rat crawling with white maggots had now quadrupled to the size of a small cat.

Since all three of the children had, at various times, vomited in the tiny chamber, the aroma in the room was akin to a lavatory on a ferry boat full of sea-sick passengers.

But Isabella in particular had other things to concentrate on. For every minute that went by, the pressure was mounting. She curled her fingers up so that her nails dug into the palm of her hand to stop herself blacking out and, helped by Old Man Wood began some calming breathing measures.

'Your sister and brother have done it. And me, too – and utterly fan-tab-ulicious it was too. So you can do it. You know it's all about that smart head of yours, littlun.'

Isabella's lips began quivering. 'But I had months of therapy because of this.' She sobbed. 'Months ... and now this ... this ... torture.'

'Come on, Bells,' Daisy said, moving in beside her and giving her a sisterly hug. 'It's simple – you know, mind over matter.'

She flashed a smile at Archie. 'If it's any help, mine was the most delicious dog poo I've ever had—'

'Don't be disgusting—'

'I'm not. It was perfectly cooked.'

'Firm on the outside with a nice soft centre,' Archie said.

'If I had half a brain,' Daisy said, 'I should have chosen a chocolate log.'

'Or lemon turd.'

'Or a big brownie.'

The twins howled with laughter.

Isabella's face, however, was set like thunder. Daisy noticed.

'Oh, come on Bells. I'm only joking. Look, all you have to do is concentrate on something you really, really want.'

'Why not try the Old Man Wood method? It was brilliant on Daisy,' Archie said, nudging the old man. 'Want to give it a go?'

Isabella nodded.

'Great.' Archie took a deep breath. 'Come on, you can do this. Now, shut your eyes. I'm sure your maggoty... er...

Daisy fired him a look.

'...your plateful, will be as delicious as, um, as, er...'

'...as mum's banoffee pie...' Daisy said, quickly.

'With an extra helping of my special thick cream,' Old Man Wood added. 'I know how much you love it.'

'With a couple of jelly babies on top?' Daisy said, licking her lips.

For the first time Isabella's lips crinkled into something that resembled a smile. Her face had more of a controlled look upon it. 'Yes. That sounds good.'

'Now, really, really believe it,' Old Man Wood said, his voice soft, deep and mellow. 'The sweet smells, how it feels in your mouth, how fabulous it looks...'

She forced herself to utterly concentrate until all she could think about was the sweet, textured, chocolaty toffee, and the dollops of cream and the squishiness of the bananas.

Old Man Wood cut out a slice off the rat and filled her spoon with a few stray maggots.

'The first amazingly scrumptious helping of thick banoffee pie coming up,' Archie said, as the old man offered up a heaped spoonful, complete with decaying dark fur, sinews and claws, to Isabella's mouth.

'With a few assorted jelly babies,' Daisy added, noticing the maggots.

The twins could hardly bear to watch.

As the spoon rose, silence filled the little room.

As Isabella's mouth closed over the spoon, Daisy let out a tiny gasp.

Then Archie emitted a kind of high-pitched squeak, a noise made not in horror, more in shock.

Isabella's mouth closed over the spoon, but she'd lost her concentration and instead of banoffee pie, the foul things she saw, rather than the toffee treat that had filled her mind, swamped her mouth.

She screamed, phleaux-ing and retching and hysterically flapping her arms, spitting endlessly.

As fast as he could, Old Man Wood draped his arms around her and held her tight, saying gentle things.

When the sobbing and moaning ceased, he released her.

Isabella looked at her plate and then across to the pale faces of her siblings.

On her plate was the maggoty rat, now the size of a fully-grown badger, dead and stinking and writhing with not hundreds, but thousands of maggots.

For the second time in only a short while, Isabella passed out.

---

DAISY SHOOK HER HEAD, her expression betraying deep worry.

'She's out cold and that thing on her plate is ... huge. She'll never do it on her own.'

'And it's beginning to stink.'

'Just like that trapped-under-the-floorboards-Archie-shoe-pong,' Daisy added, unhelpfully.

'Shut it, Daisy,' Archie fired back. He stroked a hair spike. 'Can't we just eat it?' he said. 'I mean, I'm game if you are.'

Daisy shrugged. It was a good idea considering the choices. 'OK. Nice one. What's it going to be?'

'Well, I was quite getting into the idea of banoffee pie. Those eyeballs didn't really fill me up. I think I can still feel them moving around.'

Daisy closed her eyes for a minute, imagining the Italian desert. 'Yup. Banoffee pie it is,' she said. 'Old Man Wood, you look after Bells, we're going to finish this off for her.'

The twins leaned over the table and stared at the vast meal of a deteriorating rat filled with maggots. They each picked up a fork and glanced at one another for reassurance.

'Right,' Daisy said. 'On the count of three, the most delicious banoffee pie, in the universe.'

'In the universe,' Archie agreed.

'One, two ...' and before they even got to three, the twins plunged their forks into the sticky mess.

A millisecond later, a massive electric charge shot through their forks.

Their bodies zinged and catapulted backwards. They thudded into the wall and collapsed to the floor.

Archie groaned. 'So,' he said, as he rubbed himself down, 'no sharing. That's nice and clear.'

He looked over towards Daisy who lay motionless in a puddle of vomit.

'Oh! Great! Looks like she's out too,' and then he looked at the rat which was now the size of a medium-sized dog.

'What do you suggest, Old Man Wood?' he asked. 'Because if we don't come up with some way of getting Isabella to eat this, pretty soon we're going to die in the remains of a decaying rat. And maggots are going to eat us alive. If you've got an idea, now is the time to say something.'

But Old Man Wood stared back, his face as white as chalk, shaking his head. 'I ... I don't know. It may already be too late.'

# 111 SOLOMON AND SUE

Sue made quite a fuss of Mrs. Pye.

After several minutes where Mrs. Pye stared at the wall, her body moving back and forth, Sue finally managed to get Mrs. Pye to look at her.

'It's me – Sue,' she said. 'I'm here with the headmaster and my boyfriend, Gus Williams.' It was the first time she'd ever said *my boyfriend* to anyone and the words slipped out with ease, and filled her with pleasure.

In fact she had a good mind to run around the courtyard singing: 'I've got a boyfriend and he's amazing and he loves me too-oo-ooo', adding in things like 'he's clever, he's cool, he's sweet but also hunky, la-la, in a kinda geeky way!' and then she'd whoop and scream in a stupidly high pitch fashion. And then she'd look about hope no-one was watching.

'We – Gus and me, survived the storm,' she said, barely controlling herself. 'I got a text from Bells. Amazing isn't it? Old Man Wood found them, didn't he?' she said, admiring herself in the mirror. Her skin exuded radiance. Was this from the spell of love?

'It was Bells' idea,' she continued, 'and Gus' genius at woodworking that saved us, I suppose. A, what would Old Man Wood say, "apple-tastic" miracle, Mrs. Pye, that's what it was.'

Sue sat down on the bed and took one of Mrs. Pye's hands in hers. 'The world's gone crazy since I saw you last, and that wasn't even ten days ago. I hope those men weren't nasty to you? I don't think they meant to be. I guess they're just as confused as everyone else. A horrible man interrogated me. He had stinky breath and hard, calculating eyes that gave me the shivers. Anyway, it's a bit of a fluke that we managed to get away.'

Sue stood up and wandered around the room, picking up little pictures of the smiling, often toothless, de Lowe children growing up in the assorted frames on her mantelpiece.

'You don't know where they are, do you? We reckon they left in a bit of a hurry, probably in the night or early this morning. There's a terrible mess everywhere. Have you seen it? It looks like they've been in some kind of fight. Were there other people involved?'

Sue spotted a flash of alarm in Mrs. Pye's eyes. Did it relate to the missing children or the messy house?

'Let me get you a nice cup of tea,' she said. 'You look like you could use one. If I find a crumpet, I'll bring one over. Bit of jam – would that be alright?' Sue smiled sweetly. 'Now, don't you be going anywhere. I'll be back in a bit.'

Sue headed out of the door and, as she turned back to Mrs. Pye, for the first time, Mrs. Pye looked at her and smiled in her very odd way. 'Thank you,' she croaked, her voice shallow and troubled.

Sue smiled back. 'You really don't have to thank me, Mrs P. You're the one who needs thanking – for looking after them so beautifully.' Sue went over to her and planted a big kiss on her cheek. 'Back shortly.'

She turned and slipped away with a spring in her step, down the wooden stairs, around the rim of the foggy courtyard and back into the picture-filled mess of the cottage.

---

SOLOMON LOOKED up as she walked in. He was studying a selection of older portraits on which the figure of an old-looking man with a strong family resemblance stared back. Each bore a similar, subtle-patterned background with date-marks a century or more apart. 'Any luck with Mrs. Pye?'

'She spoke two words: *Thank you*,' Sue said. 'Amazing, isn't it, the power of a cup of tea? Do you want one?' she asked.

'Yes, please. That would be lovely. Horrible tea at the hotel – a little too fancy for me,' Solomon said, returning his gaze to the pictures. 'It's really most strange.'

'Strange?'

'Well, yes. How the children and that old man have vanished without a trace. But I spotted a half-eaten toasted-sandwich lying on the floor of the kitchen. It didn't look old, if you ask me. I reckon it was discarded quite recently. Bread like that has a habit of hardening overnight and this slice seemed quite edible.'

'They call those sandwiches *empses*,' Sue said. 'Stands for *Mrs. Pye's Specials*. It's the de Lowe staple food when they're hungry – more often than not at breakfast. They're delicious – stuffed with cheese, ham, tomatoes and a poached egg. I'll try and make one if you're hungry, but Mrs. Pye's really are sensational. Have you seen Gus?'

'I believe he's somewhere upstairs, rooting around, seeing if he can come up with anything. A few odd noises coming from there. Scrapes and bashes, as if he's taken to moving furniture around. You might want to go and see how he's doing.'

Sue carried on through to the corridor that led into the kitchen. She added paper and kindling and then a couple of smaller logs into the belly of the range-cooker and, much to her joy, the fire spat into life.

Shortly, she opened the door, tossed in two larger logs, shut off the lighting vent, filled the kettle and set it on top of the range hob.

Wouldn't Gus be impressed?

She had half a mind to run upstairs and find him, but her thoughts turned back to strange old Mrs. Pye. She'd drop off a cup of tea for her and then go and find him.

She smiled at the thought. Alone with Gus at last. Sue plaited a section of hair as she let her imagination wander. *Was he,* she wondered, *at that very moment thinking the same thing?* Thinking of her? She smiled. *Of course he was.*

Sue inserted the whistle in the kettle spout and headed out of the door to rejoin the headmaster in the living room. When she saw him, she found he was comparing the portraits with the images he'd taken of the stained glass windows in Upsall church.

'Mr. Solomon,' she began, 'do you think there's something ... you know, happening?'

The headmaster took off his glasses 'What kind of *happening* are you thinking of, Sue?'

'Some sort of end-of-the-world situation, you know, like Armageddon or something catastrophic from out of the Bible.'

Solomon sighed. 'There's no doubt our flooding and plague has remarkable parallels with ancient myths and legends. The question we need to ask, I suppose, is whether these things are in any way, normal. Events that come round as part of the general cycle of life—'

'Like a freak-of-nature? You think it might be a one-off?'

Solomon raised an eyebrow. 'Actually, Sue. No. No, I don't think it is,' he said, putting on his spectacles. 'There are too many strange occurrences, too many situations that boil down to something inexplicable and very sinister indeed.'

'Then, do you think the de Lowes are pivotal? After all, I dreamt of them, and I know Isabella had nightmares about all this stuff and Stone seems to think they're important.'

'That's what I mean,' Solomon said. 'Don't get me wrong, Stone can be a nasty piece of work, but he's jolly good at his job. He has a nose for sniffing out this kind of thing, an uncanny habit of finding the truth. He's going nearly mad with the overall confusion and his desperate lack of progress. The clock is ticking ever faster. Untold pressure is building on him in a big way.'

Solomon sat down heavily in Old Man Wood's chair, removed his spectacles and sighed. 'Look, I may as well tell you, Sue. The whole situation with the flooding and Ebora is steamrollering out of control. The Americans are going to drop a rather large bomb on North Yorkshire.'

Sue gasped. 'They're going to nuke us? Why?'

'The Ebora virus reached their shores a couple of days ago. It swept across the continent as night follows day. As our American cousins woke up, boof – there it was. Ebora had already made its mark. Don't you think that's a little strange?'

The headmaster stretched his arms out and rubbed his eyes. 'The pattern is continuing like this across the globe. An pandemic of global proportions. But I did hear just before we left that the rates of infection had somewhat decreased.'

'So, you're suggesting,' Sue said, 'that the virus *moved in the dark*?'

'Yes and no.'

'Now *you're* being cryptic.'

Solomon smiled. 'I think that it has something to do with sleep. My own hunch is that it may be about dreams.'

Sue's ears twitched. 'You really think so?'

'I know it may sound ridiculous, my dear, but I'm pretty sure we have to think outside our normal areas of understanding. I hardly dare say it, but our human mind is so programmed for a certain way of thinking that "out of the box" ideas are simply shuffled out of the way as if they are entirely insignificant. As a teacher I am, I fear, partly to blame. Our role is to bring children up to speed with the world we live in – to cope with the hustle and bustle of life on our planet. Anything out of the ordinary and we learn to siphon it off. We leave it to be discarded as irrelevant or slam it as nonsense. Do you have any idea of what I'm talking about, Sue, or does it sound like meaningless clap-trap?'

'No, I think I'm running with you,' she said. 'Just about.'

'Jolly good. Because I believe there are signs just about ... everywhere. Tiny, abstract clues, so remote to our way of thinking that we cannot possibly begin to understand them.' He leaned down and picked up the portraits.

'Take these pictures. They date hundreds of years apart and yet I suspect they're one and the same thing, repeated over and over, as if they are a reminder—'

'Of what?'

'I wish I knew, dear girl,' Solomon said, examining the first and then the second. 'Now I'm struck by these rather interesting portraits. As you know, fashions change. Art, from the seventeenth century, has a totally different look and feel to art from the nineteenth century. And yet, looking at these, we find the same posture and the same background. It almost appears to be the same person. My guess is that these portraits are trying to tell us something.'

Sue peered at the pictures. 'I know it couldn't possibly be him, but you know, the nose, eyes, the kindly way he looks at everything. Don't those pictures remind you of Old Man Wood.'

Solomon leaned in and together they studied them. 'Sue, my dear, perhaps you're right, impossible as it seems. The problem is, we've got two days to figure this out and unless the de Lowes suddenly reappear and tell us what's going on, I'm not sure we've got the necessary skills or equipment – or time – to make a proper go of it. We're plucking at straws.'

'Do you think we're going to die?'

The headmaster smiled in a reassuringly head-masterly way. 'Yes, I'm afraid to say that I rather think we are,' he said. 'At the moment it looks very much like we're on a path of no return.' He sighed. 'Dying is nothing to worry about, my dear, because it is the one certainty in life – aside, of course, from taxation.' He chuckled inwardly.

'Our time may be coming a little sooner than we might have liked.' He shook his head. 'It is such a shame considering you and your friend's great abundance of talent. But enough of this depressing talk. May I suggest, that from this moment on, we absolutely believe that anything is possible. Agree?'

'Yes!'

'Good. With immediate effect we must throw away the shackles of everything we've ever been taught. Let's give our last few days our absolute all. Treat it like a fight to death!'

Sue felt better hearing a more positive tone. 'I agree,' she said. 'Where do we start?'

Solomon stood up purposefully and rubbed his chin. 'My suspicion is that this has something to do with a history that goes so far back in time that records don't exist – at least not for anyone to make sense of them. First off, let's try and find out if Mrs. Pye has noticed anything unusual—'

He was interrupted by the whistle on the kettle screeching loudly. Sue rushed off and returned with a pot of tea and several steaming crumpets. She poured a mug for the headmaster and another for Mrs. Pye. Armed with this, and a hot crumpet, she nipped out of the front door and around the foggy courtyard to see her patient.

# 112 A JOKE GONE WRONG

'Here, Mrs. Pye,' Sue said, putting the tray down on the table, 'a nice mug of tea for you and a crumpet, you must be starving. I found one of Old Man Wood's blue-coloured jams, bit of an odd colour for a jam, if you ask me, but I hope you like it.'

She removed the lid and sniffed it. 'Does he add colouring to it for a bit of fun, or is it some sort of weird blue fruit he uses?'

She handed Mrs. Pye the tea.

Mrs. Pye sipped as Sue continued to talk and soon nibbled on a crumpet.

'How's that going down?' Sue said, sitting next to her.

Mrs. Pye pulled a handkerchief out of her dressing gown pocket and blew her nose. 'Much better,' she said, before slipping it back in her pocket. 'And all thanks to you, little Sue. You're a kindly one, aren't you?'

Sue smiled. 'Well, it's a great relief to see you looking so much better. For a while I was pretty worried – what would the others say if they'd seen you in such a state, huh? They'd be worried sick.'

Mrs. Pye shook her head. 'They've gone a little in the head, you know?'

'Really?' Sue said, raising her eyebrows.

'Oh aye. I think everyone's gone a bit in the head to be honest. All these comings and goings, you know. One minute here, the next they've shot off. And then strange noises and the children pulling pictures down and making a mess and explosions. I hardly dare go over there. Don't know what I might find.'

'When did you last see them?'

'The children were about this morning. I heard 'em. Don't know how you missed them, unless they was taken—'

'But has anyone been here apart from those soldiers this morning?' Sue asked.

A little cry came from within her as Mrs. Pye turned away.

'What is it?' Sue asked quietly, moving in and holding her hand.

The older woman pulled herself together a little. 'Now then,' she snivelled, 'there was another person.' She shook her head.

'Really?' Sue said softly. 'Who?'

Mrs. Pye burst into tears once again. 'You'd never believe me!'

'Of course I would.'

Mrs. Pye shook her head. 'But he wouldn't have taken them. Couldn't have.'

'Who?'

'That boy ... my—'

'Which boy?' Sue said, confused.

'My son,' she squealed. 'My baby.'

Sue's mind raced. 'Are you alright, Mrs. P? Do you ... do you want to lie down?'

Mrs. Pye squeezed Sue's hand tight. 'My child came to me, Sue. He did, really. Then he left – but he couldn't have taken the others with him. He didn't mean no harm. Just wanted to see me. Tell me he knew.'

'Knew what?' Sue repeated.

'That I was his ...'

'His, what?' Sue said.

'You know ... mother,' Mrs. Pye said through her tears. 'That I was his—'

Sue reeled '... Mother?' she repeated.

'I always thought there might have been a child. But, you know, the accident and all that.'

Sue remained baffled. 'Are you sure? Are you sure it wasn't a ghost or something like that?'

'Don't be silly,' Mrs. Pye said. 'I know perfectly well who it was.'

'You *know* him?'

'Ooh, yes dear. Archie's friend. Don't think you girls like him so much.'

*'Don't like him?'* she said in amazement.

Sue leant back and studied her. Thick hair, fat lips.

Mrs. Pye looked up from her light blue, piggy eyes. 'You call him Kemp?' she said.

But Sue knew Kemp was miles away at Swinton Park. 'Kemp?'

Mrs. Pye nodded. 'That's the one.'

Sue shook her head, baffled, when all of a sudden the mist lifted.

'*Oh, Kemp*!' she laughed. 'But *that* Kemp only arrived by boat an hour or so ago, with me and the headmaster.'

How sweet that Gus had gone to see her first ... but then again, how incredibly nuts to tell her he was her son. Why would he do that?

Sue shook her head. 'Look, I'll let you in on a secret. That Kemp is actually called Williams. Gus Williams.' And then she added because she couldn't resist it. 'My boyfriend.'

Mrs. Pye pulled her handkerchief out once more and sobbed into it.

Sue thought the whole thing most peculiar. Was Mrs. Pye confused? Was Gus confused?

Perhaps she should find Gus and ask him if he'd been over here being Kemp. And if so, that his joke had misfired badly.

# 113 FIGHT TO THE DEATH

'Surprised? Yeah, I bet you're bloody surprised!' Kemp said.

Gus took a step back. 'What are you doing here ... you're not part of this, are you?'

Kemp sighed and sat down at the chair by the desk. 'Well, Williams, you could say I got here ... by accident.'

'What happened to your head?' Gus asked.

Kemp ran a hand over his white cranium. 'Burnt off ... it's a long story,' Kemp said, and smiled his fake, fat smile. 'Let's just say I had a lucky escape.'

'From what?'

'Death, I suppose,' he said, lifting his eyes to meet Gus'.

Gus suspected something fishy. 'What are you doing ... what do you want?'

Kemp wiped his nose with the back of his hand. 'To be honest,' he began, 'it wasn't you I was hoping to find.'

'Who, then?' Gus said, confused. 'Archie?'

'Nah. The de Lowe's are a bit indisposed at the minute. Eating for their very lives.' He grinned. 'It's quite possible they'll never be seen again.'

Gus screwed up his face. 'I don't understand. Have you done something to them?'

'Me? No! Look, there's no way you could possibly understand,' Kemp said. 'It's none of your business.' He puckered his lips. 'Thing is, Williams, what exactly are *you* doing here, rummaging about Isabella de Lowes' bedroom like a perv?'

'I'm with Sue and the headmaster,' he replied coolly. 'We've been sent by the authorities to help find the de Lowes. They're in trouble but no one seems to know what it is. You know where they are?'

'Yeah, 'course I do,' Kemp said, thickly. 'To be honest, there isn't much I don't know.'

'Then tell me!'

'They're locked in a small room, not too far from here,' Kemp volunteered, 'until they work something out.'

Gus looked confused. 'How do you know all this?'

'I have an ... associate, who's pretty worldly—'

'Worldly? I thought you were stuck in the hospital, burnt—'

'I was,' Kemp interrupted. 'But my companion had a change of heart.'

'Who is this guy?'

'He's an old man, that's all you need to know—'

Gus looked quizzically at Kemp. 'Hey! I know – I saw you,' he said, jabbing a finger at Kemp. 'You and an old man in the alleyway moments before the storm broke.' He rubbed his hands as he remembered. 'Weren't you? Someone in a long coat and a hat.'

Kemp leaned in and tapped his nose. 'As I was saying, Williams, it's really none of your business.'

An awkward silence fell between them.

'So, if you're not here for Archie,' Gus started, 'and you're not here for the de Lowes, you're here to see the headmaster, right?'

Kemp chuckled. 'Oh yeah. Hilarious. Nope, wrong again. I'm here for more ... personal reasons.'

'To see Old Man Wood?'

Kemp shook his head. 'No, you daft, lanky git,' he said. He was enjoying Gus' confusion. 'Not old man whatshisface.'

'Then who?'

'I'm here to get Sue,' he said bluntly. 'You know, sexy Sue, best mate of freak-of-nature, Isabella-de-bleeding-Lowe.'

Gus' jaw dropped, and for a brief moment his brain froze as if he'd eaten a tub of ice-cream. *Had he heard that right?*

'I'm sorry,' he said at long last, 'you said, *get* Sue. What, exactly, are you talking about?' His fingers were shaking.

'Precisely that.' Kemp creased an eyebrow. 'You got a problem with it?'

Gus composed himself. 'What,' he said slowly, trying to mask his growing anger, 'makes you think Sue would be in any way interested in you?'

'Aha. Finally, a decent question, Mr. Williams. You see, this little union I'm going to propose, is based entirely on a lack of rival suitors.'

'Union? Lack of rivals?' Gus felt himself perspiring.

'Yeah.'

'Why?'

'Jeez, Williams. Don't tell me you haven't worked it out?'

Gus shrugged. 'This disease thing?'

Kemp raised an eyebrow. 'You're finally getting there,' he said. 'It's going to kill everyone, except me and Sue.'

Gus shook his head. 'But I still don't think she'll go with you, Kemp. She totally hates your guts—'

'I didn't say she would. That's why I said I'm going to *take* her.'

Gus felt winded. 'But she's going out with me,' he said softly. 'She's not yours to take—'

'Oh dear, oh dear. Is that right?' Kemp leered back. 'Unlucky.'

The curtain swished out of the way.

'The thing is,' said a much deeper and rather croaky voice to the other side of him, 'you're all going to die.'

'Bloody-nora!' Gus said, jumping out of his skin. '*What the ...*'

'Oh,' Kemp said. 'Meet my ... associate. He's a ghost.'

Gus glanced around nervously as the voice started again.

'He'll be doing her a favour, you know.' The ghost parted the curtain and reappeared moments later wearing an overcoat and hat.

Gus gasped. 'What ... who ... are you?'

'I'm a spirit, and this young man has become my flesh and blood. Come on, boy, there's no time to lose.'

Gus tried to compose himself. 'You won't be able to take her with you,' he said. 'She'd rather die than go with you. I know her better than anyone. Trust me, Kemp.'

Kemp tutted. 'Thing is, Williams, you won't be any good to her when you're dead. Because, in a couple of days, everything here will be dead or dying and there's nothing you'll be able to do about it.'

'You don't know her!' he spat.

Kemp smiled his fat, cheesy, smug smile. 'You're missing the point,' he said coolly. 'I don't *have* to!'

'She won't do it!'

'Then I'll quite simply scoop her up, kicking and screaming. Like up a little dolly. It's as simple as that. You see, Gus, I'm going to need a woman to start a family, a very, very big family. Have loads of kids and all that.' He smiled, delighted by the agony it must be giving Williams.

'You'll do it over my dead body,' Gus roared.

'Very well. That's easily arranged. Look, I hate to break it to you, Williams, but like it or not, Sue's going to be, like, my very own *Eve*. After the annihilation of the planet, together, we're going to repopulate the world.'

Gus looked on in astonishment as Kemp casually walked over to the ghost and pushed an arm down the coat. First his legs and then his left hand morphed into a curious material.

Dust fell to the floor. Ash?

A terrible fury tore through Gus. Before he knew what he was doing, he hurled himself at Kemp, his hands going directly for his throat, crushing Kemp's windpipe.

Kemp gargled and tried to fight back but, being made of ash, his punches to Gus' midriff came to nothing more than puffs of dust.

Gus squeezed harder, gritting his teeth.

Kemp's face reddened and he fell to his knees.

'*Let go of him*,' the ghost's voice ordered.

'NO,' Gus roared, 'unless he promises not to touch Sue.'

As the ash leached up Kemp's body towards his neck, Gus was finding it increasingly difficult for his hands to stay attached. Ash flew about as though scattered by an electric fan.

Kemp floundered and Cain could feel his suffering.

'HALT!' the ghost cried out. 'This helps no one.'

Gus snarled. 'As I said, NO!'

'I will make you an offer—'

'Not good enough. Promise me—'

'Promises do not exist. I will make you the very best next thing: an offer,' Cain said. 'But only if you release him now.'

'Help!' Kemp croaked, his head puce.

Gus released Kemp and, as he did, Kemp's body crashed to the floor. Moments later, the ghost stood next to Gus watching Kemp fighting for breath.

The ghost's hat tilted upwards. 'You have no idea what you've just got yourself into.'

The tense figure of Gus stood shaking, staring alternately at Kemp and then at the ghost.

'What is your name?' the ghost barked.

'Gus.'

'Gus,' the ghost repeated. 'Good. I cannot be doing with a weakling as my companion. You have given yourself a chance to save yourself. And you may be a better match than this boy, although he does have certain qualities I admire.'

'Tell me your offer,' Gus panted. 'But before that, tell me who you are!'

'I am the ghost of Cain. I cannot die but my power was removed and my flesh stripped from me. I exist as a spirit and I am the Master of Havilah and soon to be ruler of the universe. Is that sufficient?'

Gus said nothing.

'Here's my offer—'

'Let me kill him,' Kemp said, hoarsely.

'No. In matters like this,' Cain said, 'it is important to keep one's word. However, only one of you can come along.' He addressed Kemp. 'The boy bested you. He deserves a chance.'

'A chance?'

'To survive, boy.'

'What sort of chance?' Kemp's voice hinted on nerves.

'One of you must die.'

'*Die?*' both boys repeated.

'Indeed. You will fight each other in a fight to the death. The winner comes with me and brings the "hot" girl named Sue.'

'To the death?' Gus said, shaken.

'There is no room for another.'

Gus whimpered.

'Just one winner,' Cain said. 'But you must willingly, with all your heart, and with all your soul, agree to come with me – or the deal's off. You agree?'

Kemp sat on the floor, caressing his neck. His face was purple with rage. 'I know this freak, Cain. He'll never do it – he'll never, ever, go with you,' Kemp croaked. 'He doesn't have the balls—'

'Do what?' Gus fired back. 'Go with who?'

Kemp coughed. 'Look, Williams. You have to give yourself freely to the ghost. When you're combined, he's the one in control and, believe me, he's a freaking maniac. My advice to you, Williams, is don't do it. It's one step too far.'

'But it's alright for you is it, Kemp?'

'Listen to what the ghost said: you don't know what you've got yourself in to. I promise you, Williams, for you, death would be better.'

Gus shook. 'Why do you say this?'

'Because it's true. You're giving your soul to the devil, Gus. You'd be better off dying rather than suffer what he has to offer.'

Cain tutted from under his hat. 'Well, well, well, boy. What a dramatic speech. Who knows,' he said drily, 'Gus has earned the choice, and it is a simple one; do nothing and die helplessly in the oncoming destruction of the planet. Or kill you and spend the rest of his life ruling all the known worlds with me, alongside a girl he clearly cares very deeply for.'

Cain paused. 'Personally, I think my offer is rather a good one; I know which one I'd choose. What do you think, Gus? It must be tempting? And, of course there would be so many fewer relationship issues for me to deal with.'

The ghost turned towards Gus. 'Therefore I offer myself to him right now to discover what lies ahead.'

It took a couple of moments before Kemp clicked. 'But ... you can't – what about me?'

'Be quiet, boy,' Cain snapped. 'As I said, Gus has earned the right to give our union a try. If he prefers death, then he cannot complain that he never had a fair chance.'

Gus quaked. 'What do I—?'

'Willingly put the coat on,' Kemp said, reluctantly. 'Like I was doing when you went for me. But don't struggle. Then put on the hat. Close your eyes as the feeling moves up into your head. You'll get a wicked burning feeling, so relax and don't fight it. Take a good look at my baldy head if you want proof of what happens when you struggle. Got it?'

'Sure,' Gus said.

'How else do you think I ended up in hospital covered in burns, huh?'

Gus stared at his foe.

Kemp grinned. 'It was by way of this lunatic.'

Gus examined Kemp. He hesitated.

'Look,' the ghost said, sounding a bit bored, 'if you cannot freely join with me then there is no contest. You, my old friend, win. It's as easy as that.'

'Wait,' Gus said. 'I need to think—'

'Sorry, there's no time for any of that,' the ghost crowed. 'It's now or never. Come along, Kemp.'

Kemp stood up and rubbed his neck. 'I didn't think you could,' he jibed. 'Always been just a little too much like a chicken.'

In a flash, Gus moved in front of Kemp.

Then, looking Kemp straight in the eye, he thrust one arm down the coat's sleeve-hole and, without delay, the other. His eyes rolled back and he squeezed out a long groan.

Now, the cold treacle-effect coursed through his body, along every vein and artery and down every sinew and fibre in him, thrilling him.

Kemp closed in.

'Keep away,' the ghost barked. 'We won't be gone long.'

Gus groaned ever more as the cold liquid rounded his brain.

'Dreamspinner, dreamspinner, dreamspinner,' Cain barked into the air.

'You're not going,' Kemp said desperately. 'You can't leave me here.'

'Of course we are. I have to show the boy what he would be missing. It wouldn't be fair otherwise.'

Two dreamspinners appeared out of the sky.

'Back to Havilah, right away,' he barked, and, using Gus' body, Cain bent down.

'You know,' he said to Kemp, 'it might not be a bad idea to be friendly to this "hot" girl. Trust me. You will never have a more opportune time to try.'

And with that, Cain and Gus dived off through the maghole of the dreamspinner and vanished in a tiny flash of light.

Silence filled the room. Kemp scanned the attic, the floor of which lay covered in ash.

He heard footsteps starting up from the bottom of the stairs, creaking lightly at first, then louder, step by step.

'Gu-uss,' a voice called out.

Kemp squirmed. Shit. Sue. What would he tell her? The truth? Make something up?

'Gus, honey, where are you?' she said. 'Are you hiding from me, big fella?'

Kemp looked around for somewhere to hide. In Isabella de Lowe's bed? Hell. The bloody irony.

What was he going to do?

# 114 THE DEAL

Kemp thought fast. What should he say? Could he run off to see his mother? *His mother!* Just the thought filled him with such joy that a burst of love, of joy, coursed through his veins.

But what good was that now? He'd accepted an offer of a fight to the death, against Gus Williams. *To the death*! Kemp shook. Could he do it? He had to: if he won, he would have a mother – the one thing he'd yearned for all his life.

Sure, they'd give each other a kicking, a few punches, but ... death. That was an entirely different matter. In front of him lay the currency of survival; the price of living, the ledger of life and death.

*More importantly,* Kemp thought, *did Gus have it in him to kill him?*

Already, in their short time together, Cain had done unspeakable things, but it was always Cain's doing, not his. Never his.

To Cain, every life was expendable and in their new arrangement he was the body, the muscle and he'd learnt that it wasn't worth arguing. Whatever Cain wanted, he obliged, and as such, Kemp didn't care either.

The experience was thrilling and powerful. With this attitude he felt like a king, a god. But this was Cain's hand at work, not his. When it came to his schoolmates, even if they didn't like each other, murder by *his* hands was an entirely different matter.

In two bounds he was in Archie's section, throwing himself on the bed.

The door opened. The floorboards groaned.

He heard her call out, rather sweetly, 'Gus?'

Suddenly the rings of the curtain pulled back. His heart thumped in his chest.

A gasp.

*Whatever you do, please don't scream*, he thought.

She stared as he moaned. He turned awkwardly in the bed.

She rushed towards him, concerned.

Kemp knew exactly what he had to do. He needed her sympathy.

*He needed to fake it.*

Make it look like he was a victim.

He rolled and cried out, as though in agony.

Soft hands rested on his forehead.

He groaned.

He smelt her as she sat beside him. A simple, soft, fragrance, like perfumed blossom.

'I'm sorry,' he said, sadness in his tone. He couldn't think of anything else to say. 'Please ... please don't hurt me,' he added, for effect.

Her hand moved from his forehead across his bald head. 'I'm not going to hurt you, understand?'

He nodded.

'Is it you, really you?' she said, a puzzled tone to her voice. 'I don't understand. How did you get here?'

Kemp rolled over and faced her, tears in his eyes. 'I don't know ... I ... I stole a boat ... walked ...' he stammered. 'No one was here when I arrived.'

Sue walked around the room. When she opened the curtain to Isabella's section, she stopped and kicked at a pile of ash. 'What happened in here? It's like there's been a fire – but without a fire?' she examined some of the marks in the ash. 'Do you know where Gus is?'

Kemp shook his head. 'Sorry.' He noted the disappointment in her face and pulled himself up. 'You ... you survived, you made it.'

Sue came over. 'Ssh,' she said. 'Can I get you something? You must be starving.' She smiled and held his hand briefly. 'Mrs. Pye told me your news.'

Kemp flinched. 'News?' he repeated.

Her eyebrows lifted and she smiled sweetly. 'That she's your mother,' she said. 'I think it's one of the most amazing stories I've ever heard.'

Kemp smiled. He couldn't help it. 'Thanks, Sue,' he said. 'Look, I'm so sorry—'

'Don't—'

'No ... I'm sorry about being such a terrible dick-head to you and Isabella. I've learnt my lesson.' For once, he meant it.

'That's really sweet of you,' she said. 'And it's all in the past. Let's forget about it, OK?' She smiled. 'Looks like you've been through enough to last several lifetimes.'

'Yeah,' he said in as affected a way as he could achieve.

Sue remained sitting on the side of Archie's bed. 'You sure you don't know where Gus is?'

'Sorry, I've been asleep ... for hours, I think.'

'And that ash. Any ideas? It's like Mrs. Pye filled a bucket from the fire and dumped it over Isabella's floor.' She screwed her face up. 'Weird, isn't it? Thing is, I'm sure he came up here,' she said, scrutinising Kemp's body and the similar, strange-looking, dusty marks on him.

'Oh well. Gus probably sneaked downstairs at some point.' She looked into his eyes. 'Why don't you grab a bite in the kitchen – if you're feeling strong enough – tell us about your adventures? Someone in the hospital told me all about you. They said it was a miracle you survived, said that you were the bravest person they've ever come across. There's a pot of tea just brewed if you want.'

She turned and walked round the room, inspecting it. Then she headed off down the stairs, looking back at him before disappearing out of view.

Kemp forced a smile back, turned over and exhaled. *Oh hell. Little did she know what was about to kick off in this game of survival...*

Sue looked nice enough – exquisite, if he was honest – but the thought sucked on him like a leech that if Sue came with him to Havilah, he'd ruin her, like a group of school kids carving their names on priceless artwork with penknives. Besides, wasn't she just a little too old for him? Daisy would be a better bet, for sure, but how would that happen?

Kemp wanted to cry. He'd survived and found his mother, and he'd been prepared to die for that chance, so what was the point of throwing it all away now? But if he didn't take Sue, then Gus would, because Gus loved her and was prepared to die for her.

And, he suspected, that if it came to a simple choice, Gus would indeed kill him.

So, Kemp thought, if he was to have his mother and a girl, it had to be Sue and therefore, Gus would have to die.

And when that happened, it would break her heart, and it would break his heart too.

---

'YOU'RE STAYING HERE,' a voice said, out of the blue.

Kemp sat bolt upright. 'What? Cain? Is that you?'

'I said, you're staying.'

Kemp thought he'd mis-heard. 'No, I am not. I need to get out of here, with you, now.'

'A change of plan, boy,' Cain responded. 'You will stay here until the Heirs of Eden – your de Lowe chums – either come out of there alive, or do not come out at all. You will prepare for a fight to the death with Gus. I cannot have both. There are fewer dreamspinners than Asgard thought.'

'I want to go with you,' Kemp implored. 'Girl or not—'

Cain sucked in a breath. 'You don't want the "hot" girl?'

'I didn't say that.'

'You implied it, boy.'

'I never—' Kemp thumped the pillow. 'I don't bleeding well know, do I?'

Cain's presence loitered. 'I sense confusion in your mind.' He sniffed the air. 'I sense that maybe you desire another. Perhaps it is the other Heir of Eden, Archie's twin. Hmmm. It is a better choice, but, dear boy, have you forgotten? That the Heirs of Eden are about to die in the chamber of Blabisterberry Jelly in a quite horrible suffocating death.' The ghost sighed. 'You will fight Gus at the ruin and you will win because there is something I know that you do not.'

Kemp drew in a breath. 'What?'

'Even if the children come through, the final tablet of Eden rests within the rocks of the ancient building near this house.'

'At the ruin? On top of the cliff?' Kemp said. 'But there's nothing there—'

'Beneath it,' Cain cut in, 'a structure is carved into its belly. Here, a beast has woken after a long, deep sleep. This beast, Gorialla Yingarna, the mother serpent, is my friend. We go back in time. She knows that the price of her freedom is the death of the Heirs of Eden.'

'What do you propose to do with this monster-mate of yours?'

'I cannot free it from its walls, for the ancient rules of the universe say that meddling directly with the Heirs of Eden and their quest will bring them immediate triumph. I do not wish to lose as I, like you, have a mother to save. That is why, secretly, I have chosen you to be with me, not that other boy. He doesn't have the necessary charm nor your warped sense of justice. Furthermore, he is more afraid of killing you than you are of him.'

Kemp buzzed at the thought. But if the idea of battering Gus to death filled him with dread, goodness knows what kind of state of mind Gus must be in.

'What's your plan?'

Cain, though invisible, smiled. Kemp felt it. 'We cheat.'

'Cheat,' Kemp said, 'Really?'

'Of course, you numbskull.'

'How?'

'I will show you,' Cain said. 'This way the pain will be easier for both of you to bear. Moreover, if Gus dies in, let's say, a terrible accident, where perhaps you are trying to save him, eventually Sue may, at length, give you her trust. She never needs to know there was a fight, or that we made an *arrangement*. You will fight Gus at the ruin where there is a hidden entrance that leads into the structure beneath the ruins. I will point it out to you. Get him close and Gus will fall into the beasts' lair – a little meal for the mother serpent.'

'What if he gets me first?'

'You must avoid him at all costs. I will do the final flourish for, as you know, I do have an element of oomph in my ghostly being.'

Kemp outwardly exhaled. He could live with this plan. Once again, the ghost's scheming felt neat, tight.

Footsteps – a boy's, walking up the stairs.

Gus entered, rubbing his scalp.

'Some of your hair missing?' Kemp said, grinning. He sniffed the air. 'You honk.'

Gus raised his not-so bushy eyebrows. 'All your hair disappeared, so I don't know why you're so pleased with yourself. Or hadn't you noticed?'

Kemp smiled badly. 'Think you can handle it?'

'Yeah. Course I can. No big deal,' Gus said. 'Me and the spirit got on just fine, didn't we?'

'You did well, boy,' Cain said. 'Now you know how to dance with the devil. Are you ready to live with it?

'Yeah,' Gus said confidently. 'When?'

Cain summoned Asgard and together they spoke in a low voice. Then his trilby turned towards the boys and tilted upwards.

His voice sounded victorious. 'The Heirs of Eden,' he crowed, 'are in serious trouble. Should they not succeed in their task within the next hour, they will die. In this case you will fight at noon tomorrow. If, by some miracle, they succeed and emerge from the cavern, you will engage with one another five hours after midnight at the ruin, as light breaks. It will give you a chance to say your farewells.'

'That's it then?'

'Yes. Time is running out for everyone. The end is fast approaching. One of you will live and the other will die.' Cain's voice lowered. 'Say not a word to anyone. Especially the "hot" one. Do not cross one another and do not be late. I will provide a weapon for each of you at the appointed hour. For my part, I am off to see the stage of your duel and speak with Gorialla Yingarna so she knows what to expect.'

Cain tilted his hat. 'Until tomorrow, boys.' And then he vanished, leaving his coat and hat falling to the floor.

# 115 GAIA REVEALS

Gaia, the dreamspinner, flashed from the corner of the cavern, in which Blabisterberry Jelly was causing untold havoc, and arrived in the attic room where Kemp lay in wait for Sue. She hid in a corner, invisible to the human eye.

Right now, the children looked as likely to fail as they ever had. And, with only two and a half days to go, Cain was spinning his web around them using the children's friends as his allies. Even as a spirit, Cain was a smart operator, but how far would he push the parameters of the unwritten rules?

Gaia inverted through her maghole and found Genesis. 'Mother, you seem better,' she said, walking towards her.

'Enough!' Genesis snapped back. 'We must aid the Heirs of Eden. The finding of Blabisterberry Jelly is all in the mind. Use dream powders to stimulate the girl.'

'I have done much already. I dare not meddle again.'

Genesis reared up. 'Gaia! Does Asgard care?'

'But we are different.'

'Huh! Do as you did with the old man. Dreamspinners do not want – will never want – dream-powders from Havilah. It is a nasty, short-term solution. Go now. Let the girl understand the true nature of Blabisterberry Jelly.'

Gaia inverted and flashed to the scene of foodie hell in the small room. In no time she was over Isabella, the dream powders invisibly sucked deep into her lungs with every long, deep breath.

There. It is done.

With any luck, she would dream fast, and then the girl will wake. So long as the girl interpreted the visions correctly, her understanding would be enriched. Her choices clearer.

Gaia looked at the table and the foul, rotting beast that now sat upon it.

Blabisterberry Jelly grew in proportion to the time and struggle. She knew that at a certain point of enlargement, there came a tipping point, whereby one person's eating alone would not suffice. For if Blabisterberry Jelly suspected it could not be beaten, it would grow exponentially, quickly suffocating those inside the room.

By the size of the huge, decaying monster pulsing with maggots on the table, that moment had already been and gone.

# 116 ISABELLA COMES TO LIFE

Isabella leapt to her feet as though a bolt of lightning had smashed into her. 'I've got it!' she said, pointing a finger in the air.

Archie jumped. 'Bells! You're back! You OK?'

'Couldn't be better,' she said. She turned towards Daisy. 'What happened to her?'

Archie wondered if this was the same Isabella. 'Knocked out,' Archie said, 'just like you.'

Isabella whistled, picked her way across the foul-smelling floor and picked Daisy up. 'Come on, come on, little sis. I'm going to need your help.'

'Help?' Archie said. 'For what?'

'To eat that enormous banoffee pie on the table. I can't do it on my own.'

Archie exchanged looks with Old Man Wood and twirled his finger around his temple as if she were mad. They sat down as Daisy stirred.

'OK,' Isabella said. 'Now, come on. Why don't we all tuck in?'

'Because,' Archie said, 'the last time we tried, Daisy and I were propelled into the wall *and,* believe it or not, the wall won.' He raised his eyebrows. 'Between you, me and these four walls, I'm not sure I'm ready to do it again.'

'I am,' Daisy slurred, as she joined them, nestling her head in her hands. 'Beats death-by-maggot any day.'

'Excellent, Daisy!' Isabella cried. 'Come on then! Let's do it!'

'You cannot be serious?' Archie said, nervously.

'I'm deadly serious, bro. Loosen up,' Isabella said, as she held her spoon in one hand and kissed it in a mildly theatrical way.

Daisy picked hers up and tried to do the same but it went wrong and clattered to the floor.

'Leave that there, Daisy darling,' Isabella said. 'You won't be needing it.'

Archie and Daisy exchanged glances.

'This is how we're going to proceed,' Isabella said. 'I'm going to sing a song.'

'Really? You're going to sing?' Daisy quizzed. 'Do you have to?'

'Of course. I have the finest voice in all the world.'

Archie heard a small guffaw from Old Man Wood. He found himself staring at the floor to hold back the floodgates of nervous hysterics.

Isabella stood up. 'Now, it goes like this,' she began. 'I'll stand here in front of my banoffee pie and, on my command, you lot are going to line up over there.'

'She's gone completely mad,' Archie whispered.

Old Man Wood draped an arm around him. 'She's got a plan, Archie, and no one else has a plan, and we need a plan, and apple-fast. Let's see how it goes, huh?'

Isabella turned on them. 'Be quiet you two!' she said. 'The first spoonful is for me, then, the next one is for you. I can't eat all of that banoffee pie on my own, so you're going to help me. Are you all clear with this?'

Archie and Daisy swapped glances. 'I'm not sure we're allowed to eat yours. It nearly killed us last time we tried.'

'We'll see about that,' Isabella said. 'The difference is that this time, *I'm* going to feed *you* with *my* spoon.'

'You sure this is going to work?'

Isabella looked astonished. 'Of course it is! Do you think I'm crazy, or something?'

Daisy pulled a face that implied they did.

'Anyway,' Isabella continued unabashed, 'I don't think there's another option, do you? Now, mine is delicious banoffee pie. Yours can be whatever you want it to be. But you must say it out loud.'

This time, it was Daisy's turn to question her. 'Sis, are you totally one hundred and a little bit percent sure about this?'

'Of course! The brain works far better with spoken commands rather than concealed inside the grey matter.' She sucked in a massive breath. 'Now I want you to sing with me – are you ready Daisy?'

'Sing?'

'Absolutely. Follow my lead.'

Daisy nodded, slowly.

'Archie?'

'Er, yeah. I suppose.'

'Not good enough. Yes or no?'

'Yes,' Archie said, beads of sweat bubbling on his forehead.

'Old Man Wood?'

'Absolutely. Can't wait.'

'Good. That's the way.' She shut her eyes. '*Banoffee pie, banoffee pie, I need banoffee pie*,' she chanted.

She continued, a little more assuredly, clapping slowly in time with the words encouraging the others to join her. She cut away a spoonful.

'*Banoffee pie, banoffee pie, I need banoffee pie*,' she popped the spoonful in her mouth. 'Del-i-c-i-ous!'

Isabella pointed at Daisy as she chewed. Daisy came forward and opened her mouth.

'*Duck pancake, duck pancake*' she said out loud. The others joined in. '*I need a duck pancake*.' Isabella sliced a spoonful off and fed Daisy's open mouth.

'Mmmm.'

'*Banoffee pie, banoffee pie, I need banoffee pie*,' Isabella said again, quickly popping a spoonful in her mouth.

Now it was Archie's turn, '*Steak and chips, steak and chips*,' everyone joined in. '*I need steak and chips!*' Archie munched it down, a look of blissful surprise on his face.

'*Banoffee pie, banoffee pie, I need banoffee pie*,' they sang as Isabella scoffed on her latest helping.

Old Man Wood came up to the table.

'*Starlight apple crumble with lovely thick cream, starlight apple crumble with lovely thick cream. I need starlight apple crumble with lovely thick cream,'* they laughed, as their mouths struggled with the words.

He devoured the spoonful.

*'Banoffee pie, banoffee pie, I need banoffee pie,'* they sang. Isabella demolished another mouthful.

'*Roast chicken dinner,*' Daisy tried and repeated clapping her hands. '*She needs a roast chicken dinner.*'

Gulp.

And on it went:

Archie; '*Strawberries and cream.*'

Old Man Wood; '*Fish pie.*'

Daisy; *'Liver and bacon.*' (ugh, from Archie!)

Archie; '*Scrambled eggs.*'

Old Man Wood; '*Beef stew.*'

Daisy; '*Chocolate ice cream.*'

Archie; '*Spaghetti Bolognese.*'

Old Man Wood; '*A juicy apple.*'

Daisy; '*Chicken stir-fry.*'

Archie; '*Seafood paella.*'

Old Man Wood; '*A juicy pear.*'

Daisy; *'Strawberry jelly.*'

Archie; '*Orange jelly.*'

And they looked at one another, wondering if Old Man Wood might say *Blabisterberry Jelly,* but instead he said:

*'Carrot jelly.'*

'You're so weird, Old Man Wood,' Daisy said, and in the same breath, '*lemon sorbet.*'

Archie; '*Veg spring roll.*'

Old Man Wood; '*Starlight apple crumble.*'

After each mouthful, Isabella took a large spoonful of the maggoty-rat-banoffee pie.

After a lull in enthusiasm where the pace lessened, the children and Old Man Wood puffed out their cheeks, their tummies expanding.

'We're nearly there,' Daisy announced. 'A couple more each, that's all. She clapped her hands. 'We can do this!'

The noise level increased.

'*Fillet steak, fillet steak,*' Archie said. '*I need fillet steak,*' they shouted.

Isabella tucked in again. But she was struggling to maintain her concentration.

Archie noticed. When it came round to him again he said, '*Celery, celery. I need celery.*

'Ugh. *Celery*,' Daisy quipped. 'Everyone knows Celery is disgusting.'

'... But it's mainly water, isn't it?' he said. 'I'm not sure I can fit anything else in.'

'Two more,' Daisy yelled. 'Come on, Old Man Wood.'

The children clapped repetitively. But Old Man Wood's brain had gone blank

'What is your food, Old Man Wood,' Isabella demanded.

'Hmm, there is something—'

'Another apple, perhaps?'

'Not this time,' he said rubbing his chin. 'This one's special,' he said with a big smile on his wrinkly old face. 'Yes, I know! Mammoth testicles!'

The children collectively looked at him.

'Mammoth testicles?' Archie said.

'Mammoth bollocks?' Daisy said, incredulously.

'Oh, it's an apple-tastic delicacy I believe I used to be very fond of.'

Isabella cut out a portion as the others clapped.

'*I need mammoth testicles*,' they howled, laughing.

'Last one, Bells!' Daisy yelled, 'it's all yours.'

Isabella felt so enormous that it would need a crane to move her. She took a deep breath. 'OK. Here we go.'

'What's it going to be?' Archie asked.

'There is one thing,' she said, eyeing up the goblet, 'that has to be the best thing of all—'

'Oh, no.' Archie said. 'I'm not sure that's a good idea.'

'Oh, yes it is,' she said, drawing a deep breath. '*Blabisterberry Jelly*,' she said. '*I need Blabisterberry Jelly.*' Her eyes sparkled as the others looked on with a mixture of amazement and trepidation.

'*I need Blabisterberry Jelly*,' they yelled.

Isabella gathered the last morsels onto her spoon, held it up to the others like a toast, and shoved it in.

'*Eurgh ... Revolting ...*

'*YUM ...*

'*OH NO! ... Urggugh ...*

*'... oooooh HHHH*

*'CRIKEY ... OW! ...*

*'INCREDIBLE!*

*'... No! Hang on ... good! Oh YES! ... no ...*

*'Blimey ... Yeeeessss!*

*'WOOOOOWEEE!'*

She tossed her spoon into the corner of the room and wiped her mouth.

Silence filled the room.

'God, I'm full,' Daisy said, swaying on her stool.

'Me too. Don't think I can move,' Archie replied. 'I think I'm going to be sick.'

All four sat for a minute, digesting.

Finally Archie spoke again. 'Well, I'm not sure I can believe it,' Archie said. 'Tell me, Bells, what did Blabisterberry Jelly taste like again?'

Daisy hit him on the arm.

Getting up, smiles spread across their faces. Suddenly all four of them were jumping up and down, as energetically as they could in view of the vast quantities they'd scoffed, like a football crowd enjoying a dramatic win.

Suddenly it happened.

From out of Isabella's mouth the most enormous burp they'd ever heard burst forth, like the long, unwavering note of a French horn, and it continued on and on, producing a balloon out of her mouth that looked like a mini amber-coloured tent.

Archie laughed so hard that he had to hold his sides and for a moment thought his eyeballs might come up. Then he burped again, followed by Daisy and finally Old Man Wood, who looked deeply embarrassed, the noise a cacophony of burpy trumpeting.

Daisy clapped her hands. 'Put them together. Put the burp-bubbles together. Isn't that what we've got to do?'

Carefully they stuck the strange, floating, sticky bubbles together. Nothing happened.

'Are you sure we're doing this right?' Isabella said.

'Well, I don't know,' Archie said. 'It's not like I know anyone who specialises in this kind of thing.'

Immediately, a huge...

***"POP"***

... as though a massive cork had blown out of a champagne bottle, reverberated around the room, followed by a *"PUFF"* like a firework, with a plume of colourful, showy glitter.

And there, on the table lay a stone tablet, identical to the one that had come from the fire, with matching markings.

---

THE STAIRWELL they'd come down in the first instance reappeared and they dashed up it and into the dark, foggy courtyard. Collectively they drew in a large lungful of fresh air and, when they looked back, the stairs had reverted to a normal, grey-coloured paving slabs as though nothing had happened and the room had never been.

Archie was desperate to know one thing. 'Old Man Wood, we had to overcome our worst fears. Daisy hates dog poo after the slipper episode when she was little, Isabella screams the house down if she sees rats – or maggots for that matter – and those must have been the eyes of the blind Ancient Woman from my dreams. But who, and what, were those weird kind of spiders doing on your plate?'

'Hmmm,' Old Man Wood said, a little taken aback. 'That, littlun, is most observant. That spidery-thing you saw, if I'm not mistaken, was a dreamspinner. These aren't spiders like the ones that busy themselves in the corners of a room. *These dreamspinner creatures give dreams to living things.*'

'Dreams?'

'Oh yes. There's very little known about them – humans don't even know they exist – until now, of course. They're extraordinary, remarkable things.'

'But why do you fear them so much?'

'Anyone as old as I am fears them, for they know the truth of space and time. And if you must know, I had the same nightmare involving a dream-spinner spider night after night. The dream was trying to tell me something.' He scratched his wispy hair as he wondered about it, his frown lines growing deeper on his brow.

'You see, dreamspinners control what goes into your dreams and, in a way, your ability to think, create and discover. Dreamspinners put in the seed, the germ of an idea, or thought into your head, but then it's up to the individual receiver as to how it germinates – how it's interpreted.'

Archie's heartbeat quickened as he thought about the creature he'd seen over Daisy before the storm. 'So these dreamspinner things are responsible for the crazy, mad dreams we had?' he said.

'Certainly. Those dreams were almost certainly given to you by one of those spidery creatures I gobbled up!'

Archie shivered. This explanation was a little more complicated than he felt like understanding right now. He glanced over at Daisy who looked as if she was about to throw up. 'Come on, you lot. Time to get inside. I really need to lie down.'

More than anything though, a tickling in his stomach gave him the feeling he, too, needed to be very sick indeed.

---

A NAGGING THOUGHT TOYED with Old Man Wood's mind: If Archie's "fear" was to eat the eyes of this blind, Ancient Woman he'd spoken about, then who did the other eyeballs belong to? After all, there had been *two* sets of eyes on his plate.

Old Man Wood searched the depths of his mind. Somewhere, somehow, he'd known both. One, a soft, nutty-brown set, with a look of yearning. The other two fractionally larger, with a distinct, icy, pale-blue madness about them.

Why did these warrant his attention? They were familiar – eyes from a long time ago, but whose? And as he wondered, he remembered something vitally important. Wasn't there something utterly crucial about eyes? Something brilliant and possibly sinister? Something magical that he couldn't quite lay his finger on?

Why, oh why, was Archie so desperately frightened of them?

# 117 A CURIOUS REUNION

'For goodness' sake, be quiet you two,' Solomon said. What a perfectly awful evening. While he'd tried to continue his investigations, Kemp and Gus Williams had been at each other's throats, their comments towards one another were acidic to put it mildly.

Finally he snapped. 'I'm fed up with you two,' he said. 'You're not helping me, or anyone. I rather hoped it might be a little more jolly.'

The fact that Kemp had turned up out of the blue remained Solomon's biggest shock thus far. Solomon knew that he had escaped from a toilet in the isolation ward in mysterious circumstances, leaving only – so he'd been told – a small pile of ash.

By his own admission, Kemp told them that he'd stolen a boat and rowed through the night across the floodwaters, landing – quite remarkably – at the foot of the cliff by the de Lowes cottage. It had to be balderdash, he thought. The soldiers used tracking devices for the crossing and, although it was do-able, the chances of success were highly improbable.

Aside from the general upset he caused Gus, Kemp appeared different: confident and more caring. The way he'd spent so much time helping Mrs. Pye out in the kitchen after he'd coaxed her out of her apartment. The way he smiled every time he looked at the strange woman who appeared happier than ever before. The way Kemp reached for plates and washed up without having to be asked. And then there was the way he smiled every time he looked over towards Sue. These were the actions of a young man almost ... in love. *Perhaps*, he thought, *Kemp was in love with life*.

Solomon shook his head. By the look of things, one would have thought that Kemp, not Gus, was the loved-up partner, for Gus looked pale and withdrawn and, quite frankly, ill.

Was Kemp really flirting with Sue? But why so blatantly in front of Gus? To wind him up?

His thoughts were interrupted by a noise.

'Quiet!' he said, whispering hoarsely.

They stopped and listened.

'Ssshh. There,' he said, pointing his arm. 'Outside.'

The five of them, Mrs. Pye included, listened as the fire crackled in the hearth.

Yes ... and now chatter, footsteps. A bang outside the front door.

'Hide!' Solomon whispered. 'Now!'

Sue, Solomon and Mrs. Pye edged behind the sofa, blowing out the candles that dotted the tables until only dim light emanated from the hearth. Gus and Kemp crept up either side of the big oak door, their backs leaning in to the plaster.

Jumbled voices, footsteps, laughter. A cough. A retch. Vomiting. More vomiting. Cheering.

Williams and Kemp exchanged glances, puzzled looks on their faces.

Now a hand on the door latch. It twitched upwards.

Kemp picked out a long wooden stick.

'What are you doing?' Gus whispered.

Kemp hesitated. 'You know – just in case.'

The door swung open. A strange head appeared in the dim light, dotted with weird spikes.

Kemp swore. 'It's a freaking alien!'

'Smack it,' Gus said, as he dived behind an armchair.

In a flash, Kemp swung the thick wooden stick down on top of the spiky head. But instead of incapacitating the intruder, splinters flew in every direction. The head remained quite still and then, with a growl, the body flew up, hands outstretched with such speed and precision that Kemp didn't have a chance. In an instant, Kemp was pinned to the wall, a hand tight around his neck. He gasped for breath.

Archie snapped the remains of the stick with one hand.

'Get off me,' Kemp howled.

'Who are you?' Archie roared, trying to make out who the person was in the dim candlelight.

*'P-p-p le ... eeese don't hurt me,'* Kemp squealed.

'Archie! Let go of him!' Daisy ordered.

Archie ignored her and lifted him up off the floor with his one hand that was glued to his neck.

'Who are you?' Archie repeated.

'Kemp,' he whispered. 'It's ... me ... Kemp,' he said, struggling, his eyes bulging.

'Let him go!' Daisy shouted.

'Kemp?' Archie repeated. 'It can't be Kemp – he's in hospital. We saw it on the telly.'

Archie threw him to the floor and stood over him.

'Archie? Is that you?' Kemp said, rubbing his neck. 'What happened to your head?'

'Speak for yourself. What happened to yours?'

Kemp moved a hand from his neck to his bald dome. 'Long story, Arch,' he coughed. 'I'll tell you about it one day.'

Daisy marched over and offered Kemp a hand. 'Sorry about Archie throwing you – he doesn't know his own strength.' She scoured the dark room, her eyes lighting up like car headlights.

'Mrs. Pye, you can come out from behind the door ... it's OK, it's only us.' She looked down. 'There's a girl facedown behind the sofa and someone behind the armchair. Is that you, Gus Williams? Come out now! I can see you.'

She shook her head. 'And ... er ... Mr. Solomon. What the hell are you doing here?'

Daisy's eyes started returning to normal as the people emerged, stunned.

Isabella walked over to the candles on the windowsill, clicked her thumb and finger, whereupon a flame, like a gas lighter, shot out of the end of her nail.

Gus, Solomon, Sue and Kemp backed off against the walls.

Candlelight soon filled the room.

'Oh heck,' Archie said, retching. 'Sorry guys, gotta go.' He barged past the bewildered looking headmaster and shot up the stairs, the sounds of his puking echoing through the house.

'What's the matter with him?' Kemp said.

'All that rich food at our ... picnic party,' Daisy said, smiling at him.

Kemp smiled back, looking into her eyes. His heart skipped a beat. Her eyes glowed, like beautiful rubies in the fire. Kemp couldn't take his eyes off her. Daisy had turned exotic, almost divine.

The odd thing, though, was that Daisy couldn't stop staring at him and for the first time he could ever remember, it wasn't in a sour, hateful way.

'SUE!' Isabella screamed. 'Is it you?'

'No it's an illusion. *Of course* it's me!'

They both screeched in delight and ran across the room, embracing and crying and giggling with delight.

'And Gus?'

Gus, for the first time in a while, beamed at everyone with his wonderful, toothy smile.

'Oh my god. Our National heroes!' Isabella said, embracing him. 'How... what ... how ... did ... it's impossible...'

'Headmaster Solomon can probably explain it best,' Gus said as Archie slapped him on the back. 'We've all come a long way in the last three days.'

The headmaster coughed and moved across to the children. 'Now, first off, please promise you won't set fire to me, Isabella, or see through me, Daisy, or get Archie to beat me up?'

'Don't worry, I'll try not to vaporize you,' Daisy said. 'But look out for Isabella's burps. I promise you, she has recently done the longest one ever. Definitely a world record.'

Isabella's face, even in the dim light had turned notably puce. Noticing, the headmaster roared with laughter, everyone else joining in.

Sue and Isabella eventually settled down on the sofa, Old Man Wood in his armchair, Gus and Archie on one side of the hearth and Daisy, Mrs. Pye and Kemp on the other.

'So, why are you here?' Isabella asked.

'Do you guys have any idea what's going on?' Sue said. 'Out there, the world is falling to bits and the men in charge seem to think it's got something to do with you lot—'

'You're the most wanted people on the planet,' Solomon interjected.

'It's a stroke of luck the entire valley is shrouded in thick fog, or several battalions of Her Majesty's armed forces would almost certainly be sharing this jolly scene with us.' His voice took on a softer tone. 'Sue is right, though, isn't she?'

Isabella's emotions suddenly got the better of her. 'We're caught up in a nightmare!' she said, wiping away a tear. 'A living hell.'

Sue cradled her. 'You're OK, though, aren't you?'

'Only by the skin of my teeth. I'm not very good at this kind of thing. The twins have been amazing.'

Archie shook his head. 'We have to do this thing together. We all bring different things. You won't believe how fast Isabella can run—'

'Or what she can heal,' Old Man Wood butted in.

'Or eat,' Daisy threw in. 'And burp.'

'There's a plague flying across the world, ' Sue said. 'Your hell isn't very far away.'

Solomon coughed in his most head-masterly way. 'I am supposed to turn you in to the authorities, directly. They want to know what secret you're harbouring. But I take it from what I've seen of you so far that there is something rather important you must do?'

The children looked from one to another.

Isabella piped up. 'We found some riddles which we have to solve. The deeper we delve, the more clues we seem to stumble across—'

'I knew it!' the headmaster said. 'And it is only you three who can do this – and of course you, Mr. Wood?'

They nodded.

Solomon stood up and began pacing the room, thinking. While he did this, Mrs. Pye took it as the perfect opportunity to make an announcement. 'Now then, you children must be starving.'

Isabella caught the others' eyes and together they burst out laughing.

Mrs. Pye ignored them.

Archie piped up. 'I can't speak for you lot, but we're pretty full, so don't worry about us.'

Mrs. Pye looked slightly irritated. 'Have you been eating behind my back then, huh?'

'Only a bite.'

'What?'

'It's a strange thing – you've probably never heard of.'

Mrs. Pye reddened. 'Go on. Try me.'

'Well, it's a funny thing,' he continued, 'called Blabisterberry Jelly!'

'Blabster-whatty-ellie?!'

'All you need to know is that it isn't as good as a Mrs. Pye Special,' Daisy said.

Mrs. Pye smiled, or grimaced. 'You other's want one?' She counted the nods from Sue, Gus and Solomon. 'Four emps coming up.'

'I'll help,' Kemp volunteered, following Mrs. Pye out of the room.

Solomon sat down and looked over the top of his glasses. 'You should know this,' he said rather solemnly. 'Unless there is evidence of progress, and that means finding you, a rather big bomb is due to land on this area.' He searched their faces. 'However, if you're handed over, I take it this would be bad news?'

'Extremely,' Archie said. 'We have less than three days to go.'

Solomon shifted. 'The same time as the bomb is due to go off.' He paced up and back, rubbing his chin. 'Therefore the question is this: how can we help you?'

'By making sure we aren't stopped,' Archie said.

Solomon smiled. 'Just as I thought. By the way, what on earth has happened to your head?'

'Oh! That's from when I got struck by a lightning bolt at the football match—'

'You think that's bad,' Isabella said. 'Look at these.' She removed her half-gloves and held her hands up.

Sue gasped. 'Holes? How come?'

'Another massive lightning strike. But I'm telling you, the science absolutely doesn't add up. Want to see something cool?'

'Sure.'

'Then watch this,' Isabella closed her eyes and pointed her hands at the wood basket. Suddenly a log hovered in the air and moved in mid air across the hearth to the fire where it nestled into the burning embers.

Sue swore out loud. 'Bells, where did you learn to do that? It's like you've discovered *the Force*, from *Star Wars*!'

Isabella laughed and winked at the others. 'You should see what Daisy can do! And anyway, Sue Lowden, where in hell did you learn to swear like that? At sea, perchance, with Captain Williams?'

Sue blushed.

Isabella pulled her to the side, 'Time to tell all, dear friend. And do not omit even the tiniest details!'

# 118 A SMALL REFLECTION

Stone thumped the desk.

So much didn't make sense; didn't join up. 'Let's check that camera you planted in the old woman's apartment,' he said to Dickinson.

Dickinson tuned in the receiver. The TV showed the blank wall. Dickinson fast-forwarded the screen, zooming through the footage.

On and on the film continued. 'Nothing, sir.'

Stone scratched his chin. 'Well, if they're not there, any joy from the shopping malls?'

'Most are underwater in the area surrounding Upsall. They'd have had to get out of the flood zone, and that's about a two hundred mile radius.'

Stone examined the screen. 'STOP IT – right there!'

Dickinson paused the recording.

'Back a little.'

'There!' Stone said. 'Forward a couple of frames.' He stood up and moved over to the screen. 'Can you blow this up?' he said pointing at a picture.

'This one?'

'Yes, Dickinson. The one in the frame. Zoom in on it.'

Soon the picture ballooned onto the screen. Stone clapped his hands and swore under his breath. 'I knew it. I bloody knew it.'

'It's a photograph of the de Lowes' parents on their wedding day, sir,' Dickinson said. 'One of the one's on her dresser.'

'Is it really, Dickinson. Look carefully, lad. Look very carefully.'

Dickinson peered in. 'I still can't see what you can, sir.'

'Try the reflection.'

Dickinson adjusted the settings and whistled. 'You know,' he said, 'I've been wondering where he'd got to?'

'Kemp?'

'Yes. He had to turn up somewhere. And if he's there, what's to say the rest of them haven't suddenly decided to make an appearance.'

For the first time in a long while, Stone smiled. 'Dickinson, time to get back there. And damn fast if you ask me.' He checked his watch. 'First light, fog or not. Understand? We've been way too soft on them. I think we've been played for fools.'

He leaned back in his chair and stretched his arms behind his head.

'This time, my friend, they're going to be in for a proper reality check.'

# 119 TO THE DEATH

Gus hadn't wanted to leave Sue's side. When Isabella and Daisy excused themselves for bed, he hovered around until everyone had left. They cuddled.

'You need to go, Gus,' she said softly, stroking his face. 'You'll be alright on the sofa – won't you?'

His dark eyes searched hers longingly. 'Yeah. Look,' he began, hesitantly, 'I just want you to know something.'

'What?' Sue said.

He smiled. 'That I ... um ... well, I love you, Sue. And that whatever happens, it's been fun, really fun.'

'You too,' she said, her eyes sparkling, a cloud of confusion briefly passing over her face.

'And thank you, for everything,' he said.

'Go. You're turning into a soft little bear, Gus Williams. Away to bed, my Leo. I'll see you later.'

He held her hand and prepared to leave. 'Just don't forget me in the morning, alright?'

Her face glowed like velvet in the soft candlelight and he sucked in every sweet detail, every line, remembering it.

He kissed her on the lips briefly, shutting his eyes as though savouring the moment forever. Then he slipped away, down the creaking staircase, along the corridor, the main stairs and past the rugs lying at the foot of the stairs before collapsing on the sofa.

He wiped his tears and breathed deeply, trying to control himself.

He checked his watch. Midnight. Four hours of sleep, and he'd need every minute – if he could get to sleep.

Gus lay down and pondered the last few days, and the day to come. Destiny is a funny old thing, he thought.

He'd be dead by now if it wasn't for Sue. She'd saved his life. Now, he had the chance to save hers.

He thought of Kemp with her, kissing her, fondling her, and his stomach tightened. Nothing, nothing in the world, the universe, could make him angrier.

Then he closed his eyes and drifted into a fitful sleep.

---

KEMP LAY down on Mrs. Pye's large bed.

*What a wonderful, perfect, brilliant evening,* he thought. He turned to look at his mum lying there beside him, a smile on her funny, snarly, scarred face.

She looked at him, he at her as they held hands. Breathing in unison.

Being with his mother felt as though a hole in his heart had been patched up: when he caught her watching him from a doorway, or staring at his hands or squeezing his shoulder.

Little gestures that spoke of a deeper bond, whose once loose ties had been sewn neatly back together again, gave him a new sense of wholeness.

And then, he'd talked to Daisy for what felt like hours. He'd talked about Archie, and he'd told her about Cain and the agony and the choice he'd had to make and how he'd been left in the hospital full of needles and drips.

They even talked about their animosity but agreed how amazing Mrs. Pye was. And he belly-laughed when she told him about Blabisterberry Jelly. And he had said things and opened up to her like he'd never done to anyone before. Not even Archie.

And she was hilarious and crazy and clever and beautiful and ... he couldn't help feeling that she even ... liked him. Yeah. She definitely liked him.

It wasn't a sloppy kiss, just a stretched out peck on the cheek that seemed to linger for too long – that kind of kiss. But he'd felt her breath on his cheek, her smell intoxicating, her hair brushing his scalp. A simple, perfect, neat kiss from Daisy de Lowe.

He grinned. It wasn't so long ago that she'd kicked him in the shin and he'd texted his friends to tell them to literally knock her out of the cup final.

He'd laughed about it, nervously at first, but when he reminded her that she'd teased him about fancying her, he felt himself blush. And she smiled at him and shook her head, and her hair fell wildly over her face and then she'd stared deeply into his eyes with eyes that reminded him of an erupting volcano. And, for the first time ever in life, his heart had raced, soaring high into the sky, fluttering like a bird.

And then he'd returned to the comfort of his mother's unquestionable love. Kemp lay back and stared at the dark ceiling.

And all this joy would vanish if he didn't defeat Gus.

He shut his eyes. From intense happiness to terrible despair in one brief moment. Wasn't life a bitch?

He clenched his fist. No way would he lose this feeling. Not in a million years. Not ever.

To keep it, all he had to do was beat the living crap out of Gus, and then follow Cain's plan.

---

A QUICK TAP on the shoulder was all it took.

Gus woke with a start, opened his eyes to see Kemp staring down at him, his arm raised as though ready to thrust it down.

Gus panicked. 'NO!' he yelled.

'Come on,' Kemp smirked. 'Time to go – and keep the noise down.'

They stole out of the house, the latch clicking into place as the door closed behind them.

'We'll never get to the ruin in this,' Kemp said, waving his arms at the dark, dense, soupy fog around them.

'Then we won't have to try and kill each other like barbarians,' Gus replied. 'Listen, Kemp, can't we be sensible and not do what that creepy spirit wants.'

'Watch your words, young man,' said a familiar, deep voice. Cain's voice.

Gus reddened.

'I know it is hard to believe, but unlike everyone else on this rather dull planet, one of you has the chance to survive and flourish. The other will not.'

'But the de Lowes beat the weird food test,' Gus argued. 'How come you're so sure they'll fail? I mean, what if they do succeed?'

'They can't.'

'Why not?'

Cain sighed. 'Walk with me while I tell you.' Cain hovered forward, as a bright flame flickered into life at head height. 'Follow this, but keep close or the fog will swallow you up.'

The boys walked along, every now and then turning a little to the left or pulling sharply to the right. All the while, Cain spoke.

'To open the Garden of Eden, the Heirs of Eden must do unspeakable things—'

'But so are we,' Kemp argued.

'There's a chance though, for one of you to live,' Cain said. 'For them, success is so very far away.'

'Why?' Kemp said bluntly.

Cain seemed to suck in a mouthful of air. 'We are headed towards a labyrinth, built under the hills where the old castle once stood. In this belly of rock there is a beast that has only recently awoken after a very long sleep. The beast, there since the time of the Great Closing, does not wish to die. Furthermore it is angry and hungry and bitter and desperate.'

'Yeah? Big deal,' said Kemp. 'So what makes it so special?'

The light disappeared and Gus almost clattered into Kemp.

'The beast is the snake of the Tree of Knowledge. The same serpent who tricked humankind, the beast who rules half of every kingdom; the beast who penetrates minds and toys with them, bending them to her will.

'Her skin has never been penetrated and her fangs spray deadly poison, as well as fire and ice. She is both huge and small, and can disappear like a chameleon. This beast has slain entire armies and defeated hordes of ogres and giants, werewolves and ancient beasts.

'Sometimes, she is known as Satan or Beelzebub or the Devil. Her name is Gorialla Yingarna. She is the "mother serpent", the creator of valleys and mountains.' Cain paused, for effect.

'And your dear little friends will have to kill her to get what they need. Be under no illusion, the beast is a perfect creature, an organism above others and a lethal weapon. And to survive, the beast must kill the Heirs of Eden. That is why they cannot succeed.'

Cain moved on. The boys trudged after him silently.

Then he stopped again. 'And, even if these children do, by a miracle, happen to triumph, there is another challenge that they cannot do, no matter how high the stakes, no matter how many billions will die. They must kill one of their own.'

Gus felt like being sick. 'Really?'

'So you see, a new time is coming for mankind. One of you will be there to forge it with me, and one of you won't. Be assured, the one who fails now will suffer a death infinitely less painful and drawn-out than the gruesome death inflicted upon your friends. I almost pity them.'

Soon, Cain had led them to the ruin. 'Stand behind this rock, while the fog is cleared.'

'Who's going do that?' Kemp said.

'Gorialla Yingarna will burn it out. Both of you will have a stick fashioned from the root of a baobab tree. They are hard and light and can inflict terrible damage if used in the right way.'

The ghost left them, heading off alone and, moments later, a great burning, roaring noise like a furnace bellowed into the air around them. The boys ducked as flames licked around the rocks, the heat scorching their faces.

Then the voice called out to them. 'It is time, boys.'

'Are there any rules?' Gus said.

'No. You may do as you please. If there is no clear winner, Gorialla Yingarna will decide.'

The boys grabbed their wooden clubs and moved out into the main part of the ruin, the arena lit by two burning bushes.

They faced each other.

'Good riddance, Kemp,' Gus said. And with those words, he launched a furious assault with a turn of speed that caught Kemp completely off his guard.

# 120 DAISY HEARS NOISES

Daisy stirred. Deep in her bones, an ache remained, that would not go away.

She rolled over, then back again.

She sat up and tiptoed around the attic room, glimpsing the early light of dawn that highlighted the foggy cloud like dirty cotton wool.

Inside the room, Sue slept on the sofa, her snores gentle and then petering out as she moved her head.

Daisy crept back to bed and sat up, thinking.

Quiet.

She smiled about Kemp, reddening at the memory. He'd kissed her goodnight, or did she kiss him? OK, so it was only a peck, but her heart had jumped at the sensation. And she'd wanted to... but then ... she blushed.

She closed her eyes and listened to the quiet. So still she could hear the beat of her heart.

Then she heard it; a strange talking noise. She shook her head as though something had climbed into her ear.

There, again.

She tuned in. Someone talking and then ... Gus. It had to be. And now Kemp.

It couldn't be. She shook her head.

Something about death. Something about a fight.

But they were downstairs, weren't they?

Without hesitating, Daisy shot off and inspected the living room but found an empty sofa, the blankets discarded. She checked the bedrooms.

She opened the door and searched the building opposite. Still nothing. She stood outside in the murky light and listened.

Suddenly a roar, like a dragon, burst out of the fog. She stared up the hill, and now that she thought about it, a fleck of light made the fog brighter.

Goosebumps raced across her skin.

*They were at the ruin.*

She rushed in and grabbed her boots, coat and hat, closed the door and set off into the fog.

The farther she went, the clearer the noises. She ran and jumped and skidded as fast as she could, burning a hole in the vapour with her eyes.

As she turned off the track she heard it. Sounds of grunts and cries and moans. Fighting. Wood cracking on wood.

She moved further around, where she might see into the courtyard of the ruin and slipped between a tiny gap that separated two sheer boulders, an old hiding place she knew well from games of hide and seek. It gave her a perfect view. And from experience, she knew it was impossible to be seen unless from right up close.

Now that she looked out, in the centre, a small tree burned and the fog fell away like the edges of an arena.

Gus, his dark hair matted to his forehead, teeth gritted, attacked hard, smashing down with his stick on top of Kemp.

Her heart leapt.

Kemp managed to fend off several blows, then swung but without great purpose, turned and limped towards her hiding place.

She could see how his face was smeared with blood. A gash cut angrily across his forehead, reminding her of Mrs. Pye's scar. His lip split, his ear bleeding. He hobbled.

Gus walked behind, teasing him. Ready to smash him again.

*Why?* She thought. *Why were they beating the living daylights out of each other?*

Kemp rallied and slashed back, catching his upper legs.

Now, they were only ten metres away.

Gus held his stick out and, in a flash, wallopped it down on Kemp's shoulder. Then, another blow, this time to the kidneys.

Kemp doubled over and fell. 'Stop!' he cried.

Gus moved over him. 'Sorry, mate,' he said, almost apologetically. 'You know the deal. There's only room for one. Only one can inherit the Earth.' He laughed nervously. 'And just so you know, I would rather have you die than for you to take Sue.'

Daisy pulled herself further into the crevice between the rocks. *Take Sue? What did he mean?* She scoured the area searching for something that might explain all of this.

And there it was.

Sitting on a rock to the side was a lizard the size of a lion, a forked tongue flicking in and out of its mouth. She turned back to the boys and when she looked up again, the lizard had gone. But now, she noticed, on the other side was a huge snake, like a boa constrictor, coiled neatly in a pyramid shape.

A cold, icy feeling swept through her. Was it one and the same thing?

Kemp ran, but Gus was too fast. A sickening thud over Kemp's back made him crash to the floor only yards from her hiding place.

Blood soaked his face, his head streaked with red.

Daisy winced. Tears formed. She wanted to do something but knew that whatever was happening here, it wasn't her fight.

Gus leant on a rock nearby. 'There,' he yelled out into the air as though addressing a crowd. 'What would you have me do? Beat him to a pulp? He's finished. Aren't you, Kemp?' Tears ran from his eyes. 'Aren't you?'

A cold voice answered him. 'Your requirement is to eliminate your opponent. No more and no less.'

Gus roared his disapproval. 'Come on! We're kids! Kids! This is barbarous. Is this what you would have us do, huh? Go round destroying everyone, like maniacs?'

Gus slumped to the ground and sobbed.

'The fittest of the species always survive,' the voice continued with a trace of mockery. 'The defeated never write history, so they never shape history.' And then, almost as an afterthought, the voice added, 'this sort of lack of killer instinct is why the Heirs of Eden will fail. Because they are weak. Because they, like you, are pathetic children. Show me your strength Gus, and you will prevail.'

Gus gritted his teeth in frustration and moved out into the open towards Kemp.

Daisy looked through the slit of stone at the prostrate body of Kemp. She bent her head and noticed a small rock in front of her foot, the size of a tennis ball. She worked it free with her foot.

Gus screamed. 'Come on! Please! Let him go ... this is crazy!'

Daisy levered her foot back and kicked the stone ever so gently. It rolled over the stony ground and doffed Kemp on the shoulder.

She watched, wide-eyed, as, very slowly he craned his neck and for a moment stared directly at the gap, certain that his eyes met hers.

Now his hand rested over the stone. He raised his head again.

*She could've sworn that he saw her.*

Kemp lay still.

*Was her action too late? Was he too far gone?*

Daisy desperately wanted to rush out and grab him. Wake him up, but in no time Gus returned and stood over him.

'Sorry, Kemp,' he said. 'I really don't want to do this.' He raised his stick in the air.

Daisy couldn't bear to watch and shut her eyes.

And then suddenly there was a crunching noise, like the snapping of twigs.

Gus howled and fell to the ground.

They tore into one another ... Kemp rolled on top and pummeled him once, twice, three times with the stone in his hand.

And there was Gus, flailing wildly, aiming for the throat, punching anything.

When she opened her eyes again, the two boys lay on the ground, blood streaming from their wounds.

Kemp was the first to pick himself up.

'Run, Williams,' he croaked. 'Go. Get out of here.'

Kemp eyed up the sticks and picked them up. He tossed one out of the courtyard into the fog.

'Piss off out of here,' he roared. 'Now. Anywhere.'

Gus stirred and dragged himself to his knees.

Daisy noted the damage to his face – a front tooth missing, swollen lips, his nose badly flattened.

Kemp walked away towards the far end.

Gus following. Both limping.

Kemp kept on.

Gus tried to break into a run as if to catch him.

At the far end Kemp stopped.

She heard him pleading.

'Run, Gus. Please, leave me.'

'It's too late for that,' Gus said, circling him.

Kemp shook his head. 'No it isn't. Gus, please.'

Gus smiled his big, toothless grin. 'Then you should go.'

Gus rushed him but it was slow and clumsy. Kemp had time to step aside and crack him with the stick. Gus reeled, his feet unsteady.

Daisy's tears fell. She looked away and saw, instead of the boa constrictor, a monster, similar to the dragon in the stained glass of Upsall church. The dragon flew close to the boys and disappeared.

She refocused on Kemp, who pushed Gus away, but back he came, staggering like a drunk.

Kemp shrugged. Then, with a huge swipe, he walloped Gus in the midriff, and, as he raised the stick to crack it over Gus, Gus toppled one way and then the other, and vanished into thin air.

Daisy shook, her whole body filling with grief.

Nearby, a deep, powerful roar was followed by the strange "bark" that she'd heard with Archie.

Kemp raised his hands to his face, let out a desperate cry and, very slowly, sank to his knees.

# 121 AN OFFER

Daisy moved out of her hiding place, shaking.

What had she done? Her stomach knotted, her head throbbed with white, empty pain: This was her fault.

*HER FAULT!*

She thought of Isabella and especially Sue. Could she tell them she had given Kemp a weapon with which he had slain Gus?

Brave Gus who had escaped the storm only to be brutally murdered – and she hadn't lifted a finger to help.

Worse still, *she* was party to his murder.

---

CAIN HOVERED OVER TO KEMP. 'The deed is done, boy,' he said, quietly. 'You have won.'

Kemp stared numbly at the rock.

Whispering, the spirit continued, 'you have an opportunity to seize the girl, this Heir of Eden you are so fond of.'

Kemp looked confused, but when he turned, he found Daisy looking at him, from the other end of the courtyard.

His heart sank.

'Go to her now,' Cain whispered. 'Go to her and persuade her to come with us. It is the best chance you will ever have.'

'She will despise me,' Kemp said, drawing his sleeve across his face. 'Because I have done something awful.'

Cain slapped him across the face. 'Wise up, boy. You can save her. Maybe not now, *but later*. She will go to a dark place where her life will hang in the balance. You have the power to offer her an alternative to death.'

Kemp cocked his head. 'Save her later, how?'

'All she has to remember, boy, are the words used to call the dreamspinner, Asgard. You know what they are. Asgard will know what to do.'

The corners of Kemp's mouth turned up. *Of course!* He started walking, limping towards her.

'Daisy,' he called. 'Stop.'

She wiped her tears. '*Why?*'

'I didn't mean it. You know that ... I had to.'

'But ... murder?' she cried again. She wanted to punch him.

'Because, Daisy, we're all going to die—'

'No, we're not!' she cried, her voice quivering. 'We're going to find the tablets – you'll see.'

'You won't. There's too much for you to do. Deep down you know it's beyond you—'

'Then we'll die trying.' She rubbed her eyes and faced him. 'That's all you need to know.'

'Look,' he said, 'there was only ... only room for one of us. Me or Gus.'

'What are you talking about?'

'It's the ghost. He can take only one other, to be a part of him. Soon there won't be anyone left on this planet. Just a spirit, and me and well, there's an arrangement. The winner can take one other. A girl. So it was a choice.'

Daisy glared at him icily. 'You killed him, Kemp. You're a bloody murderer.'

Kemp stared at the ground and wiped his bloody lips. Then he looked her in the eye. 'You helped me, Daisy. That makes you complicit. So you are also a murderer.'

She reeled, stunned that he understood her actions too.

Kemp's bloody face stared at her imploringly. He stepped forward. 'You don't understand. If Gus had won, he'd have taken Sue—'

'But *you* won.'

'Yeah,' Kemp replied. 'Because when I saw your eyes in the darkness of the rock where you were hiding, I realised I wanted *you*. I want *you* to come with me, Daisy – more than anything else. Nothing has ever felt so right.'

He moved in close.

Daisy noted the terrible beating he'd received. The mangled face, the deep burgundy cut across his forehead. She had a terrible urge to smack him and clenched her fists, but when he stretched his arms out to her, she reached out and took his hands.

'Come with me, Daisy de Lowe.'

Daisy stared at him and swallowed.

'Please?' he implored. 'I don't want you to die.'

Her lips flickered and she squeezed his hand. 'I can't,' she said. 'It's impossible.'

His face fell. 'Look, you don't have to come, you know, right away,' he said, bowing his head.

'I must go,' she said, knowing she needed to be back at the cottage. She turned.

He thought quickly. 'Daisy, your next task involves killing a serpent,' he said, stopping her in her tracks. 'By all accounts, it cannot lose—'

She hesitated. 'Why not?'

'Because it can be any reptile, big or small, with every power known to exist.' He shuffled closer as she tried to edge away. 'Listen to me,' he said. 'If you are near to the end, you must shout out for me. Call for me.'

'Call you?'

'Yes! If there's time, I will come, I promise, and then all of this ... this craziness will be over. I swear it.'

The strange voice Daisy heard earlier rang out. 'Time to go, boy, with or without her.'

Kemp leaned in quickly so that his breath touched her ear. 'If you're really, truly stuck, if you're on your knees with nowhere else to go, there is one other thing you can do—'

'Come on, boy, the light is growing, we must be away.'

Kemp winced and spoke with more urgency. 'Say these three words out loud. You'll feel a force field in front of you. Dive towards it — through it — thinking of me. You've got to trust me, Daisy de Lowe.'

Daisy cringed. 'What words?' she croaked.

He smiled and moved his cheek to hers, so that she could smell him and almost taste the matting blood on his cheek.

He whispered three words:

*'Dreamspinner. Dreamspinner. Dreamspinner.'*

And then, in a flash, he turned and vanished into thin air.

*... TO BE CONTINUED*

# ONE MORE THING...

Dear Reader,

Please, spare a moment to give THE CHAMBER OF TRUTH your honest **review** from the store from where you purchased it!

***I'd appreciate your help**! It might even help me finish off the series - one day!*

*Thanks-a-million.*

*JKE*

# EDEN TEAM

If you'd like to join my closed "Eden" group, on Facebook, go to Facebook, look up EDEN TEAM and request to join.

Or, send me an email.

NOTE: It's only for those of you who'd like early access to new releases in exchange for feedback and reviews. And also to converse with likeminded souls and be advance readers and cool supporters when new books come out.

To join, I would expect you to have reviewed one book and preferably to have read at least one other...

I look forward, very much, to seeing you there.

James

# A BIT ABOUT YORKSHIRE

I thought it might be helpful to provide a small map for those of you who haven't been to the amazing county of North Yorkshire in the UK.

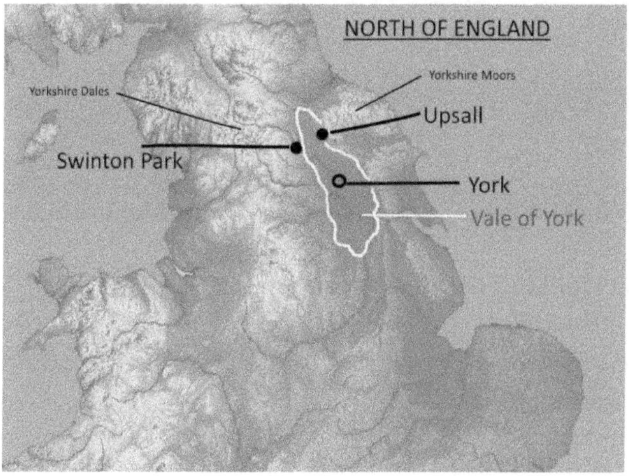


North Yorkshire, where I once lived, is an ancient, beautiful and varied landscape, studded with glorious scenery and wonderful monuments.

This area is well-known as the location for the writings and TV dramas of the famous vet, James Herriot, who lived at Thirsk. He used to attend to my wife's grandparents livestock. Some of the characters in Herriot's books are - so she says - based upon her family!

Upsall actually exists. It's a tiny village, perched on the edge of the moors. A medieval, though renovated castle overlooks the expanse of the Vale of York below.

This is typical of my idea for the setting of the Eden Chronicles, based on the cliffs and forests and rugged villages and farmsteads dotted here and there. I also liked the name of Upsall.

Nearby, lies the World Heritage site of Fountains Abbey. I have spent many happy hours enjoying the astonishing medieval ruins letting my imagination wander off...

Here's a picture so you can understand what I mean.

This is typical of the kind of buildings I had in mind for the ruins above Eden Cottage.

I hope this snippet gives you a tiny insight into the character of this evocative landscape.

# ABOUT THE AUTHOR

James was born in Suffolk in the UK. He travelled the world extensively, worked as a journalist in the 1990's and then turned to his passion for the great outdoors, designing and building gardens for several years before returning to writing.

James moved to North Yorkshire where he lived between the Yorkshire Dales and the Yorkshire Moors. It inspired him to use these beautiful areas as the location for the EDEN CHRONICLES series.

In 2013 James rowed across the English Channel and the length of the Thames to raise money for MND and Breakthrough Breast Cancer.


www.jameserith.com

james@jericopress.com

facebook.com/JamesErithAuthor

twitter.com/jameserith

instagram.com/edenchronicles

goodreads.com/jameserith

pinterest.com/jameserith

amazon.com/author/jameserith

# COPYRIGHT

**Eden Chronicles Series, Books 1-3**
**The Power and the Fury, Spider Web Powder, The Chamber of Truth**

First Edition published 2017


Cover: Tom Moore (tom@beatmedia.co.uk)


ISBN: 978-1-910134-15-3 paperback

# ALSO BY JAMES ERITH

The Dragon's Game - Eden Chronicles, Book Four

Lightning Source UK Ltd.
Milton Keynes UK
UKHW011316041120
372791UK00001B/2

9 781910 134160